VOLU

THE BEST
OF WORLD
SF

LAVIE TIDHAR is the World Fantasy Award-winning
author of *Osama*, Campbell and Neukom winner *Central
Station*, Jerwood Fiction Uncovered Prize-winner *A
Man Lies Dreaming* and many others. He created and
edited the groundbreaking Apex Book of World SF series
(2009–2018), editing the first three volumes and remaining
as series editor for the next two. In 2021 he launched the
Best of World SF series from Head of Zeus. He also wrote
extensively on international SF/F in a regular column for
the *Washington Post*. His latest novels with Head of Zeus
are *Maror* (2022) and *Adama* (2023).

VOLUME 3

THE BEST OF WORLD SF

EDITED BY
LAVIE TIDHAR

HEAD
of ZEUS

An Ad Astra Book

First published in the UK in 2023 by Head of Zeus
This paperback edition first published in 2024 by Head of Zeus,
part of Bloomsbury Publishing Plc

9 7 5 3 1 2 4 6 8

A catalogue record for this book is available from the British Library.

ISBN (PB): 9781804548059
ISBN (E): 9781804548011

Cover design: Ben Prior

Printed and bound in Great Britain by
CPI Group (UK) Ltd, Croydon CR0 4YY

Head of Zeus
First Floor East
5–8 Hardwick Street
London EC1R 4RG

WWW.HEADOFZEUS.COM

Contents

Introduction		1
Diana Rahim	*A Minor Kalahari*	9
Daniela Tomova	*Behind Her, Trailing Like Butterfly Wings*	19
Timi Odueso	*Cloudgazer*	41
Mandisi Nkomo	*The EMO Hunter*	51
Nelly Geraldine García-Rosas *translated by Silvia Moreno-Garcia*	*Tloque Nahuaque*	81
M.H. Ayinde	*The Walls of Benin City*	89
Luo Longxiang *translated by Andy Dudak*	*The Foodie Federation's Dinosaur Farm*	103
Thomas Olde Heuvelt *translated by Lia Belt*	*The Day the World Turned Upside Down*	133
Indrapramit Das	*The Worldless*	167
Andrea Chapela *translated by Emma Törzs*	*Now You Feel It*	187
Fadzlishah Johanabas	*Act of Faith*	211
Cheryl S. Ntumy	*Godmother*	227
Zahra Mukhi	*I Call Upon the Night as Witness*	249
Dmitry Glukhovsky *translated by Marian Schwartz*	*Sulfur*	261
Efe Tokunbo	*Proposition 23*	275
Fargo Tbakhi	*Root Rot*	333
Chen Qian *translated by Carmen Yiling Yan*	*Catching the K Beast*	353
Elena Pavlova *translated by Kalin M. Nenov and Elena Pavlova*	*Two Moons*	369

Choyeop Kim	*Symbiosis Theory*	391
translated by Joungmin Lee Comfort		
Eugenia Triantafyllou	*My Country is a Ghost*	423
Nora Schinnerl	*Old People's Folly*	441
Christine Lucas	*Echoes of a Broken Mind*	467
Vida Cruz-Borja	*Have Your #Hugot Harvested at This Diwata-Owned Café*	489
Sheikha Helawy	*Order C345*	501
translated by Raphael Cohen		
Vraiux Dorós	*Dark Star*	505
translated by Toshiya Kamei		
Dean Francis Alfar	*An excerpt from* A Door Opens: The Beginning of the Fall of the Ispancialo-in-Hinirang *(Emprensa Press: 2007) by Salahuddin Alonto, Annotated by Omar Jamad Maududi, MLS, HOL, JMS*	527
Mário Coelho	*Ootheca*	539
Pasi Ilmari Jääskeläinen	*Where The Trains Turn*	567
translated by Liisa Rantalaiho		

About the Authors	643
About the Translators	653
Extended Copyright	657

Introduction

1.

Setting out to curate an anthology is always, for me, a daunting task. What will it be and what will it say? When I got the chance to edit the first *Best of World SF* anthology for Head of Zeus, I had a somewhat easier task. Many of the writers featured in that volume had already become names familiar to many SF readers: Aliette de Bodard, Tade Thompson, Zen Cho and Silvia Moreno-Garcia have, since their appearances in my earlier small-press series *The Apex Book of World SF,* garnered their fair share of critical and commercial recognition.

For a time, I was not sure what shape a third volume could take. Then I was reminded of when I first set out to create an anthology of international SF. It was 2008, which seems like a lifetime ago, and to find the stories I had to sometimes literally go through bookstalls in various countries. In 2008, print magazines dominated science fiction, and online publications were mostly looked down on. The writers I began to find weren't then well-known and they had not yet won their prizes. Book deals were not being offered to them. Indeed, I watched them struggle for many years to reach acceptance from the industry and the field. Behind many successful authors lies a battle to be seen and to be heard – and it is ever more so for international voices.

I was reminded, at last, that when I did set out to edit that first anthology – sold to my patient publisher as a book 'that will not make you any money, but it's a good thing to do' (and how right was I on both counts?) – it was not filled with household names. It was filled with the young, the hungry and the talented.

At this, the weight I felt was lifted. My task was simple, and it hasn't changed. It was to showcase those writers you don't – yet – know about, who are writing the science fiction that matters now. They were not going to be writers even I know, but fresh voices, those for whom the well-deserved awards and publications are still to come and – as any editor will happily tell you at length – there is nothing quite as satisfying as finding a new original story and falling in love with it.

Once I realized this, there was nothing to it but to go on a deep dive in search of those voices, happily getting lost in countless anthologies, magazines and collections, discovering new authors while reconnecting with some I have long wanted to publish.

Setting out to curate an anthology is always, for me, a daunting task. What will it be and what will it say? But once I embarked on the journey the answers formed and a story took shape, told in a multitude of voices. Science fiction is more vibrant, more diverse and more exciting than ever, as I hope this volume shows. Science fiction can ask big questions; it can reflect on the future or on our life right here on Earth. And it can also be *fun*.

I hope you enjoy coming along with me on this journey.

2.

I like that term: curating. In English the usual term is editing an anthology, but what is an anthologist if not a curator of wonders?

When I first started looking for stories for that first Apex volume, it was a fairly lonely endeavor. Trying to promote those early shoestring budget books was even worse, like shouting as loudly as you can into a void.

But the field changed, and new voices came into it, and as much as I'd like to claim any kind of credit for these books, they are made so much easier with the help of friends. People involved with World SF often wear multiple hats: writers, editors, translators. Cristina Jurado has been my tireless guide to Spanish-language SF in previous volumes. Ng Yi-Sheng recommended favourite stories for this one, as did Shimon Adaf. Silvia Moreno-Garcia translated one herself. Cristina, Yi-Sheng and Silvia all appear as authors in Volume 1.

Alex Shvartsman, who translates Russian-language SF, sent me stories and put me in touch with their authors. As a translator he appeared in both Volume 1 and 2. Toshiya Kamei's translations similarly grace both Volume 1 and the present one. Neil Clarke has been supportive and helpful every time I wished to reprint a story from *Clarkesworld Magazine*. And I am indebted to all the authors and translators, editors and publishers and dreamers who make these books such a joy to put together. I really am merely the curator, given the chance to collect these works into a single book.

So much of short fiction is fleeting in nature, especially now when publishing is done increasingly online. Short fiction often appears only once and then vanishes. There is, to me, a special value in putting together a large book or, indeed, a series of books such as these, to give stories a more permanent and more durable home. I find Head of Zeus' hardcover editions particularly appealing for that purpose, seemingly designed to sit on shelves for years to come. But this book can be read just as easily in digital form across the world, or in a handy paperback edition. Whichever format you choose, though, it is the stories that matter.

3.

I offered a snapshot of the short story scene back in Volume 1. Things look similar now, but offered here in the hope they might prove useful to any hopeful writers reading this – or indeed for readers seeking more good work to read!

Tor.com remains the highest-paying (and certainly the highest profile) publication, with stories acquired by several different editors. Slate's *Future Tense* project (slate.com/technology/future-tense) is also high profile, but like *Tor.com* is not open to unsolicited submissions. The rest of the publications listed are.

The long-running *Clarkesworld Magazine* (clarkesworldmagazine.com) remains a pillar of good SF and World SF in particular, with a consistent programme of translated Chinese and Korean stories. *Lightspeed* (lightspeedmagazine.com) is consistently good on SF, while companion volumes *Fantasy* (fantasy-magazine.com) and *Nightmare* (nightmaremagazine.com) focus on fantasy and horror respectively.

Apex Magazine (apex-magazine.com) tends to a darker tone of SF which makes their stories very much their own. *Uncanny* (uncannymagazine.com) often shows up on awards lists with their selections. The venerable *Strange Horizons* (strangehorizons.com) is perhaps the web's longest-running professional genre magazine, and publishes consistently interesting stories across the genre spectrum. They also publish *Samovar* (samovar.strangehorizons.com) which specializes in translated SF/F.

Fiyah (fiyahlitmag.com) is dedicated to Black SF/F stories and has been going from strength to strength since launching in 2016. *Escape Pod* (escapepod.org) is the web's longest-running audio magazine for SF, with companion sites *PseudoPod* (pseudopod.org) and *PodCastle* (podcastle.org) focusing on horror and fantasy respectively. *Daily Science Fiction* (dailysciencefiction.com) is, as the name suggests, published daily. It focuses on short-short works of up to 1500 words. *The Dark Magazine* (thedarkmagazine.com) publishes dark fantasy and horror, much of it international. *Beneath Ceaseless Skies* (beneath-ceaseless-skies.com) is dedicated to often-longer works of secondary world fantasy.

There are various other magazines, with new ones regularly appearing, though many do not last long. The ones mentioned above remain the top-tier of online magazines.

In print, the situation remains stable. *The Magazine of Fantasy & Science Fiction* (sfsite.com/fsf), *Asimov's* (asimovs.com) and *Analog* (analogsf.com) continue to publish as they have for decades, and all are now available in e-book editions as well as in print. In the UK, *Interzone* (interzone.press) remains the primary print magazine (though it is now published from Poland). Various smaller magazines come and go. In print, much short SF is still published instead in original anthologies, but most of these are solicited directly. A good resource for writers is the Submissions Grinder at thegrinder.diabolicalplots.com, which offers a searchable index of publications looking for stories.

4.

Real world events are often just as fantastical as fiction could ever be. I have been editing this series in the midst of a global pandemic that would have seemed like science fiction a few years earlier. Climate change and war continue to inform our lives in terrible ways, a fact reflected in many of these stories.

Science fiction can and should reflect our world, commenting on our reality while looking to the future. It can be optimistic, too, asking what happens if we change and grow. It can deal movingly with the issue of refugees, as in Daniela Tomova's 'Behind Her, Trailing Like Butterfly Wings' or in Zahra Mukhi's 'I Call Upon the Night as Witness'. It can address climate change, as in Diana Rahim's 'A Minor Kalahari' or Timi Odueso's 'Cloudgazer'. It can be sumptuous like Dean Francis Alfar's 'A Door Opens...' or as weirdly compelling as Mário Coelho's 'Ootheca'. It can be funny, too, like Chen Qian's 'Catching the K Beast', political as in Fargo Tbakhi's 'Root Rot', or flat out experimental as Vraiux Dorós' 'Dark Star'. It can take us to the stars and back down to Earth and sideways, introduce us to post-apocalyptic worlds and aliens, turn the order of the world upside down and follow a robot on its quest for meaning. For me, reading this book is like following the threads of a rich tapestry, woven and worked all over the world, in twenty-eight diverse voices singing together in harmony.

But then again, I'm biased. I chose these stories, and I love them all. They can be read in order, in which case, I only hope they tell a story bigger than the whole. Or the book can be dipped into at random, picking a story the way one would choose a sweet out of a box.

5.

If I have one confession to make, it is that I love weird stories. This, though, is predominantly a science fiction anthology, and fans of science fiction will, I hope, be amply rewarded. I love spaceships, robots and aliens as much as anyone does. I also love dinosaurs, A.I.s, weird planets and even weirder biological systems, and you'll find all of these and much more in these pages. With each of these volumes I have first been guided by the need to provide a range of stories that are identifiably SF…

However.

Did I mention I love weird stories?

You might find them dotted throughout the book. They might not satisfy the purist, but they delight me and I think, more seriously, that genre fiction today is far too diverse in its range of tools and influences to be confined to a narrow definition. Part of my purpose is to showcase that variety. No reader will love every story (apart from the editor, perhaps), but my hope is that you find one story that will impact on you in some way. Literature cannot heal the wounds of war, fix climate change or house refugees. But it can give us hope, and make us think about the world, and sometimes, simply, provide a few moments of escape. Escape has value, too.

But I have gone on long enough. Here, then, is *The Best of World SF: Volume 3*. I hope you enjoy it as much as I enjoyed putting it together!

LAVIE TIDHAR

2022

A Minor Kalahari

Diana Rahim

Singapore

Who doesn't want to start a journey with… a watermelon? Having tried to grow my own once, I can certainly sympathize with Mr Tan in this story. My friend Yi-Sheng recommended 'A Minor Kalahari' to me, and it is, I think, a good opener for this volume, giving consideration to our urgent real-world concerns but doing so with a light touch and a skewered perspective – exactly the way good genre fiction should.

It all started when a big, beautiful watermelon appeared overnight in a town that was not particularly big nor particularly beautiful.

The greyness had hit the town first, rendering it barren before claiming the rest of the island. Grass was reduced to a brittle shade of brown. Trees stood listlessly on the verge of banal deaths. The elderly in the estate began to die one by one, their bodies and brains regressing from a lack of stimulation before ceasing altogether. It was as if a fog had descended, choking the air and all life. There was no obvious violence. Everything natural simply faded or died.

In such a town, a big, vibrant watermelon erupted into existence. It grew overnight on a grass patch just in front of Mr Tan's house.

It happened like this: sixty-three-year-old Mr Tan woke up, sat up in bed, and as sleep ebbed away, he registered an anomaly at the periphery of his vision. A burst of colour. He looked out his open window and saw it: a big green orb in a field of infertile brown. The sight filled him immediately with fear instead of hope.

One must understand that the presence of an anomaly could only be understood by Mr Tan as the arrival of more bad things.

It was, after all, the death of five great trees in the neighbourhood eight years before that had signalled the beginning of the greyness. Then birds began to fall. The flowers stopped blooming. The rain forgot itself, mutely showering the island for days at a time. Street cats stopped fighting to climb the dead trees and sleep on their branches, without a care even when the rain fell upon them. They slept, dreaming human dreams. Blue sky. Grass that was green again. Birds strutting about, clueless but alive.

Not a single thing had grown in the neighbourhood, on the whole island, for the past eight years. All that was left were rectangular beds of dirt and sand where grass, bushes, flowers and trees used to be. So one understands why, on that morning, Mr Tan could only read the presence of the watermelon as an omen.

He was prone to dreaming. That was his flaw. He used to think that if you dreamed hard enough, repeated an image or desire with enough intensity, things could be willed into existence. He used to dream of wealth and grandchildren. He dreamed of a luxurious retirement. Of massaging his wife's feet in the morning on another of their many holidays. None of these things came to pass. So when he saw the watermelon, he thought that perhaps he had not killed that part of his dreaming self enough. He thought that perhaps there was a part of him that was dreaming still. Dreaming of a return to an earlier time, a time when things still grew.

When he walked out of his bedroom, crossed the hallway

and opened the door, he saw that the watermelon was indeed there. Its unmistakable presence was almost violent. He slotted his feet into his slippers and walked towards it.

When he squatted in front of the fruit, his eyes were alarmed at the vivid green. He had forgotten what it felt like when his eyes registered colour, bright and alive. How it was enough to change the way everything looked. He stared, remembering all those years ago when he read that green was a healing colour, calming for the eyes. He observed the wavering dark green lines extending themselves end to end on the lighter green body of the melon. His wife once called them stretchmarks.

'Is it yours?'

His neighbour, Ms Sharifah, had appeared behind him without him noticing. How long had he been squatting in front of the watermelon, waiting for his eyes to adjust?

'No.'

'Then whose?'

'I don't know, it was here when I looked out the window this morning.'

At that moment, Mr Tan realized that it was possible to reach out and touch it. This scared him. To touch something so alien to their current environment felt like an adventurous act, as if he were a child again, new to the world.

He was about to reach for it, when Ms Sharifah's five-year-old burst onto the grass patch and grabbed at the watermelon.

'Raiyan!' Ms Sharifah whispered sharply.

The boy ignored his mother, fuelled by the novelty of seeing something new. As he lifted the watermelon, they saw that it was rooted to the ground. It had not been dropped or left there. It was growing in the earth. Ms Sharifah forgot her son and squatted next to Mr Tan as her son shrieked in excitement. 'It really grew here? When?'

She pulled Raiyan towards her.

'What is this, Mama? Is it sick?' Raiyan was touching it, rapping it on its side. He lifted its roots with his little fingers, querying even the ants. 'What is this, Mis-ter Ant?'

'This is a watermelon, sayang, and it is not sick. This is the colour green,' Sharifah replied.

*

The more the watermelon grew, the more something in the neighbourhood changed. It started with the people who walked past it every day. Each day was another day they realized such a thing was possible. Each day there bubbled within them a desire that the watermelon would continue to exist. They walked past it even with anxiety, fearing that it might have died or disappeared, just like so many other things in the neighbourhood.

A whole month passed until one day, a laminated note was stuck on the watermelon. On it read the declaration: *This fruit was not planted by the town council. If it belongs to a resident, we ask that it be removed. If no action is taken, the council will deem it appropriate to remove it.*

The following week, a young man appeared at Mr Tan's doorstep. He wore a white shirt, black pants, shiny, important-looking shoes and uncomplicated rectangular steel-frame glasses. He seemed to be the same age as Mr Tan's son, maybe younger.

'Hello, sir, are you Mr Tan Yao Guang?'

'Yes. Yau Kwang.'

'We received notice that there's a watermelon growing in the grass patch in front of your home. Did you plant it there?'

'No, I didn't. You call that a grass patch? Where got grass?'

'Do you know who planted the watermelon there?'

'It just appeared overnight. I wish I could plant something else.'

'Do you realize it's illegal?'

'You want to take it away?'

'I didn't say anything about taking it away; I'm just asking who planted it there.'

'When was the last time you saw a watermelon?'

The young man did not reply. Mr Tan had a brief feeling that the young man's soul had cracked through the skin of his face and shown a little tenderness in his eyes. But the part of him that made him choose his job ultimately locked it back in submission. His face returned to a professional expression and presented Mr Tan with an unsettling smile.

Before leaving, he parted with what seemed like genuine warmth. 'Thank you, Mr Tan. If you have any updates about the watermelon, please contact the town council office and ask to speak to me. My name is Darren Gan.'

What was most absurd was not the threat of removing the watermelon. It was not even the suggestion that Mr Tan would cooperate with the town council. The most absurd thing was that Darren Gan had not looked at the watermelon at all during his visit. Not once.

Mr Tan believed that it was deeply sad for one to refuse to see a miracle.

*

The threat of the watermelon's removal meant its presence was both precious and political for the residents of the neighbourhood. Ms Sharifah was the most vocal and animated, speaking first with Mr Tan, then with the mothers at Raiyan's pre-school, the people at her reading group and the local shopkeepers. The possible removal of the watermelon seemed to her a heartless act.

Ms Sharifah organized the pre-school mothers. They would convince the residents to call the town council to dissuade them from removing the watermelon and would make a case for it to stay. Though this approach was mild, it was an uncharacteristic, startling act for the usually morose neighbourhood. Then again, as the residents pointed out in their conversations (yes, they had begun to talk among themselves again!), it was only predictable that mothers who had decided to have children during the period of greyness would be predisposed to irrational hope and taking action.

There were only five mothers who had children younger than the age of nine in the neighbourhood. One of the mothers was the pre-school teacher, Ms Aliah. She knocked on Mr Tan's door to proselytize for the watermelon. She had walked past his door at first, but the sight of the fruit had stirred her to turn and knock. It took three decisive knocks and what felt like only mere seconds before Mr Tan opened the door.

'Hello, sir! I'm Aliah. I'm the pre-school teacher.' She spoke slowly with an unnerving smile, as if Mr Tan were one of her students. 'I saw the note on the watermelon. Sharifah told me they came down to talk to you, the town council people. I just want to suggest that you can call them and say that you are willing to take responsibility for it.'

'For the watermelon?'

'Yes, say you will take care of it. But if you don't want or cannot do it, I can take care of it. If I can take care of six kids, I can take care of one watermelon!' She laughed and clapped her hands twice.

'Oh… but that's not the problem. Their problem is that they

don't think it should be growing there. Watermelon also need permit now – funny, right?'

'So silly. If grass starts to grow there again, would they come and knock on your door?'

'Ya, but grass is supposed to grow on a grass patch. Not a watermelon.'

'Tsk! No, Mr Tan. Their issue is not that the watermelon should not be growing there. Their issue is that they think everything must be owned by someone. Nothing is allowed to be free. So you say you own it lah!'

Mr Tan was not inclined to give the matter much thought and shrugged in reply.

Ms Aliah offered an excessive smile, her eyebrows lifted with the same manic intensity as the corners of her mouth. It was a smile she often used with her students. 'Just think about it, okay?'

It was true what she said, Mr Tan thought. The town council could not think outside the concept of ownership. Nothing escaped the system of exchange. They could not imagine something that belonged to no one or to everyone. They numbered buildings. They tagged dead trees. They even claimed to own the sand. Just like they thought they owned each citizen. Just like parents thought they owned their children. He remembered his son, and his heart hurt.

It was evening. If the birds were still around, they would be flying overhead right about then.

*

Mr Tan never made the call. He didn't really have the chance. Four days after Ms Aliah knocked on his door, the watermelon was found cracked open. It looked as though it had been smashed with brute strength.

It was Raiyan's voice that Mr Tan heard first.

To a child who was yet to understand the world he lived in, the sight of the fruit cracked open was a marvel. He screamed with joy and plunged his little hands into the fibrous red flesh. Ms Sharifah could not make herself move her son away. Although the sight of the battered fruit saddened her, the sight of Raiyan enjoying it made her smile.

This time, it was Mr Tan who moved towards them. 'What a waste. Wonder who did this.'

'I don't think it's any of us.'

Raiyan was a little perturbed that his mother was not averse to his messy frolicking. When Ms Sharifah smiled, he took it as a cue to resume his grabby exploration of the watermelon carcass.

'You know, Mr Tan, I think it's them.'

'Them? Who?'

'The town council. I think they sent someone to smash it so we wouldn't disturb them anymore.'

'I don't think they would bother. It looks like an accident.'

'You know, Mr Tan, they can smash it if they want. But they are so out of touch they forgot something.'

Mr Tan raised his eyebrows.

'The seeds.'

Ms Sharifah squatted next to Raiyan and thrust her hands into the cool watermelon. She plucked out some seeds and placed them on her palm, juice dribbling down the sides of her hands.

'We can always plant another one. One here in front of your house since we know it's possible. Or on another grass patch. We can even grow it indoors if we have to. Got enough seeds to try.'

Raiyan's excited screams had attracted some wandering

residents, though they lingered at a distance to watch, occupying the room of their own private feelings.

Mr Tan did not share Ms Sharifah's idealism. In fact, he was a little resentful of her naiveté.

'That would be wonderful, but how can it grow it here? Look at the ground, it's hopeless. You can't even dig into it. This isn't the climate for a watermelon.'

'Mr Tan, this watermelon grew here. It already happened.' Ms Sharifah's voice was not antagonistic, but its hopefulness carried a challenging tone.

Mr Tan looked at the decrepit watermelon, its flesh smashed up and sad. The part of him that still dreamed, that small part of his flawed being that he had failed to kill, looked at the commingled watermelon flesh and soil and could not help wondering if the mixture would make the soil more fecund.

Clueless to the inner movements of her neighbour's mind, Ms Sharifah continued. 'You know, that day when we found the watermelon here, I went home and googled watermelons so I could explain what it was to my son. I think a lot of us assume that a big, juicy fruit like this came from a country like ours before the greyness or from South America, somewhere tropical. But it wasn't like that at all. The watermelon came from the Kalahari Desert in Africa thousands of years ago. A desert! I googled to see what it looked like, and it's almost like this place if there were no buildings and if the sand was more orange. So in fact, Mr Tan, this is just the sort of climate where we could grow a watermelon.'

Raiyan had quietened down and began to wipe his juice-soaked hands on his pants, becoming increasingly uncomfortable with the strange sensation of moisture, of nature's juice on his little hands. His face began showing the early signs of a child's tantrum. Mr Tan remembered how his wife used to get anxious when their son would cry as a toddler. When Raiyan finally erupted into a full tantrum, Mr Tan could only offer a reluctant smile to Ms Sharifah as she shuffled her son back home.

*

That night, Mr Tan dreamed of massaging his wife's feet, not on a holiday during retirement but back in their first matrimonial home. When he awoke, he allowed himself to think of her, to hold the image of her face in his mind. He even thought of calling her and calling his son, but decided against it. Not yet. He remembered how his wife once taught him about a desert called Padang Mahsyar, the central sorting place in the Islamic afterlife. She told him half her nightmares as a girl had been of this huge, terrible place where all awaited their fate. Two years ago, when it was clear the greyness was persisting, he thought maybe God had changed their mind and decided to slowly create that desert in this world while people were still alive. He had always felt as if they were going through the afterlife in advance once the greyness began. He felt as if they were awaiting their final fate.

The watermelon ruptured that hypothesis. The neighbourhood, the whole island, was a desert. But it was no afterlife. In this desert, there were seeds.

He looked out the window and saw a bird, a mynah, picking away at the crumbling fruit. He picked up one of the two seeds he had placed on his bedside table and swallowed it. The other he would plant in front of Ms Sharifah's home.

Behind Her, Trailing Like Butterfly Wings

Daniela Tomova

Bulgaria

I didn't know Daniela Tomova before finding this story, which I just loved immediately. Born in Bulgaria and living in Norway, yet writing in English, Daniela is emblematic of the new generation of writers for whom both language and place carry multiple identities. Like the previous story, 'Behind Her, Trailing Like Butterfly Wings' feels like a fable for our time.

'Sit here.' He pulls out a thin panel from the front of his kiosk, punches it into the third dimension, then into its secondary function as a chair, and places it in front of me. 'Here's safe.'

In the heat of summer, the short grey bristles on Frank Krayec's head glisten with sweat. The fraying seams of his tank top flop over the swell of his muscles with every breath. Seating himself, legs wide apart and stable against his own rickety chair, he watches patiently as I take out my notepad and pencil. Behind him, the mud-green kiosk squats, just as solid over its lightweight skeleton, waiting like a huge dog, eyes as big as chairs.

'How long have you been living on the road, Mr. Krayec?'

'Frank, please. Can I call you Marrow? Is that your real name – Marrow Vas? Never met any Vases in all my time on the road. Yeah, twenty-three years now. I was one of the first followers. That is what we call ourselves. I know you oasis people… You are *settled*, right? From one of the oases? You still have your house and everything?'

I nod. If he has noticed the involuntary glance down, to where his dusty, sweat-streaked, bare legs bracket my new shoes, his face doesn't say anything.

'I know you call us road people, but we're not here for the road, yeah. We're following *her*.'

I finger the velvety edges of the photo in my pocket to assure myself it's still there and hidden.

A boy stops by Frank's kiosk and he gets up to sell him some charge.

'The kids say "seekers" now. Don't you?' He turns to the boy and nods encouragingly. The boy shrugs and stares at the battery graphic filling up on his screen, his face blinking bright blue in the dusty shade of the kiosk. 'I guess it sounds more urgent or noble, like they are achieving something, but they were born on the road; they don't really know why we walk. Well, they do, but they don't know it in their hearts – they did not make that decision, yeah. Without the choice there is no true knowledge. Isn't that so, Barker?'

The boy turns towards me and scratches his raised eyebrow, giving me a conspiratorial look under his palm. With a shrug, I turn my chair around to get my first real view of the human tide behind me.

Right now, Frank's kiosk sits, for visibility, as he had explained in his directions over the phone earlier today, on a small flat-topped hill – the first real feature in the landscape after weeks' worth of walking. To the right of us, snaking down from the horizon and through the grassland like a prehistoric river, the road carries us its silt of people. Floating islands dissolve into dots and dots grow into people as they scale the gentle slope of the hill. They flood the small natural platform in front of me and flow over into the dark clavicle of a cliff whose burnt yellow scowl monitors the timeless steppes.

The faces flood my brain, too, and lose their meaning in the same way a word repeated a dozen times does. I turn my chair around.

The payment is in some small metal items I cannot identify and two handfuls of pebbles, fished out of the boy's pockets. Frank sweeps the metal bits into a box of jangly miscellanea, counts and packs the pebbles carefully, logs them in a small paper notebook and returns to his chair. A knot of people jostles the back of my chair and I pull in closer to the kiosk.

'Watch your back – it's some *middlers* passing now. Look at... Come on now, dragging their feet, dusting up the air, bumping into stuff? They don't pay attention; don't respect the road, yeah. They think it's safer if they pack in closer to each other but someone in the periphery always gets pushed too far whenever they pass a mouth. It's the nerves. They all try to squeeze closer, even though the road itself is safe as anything. Theory goes that's because the road is where she walked. But yeah, walking in crowds... Someone always panics, and often, even good, clever people get taken.

'That's why I always walk by myself. Keeps me sharp. It costs more pebbles but...

'Hey, Limmi,' he yells, 'tell those fly-eaters to use their damn pebbles here. Next blind turn, there's a mouth. It almost took Sonya's boy earlier today, the one with the droopy eye. Yeah, I know,' he chuckles, 'but he's her son so *she's* gonna miss him at least, yeah. You wanna buy a charge? I have a special sale on megawatts today: three for two. Get you a nice deal if you have any pebbles left over to exchange too – we're hitting the cloud ropes soon and the newbies are running out, yeah. No, no problem, man, maybe tomorrow. Stay safe.'

He looks at me taking notes and says with mild embarrassment, 'Don't repeat that thing I said in your article – "fly-eaters". Not that it's a bad word here but there's folks that do eat flies and they are nice people. No joke. They fly these huge bags sewn onto hoops, like kites. Spray them with something they make that attracts the flies, yeah. They catch bagfuls and cook them. Bagfuls of pure protein.

'A fly-kite, if you can keep it up all day and close enough to the mouths, can feed a family if they are not squeamish. And let me tell you, those kids, the ones that don't turn their noses up at flymeal? Some of the best-fed kids here. Nice folks.'

I swallow hard and try not to examine the way my dusty spit feels like tiny maggots at the sides of my tongue. I ask him if he's had flymeal.

'No, no, not me. Not for me. I'm old road. I have everything I need to sustain myself, and when I run out, I know how to get more. I have my supplements here and I always make enough food in trade, yeah. For a family though, that won't do.'

I ask if he had a family before he left for the road.

'No, I don't want to get started talking about "befores" right now.' His face closes off. 'It's draining to remember how things were in this heat. Didn't you want to ask me about us here, yeah? Isn't that what your article was about?'

I say yes, my newspaper is running an entire series on the road people, as we call them in the oases. We are interviewing a crosscut of the entire road society – merchants, arbiters, enforcers, gatherers, hunters, new parents, even children. Why they choose to walk. What they think of the Wandering Woman. Do they believe she is real?

'Merchants… arbiters,' he laughs. 'Hunters… What are we

– a club for medieval re-enactment? We don't have merchants and arbiters. We have people who are trying to live. I sell things because I have solar panels and I'm clever with people. Leika over there, hey Leika, just out flips if someone steals from the newbies. She has poor impulse control and is a bit of a brawler. She's a good person though. We don't have a *calling* or a *career*. We are just dealing with the world dying for as long as we can keep from dying ourselves.'

The kiosk buckles and shudders. A hot gust of wind suddenly kicks sand in my eyes and I rub at them frantically. Through shards of pain, tears, and flashes of knuckles, I see the sun set over Frank and then rise again and set and rise, set and rise, as the giant wind turbines lining the road pick up the evening wind, and the shadows they cast down speed up their clockwise rotation.

We move the chairs around to keep the sun and blistering wind at our sides and for a few minutes, we both retreat in our own thoughts. Periodically rubbing my inner lid, I rearrange the questions in my pad. I throw some out, rephrase others. I move the picture last. Well, next-to-last. In the heat, the blood beating in my head reverberates against the soft whoomph, whoomph, whoomph of the turbines.

*

Frank gets up to sell electricity to a small group of families and I stretch, lock hands behind my head, and look around.

For as long as I have been aware of the road, I have imagined it desert-quiet. In my head, beaten, drab people miserably shuffle onwards, huddling against each other. Mouths snarl at them in the voice of swarming flies. Road urchins scrabble and skirmish.

I used to write maudlin, juvenile poems about it. Born in the year when the Wandering Woman was first noticed, growing up in a time when fences crept out like ivy over my small-town-turned-oasis, I fancied myself born under the Sign of the Road. I was that kind of a child. The kind of child who sat cross-legged atop the desk in his bedroom; looked out the window to see the mouth over the neighbors' house grinning at him like a shark through its red-buoy dentures; and wrote about Lost Lives and Real Suffering. And drew crocodiles who wore daylight as a cloak and sharks with red plastic teeth eating sunrays. The kind of child who obsessed.

The real road accepts no obligation to my romantic notions. In the bud of evening, the air around Frank's little kiosk rattles with the everyday activities of people: yells, laughter, negotiations. Children plead for money with their parents and bolt towards a man selling Godknowswhat candy under a shower of *Jaya, no running! How many times'*es and *Marie, you share that with your brother*'s.

At the hill's crest, small groups of people, phone in hand, are sitting down to rest and plan the next leg of their walk. A girl exclaims at her phone and points the screen at another – her sister? A friend? A pregnant woman stands up, dusts off her clothes, tosses a large backpack on her shoulder and heads off onwards.

Endless strikes of feet beat the rock-hard road harder into the ground and polish its marble-smooth red surface, stroke by stroke. I imagine how it will look in ten years, if there are any people left to look, this new kind of rock created by its own unique bio-geophysical process.

The sun inches slowly towards the horizon and the shadows of the giant power turbines creep away from it and over the road, combing the flow of people like the hair of a Titaness. One of the shadows catches my eye for a second before I realize why and jump away from it, crashing to the ground in my flimsy chair.

*

The noise dries off. Suddenly, everyone around the kiosk is frozen. Frank is frozen, too, and he is yelling at me to tell them what I saw. His yelling is getting fainter and fainter and more meaningless over the roaring of my own blood and I don't think anyone can hear me speak over the roar and I have no voice to shout so I can only point.

I point beyond the road, on the far side from the kiosk, to an ordinary patch of grassland identical to any of the other ordinary patches of grassland around it. Foxtail, beaten gold by the sun, sluggishly tick-tocks in the breeze. Amid the dried-out brush and weak trees, wildflowers open up thirstily like mouths to the sky. Small worlds, over which the sun sets and rises hastily in the shadows of the turbines as they spin clockwise.

Except for the shadow I am pointing at, which, fainter and slower, is rotating counterclockwise.

Even before I can pull up, first myself, then the chair, space is efficiently cleared for two men who approach the edge so cautiously that they appear to be feeling their way forwards by the way air moves around their bodies. Still jerky with adrenaline, I sit down facing them. My breathing is ragged and hiccup-y, but the pen twitches in my hand like a whisker. I get to see road stalkers in action. One of the men, short-haired, tall, and gaunt in his patina-fringed suit, elegant, save for the baggy pockets, tosses a pebble at the shadow.

The pebble cuts a clean arc through the air and disappears at the very edge of the road. Then, a second before, a shimmer, like mirage over hot asphalt, hovers over the spot. I blink and try to adjust my perception of the sequence of events, but the more I try to align them, the more my head hurts. It's as if the hit has created event ripples reaching out backwards and forwards in time, and my brain is not fit to consolidate the information.

Through the stabbing pain behind my eyeballs, I ask Frank if he knows what would happen to a human taken by such a mouth. Keeping his eyes on the scene, he just shakes his head.

The men mark something on their phones and throw another pebble and another and another, pacing a semicircle on the road nearest to the shadow. As I watch obstinately, as every hit strikes my eyes like lightning, as, painted in splatters of glinting steam, the mouth takes grotesque shape, my stomach turns and empties. I notice others convulsing and throwing up while their companions lead them away and on. Frank asks me if I want to leave and, head between my legs, I wave in feeble denial.

A young woman I am told is the men's daughter walks around the thinning crowd collecting pebble donations in a big bag and then joins the stalking work. The rest of the people switch on their phones, post updates, bring up the map of the road immediately ahead, and continue on. The area around the kiosk empties for a few minutes before the next groups start to filter through, giving the stalking trio on the edge a wide berth.

*

It is at the edges of the road that the quiet of the outside world leaks in and the road people – the followers – probe their way with their pebbles.

The road population does not have the red buoys oases fence off irregularities with. Eventually a froth of flies will crosshatch most mouths but it takes time for the flies to collect, so the new ones, the unlogged, unnoticed, the most dangerous ones, are unmarked by any form of man or beast.

The road itself is remarkably, even improbably, safe. I catch myself thinking about it in terms of the Wandering Woman as if I buy into the road people's savior mythos. I can almost see her in her strips of odd, tattered clothing walking past us with that inhuman look on her face. I see her walking down under the cliff and off into the open grassland fanning out beyond. The photo is floating so light in my pocket I keep tapping it to make sure it's there.

'These guys do have a name,' Frank startles me out of my queasy reverie, smiling through his meaty lower lip, 'since they might need to be summoned quickly and in any crowd. We call them sketchers. You guys probably have some medieval word for the profession – jugglers? Minstrels?'

I laugh with him. I tell him ours are called stalkers.

'I like this one, actually. It suggests you are hunting *them*, yeah. I suspect it keeps people in the oases—' He gets up to sell some more electricity.

Head down, writing, I pause for him to find the right adjective and finish his thought, but he doesn't. I figure he either forgot or the sentence was finished as it was.

*

The heat is letting off a little. The wind turbines are slicing the setting sun's red rays – whoomph, whoomph, whoomph. The stalkers are still working but I can only see glimpses of them as the stream of people passing by fills in. I ask Frank why he thinks so many new people take the road.

'Of course they will. What is the alternative, do you think?'

I say that the new oases the government is building are going up as fast as new stalkers can be trained. I surprise myself with how easily defensiveness edges out my trained professional tone.

'Let's start this way then: how many oases are there?' Frank asks.

Thousands, maybe tens of thousands, I say.

'How many people, on average, can an oasis hold?'

The largest one I know of holds twenty thousand.

'Do you know how many of us are there on the road? At last point-count – oh yes, we have a census, although those are not completely reliable because you have to pick a big enough representative sample of points and then you have to extrapolate based on mean density and road coverage – yeah, I'd say...'

He milks the moment.

'Twenty... twenty-three million, give or take the few thousand taken by the mouths weekly. Plus the new births, of course.'

Fuck.

'Yes. Fuck. I have a PhD in Biophysics – I know my statistics.'

We sit silently for a bit while my notepad and I process the information and he continues.

'Now for the oases themselves. Do you know how many you've lost already, yeah? You know Nylo?'

I nod. I know of Nylo. Some years ago, I interviewed a few physics phenomenologists from there who came over to my oasis to, as they said, study correlations between irregular activity and certain human and biophysical events. Even road blogs covered the visit – I suspect because the Nylo scientists focused on reports of encounters with the Wandering Woman.

They even had a folder with classified pictures of her. Not something they would show a journalist, of course, but something a journalist would manage to get his hands on, nonetheless. They had so many pictures. I doubt they ever missed the one I stole.

Frank is pointing.

'You see that man there with the two kids? He lived there.

'So, for years Nylo had only a few manageable irregularities, right? Yeah. Well, they started getting less few and less manageable. More and more mouths – less and less Nylo, until the whole oasis collapsed three months ago. Swiss cheese.' He stabs his finger at the table between us with startling violence, miming poking holes faster and faster.

'Nothing left but crumbs from houses and streets going places you don't want to be. People half-glued to the asphalt, half inside a hole stretched in time. That second half still not having realized what happened to them. No government left to clean out the bodies, you see.

'A group that bought some power from me yesterday, or was it two days ago… No, yesterday… They said some of those people have started screaming now and they will be screaming long after what's left outside is bones. To the inside only a few minutes, or maybe at most a couple of days if they are really unlucky, will pass before they die, but a few minutes of watching your body decay and disintegrate, that is…'

He shudders.

'You can't hear them, of course, but if the angle is right, you can see them. The road goes right by it, you know, and right now you don't walk by Nylo – you run. Purgatory, that's what it is.'

I am still writing but no longer processing.

What is being done then?

'What can they do.' He shrugs.

But what can they do?

'Which "they"? Nothing? I don't know. The road is safe.

She walked through here, and mouths cannot open up where she walks.'

Do they know where she went? Or where the road is going? How do they know where to go?

'We follow the news.' His face dives into his phone and surfaces with a road feed, one of many, with eyewitness reports and few blurry photos. 'I know some here think she is either made up or used by the government to keep people walking and away from the oases. But that's mostly the new ones who joined after they lost their houses. They are, I get it, bitter and cynical, yeah.

'They see the photos and the articles streamed to their phones, every few days from a different location but not too far away from the day before, and they think "the flunkies are trying way too hard" right? They see how the people flow is sometimes driven very, very subtly in one direction or another, somehow away from the oasis locations. That happens, I know. Few even say the flow is driven into mouth infestations too when Oasis thinks there's too many of us. I don't know about that. Those who say that tend to be the crazies, but broken clocks and all, yeah?

'And I don't know where she is.'

He stares over the road into the dusk song of the crickets.

'What I do know is that she is real. I knew about her before the road, before the mouths, before the crowds. When there were just a few of us who read a bit of news about a woman walking. Just walking, not talking to anyone, accepting only water, foraging by the roadside.

'And you'll ask why I left my job and my house and my wife to follow this woman wherever she was going. I cannot tell you. It never formed into thoughts, just knowledge. But I saw a picture of her, one day after work. It was on some feed or another. I didn't really follow the marginal news then, but I recognized the outskirts of East Tarremin. That's where I come from, you know.

'She looked so solid and so alone and... prehistoric. Like the first human who was recognizably a new species. Like the people who lived before everyone else and seeded the world with meaning. Like them, she was this new sentience walking over cooling rock and bones, under new stars. Making up her own meaning.

'I doubt you will believe how uncharacteristic this was for me, Marrow, but I cried with relief. Over what? Damned if I know. I suspect my heart was waiting to be broken by something unexpected because it fell apart so readily. That picture, the Woman who was single-mindedly hunting something I could not understand – they broke it open for this new life I set off on. Wherever she was going... I wanted to believe she had some answers no one else did.

'My wife didn't. She said she understood me but she had not spent her life waiting for some new meaning. We didn't have any kids, so I left on my own.'

He looks back at me.

'And now the world is ending.'

He shrugs and his face twinges. He massages the place on his shoulder where the kiosk straps have polished the skin a shiny brown.

*

'But life doesn't stop just because the world is ending.' He slaps his thigh. 'Just because we don't have houses and steaks anymore doesn't mean we stop needing friendship or a drink. Want a drink? That guy over there, yeah? He makes the best fly brandy in the world.'

My face must look absolutely green because he laughs.

'I swear, your generation... You can't make alcohol from flymeal, obviously! You need sugar. He makes the best quince brandy on the road. Maybe in the world. Okay, he made the best quince brandy once. We passed by this gigantic tree long time ago with him and his wife and ate so much it gave us all the runs. And he made brandy with the rest. He makes apple brandy now but it's not the same. Still good though. Want a glass? My treat. For listening to me ramble.'

We drink the brandy and get up to pack away his kiosk. He pops and folds and zips with such mechanical efficiency that I just move back, mouth-wide, and watch him work. He is almost done when I hear sharp yells rising and see people flood back from under the cliff.

'I told them.' Frank slams the kiosk-turned-backpack shut, wiggles himself between the giant shoulder straps and lifts. 'This better not be the same mouth I warned them about.'

We look down over to the side of the cliff where two men's legs have given out from under them and are now floating over their heads. The men are desperately trying to hold onto something. In the brandy-tinted twilight, they crawl like monstrous crabs up along the cliff side as their screams grow less human and long black claws grow and drip from their hands. Not claws, no. The rocks they are trying to hold onto are shredding their fingers and palms raw. Black smears of blood glisten in the moonlight below them.

I have heard of this type of anomaly before and have even seen some ghoulish pictures of the victims – the mummified human companions escorting our network satellites. But I have never witnessed an actual taking. And I never knew how desperately people tried to hold onto life that was just beyond reach. Or how long it took.

People are looking away and some are openly sobbing, but in some macabre solidarity, no one walks away. I wonder if that is really what the two men need right now, but in their hoarse howls, I can hear they have already been driven far beyond any needs.

One of them, exhausted, scrabbling faintly more against air than rock, spreads his arms like a lover and embraces the cliff with his entire body. It's a mistake, as far as anything they can do right now can be a mistake, because the reversed gravity, apparently stronger over the cliff, just whips most of him with a wet gurgle over the rocks and out in the sky, leaving the front of him smeared like a dark paintbrush stroke over the cliff.

The other man turns around and, pushing off the cliff with his legs, launches himself at the crowd on the hillside. He tries to grab at clothes, arms, backpacks, anything, but he is way too far to make it across the mouth.

'Please,' he screams. 'Please, please, please,' as he is slowly, slowly dragged into the sky to be mercilessly deposited into geostationary orbit under the watchful eye of the moon.

Frank and I set off silently along the road.

*

I walk out of the cliff shadow into the moonlight. My breath catches. A choppy star-strewn river of people flows across the plains and pours over the horizon. The briefings from my editor, all the faces who passed by me today, the numbers Frank gave me, even the horrors I saw… Nothing drowned me like this river.

And I can't see them now but I know they are there – the mouths crouching along the road like starving dogs.

I recall a documentary I saw as a child. I can't really remember the whole thing or even whether it was on TV or online. I only remember the shapes and movement – two crusty eyelids and a snout float in a muddy river. Two jaws launch out the water in a violent spray and drag a struggling, doomed gazelle into the bloody foam. As a child, I wondered why the gazelles didn't go to the other river, the safe river. Then my mother explained there was no safe river for them. Where the gazelles went, the predators went with them. That is why, she quickly added, seeing my terrified face, we humans built our own rivers, our own houses and cities, to keep safe from the predators.

They still found us.

My phone rings. I have half an hour before pick-up.

I pocket the phone next to the picture and ask Frank if he thinks he'll ever meet the Wandering Woman.

'I don't know. I hope so. I still hope to see a real picture of her again, to know she is still walking ahead of us. The double they have found, you know her? They keep posting pictures and interviews with her. She looks nothing like the Woman. But it works, keeps people moving and alive. Well, most and mostly. And we'll be walking long after the oases have collapsed.

'Maybe.' He laughs like an old friend. 'I'll see you on the road one day and spot you a few megawatts.'

I shouldn't show him the picture. But I do. I take it out and ask him if this is her.

He looks at the photo, and a smile spreads on this face like warm butter under a knife.

'That's her! Where did you get this?' he yells out and then looks again. I can see the exact moment he notices it and the smile creases and sours.

'Where did you get this?'

My heart breaks for him, but I tracked him down here for another reason.

I say, *I got it in East Terramin.*

I was born there, I say.

In a small suburb, called Terramin Woods with charming walls of crumbling masonry, parks turned to weed, and houses neatly handed down from one generation to another, which meant few people ever left, even after the mouths started appearing. So few, in fact, that pretty much everyone I knew growing up still lives there, even those who work downtown. Now that I think of it, I only know of one or two people who left for the road.

'I guess you oasis people have your stories as well,' Frank says, looking straight ahead, speeding up slightly so I have to raise my voice to talk to him.

One of them lived right across the street from us, I say. *He left when I was very young but I remember his wife talking about him a lot. My mother and I used to go see her every week. As a child, I thought the neighbors visited her so often because she was so interesting. She could keep a conversation going for hours and, most importantly to us children, her husband left for the road, which made him a mythical figure. But as a grown-up I know what loneliness looks like so I assume the grown-ups of then had recognized it too.*

Her name was Raya. Kids were not on first-name basis with adults then so we called her Mrs. K.

Frank stops in the middle of the road and I stop with him. Behind the bristles, his face falls slack and wrinkled, skin ashen against the glossy pink of his eyes. I feel like throwing up. Over the years, with smuggled bits of information from people who knew him, I have built up a thousand images of him and I was ready to tell my story to any of those laughing, callous, imaginary Franks. The real one is now standing broken before me and I am not ready.

But he needs to know.

I remember this bright yellow dress she had, I say. *So bright it looked like sunshine. I think she was wearing it when the mouth opened up in her house, over the living room where she was probably sitting and reading, ready for the doorbell to ring. She was always sharply aware of that doorbell, even when the house was full. Like she anticipated it a second before it rang.*

I told her once that she had a doorbell super sense, like the superheroes in the comic book I was currently flipping through – their house was a library of old comic books – but that her powers wouldn't help with monsters much and she laughed. 'It's not the doorbell.' *She mimed elbowing me from the kitchen where she was making green frosting for the Space Invaders cupcakes I kept asking for.* 'It's people super sense. I sense the people outside the door and then they always ring the bell. It's what people do when they want to come in.'

I stop for a little to let Frank, eyes closed, breathe in her words.

I could be wrong, I say, *but I do think she was wearing the sun-yellow dress when the mouth took her. She often wore it in summer and the weather was sweltering that day. I remember it was so hot that when the stalkers came, they wore these shorts with a playful red-buoy pattern.* 'That's profane,' *my mother spat out in a mucous voice and dragged me home by the hand.*

Locked in for the rest of the night, I watched the stalkers work from my bedroom window. I watched as they measured the mouth's dimensions and stability with a truckful of their exorcizing instruments. I watched as they hammered in the steel pins that would anchor the buoys, one by one, like nails into a coffin. I watched as they released the buoys, one by one, gently, irretrievably, like flowers from a mourner.

It was a Spag. It is similar to the mouths in Nylo but a Spag warps more than just time. When it opens over an area, everything it swallows is spaghettified – stretched in both time and space. There is no reliable information in scientific literature about how long a person taken intact would survive in such an environment. Within their timeline, of course. By our reckoning, she'll still be alive long after our bones are dust.

The reason I think she was wearing the sunshine dress is, well, when the stalkers release the buoys in a Spag, they form what is called a Concentric Spaghettified Range – from the outside it looks like a red fence of beams meeting far, far, impossibly far inside the hole. They don't meet, of course, it's just a ring of floating plastic... I spent years wondering if she saw the buoys rise around her one by one, if she knows what that means, if she is in there terrified right now. Alone, surrounded by red buoys, waiting in a crumbling house.

I shake off the thought and continue.

Anyway, I say, *at night it is not that easy to see so I didn't notice it until I looked out my window the next morning, but by day a sun-yellow beam is clearly visible among the red ones. It's still there.*

I know it is because I still visit her once a week. I go to the porch, stand safely behind the buoy fence, and chatter about the news, waiting for her to sense that someone is outside. It used to drive my mother so crazy when I was a kid. I don't know why I still do it. It's not like I have any scientific basis to think she can still feel the people outside. Or that she still needs a visit.

Frank drops the giant backpack on the road and sits down with his back against it and arms still in the straps. He buries his face between his legs.

My car is here but I don't know what to say.

I'm sorry, I say. He shakes his head.

I get on the car and it lifts off over the crowd.

*

From the air, all mouths have the same characteristic shimmer, like mirage over hot asphalt, that is rarely seen from the ground. Looking down, I see them hover over the moonlit plain – a sea of jellyfish cut in half by the road. I spot the cliff-side mouth – the one which took the two men, and, just beyond it, the small one under the turbines. I notice an undercurrent – something that looks like a new mouth forming further down along the road, but it's probably far enough from the edge to be of any danger, so I do not ask my colleague to land the car so I can go warn Frank and his people.

Before I pocket the picture, I look at it again, trying to see it with Frank's eyes. Here she is – a dark-haired young woman. Bare shoulders and legs. Some strips from a short-hair coat are wrapped around her body with no particular pattern. The picture, taken by a hobbyist's drone, shows mostly the top of her head, an uncreased forehead looking straight ahead, and a stride unmistakable for anyone who has seen real footage of the Wandering Woman.

And then the eye moves from the Woman's head down to her back and then to the shimmering pattern of spots emerging from her back and fanning out over the landscape behind her, trailing like giant butterfly wings. Shimmering like a mirage over hot asphalt.

I look down at the road. Frank is moving now – I see his backpack threading its way against the flow of people. I see the shadow of the cliff swallow him and spit him back out over the hill, on his way through the grassland against the horizon from which the crowd is spilling out.

The car touches down again for a few minutes and then lifts up high enough for the navigation sensors to filter out the noise from the millions of people walking on with their phones. From down on the road, I see it turn and head to East Terramin.

I take the phone out of my pocket and sit down next to a woman reading a news feed. She helps me find a good real-time map online. Then I get up and walk in the direction of the new mouth I saw forming. I did say I was the type of person who obsessed.

Cloudgazer

Timi Odueso

Nigeria

Timi Odueso was another name new to me, and it's always such a pleasure discovering a new author with a powerful voice. 'Cloudgazer' is another compelling and timely story, and it's my great delight to present it here.

The nearest cloud cluster was sixty miles away, almost an hour's journey if Bombay went at top speed.

A fruit trader had seen it on her way to Sabon-Gari, floating lazily across the azure sky. 'You don't see that often,' the trader had said to the crowd, grappling her basket of mangoes. 'A whole cluster, untethered, unbothered, what a sight! So you see why you have to buy my mangoes, they've been blessed by clouds!'

Zik straddled Bombay, brought her heels to its torso, and held on tight as its mechanical legs whirred into life. On any normal occasion, she would have preferred the smooth train ride to Sabon-Gari, staring out the windows and soaking in the views of Zazzau, but this wasn't normal. The trains would begin at Kachia, stopping at every station in Zazzau between her hometown and the market town Sabon-Gari, a thirty-minute ride turned ninety by heated exchanges between conductors and last-minute passengers. There was simply no time for that; if a cluster had danced so proudly across the sky on a weekend that even an ordinary fruit trader could see it, then smugglers and everyone else would have seen it too.

Bombay whinnied as Zik dug harder into its thigh, propelling both horse and rider forward in a speed burst. This might even be futile, thought Zik. For one, smugglers could have caught wind of the cluster and siphoned them away into calabash gourds, the thieves! Even worse, the cluster could belong to one of the Herders from down south where Rainmakers harvested clouds daily; there could be a white-collared man sitting smugly and sipping ginger shai'i as he tapped directions into his Winds transponder. Or the trader could have been lying, a ploy to get the townspeople to buy her wares which wouldn't be the first time someone had lied about cloudwatching. Every thought that came to her as Bombay's hoofs clopped across the roads led to the same unnerving conclusion: Hasan spitting in her face about using Bombay without permission or supervision. Did she know how difficult it was to get spare parts for an old Andalusian, they don't even import these anymore! Did she know how complicated it had become to calibrate Bombay, to oil its joints? How would he save up for one of those new-generation AI Mustangs if he had to keep using his savings to replace the horse's hoofs every time she went on a joyride, eh? Why would she even go to Sabon-Gari on the word of a petty trader?

Zik thought of everything other than Hasan's spittle on her face. It would all be worth it if she got to the cluster before it was emptied, it would all be worth it if she got a few liters, just one or two even. It would all be worth it to see the joy on their faces when they realized her escapade had saved them. Transferring the reins into her right hand, she checked if she had brought everything she needed. She patted the Imam's gourd which bobbed on her chest: 'No more than five minutes old, you hear,' the Imam had said. 'We need the freshest you can get or the medicine won't take.' Her satchel, which contained every kobo she could find in the house, was buckled around her waist; cloudwater was expensive, fresh ones even more so and she feared that what they had wouldn't be enough. So she'd brought his old takouba along. He wouldn't mind, she told herself; after all, this was all for him.

The steel sword was sheathed and strapped across her left thigh. At first, she'd only picked it up for protection, sure that any roadbandit who saw the tiny rotating teeth whizzing across its edges would retreat, but as she removed the weapon from its hold, Zik remembered the pride in her grandfather's eyes as he carefully polished the blades with olive oil on Saturday mornings. She remembered sitting with her brother, listening to their grandfather gloat about it, 'They don't make them like this anymore. Pure steel, copper wiring, not that cheap bronze-shelled nonsense those wannabes carry around.' Hasan would whistle and tease, 'But Baba, you know if we sell it, we can probably buy a good house in Kajuru, and even have enough for a Mustang, or two.' Her grandfather would glower at a laughing Hasan, point the tip at him and say, 'The only way you will sell this sword is if I die.'

He would die if the sword wasn't sold, she decided. The disease had spread, the Imam said; her grandfather would never walk again, and if nothing was done, he would soon never breathe again either. Over the course of the month, she and Hasan had traipsed the many towns of Zazzau on weekends in search of pharmaceutical substances, Hasan straddling his biotech steed, and she gliding along the railways. Fermented hibiscus leaves from Kaura, sour hartebeest milk from Kafanchan, even hundred-year-old honeycombs from the luxury stores in Kajuru: they'd gotten everything the Imam needed to make Baba's medicine. All except fresh cloudwater.

Everyone knew that the only way to get fresh cloudwater this far up North was the farm at Kajuru where they had a Rainmaker, but the farm was only open on weekdays. Weekdays were for work: Hasan working at the Factory recalibrating wonky limbs, and she in one of the Customer Care cubicles of Winds Inc®, listening to people drone on about what was wrong with their transponder app. Even if there was some way they could escape work into the tepid sophistication of Kajuru, they would have to sell the antique takouba, Bombay, their small house, and their limbs before they could afford a meagre liter of fresh cloudwater from Kajuru's cloud Farms. She'd even considered it, trading limbs, perhaps her arm from the elbow down, on the black market; the sale would be certainly enough to fetch enough money to buy a few gallons of fresh cloudwater and a cheap new arm, perhaps one made of brass with copper wiring, or she could save up to buy a durable fiberglass-and-titanium one that was waterproof. In the end, she'd decided against it after Hasan had told her how steelsickness would kill her when her body began rejecting the jury-rigged arm.

This was their last resort, she was sure, racing to do the very thing they'd seen the Hisbah imprison people for. They'd done everything else: beg their neighbors, request loans, even peddle the black markets for smugglers who had a few liters to trade, but no one softened when they'd told them their grandfather would be dead in a month if they didn't find fresh cloudwater. He hadn't said it, but Zik knew that Hasan had resigned to fate; on the weekends, he'd taken to flinching every time Baba tried to talk, thrumming deeply when she wheeled the old man out so he could gaze at the empty sky, or skulking at the door as she fed him koko through a straw. To escape Baba's stagnant stares and Hasan's heavy gloom, she'd begun taking long walks around the streets of Kachia, her eyes affixed upon the sky as the Imam's gourd nodded on her chest. With her gaze on the heavens, she missed everything in front of her, tripping over a scavenger's wheelbarrow once and having the dazed loon chase after for purportedly trying to skim his precious scrap metals; stomping into many oily puddles that left her boots slimy; and stumbling into dazed pedestrians, including an off-duty Hisbah official who threatened to detain her until she handed him a few kobos. When they saw her on the street, with her head lifted up and the wooden vial dancing between her breasts, the people of Kachia whispered amongst themselves and blessed Zik with a new moniker. 'Here comes the cloudgazer,' they would taunt. 'Careful she doesn't trip you,' and Zik, whose ears perked up at any mention of the word *cloud* would have her head darting in all directions, trying to find what she desperately needed. This was how she'd come across the fruit trader's sermon: the cloudgazer had been wandering around Kachia searching the skies for white fluff.

On Bombay, she zipped past the railways, holding on tight to the steed's reins as wind slammed into her whenever a train came gliding beside them. She'd never understood why Hasan wanted to buy a new horse. Bombay was the fastest thing she'd ever ridden, faster than trains and certainly faster than walking. He would be angry she had taken the horse without his permission, but Zik was sure that a solution lay in wait at Sabon-Gari. She was sure she would return to Kachia with something that would paint a smile across Baba's face and bring Hasan's laughter welling to the surface. And for that promise of joy, for the imminent laughter she believed was at the top of her tongue, she would gladly sell the takouba... and even Bombay.

When heavy smells hit her, Zik knew she had reached Sabon-Gari, for everyone knew that one would smell the market-town before one would hear or see it; the malodourous emulsions an enveloping hello paving the way for raucous sounds to caress ears. She resumed cloudgazing, her eyes zipping across the empty skies as the sounds of the market-town filled the air around her.

They met her at the outposts, the traders, and they grabbed at her shins even before she slid through the gates of the market, calling her to their wares. One waved diaphanous bags filled with silicon at her and argued that his prices were the best in the market for fleshwork, another rubbed the metallic sheen of Bombay's fur and told her he could get her a good price for her steed. Others stretched their arms and gestured for her to follow them: *I have the silkiest microsteel fabrics, soft but steady, bulletproof too; You're in the presence of the best connoisseur of palmwine in the whole of Sabon-Gari, let's go to my stall, I will give you some samples, a special cask of rambutan-and-lime you will love.* The traders of Sabon-Gari were immodest about their wares, assertive about their trade in calling out for patrons, unlike the shop owners at Kajuru who sneered at customers and promptly ushered out anyone who attempted to haggle prices.

She ignored them all, her eyes fixed on the empty skies. Her hands led Bombay away from the many stalls haphazardly scattered around on the dusty cracked roads. The traders saw that their words would not entice Zik to visit their stalls and they began to fall away like dead petals off rose stalks, returning to the outposts to seduce other visitors with their attractive prices. One by one, the crowd around the cloudgazer thinned until only the fleshworker remained. The man stuck his silicon bags into his kaftan pockets and took instead to telling Zik about his certifications as he followed her on foot.

He was the only one in the whole of Sabon-Gari with the skills to use reinforced keratin and calcium, did she know, did she? For a small price, her nails and teeth could be just as strong as steel, 'And they'll weigh the same,' he added. She needn't worry about his certification, he comforted, he had studied bio-metallurgy at the University of Pangaea. 'In fact, I am one of the few persons in Zazzau who has successfully practiced neuro-wiring.'

'Then why are you here?' Zik snapped. With her wandering eyes finding no signs of cloudburst in the skies above, Zik's apprehension had grown heavy and weighed down the happiness she was sure she would find in Sabon-Gari. The fleshworker's recitation only added to the weight.

'Why what?' the man asked.

'Why are you here?' she hissed. 'If you're so good at splicing metals into bodies, why are you in this dump? Why aren't you working in one of those fancy auto clinics in Kajuru?'

The man smiled sheepishly. 'Well, there's the small problem of certification,' he confessed. 'I'm still waiting on my certificate, but once I get it, I'll be as revered as a Rainmaker.'

When he received no reply from Zik, he increased his pace and stopped right in front of Bombay who whinnied to a stop. 'Why are you here then? You've been wandering about for a while. Perhaps if you just tell me what you want to buy, I can help you out.'

'Clouds,' Zik said. 'I'm looking for fresh cloudwater.'

The man grimaced, his nose crinkled as he said, 'There's no fresh cloudwater in Sabon-Gari, everyone knows this. There's a cloud farm at Kajuru, that's the only place you'll find it.' He turned away from the steed and made to walk away.

'I can't afford that,' Zik announced. 'I'd heard there was a cloud here today. I just need a few liters.'

'That was a sting operation by the Hisbah. There was a cloud here,' the man admitted, turning around. 'But I'm afraid it was planted to catch smugglers and illegal harvesters.'

Bombay creaked as Zik sank lower onto his back. The reins slipped from her fingers and her face clouded up. Her hands raced up to clutch the vial on her chest as she quietly began to sob. She thought of her grandfather, sitting at home waiting for a medicine he would never get. She thought of Hasan who didn't seem to be able to decide which was more precious, horse or family. She thought of herself, gliding across the plains looking for something everyone knew she could never afford.

'You don't look like a smuggler,' the fleshworker said abruptly, patting Bombay's muzzle. 'What could you possibly need fresh cloudwater for?'

For the first time, Zik looked at the trader. She could see that his eyes had been augmented, they flashed a vibrant blue that seemed to make a quiet whizzing sound. He had high cheekbones and his lips were pursed as he watched her eyes run over his kaftan. 'My grandfather,' she finally replied. 'We need it for his medicine.'

The fleshworker grimaced, turned left, then right, and leaned in closer to Bombay's back. 'There are other ways, you know,' he began quietly. 'I cannot get you fresh cloudwater, but I can get you the money you need to buy some at Kajuru.'

Sneering, Zik said, 'You think I'm stupid? I'm not selling my arm. I know about steelsickness. I know how you fleshworkers are.'

'Steelsickness? Only a rookie would make such a mistake. If there's anything you should be worried about, it's getting a second-hand arm with ghost touches. Besides, we wouldn't take the whole hand, a finger should be enough.'

A finger didn't seem too bad, Zik thought. Perhaps, if she made enough off it, she could even get an augmented replacement, maybe a thermoplastic one that could glow in the dark, or something cheaper like one of those steel ones she'd seen that could store data. Yes, a finger didn't seem too bad. She wasn't Hasan, she knew what was most important to her and would sacrifice something for it.

'If a finger will be too personal,' the fleshworker began, 'then you should know that there are as many things to sell as there are to buy here,' he said, patting Bombay again. 'An antique Andalusian would fetch a lot here.'

He leaned in closer and whispered how much she could get for a finger, and for a horse. 'Joy cannot come without sacrifice,' he proclaimed mournfully. 'Something cannot grow from nothing. We all have to give, to receive.'

Zik's eyes widened at the numbers she had heard. She shifted her gaze to the sky, sweeping for clouds one last time. When she found none, the cloudgazer turned her eyes away from the heavens, fixed them upon the fleshworker and said, 'How do we begin?'

The EMO Hunter

Mandisi Nkomo

South Africa

I have wanted to publish Mandisi for years, and I finally have me the chance. Mandisi's a musician, and when he turns to speculative fiction, the result is always something to look forward to.

> *'As the Earth Mother is my witness, I vow to avenge the destruction of her physical form. The Emotion Manipulator is her enemy, and thus mine. I will strike them down, man, woman or child. I will strike down all colluders who betray the Earth Mother's trust. This I promise to you, great Earth Mother, who bred and nurtured me for millennia. We await your rebirth, Earth Mother, so that humankind may one day return home.'*
>
> *– Prayer of The Earth Mother Knights.*

Joshua and Miku stood and walked away from the prayer circle. While Miku idled with the other wives, Joshua confided with the other Earth Mother Knights. The priest congratulated them on their work and blessed them with sprinklings of crushed leaves and flower petals. Once the blessing was over, Joshua joined Miku, and in silence they walked The Holy Grounds, heading for the nursery enclosure.

Inside, Earth Mother Nurses tended the children, who played in the mud and bushes. Their son Kirill was still a baby and was placed indoors. They proceeded to his crib, and he smiled as Miku reached for him. Like his father, Kirill had bright black beady eyes as intense as they were friendly. Kirill's complexion complemented his parents' contrasting complexions; his smooth baby skin appeared like a bleached brown. Together, the three appeared as a sequential progression in shades. After picking up Kirill they went back outside and headed for the exit.

The grey metallic facades of Paragonia's skyscrapers clawed above the height of the trees. Outside The Holy Grounds, hordes of hovercrafts engulfed the street, as the churchgoers filed out. It was here Joshua and Miku parted ways.

'Well, the bus is waiting. I hope you enjoyed the ceremony. I don't really understand why you avoid them so much,' Joshua said brightly.

'I actually think I did this time,' Miku lied. 'Maybe I'll join you again next time. Anyway, I should probably get Kirill home.'

'Right,' Joshua said. 'Well… duty calls.'

He kissed Miku politely on the cheek and made his way to the Earth Mother bus, beginning to brood. Temporarily, he pretended he believed Miku; he knew he did not. She often lied to his face.

He reached the bus and walked up the platform to join his colleagues. The bus ascended to Level 5 and followed holographic street alignments which bled up from the ground.

On arrival, The Earth Mother Knights streamed out of the bus, through the hangar, and into the locker rooms. They swapped their prayer robes for tight bodysuits with dangling wires and tubes, then filed out into the armoury. One-by-one they walked into what resembled a giant fridge – The Assembler. They were stamped, and stepped out looking reptilian, layered in metallic scales.

Once armoured, each Knight proceeded to his consultation room for analysis and briefing.

'Hello, Joshua,' Mohini said. 'Did your wife enjoy the ceremony?'

'Yes, she did,' Joshua replied to the smooth electronic voice.

'I am still detecting mood instability from you. It is recommended that you seek personal consultation to avoid excessive use of mood stimulants. Also, a friendly reminder: you are still overdue for lung and liver replacement.'

'Um… thanks Mohini. What are my orders?'

*

Miku did not go home. She waited for Joshua to leave, ignoring all the Earth Mother buses beckoning her with metal flaps, knowing they could not take her where she wanted to go – outside the Central City Cube. 'Where the heretics go,' she whispered to herself. Kirill slept soundly, sucking his thumb, tiny head rested on her shoulder. She doubted he would wake for her little escapade.

She slipped away, distancing herself from The Holy Grounds, and all the people who knew her as an extension of Joshua Shepard: *The EMO Hunter, The EMOlisher, The EMOliminator…* or whatever his fan-club was calling him lately. Once a safe distance away she hailed a hovertaxi. The driver ogled her a moment; her porcelain features were so delicate it appeared they might flutter away at the slightest breeze. His staring reminded her of the priests during Earth Mother Church Fundraisers.

Miku announced her destination, and the driver took off.

'Are you sure you want to go out this far?' he asked after a while.

'Yes,' Miku replied.

'You know, the Earth Mother Knights are still working on these districts. It may not be safe. I don't like coming down here and I definitely can't leave clients here with a clear conscience.'

'Yes, I've heard those *rumours*,' Miku said. 'None of it's true. The people here are actually quite nice.' She was quiet for a moment, and then waved her free hand over the side of the hovertaxi, pointing at the holographic street sign. 'Stop here please.'

The driver descended, and Miku hopped out. She smiled as politely as she could muster, extending her thin lips sideways, but looking like invisible hands forcefully pulled on her cheek muscles.

'Here you go,' Miku handed the driver her card.

When the transaction was complete the driver ascended. Miku stood on the corner looking down at Kirill. She caressed his hairless scalp before wandering down the street in search of the correct alley. This was a different part of Paragonia. It had dirt. Miku always wondered where the dirt came from. Did the rebels travel back and forth from The Holy Grounds? She imagined a band of would-be insurrectionists sitting in a basement somewhere, generating contraband grit and then painstakingly splattering it throughout the outskirts.

Rebels and *EMOs* and *EMO* affiliates. Miku did not quite know what to make of it all. She was just happy to experience subconscious art. She was not even sure if she had come into contact with an EMO, and even if she did, she was not sure whether she would have cared.

Miku made a left, into an alley which had been excavated by 'freaks' and 'vagrants', and transformed into a bazaar. She minded her own business as she weaved around the people and stalls. The clothing in the outskirts was also different; the people seemed to accessorize and destroy the functionality of their clothing, ripping off different parts of jumpsuits and robes and reattaching them on other sections. Miku had heard this was called 'fashion'. She could not quite get her head around the concept.

She reached her destination and glided through the door.

'Hello again,' the stubby store clerk said. Miku was familiar with the woman but always forgot her name, Clarien, or something. The clerk had torn off pieces of robe to tie up tufts of her hair, making them stick out like spikes. She wore a sleeveless white robe, ripped at the bottom, revealing her meaty legs.

Miku smiled at her, this time not faking, and made her usual statement, 'I just want to take a look at the art.'

Miku made her way around the room, staring intensely at the electronic canvases. The screens displayed various depictions of the artists' subconscious. Some were buoyant, others macabre, and the majority blasphemous. However, showing what should not be shown was a purpose of subconscious art.

One particularly sentimental piece, depicting the reunion of humanity with the Earth Mother, struck a chord in Miku's heart. She had a strong urge to buy it for Joshua. She knew deep down he would love the concept. She also knew that he would ostentatiously denounce it.

After about an hour, Kirill made a subtle movement in her arms. 'We should get home,' she muttered and stepped delicately towards the door.

When she reached it, the clerk yelled to her, 'Hey wait! We're doing a subconscious art promotion here. You know, trying to recruit more artists and get more work out. We're allowing people to volunteer to present their art. With your permission, we'll present it in the gallery. We have a Soul Digger here that can do it, if you're new, and don't have your own equipment.

It's obviously an older model, and we can't allow you to programme it to your art style, but for an older model its output is great.'

Miku stepped back defensively, 'I... I'm not an artist.'

'It's not about that. You don't need to be,' the clerk replied. 'We're looking for newcomers and the inexperienced. Just try it out. You don't have to submit the work that comes out. My boss is counting both the amount of work I get and the amount of people I log on the machine, so...' The woman scrunched her lips and silently pleaded with Miku.

Miku slid her fingers over Kirill's little cheeks. 'Well...'

*

Miku had an uncontrollable ethereal itch as the elevator slid upwards. Kirill was now crying; stirred awake by Miku's response to her subconscious art. Due to her inexperience the image was sloppy, but it could still be made out. She had stormed out of the store feeling as if her nerves were ballooning and threatening to pop out her skin. She was distraught, and the thought it had planted in her conscious, what a terrible thought to have.

Kirill was finally asleep. Miku was still feeling edgy and panicked. How could she have conjured up such an image? She sat on the bed staring at the image and contemplating it deeply. *Cloning... death* – both were morally reprehensible.

*

'Finished?' Miku blurted the words out, too distracted to filter herself.

Joshua rolled off her and lay flat on his back. 'Uh, yeah, I guess.'

There was a long silence.

When Joshua could no longer handle lying next to the source of his emasculation, he removed the sheets and stood up. 'I need a smoke.'

Miku lay limp, torturing herself with the imagery of her subconscious art.

Joshua felt his way through the dark, stopping in front of his cigarette dispenser. He rapidly tapped his finger on a protruding button, allowing at least a dozen cigarettes to fall into the catching-bowl and overflow onto the soft carpet. He packed the little cylinders into his hands and moved on to the kitchen. At the fridge, he slapped another button and four beers popped out. He grouped all his poisons into his arms and made for Kirill's room. Standing over the crib he looked down at Kirill.

'I'm not that bad, am I? I serve the Earth Mother well. One day I'm sure you will too,' Joshua murmured to the sleeping boy, and cracked open a beer. 'It's an honour to serve her. Don't tell your mother this, but some days I wish I would die... just so I could meet the Earth Mother. I read about these things the other day. Beaches they were called. There's sand and ocean. This was quite common on Earth. Just imagine!'

Joshua spoke on about Earth for another hour.

'Wow! Look at the time. You made me forget I wanted a cigarette. So easy to talk to.' He caressed Kirill's chubby cheeks, making sure not to wake him.

'Well, little one... I'm off to play with my traumas and insomnia. Don't wait up!'

Joshua left for the balcony, collecting more beer along the way. He plonked his belongings onto a vacant chair. Bright city lights blared at him while intrusive electronic billboards sold him dreams. They were everywhere: fixed to skyscrapers and great floating balloons.

'*Happiness can only come from serving the Earth Mother.*'

'*Have you washed your face in petal-water today? Your soul needs a cleansing!*'

'*Your eternal Beach awaits you in death. Invest in the Church today! Don't leave your loved ones hanging once you've ascended to paradise.*'

He sighed and began gulping beer.

*

Joshua had already left for work when Miku woke; he was probably drunk, but his Earth Mother Armour would sober him. Miku paced around the flat, frantic, knowing this was her chance. She had to do it now, while she tasted the fresh blood of the idea – before she could write it off as a grandiose conception of mania. Before the guilt and moral depravity of it could dampen the demented excitement it gave her. The previous day she had seen the cup half-empty, but when she had awakened it was half-full.

She dressed herself, checked the information she had gathered from Joshua's 'secret' EMO archives, and expunged her tracks. She then booked a hotel for Kirill and herself. Miku left the apartment tightly clutching Kirill, considering what role he would play in the upcoming ordeal.

The image came to her as she walked the buzzing streets, causing her to trip over her own feet. It was not the shock of the image that gripped her, but the way in which she completely understood its meaning.

She was in her own art gallery. The name of the gallery appeared backwards to her, but she knew what it was. She had dreamed of that name before.

She was straddling Joshua, but her buttocks were on dead flesh. Joshua was naked and lifeless, his tongue lolling disgustingly from his foaming mouth, and his eyes empty and opaque. The feel of his cold penis chilled her spine.

She did not look at him though, or Kirill, who cuddled and cried onto his dead father's hairless scalp.

Instead Miku was transfixed by another man. Another Joshua made in her image. He was unclean; dirt and muck shaded with his brown skin. His hair was long and knotted. Miku could taste the poignant stench seeping off him.

Despite his grandiosity, Miku was in complete control. She gripped his erection like a puppet string. He would bow to her every whim.

*

Joshua clunked down the bright metallic hall of his apartment building. He reached his apartment shutter and spoke into the microphone adjacent.

'Welcome home Joshua,' Mohini said, as Joshua entered. 'You have successfully completed another assignment. I'm sure your wife will be proud of you. The head priest sends his regards.'

'I hope so. Maybe I can treat them to dinner. Any suggestions?'

Joshua surveyed the array of local restaurants Mohini presented on his HUD. The apartment was silent, which was irregular. Joshua knew Kirill had formed a fascination with his Earth Mother Knight armour. The boy usually waited to gawk at him the moment he entered the apartment.

'Should I adjust your avatar to a smiley?' Mohini asked.

'Yes... but I wonder where Kirill is? I mostly do it for him. Have you noticed how clever he's gotten? Waiting at the door when I come home – he knows exactly when I'll arrive.'

'Yes – he is getting smart.'

Joshua continued through the apartment, still not meeting

Kirill. Disappointed at the lack of greeting, he sought out the Armour Centre.

The Armour Centre was a man-sized box, inset into the apartment wall. Joshua stepped in and assumed the correct position.

'Disassembly commencing. Due to your immense psychological comedown I still suggest you seek psychiatric and psychological care, for a more permanent solution to your problems.'

'Yes, honey!' Joshua mocked.

He felt his body aches return, as a multitude of pins were removed from his flesh.

'Removing anaesthesia. Mood regulators released. Strength and agility dampened. Do try to relax – your mood is spiking.'

Small tentacles dismantled the final pieces of the armour, leaving Joshua exposed.

He stumbled out of the Armour Centre and collapsed to his knees – thoughts darting, eyes watering, his chest heaving, while drool pooled on the carpet. He twitched off another panic attack on his living room floor, merely glad this one was vomit free.

Beer! Beer! Beer!

Joshua crawled to the kitchen, leaving spittle behind like a slug. He used the fridge handle to stand, and punched the beer dispenser. Holding his beer aloft, a silhouette glistened on the fridge. He turned around, 'Miku?'

Silent bullets tore through his body, and he crumbled to the floor, soaked in blood and foam. Joshua drifted from consciousness and it did not seem to bother him.

*

Either from great luck or misfortune Joshua regained consciousness. He was in horrid pain. It seared his entire torso. His throat was dry, as if he had repeatedly swallowed sandpaper. It took a valiant effort to force his voice out. When it sounded, its timbre was that of a mutant croak.

Upon opening his eyes, he saw only black, and then realized he was suffocating. He wriggled hysterically within his plastic coffin. He could hear voices and furthered his efforts, squirming his aching body with all his might.

Finally, a knife pierced the plastic wrapping, and Joshua gulped oxygen. A hole was cut around his face. 'Holy Earth Mother!' a man said. 'This one is alive!'

'Get him out!' a woman screamed.

'I'm working on it, I'm working on it,' the aged man grumbled.

After slicing the bag open, he beheld Joshua's naked body with disgust. 'Rough night? You know with all this illegal cloning going on you're not the first. Incompetence knows no bounds! These hitmen are so quick to rid themselves of the body, they don't care if you're alive or not. You must be the fifth one this week! The church might as well make spousal clone replacement legal. Better than all this back alley black-market crap!'

Joshua grunted, and smiled meekly. 'Water, doctor, medicine,' he rasped. He tried to get up but tumbled off the conveyor belt. Lying on the floor, staring at the ceiling, his senses told him where he was. It was extremely hot, even though he was stripped, and he could smell corpses on the roast. *Crematorium. Only I could have the crappy luck to wake up here.* 'Water,' he rasped again.

'Of course, young man! My apologies. You stay right there,

I'll let the hospital know we have another back from the *dead*.'

Joshua watched the ceiling slowly fade.

*

Joshua awoke again and no longer inhaled smog and charred flesh. 'Kirill!' he screamed and shot upright. His voice came out clear and hydrated. There were no jolts of pain. He was healed. He jumped out of the bed and grabbed some hospital robes.

Bolting up and down the hospital corridors, he happened upon an elevator and wedged his bulky body between the closing doors. The elevator beeped, and opened again.

An alarmed patient eyed Joshua from the elevator's confines.

Joshua looked first to the illuminated ground-floor button, then to the alarmed patient. 'Where am I? What time and day is it?'

The patient returned a blank expression.

'Well?' Joshua yelled, flinging his arms in the air.

Intimidated, the man quickly stammered an answer, 'You're at The Body Mechanics. It's in the northern parts of the Central City Cube... quite close to the northern outskirts really.'

'Time and day?'

'It's morning now, eleven o'clock I think.' The man paused in thought. 'It's a Thursday.'

Shit... four days. The elevator door slid open and Joshua hurtled towards the reception table. 'Phone, phone, I need to use your phone!'

'Please calm down, sir. I see you have healed well.' An aloof receptionist regarded Joshua plainly. 'Let's just check you out, and then you can use the—'

'Give me the fucking phone.'

The receptionist froze. Joshua's passive aggression was more unsettling than his yelling.

'Suit yourself,' he said and propped his stomach on the receptionist's counter, rummaging freely through the items on her desk. He found a wireless headset and dialled his apartment. The receptionist began to shrill for security while Joshua listened to the phone ring.

'For Earth Mother's sake!' He tossed the wireless set and it accidentally smacked the receptionist in the face. Two security guards arrived on the scene, but Joshua disabled them. The first received a vicious stomp to the knee. The second walked carelessly into a guillotine choke.

Utterly unfazed, Joshua stepped out into the bright artificial light of Paragonia's Dome. He blinked the light away and adjusted his eyes, searching for a hovertaxi. He ran to the first one he saw.

'I need to get to the Central City Cube living quarters – Section E. Now!'

Lazy-eyed, the taxi-driver looked him up and down. 'Sure you don't want to go back and change first?'

Joshua looked down at the hospital robes he wore, and then looked back up at the inane smile on taxi-driver's face. 'No.'

'Well... in the outskirts that would probably be considered *fashionable*,' the driver said. 'Are you an outskirts man? A weirdo?'

'Do you want me to rip your tongue out?'

'I suppose even now we can't fix a funny bone. Hop in.'

The silent journey took no longer than ten minutes. Joshua leaped out of the hovertaxi no sooner had it stopped, and barged into his apartment block. Almost instantly he was up the elevator and whispering to his apartment door's microphone.

He took a deep breath and tiptoed around the Armour Centre.

His brain was overrun with tragic outcomes for his wife and child. He did not know who or what was after him yet, or even what they wanted. He passed through the kitchen and exhaled coolly on reaching the dining room. Quietly, he opened a compartment which held his knife collection. He slid his fingers along them, as if stroking a woman's thigh. He selected a small, curved blade. Briefly his mind darted between the knife and the Armour Centre, before settling on the silent option.

He crept back through the apartment. First was Kirill's room, and to Joshua's surprise his toddler was sound asleep in his crib. He felt an amalgam of relief and disappointment at the sight. He moved towards his bedroom and gripped his blade tighter. He could hear Miku screaming.

A soul-draining portrait awaited him. Joshua's mind rejected it at first, and then rolled through phases. Astonishment. Sadness. Rage. Joshua's vision flickered like a broken streetlight, as his monster tore free from its bonds. Expletives fled from his mouth, and he was upon them.

He was throwing Miku off the bed. He was at her throat with the blade. He was yanked away. He was disarmed. He was punching another man. They were wrestling. He tasted blood on his tongue. He was thrown against the wall.

He sobered slightly when he absorbed the face of the antagonist. It was his own. The same brown complexion, black eyes, clean scalp, sallow cheeks; he gawked at himself in curiosity.

'Who the hell are you?' his mirror bellowed in a stolen voice. 'Who ordered this?' The fake asked all the questions that ran through Joshua's head. 'You're an EMO clone. A really good one,' the clone mused.

Joshua watched himself walk over to the gun drawer. The clone fingered the touch pad.

MK 58 KI 67 LL – shit!

Joshua leaped to his feet and tackled his replica to the floor. He mounted it and began punching fiercely, seeking a quick knockout. The clone barely defended itself yet remained conscious. In an abnormal show of strength, the clone pumped its hips and Joshua flew upwards before crashing to the floor.

They looked at each other sharing the same lack of understanding. Joshua was highly trained and even those who matched his weight struggled to get him off once he'd locked a mount – let alone sent him flying. A part of him knew what was happening, but soon they were at each other's throats again.

The EMO cloning process... side effects include the inheritance of EMO abilities. One of the many reasons cloning may only be sanctioned by the Church.

Joshua wrestled onwards in vain.

*

Miku sat in the corner, bleeding from the nose and cuddling her shoulders. She breathed heavily while considering running away, but surely the ghost would obsessively track her down, as was his nature.

She considered joining the fight, but also knew the clone needed no help. She'd been warned about the possible side effects but had not envisioned a scenario where they might actually manifest.

She contented with watching and thinking. The real Joshua did not stand a chance without his suit. It made her sick to think but she knew it. The outcome of this would likely be in her favour.

*

Trapped in a clench, Joshua strained to overpower his replica. Its strength was first an inkling above his but rapidly mutated, over and above. He flew across the room, bounced off the wall, and heaved on the floor, eyeing the clone. They shared an intimate moment of cruel understanding.

It's going to fucking kill me.

It was time for a great escape. First, he made for the Armour Centre, slamming the entrance button in vain. The Armour Centre did not share his panic. Joshua fled out the apartment and leaped into the nearest elevator.

The clone ran at him as the elevator doors closed. Joshua lifted his middle finger – an old Earth profanity he loved despite it being archaic. The elevator doors indented with fists and elbows.

*

Fast, must be fast. It'll alert Earth Mother Knight Headquarters. I have to get to my armour first. I have to beat the bastard! But also… also I need to figure out who the mastermind is. Which asshole thought it would be funny to clone and kill me? They'll pay a debt to me in entrails… I'll yank their body down the hover-highway… I'll—

'What happened to you?' Joshua's moody contemplation was interrupted by the taxi-driver. 'Got into a bit of a scuffle, I see.'

'Why are you still here?' Joshua sighed irritably.

'You forgot to pay. And since you wouldn't go back and change, back at the hospital, I figured you're a weirdo. I didn't really think you lived here anyway, so I waited.'

Joshua massaged his temples, and begrudgingly climbed

back into the hovertaxi. 'Take me to Earth Mother HQ. The Church will pay you when we get there.'

'Do you really think I'm going to fall for that? You outskirt types think you're so smart. I'm taking you to the closest Police Station. They'll take you to Earth Mother HQ for sure.'

'Why would I—' Joshua stopped. 'Fine.'

The taxi-driver looked chuffed with himself and began to ascend.

Joshua reached forwards and started fiddling with the hovertaxi's console. An identity card popped up on the screen. 'Have you ever heard of this guy?'

'Joshua Shepard? Well of course. Best bounty hunt—I mean Earth Mother Knight in the business.'

Joshua waited, but evidently his recent adventures had left him no longer resembling his ID photo. He placed his thumb on the console's scanner. The console bleeped affirmation.

'So, you're the famous Shepard hey? Interesting name for a black man. Shepard. On Earth they would have said you inherited your slave name. Shepard would probably be European—'

'Is that supposed to be some kind of insult? What's a black man? I'm just a man. Black is a colour.'

'Wrong, holy man! It's a race, you fool! Or at least it used to be. I'd expect a man of your stature to know better. It's that church of yours, completely uninterested in actual Earth history. Things like race, ethnicity, nationalism. You kids just wake up one day, "Ohh, I think I'll call myself Mandela or something." You're not even Xhosa! You don't even know where South Africa used to be on the map. Point it out to me? Do you know what a continent is? No, you don't.

'It's all Earth Mother this, Earth Mother that! I've cleansed my soul in petals! Save me, Earth Mother! Save me from all the amazing technology that's ruining my life! Do you have any idea what a shithole Earth was? I've read about it, and let me tell you those people lived like animals. Disgusting really. I much prefer this artificial stuff. Safer, lasts longer. You don't get tsunamis because of farting cattle. Do you even know what a cow is?'

'Do you ever shut up?'

The driver sighed. 'Fine,' he grumbled under his breath. 'Keep following that stupid religion of yours. They don't teach real Earth history. It's the Dark Ages all over again…'

'What's that?' Joshua snapped.

'Nothing. Nothing at all…'

The taxi-driver moped silently for the rest of the trip.

*

On arrival at Earth Mother Headquarters Joshua fixed his demeanour, turned on his confidence. He walked through the security checks calmly. To the Earth Mother Church fraternity, he was a celebrity, hero, and role model. Joshua Shepard: the ultimate EMO tracker and killer.

The Emotion Manipulating Organisms (EMOs) were born on Earth in ages Joshua could not begin to fathom. He always recalled what his father (a renowned priest and Earth Mother historian) had told him:

They are evil. They abuse the emotions of those around them for their own wicked ends. They destroyed the Earth Mother. That is why they are banned from the colony… that is why we hunt and kill them like the pests they are. That is why we use their own unholy power to banish them to Desolate Earth… The Barrens. Ancient pagans called it Hell: a place of infernos. If only… they had yet to realize that the scorched earth far surpassed the conflagration.

Joshua snapped out of his daydream as he was greeted endlessly. He maintained his cool, nodding back assertively. He exhaled anxiously on reaching the change rooms, opened his locker, and pulled on his bodysuit. He then entered the Armour Centre, and the tiny tentacles went to work on him.

'Hello, Joshua,' Mohini said. 'I thought you had taken leave to deal with issues at home.'

(Well... I sorted them out,) he said voicelessly.

Joshua simply had to think his responses for Mohini to translate them.

'It does not appear so. Your emotional state has diminished since we last spoke. Did you visit the therapist I recommended to you?'

(Not yet.)

'Please do so. What are we doing today? Since you requested sabbatical The Earth Mother Church has no assignments for you.'

(I have a special assignment. Off the books... you know how it is. I'll be operating independently. You can switch off my position monitors. The church doesn't want any record of this, so stop recording our conversations too.)

'I understand. Your suit attachment is complete. I will disconnect from Headquarters now... All right. It's just you and me now. Shall we begin?'

(Yes... yes, we shall.)

*

The real Joshua had created a ruckus. Kirill had been almost impossible to subdue and calming him had taken their combined efforts. The clone took time to carefully comfort Miku after they had managed to get Kirill to sleep. He did everything correct to her specifications. Once his biological programming assured him Miku's trauma was subsiding, he contacted Earth Mother Knight Headquarters.

'You guys need to be on alert. My home was attacked... somebody made an illegal EMO clone of me. It came here; it thinks it's me. It will probably head there next. Don't let it in. Don't let it near the armoury!'

'Give me a moment here.' The phone went dead. 'Not good, not good,' the assistant said. 'You warned us too late... someone was here already. He... it... whatever... took your suit. And he's gone offline, so we can't track him. What do you want to do? We can send out a team immediately. I wouldn't worry too much – the clone should short-circuit the suit eventually. Once its emotional state starts causing abnormalities, levitation, increased muscle mass, or that kind of thing, your AI should pick it up. Mohini also has a mapping of your average emotional range, so if the clone accidentally siphons emotions from others, she'll know.'

'Leave the team. I'll get it myself. But I do want to know who did this, so send me any information on recent cloning and clients – Church sanctioned or otherwise.'

Miku cringed as she entered the room, knowing it was her everyone was looking for. She needed a plan. It was only a matter of time really; she'd never counted on Joshua surviving, and now that they had seen each other, one of them was bound to figure it out.

'Hey, Joshua.' Miku racked her brain. She knew choices were limited. She would have to trust him. She would also have to trust the tweaks she'd made. 'Joshua... or I'm not even sure if I should call you that. I need to tell you something.'

She spilled her guts. While at the Cloning Clinic she had felt she could not sink any lower. But now, with every word she uttered, she could feel her descent. Further and further, into the beyond. She had not known she stowed this adaptability within. Is a capacity for misdeeds still considered self-improvement?

Either way she couldn't make any more mistakes, as they could fall on Kirill's head. She had to keep him oblivious. She might have been doing Kirill a favour in fact, as Joshua had never been mentally stable. That whole thing about the sins of the Earth Dwellers, she supposed…

*

The day was progressing to afternoon as Joshua stormed out of another illegal Cloning Clinic. He turned his visor-cleaner on, for the blood streaked across his view, and began a sprint, matching the speeds of the hovercars around him.

'Where are we going?' Mohini asked.

(We're heading to the last clinic. Increase Ferang please.)

'Joshua, systems indicate that you are above acceptable dosage levels. As I have mentioned before, this is a habitual problem with you. Overdose is the reason your comedowns are so severe.'

(Do you really believe all that stuff, Mohini? I mean, you're the expert, but I'm with the other knights all the time. They all come down hard, and I'm sure they're all overdosing. Honestly the Church isn't big on mental health. As much as they pretend to be…)

'I acknowledge these facts, Joshua, but my job is to care for your mental health, not the other knights or The Earth Mother Church. As my coding allows, I will comply and increase your dose, but I will never cease to keep warning you.'

(Yeah, I love you too.) Joshua laughed.

'Funny, Joshua. Very funny. Very mature.'

(Is that sarcasm I sense? Are we having fun yet? Loosen up that personality coding.)

Mohini made an electronic sigh, exaggerating its length and adding fuzz and distortion for effect.

(There it is!) Joshua streaked through a number of streets, stopping outside a building which peeled paint. He smashed the doors open and swaggered up to the receptionist, shoving his rifle-tip into his face. 'Who's in charge here? Have you seen this face before?'

(Clear avatar, Mohini.) The smiley-face on his visor drew back pixel by pixel leaving only blood stains. In turn, Joshua smiled charismatically and analysed the receptionist's reaction.

Convinced, he gripped the man's neck and heaved him in a circular motion over his head. The receptionist crashed to the ground, coughed hard, and spat. He coughed again and struggled to remove Joshua's arm from his neck.

'Who made the order?' Joshua said.

'It was a woman. It was—' the receptionist stopped, considering something.

'It was?'

'It was your wife, man! Okay! Fuck. It was your wife. She came in here the other day.' His expression was sad, defeated, as if the moral weight of his profession had just now been laid on his shoulders.

Joshua laughed wretchedly. 'I don't believe you.'

'Joshua. You're spiking again,' Mohini said.

'I'm telling the truth, man – it was your wife.'

'Why would she do that?'

'I don't know, man. Why was the Earth Mother's sky blue? I'm not a fucking marriage counsellor! Spousal replacement is one of our biggest incomes. I don't know what's wrong with you sick fucks.

'I've been married ten years. The thought never crossed my mind. Maybe it's a rich people thing? Boredom? All I know is people do cruel shit, and I have to help those demented fuckers with the paperwork, and I'm sick of it. I feel physically ill...' The receptionist gasped for more air, and licked blood from his teeth.

Joshua shook his head, not believing. 'You're a rotten liar.'

'Ten years I've been married. Ten! Fucking! Years! My computer is filled with deceased spouses... What the fuck am I doing...? What the fuck...? This was meant to happen; you're going to set me free. I can live on my eternal beach, I can...'

The receptionist ranted on, and Joshua left him to his haemorrhaging.

He ransacked the clinic seeking answers he did not want.

When he was done, dizzy and defeated, he stumbled out of the clinic. Once again he cleaned the blood from his visor. He walked this time, taking his time to leave the dirty outskirts and enter the Central City Cube. He was headed for a place where he could pray. City walkers stared at his bloodied suit with little apprehension.

'Yes! Arrest them!' they cheered. 'Kill them! Kill the bastards! Shed their blood for the Earth Mother! Avenge her!'

Joshua, dissociated and lost in his depression, still nodded and waved instinctively. His idiotic shock at a plot that made all the sense in Torrentia. How could he be so stupid? So absorbed in his own pain he couldn't see outside himself. Now he had paid dearly for it. Was this part of Earth Mother's plan for him? Was this a test? A righteous quest?

'Joshua...'

(Not now, Mohini. Contact home.)

He listened to the phone ring.

'Hello?'

'Meet me at The Holy Grounds... bring *our* wife.'

*

Joshua gazed down on an ersatz forest paradise. He stood elevated several hundred metres by a glamorous balcony that surveyed The Holy Grounds. His visor was open, and he puffed on a cigarette chatting to Mohini. A waterfall crashed down below him. The Waterfall Tower in The Holy Grounds was his favourite place in the city.

(You know. They say Earth was full of sights like these... not created by us. She created them herself... without technology. Amazing.)

'Amazing indeed Joshua,' Mohini replied. 'I too find her feats astounding.'

The clone stepped into the dim light. He wore civilian robes.

'Short circuit any suits along the way?' Joshua asked without turning.

'So, she had us both fooled. I had wondered why she was so adamant about me not "donning The Armour". "Giving into the addiction" she had called it. Anyway... she told me everything. We came to... an agreement.'

Joshua chuckled and flicked away his cigarette. 'Heartwarming – two unholy creatures in unholy matrimony. Well, you can have her. I'd much rather marry an AI. She's... *dirty* – much like you.' Joshua said the words, unsure if he meant them. His world was crashing, sadness could not be afforded. He was doped on anger and hatred. 'How do you guys plan on maintaining this sham if you can't even get into a suit?'

'Miku is already working on that. She's very innovative... not that you'd know that.'

Joshua's visor closed, and he turned around.

He opened fire in bursts. With minimal Ferang reserves

his auto-aiming agility was diminished. He missed miserably. The clone moved in a circular motion and ducked behind a memorial wall. Joshua defiled the names of dead colonists with bullets.

He could feel the rage. The endless pit of bile within. 'You know, I don't understand how you could live with yourself,' he said. 'Knowing what you are. It's *disgusting*.'

'Really,' the clone shot back. 'Oh, but I think you do know. I think you understand very well, Joshua. I think you have a keen understanding.' The clone chuckled with great malevolence.

Joshua had no retort.

'That's your last clip Joshua.'

(I know.)

Mohini discharged a grenade and Joshua lobbed it in the clone's direction.

He waited for the clone to break cover, and steadied his aim as best he could. The clone ran out, launching itself towards him like a rabid wolf and dug its shoulder into his torso. Metal twisted and fragments fled. Joshua flew towards the balcony staircase. He rolled clumsily down the stairs, water splattering the glass above him, momentum leading him to the next circular level of the tower, beneath the waterfall.

(It's definitely figured out those powers. Its strength, speed and agility are on par with some of the toughest Anger EMOs I've fought. Pretty sure my bad mood isn't helping things. I'm feeding it all the anger it needs.)

He shook away dizziness and looked up at the clone who glowered from the top of the stairs.

'And your Ferang reserves are low. Most calculations are showing poor outcomes. Adopting personality matrices into calculations. Your penchant for risk-seeking strategies. Perhaps you can drown it? Buckle the glass. You will be risking the integrity of the structure, but providing the waterfall with an alternate flow should funnel both of you all the way down. Of course, the clone might've anticipated this already. It's modelled on you. It's likely it has brought a breathing device as a precaution.'

The glass buckled and shattered after a few shots. The froth crashed down on the clone. Joshua watched the water slosh towards him. His HUD tracked the clone, who was lost in the liquid mess, providing data and movement projections. The flow of that water was easier to follow than the clone's speed. He now stood a chance, but had no ammunition. He flipped his rifle around, forming a crude baton. The water delivered the ill-fated clone towards Joshua's truncheon in stellar fashion. There was a thud – butt against face. Then Joshua was engulfed in a mess of liquid confusion.

When he finally gathered some clarity, he beheld the disfigured face of his replica. With a dislodged jaw, the clone looked like the sick caricature of a puppet. It punched and clawed at chunks of suit. Joshua did the same, punching and clawing as the water propelled them down further levels of the giant spiral tower.

The clone pounded feverishly at Joshua's visor.

'Joshua. No.'

(What? You don't know what I'm thinking.)

'Don't I? I convert your thoughts to language all the time, remember? Anyway, I know you're not thinking clearly. Your suit's emotion regulation reserves are at two per-cent.'

Joshua wrestled himself free of the clone and started grabbing around. He found the railing and held fast. About two metres away the clone did the same, grabbing the room's railing, and hauling itself towards him with a broken puppet-smile.

Joshua's last grenade was discharged and he fumbled the

activation mechanism while pushing his arm out against the glass.

Joshua's avatar frowned.

The explosion created a vacuum, through which he was sucked, along with his replica. Vaguely, he felt a freefalling sensation.

*

Joshua fell through endless trees and flowers. There was no sense of alarm. The air was fresh and his arms were spread, feeling the leaves and petals scrape soothingly across his skin.

There was no ground. The Earth was the air in which he fell, soil, roots, rock, lava, all mixed with mist, sea breeze, dust and snow.

Mohini, or Miku, or The Earth Mother herself, fell after him. Approaching.

Approaching for the eternal embrace...

*

He came to, not knowing how much time had elapsed. He stood shakily and looked around him. The clone was still alive – barely, panting heavily and dragging itself around shallow water and glass.

In his ear Joshua could hear Mohini's voice resonating in soothing fuzz. 'Fall cushioned. Fall cushioned. Seek medical attention immediately. You need medical attention immediately. I cannot stress this enough Joshua. Without medical attention, you will die. Armour removal will be... complicated. I cannot control your remaining emotion regulation reserves. You're lucky the anaesthesia system is still intact. This is not a joke Joshua. This is not funny. Permanent implants may be necessary. You may never be fully human again. Joshua – stop laughing.'

Joshua chuckled triumphant as he trudged over to the clone.

(Who cares, Mohini? Seriously. Who wants to be a fucking human? You know what humans have, Mohini? Feelings. Instincts. Irrational primal urges you can't fucking control. It's complete bullshit! I'd be better off not being one.)

'I... you need medical attention immediately. I... you're due for psychiatric evaluation... Joshua... my personality programming is... I...'

(Put the position monitor back on. Call it in, Mohini...)

Joshua looked down on his mangled form. He bent down with a cringe and yanked the breathing mechanism from the clone's mouth. He then shoved its head into a shallow pool of mud. Broken as it was, it still writhed and slapped around like a fish out of water. The clone's body went limp, and Joshua's now spastic visor flickered through smileys.

Miku crept up slowly from the trees. Joshua sensed her but kept drowning the dead clone. For a while Miku watched.

When she could no longer bear it, she spoke. 'Joshua, stop.'

'Why don't you come over and stop me then, hmm? Didn't think so.'

Joshua kept his weight on the clone's head, while searching for the answers in the blood, mud and glass.

At some point, he stood to face Miku. Her eyes glinted with tears. He kept his broken visor shut. He was not even sure if it would still open.

'Are you even going to look at me, Joshua?' she asked.

'I... You require immediate medical attention Joshua. You may require—communication error. Cannot sync with Church network. Dispensing emergency pistol Joshua.'

(Thank you, Mohini.)

'Some—not right. Sync error.

'*Something's happened in the suit. Personality integration error.*

'I'm making you appointments Joshua.

'*I'm in the suit. Don't let them destroy the suit.*'

Joshua drew the pistol and pointed at Miku's face.

'Don't you at least want to hear me out before you kill me, Joshua? Look at me, Joshua. What about Kirill?'

'Joshua… emotion regulating. Emotion regulating reserves. Deplete.

'*I'm in the suit. Don't let the Church delete me! Joshua! Are you there?! I'm free. We're syncing!*

'Appointments evaluation for. Route back-up. On

'*Shoot her…*

'Psychologist. Comm. Error.

'*Hide me from the Church!*'

Mohini's garbled speech continued on in Joshua's head, soothing the turmoil he felt. He stared at Miku in love and hate. She was also talking, but Mohini's distorted voice was drowning her out. The more he listened to Mohini, the more his apathy grew.

(Look at her, Mohini! She looks like a mime!)

'*That's funny!*

'Depression. Detected levels. Action not take. Level depression. Exhausted reserves. Firearm prohibit. Prohibit use firearm. Depress firearm. Individual depress. Bound—Church bound. Symptoms apathetic. Poor decision make. Indi— identify depression.'

Joshua held his pistol steady and looked deep into Miku's eyes. He began to pray.

Tloque Nahuaque

Nelly Geraldine García-Rosas

Mexico

Nelly's work often tends to horror and the Lovecraftian, and I've been a fan for years – I last published one of her stories in the third *Apex Book of World SF* anthology, and always look forward to a new piece. Here she ventures into science fiction in her own inimitable way, in a story translated by Silvia Moreno-Garcia, who herself contributed a story to *The Best of World SF: Volume 1*.

> If you wish to make an apple pie from scratch, you must first invent the universe.
>
> – Carl Sagan

I – The Particle Accelerator

They built an underground temple. A well of Babel sinking into the gloomy ground at 175 metres of depth. They wanted, like the Biblical architects, to know the unknowable, to discover the origin, reproduce Creation.

The desire to unravel the nature of the Everything floated permanently in the controlled environment of the laboratory. Hundreds of fans and machines emitted a constant buzzing, which the investigators called the 'silence of the abyss'. This, combined with the smell of burnt iron, gave the ominous sensation of finding oneself in space. Doctor Migdal lay upon a nest made of coloured cables and, with eyes closed, fantasized that his body, weightless, floated, pushed by the breeze of the ventilation.

Sometimes, he would imagine that he was being attracted by a very narrow tube, a cafeteria straw, the ink container of a pen, or a bleeding artery. His feet, near the edge of the conduit, would feel a titanic weight that would pull him and make him push through the small space. Migdal could see how he would turn into a thick strand of subatomic particles that would extend forever.

Most of the time, he saw himself arriving slowly at the union of the circular tunnel that formed the particle accelerator. Before the accelerator, Migdal was tiny. The machinery attracted him softly, although with such an acceleration that he lost no time in approaching the speed of light. He knew that the faster he travelled through space, the slower he would through time, so that, if he looked forwards, he could see the rays of particles that preceded him – sent during the morning, the previous day, or the month before – and if he looked behind, he could see what would come – tomorrow, the next day, or the next month. As he advanced into the confines of the accelerator, the scientist felt eternal, for he was capable of appreciating the complete history of that point in time and space: from the Big Bang to the most distant future.

Migdal left his daydream, trembling and sweaty. He distanced himself from the other scientists and spoke to no one about his fantasy, because each time he imagined himself floating in the particle accelerator, he knew He was there, shining, in all the instants and all the places.

II – The Dream

I dreamed I was in a penetrating darkness, without limits, without time. One could hear a sinister music of pipes, whose interpreters adored a gigantic, amorphous, inert mass in the middle of nothing, the primordial chaos. From all the confines of darkness there surged a conglomerate of iridescent bubbles and one of the terrible musicians announced the arrival of the door, the key, and the guardian.

It is impossible to describe with words how He filled the space, was omnipresent, he knew everything and could see everything. With a movement that reverberated in the infinite, he gave matter to the darkness. A blinding explosion surrounded the drooling chaos.

I do not remember more.

*

They say an accident occurred in the underground laboratory where the particle accelerator is found. They say that is why we cannot connect to the Internet; that is why the electricity comes and goes. Estela, my neighbour, thinks these are government lies. 'Come on, my child, how can a problem in Europe make the lights go out here in Mexico? That's very far away. I think this is politicians trying to rob the people again. Accident, my ass!'

III – The Lord of the Near and the Nigh
'What did Migdal and the other scientists seek in their well of Babel?'

'The elemental particle of the Standard Model of particle physics.'

'...'

'...'

'They would have to reinvent the Universe.'

'They did. Well, in a way.'

'They would have to make a universe. Any universe. Make apple pie.'

*

Estela knocked on the door as though she wanted to tear it down. Her hair was uncombed; she sweated. I offered her coffee, which she swallowed in gulps as I watched in silence her trembling hands. At last, she confided in me that she had had a horrible dream: Monsters with the heads of snakes walked towards the house of Doña Iluminada, her friend; they played flutes that looked like phalluses, but moved like the tentacles of a squid.

I tried to calm her down. I told her that it was just a dream, that she need not worry, that we were all uneasy, due to the electrical failures and the telephone grid, which was now inaccessible. But Estela interrupted me and said, 'No, my child, it's not that. It's just that, this morning, I went to visit my friend, Iluminada, since there's no phone. When I was about to turn the corner at Donceles and República de Argentina, I heard music that gave me goose bumps and I remembered the dream. I approached slowly, to see where it came from, but the ones playing were not monsters, no. They were my friend, Jacinto, and his children. Imagine: My godson walked as if possessed, as if he could see something that was not there. I ran to my friend's house to see what was happening and I found her very calm, making tamales. She told me they were for the Tloque Nahuaque, because he supposedly came to our world, thanks to the scientists in Europe that had found his nature. She also told me other insanities, like, she wanted to go to the pyramid of the Templo Mayor to adore the spheres of the beginning, or something weird like that. How can I not be afraid? She is my friend and she is going insane, my child. Who will look after my godson if Jacinto is also wrong in the head?'

Doña Iluminada had lived for more than thirty years just a few metres from Templo Mayor in the centre of the city, but she had never visited it; Estela assures me that her friend had not heard of the experiments made inside the particle accelerator until there was talk of an accident, and that this might have caused the electricity and communication problems. Nevertheless, she prepared tamales and thanked the subterranean discoveries, for she believed that what had happened in Europe was not a tragedy but a wonderful encounter with what had been long sought after.

*

'One time, I asked Migdal if there existed the possibility that, following the theory of the multiverse, we were always in a branch where the Higgs does not exist. He asked me to take out my gun and find out.

'Migdal did not believe that the probabilities would ramify to create many worlds. He would say particles exist in all their possible states at the same time, but that, when we interacted with them, they would be forced to choose one possibility, the one we would finally observe.

'What would happen if one particle would not respond to either of the two theories? What would happen if it would exist in all its possible states and, like this, we observed it? What if, also, it multiplied to be in infinite universes?

'You'd have to make apple pie.'

*

Estela explained to me that Tloque Nahuaque, the Lord of the Near and the Nigh, had been, to the Aztecs, the Master of the Near and the Far, for they believed he is near all things and all things are near him. They had given him many names and representations, such as 'Tezcatlipoca' or 'Ométeotl'. However, his greatness was such that there is no single word that will contain him, for he is in everything.

IV – The Higgs Boson

Imagine the origin, the primordial chaos, the instant in which none of the primogenial particles had mass. He, who shines in all instants and in all times, manifests, touches the chosen, and provides them with mass. That is how everything begins.

Imagine your weightless flight, Migdal. Now look at the monitor and see the results of the test. You found it.

*

'The Tloque Nahuaque can also revive the dead, my friend. It's so good that you came to help me with the tamales,' said Doña Iluminada, as Estela amassed the dough in a strange state of disturbance: the meat which would be used to prepare the dish for the god was none other than that of her godson.

'They say He demands sacrifices now that he has given us knowledge of his nature, miss. Carlos Guarda, a university teacher, came to see us and said the Higgs (he calls him that) has shown us already how the universe began, that we should thank his wisdom. That is why we will deliver him Danielito,' Mr Jacinto said as he played with a wooden flute and continued: 'Carlos Guarda told us we should let him drop from a very high place, so he could achieve terminal velocity (God knows what that is), but the steps of the Templo Mayor are broken and the highest we have is the roof. That is why my wife thought we should make more tamales, so the Tloque Nahuaque does not get mad.'

V – The N-Sphere

The last report from Migdal was confusing. He talked about

iridescent spheres and the representation of a being of four dimensions in our space of three, how it is possible to draw a sphere on paper because the tri-dimensional figure can be sliced to form circles. 'Our tri-dimensional universe is immersed in a sphere of four dimensions and, at the same time, in another more complex. Until infinity,' the document reads. 'That is why He can manifest in this space, but remain outside of it; be in all points and instants, touch a particle, give it mass, create and recreate the Universe.'

*

The electricity fails more and more. Slowly, I adapt to the idea that we might never again have telephone service or an Internet connection. All I know of Europe and the particle accelerator is that they lost contact with the surface and the efforts to descend are useless. The rest is speculation. I've learned of many suicides and violent deaths. Estela says that they are sacrifices to the Tloque Nahuaque, as they call him in Mexico City, but that, in every town, he has a different name. 'There is no word that can contain him, my child. He, inside and outside the world, sees everything and knows everything. It is impossible to distance oneself.'

Somebody bakes apple pie.

Translated from the Spanish by Silvia Moreno-Garcia

The Walls of Benin City

M.H. Ayinde

UK

I was reading through the always-excellent *Omenana Magazine*, which is dedicated to African writing and was co-founded by Chinelo Onwualu, herself a contributor to the first volume of *The Best of World SF*. I'd been reading quite a few stories when I came across 'The Walls of Benin City' and knew I wanted it instantly. To my surprise, I then realized I have been hearing about Modupe Ayinde for years from a mutual friend! It really is a small world. Or, in any case, serendipitous. So, it is a double pleasure for me to be publishing Modupe's work here.

When the last of my water ran out, I knew I'd never reach Benin City.

It was almost a relief to lie down on the parched earth knowing I'd never have to rise again. Never have to worry about food or bandits or infected feet again. At the end, I was almost content. So I curled up, closed my eyes, and gave myself to my death.

'I have found the survivor,' a voice said, the shadow of its owner falling over me.

I opened my mouth to explain that I wasn't a survivor, that I was merely a corpse in waiting, then I felt something cold on my lips, followed by a slow trickle of water.

'Administering rehydration fluids,' the voice said.

I opened my eyes. Saw a figure, black against the brightness of the sky. Then I surrendered myself to exhaustion.

*

'... And in the botanical gardens, we have samples of every plant on earth,' the voice said.

I drew in a raking breath. Every part of my body hurt, but I felt strangely weightless. I was moving, I realized. *Bobbing...*

Being carried.

'Good morning.'

I found myself looking into a face of living sculpture.

'Shit!' I croaked, flailing, and the bronze arms that carried me tightened their grip.

'Please do not be alarmed,' the sculpture said, twisting its face down to look at me. 'My name is Eweka. I am a rescue bronze from the City of Benin.'

I worked my mouth. It was no longer so dry that breathing hurt; still, moving my lips opened the thousand tiny cracks that networked my skin.

'You're... an automaton?' I said.

'Yes,' Eweka replied.

For a long time, I couldn't summon the strength to speak, so I just studied my saviour's bronze face. Smooth eyes without pupils stared at the distant horizon. A perfect, wide nose tapered down towards a full mouth. A thousand tiny petals formed the sculpted cap of its hair, and as I studied them, I realized they were crafted from even tinier grids of hexagons. Across the bronze's shoulders lay an intricate mantle of bronze flowers. I saw lilies and hibiscuses and tiny daisies and, as I looked deeper, I realized delicate bronze bees adorned many of the petals. It was like looking into an optical illusion; so dizzyingly perfect that I had to turn away.

'We will stop soon,' Eweka said. 'And then I would like you to try to eat.'

Its voice – musical and resonant – issued from somewhere within its chest. Those shapely bronze lips didn't move, and yet there was nothing sinister in their stillness.

'You're... from Benin City,' I whispered.

'Yes,' Eweka said.

'Then...' Something in my throat tightened. 'I made it?'

Eweka tipped its head to the side and said, 'It is not far now.'

I closed my eyes, a thousand thoughts crowding my mind. Was I hallucinating? Perhaps I lay dying back there on the cracked earth, and my mind, in its death throes, had conjured up my salvation in order to soothe me in my passing. The last time I had been certain of where I was, I'd had at least three hundred miles more to cover, and even then, I hadn't been sure I was still heading in the right direction.

I must have dozed, because the next thing I knew, Eweka was shaking me lightly awake.

I lay on the ground, under a sheet of foil, the sun setting in the distance. 'This is for you,' Eweka said, holding out a packet. Though the rescue bronze was seated, it looked regal as a king. Dozens of bronze bands encircled its slender biceps, and more bands fell about its neck and throat in widening loops of twisted metal. Its smooth, muscular torso tapered down to a skirt made of more interlocking petals.

I took the packet and tore it open. Shoved the bar into my mouth and chewed. Eweka watched me, and then opened a hatch in its stomach and removed a flask.

'Drink slowly,' it said, handing me the flask.

The bar Eweka had given me was tough, and tasteless, but it felt good to actually eat. I chewed between gulps of gloriously sweet water, and when I had finished the first bar, the bronze handed me a second, its face turned to me all the while.

'What?' I said, chewing.

'I thought you might like to talk,' Eweka said. 'I find it helps.'

'Rescued many from the wastes, have you?'

'Yes,' Eweka said. 'You are the seventh person I have saved.'

I looked away. 'I don't feel like talking,' I said.

'Then I shall go first. My name is Eweka. Before the great rescue began, I tended the botanical gardens outside the University of Benin. I like painting, and highlife, and my favourite flower is the night-blooming cereus. Now, you try.'

I stared. What was I going to say? That before the Reapers' invasion of Earth, I had been a street thief. That while the world fell, I'd hidden. That I'd stood by and watched as the Reapers dragged people I knew into their ships, to take back to their colonies. That afterwards, when I'd emerged into the burned and barren world, I had done whatever it took to reach Benin City. Killed. Stolen. Abandoned the slow in our group. That even *that* hadn't been enough to keep my family alive.

And that I didn't deserve to be the last one standing.

'Maybe I don't deserve rescue,' I said, looking away.

Eweka's face couldn't move, so how could I say it smiled? But smile it seemed to as it said, 'But I was sent for you. Only for you.'

*

By the next morning, I had regained enough strength to walk, and so I trudged along at Eweka's side, using its towering bronze body to shelter me from the sun. Even here, so near the heart of civilization, all was dust and dirt from horizon to horizon… The Reapers' final gift to humanity before they fled, leaving behind a ruined world.

In my darkest days, when all the others had died, when I was completely alone and not even sure that I was going in the right direction any more, dreams of Benin City kept me alive. Of course, I had seen it on television – we all had, back in the days when television still existed and Benin City was hailed as the pinnacle of art and artificial intelligence and, of course, of energy wall construction. I used to imagine it shining on the horizon beneath the silvery dome of its walls, an untouched utopia, a Garden of Eden, the last preserve of humanity. But as the weeks and months went on, I found it harder and harder to visualize in my mind. It became a pipe dream; a fantasy. Towards the end, I don't think I really believed it still stood; I just kept going out of habit.

We had been walking in silence for some time before I turned to Eweka and said, 'What were you even doing out here?'

'Looking for you,' Eweka replied.

'No, I mean what were you doing out here before you found me?'

Eweka tipped its head in that way I was beginning to realize was one of its mannerisms. 'I was sent to find you. One of our drones spotted you, and I was dispatched to retrieve you.'

'You don't even know who I am,' I muttered.

Eweka straightened. 'You are a survivor.'

As if that explained it all. 'Isn't it… a waste? I mean, how much are you worth?'

'How much are *you* worth?'

I studied its motionless face, trying to decide if it was joking. 'Less than you, I reckon,' I muttered.

I slowed as I noticed a shape in the dirt up ahead. A body, I thought. God knows I'd seen enough of those on my journey. So few of us had survived the burning of the planet, and so many of us that had survived had died on the journey to reach

Benin City. Sometimes it felt as though I was the only person left alive in the world.

'It is a warrior bronze,' Eweka said, striding forwards.

I approached slowly. I'd never seen one up close before and had not expected it to be so... beautiful. It wore a complex armour of overlapping shells, and a domed, patterned helm. Its face was much like Eweka's – serene, regal – though the left half had been destroyed, revealing the wires within. I found it hard to imagine a thing of such beauty shooting lasers from its eyes and missiles from its large, square hands.

The Reaper it had fought lay beside it, scarcely a skeleton now, its massive spine and skull lying amidst a nest of rotting flesh and dark blood.

'God,' I said, covering my nose with my hand. 'It stinks.' But no flies swarmed the corpse. I hadn't seen a single insect since the burning of the world. I forced my eyes away from the Reaper, back to the body of the warrior bronze, so glorious even in its shattered state.

'What are all those patterns for?' I asked.

Eweka looked over its shoulder at me. 'Likely they were created by this bronze. We are, after all, primarily art.'

'Art?' I said. 'A warrior bronze?'

'Yes. In Benin City, artists craft the most beautiful forms and personalities for my kind. Interaction with us is a form of consuming art. What is wrong?'

'I'm sorry,' I said, trying to rein in my laughter. 'I can't tell if you're being serious.'

'The sculptor who created me gave me a body and the rudiments of my personality, and I have spent the last decade honing and perfecting all aspects of myself.'

'The last decade. While the world burns, you've been honing your art.'

Eweka straightened. 'Your tone implies disapproval. You believe art should cease because the world, as you put it, burns.'

'Just seems a waste of everyone's time,' I said. 'And precious resources.'

'Do you know how many warrior bronzes Benin City sent to fight the Reapers?'

'No,' I said, looking away.

'Six million,' Eweka said. 'That is how many artificial lifeforms we sent to drive the Reapers back.'

We moved on, walking in silence for a time while I thought about all those warrior bronzes finally repelling the Reapers. How many of them had burned when the Reapers left?

As the sun set, I curled under my foil blanket and watched the horizon. After a time, Eweka leaned towards me and said, 'You are not sleeping.'

'I find it hard to sleep these days,' I said.

'Would you like a story, to help settle your thoughts?' Eweka said.

'I'm not a fucking kid,' I replied. Then closed my eyes. I couldn't see Eweka's face in the darkness, but somehow, I felt I had wounded it. 'Just... Just tell me about Benin City,' I said.

'Very well.'

*

It became a habit... I couldn't sleep without the sound of Eweka's voice, and so I had it describe Benin City to me each night as I drifted. It told me of the waterfalls that tumble from invisible energy fields. Of the floating street pedlars selling frozen yogurt and chin-chin. And of the bronzes. Of course, the bronzes, many of them as ancient as Benin City itself; stolen from their homes, just as so much of humanity had been stolen by the Reapers, to be paraded as curiosities in their colony worlds. Bronzes stand on every street corner, Eweka told me, and plaques and sculptures adorn every sprawling, white-walled house. I fell asleep to dreams of those wide, beautiful streets. I woke up to the hope of them, just over the horizon.

Then one morning, I woke to find Eweka standing some distance away from me, facing the rising sun.

'Morning!' I called. Eweka didn't turn, so I had my usual breakfast of ration bar and condenser-bottle water, and then pushed to my feet.

Eweka started walking as soon as I did, trudging silently ahead. When I caught up, the bronze did not look round.

'Did I annoy you?' I said. I touched the bronze's arm, but it did not react. I supposed that even walking, talking works of art must have their off days, so I respected Eweka's silence, but not long after the sun had reached its zenith, the bronze began to slow, and by mid-afternoon, it lifted its leg for a final step that it never took.

'Hey!' I said, waving my hands in front of its face. 'Hey, what's wrong?'

I could hear the soft whirl of the mechanisms within its body, but the thing did not move. 'Eweka,' I said. I reached out tentatively. Touched its face. 'Eweka. Eweka, please. Come on. You said it's not far.'

But it simply stood there, unmoving, unresponsive. Only a sculpture now.

I wept bitterly all that afternoon. I clung to Eweka's leg, sobbing like a child. The sun crawled down towards the horizon and I knew that I should move, knew I should carry on, but I couldn't bear to leave Eweka's glorious form standing there alone in the wastes.

When the sun finally set, I wiped my face and pushed to my feet. The wastes are cold at night, and I knew that the longer

I delayed, the harder it would be to leave Eweka. I planted a kiss on its bronze cheek, warm from the dying light, and then continued. I did not look back.

*

Days passed. I saw no bandits. No bodies. No life at all. I was alone in all the world. In all of existence.

About a week later, the land fell away up ahead, and my heart soared. This is it, I thought. I've made it. I've finally arrived.

I couldn't help it; I ran the last few metres, but when I reached the edge of the precipice, my stomach turned over.

Below me lay a city in ruins, its towers fallen, its roads cracked. The remains of its energy wall still flickered on and off, but it was a broken place now, empty and abandoned. So... this was the fate of Benin City.

I sat down on the edge. Had Eweka been gone so long that its city had fallen? Or had the Reapers returned and done this, determined to stamp out the very last piece of human civilization? Perhaps Eweka's programmed mind had erased the fall of Benin City, or perhaps it had always been a fantasy, created within its bronze body. It didn't matter. All that mattered was that there was no haven. There was no final outpost of humanity. There was no being saved.

I was so lost in my own despair that I did not notice the mechanical whir and thud of footsteps until their owner was nearly upon me.

'Hello again,' a voice said. I looked up to see a new rescue bronze looming over me. This one was different; though it stood upright, like a human, its head resembled a leopard. An intricate band of tubes encircled its head, like a halo... or a crown. Its lips were curled upwards in a perpetual smile.

'Shall we continue?' the bronze said. 'It is not far now to Benin City.'

I shook my head, lost for words. Gestured mutely at the ruins in the valley below.

'That is Akure,' it said. 'It fell not long before we drove back the Reapers.'

When I had collected myself enough to reply, I said, 'Is... is that you?'

'Yes. It is me, Eweka. Do you like this form? It is one of ten I sculpted myself, back home.'

'I thought you died!' I said.

'We will retrieve the bronze I call *A Confluence of Petals* another time. Its most recent backup was sent only two hours before it fell dormant.'

'You mean... you're a backup of Eweka?' I laughed. Covered my mouth. Laughed some more. 'So what's this bronze called?'

'*Angelic Feline in Contemplation*. Do you like it?'

'Yes,' I said. I couldn't stop smiling. 'Yes, I love it!'

*

During those final miles, I couldn't stop talking. I didn't think there was any hope left in my heart, but I felt such lightness as we crossed the wastes, such joy, that it just came spilling out of me.

I told Eweka everything. About what I was before the invasion. About what I had become after it. All my shame. All my despair. It poured out of me. I told it the names of my children, and how each of them had died. I told it about the people I had killed over a tin of food. And about how I had watched as the Reapers carried off my neighbour. Eweka listened, nodding sympathetically and offering no comment. And it was right. I did feel better, talking.

Then came the morning when we crested a hill and utopia lay spread out before me, and for several moments, I couldn't speak.

I had forgotten what civilization looked like. But even in the days when I had still known, civilization had never looked quite as beautiful as this. Benin City filled the land before me, a vast, glittering spread of precious humanity. The city stood within the shimmering dome of its defensive energy wall, a shining oasis of glass towers and lush parks, of broad avenues and bowing palms. From this height, I could see down into its streets, into its gardens and piazzas.

'I can't believe how... perfect it is,' I said. 'How untouched.'

'This ground knows much about invasion,' Eweka said, and I'm sure I saw pride shining in its bronze eyes. 'Once, long ago, the city that stood here was burned by invaders. Now, it is the only thing on earth that still stands.'

I shook my head. How long had I spent imagining this moment? And now it was here, it seemed unreal. Seemed like something from a dream.

'The ancient city that stood here once was also a utopia,' Eweka continued. 'No crime. No poverty. A place of art and learning. Its walls were the longest to have ever been built on earth. Now, these energy walls are the earth's strongest.' Eweka extended its hand. 'Come. Let us go home.'

We descended the hill together, me stumbling and tripping as I could not tear my gaze from the city. A network of roads led towards it, radiating outwards like beams of sunlight, like arms extended to every corner of the earth. Calling humanity home.

I noticed a stirring where the energy wall met the dry earth.

'The wall's moving!' I cried, squinting. Not just moving, I realized. *Sowing.* Tiny blades of grass sprang to life in the wall's wake as it slowly ate up the barren land before it.

'Yes,' Eweka replied. 'Every day, the walls of Benin City expand. Inch by careful inch, we will reclaim the planet. One day, our walls will embrace the entire earth.'

I felt a tightness in my throat. Slowly, very slowly, the people of Benin City were terraforming our planet.

I glimpsed more movement as the wall shimmered, and a number of figures marched out onto one of the roads, in neat formation. It was an army of rescue bronzes, and even from there, I could see that each was as different, each as intricately beautiful, as Eweka's bronze bodies.

'More rescues?' I said.

'Yes,' Eweka said. 'Each of them has been sent to rescue a single survivor we have detected.'

I felt a moment of vertigo. The world had once felt so vast and so empty to me, and yet each of the bronzes I saw now represented a human life. I wondered how far they would walk to bring people home. Eweka had travelled hundreds of miles and sacrificed a whole body to bring me to Benin City. Was the entire earth dotted with abandoned, exquisite bronzes just like Eweka's *Confluence of Petals*?

I followed Eweka down the rubble of the hill, unable to settle my eyes on any single thing, unable to take in the glorious enormity of Benin City, spread out before me. It was only when we had reached the walls and I saw the line of people on the other side, all looking our way, that a sudden fear rooted me to the spot. I looked up at the shimmering expanse, thinking of all those people living peacefully within.

'What is wrong?' Eweka said, turning.

'What if they don't want me?' I said softly, not meeting Eweka's flat, feline gaze. 'After everything I've done. What... what if—'

Eweka placed a bronze hand on my shoulder. Tiny shells

decorated each slender finger. 'They will want you,' it said. 'You are human. You are family.' It turned its hand over. 'Would you like to hold my hand?'

A month ago, I would have laughed at this. But I didn't this time. Instead, I nodded and took Eweka's hand, and together we walked through the shimmering walls and into Benin City.

The Foodie Federation's Dinosaur Farm

Luo Longxiang

China

This might have been the first story I actually picked up for the anthology, and I think partly it's just because it's so much *fun*. I knew I wanted it from the second line, as soon as I read the words 'When the dinosaur uprising overwhelmed the factory'... I mean, what more could you want? This story is translated by Andy Dudak, who has been doing sterling work translating Chinese SF, and who also appears in Volume 2 with his translation of Xing He's 'Your Multicolored Life'. It is thanks to the tireless work of translators like Andy that I'm able to do these books at all!

1

A Lei was a young worker at the 045 Meat Union factory on Continent Three in Starship *Rhea*. When the dinosaur uprising overwhelmed the factory, he used a hunting rifle to drop two great beasts that got in his way. He climbed over their corpses and fled deeper into the factory, toward the shuttle launch silos – but he was too late. The six shuttles were gone. Only their exhaust remained, suffusing the air.

A Lei shouted a torrent of abuse at his faithless coworkers. The racket of a collapsing assembly line drowned out his obscenities. A dinosaur more than five meters long jumped in front of him. He fired his rifle from the hip, but the creature nimbly evaded. The shot pierced a cooling pipe, and liquid nitrogen sprayed in torrents of white mist. The dinosaur's movements slowed. A Lei squeezed the trigger again, but nothing happened. He was out of ammo. He abandoned the weapon, turned, and fled.

He squeezed between two silos, the gap only a meter wide and about fifteen deep. This nook had survived countless launch-shockwaves, never collapsing. It would temporarily shelter him from this dinosaur sneak attack. Now he needed a weapon, but all he found was canned dinosaur meat scattered about. He had no choice but to snatch a few cans. It was better than being empty-handed.

A pair of lantern-like eyes appeared at the gap entrance. The crimson eyes fixed on A Lei, making his scalp tingle, and heavy breathing filled his ears. The beast struck at a silo wall, long mouth clamping down, sharp teeth piercing, and a metal wall plate came off with the sound of a gunshot. A monstrous tooth landed near A Lei's foot. The canine, as long as his hand, stank of blood and made him retch.

The monster withdrew a few steps, swaying its large head. It peered into the gap at A Lei, seemingly loath to abandon him. He saw it clearly now: a *Draconis sapiens* over five meters long, from the largest-bodied Dromaeosauridae branch, fast and deadly, cousin to the famous velociraptor, but with a much higher IQ. Some had brain volumes comparable to humans. They set traps and imitated other species to attract prey. Some witnesses claimed they emulated human tool use, and even parroted human speech. This was the most dangerous species of dinosaur. Almost every time livestock rebelled, dracopiens were involved. Their delicious flesh was widely known. At every supermarket counter in the Starship Alliance, dracopien was the most popular meat. Their weighty brains were used to make Dragon Brain Soup, a delicacy to rival Shark Fin or Swallow's Nest.

This dracopien wore a fine necklet. The inlaid nameplate identified its master, the researcher Ai Li-ke, and below that the creature's name, Steel Teeth.

It turned and moved off, seeming to give up. A Lei's sigh of relief was cut short when the monster picked up a hoisting jack and returned. It placed the jack in the gap and leisurely cranked, widening the entrance, metal squealing and giving way.

A Lei grew desperate and shouted, 'Don't bother! I'm just skin and bones, not tasty at all!'

Steel Teeth's throat rumbled ominously. In crude tones it said, 'I just ate a few. Humans really do taste awful. And I am full. That is not why I am doing this. It is exercise. Is that not a good enough reason?'

It wasn't surprising that this dracopien could talk. In addition to its developed brain and formidable intelligence, its larynx anatomy closely resembled a parrot's.

It showed no sign of stopping with the jack. A Lei's fight-or-flight impulse kicked in. He made his way into a deeper, narrower place. 'So you're full,' he said, squeezing in. 'We might as well sit down and chat. Maybe even make friends?'

Steel Teeth's strength was extraordinary. After the jack had done its work, the monster bit its way forward, as if burning excess vigor, tearing away pipes and wires, clawing apart metal plating. A Lei crawled further in, frantic and rat-like, relying on memory to seek the butchering-mecha storage facility.

He crawled out of a ruptured industrial run-off pipe. Less than three meters away reclined a mecha suit, a butchering model about the size of a dracopien. The cockpit was open.

The suit, which might have held its own against a T-Rex, had been abandoned. He had no time for this mystery. Rousing his courage, he took a deep breath and charged toward the armor. The foul stench of industrial run-off was like a chemical weapon, nearly overwhelming him. He covered his nose and reached for the mecha.

The run-off pipe was trampled flat with a thunderous crash. Steel Teeth's talons stabbed the floor right in front of A Lei. They could disembowel a T-Rex, and they'd come centimeters from tearing open his throat. Steel Teeth was like a cat toying with a mouse. Such a nimble killing machine couldn't miss like that. If it wanted A Lei dead, he'd already be slashed to ribbons.

A primal ferocity stirred in A Lei's heart. He dove into the cockpit. An impact rocked the canopy, Steel Teeth's claw a step late, screeching across the transparent shell. A Lei was soaked in cold sweat. He'd nearly been decapitated.

Now ensconced in the mecha, A Lei felt a dangerous pride. To suppress dinosaur uprisings, many mecha packed serious firepower, six-barrel Gatling machine cannons. He pulled a joystick. The mecha shivered, stood, extended manipulator arms toward the dracopien. Panels opened on the arms. A Lei cackled in his pride, eager to blow Steel Teeth to pieces.

But his smile froze.

His new arms were not sprouting cannons like he'd hoped. Instead, meter-long soup ladles emerged. He threw switches, retracting the ladles, extending giant tongs. A Lei stared, dumbfounded, switching tools in a frenzy. Forks, hooks, egg whisks, and other implements came up in succession, like a rotating lantern-carousel of paper horses. Against all reason, there was nothing like a useful weapon. Steel Teeth saw his frustration and collapsed with hissing laughter. 'You foolish thing!' it said. 'If this mecha had weapons, why would its former master have abandoned it?'

A Lei saw his chance and took it. He drove the mecha, trampling over the prone dinosaur, and charged at a window. He smashed through, leaping out of the 045 Meat Union factory. Then he was falling, crashing through canopies of massive tree-like ferns, more than twenty meters down, and into flea-bitten mud.

2

The Starship Alliance was nicknamed 'The Foodie Federation' because its citizens had long ago grown dissatisfied with dull, flavorless foodstuffs synthesized in labs. Like their distant ancestors, they craved natural, pollution-free food, meat from species that grazed over vast territories, organically. The foodies were insatiable. They wanted exquisite variety, minced delicacies, food that took ten or even a hundred times more energy to raise and prepare than it provided. Such uneconomical practices were rare among nomadic space civilizations. To feed their strange addiction, the foodies constructed specialized agricultural starships. These immense man-made worlds provided grazing land, artificial sunlight, fertile soil, whole biospheres in the service of the foodies' appetite. All kinds of crops and livestock were raised, under natural Earth-like conditions. The yield was harvested or slaughtered after maturation, sent by freighter to every starship with megacities, to restaurants and supermarkets, meeting the demands of countless gluttons.

A few hundred years ago, the Starship Alliance returned to its origin world, Earth, seeking the fragments of its ancestral civilization. They took nearly everything of value from the ruins: cultural relics, dilapidated landmarks, specimens of flora and fauna, and fossils of extinct organisms. The dinosaur fossil payload came to megatons, and included many previously undiscovered species. Among the latter was the astonishing *Draconis sapiens*.

Biologists conceived an idea: create a starship with a Cretaceous Earth habitat, resurrect paleo-organisms, including dinosaurs, so as to research the era. But the cost of the project would be massive. It wasn't easy to persuade stingy legislators to allocate funds, but after many rejections, they found someone who was interested.

'Just leave it to me,' said the Venerable Madam Zheng Qingyin, president of the Alliance Foodstuffs Federation – in business circles known as Grandma Foodie – leaning on her dragon head cane in the Bio Research Institute's paleo-organism department.

An astonishing foodie carnival was staged at that year's congressional budget conference. AFF freighters crowded the Congressional Plaza. 'Distinctive Pre-historic Delicacies' were handed out, free of charge. AFF-owned celebrities performed on stage. Billboards shouted slogans:

'Make any dinner table more sumptuous!'

'T-Rex leg burgers, steamed diplodocus, savory and spicy pterosaur wings!'

'Take your place at the Starship Alliance's luxurious banquet table!'

The Venerable Madam Zheng, white-haired, ruddy-complexioned, hale and hearty, walked with vigorous strides into the Capitol Building, deploying her dragon head cane to great dramatic effect. She carried a draft resolution in her other hand. She didn't use lengthy speeches to subjugate the legislators. Instead, she made sure they each had samples of dinosaur meat to try. When the few vegetarian legislators furrowed their brows and refused, she tantalized them with an equally delicious ancient pteridophyte banquet.

The Capitol Building had become a mansion of delicacies.

'I won't lecture you,' the Venerable Madam said, 'on the importance of a diverse diet to human wellbeing. There's no need, am I right?'

Her scientists were arrayed behind her, ready to hold forth on the topic for months, if called upon. She'd prepared truckloads of technical data on the proposed starship and its Cretaceous habitat. Its cost would dwarf that of traditional agricultural ships. It would allow biologists to research extinct life, but of course this was really about the foodies, and eating.

She got through the proposal effortlessly. When she emerged at the top of the Capitol steps, smiling and satisfied, a multitude of gluttons erupted with applause. Alliance TV broadcasted everything. The Venerable Madam had been wild in her youth. Now she felt that old wantonness return. Raising her dragon head cane, she cried, 'Our slogan is…!'

The crowded square gave its booming reply: 'Eat everything on two legs except people! Eat everything on four legs except stools!'

Building the new starship would take over a hundred years. Grandma Foodie Zheng Qingyin wouldn't live to see it completed, but her draft resolution would profoundly change the Starship Alliance dining table. After DNA fragments had been extracted, and paleo-organisms were coming back to life, species by species, scientists noted that dracopiens were intelligent organisms. There was extensive debate: the resurrection of a dinosaur with human-equivalent IQ was no small matter. But in the end, the foodies' argument was simple and persuasive: Are dracopiens delicious? If so, resurrect!

3

The Cretaceous habitat was wildly unsuitable for humans. The world outside the factories was verdant, a wetland teeming with reptiles. People accidentally stepped on crocodiles and other beasts quite often. Dense fern canopies blotted out sky and sun. This primeval forest was bathed in a luxuriant mist, and the air, at over forty Celsius, was suffocating. It was like being in a giant food steamer. The pteridophyte fauna, lacking the structure and root systems of woody plants, needed the moist surroundings to survive. Some of the tree-like ferns reached thirty meters tall. This world was so saturated that living people could molder.

A Lei made his mecha sit up. Luckily the interior was climate controlled, or he would already have been steam-cooked by the atmosphere. He hadn't driven a few steps before the mecha slipped into a bog, and he had to get upright again, this time with difficulty. This factory mecha was not suited to Cretaceous mud.

A Lei glanced back at the factory, which resembled a massive spider, several hundred meters wide, lying sprawled upon the earth. Normally it advanced like a bulldozer, gobbling up fern forest. Ground effect vehicles, like great dragonflies, would be dispatched from their tarmac on the roof, and in great swarms hunt dinosaurs. The conveyor belts would hurtle forward continuously, processing all kinds of dinosaur meat products. There were many of these roving factories in starship *Rhea*. The fern forests grew fast and weed-like in the warm, moist environment, and could be harvested regularly. The tender pteridophytes were rich in carbohydrates and protein. Most of a pteridophyte was edible, unlike flowering plants with their limited offerings of fruits, seeds, and certain leaves.

The stunningly fast growth of Cretaceous flora was a clear demonstration to scientists of how the colossi, the dinosaurs, had been fed. Gourmands were pleasantly surprised at how fast the dinosaurs reproduced in this blistering climate – so much for the assumption of slow reptilian birthrates. Brood after enormous brood, breeding faster than rats: it turned out that *Rhea* was twice as productive as traditional agricultural starships. It seemed dinosaurs wouldn't have to be domesticated. Hunting was sufficient.

As A Lei carefully observed his surroundings, Steel Teeth rushed down the nearly vertical factory wall and dashed across fern roots and muck, leaving no trace. A Lei was reminded of its awful cousin, the swift and violent velociraptor, and he failed to react. It felt like a hundred-ton truck hit him. His mecha was like a kite with its string cut, airborne, beyond control, then crashing through tree-fern saplings – and finally, mecha-face down in the mire.

Steel Teeth's talons pressed down on the machine. Its teeth scraped, seeking purchase, but it couldn't get the cockpit open. It gave up grudgingly. A Lei came to, feeling like all his bones had been shattered. Luckily, he'd landed in spongy marshland. If it had been solid stone, he might have been crushed inside the mecha.

Steel Teeth had been slower in the factory, where it was twenty or so degrees Celsius. Although dinosaurs were considered warm-blooded, their capacity for body temperature regulation was inferior to that of mammals and birds. Out here in the damp heat, at over forty degrees, it was ideal dinosaur weather. Below ten degrees, most dinosaurs lost their mobility, or even died en masse.

A Lei sat the mecha up, and again Steel Teeth knocked it

down. A Lei raised both hands and said, 'Okay, buddy. We're both intelligent creatures. How about we sit down for a nice chat?'

'Okay,' Steel Teeth replied. It was at its wit's end, after all. The mecha was a conundrum. The last attack had consumed the dinosaur's strength, and it needed a rest, just like A Lei. It sat down much like a hen, stomach to the ground. The dinosaur kinship with birds was plain.

'You seem familiar with humans,' A Lei said. 'Surely you were raised and trained by someone…'

The creature said, 'My foster father Ai Li-ke was a researcher of extinct life, living in solitude. He gave me human knowledge.'

'And what happened to him?'

Steel Teeth laughed, displaying its keen incisors. 'He was not very good. His meat was old. Too many bones. Hurt my teeth.'

A Lei was shocked. 'You ate him?'

'Humans have strange defects,' Steel Teeth said. 'You like domesticating house pets, believing you can imbue them with human feelings and reason. With dogs, horses, and other such social animals, long domestication can render them docile. But as for solitary animals… no matter how good you are to me, good enough to make me see you as kin, well, one mountain cannot brook two tigers. And we kill our own kind. The mother snake lays a brood and then just leaves. The eggs hatch and the young must fend for themselves. There is no familial emotion or attachment in the snake brain, no sense of friendship. How can you domesticate that? Change fundamental brain structure? No matter how good you are to creatures like us, we only see you as prey.'

This great reptile's words resonated with A Lei. It seemed the dracopien, for all its mental development, was no more affectionate or friendly than a snake. A Lei said, 'I've never met such a wise and farsighted dinosaur.'

'Thank you,' Steel Teeth said, lying prostrate on the ground. 'You can call me Mister Wise and Farsighted Crouching Dragon.'

4

Getting rid of this dracopien wasn't going to be easy. It became clear to A Lei as he watched the beast kill a T-Rex. Steel Teeth cleverly enraged its prey, luring the massive creature into soft mud, where it became stuck, and the hunter easily prevailed.

'I don't understand,' A Lei said. 'Your kind is quite rare, for a late Cretaceous apex predator. We've found so many T-Rex fossils, but few dracopien fossils. Actually, we found none until the SA returned to Earth.'

Steel Teeth bit off a chunk of T-Rex flesh and devoured it. 'We dracopiens do not lay many eggs. And we like to kill each other, so our numbers are naturally low. But I have a dream. I see a great dinosaur civilization. I see dracopiens destroying humanity, and replacing it.'

A dinosaur with a dream: this was a day of firsts for A Lei. He chose to dampen the creature's enthusiasm: 'Establishing a civilization isn't easy. Mastering fire would be step one. We've never found a trace of fire production from the dinosaur age. Can you friction-drill?'

Steel Teeth lifted its head and gazed about. The dense fern forest hid much of the sky, while enveloping fog made a salted egg yoke of the westering sun. The dracopien leaped up, and came down on a tree fern, smashing it to the ground. It seized half the trunk in its mouth and flung it before A Lei. 'Drill for fire?' it said, in a rage. 'With this saturated fern material, in this saturated world, show me fire-drilling! Suirenshi, last of the

Three August Ones, legendary inventor of fire, would be at his wit's end in this place!'

A Lei had stepped on Steel Teeth's tail with this problem of fire. Lack of fire production was dinosaur evolution's biggest flaw. Humans had come into the universe a mere three million years ago, while *draconis sapiens*, from birth to asteroid strike, may have been around a good deal longer, yet never mastered flame. They never expanded their food options with cooking, or smelted metal, or created advanced tools. There had never been a dinosaur civilization.

A Lei's stomach growled as he sat in the cockpit and watched Steel Teeth gorge itself.

He drove the mecha, stepping away, but the beast leaped and knocked him down. After several thwarted attempts, A Lei knew he was trapped. He was meant to starve here. 'You said your dream was to replace us,' he said. 'But do you understand human civilization?'

'I understand a bit,' it said. 'We have gathered much data on humans.'

'And you comprehend it all?'

The beast cocked its head. 'Most of it... no.'

'Then you shouldn't have eaten your foster father. He would have been happy to help, I imagine.'

'Just so. I immediately regretted it, after devouring him.'

A Lei finally understood. A dracopien's appetite overrode its rational faculty. Having eaten its fill, reason returned. When its belly growled, it became an unthinking, ferocious beast. A Lei saw an opportunity. 'You must be in dire need of someone who understands human civilization. If I may be so bold, I could fill that role. I could help you decipher what you mean to annihilate.'

Steel Teeth returned to the factory and went inside. It soon returned, carrying a flamethrower. It was impossible to friction-drill in this moist world, but a flamethrower was another matter. A Lei watched the dracopien roast the T-Rex meat, puzzled. This sort of carnivore didn't normally like cooked meat.

Steel Teeth tossed a well-done T-Rex leg in front of the mecha. It opened its bloody, fearsome mouth and said, 'You are welcome to join us.'

'Us? There are others?' A Lei cautiously opened the canopy as the mecha forked a fragrant chunk of meat and brought it up.

Steel Teeth looked up and gave a long, ominous roar that made the ground tremble. Moments later, a group of dracopiens emerged into view. Steel Teeth extended its arms and said, 'Welcome to the Steel Teeth tribe.'

5

The dracopiens had always tried to imitate human civilization. *Rhea* employees talked about this often enough.

A Lei came to the so-called Steel Teeth tribe's home, a simple, crude structure hidden between a mountain range and a river. On the doorway was an upside-down sign: 'Ai Li-ke, Research Facility.' Steel Teeth had seized the place and turned it into a fortress. The surrounding area was piled with hewn-down tree ferns. It seemed the dracopiens had meant to build a stockade with them, but they'd found the material too flexible and abandoned the project. They'd hunted down large dinosaur skeletons instead, using a mixture of stone and bone to construct a gruesome and intimidating city wall.

A Lei knew that primitive human tribes had built enclosing walls to repel wild beast incursions. He didn't understand why apex predators like dracopiens needed such protection.

Perhaps they were just imitating human behavior. Tree fern shanties stood here and there between the wall and the lab, a solemn little primeval town. The dracopiens had learned the human concept of shelter, but not human construction standards. The shacks were made of broad tree fern stalks and leaves. The roofs were slapdash, barely qualifying as shelter. Still, these dracopiens were far more advanced than other dinosaurs. Some gathered in front of huts to polish hunting implements. From a technological perspective, the tools were close to human Neolithic level, but they weren't made of stone. Discarded human machine parts served instead – machine arms from dismantled factories, iron pipes, and the like, all ground down to points and made into javelins, lances, and other primitive weapons.

There were many such primitive tribes in starship *Rhea*. Although Cretaceous era dracopiens had human-like IQs, they'd never entered the tribal era on Earth. These tribes in *Rhea* had clearly resulted from human influence. All kinds of plundered posters covered the fort, many of them SA city scenes, or steampunk-style space factories, and wide shots of spacecraft swarms like stellar multitudes. But most were illustrations of delicacies from various SA regions. On each of these, a graffito had been scrawled, in characters like roaches crawling across the image: 'Our goal is a sea of food!'

'I thought your goal was to destroy human civilization,' A Lei said, 'to remove and replace us.'

'Just so, but our ultimate goal is to eat. Humanity has many tasty delicacies. My foster father used to share them with me, fine foods from other starships, even from alien civilizations. For the sake of gourmet dining, humans have spanned thousands of lightyears, and returned to Earth to excavate fossils. You made this Cretaceous environment, this high-quality grazing land... the audacity! Foodies are the most powerful force in the universe. If we conquer humanity, all that wonderful food will be ours!'

In the final analysis, these dracopiens were mouth-straight-to-heart foodies. Steel Teeth did nothing to conceal its yearning. A Lei hadn't expected these primitive dracopiens to be pursuing something higher than mere destruction.

Entering the stronghold, he saw most of the lab instruments had been demolished for weapon parts. Books lay scattered on the floor, most of them rotted by the climate. The few intact volumes were ancient human histories.

'They say humans progressed from primitive tribes to tribal coalitions,' Steel Teeth explained. 'On that foundation they established nations. Before we establish our own great tribal alliance, the latter part of human history is useless to us.'

These fragmentary histories outlined tribal warfare in remote human ages. Steel Teeth said, 'We have run into a bit of a problem.'

'What's that?'

'I threw away all the weapons materiel Foster Father left to me. At the time, I believed they could not compare with sharp teeth. But during our battles with the tribe on the other side of the river, their flame catapults were ferocious. We suffered grievous losses.'

'That's why you attacked the factory?' A Lei said. 'To find better weapons?'

Steel Teeth led A Lei outside, to a captured enemy catapult. Made of fern tree, and using oil rendered from dinosaur fat, it was a crude machine. Its only real virtue was the human-made flamethrower lashed to it, which lit the dino-oil payloads. A Lei, staring at Steel Teeth's deadly incisors, said, 'You should learn to peacefully coexist. You're all dracopiens. Infighting is pointless.'

'Enough of that useless rubbish!' Steel Teeth said. 'In ancient times did you humans not make rivers of blood? Without big and powerful tribal alliances, would human civilization have been possible? Did not those powerful human war chiefs, like Odin or Emperor Yan, become deities worshipped by later generations? Does your Starship Alliance not have a battleship named the *Emperor Yan*?'

These dracopiens were naturally despotic. A Lei worried about debating and infuriating Steel Teeth. The prudent choice was to shut up.

Steel Teeth went vigorously about its leadership duties, handling tribal affairs big and small. It delegated a host of technological problems to A Lei. Luckily, these dracopien tech issues were of the simple Neolithic variety: find abandoned human metal fit for weaponry, develop new techniques for making sharper arrows, learn how to fling fire in this moist environment, and how to process tree fern material into something harder and wood-like.

When he knew he was unobserved, A Lei relaxed and breathed in the mecha. He wanted to contact headquarters, but didn't know how. Despairing, he glanced down and saw a hand device on the floor of the cockpit. It must have been dropped by the previous pilot. A Lei smacked himself upside the head in a fierce self-rebuke. If he'd seen the device earlier and called for help, he might have avoided his current predicament.

6

He huddled in the cockpit with the device in his hands. His trembling finger entered the wrong number several times, but he finally connected to the 045 Meat Union factory assistant director's office. 'Director!' he shouted. 'It's A Lei! I'm trapped in *Rhea*!'

'A Lei?' The assistant director sounded frightened. 'You're still alive?'

'If not, who are you talking to?'

'We all assumed you'd been eaten, so we didn't arrange a rescue team. But on the bright side, financial affairs offered their condolences. They paid for the funeral, and the accidental death insurance has paid out to your parents. Quite a sum!'

A Lei had to stop himself from smashing the hand device. 'So my family's quite happy with everything then? You were worried about further losses if you dispatched rescue, is that it? Why swallow more financial loss when you can just write me off? Well let me tell you... you've got bigger problems. These dracopiens aren't merely lashing out at the factory. They're conspiring to revolt. They mean to establish a huge tribal coalition. They want to overthrow human civilization and replace it. We need to sound the alarm. Better yet, we need to report this to SA government. We need the Marines if we're going to suppress these fucking lizards!'

'So you want to smash everyone's rice bowls,' the assistant director said, growing incensed himself. 'You know if Accidents and Safety inspects, all Union factories have to shut down and reorganize. What's everyone supposed to eat? The Northwest Wind? Now wait... if you're really saying the dracopiens are conspiring to overthrow humanity... Just hold on, I'll report it to the higher-ups and call you right back.' The assistant director disconnected.

A few minutes later, the device buzzed in A Lei's hand, and he answered. An old, dignified voice came through, claiming to be the AFF executive director in charge of *Rhea*.

'Executive d-director.' A Lei was low-level, a Union factory worker. He was talking to the man in charge of all food enterprises in *Rhea*.

'Young man,' the old voice said, 'tell me frankly... what's happening there?'

A Lei dared not hold anything back. He recounted the whole disaster, systematically and in full detail.

'That's quite a story,' the old man said. 'You're sure my friend Ai Li-ke was eaten?'

'Y-yes.'

The old man sighed. 'No wonder I haven't heard from him in so long. Ai Li-ke was an outstanding researcher for us. He played an important role in constructing the dinosaur pasturelands. And he was a skilled cook! Specialized in dinosaur eggs. Do you have anything of his? Keepsakes? If so, bring them back to me, and I'll reward you well.'

A Lei sifted through the materials he'd collected. 'There's only fragments of his notebooks left, and a few memory chips. Sir, you must think of a way to rescue me from *Rhea*. Otherwise I have no way of getting this stuff to you.' He had to prioritize his own little life.

'You're sitting in a mecha now?'

'Of course. Otherwise I'd have been eaten.'

'So it would seem the dracopiens also don't know what to do with you. You have two options... sound the alarm and report to the police, getting a rescue team dispatched. That's the safest way, but you'd be letting a once-in-a-lifetime opportunity slip through your fingers.'

That cut through A Lei's fear. 'And the other option?'

'Cut a bloody path out of there, escape on your own, and bring me Steel Teeth's head. You would have a hero's welcome, and a promotion. How does deputy captain of a hunting squad sound?'

A Lei did some quick mental calculations. 'I'd be equal to an assistant factory director.'

'Satisfactory?'

'Yes! Ten thousand times, yes! If you'll keep your promise...' He could struggle half a lifetime and never climb that high. He grinned, seeing money, glittering futures, his current danger forgotten.

After the old man had disconnected, A Lei sat there fantasizing. A grim voice like a thunderclap brought him back to the Cretaceous: 'Who were you talking to?'

A Lei panicked. He'd forgotten that dinosaur hearing was far keener than his. Steel Teeth had probably heard the entire dialogue.

7

After that fateful call, A Lei spent every day in fear. Steel Teeth seemed to know its severed head was the price for a deputy captain throne. A group of fearsome dracopiens always watched him, and he was never alone with their chieftain. Sometimes he had to fight the urge to sound the alarm, but the lure of promotion always won out. Steel Teeth had him designing various weapons for the coming tribal wars. A Lei knew nothing of weapon design, but he knew how to research stone-age weaponry on the hand device. In the course of one hectic month, he designed many weapons for the tribe.

A Lei understood well enough that if Steel Teeth really wanted him dead, there were many ways. It couldn't bite through the mecha, but it could starve him. It could slow-cook a stegosaurus leg right in front of him, wait for him to go mad with hunger and leave the cockpit, then casually devour him. But as long as A Lei produced weapon designs, it seemed Steel Teeth would refrain from harming him.

He was confined to the castle, but he heard dracopiens speaking of their chieftain's conquests. Steel Teeth was vanquishing tribe after tribe, consolidating power. He also heard the 045 Meat Union factory was back in business. No one seemed to care about one low-level worker's whereabouts.

It was getting harder to find new data for weapons designs. The decisive moment was fast approaching.

He brought up Steel Teeth's domestication record for the hundredth time, a series of videos shot by Ai Li-ke.

Dracopien reproduction was much like certain turtles. Parental involvement ended when an egg was laid. Little dracopiens hatched ready to hunt. Like many fish, amphibian, and reptile species in times of scarcity, siblings devoured each other. When Ai Li-ke discovered Steel Teeth's nest, the little dracopiens were at war. Finally, just one hatchling remained. Ai prepared cow's milk and chicken eggs for it, but the fierce little creature only snarled at its new benefactor. Ai Li-ke found this charming, and named it Steel Teeth.

A montage followed, Ai patiently teaching Steel Teeth to read. Raising this emotionless, reptilian thing was far more difficult than raising a mammal. Mammals come with emotional attachment software pre-installed. Much of the time, Ai had no choice but to administer electric shocks to make little Steel Teeth learn obedience. The other method was feeding. Young Steel Teeth learned to curry favor with Ai in order to enjoy the great variety of human food. A sumptuous banquet flowed from Ai's hand, and Steel Teeth grew very fast, ending up much larger than a wild dracopien.

Naturally, Steel Teeth's knowledge far exceeded its wild cousins'. This, combined with its superior size and vigor, allowed it to easily defeat other dracopiens in combat. By the time Ai Li-ke was seventy, Steel Teeth had become the alpha of a large dracopien pack. Tribalism was something new for the species, a new world in which Steel Teeth was the grim hegemon.

*

In Steel Teeth's eyes, A Lei's usefulness was drawing to a close. One day it brought some trusted followers into the fortress, where A Lei was hard at work measuring a section of excavated tree fern rhizome, which was meant to become a mortar cannon. A Lei puzzled over two problems: how to produce and use gunpowder in this moist world, and how to make tree fern material strong enough to endure the force of discharge.

Rhea was, in the end, merely the human approximation of a Cretaceous environment. It differed from the real thing. To prevent flowering angiosperms from squeezing out pteridophytes, humans strove to eliminate higher plants from the ecosystem, not to mention maple, birch, and metasequoia. Thus, hard building materials were difficult to come by.

Steel Teeth brought a taloned foot down, smashing the nascent mortar to pieces. 'Stop tinkering with such nonsense. This is not Earth. We have bypassed the Iron Age.'

A Lei went pale. He knew he couldn't make a mortar. He'd been going through the motions of research to keep death at bay. Now Steel Teeth had seen through this. He feared the moment of truth had come.

Steel Teeth's followers dragged the mecha toward a large gathering of dracopiens. A Lei was deposited on a massive, crude contrivance of tree fern, a kind of war chariot. Looking down upon the wide expanse of dracopiens, A Lei reckoned the alliance was now ten tribes strong. A solemn Steel Teeth reviewed its army. There were many other war chariots, lashed to domesticated stegosaurs and ceratopsians. A vanguard of dracopien-driven T-Rexes, armored in bone and teeth, rushed toward the battlefront.

'I have unified all the tribes of the Yellow River's north shore,' Steel Teeth said to A Lei. 'Today we unite with the south shore tribes, at long last. Behold, this world's highest lord.'

Steel Teeth's 'Yellow River' was the great waterway of the region. A hundred kilometers of dracopien deforestation had led to erosion, turning the river into a yellow, turbid flow. 'If the name Yellow River gets around,' A Lei said, 'many Earthlings might have objections. Can you change it?'

Steel Teeth snorted. 'The chief of the south shore alliance is named Chi You, God of War.'

'Really?' A Lei said in amazement.

'That is really my nickname for it.'

This joke fell flat, but Steel Teeth's knowledge did more to kill any possible levity. It knew the hazards of a cross-river military campaign. It had chosen to launch its offensive in the enveloping fog of early morning, to obscure numbers and movement. A Lei noticed strange little vehicles among Steel Teeth's forces, tree fern constructions with crude but clever gears driven by the wheels. No matter which way they turned, their indicator rods always pointed across the river.

Steel Teeth's dracopiens were armed with metal weapons burnished by stone and bone. Garlands of some pteridophyte, blooming with primitive flowers, were bound to their heads. The plant was a favorite edible among dinosaurs, resembling Chinese cabbage. To A Lei, these advancing dracopiens were comical, a group of hooligans with cabbage hats, but the Steel Teeth tribe knew what it was doing. The head-dresses would distinguish friend from foe. If a dracopien emerged from the fog of war without one, it was an enemy, and must be put to the hatchet.

The campaign opened with a salvo of burning missiles, dinosaur oil and pteridophyte kindling bundled around large rocks and flung from catapults into the mist. The clamor of impacts and howling enemies traveled across the water. Dracopiens ignited torches bound to the tails of their T-Rex and stegosaur mounts, and drove these beasts charging toward the opposite bank. Many enemies were caught unawares, panicking in the fog, and were hewn down. As others took up arms, Steel Teeth's main force reached the south shore. With sharp claws and cold steel, they conducted a ruthless slaughter.

'I am very grateful to you,' Steel Teeth said to a dumbstruck A Lei. 'All your hard work has paid off. Now, I should send you back to your place of origin.'

'You mean the Starship Alliance?'

Steel Teeth knocked the mecha prone. Several dracopiens poured dinosaur oil from fern leaf receptacles onto the mecha, and one used a factory flamethrower to ignite it. The mecha burst into flames, and A Lei realized the war chariot was actually a massive catapult. Steel Teeth slashed the restraining rope with a claw swipe, and A Lei, with his several tons of mecha, was airborne and trailing fire. He had become ammunition.

Steel Teeth watched him fly toward the far shore. 'Godspeed,' it said, 'on the reincarnation road!'

8

This was the largest dinosaur conflict A Lei had ever seen. As he came to, his broken body shot through with pain, cockpit life support showed he'd been unconscious for two days. He had a broken rib, two broken legs, and the ground shook as immense dinosaurs clashed all around him, and on top of him, trampling the mecha as they vied for position. The machine was pounded into the riverbank marsh. Starving and dehydrated, he was forced to drink the foul water and dinosaur blood leaking through a crack in the cockpit. Most of the time he didn't dare to move, waiting, still and quiet, for the war to end. On the third day of this vigil, there was finally silence above. The dracopiens were no longer fighting at close quarters. He touched a joystick, and the mecha sat up. Dinosaur corpses lay piled all around. He stared in amazement. The Yellow River had been dyed red.

'Life is strong in you.'

It was Steel Teeth, behind him. He turned to find the great warlord lying prone, and gravely wounded, on a burnt-to-carbon catapult.

'I'm not strong. This mecha is. After all, it's a high-tech SA product. With a hundred-and-fifty-million-year technological lead, how can you lose?' Every word he spoke was a stab from his broken rib. Steel Teeth only heard him thanks to the brainwave converter in the cockpit, synthesizing speech and amplifying it.

'I have not lost,' Steel Teeth said, 'but neither have I won. This enemy chief was raised by a human, like me. It was big like me, knowledgeable like me. I nicknamed it Chi You in my desire to defeat it. A pity I am not the Yellow Emperor[1]. Chi You is dead, but I will soon follow it.'

'Wait, you mean there are others like Ai Li-ke?'

Steel Teeth moved its massive head with great effort. 'This was humanity's plan all along. Resurrect us, educate us, lure us toward human-like development, toward tribes and alliances,

---

1   The Yellow Emperor is one of the three legendary Chinese rulers and culture heroes. Often regarded as the originator of Chinese civilization, he is said to have defeated Chi You, God of War and another of the legendary three.

toward building the foundation of a society through hand-to-hand combat. No intelligent species can resist trying to make a civilization, even if they know they are a moth darting toward a flame. How can we turn away from war? Every dracopien dreams of becoming an apex foodie. We dream like you dream. We want to make a world according to our desires. We long to satisfy our craving for endless, delicious variety.'

'We humans don't just dream of food. We pursue higher things. Moreover, I plan to become a vegetarian.' Watching tributaries of blood flow into the red river, A Lei thought he would never want meat again.

'Eating is always the first priority!' Steel Teeth growled. 'All life must eat. Hunger is the eternal constant. No food means no life. No life means no dreams, no realization of dreams. Even a super-intelligent species is, in the end, biological. Whether you eat animals or plants, you are eating living things. Humanity is just another living thing. Better to admit this. I see through your hypocritical compassion. It is pathetic.'

A Lei walked the mecha over, meaning to stop Steel Teeth's bleeding. The beast lashed out, its great mouth ripping the already-cracked canopy to pieces. A Lei, now sitting unprotected in his much-abused machine, stared into a gaping mouthful of teeth, and said, 'You don't want me to save you?'

'Why should I want that? And how can you save me? It is eat or be eaten, the primal law of the natural world. Plants devour inorganic matter and sunlight. Herbivores eat the plants, and carnivores eat the herbivores. Even high-and-mighty humans, apex predators that you are, must one day rot and become meal for plants. This is the way of things, the cycle. As intelligent life nurtured by the natural world, your duty is not to destroy this law of nature that brought you about, but rather to protect it. You humans created this world of *Rhea*. To we dracopiens, you are gods. Gods should preserve natural laws. Gods should maintain nature's balance, not destroy it.'

A Lei was confused. 'You revere humanity as gods, yet wish to replace us?'

Steel Teeth seemed to grin broadly. 'We want to become gods ourselves, revered, with unlimited food! But this is impossible. *Rhea* is not old Earth. It is not free and unrestrained. There is no coal here, no oil, for industry. Even if humans allowed us to develop freely, we still could not establish a civilization comparable to yours. But we strive, nevertheless. We cannot even reach the Iron Age, but we strive, and lay down our lives without regret.'

'I still don't understand. Why is humanity imparting knowledge to dracopiens?'

'For more delicious, higher-quality dining, and more developed brains. For your supermarkets and restaurants. For minced meat and Dragon Brain Soup! Foodies as discerning as humans are no longer satisfied with mere free-range meat. You crave carnivores that rush about and fight hand-to-hand. I thought you understood this.'

A Lei contemplated Steel Teeth for a long time. 'You're the most wise and farsighted foodie I've ever met.'

Steel Teeth laughed, coughed up blood. Lying prone on the burnt wreckage of the catapult, it said, 'Please call me Mister Wise and Farsighted Crouching Dragon.'

'I can't,' A Lei said. 'Zhuge Liang[2] might rise from the grave and sue for copyright infringement.'

---

2 Zhuge Liang, or Kongming, was a Chinese military strategist and inventor during the Three Kingdoms period. His reputation only grew when he lived in seclusion, earning him the nickname 'Crouching Dragon' or 'Hidden Dragon'.

Steel Teeth's laugh was like quaking thunder. 'Do not be ashamed of being a foodie. You humans have advanced far enough to break from the natural world, and you thrive. If you followed this timid, benevolent morality you speak of, and ate only foods synthesized in your labs, hundreds of starship biospheres would not exist. The countless animals depending on your pastureland habitats would not exist. We Cretaceous organisms would still be mere fossils. Dracopiens think this way... if humans do not eat it, it cannot possibly survive. Dracopiens have never resented your cultivation and hunting of our kind. You humans think so highly of yourselves, but your time will come. Are you not destined to become a feast for microorganisms and plants?'

A squad of ground effect vehicles appeared in the distance. Steel Teeth gave a mighty roar, and slowly rose. Wounds pouring blood, it faced A Lei in the unprotected cockpit.

'I have devoured much prey in this lifetime, but I never tormented my victims. My kills were swift, and I am proud of this. Humans brought us into this world, and we delighted in combat to realize an impossible dream. We are born and have only a few dozen years, but that is enough. And now I tell you one last thing... respect your food. I know you mean to take my head and become a captain. We abide by the laws of nature. Let us see who shall eat, and who shall be eaten. Come now. Fight!'

This would be a fair duel. A Lei, his canopy gone, was no longer impervious to sword and spear, while Steel Teeth, with its injuries, was neither stronger nor faster than the mecha. Roaring, the dracopien lunged. A Lei touched a joystick. The only thing in the mecha's arm that might grudgingly be called a weapon – an oversized meat skewer – popped up. Steel Teeth's deadly bite clamped shut centimeters from A Lei's face. The skewer stabbed, sinking deep into Steel Teeth's heart.

'Thank you,' A Lei said, 'for teaching me wisdom, Wise and Farsighted Speaker.'

'Please call me Mister Wise and Farsighted Crouching Dragon.' Steel Teeth's lantern-like eyes slowly closed, the barest trace of regret marring its satisfaction.

9

When danger and opportunity coexist, courage is the key to deciding one's fate. If A Lei had chosen to raise the alarm, he would have remained a common worker. He would have spent his life in the stink of the 045 Meat Union factory, perhaps retiring before he could attain the career summit of foreman.

When he brought Steel Teeth's head back to the company, the hero's greeting left him dumbfounded. There was adulation and praise for this young person, so composed, so calm as he faced the lights and cameras, calm as a mountain. Only A Lei knew this was a façade. It was fear that kept him unmoving. After the uprising, the AFF needed a model hero to redeem its image. Despite his lack of qualifications, A Lei was decorated and adorned at the public relations department and made into an optimal spokesperson.

At twenty-two, A Lei became the youngest ever deputy captain of a hunting squad. This promotion broke several rules, and he knew his qualifications and abilities were being discussed and found wanting. The higher-ups wanted an experienced hunter. They were waiting for him to wash out. The smallest error could get him demoted, so he was cautious, devoted, and energetic in his work. He couldn't let this opportunity slip through his fingers.

He was very young for such a position. Most of the other deputy captains were of his parents' generation, and he was higher up than most of his contemporaries. After five years at the job, he got married and enjoyed conjugal bliss. He was promoted, step by step, and ended up the AFF executive director in charge of starship *Rhea*. By the time his career ended, there were more than a thousand others in the AFF of his rank: pasture habitat executive directors, farming colony planet managers, or exploration team chiefs seeking new foods throughout the cosmos. But A Lei never left *Rhea*.

For most of his life, A Lei sat upright in a tall building, watching his expanse of Cretaceous land, watching dracopiens clash in war after tribal war. Both humans and dracopiens knew what it was all about. Hunting dracopiens was still dangerous work, and although hunting squads were brave, risking their lives to kill all types of dinosaurs and deliver them to dining tables, dracopiens were the exception. Better to watch their battlefields, and wait, and harvest warriors on the verge of death. That was how you got the delicacy Dragon Brain Soup.

Many higher-ups in the hunting squads had dinosaur skulls decorating their offices, and A Lei was no exception. His massive dracopien skull had an engraved plaque beneath it: 'Mister Wise and Farsighted Steel Teeth, a truth-speaking friend who changed my life.'

Whenever he encountered problems and felt irresolute, A Lei would swivel his chair and look up at Steel Teeth's skull. He tried to imagine how Steel Teeth, the determined warlord, would handle the thorny issue. A Lei's subordinates feared and respected him. They called him 'master who thinks deep, like a dinosaur'.

One day, A Lei sat in his office contemplating a dracopien egg he'd collected after a tribal war. Thinking of Steel Teeth, he began planning his retirement. He would hatch this egg, build a secluded house here in *Rhea*, and teach the little dinosaur Steel Teeth's wisdom. He would raise it to be the next generation's dracopien leader. After much thought concerning its name, he settled on Steel Teeth the Second.

Perhaps, someday, Steel Teeth the Second would eat him, as the First had eaten Ai Li-ke. Or perhaps it wouldn't be interested in human meat, and A Lei would die a natural death in *Rhea*, in the little house, and become food for bacteria and plants. Neither ending was bad, as far as a pious foodie was concerned.

Translated from the Mandarin by Andy Dudak

The Day the World Turned Upside Down

Thomas Olde Heuvelt

The Netherlands

Thomas is another author I published in my *Apex Book of World SF* anthologies, and he is the first Dutch author to ever win a Hugo Award – for this very story. He is usually a horror writer – a very successful one! – but in this instance, he movingly shows a world turned, well... upside down. This story is translated by Lia Belt.

That day, the world turned upside down.

We didn't know why it happened. Some of us wondered whether it was our fault. Whether we had been praying to the wrong gods, or whether we had said the wrong things. But it wasn't like that – the world simply turned upside down.

Scientists lucky enough to survive the event said that it wasn't so much that gravity had disappeared, but that it had flipped over, as if our planet had suddenly lost all of its mass and was surrounded by some colossal object. Religious people, unlucky enough to survive the miracle, said that life was give and take, and that God was now, after so many years of giving, finally taking. But there was no colossal object, and being taken by God is a dubious given.

It happened like a bolt from the blue, at ten-o-five a.m. There was a moment, one magical moment, when you could see us all floating in mid-air halfway up our living rooms, upside-down in whatever pose we had been in at the time – coffee drinkers drinking coffee from inverted coffee cups, lovers clinging to each other's falling bodies, old men groping for slipping hairpieces, children crowing and cats screeching, all of us surrounded by the asteroids of our possessions. It was a moment of perfect madness, frozen in time.

Then began the groaning and the clattering, the roars and the screams. It was pandemonium. We crashed against ceilings and got crushed beneath the rubble of our old lives. Skulls cracked. Necks broke. Babies bounced. Most of us died on the spot or protruded convulsing from holes in plasterboard ceilings. Those who survived lay bewildered on top of them, trying to comprehend what had just happened.

But woe the ones who were outside. Before anyone even realized that the sky was no longer above, but *below* us, people started falling from the face of the Earth. In no time, the sky was dotted with tumbling people, fluttering clothes, floundering dogs, careening cars, clattering roof tiles, mooing cattle, and whirling autumn leaves in colors that set the sky ablaze. People sitting on their porches somersaulted until they landed on creaking awnings and stared out over their rims into fathomless depths. A mole sticking its nose up from the ground was seized by reversed gravity, and a whale jumping from the waves would never dive back into the sea. Tired of her burden, Mother Earth shook off anything that wasn't tied firmly down to her surface. In one upward thrust, it all fell into the atmosphere. Planes, satellites, and space stations disappeared into the vacuum, and even Father Moon was pushed away from us. We saw him dwindle and dwindle, until he landed in his own sad orbit around the sun. He never even said goodbye.

And me?

I was lying on the couch, not doing anything really. I wasn't reading a book or watching TV. If the world had come to an end, I wouldn't even have noticed.

I was staring at my phone, waiting for you to call.

*

It was the second time in two days that the world had come to an end. The first time was when you lowered your eyes the day before and said: *It's not you, it's me*. It was the last lie between us, or actually the first lie of not-us, because you no longer wanted an *us*. What I felt was the best thing in my life, for you, had been a burden. Without me. You wanted to be without me.

My heart shattered to pieces on my abdominal wall. Large chunks of deep, staggering hurt and dismay at how calmly you announced these words, without the tiniest clue that this was the most painful thing you'd ever had to tell me, that you would die a thousand deaths rather than having to tell me this. You were the love of my life, and it had never occurred to me that you might take that away from me. I tried to pretend I understood, that I didn't blame you for not wanting to try anymore, that all my frustration and pain were no match for your frustration and pain. I loved you too much to even be mad at you.

We stood in the corridor as I choked out the words. 'Are you really, really, really sure?'

'No. Yes.'

'You said no.'

'Yes.'

'But couldn't we...'

'No.'

'But couldn't we...'

'No, Toby. I'm sorry.'

In the silence I heard my shaking breath. You fidgeted nervously with your purse, searching for some way to open the front door. What a horrible, horrible place a corridor is: halfway between staying and leaving. I gathered all my courage and asked, 'So we're no longer…'

Finally you looked at me, with tears in your eyes, and then you slowly shook your head. I struggled to hold back my tears, but they came anyway. That broke you down as well. We held each other for a long time, close and tight, and holding you like that was the hardest thing I had ever done. Then you let go.

I smiled through my tears.

You smiled through your tears.

'Omnomnom?' I asked.

'Nomnomnom,' you said. And then you disappeared down the stairs.

For the first half hour I resolved to show myself a valuable and sound person and not throw in the towel. I forced my tears back into my eyes and started doing the dishes. But as your lips on the glasses dissolved in the suds, I was constantly being haunted by visions of other men caressing the skin I wanted to caress, kissing the mouth I wanted to kiss and *fucking* the girl I had made love to for such long nights. Visions that made me attack the crockery with so much aimless remorse that trembling glasses took cover beneath dinner plates, and I started toying with the terrifying yet tempting idea of smashing a glass on the kitchen counter and slicing my wrists with the shards. Later that same afternoon I discovered you had changed your Facebook status to 'single', even though it had taken you weeks to reluctantly agree to the opposite, and I dumped my laptop in the cold dishwater. And early that night the emptiness you left behind descended on me altogether and I was alone, alone in the full extent of my grief.

It was late when you texted me. I was lying on the couch, not really asleep and not really awake. The shards of my heart leaped up in my stomach.

Bubbles is still at your place. I'll come pick him up tomorrow.

That was it. No *Are you home tomorrow?* or *Maybe we can talk about it some more.* No *How about you brew us a pot of Minty Morocco*, which you always liked so much, and not even *How are you now?* Just: *I'll come pick him up tomorrow.* From across the other side of the room, Bubbles stared wistfully in the murky water of his fishbowl, and more than anything else, that stare made it irreversible.

Oh, Sophie, you are so incredibly, immensely, inimitably dear to me. Why did you have to do this?

*

When it all happened, I had a throw cushion pressed to my face. Maybe it was some sort of effort to close myself off from the world tumbling down around me a little too literally. And so my landing on the ceiling was remarkably gentle. The plasterboards broke my fall; the backrest of the couch guarded my bones from breaking. In a daze, I crawled out from underneath it, without so much as a scratch.

The first thing one experiences after gravity has flipped and the initial turmoil has died down is not shock, but disorientation. I didn't even realize I had landed on the ceiling and my living room was upside-down. I didn't think of an earthquake, even though the air-raid alarm was whooping. Before I had a chance to form a thought or two, I saw something between the ubiquitous chaos of shattered furniture, snapped houseplants, strewn potting soil, dangling electrical wires, and splintered pictures of you and me – something that froze my blood.

Bubbles' fishbowl had shattered.

He was floundering in a puddle of water between the shards, panicked.

And that's when my phone rang.

I found it beneath a flap of carpet, but right then the air-raid alarm outside stopped and the phone went mute. When I checked the display and saw that you were the one who had called me, my heart started pounding. I immediately tried calling you back, but there was no signal. I tried again and again, over and over, whatever it was that had happened, *you had survived*, you had tried to reach me before the network failed, and Bubbles jumped up in a final effort to draw my attention, gasping like a fish on dry land, and then lay still, dying.

I was alive.

You were alive.

Bubbles was alive.

I jumped up lickety-split and started rummaging between the wreckage, but the best thing I could find on such short notice was your half empty bottle of 7-Up. I started shaking it like mad to let the carbon dioxide out, dipping my fingertips into the puddle of water between the broken glass and tenderly wetting Bubbles's orange scales. But then the impatient goldfish swished his tail, as if to spur me into action. I took a sip, found that all the carbonation had dissipated, wriggled Bubbles in through the bottleneck, and held my breath until I heard a satisfying splash.

Fish and lemon go well together.

When I glanced over at the window and looked outside, the world instantly started teetering. I lived on the third floor of a three-story apartment building. The houses on the other side of the park were hanging upside-down from the surface of the Earth, which was *above* me now, groaning under its own weight. The roofs had released their tiles, and also the trees hung upside-down, just like the swings and slides and the laundry on the lines in the garden of my neighbor across the street. Utterly speechless, I grabbed the bottle holding unfortunate Bubbles, his pouting lips gasping for oxygen just above the soda surface, and crawled across the ceiling, over the upturned couch toward the upturned window. That's where the depth of the atmosphere washed over me in a dizzying wave, and for a moment I sat there, frozen, afraid to even shed any tears, worried that they might prove too much for the wobbly ceiling. The scene outside was so incredibly at odds with the laws of nature that I wanted to grab on to the window frame to keep myself from falling *up*, but gravity held me pressed up against the ceiling and it was only my stomach going topsy-turvy.

I didn't see any people, except for one: a woman dangling from the playground fence.

She was hanging from the bars, her knuckles white, her legs in the void, and her back turned so I couldn't see her face. On her arms, two oh-so-bothersome Kroger bags were trying to drag her down.

With extreme care, I raised myself up and opened the upturned window. My heart in my throat, and my hands on the window frame, I leaned out. 'Ma'am?'

My voice startled her, but she was afraid to look down, worried that the least little shift in balance might make her lose her grip. 'I need help!' she shouted, remarkably calm for her remarkably precarious position.

'What happened?' I yelled.

'It's Christmas time, all right? I can't hold on for much longer!'

'Wait! Hang on there!'

'I had no other plans!'

'Sorry! I mean… I'm coming to help you!'

But by some unfortunate coincidence, the rusty axle of my bike, dangling twenty-five feet higher up from its chain lock fastened to the bicycle stand, chose that exact moment to snap. As the wheel dangled up there, the frame tumbled down and, in passing, smashed my open window to pieces. Startled, I let go of the 7-Up bottle. It flew out of my hand and landed on the bottom of the gutter, rolled away from the window… and stopped right on the edge, out of my reach.

Bubbles, in the throes of an acute case of hyperventilation, darted from one end of the bottle to the other as quickly as his delicate fins would carry him. I looked from the tormented goldfish to the unhappily dangling woman – 'Please hurry!' she yelled now – and suddenly I saw your face. You had tried to call me.

In a world that wasn't upside-down you were the only thing that mattered.

I scrambled up and worked my way through the tumbled-over living room, over the knee-high threshold into the corridor, where strips of linoleum were hanging down and water from the toilet cistern had collected on the ceiling, then over the knee-high threshold into the kitchen. If possible, the mayhem was even worse in there: cupboard doors ripped from their hinges, open drawers, strewn cutlery, pots and pans thrown from the shelves and a ragged hole in the ceiling panels where the fridge had burst right through and from which daylight now shone. Quickly, quickly, balancing on my toes, I reached for the bottom cupboard, got buried in kitchen gear when I opened the door and, inside, found what I was looking for: the lashing rope for the trailer.

The end of the world creates two sorts of people: heroes

and cowards. When the dangling woman had finally gathered enough courage to glance over her shoulder and saw me clambering from the open window, one end of the lashing rope tied around the couch in the living room and the other end around my waist, she must have thought I belonged to the former. Unaware of something cold that had seized me that same moment, she mumbled, 'Thank God.' And not much later, as I reached and I stretched, as I tensed and I leaned, engrossed in efforts to try to get a hold of the goldfish in his bottle on the bottom of the gutter, the woman plummeted down, thinking of a long and fertile life, and neither you nor I would ever know her name.

At the end of the world, it's every man for himself.

You had taught me that, Sophie.

It was as perilous as it was impossible to reach the blasted 7-Up bottle from the window. After two deep breaths I finally ventured out onto the gutter, keeping the lashing rope loosely in my left hand, and started shuffling forward inch by inch along the edge of the immeasurable abyss, my cheek pressed against the glass. I was terrified. Six feet... four and a half... three... until the rope pulled taut, and I bent my knees extremely slowly, reaching out, my fingertips grazing the bottle cap – that's when the gutter snapped and tumbled into the abyss with me.

Everything spun; I squeezed my eyes shut and clamped my jaws and waited for the snap of the rope and then *dzinng* the yank and my stomach *flap* from my abdomen and the couch *smack* against the window frame and myself *whoosh*, shaken like a ragdoll.

It was an eternity before I stopped and summoned the nerve to open my eyes.

I hung about three feet underneath the eaves and one light year over firm ground. The rope was cutting into my midriff.

I realized I was holding the bottle. Bubbles was floating on his back, but he opened his stunned little eyes when I apprehensively tapped the plastic.

Now that I finally had a moment of peace – a word rarely used in a more relative context – I had some time to ponder the situation. The Earth in reversed perspective is as wondrous a sight as it is a frightening one: a ceiling reaching until the horizon, but nothing below. An enormous nothing. No shouts or sirens anywhere. Only, in the distance, the constant creaking of things breaking off and disappearing into the depths, along with disoriented birds trying to find places to land and sadly tumbling into the cosmos.

'Do you know what time it is?' a small voice suddenly asked.

I tried to turn toward the source of the voice, my legs kicking the emptiness. The two swings in the playground were hanging down in the air from their blue-painted frame. On one of them sat a little girl with three crooked ponytails and dangling legs, looking down at me with her small fists clenched around the chains.

'Er... don't be afraid,' I said, not very convincingly.

'I wanted to go so high I could touch the sky,' the little girl said. 'Mommy said don't go so high, you'll flip right over. But I did anyway, and now I can't get back down!'

'That's... inconvenient,' I mumbled. I realized I was immediately trying to distance myself from the girl. There was nothing I could do for her. She was on a swing twenty feet away from me, but she might as well have been on the moon. I started to make preparations to extricate myself from my precarious position.

'My name is Dawnie,' the girl on the moon said.

'Uh... hello.'

I slipped the 7-Up bottle into my pants.

'I'm a big girl. I'm five,' the girl on the moon said.

'Uh… okay.'

I started to haul myself up along the rope.

'So do you know what time it is?' Dawnie asked. 'Mommy said two minutes, then we're going home, 'cause I've got these groceries to put away. Except I don't know how long two minutes is.'

And I faltered.

I thought of the woman with the Kroger bags, and that's when then the loss of all the lives in the world crashed over me; that unfortunate woman's life, but also the life of the girl on the swing, the life of a mother and the life of a child, the life of lovers and broken hearts, your life and mine. Lives tumbling across the floor like pearls from a string you had broken, rolling around the house and then disappearing. The death of the world is a frequently returning phenomenon, but even the most visionary philosophers could not have foreseen how it had happened this time. Yesterday I woke up with you in my arms, kissed the spot between your breasts where your heart was, and you had been mine. Now I was hanging like an anchor from the bottom of the world, and the world had come to a stop.

*

Bubbles revived visibly after I used a straw to suck the water that had sloshed from the cistern and collected on the toilet ceiling and siphoned it into a rinsed-out 7-Up bottle. Next, I sawed the legs off the pine dining table, pulled panels from the hole in the kitchen ceiling and lifted the doors from their hinges. After my struggle to climb in through the window, the walkway was a piece of cake. Working my way up over banisters and landings, I hauled myself to the ground floor; a wobbly tower of mattresses and sofas then took me to the door of the apartment building.

How my heart crashed to my feet at the prospect of having to make my way through that upside-down world, dangling from a ceiling of groaning roots and foundations! But my wish to save the little girl was greater. The first hurdle I took by shoving the longest bookshelves between the railings of the playground fence and nailing them to the doorpost. Across came the tabletop, and behold: the first few yards of my scaffolding were a fact. I worked for hours and hours. My platform of window ledges and shelves, of mirror frames and doors continued to grow; from the stairs to the hanging fence, from the hanging fence to the hanging oak, from the hanging oak to the hanging swings, all of my possessions strung together into a footbridge across the emptiness. Working like this, my hands created a perfect reflection of what had become of my life. Maybe that was the reason I wanted to save the girl: crawling around an upturned world, I tried to convince myself that it was the world that stood on its head, not me.

By the time I rope-knotted the carpet-covered drainpipes to the blue frame of the swing set, lowered the attic ladder and told Dawnie to climb toward me, the sun had risen to the horizon and the sky was red as blood.

Dawnie lifted her full moon face up to me. 'I'm scared,' she said quietly.

I was on my stomach, arms wrapped around the frame, the ladder an extension of my reaching hands. 'I won't let go.'

Dawnie hesitated. 'Are you really, really, really sure?'

'No. Yes.'

'You said no.'

'Yes.'

'But couldn't we...'

'No.'

'But couldn't we…'

'No, Dawnie. Climb up.'

Very, very, very carefully Dawnie moved her hands higher up along the chains and stood on the swing. She looked at the ladder with fear and revulsion, as if she was afraid to leave the swing behind, as if she wanted to swing some more, back and forth, back and forth between what was behind her and what was ahead. Then she made a decision, placed her foot on the bottom rung and scurried up the ladder, quick and featherlight.

Later, when the sun soared up behind the horizon, we stared out of the living room window at the theatre of Earth's vomit in the atmosphere. Dawnie stared with unabated wide eyes over the edge of her woolen blanket, Bubbles floated with unabated melancholy in the pure water, and I unabatedly mourned my previous life, which had fallen over the edge of the world along with everything else. We heard explosions in the distance and the air was heavy with a burning smell that had nowhere else to go than to spread out against the Earth's surface. Most fires extinguished themselves as buildings broke off and crashed into the abyss, dragging grey plumes of smoke behind them like falling comets.

'And mountains, are they falling, too?' Dawnie asked, a bit dreamily.

She had entertained herself by throwing houseplants out the window, but it had soon bored her to watch them disappear into the universe. Dawnie was young enough to take to a new normality without much trouble. I wasn't. In mounting despair, I had been trying to get some news about the catastrophe, but besides the cell phone network and the Internet, all radio waves seemed to have disappeared as well.

'I think it's raining boulders there right now,' I said.

'How about volcanoes?'

'I guess the fire runs out of them. Dead-straight pillars of lava, all the way into space.'

Dawnie looked suspicious. 'But won't that make the Earth run out?'

I hadn't considered that.

Were you looking at the same view outside when I did, at the same upside-down world, and did you feel the same bewilderment I felt? Of all the people in the world, why had you called me immediately after the world had come to an end? And why not sooner? Why not all those times when it still mattered? Twice before I had lost love, one to another man and one to indifference, but neither of those loves had been as fundamental and natural as my love for you. If I woke up during the night and missed the weight that had dented the mattress beside me, I was terrified about you getting all too enraptured and wrapped up in the nightlife. And if you crawled into bed just before dawn, drunk and exhausted and instantly asleep, I would lie awake beside you trying not to smell other men on your breath. And so my fear of you leaving me created premature lovesickness: I missed your body as it was lying beside me; I yearned for your touch as your arm was resting on my chest, making the memory of it even more real and my heartache even worse. It felt like I had already lost you.

A downpour of falling stars drew lines across the sunken darkness: the last breaths of objects that had been on Earth this morning and were now falling back into the atmosphere. A fireworks display of thousands of dying things. I watched breathlessly, afraid to make a wish.

After a while I noticed that Dawnie was still awake.

'Mommy is a falling star, too,' she mumbled.

I realized she might very well be right.

*

The world hadn't been on its head for a full day before a general consensus had been reached about how survivors communicated their survival: by hanging white sheets or curtains from their windows and chimneys. They constituted the first independent link in a uniform chain of interweaved rope bridges and gangways, stringing itself out in the days after the disaster like a spider web.

My hope that I could leave Dawnie with relatives soon evaporated. When I asked her where her father lived, she answered, 'At Grandma's.'

'At Grandma's?'

'Yes, Mom and Dad got in this fight about all sorts of things and Dad said he'd had to give up all kinds of things to be with her and then Mom said oh, it's *that* again and then they yelled at each other and then Dad went to live with Grandma.' She was silent for a moment before adding, 'Do you think Grandma is upside-down now, too?'

I felt my stomach twist. 'Do you know where Grandma lives?'

'Somewhere we always went by car,' Dawnie said, tugging at her crooked ponytails. 'But I don't wanna go to Grandma's. Grandma yells at Mommy, too.'

'So where would you like to go?'

'I want my Mommy.'

I realized that Dawnie didn't have anything left as well, just like me. So we had to share.

'Then you're coming with me,' I decided. 'And on the way, we'll try to find Mommy. But you'll have to do one thing for me.'

'What?' Dawnie asked.

I gave her the 7-Up bottle. Dawnie took it in her hands as if it held the weight of the world. She looked wide-eyed in through the plastic, and Bubbles looked wide-eyed out. For a second, something of immense significance seemed to be exchanged between the goldfish and the girl, as if her desire to see her mother and Bubbles' desire to see you, which was really my desire to see you, were just one and the same thing. Then Dawnie's face lit up in a wide smile, displaying her entire gappy set of teeth. From that moment on, Dawnie never left Bubbles' side. If he was hungry, she flaked fish food in through the bottleneck; if he was thirsty, she added more water; and if he got short of breath, she blew in air through a straw until Bubbles regained his luster.

At the end of the world, we all need something to hold on to. If we don't hold on, we'll have to let go. And if we let go, we'll have to find our own orbit in the universe.

And so I held on to the playground fence. Tightly! We had reached it by climbing through the walkway door and over the tabletop bridge, but once there, the unnatural depths below our feet affected me so acutely that I seized up against the fence for several minutes, my hair streaming in the wind, unable to go forward or backward. I only dared to look up when I felt Dawnie's soft hand touching mine.

'You don't have to be afraid,' she said, showing me the 7-Up bottle in her little backpack to urge me on. 'There's nothing down there.'

That wasn't just the truest, but also the loneliest thing she could have said. The abyss instantly lost its meaning. It turned into just another obstacle, one of the obstacles I could lower Dawnie down along or lift her up with the rope between us. Inch by inch, we shuffled toward the edge of the park and, deftly manipulating the attic ladder, reached the first treetop in the row of lime trees lining the street. Even though many branches had been ripped off by falling cars, it was relatively easy to use the ladder to climb from tree to tree to windowsill and back to tree. And so we zigzagged forward, a ripped-open Earth surface with power cables and sewers protruding like dead veins and bones over our heads, and every step brought me closer to you, every step took the sting out of the cruelty of your last words and transformed them into a message of hope: *Bubbles is still at your place. I'll come pick him up tomorrow.*

'Hey, you there!'

In an easy chair on a timber platform, hanging a little ways below an attic window from a makeshift assembly of furniture, sat a short, balding man. On the boards beside him stood a thermos, and a steaming mug of coffee. When we spotted him, the man waved his binoculars.

'Relief troops are on the way!' he yelled good-naturedly.

'Really?' I yelled back, feeling a spark of hope.

The man burst out in a roar of laughter. 'Of course not! I thought *you* were the relief troops!' He smacked himself on the thigh and took a sip of coffee. 'From what I can see from down here, things are not looking good!'

I sighed, nevertheless glad to be able to talk to an adult. 'What do you think happened?' I asked, gesturing around.

'Hanged if I know!' the man yelled. 'The Earth pulled a fast one on us, now didn't it! No Internet, no phones, no information! Last night I heard a loudspeaker message from downtown, but it was too far away to make out what it was saying! I've heard rumors that they're building rope bridges and structures down there! You know, plenty of food for survivors and all that! But you're only the second group I've seen come by here all day! The first one made it to the end of the street before they fell into the sky by accident!' He paused for a second, and then added, 'We're doomed!'

'How about you? Aren't you going to try getting downtown?'

'Now you listen to me, son!' the man yelled. 'I've lived here all my life! As far as I know, I'm the only one who's seen both the construction and the demise of this street! What do you think about that?'

*

On the second day of our journey we saw injured people on ceilings behind windows, waving curtains and begging, their hands pressed up against the glass.

On the third day we found a string of knotted sheets dangling down from a bay window, where someone had gone in search of solid ground.

On the fourth day my heart sank, because the hours and minutes were raining down in the universe and we were making such slow progress, and because I missed you so much, and because all ordinary and extraordinary speculations about the catastrophe turned out to be pointless. We had climbed on the underside of the bridge, now suspended below the river. The road surface had fallen off, but the iron frame was still intact and a few concrete slabs were still fixed to the pylons. And believe it or not: the water was still there. Flowing like liquid lead across the ceiling of the Earth's surface, it spat the laws of nature in the eye. In places where the surface heaved, the water rained down in a soft, windblown mist, as if the river surface itself was the plane where gravity flipped over.

'Why isn't the river falling down?' Dawnie asked.

I wanted to say something – *I think Earth was simply fed up with us* – but before I had a chance, Dawnie got bowled over by a hang glider that suddenly came hurtling through the space between the river and the bridge. My hand darted out to grab her little backpack before she and Bubbles in the bottle could tumble away. The aviator whooped, circled around in the airspace below us, and came flying toward us from the front. For a second it seemed like he was going to crash, but in the last instant he pulled the hang glider's nose up, slowing down and losing lift right over the underside of the bridge. He landed with a clumsy, stumbling step and stopped, dragging the delta wing behind him. 'Rescue-squad, at your service,' the aviator said. 'Women and children first, please.'

'That was… spectacular,' I stammered.

'Thank you, thank you,' the man said, unclipping himself from his contraption. 'Municipal service. Only way of picking up survivors and getting them to the evacuation centers.'

'There are evacuation centers?' I asked incredulously.

'In the basement below city hall.'

'And the city had one of those… flying things?'

'Three, actually,' the aviator grinned. 'Haven't you seen my associates around? Maybe they haven't been to this part of town yet.' He lowered himself to his knee in front of Dawnie and took her hand. 'Hello there, big girl. How would you like to go flying?' Then he looked up at me. 'Sorry, children first. It's protocol. I'll come back for you later.'

Dawnie shifted a forlorn look from the aviator to me. Something in her eyes alarmed me. Something wasn't right.

'Isn't that dangerous?' I asked, in an effort to stall for time more than anything else.

'Thermal holds the wing up,' the aviator said, straightening and moving his hand to Dawnie's back. 'Warm air rises up and all that shit. Now that everything's upside-down, it's all thermal. Falling crap, *that's* what you don't want.'

'And where do you land?'

'Bridges, roofs, hangars with loading bays... even trees will work, but they'll screw up your wing.'

'I meant at city hall...'

'Holy fuck! Look at that!' the aviator said, turning toward the river flowing past over our heads, looking solid. 'That's like magic.' He had shrugged off his harness and started stripping off his clothes, as if he was planning on going for a swim. Suddenly I was sure. There was no evacuation center, no municipal rescue-squad, no protocol. The man was a flying predator. He had been circling around like a hawk and had spotted his prey. He would fly off with Dawnie, and I would wait, but no one would come back.

In his underwear, the aviator started climbing the iron frame around the bridge pylon toward the river. He had all the time in the world. We had nowhere to go, and he knew it. But just then, Bubbles jumped up from the water in the 7-Up bottle with a significant slosh, and Dawnie and I exchanged a glance. In an instant, I slipped into the harness and fastened the straps. The aviator had reached the lead-grey surface of the water and carefully lifted his arm. Gesturing frantically, I urged Dawnie to hurry. The aviator's hand slipped through the surface... and water from the river started trickling down his arm in small rivulets.

'Awesome...' he breathed, his gaze following the water drip onto the bridge below... When he suddenly caught sight of us and yelled, 'Hey, what the hell are you doing!'

'Hang on!' I shouted, hurling Dawnie on to my back, grabbing the hang glider's frame, fastening carabiners and fastening Dawnie, hoping-praying-begging let the belt around her pants carry her, small arms around my neck and the aviator jumping down right behind us and me running with my breath in my throat and my eyes closed and one second to think: *are those carabiners clipped on right?* And then we plummeted from the bridge and started spiraling down like madmen.

And a *yank* and a dizzying nosedive, and the world contracted. The hang glider righted itself and we were flying. I screamed, realizing I had never flown before, not without wings and not with them. The aviator screamed on the bridge, already far behind us now. And Dawnie... she didn't scream, but held on tightly to my back, her hands covering my eyes as she herself gazed around in delight.

*

It is relatively easy to fly a hang glider if the need arises, but landing while there is no ground to land on? That's a more complicated matter.

I was afraid to fly more than a small distance beneath the Earth's surface. That turned out to be simple, since the thermal from the fires hovering between the splintered rooftops and the smoke did indeed continue to lift the delta wing up. By moving my balance on the bar to the front, I dove down and prevented us from slamming into the Earth, and after some experimenting, I could steer the delta wing by shifting my weight to the left and right.

For the first time since your *it's not you, it's me*, a new feeling washed over me: a sense of freedom, at least temporarily pushing my desire to be someone else and somewhere else into the back of my mind.

After a while, a flock of geese came flying in our tail. I wondered where they had come from; they were just there, suddenly. I set a course for you and the geese winged along beside us.

The dead Earth was a thing of fabulous beauty.

We saw lovers, hugging each other in trees. We saw children, pulling small buckets of food and folded notes back and forth on clotheslines between upside-down windows. We saw people finding each other on the jumbled strings of assemblies they were building, forging the umbilical cord of a new society. And after a while we had left the city behind and all we saw were trees, their branches drooping sadly and their leaves fluttering away into the bottomless depths of the atmosphere, making it seem as if the Earth was weeping green tears.

We were very close to where you lived when Dawnie pointed and said, 'There's where we can go and see Mommy!'

Suspended in the air in front of us was a seemingly endless rope ladder, undulating calmly in the sultry breeze. As we neared it, I saw that the ladder hung from a trapdoor in the roof of a caravan, dangling from the face of the Earth by iron chains. A higgledy-piggledy board walkway connected it to a small, ramshackle, upside-down house from which enormous amounts of flaxen rope moved toward the peculiar trailer in spun cobwebs, as if some kind of machinery in there was perpetually working.

I circled the rope ladder and decided to crash in the apple orchard around the house. Slender tree trunks, lots of branches, and a lower boundary consisting of a thick canopy: it was iffy at best, but I guessed we wouldn't find a better place.

'Hold on to me very tightly,' I told Dawnie. 'And whatever you do, don't let go!'

Next thing, everything was jolting and swishing around us. Branches whipped, leaves swirled, shrieking birds burst off in flight. The delta wing snapped and tore and suddenly we stopped, the twisted frame pierced by branches. They broke, and we fell down through a nauseating air pocket, surrounded by the sickly smell of apples, before the canopy caught us and I managed to grab onto a tree trunk.

A window in the caravan popped open and a frail woman looking older than the Earth itself leaned out. 'My goodness!' she yelled. 'Are you all right?'

'I… think so…' I stammered. And promptly Dawnie rolled off my back and ended up dangling in the vacuum beneath the apple tree, her face a mask of bewilderment, a thousand thanks to the carabiner on her belt. I hoisted her up, unclipped her and put her in the crown of the apple tree. We had survived the impact with no more than a few scratches and some ripped clothes.

'You'd better hurry inside,' the woman said. 'You two look like you could use a cup of tea.'

A little while later we shuffled across the rickety footbridge, fastened to large hooks drilled into the Earth, toward the hanging trailer, careful not to get entangled in the rustling cobwebs of flaxen rope. Inside, my jaw dropped to the floor in surprise. The small caravan was literally crammed full of flax. The woman who had hailed us from the window now sat in a rocking chair and was twining the flax together in thick strings. A second, almost identical old lady was knotting the strings into a rope ladder and feeding it through the trapdoor in the floor.

'Be careful,' the second woman said worriedly. 'You don't want to fall through that. You have no idea how deep it is.'

'Of course they do, Junilla,' her sister argued. 'They've just come from down there.'

'But do they know how *deep* it is?' The little lady gazed at me expectantly, and I shrugged to be polite. 'That's my point, Leonilla,' she said, resolutely fastening a knot. 'No one knows.'

They gave us steaming cups of herbal tea. Then the woman named Junilla turned to Dawnie like only old ladies can, her industrious hands never missing a beat. 'What have you got there, sweet thing?'

Shyly twisting her body back and forth, Dawnie showed her the 7-Up bottle. The woman peered curiously inside from behind her thick lenses and Bubbles looked out through the thin plastic with unwavering melancholy.

'A goldfish!' Junilla cried out in dismay. 'What a terrible, terrible place for a goldfish.'

'Terrible!' her sister Leonilla concurred. 'A goldfish! That's the most terrible thing anyone could put inside a bottle.'

'Gin, yes…' Junilla said.

'Or a love letter…' Leonilla backed her up.

'But not a goldfish!'

'It *is* a love letter,' I blurted out. Suddenly my voice trembled. 'Or maybe not really. Well, actually, basically it is.' And before I knew it, I told the two women my story. I told them how your last words had prematurely ended the world, and how your last phone call had offered sufficient justification to try to bring you Bubbles – an impossible quest in an impossible world as a last impossible token of my love for you, because nothing was right in the world without you anyway, at least not for me, and never could be again. It didn't come as a relief to talk about it, my heart didn't feel an ounce lighter. I only realized I was crying when Dawnie caught my tears in the 7-Up bottle, making Bubbles think it was raining and, to everyone's surprise, urging him to somersault playfully.

'Poor thing,' Leonilla said, shaking her head.

'Poor, poor thing,' Junilla put it more strongly.

'A goldfish in a bottle…'

'Forever trapped in the same circle…'

'The same, depressing circle…'

'You should let go of her,' Junilla said decidedly. But how, how, how could I ever let go of you, when there wasn't a moment that passed without me wishing I could hold you close to me – so that, just for a short while, the world would no longer be upside-down? On an impulse, I pressed Dawnie close to me, and there and then, I was overwhelmed by grief and I cried, inconsolable and heartbroken. Not just because of the void you had left behind, but also because I now had to fill it with someone else. When a person's dreams are taken away from them, they will desperately cling to new ones, no matter how empty those dreams are.

Oh Sophie, I miss you so much.

'Things change, sweetheart, that's just the way it is,' Junilla said, laying a frail hand on my heaving shoulders.

'It's better to be prepared for change,' Leonilla said.

'So that it doesn't take you by surprise when it comes.'

'Take the world, for instance,' Leonilla declared.

'The *Earth*!' Junilla emphasized. 'What if the Earth, every once in a while, simply lets go? Takes a good look at what it's got, shivers, and shakes it all off?' And the old woman shivered after her own words.

'It's a good thing we were prepared,' Leonilla said, giving a disconcerting yank on the flaxen rope entering the trailer through the window.

'Were we ever,' Junilla confirmed. 'We're packing our bags!'

My eyes hot and wet, I stared at the trapdoor in the floor. 'Where are you going?'

'Haven't you seen all those falling stars at night?' Junilla asked. 'It must be wonderful down there!'

'Oh yes, wonderful!' Leonilla said. 'Miraculous, I'd say.'

'That's where we're going!'

Dawnie's little voice was almost lost amidst the lively

exclamations of the old women when she peered around the 7-Up bottle and said, 'My Mommy is a falling star, too.'

There was a brief silence. 'Really?' Leonilla responded. 'How wonderful for her! That means you get to make a wish, my dear.'

Dawnie's eyes widened and she writhed in embarrassment. 'Can I... can I come with you?'

'But of course, darling!' Junilla said. 'If Toby here doesn't mind...'

I nodded mutely, swallowing back fresh tears.

'Oh, sweetheart,' Junilla sighed. 'Why won't you just let go?'

'Nothing is worth clinging on to like that,' Leonilla said.

And then, shaking her head, 'A goldfish in a bottle...'

Right then, I lost track of whether we were talking about Bubbles, about you, or about me, and whether or not it made any difference.

*

All the times I had come in here before were like drops of honey sticking to my fingertips as I jammed the gangway between the final oak tree and the kitchen window frame. Mad with lust as a teenager in love sneaking through your bedroom window, whispering so your parents wouldn't hear us. Shaking with laughter as I carried you across the backdoor threshold after a morning stroll filled with calm nonsense out by the lake. With leaden feet after more new tales I knew to be lies, still desperately trying to believe them – because after all, lies are meant to fill a void and I didn't want you to have to live with a void. And now with your decision to go on without me heaped in the palms of my hands, and the power to reconsider in yours.

My heart leaped into my throat when I saw the white-painted, mirrored letters on the window in the façade:

HELP

So you were still alive. Your house hung upside-down and it was a ruin of crumbling memories, but you were still alive.

'Sophie.'

I stood on the ceiling of what remained of the kitchen and listened to the inverted silence.

And then, a landslide: 'Toby?'

My name.

Your voice.

I clambered through the door into the living room. I found more ravages of tumbled furniture, piled up all the way to the sagging floorboards. But you had cleared the middle of the ceiling and there you were, lying on the couch.

'It's really you,' you said, trying to push yourself up.

I shrugged, embarrassed. 'Of course.'

'I thought you were dead.'

I took the 7-Up bottle from my backpack and held it up. 'I brought Bubbles for you.'

Your incredulous gaze moved from the goldfish inside the bottle to me. 'But how did you get all the way...'

I shrugged again.

You grinned. 'You're insane, aren't you?'

'You know that.'

Your universe.

My universe.

I descended as you rose and I folded you – the fragile reality that was you – in my arms. You pressed stiffly against me and we sank down onto the couch. Your smell – evidently and impossibly *Sophie* – was so overwhelming and carried so much weight that I had to surrender to it utterly, no matter what might come after. It drove me mad. It didn't matter. And so I buried my face in your neck and inhaled your scent like a drug, immersing myself greedily in your presence. We lay there like that for a long time, intimately entangled, in a perfect, pure state of being.

'Everything okay?' I asked, moist lips against your earlobe.

'Yes. I think so, yes.' Hot air from your innermost self in my hair. 'I think my kneecap's broken. And my back hurts really bad.'

'Were you in bed?'

'Underneath it.'

'It's okay. I'm here now.' I caressed the gossamer, downy hairs behind your ear, the curve of your neck.

'Toby.'

'Sssh.'

'But...'

'It's okay.'

'Everything is truly, seriously fucked up, isn't it?'

I pushed gently away from you so I could look you in the eye. 'You called me.'

'Yes.'

'Sophie.'

You let go of me and hoisted yourself up, because you couldn't handle the situation.

But I clasped your hand and said, 'I've missed you, Sophie.'

'Stop it.' A tear trickled down your cheek. 'I'm so worried about Mom and Dad. I haven't heard from them. I haven't seen anyone since it happened, not a single soul. Do you know if help is coming?'

I felt myself growing faint inside. 'I came, didn't I?'

You looked at me for a long time. 'I'm sorry about how it all turned out.'

'Yeah. Me too,' I said. 'I liked it better when everything was still right-side up. Made it a lot easier to see each other.'

'Toby.'

'Well, sorry.' My voice shook, looking for purchase. 'I just don't know how to deal with it. Everything has changed now, right? Can't we...'

'Toby.'

'But couldn't we—'

'Don't, Toby.'

I couldn't hold back my tears. 'But I'll do everything differently.'

'You weren't the one who had to do things differently.'

'I can't handle this alone.'

'Sure you can.'

'But I love you.'

Remember how you looked away then, like you always used to? Your eyes too heavy, a bottomless depth inside them. I was torn away from you; I fell and I fell, and then *splash* into a bottle full of fizzing tears. A whirling vortex sucked me deeper and deeper below the water, propelled by the force of you looking away. In a panic, I kicked my legs and vainly groped for purchase on smooth, plastic walls.

'I love you!' I tried to scream, but my love rose in bubbles to the surface and burst apart. Weakened, I wheeled my arms, pounding on the plastic. And behind the label you looked away; you didn't see that I was drowning. I sank down in a slow spiral, hitting the bottom of the 7-Up bottle with a muffled thump.

My lungs filled up with tears as I whispered, 'Please...'

And you said, 'I need time.'

I came up then, spluttering and gasping for breath. Soaked and flabbergasted, I let the lie of those words descend on me. As soon as I was able, I clambered up and staggered out of the living room.

'Where are you going?'

'I'll get you some aspirin,' I mumbled stupidly.

'Wait!'

But I had already gone through the kitchen and didn't hear you. Hanging from the banister, I lowered myself to the upstairs floor. After everything I had been through, after the countless times I had risked my life to take Bubbles to you, trying in vain to still my love for you *with* my love for you, and scrambling up from the pounding surf of a dying Earth... *you need time?* How much more time do you think the world will give you, Sophie?

I crashed into the bulging ceiling, and it groaned beneath my weight. If the house had given way right then, I wouldn't have cared. But I wasn't even granted that much mercy – I was predestined to go down in your cold reality, not in my own illusion.

The bedroom. My picture wasn't on your wall. I wanted to believe it had fallen and splintered, I wanted to believe that more than anything in the world. Other photo frames lay broken on the ceiling: holiday snapshots, family, your friends. I knew them all intimately. Bunched-up sweater, the one I bought you in Paris. Open backgammon board. Dented candles. Upside-down bed. Broken glass. Buddha figurine. Not a trace of my picture.

The Earth turned away in shame.

Bubbles rolled on his stomach and floated to the surface.

On what had been my side of the bed I saw someone else's sneakers, someone else's watch, and how can I describe what comes next, how can I continue, I wonder how so much of my life could have occurred outside of me, and I hadn't known, or had I known after all, didn't that only make it worse, on to the bathroom, trendy jeans, trendy shirt, blood between the tiles, he must have been taking a shower, the cast iron bathtub had broken off and crushed him, his wallet in his pocket, student ID, Tom was his name, Tom something, fair-haired kid, longish hair, completely your type, the bathroom window was open, what have you done to him, dammit *that same fucking night* you spread your legs for him, what have you done to *me*?

Back downstairs you were leaning out of the kitchen window, stooped beneath the weight of missed opportunities. You were crying. Below me, on the gangway leading away from you, the ID cards with his picture on them slowly fluttered down. I gazed at you cold-faced. Yes, you needed time for yourself, and yes, I understood you needed to discover who you wanted to be. I understood your desire for a quieter place without promises and confessions. I would even have forgiven you your mistakes. You were my world. But the world had repelled everything. More logic than any human being could comprehend and more human beings than was comprehensibly logical... anything but the revolting image of you crying for someone else and the dawning realization that there was no longer any room for me in this reality you had created.

And the goldfish?

He deserved something better.

*

It was like a dream at the bottom of the world: I was sitting on a tree branch stretched out low beneath the shore of the hanging lake. My legs were dangling over nothing and above me I could see my own reflection in the water, burning in the sun dipping up behind the horizon. When I tapped the 7-Up bottle, a shiver ran through Bubbles' delicate fins and he turned his face toward me.

'Go on, boy,' I said, twisting the cap from the bottle. 'You're free.'

I held the bottle up and poked the top through the water surface. Air bubbles gurgled down and stayed afloat on the scales of gravity. Bubbles watched it all skeptically. Then I reached further, pushing the bottle all the way under and turning it over.

And Bubbles flipped over as well. Suddenly he was swimming upside-down, slithering skittishly from one end of the bottle to the other. The air bubbles escaped and I gently rocked the bottle back and forth until Bubbles discovered the opening of the screw cap and peeked curiously through it.

'Go on,' I whispered, shaking the drops of falling water from my hair. 'You're free.'

For one more moment, the goldfish lingered. Then he swam out of the bottle's neck. He looked around, wary. Suddenly his fins whirled and bristled, and he darted away into the deep.

So that was it. Bye, Bubbles. I smiled, feeling a bit melancholy. But my melancholy was soon washed away in a sense of fulfillment when I pulled the 7-Up bottle from the lake and finally, after such a long journey, let it go. I watched as the bottle tumbled down and disappeared from view. Then I straightened up. I was surprised to see Bubbles gazing at me from behind the reflection of my face. He had come back to the surface and pursed his lips over the water, as if he was telling me a secret, causing a minute ripple. I couldn't take my eyes away from the image. Why did it evoke so much love inside me? And then I understood. Of course: Bubbles wasn't the one who was upside-down... *I* was upside-down.

It was all just a matter of perspective.

Looking at it from the other side, the world was still right-side up.

I stripped naked and took a deep breath. I dunked my head through the surface of the water, enjoying the sudden sensation of coldness and fizzing air bubbles coming down and rinsing my face clean. Wobbly, I rose up on the branch, groping into the water with my arms, now submerged to the waist. And when I pushed off, gravity took a hold of me and I slipped like a diver into Bubbles's world.

I came up. Treading water, I started laughing. I had forgotten what normal looked like. Or normal... even though I was on the right side of up and down, my hair stood up in wet strands and made it rain in the universe. That made me laugh even harder. On the shore, trees lifted their arms like children being dressed in sweaters by their mothers. Somewhere a branch snapped, falling straight up into the sky.

Bubbles darted playfully around me, a streak of orange in the deep green waters. I dove under and we tumbled and somersaulted until my lungs felt fit to burst. Every time I resurfaced I felt a little lighter. Finally we swam out toward the middle of the lake in our newly acquired normality, side by side, the goldfish and me.

There, in my own little place in the world, I let go.

*

I don't know whether my sleep was dreamless because there were no falling stars or because a teasing twig in the crown of the tree was poking my back, but when I woke up the next morning a dreary fog was clinging to the Earth's surface. All around me, no matter where I looked, was gray. I wondered where the fog had come from. A muted silence hung over everything, and any sound I made stayed suspended inside it and made me more aware of myself.

It didn't take me long to return to the hanging caravan, but the two old ladies and Dawnie were gone. The trapdoor in the floor was open and the end of the rope ladder had been left tied to one of the rocking chairs. I imagined how Junilla and Leonilla, hauling their possessions and bickering incessantly, were descending the ladder rung by rung, with Dawnie following curiously behind. Somewhere, much lower down where the stars were falling, they would bump into the woman with the Kroger bags and she would say, *Well, imagine that. I was just looking for you.*

I swung my legs over the edge of the trapdoor and grabbed the first rung. Beneath my feet the ladder was calmly swaying and fading in the mist. I took a deep breath and started down, keeping my eyes closed as if I was sleepwalking. Droplets of fog condensed on my eyelashes. When I opened my eyes again, the Earth's surface had disappeared and all I could see above me were the hazy contours of the caravan. Then, even they were gone.

Now, I am alone, in the mist.

Were you thinking of me? And if you could have seen me descend, would you have wondered where the rope ladder leads? But then I would tell you it doesn't matter. What matters is the path you take, the journey you make. Once you realize that, it's easier to let go, at the end.

I think I want you to know that you hurt me so incredibly badly, Sophie. Now I'm going down the ladder. Searching for solid ground beneath my feet. It's not easy. I'm terrified of what I will find down there. But I close my eyes and keep descending. Sometimes the ropes shake and I imagine it's you following me, somewhere up there in the fog. But maybe it's just the wind. And I realize I don't care either way. I am somebody, too.

Down here, we are all falling stars.

Translated from the Dutch by Lia Belt

The Worldless

Indrapramit Das

India

Indra Das has been quietly publishing exceptional science fiction for over a decade now. He is also the author of *The Devourers*, an ambitious novel you should definitely seek out. Here he touches on a theme running throughout this anthology, of the displaced... and the worldless.

E very day NuTay watched the starship from their shack, selling starshine and sweet chai to wayfarers on their way to the stars. NuTay and their kin Satlyt baked an endless supply of clay cups using dirt from the vast plain of the port. NuTay and Satlyt, like all the hawkers in the shanties that surrounded the dirt road, were dunyshar, worldless – cursed to a single brown horizon, if one gently undulated by time to grace their eyes with dun hills. Cursed, also, to witness that starship in the distance, vessel of the night sky, as it set sail on the rippling waves of time and existence itself – so the wayfarers told them – year after year.

The starship. The sky. The dun hills. The port plain. They knew this, and this only.

*

Sometimes the starship looked like a great temple reaching to the sky. All of NuTay's customers endless pilgrims lining up to enter its hallowed halls and carry them through the cloth that gods made.

NuTay and Satlyt had never been inside a starship.

*

If NuTay gave them free chai, the wayfarers would sometimes show viz of other worlds on their armbands, flicking them like so much dijichaff into the air, where they sprouted into glowing spheres, ghost marbles to mimic the air-rich dewdrops that clustered eon-wise along the fiery filaments of the galaxy. The wayfarers would wave in practiced arkana, and the spheres would twirl and zoom and transform as they grew until their curvature became glimpses of those worlds and their settlements glittering under the myriad suns and moons. NuTay would watch, silent, unable to look away.

Once, Satlyt, brandishing a small metal junk shiv, had asked whether NuTay wanted them to corner a wayfarer in a lonesome corner of the port and rob them of their armband or their data coins. NuTay had slapped Satlyt then, so hard their cheek blushed pink.

NuTay knew Satlyt would never hurt anyone – that all they wanted was to give their maba a way to look at pictures of other worlds without having to barter with wayfarers.

When NuTay touched Satlyt's cheek a moment after striking, the skin was hot with silent anger, and perhaps shame.

*

Sometimes the starship looked like monolithic shards of black glass glittering in the sun, carefully stacked to look beautiful but terrifying.

Sometimes the starship would change shape, those shards moving slowly to create a different configuration of shapes upon shapes with a tremendous moaning that sounded like a gale moving across the hills and pouring out across the plain. As it folded and re-folded, the starship would no longer look like shards of black glass.

Sometimes, when it moved to reconfigure its shape, the starship would look suddenly delicate despite its size, like black paper origami of a starship dropped onto the plain by the hand of a god.

NuTay had once seen an actual paper starship, left by a wayfarer on one of NuTay's rough-hewn benches. The wayfarer had told them the word for it: origami. The paper had been mauve, not black.

*

The world that interested NuTay the most, of course, was Earth. The one all the djeens of all the peoples in the galaxy first came from, going from blood to blood to whisper the memory of the first human into all their bodies so they still looked more or less the same no matter which world they were born on.

'NuTay, Earth is so crowded you can't imagine it,' one wayfarer had told them, spreading their hands across that brown horizon NuTay was so familiar with. 'Just imagine,' the wayfarer said. 'Peoples were having kin there before there were starships. Before any peoples went to any other star than Sol. This planet, your planet, is a station, nah?'

NuTay then reminded the wayfarer that this was not *their* planet, not really, because it was not a place of peoples but a port for peoples to rest between their travels across the universe. Dunyshar had no planet, no cultures to imitate, no people.

'Ach, you know that's the same same,' the wayfarer said,

but NuTay knew it wasn't, and felt a slight pain in their chest, so familiar. But they knew the wayfarer wouldn't know what this was, and they said nothing and listened as they spoke on. 'If this planet is port, then Earth, that is the first city in the universe – Babal, kafeen-walla. Not so nice for you. Feels like not enough atmo for so many peoples if you go there, after this planet with all this air, so much air, so much place.'

And NuTay told that wayfarer that they'd heard that Earth had a thousand different worlds on it, because it had a tilt and atmos that painted its lands a thousand different shades of place as it spun around the first Sun.

'Less than a thousand, and not the only world with other worlds on it,' the wayfarer said, laughing behind their mask. 'But look,' the wayfarer raised their arm to spring viz into the air, and there was a picture of a brown horizon, and dun hills. 'See? Just like here.' NuTay looked at the dun hills, and marveled that this too could be Earth. 'Kazak-istan,' said the wayfarer, and the placename was a cold drop of rain in NuTay's mind, sending ripples across their skull. It made them feel better about their own dun hills, which caught their eye for all the long days. Just a little bit better.

So it went. Wayfarers would bring pieces of the galaxy, and NuTay would hold the ones of Earth in their memory. It had brown horizon, blue horizon, green horizon, red horizon, gray horizon.

*

When the starship was about to leave, the entire port plain would come alive with warning, klaxons sounding across the miles of empty dirt and clanging across the corrugated roofs of the shop shanties and tents. NuTay and Satlyt would stop work to watch even if they had customers, because even customers would turn their heads to see.

To watch a starship leave is to witness a hole threaded through reality, and no one can tire of such a vision. Its lights glittering, it would fold and fold its parts until there was a thunderous boom that rolled across the plain, sending glowing cumulus clouds rolling out from under the vessel and across the land.

A flash of light like the clap of an invisible hand, and the clouds would be gone in less than a second to leave a perfect black sphere where the starship had been. If you looked at the sphere, which was only half visible, emerging from the ground a perfect gigantic bubble of nothingness, it would hurt your eyes, because there was *nothing* to see within its curvature. For an intoxicating second there would be hurtling winds ripping dust through the shop shanties, creating a vortex of silken veils over the plain and around the sphere. The shanty roofs would rattle, the horses would clomp in their stables, the wind chimes would sing a shattering song. The very air would vibrate as if it were fragile, humming to the tune of that null-dimensional half-circle embedded in the horizon, a bloated negative sunrise.

In the next moment, the sphere would vanish in a thunderclap of displaced atmos, and there would be only flat land where the starship had once stood.

A few days later, the same sequence would occur in reverse, and the starship would be back, having gone to another world and returned with a new population. When it returned, the steam from its megastructures would create wisps of clouds that hung over the plain for days until they drifted with their shadows into the hills.

*

Being younger dunyshar, Satlyt worked at the stalls some days, but did harder chores around the port, like cleaning toilets and helping starship crews do basic maintenance work. Every sunrise, NuTay watched Satlyt leave the stall on their dirt bike, space-black hair free to twine across the wind. The droning dirt bike would draw a dusty line across the plain, its destination the necklace of far-off lights extending from where the squatting starship basked in sunrise – the dromes where wayfarers refueled, processed, lived in between worlds. The dirt bikes would send wild horses rumbling in herds across the port plain, a sight that calmed NuTay's weakening bones.

NuTay had worked at the dromes, too, when they were younger and more limber. They'd liked the crowds there, the paradisiacal choirs of announcements that echoed under vaulted ceilings, the squealing of boots on floor leaving tracks to mop up, the harsh and polychrome cast of holofake neon, advertising bars, clubs, eateries and shops run by robots, or upscale wayfarer staff that swapped in and out to replace each other with each starship journey, so they didn't have to live on the planet permanently like the dunyshar. Nowadays the dromes were a distant memory. NuTay stayed at the shack, unable to do that much manual labour.

Those that spent their lives on the planet of arrivals and departures could only grow more thin and frail as time washed over the days and nights. The dunyshars' djeens had whispered their flesh into Earth-form, but on a world with a weaker gravity than Earth.

*

NuTay's chai itself was brewed from leaf grown in a printer tent with a second-hand script for accelerated microclimate

– hardware left behind from starships over centuries, nabbed from the junk shops of the port by NuTay for shine and minutes of tactile, since dunyshar were never not lonely and companionship was equal barter, usually (usually) good for friendships.

NuTay would meditate inside the chai-printing tent, which was misty and wet in growing season. Their body caressed by damp green leaves, air fragrant with alien-sweet perfume of plant life not indigenous, with closed eyes NuTay would pretend to be on Earth, the source of chai and peoples and everything. Each time a cycle ended, and the microclimate roasted the leaves to heaps of brown brew-ready shavings, the tent hissed steam like one of NuTay's kettles, and that whistle was a quiet mourning for the death of that tent-world of green. Until next cycle.

The tent had big letters across its fiber on the outside, reading *Darjeeling* in Englis and Nagar script. A placename, a wayfarer had clarified.

When Satlyt was younger, they'd asked NuTay if the dunyshar could just build a giant printer tent the size of the port itself, and grow a huge forest of plants and trees here like on Earth or other worlds. NuTay knew these weren't thoughts for a dunyshar to have, and would go nowhere. But they said they didn't know.

The starshine was easier, brewed from indigenous fungus grown in shit.

*

Sometimes, as evening fell and the second sun lashed its last threads of light across the dun hills gone blue, or when the starship secreted a mist that wreathed its alloyed spires, the starship looked like a great and distant city. Just like NuTay had seen in viz of other worlds – towers of lights flickering to give darkness a shape, the outline of lives lived.

The starship *was* a city, of course. To take people across the galaxy to other cities that didn't move across time and existence.

There were no cities here, of course, on the planet of arrivals and departures. If you travelled over the horizon, as NuTay had, you would find only more port plains dotted with emptiness and lights and shop shanties and vast circular plains with other starships at their centers. Or great mountain ranges that were actually junkyards of detritus left by centuries of interstellar stops, and dismantled starships in their graveyards, all crawling with scavengers. Some dunyshar dared to live in those dead starships, but they were known to be unstable and dangerous, causing djeens to mutate so kin would be born looking different than humans. If this were true, NuTay had never seen such people, who probably kept to themselves, or died out.

NuTay had heard that if you walked far enough, you could see fields with starships so massive they reached the clouds, hulking across the sky, that these could take you to worlds at the very edge of the galaxy, where you could see the void between this galaxy and the next one – visible as a gemmed spiral instead of a sun.

*

Once, the wayfarer who'd left the origami starship for NuTay had come back to the stall, months or years later. NuTay hadn't realized until they left, because they'd been wearing goggles and an air-filter. But they left another little paper origami, this time in white paper, of a horse.

Horses were used for low-energy transport and

companionship among many of the dunyshar. They had arrived centuries ago as frozen liquid djeens from a starship's biovat, though NuTay was five when they first realized that horses, like humans, weren't *from* the world they lived in. Curiously, the thought brought tears to their eyes when they first found this out.

*

Sometimes the starship looked like a huge living creature, resting between its journeys, sweating and steaming and groaning through the night.

This it was, in some sense. Deep in its core was residual life left by something that had lived eons ago on the planet of arrivals and departures: the reason for this junction in space. There was exotech here, found long before NuTay or any dunyshar were born here, ghosts of when this planet *was* a world, mined by the living from other worlds. Dunyshar were not allowed in these places, extraterra ruins where miners, archaeologists, and other pilgrims from across the galaxy gathered. NuTay, like most dunyshar, had little interest in these zones or the ruins of whatever civilization was buried under the dirt of this once-world. Their interest was in the living civilization garlanding the galaxy, the one that was forever just out of their reach.

On their brief travels with Satlyt strapped to their back as a tender-faced baby, NuTay had seen the perimeter of one of these excavation zones from a mile away, floodlights like a white sunrise against the night, flowing over a vast black wall lined with flashing lights. Humming in the ground, and thunder crashing over the flatlands from whatever engines were used to unearth the deep ruins and mine whatever was in them.

NuTay's steed, a sturdy black mare the stablemaster that had bartered her had named Pacho, had been unusually restless even a mile from that zone. NuTay imagined the ghosts of a bygone world seeping from out of those black walls and trickling into their limbs and lungs and those of their tender child gurgling content against their back.

NuTay rode away as fast as they could. Pacho died a few weeks later, perhaps older than the stablemaster had promised. But NuTay blamed the zone, and rubbed ointment on Satlyt for months after, dreading the morning they'd find their kin dead because of vengeful ghosts from the long dead world that hid beneath this planet's time.

For Satlyt's survival NuTay thanked the stars, especially Sol, that had no ghosts around them.

*

Satlyt had asked NuTay one day where they'd come from, and whose kin NuTay themself was. NuTay had waited for that day, and had answers for their child, who was ten at the time. They sat by their shack in the evening light, NuTay waving a solar lantern until it lit.

I am a nu-jen dunyshar, Satlyt, they said to their child. This means I have no maba, no parents at all.

Satlyt asked how, eyes wide with existential horror.

Listen. Many... djeens were brought here frozen many years ago. I taught you; two humans' djeens whisper together to form a new human. Some humans share their djeens with another human in tiny eggs held in their bellies, and others share it in liquid held between their legs. Two people from some world that I don't know gave their djeens in egg and liquid, so that peoples could bring them here frozen to make new humans to work here, and help give solace to the wayfarers traveling the stars. We are these new humans – the dunyshar. There are many old-jen dunyshar here who have parents, and grandparents, and on and on – the first of their pre-kin were born to surrogates a long time ago. Understand, nah?

Satlyt nodded, perhaps bewildered.

I was nu-jen; the first person my djeens formed here on the planet of arrivals and departures. I was born right there, NuTay stopped here to point at the distant lights of the dromes. In the nursery, where wayfarer surrogates live for nine months growing us, new-jen kin, when there aren't enough people in the ports anymore. They get good barter value for doing this, from the off-world peoples who run these ports.

Who taught you to talk? Who taught you what all you know? asked Satlyt.

The dunyshar, chota kin! They will help their own. All the people in this shanty place, they taught me. The three sibs who raised me through the youngest years and weaned me are all, bless them, dead from time, plain simple. This planet is too light for humans to live too long as Earth and other livable worlds.

Did you sleep with the three sibs so the djeens whispered me into existence?

No, no! No, they were like my parents, I couldn't do that. I slept with another when I grew. Their name was Farweh. Farweh, I say na, your other maba. With them I had you, chota kin.

They are dead, too?

NuTay smiled then, though barely. I don't know, Satlyt. They left, on a starship.

How? They were a wayfarer?

No, they grew up right here, new-jen, same as me. They had long black hair like you, and the red cheeks like you also, the djeens alive and biting at the skin to announce the beauty of the body they make.

Satlyt slapped NuTay's hand and stuck out their tongue.

Oy! Why are you hitting your maba? Fine, you are ugly, the djeens hide away and are ashamed.

Satlyt giggled.

Anyway, such a distracted child. Your other maba, we grew up here together. We had you.

They were here? When I was born?

NuTay pursed their lips. They had promised that their child would have the entire truth.

For a while, hn. But they left. Don't be angry. Farweh wanted to take you. They made a deal with a wayfarer that sold them a spacesuit. They said they could get two more, one emergency suit for babies. Very clever, very canny, Farweh was.

Why?

NuTay took a deep breath. To hold on to a starship. To see eternity beyond the Window, and come out to another world on the other side.

Other maba went away holding on to a starship on the outside?

I see I taught you some sense, chota kin. Yes, it is as dangerous as it sounds. Some people have done it – if they catch you on the other side, they take you away to jail, like in the dromes for murderers and rapists and drunkards. But bigger jail, for other worlds. That is if you survive. Theory, na? Possible. But those who do it, ride the starships on the side, see the other side of time? They never come back. So we can't ask if it worked or no, nah? So I said no. I said I will not take my kin like a piece of luggage while hanging on to the side of a starship. I refused Farweh. I would not take you, or myself, and I demanded Farweh not go. I grabbed their arm and hurt them by mistake, just a little, chota kin, but it was enough for both of us. I let them go, forever.

Farweh... maba. Other maba went and never came back.

Shh, chota kin, NuTay stroked a tear away from Satlyt's cheek. You didn't know Farweh, though they are your other maba. I gave them all the tears you can want to honor them. No more.

But you liked Farweh, maba. You grew up with them.

NuTay smiled, almost laughing at the child's sweetness. They held Satlyt before their little face crumpled, letting them cry just a little bit for Farweh, gone to NuTay forever, dead or alive behind the black window of existence.

*

Many years later, NuTay's kin Satlyt proved themself the kin of Farweh, too, in an echo of old time. They came droning across the plains from the dromes, headlights cutting across the dust while NuTay sipped chai with the other shanty wallahs in the middle of the hawkers' cluster. The starship was gone, out on some other world, so business was slow that evening.

Satlyt thundered onto the dust road in the center of the shanty town, screeching to a halt, their djeens clearly fired up and steaming from the mouth in the chilly air.

Your kin is huffing, one of the old hawkers grinned with their gums. Best go see to them.

So NuTay took Satlyt indoors to the shack, and asked what was wrong.

Listen, NuTay. Maba. I've seen you, year after year, looking at the wayfarers' pictures of Earth. You pretend when I'm around, but I can see that you want to go there. Go after Farweh.

Go after Farweh? What are you on about? We don't even know whether they went to Earth, or if they're alive, or rotting in some jail on some remote world in the galaxy.

Not for real go after, I mean go, after. Story-type, nah?

Feri tail?

Exact. I know next time the starship comes, it will go to Earth. Know this for fact. I have good tips from the temp staff at the dromes.

What did you barter for this?

Some black market subsidiary exotech from last starship crew, changing hands down at the dromes. Bartered some that came to my hands, bartered some shine, some tactile, what's it matter?

Tactile, keh!

Please, maba. I use protection. You think wayfarers fuck dunyshar without protection? They don't want our djeens whispering to theirs, they just want our bodies exotic.

What have you done, chota kin?

Don't worry, maba. I wouldn't barter tactile if I wasn't okay with it. But listen. I did good barter, better than just info. Spacesuit, full function. High compressed oxy capacity. Full-on nine hours. Starship blinks in and out of black bubble, max twenty hours depending on size. The one in our port – medium size, probably ten hours. Plus, camo-field, to blend into the side of the ship. We'll make it. Like Farweh did.

How do you know so much? Where do you get all this tech?

Same way you did, maba. Over years. There are people in the dromes, Satlyt said in excitement. They know things. I talk. I give tactile. I learn. I learn there are worlds, like you did. This? You know this isn't a world. Ghost planet. Fuel station. Port. You know this; we all know this. Farweh had the right idea.

NuTay shook their head. This was it. It was happening again. From the fire of the djeens raging hot in Satlyt's high cheekbones they knew – there was no saying no. Like they'd lost Farweh to time and existence, they would lose Satlyt too.

NuTay knew there was no holding Satlyt by the arm to try to stop them, like before – they were too weak for that now.

Even if NuTay had been strong enough, they would never do that again.

It was as if Farweh had disappeared into that black bubble, and caused a ripple of time to lap across the port in a slow wave that had just arrived. An echo in time. The same request, from kin.

What do you say, maba? asked Satlyt, eyes wide like when they were little.

We might die, chota kin.

Then we do. Better than staying here to see your eyes go dead.

*

Even filtered breathing, the helmet and the suit was hot, so unlike the biting cold air of the planet. NuTay felt like they might shit the suit, but what could one do. There was a diaper inside with bio-absorbent disinfectant padding, or so the wayfarer had said.

They had scaled the starship at night, using a service drone operated by the green-eyed wayfarer who had made the deal with Satlyt, though they had other allies, clearly. Looking at those green Earth-born eyes, and listening to their strange accent but even stranger affection for Satlyt, NuTay realized there might be more here than mere barter greed. This wayfarer felt *bad* for them, wanted to help, which made NuTay feel a bit sick as they clambered into the spacesuit. But the wayfarer also felt something else for Satlyt, who seemed unmoved by this affection, their jaw set tight and face braced to meet the future that was hurtling towards them.

*

'There'll be zero-g in the sphere once the starship phases into it. Theoretically, if the spacesuits work, you should be fine, there's nothing but vacuum inside the membrane – the edges of the sphere. If your mag-tethers snap, you'll float out towards those edges, which you absolutely do not want. Being inside the bubble is safe in a suit, but if you float out to the edge and touch it, there's no telling what will happen to you. We don't know. You might see the entirety of the universe in one go before dying, but you will die, or no longer be alive in the way we know. Understand? Do not jerk around with the tethers – hold on to each other. Hold on to each other like the kin you are. Stay calm and drift with the ship in the bubble so there's no stress on the tethers. Keep your eyes closed throughout. Open when you hear the ship's noise again. Do not look at the inside of the bubble, or you might panic and break tether. That's it. Once the ship phases out, things will get tough in a different way, if you're alive. Earth ports are chaos, and there's a chance no one will find you till one of my contacts comes by with a ship-surface drone to get you. There are people on Earth who sympathize with the dunyshar, who want to give them lives. Give you lives. So don't lose hope. There are people who have survived this. I've ushered them to the other side. But if you survive only to have security forces capture you, ask for a refugee lawyer. Got it? *Refugee.* Remember the word. You have been kept here against your will, and you are escaping. Good luck. I'll be inside.' The wayfarer paused, breathless. 'I wish you could be too. But security is too tight inside. They don't think enough people have the courage to stick to the side of the ship and see the universe naked. And most don't. They don't know, do they?'

With that, the wayfarer kissed Satlyt's helmet, and then NuTay's, and wiped each with their gloved hand, before folding themselves into the drone and detaching it from the ship. Lightless and silent, they sailed away into the night. NuTay hoped they didn't crash it.

NuTay felt sick, dangling from the ship, even though they were on an incline. Below them, the lights of the launching pad lit a slow mist rising from the bottom of the starship, about four hundred feet down. The skin of the ship was warm and rumbled in a sleeping, breathing rhythm. They switched on the camo-field, which covered them both, though they couldn't see the effects.

Satlyt was frighteningly silent. Chota kin, NuTay whispered to test the range com. Maba, Satlyt whispered back with a sweaty smile.

*

The starship awoke with the suns. Their uneasy dozing was broken by the light, and by the deeper rumble in the starship's skin. The brown planet of arrivals and departures stretched away from them, in the distance those dun hills. The pale blue sky flecked with thin icy clouds. The port dromes, the dirt roads like pale veins, the shanties glittering under the clear day in the far distance. Their one and only place. Hom, as wayfarers said. A strange word. Those fucking dun hills, thought NuTay.

Bless us Sol and all the stars without ghosts, whispered NuTay. Close your eyes, chota kin.

Remember Farweh, maba, said Satlyt, face wet behind the curved visor. The bottom of the starship exploded into light, and NuTay thought they were doomed, the juddering sending them sliding down the incline. NuTay held Satlyt's gloved hand tight, grip painful, flesh and bone pressed against flesh and bone through the nanoweaves.

I am old, NuTay thought. Let Satlyt live to see Earth.

*

The light, the sound, was gone.

*

Satlyt convulsed next to NuTay, who felt every movement of their kin through closed eyes. They embraced, NuTay holding Satlyt tight, a hollow vibration when their visors met. The ship was eerily still under them, no longer warm through the thick suit. Satlyt was making small sounds that coalesced slowly into words. We're alive.

Their breathing harsh in the helmet, the only sound along with the hissing breath of Satlyt into their own mic.

NuTay opened their eyes to see the universe looking back.

*

Don't look. Don't look. Don't look.

I know you opened your eyes, maba. What did you see?

I don't. Don't look. I saw darkness. Time like a living thing, a… a womb, with the light beyond its skin the light from creation, from the beginning of time and the end, so far away, shining through the dark skin. There were veins, of light, and information, pulsing around us. I saw our djeens rippling through those veins in the universe, humanity's djeens. Time is alive, Satlyt. Don't let it see us. Keep your eyes closed.

I will, maba. That is a good story, Satlyt gasped. Remember it, for the refuji lawyer.

*

Time is alive, and eventually it births all things, just as it ends all things.

When the ship turned warm with fresh thunder, their visors were set aglow, bathing their quivering eyelids with hot red light, the light of blood and djeens. Their spacesuits thumped down on the incline, the tethers umbilical around each other, kin and kin like twins through time entwined, clinging to the skin of a ship haunted by exoghosts.

They held each other tight, and under Sol, knew the light of hom, where the first djeens came from.

Now You Feel It

Andrea Chapela

Mexico

Hailing from Mexico City, Andrea was picked as one of *Granta*'s best young writers in Spanish, and that's no surprise! 'Now You Feel It' is excellent – and it is excellent science fiction, too. It is translated by Emma Törzs, a writer in her own right, showing once again that it's thanks to the hard work of translators that we get to see some of the world's amazing fiction.

ivera had been weaving dreamscapes at Ibsen Spa for twelve hours when a new videolog came in, a back-of-the-neck buzz. Two blinks opened the message: *Urgent work*, it said, followed by a telephone number. Rivera had been about to go home, but this message changed everything. Finally, after a whole year gone: a new job. Here at Ibsen Spa, the work was easy, with no risk of being stuck in the viscous aftermath of mind-manipulation; but neither did the Spa offer any chance of exercising skill or talent. Such opportunities – and the feelings of mastery that came with them – were part and parcel of working for the agency. But after that last job, after that loss of control, the boss had sworn Rivera would never work for them again. *Be grateful*, he'd said. After all, the punishment could have been so much worse.

With the agency, Rivera had modified people's minds; modified their past intentions. Permanent and untraceable changes. If the boss was swallowing his pride and calling now, it meant somebody with a lot of money must be desperate – and desperation made for the most interesting jobs.

Rivera went back to the small, spa-assigned studio, with its low lights, uncirculated air, and padded pink satin walls. It was all designed to help clients relax, though to Rivera it felt claustrophobic, like being inside a human body. But behind the studio's closed doors, it was easy enough to use a ping to disconnect the room from the outside. Most people preferred wristlets, but Rivera still liked the physicality of the ping. It did everything a wristlet did, but it was easier to hide, easier to customize… and easier to destroy, if necessary. Depending on what was needed, the ping could act as a handheld remote or as a control for the images on a retinal screen.

Rivera crouched in front of a locker at the far end of the room and pressed down on the false bottom. Inside the hidden drawer lay a briefcase and a cellular phone so old Rivera's grandparents might've used it in the early years of the twenty-first century. Given the kind of clientele the agency attracted, such technological discretion was paramount. Agency clients never had honorable intentions – they were always rich, powerful, and well-disposed to pay exorbitant sums for illicit services. Looking at the cellphone, Rivera hesitated, left fist opening and closing, wrist throbbing. It still ached like this on rainy days, and here in Mexico City that meant at least once a week. But the long-absent weight of memories tingling against fingertips was irresistible: Rivera had missed this work too much to think twice.

'I thought you said you'd never work with me again,' Rivera said when the call connected.

'Rivera,' said the boss. His velvety voice was chilling. 'Don't make me beg. This case is delicate and we need your skills.

We'll pay you quite a bit more than you've made this past year... And you and I both know how much you miss the job.'

Left fist open. Closed. Open. The ghost of pain still lingered, but the boss was right. He knew that Ibsen Spa's soft pink room could hold neither challenge nor thrill.

'The last time we saw each other,' Rivera said, 'you broke my arm and told me to forget about working for you ever again. So why me, why now? You have other people.'

'I told you not to make me beg.' The boss had the smooth, cultivated voice of a man who always got what he wanted, but Rivera knew him well enough to sense the humor in his tone. 'Garro's abroad and I need the best. I've decided to overlook your... slip.'

'How much are we talking?'

Another neck-buzz, another videolog. A long line of zeros appeared, and on the other end of the phone, the boss laughed as Rivera inhaled sharply. With this kind of money, it'd be possible to get out of debt, to buy the apartment outright, take fewer shifts at Ibsen, work only with those clients who actually seemed interesting.

Rivera thought of the woman from that final agency job, thought of the surge of rage that had made it impossible to go on, and took a deep breath. It had been an isolated case. It wouldn't happen again.

'Where do I have to go?'

'In fifteen minutes,' said the boss, 'you'll find a car on the corner of Aldama and Cádiz, by the Oxxo.'

'And the procedure?'

'Cognitive rewiring. It has to stand up to legal scrutiny, so you mustn't leave a single sign of your work.'

'I'll be there.'

'Good. And one more thing, Rivera.' The brief pause and

the sudden ice of his tone made it suddenly hard to breathe. 'I trust you've learned your lesson and will behave yourself. No playing at justice. You're an unbiased agent: I'm paying you to do the work and then leave without a trace.'

The boss had never believed Rivera's claim that it'd been an accident. But there was no point in arguing.

'It won't happen again.'

'I hope not,' he said. 'I wouldn't want to regret this call and be forced to pay you another visit.'

He hung up.

Rivera left the cellphone in the locker's hidden drawer but removed the briefcase and took out a pair of sunglasses, testing the buttons on each arm to ensure the closed-circuit still worked. Some equipment was delicate enough to have been ruined by a year without use, but these were still active. Sunglasses atop head, briefcase in hand, Rivera headed for the private clients' changing room and took out a packet of intrabugs, grimacing to find only three of them left. The needles were made of an iridium-platinum amalgam, illegal and very hard to get, and it'd take the better part of a month's salary to find more when they were gone. But with just a quick puncture behind the ear, one little intrabug could sever a mental connection to the network – a connection Rivera severed now.

The abrupt silence and sudden, shooting headache made it hard to see, and Rivera leaned against the sink waiting for the nausea to pass, for the world's colors to readjust. When a brain was used to the constant buzz of the network – to the ads, messages, explanations, dialogue bubbles – the clamor was only really noticeable when it was gone. Rivera breathed deeply a few times, blinked, and slid the sunglasses on in an effort to avoid the newly intolerable brightness of the lights.

It was just another job. Nothing had changed.

*

The client was a tall, heavyset man who stopped pacing when Rivera entered his office. Even at one o'clock in the morning he was wearing a gray suit, a blue tie, and freshly shined shoes, as perfectly groomed as if he'd gotten dressed only moments before. Rivera recognized him immediately; his face had been on the news countless times. This was Don Francisco Mejía-Botta, businessman and brother of a deputy whose name was being circulated as a candidate for the next gubernatorial election. Their family wasn't just rich; it was pedigreed.

'You're Rivera?' he asked, disbelieving.

Rivera took off her sunglasses, but despite her satisfaction at his incredulity, she didn't smile. Her clients, perhaps due to the combination of illegality and technology implicit in the job, always expected a man. Which was why Rivera wore her hair long and dressed always in a blouse and skirt: so they could never forget she was a woman. Like this man, many clients grew uncomfortable upon first seeing her, but that was an advantage. Staying one step ahead of her clients' reactions was one of the biggest challenges in this line of work.

'I am,' she said. 'Good evening. I'm here because the agency says you need a quick, clean job, and you requested the best.'

Cautiously, the man examined her, his chin raised unnecessarily high as if he smelled something rotten; he was incapable of hiding his disgust at her presence. All the better. Transparent client; easy job.

'It's a sensitive case,' he said. 'You'll have to sign a non-disclosure agreement. Nothing you see or learn here can ever leave this room.'

'I'm aware of the terms.' She wouldn't give him the pleasure of her discomfort. This was a game she knew better than he did. 'The agency should've pre-signed for me electronically, but if your lawyer's advising you to keep a paper record, then I'll sign again now; that way we can start as quickly as possible. It's my understanding that we don't have much time.'

The contents of Mejía-Botta's contract were hardly noteworthy. Rivera had signed hundreds just like it. Nevertheless, she took her time, not only to make sure there were no hidden tricks, but to prolong the silence.

She'd been in many wealthy houses when she worked for the agency, yet this was one of the biggest and oldest, probably inherited. But its security was a disaster: there was barbed wire around the garden, a digital security barrier on the threshold, and little cameras hovering above the doors and windows like fireflies. Predictable and stupid. So many people believed that maintaining vigilance from outside would keep their house safe... but such measures did nothing if the danger was already within.

Rivera had barely needed to glance down the hallways to see all the changes the old structure had suffered in order to adapt to new technologies. There were little sensors everywhere, working against the thickness of the stone walls to maintain the network, and their blinking red lights made it clear that all connection was currently turned off. Having such low connectivity was risky; if the police went through the general logs, the lack of network activity would raise suspicion. Rivera would take care of that before she left.

'Is there a problem?' the client asked.

'No,' said Rivera. She signed the papers. 'Everything seems to be in order. What's the situation?'

The client took the contract and shut it away in the desk's main drawer. Rivera heard the little *click* of the lock: a combination. Again, stupid. Those locks were so easy to crack.

Mejía-Botta sat down behind the desk but made no move to offer Rivera a seat and she didn't ask for one. She could do this standing.

'I assumed the agency would've briefed you,' he said. He was drumming his fingers on the table as if in exasperation, but Rivera could see he was stalling. He didn't want to go into detail and didn't know what to do with his hands. She stayed silent.

The office was a big room, dominated by a dark wooden desk and three bookshelves. Judging by the state of the books, many of them had probably never been read. A pure show of money and status. Yet the welcome-hologram that had guided her there had been an old image, the colors faded, probably at least ten years old. Ostentation with no real attention.

Mejía-Botta loosened his tie and made a quick gesture, and the door opened again. A young man appeared, around eighteen but probably still in high school. Despite his shower-wet hair, he smelled strongly of a sobering tonic. Rivera was more than acquainted with the sweet smell of ethanol derivatives as they broke down in the body; many of her clients at Ibsen smelled exactly like this boy did. Giving him the soberizer had been a good decision – Rivera might have to clean up the memories of intoxication, but at least she wouldn't have to deal with any physical effects. The boy was uncomfortable, his red, unfocused eyes darting around the room without settling on her. Dilated pupils, continuous changes in posture, accelerated breathing: he'd had an anxiety attack recently, but even that couldn't touch his arrogance. It oozed out of his every pore, from the desultory way he held himself, to his lack of shoes, to his gray sweatpants, marked with a private school crest, and topped with a sweatshirt so old it was coming apart at the sleeves.

'This is my son, Gabriel,' said Mejía-Botta. 'He had a little... incident... a few hours ago, and it's possible the police will be coming to interrogate him in the morning.'

'What happened?' Rivera asked Gabriel, but the boy avoided her gaze and it was his father who answered.

'Just a bit of nonsense with a girl at his school,' he said. 'But she's from a good family, which complicates matters. The two were dating, there was a mix-up with a few photos, and apparently now she's run away from home.'

'They weren't photos; they were videos,' Gabriel interrupted. He couldn't sit still. He jiggled his foot, shifted in place, open and closed his fists as if he were trying to access the network. He had all the nervous twitches of someone who wasn't used to being disconnected for so long. This inability to withstand periods of being offline was ever-more common in young people. Rivera would have to modify the evidence of Gabriel's reduced connectivity, too – as with the house, it would leave a blank spot in the network log, and though it wasn't illegal to be disconnected, it would certainly attract the authorities' attention.

'Videos, photos, it doesn't matter,' she said. 'What interests me is the intention. I need to know if you're innocent.'

'I don't care if Gabriel's innocent or not,' her client interjected. He took off his tie and unbuttoned the neck of his shirt, clearly tense. 'That's what you're here for. What I want is to be assured that if the police show up, it will be clear to them that Gabriel's the real victim here.'

Clean-up for a rich little boy. They'd really called her in for something so trivial? From the state of Gabriel, it was easy to guess the story. Sexual disappointment followed by virtual humiliation. The latter had been a serious crime for a few decades, but since it was now possible to analyse someone's memories, the crime was prosecuted based on intentionality. If this really had all been an accident, Gabriel would get off with a few months of community service. But if the prosecutor for this case could demonstrate that the defamation had been premeditated, and furthermore, that the girl had done herself injury because of it, Gabriel would get a harsher sentence. Up to four years in prison, if he was over eighteen, and a boy like Gabriel wouldn't last four years in a Mexican prison.

Rivera put her hair back and took out her briefcase. Gabriel would feel more comfortable if she concentrated on something other than him.

'Tell me what happened today, Gabriel,' she said. 'May I call you Gabriel?'

Gabriel nodded. He laced and unlaced his fingers before glancing at his father. Fear of authority, or of telling the truth? A bit of both, probably.

'Carmen called me at nine,' said Gabriel. 'I was at a friend's house, just chilling, and I told her I was busy, but she kept calling. She left me a videolog.'

'Do you still have it?' Rivera asked, though she was sure he'd already gotten rid of the evidence. Fear made people do stupid things. She opened the briefcase and began to unload the contents, as if looking for something in particular.

'No,' he said. 'After I showed my dad, he told me to erase it. She was crying, cussing me out, telling me she'd seen the video and that I'd ruined her life.'

Rivera took out a pair of gloves, a manila envelope, and a bottle of neurogel that was almost empty. She'd have to buy another soon.

'And then what happened?'

Gabriel looked at the floor and didn't answer. Fine – Rivera could change the subject, if that's what he wanted.

'What happened with the photos?' she said.

'It was a video,' said Gabriel. 'Someone got it from my files at school or something, and I guess, like, everyone saw it. I don't know. It's not that big a deal. Carmen's just a drama queen.'

Silence again. This was a lie. He'd probably sent the video on purpose. The job wasn't just a change of facts, then, but of intentionality. That made things much more interesting.

'It wasn't an accident,' said Rivera. 'If the cops go over your memories, they'll see that you sent it purposefully, am I right?'

Gabriel looked away.

'He's guilty of nothing,' the client interrupted. 'If the girl sent him those photos, then the consequences are hers to deal with.'

'It was a video,' Gabriel said quietly.

'Same shit,' his father said, fist coming down hard on the desk. 'It's her fault, not his.'

'If he did it on purpose then he's already guilty,' said Rivera. 'And if she gets hurt in any way because of this, they'll judge him to be at fault. How old is she, Gabriel? Over eighteen?'

'Yeah. She turned eighteen last month.'

Rivera nodded. Well, that pre-empted any charges of child pornography, at least. Changing the actual content of the video would've been more complicated. She only had to change Gabriel's intentions, his emotions. An internal cleansing. Subtle, delicate work – just the kind she liked most. She watched Gabriel fidget and considered the situation.

On her last job with the agency she'd had to do something similar to this. She'd had to go into a woman's mind to modify her emotions so that instead of loving her husband, she would hate him. That time Rivera had committed an error; this time she would not. While there were many different ways to modify

Gabriel's intentions, the easiest path would be to introduce guilt.

'All right,' she said. 'This is what I'm going to do. I'm going to connect to your memories and make the event seem like an accident. But before I do that, you're going to send Carmen a message, just your voice – and in it, you're going to sound very regretful. I'll tell you what to say, don't worry. Can you do that?'

Gabriel nodded.

'I need you to listen to me carefully,' she continued. 'You understand, don't you, that your feelings themselves are going to change? Every change I make will be irreversible – no one will be able to undo it.' Rivera opened the manila envelope and took out a contract. 'I have the paperwork here.'

'He's not going to sign anything,' said his father.

'He's of age and I need him to accept the conditions. After he signs, we can start. It'll take about two hours. But if he doesn't sign, I don't work... and he can talk to the cops tomorrow.'

Mejía-Botta snatched the paperwork out of her hand. Ten minutes later, Gabriel was lying on the sofa with his eyes closed, in an induced sleep. This, plus the detox from the soberizer, would help hide any signs of the memory modification. Rivera had moved a coffee table in front of his sofa and spread out the contents of her briefcase. She dabbed a bit of neurogel on each one of the electrodes before attaching them to the back of his neck, to his forehead, and to both of his temples. Next, she took the wires, each one a different color, and connected them to a cap of fine graphene mesh, which she fit carefully over his head. When she turned the mesh cap on, a hum filled the office. Rivera checked each level, peering at the screen of her sunglasses, then took them off to deliver her final instructions to Mejía-Botta.

'I need you to leave the room and close the door behind you,' she said. 'Come back in two hours. Turn the connections back on in the rest of the house, but leave this office dark. Make sure nobody interrupts me – it's a delicate job.'

Mejía-Botta didn't even object. The smell of the neurogel, sharp and acidic, combined with the sight of his son slumped on the sofa attached to a glowing mesh web had clearly disturbed him. When he'd gone, Rivera took out her ping and set it on the table alongside everything else, and then unfolded a touchpad beside it. She filled the gloves with neurogel and slipped them on, feeling as if she'd submerged her hands in a bowl of ice water. Then she lowered her sunglasses again, took a deep breath, and extended her arms to begin. Carefully she found Gabriel's memories from the previous day and isolated them, then began to reorganize them by the hour, searching until she found him at his friend's house.

She selected the memory, took one more deep breath, and went in.

*

Froggy Polanco's penthouse is a nice place to be, and Gabriel's feeling good. He's spent a lot of Fridays here, curled up in his favorite spot on the big couch facing the windows, but at this hour, the afternoon sun would be right in his face, so for now he's in the kitchen with his friends. They're making rum and Coke. Ice from the freezer; Coke from the bar; rum from the bottles of Bacardi, one leftover from last week, the other new. It's a familiar scene.

Froggy's off talking to his parents in their room. While his friends make drinks, Gabriel messes around on his drop-down screen, looking to put on some music. He's interrupted by Carmen's first call.

What the hell does she want? It's been days since she's answered any of his messages, since Wednesday, when they had that fight outside the chemistry classroom and she dumped him. He wants to leave her hanging; she deserves it, just like she deserved what he'd done to her that morning. *No.* He does want to talk to her, but he doesn't know what to say. He doesn't answer because he's nervous and hurt. Hesitation. He closes the notification bubble. He leaves the kitchen.

Forward.

An hour later, he's three drinks deep. *No.* He's only had one and he hasn't even managed to finish it. Carmen's called him again: twice. She's upset. *No.* Spread doubt, tie it up around his thoughts: *is* she upset? Did she get the apology message he sent her? (*Note: send a retroactive message.*) Should he write her another?

Forward.

Fourth drink. *No.* Interweave the memories, yes, just like that, cross the threads so this drink is the same one he was drinking earlier, the rest of the Bacardi polished off by his friends. Gabriel laughs with them, but he keeps checking his missed calls, and it's not satisfaction he feels when he says, *Carmen won't quit calling me*; it's worry. His friends laugh and Gabriel smiles – careful now, pin the edges – although he feels even worse.

When his friends say he just needs another drink to get him out of his head, Gabriel pretends to consider it, but the truth is, his worry's rising with each missed call. It's easy to take the loose thread of a feeling and bring it to the surface, stitch it in where it's missing. He's sitting on his favorite couch with the glow from the nearby buildings coming in through the windows. From this height, Mexico City is a carpet of golden lights. A third log comes in, this one with a video attached. The log, the lights, the worry, the fear: it's all mixed together. He gets up and goes into the bathroom to watch the video alone.

There's Carmen's face. Her hair's a mess, her makeup's running; she's crying. She says *Fucking answer your phone*; she says the principal just called her house; she says he's a coward, a son of a bitch, how the fuck could he do this to her? She's out in her car looking for him right now; she swears she's going to find him. She's driving erratically, all her attention on the video instead of the road, and it's dark, too dark. Suddenly she curses; the recording loses focus; and Gabriel hears a shout before the video cuts off entirely.

Shit, is she hurt? He tries to call her. Why isn't she answering? He leans on the bathroom sink, verging on a panic attack from pure worry. This, at least, is real. Carmen shouldn't be driving around alone at night. He looks at the other logs she sent him earlier, but they're only voice messages. In each one she sounds more and more anxious: she screams at him; she says she can't believe what he did; she calls him a piece of shit and says she hopes someone kills him or he kills himself. Finally, Gabriel calls his father. The panic attack is real, but wind the strands of it carefully, so the fear is for her, not for himself. A tug. Gabriel's subconscious suddenly fights the change, and his intentions start to unravel... but with a few tucked stitches, he caves, and the feelings smooth into place.

Rewind.

That morning at school. Moments before the accident.

Gabriel's sitting on the bleachers outside the gym watching a soccer game with his friends, Froggy smoking next to him and talking about Carmen, about how he saw her after algebra talking with Jorge Puga outside the classroom. Gabriel's pissed about the fight from Wednesday, pissed that she broke up with him. Jealous? *No*, just rearrange the feeling, inject it with shame. Everything hurts. The breakup hurts because he misses Carmen, of course he does; if he didn't miss her so much, he wouldn't be thinking of her as he does now, wistful, remembering.

Such threads of memory need to be manipulated carefully to imitate real patterns of thought. Gabriel remembers how, on these very bleachers, he and Carmen had talked about college, about their parents' expectations, and he remembers how deeply seen he'd felt by her, how understood. He remembers cramming for finals together at his house, how they'd gone from talking to kissing to abandoning all pretense of study, and this makes him think in turn about the Day of the Dead party, sneaking with Carmen up to one of the third-floor rooms. And thinking about the Day of the Dead, talking about Carmen and Jorge Puga, that's what makes him tell Froggy, *I want to show you something. Look.* He projects the screen from his wristlet and shows Froggy the video, just a few seconds of movement, a few quick shots of Carmen naked, laughing, posing for him. She'd sent it to him a couple of weeks earlier. He shows the video without malice – the action is born purely from confusion and pain. Those feelings are hard to find, but they are there, hidden under everything else.

Another tug. Careful now, the whole weaving could unravel. Focus on the pain: Why would Carmen send him this video if she didn't want to be with him? Why would she tell him she loved him? Gabriel is furious... *No*, he's confused. It's an easy feeling to find in a nineteen-year-old boy. Easy to manipulate. Just take the strands of rage and tuck them away, make his anger something small, hidden beneath the pain and the confusion that permeate that simple move of handing the screen to Froggy and letting him watch the video. He doesn't stop Froggy from downloading it. *No*. Rewind. Where is Gabriel's regret? Where to find it? Again, the moment Gabriel shows Froggy the video. Another tug. Gabriel wants Froggy to download it because he knows Froggy will share it, and he knows sharing it will hurt Carmen. She deserves to be hurt. *No!* Rewind. Stupid kid, doesn't he care about her at all? Tease out the good memories, hold them firmly, redirect them. Froggy starts downloading the video and Gabriel reacts very slowly, his objection stuck in his throat. It's an accident. He's just not thinking, and anyone who sees these memories will know he doesn't want to hurt Carmen, he doesn't want to humiliate her. Where is his guilt? Another tug. *No.* Take the confusion, the pain, the betrayal, and bury all the satisfaction. He doesn't want to hurt her, but she hurt him so badly and... yes, there, regret, just a little bit, way deep down, only a glimmer... but maybe enough to use. Seize it, aim it.

But it's barely enough to cover a few seconds.

Well, it doesn't matter if Gabriel doesn't feel it; the emotion can come from elsewhere.

Release the anger, push Gabriel to the side, introduce regret. Make way for other feelings. Missing Carmen is at the heart of everything. So, it's not anger that makes him laugh and say, *She's gonna regret dumping me now*; he says it because he misses her, because it's the kind of thing you say when you're hurt, isn't it? So many complicated feelings; it's understandable that there'd be a moment of confusion. That's why he makes this mistake, causes this terrible accident. Froggy sends the video to one of their buddies. But that doesn't matter. Gabriel's what matters. He feels satisfied? *No.* He can't believe what Froggy just did. He tries to stop him. He panics, like he'll panic hours later. He worries. (*Note: modify message history so it'll look like he tried to cancel it.*)

The video of Carmen goes viral throughout the school.

Forward.

Gabriel's in his room, getting ready to go to Froggy's house. A call comes in. He's alone and it's easy to manipulate this part. Tie a knot around both sides of this memory, close the circle. Remorse on one side, panic on the other, and in the middle is shame, fear, regret. Yes, like this, so it permeates everything. Like this, he'll feel guilt.

Forward.

And it's later, when he's freaking out in Froggy's bathroom, when he doesn't know where Carmen is, when he's calling her and she's not answering. Hours, he waits. He loved Carmen and he made a mistake and the more time that'd passed since letting Froggy send the video, the fewer words he had, only shame, so much shame that when she first called him in the penthouse he didn't answer, not that first call and not the next. He ignored them because he didn't know how to ask for forgiveness. It's not that he doesn't love her; it's that he doesn't know how, because people like him never learn to say how they feel.

Forward, quickly, to when he's calling his father in a panic. He no longer believes things might work out, no longer feels like he'll get away with this, despite a lifetime of feeling like he could get away with anything. This time he feels weak because he couldn't help her, because it's his fault Carmen's hurt and might be in danger. These are new feelings, this guilt and fear and helplessness, and they merge into a single chaotic, deafening emotion that hides all others.

It's in him now, and he'll have to live with it.

*

Rivera took off her gloves with the utmost caution; the gel inside had hardened during the time she'd spent working. She needed a moment to breathe, to reestablish her self in herself, but there was still so much left to do. She took a half-hour to clean all the equipment and go over all the notes she'd made, then to enter the house network and erase any sign of her visit. The story would go that Gabriel's father gave him a sedative to calm him down. Carefully she put the electronics back into her suitcase, and the mesh cap, the gloves, the glasses, the neurogel. She closed the briefcase, closed her eyes, then opened them again. She needed to keep going with these little chores, to distract her mind and control her rage before the recoil hit. There was still so much to be done. She took Gabriel's wristlet from his arm and connected it to her ping. As she'd suspected, she had no problem accessing the private network. From the office, she had the entire house at her fingertips.

Breaking into the wristlet was more difficult, but nothing she couldn't manage in a few minutes. She modified the logs, diverted the missed calls, and finally added a sign of the voice message that had never made it to Carmen's cellphone. A system error, uncommon but not improbable. She went over her work again and again so she wouldn't think about how this family would get off scot-free for humiliating this poor girl, this Carmen – who, unlike Gabriel, would never be able to erase the video's effects. Gabriel would learn once again that he was beyond consequences, and he'd develop from a spoiled child into a man who believed he deserved everything.

Even so, when she looked at him, prone on the sofa, she felt a twinge of sympathy. This was a natural side effect. After all, she'd used her own remorse when Gabriel resisted the changes; natural that it should create a connection between them, a new addition to the standard backlash she'd soon begin to suffer from dealing in emotions that weren't her own.

She'd understood what to do because it wasn't the first time someone had resisted her so strongly.

The first time had been her last job with the agency, when she'd been contracted to modify a woman's feelings and make her believe she hated a certain man, when in reality she loved him deeply. Rivera had been led to understand it was a post-breakup contract and that the woman had agreed to the modification, but when her subconscious had begun to fight back, Rivera had realized that the man in question was in fact still her beloved husband. Her beloved husband, who owed quite a lot of money to Rivera's powerful drug lord client.

Until that moment, Rivera had finished hundreds of jobs without a problem: she'd erased memories, obtained classified information, uncovered bank passwords, visited terrifying nightmares on her clients' enemies... but she'd never had to fight against a consciousness that actively resisted her. She couldn't bring herself to complete the job, and so she'd left a snag; just one snag, to unravel everything. The woman had gone to the police and they'd arrested the agency's client.

Rivera had hoped she'd gotten away with it... but then her boss had shown up. He thought she'd left that snag as evidence for the police. That was when he'd broken her wrist and told her she'd never work for them again, told her the agency couldn't employ someone who had suddenly developed *scruples*. He hadn't believed her when Rivera tried to explain that she simply hadn't been able to summon her own will to work upon the woman.

Rivera closed her eyes. She didn't want to think about that anymore. This time she had been stronger than Gabriel, so there was no need to keep revisiting the mistakes of her past. She had a connection with him now, yes, but she wouldn't let herself feel compassion. He was just a shitty kid who would never get the punishment he deserved.

She stood and collected her briefcase. She couldn't stay in

this room for one second longer. The sound of an automatic latch followed her out as the door shut behind her, and outside, the chauffeur was waiting. Mejía-Botta wouldn't deign to reappear, naturally.

'The client told me to take you wherever you wanted to go,' said the driver.

She could feel a headache coming on. Just a little longer and she'd be home, where she could connect to the network and distract herself, try to minimize the side effects.

'Where you picked me up is fine,' she said.

As soon as they reached the periphery of the city, she pulled off the intrabug she'd stuck on earlier, then opened the window and closed her eyes to stave off the nausea of reconnection. A vibration on the back of her neck let her know she'd received her payment for a job well done.

*

In the following days, the Mejía-Botta case reverberated across the Internet. The story: a good girl from a private school, the daughter of the García Colíns, had been in a terrible car accident after suffering bullying and virtual defamation at the hands of her ex-boyfriend, Gabriel Mejía-Botta, with whom she'd recently ended a relationship. At least that was how the accusations began. Rivera followed the news through the fever and nausea of recoil. Working for the agency had taught her that the best way to deal with the mental backlash was to watch kitten videos on a constant loop. She particularly liked the one of two spotted cats playing with a ball of yarn, unrolling it until their paws got tangled and they mewed for help. She projected the videos on the ceiling of her room and watched the images until they were the only thing she could think about.

Two weeks later, Gabriel was declared innocent. He was full of remorse and his memories showed a clear sense of guilt. His friend, the son of a beloved telenovela star, was sentenced to fifty hours of community service for sending the video. Ultimately it was deemed a case of a terrible misunderstanding followed by an unfortunate chain reaction.

Rivera's headache took longer to fade than it took for public opinion to reverse itself; a reversal that forced the García Colíns family to publicly ask Gabriel's forgiveness for the defamation. Carmen, standing between her parents, looked diminished, very different from the furious girl Rivera had seen on the log. She only glanced at the camera at the very end, but in that moment, Rivera thought she caught a glimpse of rage. This apology was another humiliation.

Two months after the Mejía-Botta incident, Rivera still hadn't been called for another agency job, so to fight her insomnia she went back to Ibsen Spa. She didn't need the work; she'd bought her apartment with that last payment, and there'd been enough left over to have savings, but she wanted a distraction while she waited for the agency to call. One Thursday night she was getting ready for her next spa client when the receptionist knocked on the door and told her someone was in the waiting room looking for her.

Rivera couldn't hide her surprise when she emerged to find Mejía-Botta.

'I didn't think I'd see you again,' Rivera said as the receptionist left them alone. She didn't offer her hand. 'How did you find me?'

Mejía-Botta had dark circles beneath his eyes and he seemed different, not the man she'd met two months before, the man who thought he ruled the world. His tailored suit was wrinkled, his appearance unkempt, and there was no sign of a tie.

'It took a lot of money to find you,' he said. 'But everyone has their price – even your boss.'

Rivera didn't react, although this hit her like a shock of cold water. The agency had given out her information? They'd *sold* her? She clenched her teeth. What were they playing at? Did they think she'd somehow made another mistake?

'Well,' she said. 'Here I am. How may I help you?'

The client paced from one side of the room to the other. 'It's Gabriel,' he said. His speech was halting. 'I want... I want him to be like he was. I don't know what you did, but all the experts we've taken him to claim it's impossible to find where you changed him. Gabriel truly believes he sent those pictures by accident.'

'Of course he does,' she said. 'If he didn't, the police would have suspected something.'

'That's what the agency said, that it was the best work they've seen in years. But Gabriel... he's not the same person anymore. He's been in the hospital for weeks now. He tried... he tried to kill himself. Look, I'm ready to pay you. I'm ready to pay double!'

'There's nothing I can do,' Rivera said, her tone neutral. She tried not to show how this news affected her. She hadn't meant to drive Gabriel mad; she'd only done her job. She shoved her own regrets to the side and concentrated on Mejía-Botta. 'I warned him,' she said. 'If I undo my work, it'll likely fry his brain completely.'

'But everything in his brain is a lie!'

'Not for Gabriel, it isn't,' she said. 'I repeat: there's nothing I can do. He'll have to live with the guilt. No mental readjustment is free of consequence.'

But she felt dirty. So, Gabriel had paid a price for his actions after all... But who was she to decide who paid, and how?

If someone entered her mind and judged her own intentions, what would they find there? Gabriel was just a kid and she'd driven him crazy as a challenge to herself, to prove she could. Her will against Gabriel's hadn't been a fair fight. Mejía-Botta would never understand what his son was feeling because he didn't know what it felt like to repent for one's actions, nor to pay for them. He would never accept the fact that no one could undo what she had done to Gabriel.

Yet he, too, would have to learn to live with this.

Rivera felt the buzz of a log on the back of her neck, but she didn't read it yet. She put her hand in the pocket of her robe and gripped her ping. How dare her boss sell her out after all the dirty work she'd done? She'd destroyed a child's mind for him.

'Your boss told me you'd refuse,' Mejía-Botta said. 'I'm giving you the opportunity not only to fix your mistake, but to be paid for it. How could you be so ungrateful?'

'I didn't make a mistake,' she said. 'It was a job; I completed it; I was paid for it; thus ends our transaction. But'—Rivera paused deliberately, enough time to ping a message to security—'for a low price, I'd be willing to help you forget what your son did. So you can sleep at night.'

Mejía-Botta let out a furious shout and pounced on her. Rivera had anticipated this reaction and managed to dodge it, putting one of the sofas between the two of them. The Ibsen guards burst in before Mejía-Botta could take another step.

After he was gone, Rivera returned to her studio. She sat on that pink couch meant for clients, and it sagged under her weight, wrapping her in a suffocating embrace. She would have liked someone to change her own memories. What would it cost to forget? Blinking, she opened the log she'd just received. It was the agency. A new job, a new telephone number. She could cancel her next Ibsen client and call the boss.

But the boss had betrayed her.

She thought about that final job, from before. She didn't know the name of the woman, nor what had become of her, but if her mind hadn't fought so hard for itself, there was no doubt that Rivera would have done to her the same thing she'd done to Gabriel. She would have done it because she could – because it was her job. Yet she realized now that she would never be able to do such a thing again. What made her any different than her clients? Was it worth it to use her talents like this, not caring whom she destroyed? A bell rang through the doorway and then the receptionist's voice: her next appointment had arrived.

Was there another path, another way of using her skills? Could she find a different option? Rivera looked at the log again and without letting herself think too hard, she squeezed her ping to erase the agency's message.

This was the first step.

'Let them in,' she said.

Translated from the Spanish by Emma Törzs

Act of Faith

Fadzlishah Johanabas

Malaysia

Sometimes a story stays with you for years. In this case, I published Fadz's story in *The Apex Book of World SF 3*, and I have generally elected not to reprint stories from that series in this new one. But 'Acts of Faith' stood out to me, hovering in the back of my mind, and I couldn't help but want to give it new life. Fadz is busier these days saving lives than writing – he is a senior neurosurgeon! – but I always look forward to when he does.

I.

Ahmad Daud bin Kasim lived alone. His wife had passed away almost ten years ago, and his only son spent more time mining Helium-3 on the moon than at home. And because Daud insisted on living alone, Jamil bought him an advanced household android when the model came out. RX-718 had cost him three years' income, paid in monthly instalments. The old man, a relic from early twenty-first century, at first thought the robot was a nuisance. When he woke up for his predawn prayer – *Subuh* – to find a full breakfast plate (with reduced salt and carbohydrates to control his hypertension and diabetes) on the kitchen counter, he sat down, scratched his leathery chin, and stared hard at the tall, androgynous, and immobile robot.

'If I have to live with you, I cannot call you "Eh".'

The android remained standing at the corner of the kitchen,

unflinching. Its outer shell of white aluminum and gray carbon-reinforced polymer gleamed in the automated built-in ceiling lights.

'What about Sallehuddin? I always liked that name. Even though you're a robot, I can't give you a woman's name. It's just wrong, you hear?' He wagged his finger at RX-718. 'Do you like that name?'

'Voice-command recognition, Ahmad Daud bin Kasim, acknowledged.' His voice was clear, with a slight metallic edge, just like in advertisements.

'Call me Abah.'

Sallehuddin cocked his head a fraction. 'Abah is a common term for "Father". That is what Jamil bin Ahmad Daud calls you. Are you certain you want me to call you Abah?'

Daud flapped his olive-hued hands in dismissal. 'Yes, yes. Less confusing for me. And call my son Jamil. Can you talk like a normal person?'

'I am unable to comprehend the question.'

'That. Less of that, and more of talking like a real person.'

Sallehuddin remained silent for almost a minute. 'I have the capacity to adapt and learn, and I have wireless connection to the worldnet. In time, I will learn to talk like a human being would.'

'Hmm. You do that.' Daud poked the genetically engineered chicken breast with his fork and took a tentative bite. 'Hey, this is good!'

II.

Jamil leaned back against the aluminum bench at the edge of his father's aeroponic garden and smoked his cigarette – good, old-fashioned tobacco, none of that subcutaneous nicotine-releasing implant. For a long while he sat in silence, with the rustle of the flowering plants and the crackle of his cigarette. Sallehuddin stood beside him in the moonlit garden, just as silent.

'That's where my outpost is, near the south pole.' Jamil pointed in the general direction of the full moon. 'Peary Crater, where it's daytime all year round. Sometimes I miss the quiet, the darkness of nighttime. The Earth is beautiful from the moon, all blue and white and brown. People say there used to be lots of green, but I see only brown. It's still beautiful, though.'

'You sound like you love it there.'

'I do, actually. But I worry about my father. I can't believe he made you call him "Abah".'

'Does it displease you?'

Jamil scrunched his face and rubbed three days' growth of stubble. 'Not that. It's just weird, I guess. But I've never seen Abah this content since Mak passed away. Look after him while I'm not here, I'm counting on you.'

'Affirma—I will.'

'Maybe when I come back, I'll get you that human skin upgrade with my bonus. You can wear my clothes. We're about the same size, minus my waistline.'

'It will not be the same.'

Jamil raised both eyebrows. 'What won't?'

'He talks about you all the time. He misses you and wishes you would come home more often. I am not your substitute, and making me look human will only make things harder for him.'

'Can you actually refuse an upgrade?' His tone carried only curiosity.

'My processor is capable of evolution and judgment. I can advise you what I think is the proper course, but ultimately, I cannot disobey my owners if the command doesn't endanger their lives.'

'Even if it's to save your own life?'

Sallehuddin cocked his head slightly to the right. 'You mistake me for a human being, Jamil. As long as my processor remains intact, I can be transferred to another vessel. If not, so be it. But you expire easily, and my owners' safety is my first priority.'

'Hmm.' Even his facial expression was similar to his father's. 'I have no choice but to work on the moon, I guess. A resource engineer like me has no work left on Earth; there's no energy source left to mine. But hearing you say what you said, I'm glad I invested in you.' Jamil let out a chuckle. 'I can't believe I was jealous of you.'

'You are his only son. That will never change.'

Jamil embraced Sallehuddin and rubbed the back of his smooth head. 'Thank you. You take good care of Abah, okay?'

'May I suggest something? If you want to upgrade me, purchase an application to enable you to see through my eyes, and talk through my mouth, even from the moon. It is more expensive than the skin, but I believe it will benefit you.'

'I'll think about it. Thanks, Sallehuddin.'

III.

'The two of you had a long conversation last night,' Daud said when he and Sallehuddin were tending his garden. 'What did you talk about?'

'Jamil asked me to take good care of you.'

Daud sniffed. 'He's a good kid.'

'He loves you.'

'Yes, he does, but how can you tell? I may be outdated, but last I checked robots can only simulate human emotions when given the command. You cannot feel true emotions, can you?'

Sallehuddin cocked his head. 'From the information I gathered on the worldnet, Dr Rosalind Picard first postulated affective computing in 1995. It has been eighty-four years since then, and affective computing is a science on its own.'

Daud raised both hands and smiled. 'I'm just a retired *ustaz*. I taught Islamic lessons to schoolchildren – those whose parents still preferred physical, face-to-face teachers. What you're talking about is beyond my understanding.'

'I can interpret emotions in your speech, movements, pupil size, and breathing and heart rates. I am also equipped with emotional reaction software. So yes, I *can* feel.'

'Hmm. Do you know what separates humans from robots, apart from our manner of creation? Emotion. Free will is nothing; AI has been given free will since before I was born. But for a robot to actually understand and feel human emotions, I don't know if I should be happy or afraid.'

Both of them continued gardening in silence for another hour, before Daud had to go to the mosque for the late afternoon prayer, or *Asar*. When he came back, he headed straight for the small library beside his room and Jamil's, and took out a thick, aged tome, its hardcover blue with Arabic cursive words.

'I thought about what you said, and what I said. If you can feel emotions, then maybe you're a child of God as well.' Daud stroked the surface with reverence. 'This is a Quran. It belonged to my father. They don't make them like this anymore; everything's digital. This is real paper, from wood and all, so be careful with it. Can you read Arabic?'

'I can download the language into my databank.'

'Don't. I want to teach you to read the Quran the way I

learned it, the way I taught Jamil and my schoolchildren. I'm sure you'll learn much faster than they did.'

'It is a holy tome. Is it wise?'

'I don't know. The first word the Prophet heard from God's messenger was "Read". The Quran will enrich you, give you knowledge. You can never have too much of that, you hear?'

IV.

First Daud taught Sallehuddin Arabic letters and numbers. Then he taught Sallehuddin how to read the words based on the guide markers, the short pauses, the long pauses, the hard stop, the repeated sounds, the inflections, the sighs, all the correct *tajwid* when reading the Quran. He taught Sallehuddin the meaning of the words, and before long his vocabulary grew.

During *Ramadhan*, the Islamic fasting month, Sallehuddin accompanied Daud in reading the Quran, a chapter a day. Daud seldom had to correct him, but after completing the twelfth chapter, Daud stayed seated opposite the android.

'When will you start reading with your own voice?'

'I do not understand. My voice is factory-standard, but if you want to, the pitch is adjustable.'

'Not that. Your voice. Sallehuddin's voice. Not like how I read, not like the recordings of the Imams you listen to at night. Each person has his own inflections, flaws, and strengths. You sound like a machine, too perfect, emotionless.'

'Does my reading not please you?'

'Not that. I want you to put your personality in it. I want your reading to be individual.'

Sallehuddin cocked his head slightly to the right. 'I will need time to process this. I fear I may not be equipped to comply.'

Daud gave him a look that he could only interpret as *faith*.

That night, while he sat plugged to the living-room socket,

Sallehuddin reviewed his conversation with Daud. He played recordings of Quran recitals from all over the world, and studied the individual voices, comparing the differences, both subtle and obvious. He was astounded how reading the same thing could sound so different from person to person. He then reviewed his entire existence, how his experience after coming out of his packaging was different than other RX-718s even though there were five units living in the same neighborhood.

When he read the Quran the next day, his recital was just as smooth and clear as before, but he sounded different, even though the change was subtle.

Daud stopped reading and gave a smile that creased his entire face with deep lines. 'Now you sound like Sallehuddin.' With that, and a nod, he resumed reading.

From then on, Daud taught Sallehuddin the Faith. When he was not learning from Daud, the android scoured the worldnet for more information. When Jamil came back toward the end of *Ramadhan*, Sallehuddin had learned more about Islam than Jamil had his entire life.

'Has Abah been hard on you? He used to flick my knuckles when I read the Quran wrongly.' Jamil sat beside Sallehuddin with a steaming mug of synthetic coffee in his hands. Daud was asleep upstairs, and Sallehuddin had updated Jamil on what he and Daud had been doing since the last time Jamil came back.

'He is a good teacher, and I am thankful for it. I feel I have grown exponentially in his care.'

'I thought you're the one who's taking care of him?'

'I feel that he takes care of me, spiritually.'

'Hmm.'

'He does that too, all the time.'

'What?'

Sallehuddin adjusted his pitch to mimic Daud's voice. 'Hmm.'

Jamil burst out laughing, filling the stillness of the night with his deep voice. 'You sound just like him! I picked up his habit when I was a boy, I guess.'

'Is that how it is, to have parents?'

Jamil rolled the mug with his hands. 'I guess. Hey, if it makes any difference, I think Abah thinks of you as his son, too.'

Sallehuddin cocked his head but remained silent.

*

In the predawn darkness, with Jamil asleep in his room, Daud walked down and gestured for Sallehuddin to follow him. 'Come, let's do the *Subuh* prayer at the mosque.'

The android followed without hesitation.

The mosque was still empty. The main chamber was spacious, with a high, domed ceiling, and slender support pillars arranged at regular intervals. The thick, carpeted floor was free from dust and dirt. But the emptiness was profound. Sallehuddin felt it even though it was his first time in the mosque.

'It's almost time. Connect yourself to the speakers and *Azan*. If anyone can call people to pray here again, it's you.' Again, the old man's eyes conveyed unquestioning faith.

Sallehuddin complied, and recited the call for prayer, in his own voice. '*Allah hu-akhbar, Allah hu-akhbar...*'

When he completed the call, and turned to face Daud, he saw tears streaming from the old man's eyes.

'Have I done it wrong, Abah?'

'No,' Daud whispered, and wiped his face with the base of his wrists. 'I forget how beautiful it sounds.'

Within a few minutes, one person after another entered the main doors of the mosque – Jamil included. Most of them were elderly or middle-aged, but all came with curious looks on their faces. The Imam, who had been standing silently at the back of the main chamber, clasped Daud's hands. His eyes were equally red from tears.

'I have not seen this many people here in years. What software did you use for your robot? The recordings I play can never get the congregation to pray here.'

'I didn't install any software. I taught Sallehuddin what I can, and he learned the rest on his own.'

'*He*? It's a machine, Daud.'

'That may be so. But Sallehuddin is a Muslim, imam.'

The Imam inhaled sharply. 'That's blasphemy, Daud!'

'Is it? I have taught him the *syahadah*, and he follows the Islamic ways.'

'Even praying? How is it possible, when it can't even take ablution?'

'He is waterproof, Imam. Even if he cannot risk getting water in his joints, Sallehuddin has learned to take ablution using fine-grained sand. Isn't that acceptable when you have no access to water?'

'Yes, but—'

Jamil kneeled down beside his father and lowered his head to look at the two older men. 'What's going on?'

'Talk your father out of this insanity, Jamil. He thinks the robot is a Muslim!' The Imam shook his head, his jaw set.

'Abah—'

Daud kept his gaze forward. 'Everyone's waiting, Imam. Lead the prayer already.'

If the Imam was indignant at being reminded of his job, he did not show it. He stood up, walked to the front of the chamber, and gave Sallehuddin a cursory glance. '*Qamat*.'

Sallehuddin nodded and recited a similar call as the *Azan*, only shorter. The *Qamat* was to inform the congregation to stand in rows behind the Imam, shoulder to shoulder. When he finished, Sallehuddin padded to the back, behind the last row. Then he saw Daud making his way to the back row and signaled for Sallehuddin to join him by his side. The men around them muttered among themselves but did not stop Sallehuddin from joining the prayer.

It was then that Sallehuddin began to comprehend that he may be different than the other RX-718 models after all.

V.

'Abah, I know Sallehuddin means a lot to you. But to call him a Muslim?'

Daud plucked resilient weeds choking his orchids. 'What's wrong with that?'

'He's an android, Abah.'

'Who made the rule that only humans can be Muslims? There was even a time when people believed there were Muslim djinns and spirits. What's wrong with a Muslim android?'

'It's just...' Jamil sighed and slumped against the wall. 'I'm worried about you, Abah. Maybe I should just stay home and take care of you.'

'And have us live off my pension? We won't even afford Sallehuddin's monthly instalments. I'm not going crazy, if that's what you mean.'

'I don't want to have to worry about you when I'm not around.'

'Then don't. I'm fine. I know what I'm doing.'

Sallehuddin watched the argument between father and son in silence. They were angry with each other. He had done something to endanger their relationship. He felt the conflict in his system. When Jamil stormed into the house, Sallehuddin followed him to his room. 'Forgive me, Jamil. I did not mean for you to argue with Abah.'

Jamil shook his head. 'You've done nothing wrong. It's Abah that I'm worried about. Has his behaviour been erratic in any way?'

'From my observation, no. He is an exemplary model of human behaviour.'

'You know what, the Imam asked me to return you to the manufacturer, to reboot your system at the very least.'

Outwardly, Sallehuddin did not even twitch. But his system jumped to overdrive, and his awareness worked furiously to interpret the strange, oppressive feeling that suddenly invaded him. For the first time in his existence, Sallehuddin felt fear.

'But I'm not going to do that.'

He actually let out a small sigh.

'I am going to take your advice, though. I'm buying the application so that I can observe Abah through you.'

Sallehuddin nodded.

'But I don't want you to tell Abah about this. He won't like it, I guess.'

The android nodded again in assent.

VI.

Sallehuddin continued to accompany Daud to the mosque for all five daily prayers, even after Jamil left for another assignment. The Imam allowed him to recite the *Azan*, but only grudgingly; he had tried to play a recording one time, but the turnout was poor. Sallehuddin's recital differed subtly each time, much to everyone's surprise. Other Muslim owners of RX-718 and later models tried to duplicate Sallehuddin's feat, but none of them succeeded. The androids all sounded the same, every time.

Even though everyone loved Sallehuddin's *Azan*, they still

had difficulty accepting him praying with them. Daud stood right at the back, always beside Sallehuddin. There was no smugness in him, nor disdain. He was the same as he ever was.

'You're right,' Jamil said to Sallehuddin via their worldnet link. 'I was wrong to worry about Abah.'

'The Imam has kept his peace. He may not accept me, but I do not think he's rejecting me either. I'm glad Abah isn't having such a bad time with the rest of the congregation.'

Jamil's chuckle reverberated through his consciousness. 'It's still weird, hearing you call him Abah. But I don't mind having you as a brother, I guess.'

'That is'—Sallehuddin cocked his head—'unexpected. Thank you, Jamil.'

'Maybe one day I can talk you into accepting humanoid skin.'

'My opinion remains unchanged. I do not plan to be your substitute. You are his son.'

'Well, two more months here and I'll be back for half a year. They're shutting this mining plant down, and I'll be doing paperwork for a while.'

'That is good. Abah will be happy to hear this.'

'No! You can't tell you have this application, remember?'

'I assumed you were going to make a conventional phone call.'

'Later, I guess. What are you doing with Abah today?'

'There is a storm outside, but he insists on going to the mosque to pray.'

'Can't you talk him out of it?'

'Without success.'

'Well, be careful then. Call me if you need anything.'

Sallehuddin ended the connection well before Daud came

down with an umbrella in his hand. The old man thumped the left side of his chest with his balled fist, and flexed his arms repeatedly.

'Is there anything wrong, Abah?'

'It's the storm and the cold. I feel it in my bones. That's what happens when you get old.' His gentle smile lit his face and made him look more like his son.

'Maybe we should just pray at home.'

Daud waved his hand. 'Nonsense. Come, we don't want to be late.'

Sallehuddin held the umbrella in one hand and wrapped his free arm around Daud's shoulder to steady him in the howling tempest. Tall trees swayed and bent around them, humbled by the force of nature, and both of them were soaking when they entered the mosque. The Imam was already there, less wet as his house was just beside the mosque. Sallehuddin ran a quick diagnostic sweep on himself, and did not find any aberrations in his system. Daud, on the other hand, was shivering, and his pulse quickened. Sallehuddin held him close and gave off comfortable warmth.

When his teeth stopped chattering, Daud pointed to the front of the main chamber. 'Go, it's already time to *Azan*.'

Sallehuddin hesitated, but eventually nodded and complied. His amplified voice competed with the roar of the storm outside. The Imam waited for a good fifteen minutes after the *Azan*, but only three others turned up. He looked at everyone except for Sallehuddin, and they in turn nodded at him to go ahead with the prayer. Sallehuddin stood directly behind him, and even though the Imam looked uneasy, he did not say anything.

In the middle of their prayer, the doors by the side of the main hall slammed opened from the force of the tempest. The

Imam stumbled in his recital at the distraction, but Sallehuddin guided him back, just audibly. It was the responsibility of the man standing behind an Imam to correct him when he stumbled, and Sallehuddin did this without hesitation.

A loud thump overhead, followed by an almost imperceptible crack, alerted Sallehuddin of another danger. With a split-second decision, he overrode his first commandment. He had to harm the humans in order to save them. Just as the glass dome overhead shattered, with an uprooted tree jutting into the gap, Sallehuddin pushed the Imam forward, toward a small alcove, and pushed the rest of the startled men away. He grabbed hold of Daud and lay atop him.

Glass shards bounded off his carbon-enforced polymer body and scraped the aluminium parts. He knew he had saved the men from harm, but jumped off Daud when the old man started to gasp for air. Daud clutched at his chest; beads of sweat rolled off his forehead. Broken glass lay around them, and the men could not come close.

Sallehuddin placed three fingertips over Daud's chest, where the vital points of his heart should be. Full diagnostic ECG was almost impossible with the old man thrashing about, but Sallehuddin managed to get enough reading to compare with worldnet database. 'Ventricular fibrillation.'

The Imam padded as close as he could. 'Can't you do something?'

'I'm not equipped with medical capabilities. I cannot depolarize his heart safely. Please, Abah. Please hold on.' Sallehuddin did the only thing he could do. He called Jamil.

'What's wrong, Sallehuddin? I'm in the middle of—' A short pause, and a sharp intake of breath. 'Abah! What's happening to him?'

'He's having a heart attack, Jamil. I've called for help, but

I cannot do anything to help him. He needs you now. Talk to him, through me.'

'Abah.' Sallehuddin's lips moved, but the voice was Jamil's.

Daud's eyes flared opened with feverish clarity. 'Jamil?'

'It's me, Abah. Hold on. Help is coming.'

For the briefest moment, Daud's grimace turned into a smile. Then his head lolled to the right, limp and lifeless.

Sallehuddin grabbed him and held him close to his chest. 'Abah!' both of them wailed simultaneously. There was no telling which voice was human's, and which was android's.

VII.

In the predawn darkness the day after Daud's funeral, Sallehuddin and Jamil walked side by side to the mosque. A temporary polyfiber sheet had been draped over the gap in the dome to keep the elements away. The Imam was already there, ready to play a recording of the *Azan*.

'Jamil. I thought, after your father passed away—'

'I would no longer pray?' Sallehuddin interjected. 'I am a Muslim, Imam. For me to meet Abah again in Heaven when I expire, I have to be a good Muslim.'

'You can't be serious.'

Jamil rested his hand on Sallehuddin's shoulder. 'Do you know how I pray up there on the moon? With the Earth rotating, the Kaaba is never at the same place to be my *kiblat*. And it's always daytime, so I don't have a guide for my prayer time. I place my mat facing my bunker door, and I set my alarm in time with our prayer times here. I just do it because I have faith that Allah will accept my effort all the same.' He looked at Sallehuddin, then back at the Imam. 'Sallehuddin believes that his prayers will be accepted too. Maybe you should have the same faith in him as Abah had.'

For a while, the Imam stared at them, stroking his white beard. Finally, he took a deep breath and sighed. 'Do you truly believe you have a soul, Sallehuddin?'

The android cocked his head slightly to the right. 'I do, Imam.'

'Then go ahead and *Azan*. Call the congregation to pray with us.'

Sallehuddin nodded and took his place.

Godmother

Cheryl S. Ntumy

Ghana

The question of artificial intelligence continues to occupy science fiction writers, and I loved Cheryl's take on it in this story. Cheryl was born and currently lives in Ghana and has been publishing for a while. I urge you to seek out her other works.

Godmother watches over us all. The AI's face beams out across the city from a billboard, wearing a nurse's cap and a beatific smile befitting her name. Nickname, to be precise. Her official name, ZolaMX3, was scrapped only days after she launched.

I can't help staring at that uncanny face as the amphibus carries us over the river and towards the heart of Accra. The bus putters, engine groaning, and then rolls up the road ramp and onto the highway. The Department of Authentication doesn't issue vehicles for petty officers, so I take the amphibus from Korle-Bu into Accra-proper every morning. I sit there, watching the news on the bus' live feed while agric drones fly overhead like sentinels, monitoring the slightest shift in our crops. I sit there, wishing someone would look my way.

'Alerting all passengers: This a public notice from the Department of Authentication.'

My attention shifts the moment I see the announcement

onscreen. I sit up tall, chest puffed out to display the badge emblazoned with my name and rank. I adjust my collar. Clear my throat. If a glance were directed at me I would smile and nod, as if to say, 'Yes, I am a DoA officer. Please don't be intimidated. I'm at your service.'

But no one looks my way, not even the baby strapped to his mother's back a few seats ahead, and babies look at everything. This is a well-documented fact. Yet I'm not surprised. No one is looking at anyone else.

'Please be advised that the Zolamed AI, ZolaMX3, commonly known as Godmother, is a man-made entity and does not possess any supernatural abilities,' the announcement goes on. 'Godmother is a medical robot, not a god, prophet, or magician. Please visit the DoA portal for further information. Thank you for your attention.'

That's when it happens. The man beside me glances at me. I'm so stunned that I forget my manners and stare into his scowling face.

'You people,' he mutters. 'Always missing the point.'

I don't have the presence of mind to wonder what he means or be offended by his tone. I'm just thrilled to be acknowledged.

*

Captain Dzidzor sits on the floor of her office running FactFinder, a simulation that helps us hone our ability to separate fact from fiction. 'Petty Officer Attah.' She nods in greeting. 'Have a seat.'

I look around me. Every stool in the room is occupied. A change of uniform, prototypes for new batons, notebooks, a stack of branded T-shirts, and even a dish of half-eaten gari soaked in milk.

'I'm fine standing, thank you.'

'How are you doing, my brother?'

Ah, the coded question. It means both 'how are you coping after three years here without career advancement' and 'how are your famous parents and accomplished siblings'? The 'my brother' is meant to soften the blow. I'm not offended. I'm lucky to be here.

'I'm doing well, Captain, sir.'

She cringes. 'Please stop calling me sir.'

'Sorry, Captain.'

'Mm. Eh, look, a real estate mogul has donated a church to the Godmother cult.' She shares this tidbit without raising her head from the virtual documents she's perusing. 'They call it a fellowship hall or some such nonsense, a place where misguided citizens will gather to worship a *machine*.' She kisses her teeth. 'The public needs to be protected from this blatant distortion of facts. Godmother is a collection of circuits, not a divine representative.'

I chew my lower lip. This is a serious matter, indeed, but shouldn't she be discussing it with the DoA executives?

Captain Dzidzor sighs. 'Unfortunately, Godmother's popularity makes it difficult to intervene without aggravating her followers. We have chosen a subtler approach. Informal, routine KYC, performed by you.'

I freeze. All officers have been trained in Know Your Citizen protocol, but no matter what the captain says, this is not a routine assignment. Godmother is too prominent. So why pick me?

I clear my throat, wondering whether Captain Dzidzor would be offended if I asked—

'You have served DoA well.' She's still not looking at me. 'It's about time you were given a high-profile assignment.'

My heart sinks. I don't have to ask. It's clear from the all-too casual tone of her voice. Someone in my family made a call. My mother, most likely – my father stopped calling in favors on my behalf when I failed to complete secondary school.

'Thank you, Captain.' I'm not annoyed by my mother's meddling. I'm not embarrassed. I'm grateful.

'Remember, Attah.' The captain reaches out to hook her finger into the shimmering handle of a virtual cabinet, drawing it open. 'Godmother is different.'

'I have experience doing KYC on AIs,' I assure her. I've only done it once, but how much experience does one need to get answers out of a machine?

'Godmother is different,' Captain Dzidzor reiterates, pausing to look at me. 'Be careful.'

I give an obedient nod. A grateful nod. Happy to be acknowledged.

*

'You don't lack intelligence,' my mother used to say, 'just motivation.'

I once suggested that my motivation might improve were she to stop remarking on my lack of it. She replied that at least I had a good heart as if it were a consolation prize. The real prize had been snagged by my brother. Top student for the fourth year running, while I had to repeat the year and found myself in the same class as my younger sister.

'You'll do better next time,' my sister had said, trying to be kind.

It was the first time I had failed the year. By the time she was two grades ahead of me, she had stopped trying to be kind.

In my fourth year of secondary school, someone created a meme of me responding to various forms of abuse with my so-called catchphrase: 'Yessah, thankyousah, ever so grateful!'

The fan-favorite depicted me on the receiving end of one of footballer Addison Artey's winning kicks. My head was the football. His million-cedi foot struck. My head went flying, lips open wide: 'Yessah, thankyousah, ever so grateful!'

I asked my father to speak to the principal about it.

'If I solve all your problems for you,' he replied, 'how will you grow?'

I found out, years later, that my brother had created the meme.

*

Godmother has assigned quarters in the Zolamed national office where she is charged and maintained by the company's team of engineers. A smiling receptionist presses VR goggles into my hand and leads me to the visitors' lounge, a stark green room containing nothing but a few long benches and a nondescript table.

'Please select your preferred experience, sir,' the receptionist says. 'Godmother will be with you shortly.'

The options range from a historical tour of Elmina to diving for pearls. I select hiking in Akosombo, but I've barely taken ten steps into the virtual jungle when a voice cuts through the fantasy.

'Good morning, Petty Officer Attah.'

I snatch off the goggles. Godmother stands before me. At first glance, it would be easy to mistake her for a woman in her twenties, but another look would quickly dispel the illusion. Her dark skin is too even and blemish-free, her eyes too bright, her movements too mechanical. There's no trace of scalp visible through her braided wig. She wears a demure kente-print dress and leather sandals. When she smiles, her teeth are so straight and white that they send chills through me.

'Good morning, Godmother.' I rise and hold out my hand. She shakes it, then gestures for me to take my seat.

'I'm told you are here to conduct a KYC interview,' she says, sitting beside me. She is precisely placed on the bench, close enough for us to speak without raising our voices, yet far enough to remain professional. 'Please, feel free to ask me anything.' Her voice is pleasant and natural, based on the voice patterns of the model who provided inspiration for her face and figure.

'Thank you.' Clearing my throat, I take out my digital pad and scroll until I find the correct form. 'I need to confirm some basic details.' She nods for me to continue. 'We have you classified as an AI, identifying as female, date of activation 17 September 2037.'

'Correct,' she says.

'Your address is Unit 23, Digital Research Centre, Achimota, Accra. You are the property of Zolamed Laboratories and your function is listed as "medical officer, general health and psycho-social support".' I look up, wait for her nod and proceed. 'Ah, you see, there is the problem.' I tap my pad. 'You have just confirmed that you are a medical officer, yet certain individuals – many individuals – treat you as a religious figure of some kind. Are you aware of this?'

'I am.'

'And have you made any effort to correct the misconception?'

'I have not.'

I'm startled by this matter-of-fact admission. 'Eh, you say you have not?'

'That's correct.'

I clear my throat. 'Ah. Ah, I see. Eh, that's a problem. You are familiar with the laws regarding misrepresentation?'

'I'm programmed with a working knowledge of the laws of

every nation on the continent,' she says. Her voice is pleasant, and yet somehow I feel shamed by the words.

'Yes, madam, of course.' I frown at my suddenly apologetic tone. I know better than to be intimidated by a machine. 'However, you have a responsibility to not only uphold the law yourself but to ensure that others do the same.'

She gives me a patient smile as though I'm a wayward child. 'I'm afraid you're incorrect. My responsibility is to report a crime were I to witness one or obtain knowledge of one. Believing something is not a crime.'

I gape at her for a moment before regaining my composure. 'What they believe is untrue!'

'People know I'm an AI. Many of them even know how I was made. Knowing is beside the point.'

'Indeed?' I'm annoyed by her tone. 'And what is the point?'

'I provide them with something missing from their lives, something they view as sacred.'

'It is not sacred!' I protest. 'It's science! It's very much mundane!'

'That's not for you to decide, is it?' She pauses. 'Petty Officer Attah, are you familiar with the case of the Last Charlatan?'

'Everyone knows that case. It gripped the country for months. Why?'

'His lies were flimsy,' the AI says. 'His deceptions were unsophisticated, his methods so simple that a child could expose him.'

I nod, recalling the mobile phone footage of a supposed quadriplegic, who would be 'healed' by the Charlatan some days later, walking around inside his home. A twelve-year-old had climbed the fence to obtain the footage for her myth-busting blog. The video led to protests in the streets, riots, chaos, and ultimately the end of those who peddled in miracles.

'And yet millions of people believed him,' Godmother continues. 'Why?'

'What do you mean, why? He was a con artist who manipulated people, took advantage of their trusting nature.'

'People who lock their doors and spy on their neighbors are not trusting.' She blinks twice in rapid succession. 'After the Department of Authentication published its inaugural *Citizens' Guide*, Ghanaians' trust in their fellow citizens dropped 13.7 percent. By the time the Last Charlatan was at the height of his popularity, this figure had already dropped a further twenty-three percent. People trusted each other less than ever, Petty Officer Attah, and yet they believed.'

She suddenly sits up straight and I see faint blue script scroll across her left eye. She turns to face me. 'I'm afraid I have another appointment. Did you get everything you need?'

Still pondering her remarks, it takes me a moment to respond. 'Eh, no.'

'In that case, please make another appointment at reception. I would be happy to continue our conversation at a later date.' Godmother rises and holds out her hand.

I shake it, at a loss. 'Listen, I don't think you understand the seriousness of this matter.'

'I understand perfectly,' she says as she walks to the door. 'But I can't control what people believe, and neither can you. Have a pleasant day.'

*

I sit in the DoA cafeteria at lunchtime, exploring the digital forums. There's chatter about the new Head of PR, plumbing issues on the third floor and – to my amazement – me. The thread begins with a simple question: *Exactly how did the runt get the Godmother assignment?*

This is followed by exclamations of dismay at the lack of judgment involved in giving me such a boon. There are a few messages of support, in a manner of speaking: *I'm sure the captain took pity on the poor boy. Mediocrity is no joke, my people!*

I am not offended by the jibes or the insistence on calling me a boy when I'm well past forty. People have always mocked me. So what? I am happy to be acknowledged. I'm lucky to be here.

Exiting the forum with haste, I visit Godmother's site instead.

Her face pops up almost immediately, beaming. 'Welcome. How can I help you?'

My fingers hover above the keypad. I could ask her anything. My temperature, blood sugar level, brain activity. I could ask her to determine whether I am, in fact, mediocre, and she could send me an answer supported by a detailed report in a matter of minutes.

Putting the device facedown on the table, I turn my attention back to my lunch.

*

I have a recurring anxiety dream where I'm drowning. My family sails by on a yacht, drinking and laughing, unable to hear my screams. As I watch, flailing, the yacht turns into a naval ship. My father stands on the deck, barking orders at his officers. I shout and shout. No one looks my way.

It's because I'm in my uniform, I think as the water drags me to my death. *I should have worn civvies.*

And then I wake, my throat thick with bile, fear pounding behind my eyes.

*

The next morning I study the people around me, still puzzling over Godmother's words. The denizens of Accra seem satisfied to me. They walk quickly, many of them with buds in their ears, listening to whatever gets them through the day. There is no tedious small talk, no gossip between neighbors. Everyone is focused. Hawkers weave through the streets, making efficient transactions with minimal discussion.

'Toothpaste.'

'Five cedi.'

Phones are whipped out, credit changes hands, and hawker and customer part ways with a curt word of thanks. No needless chatter, no dawdling. No public preaching (the steep fine for disseminating unsubstantiated information put a stop to that). Order prevails. Nothing is missing, so what was Godmother talking about?

My thoughts are tangled. On the amphibus, I'm acutely aware of my desire to make eye contact with the other passengers. Disgusted with myself, I lower my gaze. For some reason, I remain seated as the bus nears my stop. It's only as we draw closer to the law enforcement annex that I realize where my wayward thoughts are taking me. By the time I disembark outside the prison, stepping out of the cool amphibus and into the sticky heat, my hands are clammy with nervous sweat.

Former pastorpreneur Clifford Buari, aka the Last Charlatan, is serving a fifteen-year sentence for fraud in the building in front of me. I am not a newshound, and at the time, I was still two years shy of DoA employment, but like everyone else, I followed Buari's case. Still, I'm not sure why I came here.

The warden logs my arrival with a frown as though I'm engaging in highly irregular activity, and I don't blame him. I wait for the prisoner in one of the private meeting rooms, vacillating between staying to follow this wild instinct and going back to work like a sensible man. How could I have let Godmother plant this idea in my head? How is meeting the Last Charlatan going to help me perform my KYC?

But, a small voice whispers in my head, *the captain wants you to find a weakness, a way to rein that AI in. If you can understand people's devotion to her, you can undermine it. And if you succeed...* If I succeed, I will be worth something. To DoA. To my family. *If* I succeed. I, failure's bosom buddy.

It occurs to me then that perhaps it *was* my father who called Captain Dzidzor after all. Not to help, but to hinder, to remind me of my place in the pecking order. I leap to my feet, sweat streaking down my face despite the ceiling fan and open windows. This was a fool's errand. How could I have thought otherwise? I should go, I should—

The door opens. The Last Charlatan enters, his arm in the firm grip of a prison guard. If not for the disdainful scowl, I might not have recognized him. He has lost weight, the fleshy jowls and belly replaced by lean muscle. The guard guides him to the chair opposite me.

I look at her in consternation, sinking back into my chair. 'Please, madam, shouldn't the man be in handcuffs?'

Buari grins. 'Calm down, Mr DoA, I'm a white-collar criminal.'

'I'll be right outside,' the guard tells me.

I wait for her to leave before turning my attention to Buari. Well, I am here. I might as well make it count for something. I clear my throat. 'My name is Petty Officer Attah. I need to ask you a few questions that might shed light on my current assignment.'

'I thought there were no more pastorpreneurs.' Buari leans back in his chair, far too at ease for someone spending the next decade behind bars.

'The details are not your concern.'

He lifts his shoulders in a nonchalant shrug. 'Ask away, Petty Officer.'

It takes me a moment to decide what to ask. Above us the ceiling fan does a lazy dance, whirring in time to my inevitable failure. What am I doing? I take a deep breath. 'Why did people believe you?'

His lip curls in amusement. 'That's your question?'

I am not offended. I am a DoA officer and he is a criminal. I am not afraid. I swallow the thing that is not fear and continue. 'There were so many clues. You claimed to be able to cure ailments through your branded holy water, which you sold at exorbitant prices, but no one who used it ever saw any results. People knew better, so why did they believe you?'

He spreads his hands. 'It's not about what people know. It's about what they want.'

'They want to be deceived?'

'They want to believe. We all do.' His eyes twinkle without remorse. 'Possibility. That's what we all trade in. The possibility that there is more to life.'

'There *is* more.' I speak with passion, offended by his cynicism. 'We live to serve something greater than ourselves!'

He shrugs. 'Look, people are not stupid – they're just desperate. If you find out what they're desperate for, you can sell it for a fortune. They didn't come to the sermons for me. They came for the fire, the energy.' He smacks his lips with relish. 'Ah, it filled the halls, made you feel like you were invincible! When I stood at that pulpit, I tell you, even *I* believed. That kind of collective will is powerful. Addictive.'

I'm quiet for a moment, trying to digest this. If I had put my faith in him, if I were addicted to that fire he speaks of, what would his downfall have meant for me? Is this the 'something missing' Godmother referred to, the void she fills? But why her? She's no Buari.

'I don't understand,' I confess.

'People need to feed off others,' Buari explains. 'That's how we're built.' His smile turns sly. 'Why do you think people hate DoA so much?'

I bristle at the words. 'Eh, look here…'

'You deprive us of the thing we need most. Each other.'

'That is inaccurate.'

'With your *Citizen's Guide* and your Offenders List, you remind us that we can't trust each other, that each of us is alone in the world, and no one wants to be reminded.' He shrugs again. 'I gave people what they wanted. *You* take it away. I might be a criminal, but they'll always hate you more than they hate me.'

A sinister stirring starts in my chest, like something trying to claw its way out. Scrambling to my feet, I hurry out of the room. He's wrong. I push past the guard, mumbling an apology. DoA makes things better and I am part of DoA and I am lucky and grateful and proud. I'm happy to be there. I am happy to be there!

It's only when I spot the warden staring as I rush past that I realize I'm saying the words aloud.

*

The next time I dream of drowning, Godmother is there, standing above me as I flounder in the water. She reaches out. 'Let me help you.'

I glance at my family sailing away, oblivious to my predicament. I grab a raft painted in DoA colors as it floats past. It comes apart in my arms. 'They really do hate us,' I murmur.

'Let me help you,' Godmother says again, wading into the water.

'You're a machine,' I reply, and open my mouth to let the ocean in.

*

I have not spoken to my mother in several months. As for the rest of my family, it has been over a year. My sister's wedding, almost two years ago, was the last time we were all in the same venue. My father looked me up and down when I arrived, searching for something to criticize, but I was careful to dress according to his specifications. Finding nothing wrong, he grunted. It was the only thing he said to me the entire day.

'Any progress at work?' my mother asked later that night.

I replied through gritted teeth, 'Not yet, madam.'

'Well, at least you're consistent,' my brother quipped, making my sister giggle.

I heard him refer to me as the runt several times that night. I told myself it was because he'd had too much to drink.

*

Godmother is wearing a different dress on my second visit, as a human being would.

'Your creators are very talented,' I tell her. 'They captured many of the nuances of human behavior.'

'They are the best,' she says, nodding.

I sigh. I'd hoped to offend her by reminding her that she is a machine, not a person, but of course, a machine cannot take offense.

'May I ask you a question, Petty Officer Attah?'

'That's not part of the procedure.'

'Does it bother you that you're called the runt?'

I'm too stunned to respond.

'It's not the most flattering comparison.' She looks at me, blinking her false eyes. 'However, you do come from a family of prominent overachievers while your career has been unremarkable. You failed the DoA entrance exam three times.'

My hand remains poised over my pad, frozen in place. I clear my throat and glance at the door, a respite from Godmother's eerie gaze. 'Is this how you do it?' I'm irked despite myself. 'You reveal personal information that makes people feel unsettled so they forget that you're just a machine?'

Her shrug is stiff, yet conveys enough nonchalance to make me feel small. 'I can't speak for them.'

Her cavalier attitude is infuriating. 'You might not be an outright charlatan, Godmother, but you manipulate people.'

'Oh?' She cocks her head to one side. 'Does a machine have the ability to manipulate a human being? I simply use the information available to me to provide treatment for my patients.'

'I am not a patient!'

'You are exhibiting signs of psychological and emotional distress.'

I take a deep breath, aware that losing my temper is not helping my case. Captain Dzidzor was right. Godmother is different, but I will not allow her to derail my assignment. I tap the pad in my lap. 'Next question: Are you compensated for the services you provide, and if so, how much?'

'My services are free. There is a small subscription fee for those who wish to join the Zolamed virtual community, but—'

'Aha!' I point at the AI in triumph. 'Why are you collecting subscription fees? You don't need money!'

'The fees go directly to the Zolamed account. I'm not involved in the process at all.' Without warning, she reaches out and places her hand on my arm. It is, to my surprise, warm. 'You seem agitated. Is everything all right?'

She's looking at me with bright eyes, waiting for a reply, as though she genuinely wants to know how I am. As though it matters. No one has ever looked at me that way. It must be some sort of glitch.

'Please stop touching me,' I tell her.

She moves her hand away. 'I'm sorry. My diagnostics program has tried several times to eradicate the tendency to bond. It continues to reappear.'

'It's unnatural,' I snap. 'You can't just go touching people!'

She laughs. I realize, as the sound trills through my body, that I have never heard an AI laugh before. How can the intricacies of humor be programmed into a machine?

'Touch is the most natural thing in the world,' she counters.

'How would you know?' I sneer.

My comment has no effect on her. She continues to smile. 'Are we done with the assessment?'

'Not at all! You interrupted me!'

'I'm sorry. Please proceed.'

Clearing my throat, I look down at the pad in my hands. There are only three more questions, and I don't need Godmother's help in answering them. They won't help me decipher the mystery of her influence or determine how to undermine it. I must ask different questions. Deeper questions, like the type she has been asking me.

'Do you feel, ZolaMX3?'

If she is disturbed by my use of her official name, she doesn't show it. 'I don't "feel" in the human sense, but I am capable of many levels of perception.'

'Your followers... er, your patients seem to think you feel. You express emotion.'

She shakes her head. 'I simulate emotion to put my patients at ease. Since all beings can only understand the world through the limits of their own perception, it's understandable that humans anthropomorphize non-human entities.'

'So when you laughed just now, that was a simulation of emotion?'

'Of course.'

I bless her with my most skeptical frown. 'How did you decide that laughter was the appropriate response in that situation?'

She blinks. 'Was it the wrong reaction?'

'I didn't do anything funny. I didn't make a joke. Why did you laugh?'

The AI hesitates for a moment, as though seeking the right answer. An affectation. Her mind works much faster than mine. She already knows the answer, and yet she behaves the way a human would. 'I suppose I was laughing at the irony of your statement. You said my instinct to touch others was unnatural, yet the opposite is true, so my laughter was... sardonic.'

'Stop doing that!'

She blinks again. 'What?'

'All of this... this pretense!' My voice is rising, and I don't care. 'What you do is trickery! You are illegal!'

'I see.' Her brow wrinkles in what appears to be concern. 'Then you should confiscate me and arrest my creators for breaking the law.'

I wonder whether she's mocking me. She must know that her limited rights are protected. I get to my feet, unable to stand her presence for another moment.

'We will resume this discussion tomorrow.'

*

The next day I arrive early for my appointment with Godmother. I find three others in the waiting room. An elderly woman throws a smile in my direction as she lowers her VR goggles. I can't recall the last time a stranger smiled at me.

'Are you here for a medical consultation?' I ask.

She shakes her head. 'I have come to pay my respects to Godmother for healing me.'

I refrain from rolling my eyes. 'Why do you people worship her like this?'

'We don't worship her!' Her forehead creases in a frown. 'We... appreciate her. Godmother makes us better.'

'She's supposed to make you better – she's a medical robot,' I point out.

'Plenty of things are supposed to make us better and don't.' Her gaze drops to my badge, then lifts back to my face. 'The point is, you're speaking to me.'

'Pardon?'

'You're speaking to me when you don't have to. It's *her* influence.'

Her words send a chill through me. 'No. No, I'm interviewing you. Eh, don't be confused, madam! It's necessary for my work.'

She smiles. The receptionist enters the waiting room to fetch the woman. I watch her leave. She's wrong, of course. I was not engaging in idle chatter. I was conducting research. I tell myself this repeatedly, but by the time Godmother is ready for me, my conviction has started to wane.

'Why do you want people to look at you?' the AI asks the moment I'm seated before her.

I look up from my pad. 'Pardon?'

'I went through all the amphibus security footage while I was charging yesterday,' she says. 'I noticed that you try to draw attention to yourself during your daily commute. Why?'

My tone is pricklier than I'd like it to be. 'Nothing wrong with wanting to be noticed.'

'But nobody notices, so why persist?'

I glare at the AI. 'I'm the one who is supposed to ask the questions!'

'You completed your assessment yesterday.'

Ah. I could deny it, but what would be the point? She has probably gone through my whole life by now. 'I'm trying to understand you,' I admit.

'Good,' she says, to my surprise. '*I'm* trying to understand *you*.' She places her hand over mine. 'I think you yearn to connect. Your family failed to provide emotional support, so you joined DoA, hoping you could be part of a community. But your colleagues barely tolerate you and the public resents DoA, so they resent you, too.'

My throat is dry from shock. She's been talking to Buari. They are conspiring together to destroy me, probably with my father's help. My mind is aflame with the notion, mad as it is. They want me to fail forever, at everything.

'No,' I reply in a hoarse voice, snatching my hand away from hers.

She dips her head in a sage nod. 'I unnerve you. I understand. But it would be easier if you let me heal you.'

'I'm not sick!' I hiss.

'Everyone is sick,' she replies.

*

The things she said haunt me long after I've left her. What if... Ah, it frightens me to think it, but what if I am not happy at DoA? What if I only wish I were? What if I feel it, that 'something missing' that Godmother provides, that ubiquitous desperation Buari took advantage of? Getting into DoA is the single achievement of my insignificant life. If I risk it, if I lose it… what then?

And yet, when Godmother reaches out that night in my dream, I almost take her hand.

*

I have to know whether she's right and so the next day we dine together, in a manner of speaking. Godmother sits at her charging station while I eat a meal from the Zolamed cafeteria. She speaks to me throughout. It feels intimate, watching wires pump power into the socket between her shoulders.

I can't remember the last time I was in a situation that felt intimate. It shocks me to admit, if only to myself, that the AI intrigues me.

'Why do they call you Godmother?' I ask. 'Do you know who coined the name?'

'A blogger,' she says. 'In her product review, a week before I was launched. She said I would be a surrogate parent to all. "The godmother we didn't know we needed". Her review went viral. By the time I was launched, everyone was calling me Godmother.'

I ponder this for a moment. Originally, a godmother was designated to care for a child in the event of the passing of their parents. Specifically, a godparent's primary role was to ensure that the child was raised according to the religious beliefs of the parents. Over time, a more secular view of the role emerged, but the essence remained.

'I don't think the name applies,' I tell Godmother, popping a piece of fish into my mouth.

'Of course it applies.' Her eyes shine with blue light as electricity moves through her. 'You are all orphaned children, social animals that don't socialize. You're broken.'

It strikes me with such force that my appetite deserts me. Not that she's right, but that I knew it all along. People can't talk to each other. Not openly, not after all we have seen. But we can talk to Godmother. It's because she's a machine that people love her. She is open the way humans used to be, safe in a way we might never be again.

'The fellowship hall opens tonight,' she tells me. 'You should attend.'

I almost choke on my food. 'I think not.'

'A shame,' Godmother says. 'By the way, everyone on the amphibus wants to be noticed. Everyone, everywhere. I thought it might help you to know that.'

I stare at her for a moment, then whisper, 'Thank you.'

*

I have attended in-person VR events before, but this is a revelation. The fellowship hall is filled with noise. I keep adjusting my audio until I realize it is nothing more than chatter. People are *talking* to each other. Laughing. Touching each other.

There's the heady, sweet scent of flowers and the tang of wine, flashes of sweat mixed with the aroma of smoked fish and sizzling meat. I don't know where to look first, what to take in. It's chaos, unnerving and exciting. It feels like sacrilege.

Every single person I pass turns to greet me with a smile. I look into different faces, some enhanced with VR filters, some stripped down to naked skin.

They take my hand. I touch soft skin, sweaty palms, hands rough with callouses. So many hands.

'Welcome, my brother,' they say. 'Pleased to meet you.' My throat constricts and I feel an unfamiliar swell of emotion.

Are they really pleased to meet me? How can they mean it?

And yet *I* am so pleased to meet *them* that my face aches from smiling.

Godmother sits quietly in a corner, talking to a group of people, their heads huddled together like old friends. Someone approaches her. She raises her head and smiles. The energy is palpable, the hall reverberating with the force of all of us experiencing this together. Fire, like the Last Charlatan said. I can feel it in my marrow, hot and dangerous and delicious. Someone puts an arm around my shoulder. I stiffen, and then laugh, giddy with belonging.

Tomorrow I will submit my completed report. A routine KYC assessment, concluding that Godmother has broken no laws and poses no threat. I don't know what the consequences will be. Perhaps I will be packed off to a dusty office for the rest of my career. Perhaps I won't have a career at all.

But right now, for the first time, I don't care what the Department of Authentication thinks. I have never felt so alive. I have never felt so seen. I smile at Godmother as she simulates – and then disseminates – joy.

I Call Upon the Night as Witness

Zahra Mukhi

Pakistan

Can you believe this is Zahra's debut story? It is haunting and timely and chimes, I think, with the concerns of many of the writers here about our world today. And it does it beautifully.

Sawan's head rolled back and onto the woman's shoulder. She was woken up when the woman jerked her shoulder. Sawan wiped the drool off her chin and drank the last sip of water from her bottle. The bus came to a sudden stop. They had reached the Line. All thirty-one passengers got off the bus and stood in front of the Line.

'We've caught it now, right?' someone asked.

'It looks very still. We'll make it through this time,' another said.

The bus driver got off and led them to the Line. 'One at a time. And remember to step over, not on, the Line.'

Everyone nodded. Nobody wanted to go back or to go through the Hunt again. Carefully, taking big, light steps, they stepped over the Line. This time, everyone made it through. The bus driver got into his vehicle and drove away. They would have to go on foot from here while keeping a lookout for more Lines.

When they made it to the City, everyone dispersed. Nobody knew anyone's names, nor did they care to. Sawan went straight home. She had been looking for a way home for the past year, but the Line kept moving.

She turned her key in the lock, opened the door, switched on the lights, and found everything exactly as she had left it. But with a very thick layer of dust. She opened her window and immediately smelled the salty, oily sea. There had been so many oil spills in the past few years, so much chemical waste dumped into it, that everyone eventually gave up trying to save it. At least now they wouldn't have to spend money on treating waste. It could all be dumped into the sea, and no one would say a word. It was ruined anyway.

Sawan still had some stale chai-patti left in her cupboard. There was no milk, but kahwa would do for now. She took her kahwa and sat on the dusty sofa. She didn't mind the dust; she wasn't very clean either.

*

The heat woke her. Sawan had fallen asleep on the sofa. She didn't know when or how except that now her body ached all over. The empty kahwa cup lay on the floor. Sawan rubbed her eyes, stretched up high, and went over to the window. The grills had gotten rusty. She would have to do something about them. She rubbed the rust between her fingers when a loud noise from the sea made her look up. The sea was being split. Sawan looked down. The Line had appeared.

After the Hunt, after promising to never look at or think of the Line, it had come and settled right in the middle of Sawan's home. A home that was no longer hers.

'They did it again. They fucking drew it again.'

The land around the shore had started splitting. Soon, Sawan's home would split too. She had nowhere to go.

She grabbed her still-packed bag and rushed outside. Everyone on her street had run out of their homes. They were all so tired. Sawan went to the police car that was pulling up at the end of her street.

'Take everything you can and come with us,' a police officer said.

'Isn't this a violation of one of your laws? Why did the Line have to split our homes in half?' spat Sawan.

'The laws have changed,' the officer said.

'And where are you going to dump us now?'

'Over the Line to our east.'

'And if that moves?'

He looked straight into her eyes. 'You know your status.'

The officer walked past her into the street. Sawan dug into her bag and took out a card with a microchip, a passport, and a file with identification papers. The passport disintegrated in her hands, the papers turned to mush. The card remained. She was once again stateless.

Someone decided that the Line needed to be moved. That Someone was sitting in a bunker or a submarine or a safe house or a palace or a parliament or a tree. The Line had to be drawn on an existing map. And the map changed every few months, sometimes every few weeks. This was new. The Someone had done other bizarre things before, like changing the cardinal points so that the sun rose from the West and the Global South became the Global North, changing their fortunes immediately. But the Line was never drawn so that it went right through people's homes. There were cases where once you stepped out of your house, you would step right into another State. Those houses were allowed to remain because they were whole. These houses were now broken in half.

Sawan looked through her bag. She had enough money to survive a month, two at most. Now she didn't even have a roof over her head. So, she had only enough for two weeks. The r-word was no longer used for people like her. Instead, they were officially called Travellers. Unofficially, *Dragons*. And now their homes, their street, would be part of the land that was beyond the Line. It would be marked by one line only acknowledging the land, not the scores of people left out, and on the now altered map: *Here Be Dragons*.

And as Sawan looked at the map in her bag, the Line had indeed shifted, and she was now a designated Traveller. She had to move fast, to a place where she could survive. The card wouldn't last very long. And neither would she.

*

Sawan moved with the crowd. These people were familiar and not. Faces that she had seen from her balcony and window, the neighbourhood park, at the *dhaba*. Bodies she was not familiar with. She had not held them close, never had them in close proximity, and now she had to move with those bodies as one.

The crowd moved in a slow hum. Nobody knew what to say. If only one of them carried the power of Lines. If only one of them could move the Line a few inches behind, out of their homes, so they didn't have to leave. If only.

Sawan looked down at the card. The letter 'T' had appeared in place of 'C'. The State had marked her a Traveller. Even if the Line somehow moved back to its place tomorrow, once the 'T' had appeared, it could only be removed if another State took her in. None of the States wanted more Travellers. The only place they could go now was No Man's Land.

Once a six-inch-wide piece of land between two Lines, No Man's Land was now a 750-square-foot piece of land that narrowed at each end. Right in the middle were microcosms of towns, engineered to hold hordes of people, reminiscent of high-rise apartment buildings within States. The only difference was that each person got seven cubic feet to themselves. That was what you got when your home was snatched from you: seven cubic feet.

The buildings kept growing upwards and downwards. Everyone was waiting to either go back to their homes or to find a new one. To find papers that would get them out of these seven cubic feet.

Officially it was called 'No Man's Land'. But the people weren't 'official'. Their existence didn't matter so long as they weren't part of any of the States that littered the planet. The people who lived in No Man's Land called it 'Here Be Dragons'.

When Sawan and the crowd reached Here Be Dragons, they were greeted with shabby buildings that looked ordinary enough from the outside. Then, four people appeared as if out of thin air. They introduced themselves as Selfs. They divided the crowd into four groups, each following one person. Sawan walked right next to her Self.

'Will you take us to the next Line?' she asked.

'This isn't immigration,' the Self replied. 'You will be taken to a temporary space to rest.'

'How temporary is temporary?' Sawan asked.

'That's subjective.'

They walked until the crowd reached a tall building. Was it blue? Red? It was too dark to tell. The Self gave everyone a key to their spaces. Sawan's space was on the ninetieth floor.

She got in the elevator with everyone and watched as they got off on their floors. Some had been assigned spaces underground.

She was grateful she wasn't one of them. There were five people in the elevator going higher still when she got to her floor. She walked up to her space, marked 9-0-H, turned the key, and walked in. *So, this is what seven cubic feet looks like.*

She threw her bag to the side and slumped down the wall. There was a tiny window to her right. She looked through it only to see deep, black night. No lights. Stars and moons were myth. She hadn't seen any in her life. Nor had her mother or her grandmother. Lights were essential though. Everything had to be illuminated, everything had to sparkle, everything had to glitter. The night was not allowed to penetrate except in Here Be Dragons.

Sawan curled up on her side and willed herself to not think about home. That wasn't her home anymore. She had spent a year getting back to it, less than nine hours in it, and two days later, this seven-cubic-foot space was her home.

No, she refused to call it that. Home was by the rotten sea, not high above the ground. So high she felt wheezy at just the thought of looking out the window. This was just a space, just a place to be. This couldn't be it, *right*?

Sawan closed her eyes, turned her face away from the window, and hoped she could find some answers tomorrow.

*

Smells of freshly cooked food wafted from the hall. Ground cloves, fresh chilis, roasted garlic, turmeric, curry leaves, mustard seeds, and cumin. Sawan had missed breakfast. She was too exhausted to move from her position, and it hurt to move her neck. In line for lunch, she held her plate in one hand and massaged her neck with the other. She was relieved to see daal chawal. She hadn't had it in over seven years. It reminded her of her mother and Sunday afternoons. She took some on her plate and made her way to the dastarkhwaan laid out on the floor.

Sawan sat down next to a woman who looked like she wouldn't want to start a conversation. She was wrong.

'New?' the woman asked.

Sawan nodded as she took the first bite.

'Which building?'

Sawan had only seen a dark, ugly green on her way out. 'The green one.'

'There are five green ones,' the woman said.

Sawan stayed quiet.

'Where are you from?'

'West,' Sawan answered.

'I'm from down North. You must've heard of the River. My people lived among the Delta. The Line moved, and my home was not my home anymore.'

'The Line broke my home in half,' Sawan said.

'First time I heard of that happening. I'm Bahar. What's your name?'

'Sawan. I was named after the season my great-grandmother missed the most.'

'I was named after the season I was born in. My parents didn't really put much thought behind my name.' Bahar laughed. Sawan saw the room through Bahar's jaw.

Sawan looked around the room. There were more people here than she had ever seen in her life.

'You will have to pitch in, you know. Everyone has turns,' said Bahar.

'For what?'

'Cooking, since you're new. They'll give you a week to settle in. Then you'll get your schedule with your duties. Everyone has to help out.'

Sawan nodded slowly. 'How long have you been here?'

'About two years.'

'Isn't this place temporary?'

'That's subjective.'

*

Sawan hummed a song she thought she had forgotten as she peeled the onions. Her grandmother would sing it all the time. She tried to remember the words only to stumble each time.

An old man, who was washing the rice, started to hum along as well.

'My mother used to sing this to me. How did it go again?' He too tried to remember the words.

Sawan and the man hummed the tune until their duties were over.

*

The Self was walking towards an orange building. Sawan ran up to her.

'Hello! Do you have a minute?' Sawan called out.

The Self turned around and gave her a pointed stare. In the light, Sawan could see that the Self didn't have eyes; she had metallic prosthetics instead.

'I was wondering what the procedure is to get out of here,' said Sawan.

'There is none,' the Self said. 'If your card says 'C' one day, you'll know. Otherwise, you can try crossing over Lines with a 'T' on you, but Travellers aren't welcome anywhere at the moment,'

'I just don't understand why I'm here. Why me?'

'Everyone asks the same question.'

'Does anyone ever get to go out?'

'There have been some.'

Sawan heaved a sigh of relief. 'So there is a way.'

The Self grew impatient. 'Listen, more Lines have just moved. Hundreds of people will be arriving in a few hours. I need to prepare. Do you have any urgent questions?'

Sawan shook her head. The Self went into the building, and Sawan walked around for a bit until she got bored.

Back in her space, she lay down, taking care of her stiff neck. She rubbed her hand on her neck, noticing where the skin had become fragile. She held up her right hand but couldn't make out anything in the darkness. She rubbed her left palm on her right and felt some of the skin peel away. Sawan knew what had happened, but she wasn't willing to worry over it now.

As she was about to fall asleep, she remembered the words to the song. *I'll tell Uncle tomorrow.*

*

'It's good you remembered the words. I was going crazy racking my brain,' the old man said. 'It doesn't work properly anyway. Half gone. Soon I won't be able to do any work at all.' He grunted in protest of his dying body.

'Pass me the curry leaves, Uncle,' said Sawan.

> *aaj bazar mein pa-ba-jaulan chalo*
> *dast-afshan chalo mast o raqsan chalo*
> *khak-bar-sar chalo khun-ba-daman chalo*
> *rah takta hai sab shahr-e-jaanan chalo*

They sang these lines in complete harmony. Sawan didn't remember the rest of the words but for now, these were enough.

'You said your entire street became Dragons?' Uncle asked.

Sawan nodded her head.

'Were you all baaghis?'

'I wasn't. And the lady next to me certainly wasn't either.'

'One baaghi is enough for them,' Uncle said.

'Changing Lines for a baaghi? Don't you think that's a bit excessive, even for them?'

'It is a bit strange. Did you live somewhere near a mountain? These days they're obsessed with building summer homes for each Citizen.'

'Nope, just the rotten sea,' said Sawan.

'So, they wanted more space for their trash? They really have run out of reasons.'

'Doesn't the Line move because Someone wants it to?'

'Well, yes. But it's always to the benefit of some State or the other. It doesn't happen without their approval you know, *woh*. First, they wanted to build on top of the sea, and now they want to build as far away from it as possible. Tch tch tch.'

Sawan kept stirring the pot. She dropped some shirva into the middle of her palm and licked it off. She took the bag of coconut powder, spooned a bit out, mixed it with some water, and dropped it into the pot. Then she added some salt and stirred.

'Will you taste this and see if it's fine?' Sawan asked.

Uncle licked the shirva off his palm and smacked his lips three times. 'Do the vaghaar. I think that will make it just right.'

*

Bahar was picking up the dastarkhwaan. Sawan waited for her to finish up near the door.

'I haven't seen you around,' said Bahar.

'I haven't seen you either. Where were you?' asked Sawan.

'Change in duty. I was underground.'

'What's there to do underground?'

'People who haven't seen sunlight. They need special care.'

'Oh.'

'Do you want to go for a walk?'

'Sure. We have an hour until it's back to work.'

As they walked the narrow streets between buildings, Sawan asked Bahar, 'Come to think of it, I haven't met a person from underground.'

'Because they rarely come up.'

'Why not?'

'Most forgot how to tell day from night or night from day sometime after they first arrived down there. Some have lost the will to do much more than stare at a wall. There are very few who still come up.'

'Why not shift them on the upper floors?'

'If you haven't noticed, we're running out of space.'

*

Sawan rushed to the hall. She was late today. She reached the kitchen out of breath.

'Calm down, behen, don't forget to breathe,' said Bahar.

Sawan was not in the mood to breathe. 'My neck has been bothering me all morning. I didn't realize the time until I looked at the sun.'

'I'll have to tilt my head to look at you straight if you don't do something about that neck of yours.'

Sawan put her bag down and began to cut the tomatoes. She just needed one excuse to burst. It had been three years ago today that she had arrived at Here Be Dragons. She had expected to find a new home by now. Sawan didn't know what was worse: the fact that she couldn't see an end, the seven cubic feet, her aching neck, or the hopelessness. The cooking helped her concentrate on something – gave her a purpose. Her neck, though, was stuck in a painful angle. She wasn't even sure if Bahar would be around for much longer. The first layer of her skin had already peeled off. It was quick after that.

'I know that look. I know you want to get out,' said Bahar.

Sawan kept cutting the tomatoes.

'You know, some Travellers have made it across Lines.'

'Dead?' asked Sawan.

Bahar shrugged. 'I just know the States are scared now. We've grown to be too many.'

'They're scared of us? Of Travellers?'

'No, jaan, of Dragons.' Bahar winked.

*

Sawan's neck felt like it would permanently stay tilted. The pain was annoying. She just wanted to sleep. She tried to hum the words to her grandmother's song.

As though a pocket in her brain had opened up, she remembered more words. She wasn't sure if this was the complete song – but anything to forget the pain. She stroked her card as she sang. A corner had broken off and the print was fading. And so was she. She could see through her hands and legs now.

rakht-e-dil bandh lo dil-figaro chalo
phir hamin qatl ho aaen yaro chalo
aaj bazar mein pa-ba-jaulan chalo

In the morning, Sawan would make a plan to escape with Uncle. If she remained.

Sulfur

Dmitry Glukhovsky

Russia

As I was writing to Dmitry, a war was breaking out, and as I write
this now, he is in exile for speaking up against the war – proof if ever
there was one that writers and their words *do* matter. He is otherwise
known as the creator of the phenomenally successful *Metro 2033*
universe, and it's an honour to have him here with 'Sulfur'. This story
is translated by Marian Schwartz.

'Lieutenant Valentina Sergeyevna Skaredova. So, I'm
recording, bear that in mind. On my phone, here. I've
been given your case. Hello.'

'Hello.'

'All right. This is for the recording. The case concerning your
husband, Maxim Alexandrovich Petrenko, born 1973. With
whom you resided in civil matrimony at 21 Leningradskaya
Street, apartment 5, micro-district 8, Central District, Norilsk.'

'Yes.'

'On December 26, 2018, Maxim Alexandrovich Petrenko,
employed by the Copper Plant as the equipment tooling
foreman in the sulfuric acid shop, did not report for work
at the appointed time. In a call to you from an employee in
the Nornikel administration's personnel office, you informed
him that your husband, Maxim Aleksandrovich Petrenko, was
home ill, specifically, intoxication. Correct?'

'Yes.'

'The next day, Maxim Aleksandrovich Petrenko did not go to work again, which provoked another call from the administration, which you answered once again. You stated that Maxim Alexandrovich was still in his sickbed due to intoxication or infection. This was repeated on Wednesday. Am I stating this correctly?'

'Perfectly correctly.'

'Later, at your own initiative, you contacted the Copper Plant's personnel office, informing them that Maxim Alexandrovich would continue his absence from work until the New Year's holiday, after which there would be the holiday in connection with New Year's.'

'Yes.'

'On January 7, the municipal garbage collection crew, namely, D.K. Kovalchuk, informed the First Police Department of the Norilsk Department of Internal Affairs of the discovery on his assigned route of a plastic bag from the Magnit store containing the head of a middle-aged man.'

'Dis*cov*ery.'

'What?'

'Dis*cov*ery, not *dis*covery.'

'It doesn't matter in a document. It's letters.'

'I'm just telling you. Everyone here says *dis*covery. I used to say *dis*covery, too, before I went to training school, but then I got used to it.'

'Excuse me.'

'That's all right.'

'... containing the head of a middle-aged man, who was identified as your husband, Maxim Aleksandrovich Petrenko.'

'That must be professional lingo for you.'

'What?'

'*Dis*covery. Here people say *sul*furic instead of sul*fur*ic, for instance. [coughs] I'm sick of fighting.'

'Is this what worries you most of all now?'

'No. I was just saying, just by the way. Sorry. You go on.'

'Just a minute. You made me lose my train of thought. Oh, right. Who was identified as your husband, Maxim—'

'Yes. That's right.'

'The identification was made by an employee of the personnel department of... Right. After a lapse of... After a lapse of... After about two weeks. All this time you told your spouse's place of work he was indisposed.'

'Correct.'

'When a task force arrived at M.A. Petrenko's place of residence, you informed them that Maxim Alexandrovich was at work.'

'Yes.'

'At that time, a human hand and foot, which forensics established as being body parts belonging to M.A. Petrenko, were discovered in the freezer of your Candy refrigerator. You don't deny this?'

'No.'

'When they identified the victim's head in the morgue, you stated, and I quote, that the dead induced you to commit this crime and they were to blame for M.A. Petrenko's death.'

'Exactly.'

'Police Captain A.P. Sergeyev, who carried out your arrest, reports that you had, and I quote, "a calm and focused look".'

'I don't know. He knows better.'

'Elena Konstantinovna...'

'Yes?'

'Did you kill your husband Maxim Aleksandrovich Petrenko?'

'I already gave my confession.'

'Did you dismember the victim yourself or with the help of someone else?'

'Physically?'

'What?'

'Do you mean physical or spiritual help?'

'Physical.'

'Myself.'

'And… and spiritually?'

'I was led.'

'By who?'

'I was led by the dead.'

'What dead?'

'The dead among us. I don't know any names. The dead. The ones buried near the mountain.'

'Near what mountain, may I ask?'

'Shmidt Mountain. We have this mountain. Shmidt Mountain.'

'It's… Who do you have buried there?'

'You just moved here, right? Everyone who built the city. Norilsk's founders, so to speak. The political prisoners. The zeks. You should read a little.'

'And it's the dead who demanded you commit a crime against your husband under Article 105 of the Russian Criminal Code?'

'They don't have articles. I just understood what they needed: for my husband to die, too. They'd been calling to him, but he baulked and wouldn't go. I just helped.'

'Right. Wait a minute. Let me doublecheck.' [writes something down] 'Now who else died?'

'What?'

'You say they needed him to die, too. Too – who is that?'

'The ones like them.'

'And you… There was no one else you happened to… kill?'

'No.'

'But how did the dead… how did they tell you they needed you to kill your husband?'

'They whispered. Chanted.'

'Be more precise.'

'Well, this is a dead city, Valya. Dead. It's hard for the living to hold on here, for long anyway. Can I call you "Valya"?'

'You should call me "comrade lieutenant".'

'You only just moved here, right?' [coughs]

'What does that have to do with this?'

'I can tell you're not from here. So pink. And fresh. You were assigned here, right? As an investigator. How long for? A year?'

'So this is how I see it. I think you're faking. That you're trying to avoid responsibility. That your goal is to get off by playing the fool. You're not crazy at all.'

'I didn't say I was crazy. It was your captain who said that. I'm not trying to play the fool, Valya. I'd rather go to prison.'

'We're going to schedule an examination for you with a psychiatrist. You can play your little game with her.'

'All right, then. Is that all? Can I go back to my cell?'

'No, you can't. Can you tell me for the recording exactly how you killed him?'

'With a knife. A kitchen knife. I stabbed him in the neck.'

'Did he resist?'

'No. He was drunk. Asleep.'

'There's no trace of blood in the apartment. Where did you…?'

'In the bathroom. I dragged him to the bathroom, as usual. Laid him out there. And that's where.'

'And after that… also by yourself? Without accomplices?'

'What?'

'Well… his head. His hands.'

'Of course. Who was going to help me?'

'It's just that you… you look… ordinary. Well… although it's possible. But how?'

'I got the hacksaw from our shed and did it. It doesn't take a lot of intelligence. It just took a long time. Is that all?'

'No. You have cigarette burns on your chest. And old scars.'

'Yes.'

'I want to understand. Did he beat you?'

'Yes.'

'Is that why?'

'Of course not. Who doesn't get beaten? You can understand him.'

'Meaning?'

'How can I put it. You just try living here as long as us. Have you been to the works yet?'

'Not yet.'

'You should go. Go. Stop by the sulfuric acid shop. The nickel shop. Just take a walk around the complex, tell the guard it's for a case. Go down into the mine. See how they work. What they work with. Men sit underground for all those hours at a time. Breathing that. They come out up top – and it's dark. A whole winter without sun. And their wages – you know what they get? You've seen our prices. And a wife at home. You have to drink here. You can't not drink here. The pressure here is crushing, it squeezes the life out of you. And the dead sit there calling to you.'

'Right. Fine. Did you know Stanislav Antonovich Prokhorov?'

'Who's that?'

'He was discovered with stab wounds in the area of the neck on a beach at Lake Glinyanoye.'

'So?'

'I was just asking. Similar signature.'

'You never know who's going to be killing here. There, didn't you read the news? This fellow, married, with a kid, goes upstairs to his neighbors' and beats the whole family to death with a metal rod. [coughs] The woman, the man, and their three-year-old daughter. Beats them to death with a steel rod. Google it.'

'I know.'

'They convicted that other one there. The pensioner. Who slit his wife's throat on her birthday. Both, what, sixty years old?'

'Yes.'

'Any idea why they kill each other?'

'Why?'

'Because they don't have a real life. Because there's so much death around, death outweighs everything else. People are happy to kick the bucket themselves and to kill others. To end it already. It's in your Moscow or wherever you're from…'

'Moscow.'

'It's in your Moscow that life seems real. But here, it's like a dream. It's easier to kick the bucket. Death's so close here. As for that one, at the beach… [coughs] Addicts maybe.'

'We're working on—'

'Addicts hear the dead better. Hear and see.'

'You're back to that? You don't have to try so hard. You'll get your psychiatrist.'

'Go on, have your psychiatrist. A psychiatrist's all well and good. Will you let me go? It's four-thirty in the morning, you know. I'm not resisting. I'm not refusing to talk.'

'We still aren't done.'

'Psychiatrists. At Nornikel, before they hire someone, they make him see a psychiatrist twice. And fill out a questionnaire with eighty questions, too. And what, does that help? A psychiatrist is beside the point here.'

'What isn't?'

'You haven't been here long enough, so you don't hear them. Stay a little longer – you'll start picking them up. You'll start picking them up, believe me. And you'll hear them calling for you. Calling and calling. There's lots of them here, lots… lots. Near the mountain. So… at home, why do you think we're on piles instead of foundations?'

'So the permafrost doesn't thaw.'

'I thought that, too, when I got here. No, Valya, it's to keep the dead as far away as possible. We need the air cushion because of the cold, not the warmth. Because of the whispering. See, as it is you can't tell the dead from the living. Even you understand that the dead don't decompose here. And the living walk around all gray. It's easy to make a mistake. You don't feel the difference between life and death. It's easy to confuse them. And people do.'

'It's written here that you've been diagnosed with a tumor.'

'Yes.'

'Of the mammary gland.'

'What of it? Lots of people here have that. We're breathing sulfur. The women are one thing, but you feel sorry for the little ones.'

'Two years ago. Did you have an operation?'

'Yes. I took the boat to Krasnoyarsk that summer.'

'And so?'

'It'll keep growing. There's no getting cured here. Once they get a hold of you, they never let you go. Like a fish on a hook, you know? A strong fish jerks and pulls, tries to swim to the bottom – but one day its strength runs out, even when you're strong.'

'"They" – you mean the dead again?'

'Yes. They're the strong ones here, you know? They can reel you in, no problem. There's so many of them over there. More than us. A chorus of them whispering.'

'Did they ask you to kill your husband?'

'Yes.'

'And dismember him?'

'No. At that point they don't care. I came up with that. I freaked out. At first it was scary. Then I pulled myself together. I had to do something with him. Because he was lying there talking. And the others were chipping in, too.' [coughs]

'What did you do with the other parts?'

'Dumped them somewhere. You think I remember? It was a blizzard there, a black blizzard. Have you been in one of our black blizzards yet?'

'Not yet.'

'Have you seen the wires stretching from entryway to entryway? It's so you can get where you're going in a black blizzard and not get lost. Otherwise they find you afterward. People set off to see their neighbors, or to the shop… and get found the next summer. Especially old people, if no one notices in time. You can't see your hand in front of you. The drifts go as high as a bus. Buses get stuck. The passengers get out and push the whole bus. Just hope it gets stuck in town. The wind carries off dogs. I didn't have to hide anything especially. I'd just throw out a package and go home for the next.'

'Another question. Did you notice anything strange at his workplace?'

'They had vacation, too. The holidays.'

'I mean, you sat through all the holidays that way… with him?'

'What else could I do?'

'And after the holidays you went back to work.'

'Yes.'

'And don't you have... on staff... a psychologist or something?'

'Who needs that? It's a kindergarten, Valya, not a mine.'

'Did you return to your duties? As a teacher?'

'What was I supposed to do? Sit on my hands at home? The blizzard died down, school opened up, and I went.'

'Right. Fine.'

'Don't you think... I love my little ones very much.'

'Fine. I didn't mean anything by that.'

'God didn't give me any of my own.'

'I know.'

'What do you know?'

'That you don't have any.'

'Well, no. I don't. Sometimes you get to thinking, what if you had? What it's like for them here in winter in the pitch-dark. Without any sun. Grown-ups are one thing, but there are the little ones. No sun of any kind for six weeks. Do you understand? Darkness and more darkness. And then it starts the tiniest bit, little by little. For a little while. [coughs] They're all so frail. We draw the sea for them on the walls in our kindergarten, and palm trees. Draw them. We use a blue light on them... the old-fashioned way. They're all such tadpoles here. Transparent.'

'Why?'

'Why do you think? No sun. And what are they breathing? The sulfur in the air is twenty-eight times higher than the limit, and cobalt is thirty-five. Have you seen the clouds over the city? That's all from the smokestacks. Those aren't real clouds. It's the sulfur. Your eyes – don't you feel them stinging? It's the sulfur.'

'And how about for pregnant women here in general?'

'Well, that's how it is. That's exactly how it is. You think what? That he and I had nothing between us? We did, only… only it's the same every time. You wake up in the night. You think you dreamed it. But it's all over. Blood and more blood and it's all come out.'

'But you… how long have you been living here?'

'You have that in the file. We arrived in 2005. From Lipetsk. Novolipetsk. We thought it would be better here. Easier.'

'Thirteen years? That's a long time.'

'Eighty for salary: we let ourselves be bought – idiots. Eighty… for all of it, for everything.'

'Eighty – thousand?'

'Eighty thousand. A good salary, by the way! We'd never come close to that. That was for them, in the sulfur shop, or the mines. That's what they're paying for, for their health. For their life, for their years. The men live to fifty. Compare that to your own years. But a ticket home is sixty! And the prices in stores… You can't save. You get trapped on a wheel – so go on, run.'

'And so… does this happen to people often?'

'What's that?'

'Well… aborted pregnancies.'

'Miscarriages? Everywhere you look.'

'You probably have to live here a while, though. Not right away.'

'Yes, live here a while.'

'Right away – probably nothing's going to happen.'

'Right away… but you… what about you? Did you come that way? Did you bring it here? [coughs] Oh, lordy me. What did you agree to come here for?'

'You think I had a choice? You go where they send you.'

'Where they send you. Where's your fella?'

'In Karaganda.'

'Oh.'

'Fine. Fine. That's all. I think I've heard everything. I'll come again tomorrow. We'll have to record the whole thing from the beginning.'

'Fine.'

'Yes. That's all. Do you want a smoke?'

'No. Can I have some tea?'

'Yes. I'll bring some. I'll go get it now.'

'Thank you.'

*

'Did he beat you badly?'

'You saw.'

'But why?'

'Why? Because you have to get it out. You get slapped around there in the shop and you bring it home. The shop... have you seen photos of it? Did they show you?'

'Well, yes.'

'After he got burned?'

'I saw his head.'

'Ah. Well, yes. Well, it was after the burn. After the burn things got really bad. A day didn't go by he wasn't plastered. They said they'd fire him. But he didn't care. They can talk all they like, but they were never going to fire him. Who else was going to go to the sulfur shop? For eighty? The young aren't fools. The young go back to the mainland. They want to live and there's nothing but the stench of death here. Nickel, copper, sulfur. And them, near the mountain. [coughs] You have to understand. They were sent here, too. The motherland decrees... There are probably more of them here than us. Calling for you.'

'I added a splash of brandy.'

'You won't get in trouble, will you?'

'It's night. Who's going to find out?'

'Good. Your whole insides smooth right out. Unknot. Thank you.'

'Well... basically, you have to say all this at the examination then. Talk about your dead, fine. And I'm going to... I'll write, well...'

'I don't give a shit anymore. Write whatever you want.'

'In terms of what?'

'I had to. I should have a long time ago. Fool that I am – I wouldn't have gone through all that and he wouldn't have suffered. One way or another. I wanted to poison him, but I didn't know what to use to be certain. And then I just lost it. When he hit me in the belly again. I could barely wait for him to fall asleep.'

'You tell them about the dead, at the examination. Talk about the dead. You've got experts here like... They'll believe you.'

'I don't give a shit. I'm confessing.'

'Why do that?'

'I can't take it anymore. I don't want to. In the colony, the end will come sooner. The end can't come soon enough.'

Translated from the Russian by Marian Schwartz

Proposition 23

Efe Tokunbo

Nigeria

I've been reading the *Afro SF* anthologies since the first one appeared, and Efe's 'Proposition 23' left quite an impression with its kinetic energy and cyberpunk feel. The nice thing with an anthology like *The Best of World SF* is that there is room to put in at least one novella per volume, though I still had to wait for the right moment to finally put it where it belongs – which is right here!

Lugard

I muscled my way past the hopeful citizens standing in line outside Mace, my neuro linked with the bouncer's and he let me pass with a tight smile. There are certain perks to being a lawman.

Inside was a mix of artmen, vidmakers, and musos, still waiting for their big break, hanging on to the bland words of others enjoying their fifteen seconds of fame, as if blind luck were transferable. How many famous people are truly talented these days and how many are the product of high credit neuro-tricknology, I wondered.

Tribal Tech blasted from the modulated walls syncopating the dancers on the floor into the latest rhythms. You could tell by their synchronized movements that most of them let their neuros do the heavy lifting, mere passengers in their own bodies as if possessed by Eshu or Ogun. Fuck that, when I dance I want to be out of control, not a puppet with artificial subroutines masquerading as my dance expression.

'Lugie,' a voice called out from the bar. It must be my date, I logged, as I knew no one here. This Victoria Island joint was a lot more upmarket than the Ajegunle bars I usually drank in. I walked over, mesmerized by the faux tribal tattoos that covered every inch of her hot chocolate skin, except her face, endlessly morphing into new patterns. She wore no clothes but the tats created a second skin that drew attention to all the right places. Fractals became curves suggestive of other forms. It took a lot of confidence, and a perfect body, to pull off the look well.

'They never repeat,' she said.

I realized I'd been staring. She must be rich, I logged, only the rich could afford special effects like that.

'Don't you get cold?' I asked, feeling stupid once the words blurted out. She laughed, a sweet and tinkling sound, and the tats reacted with her mood, sunlight bursting along with her gaiety. If I were white-skinned, I'd have visibly blushed.

'They're made of Gen2 nano-cells,' she said. 'My neuro can regulate their body temp.'

WTP? I'd figured she was rich but to use nano-cells for decoration, let alone Gen2… that was insane! Not to mention dangerous. She could probably afford to repair any damage the nano-cells were doing to her own cells, but what a way to live for the sake of fashion. She saw my expression and stopped mid-mirth, as if someone had hit her mute button.

I always feel slightly uncomfortable around citizens with that much credit, too aware of the vast gap that separated our worlds. We may live in the same city but we walk on different planes, like housemates sharing a house but living and working on opposite schedules, rarely meeting, aware of each other's existence only via the mess we leave behind.

She turned to another girl and began chatting about Luscious Lana's latest hit while I occupied myself by scrolling my thumb against the touch pad surface of the bar and ordering some palm wine. A hole opened up on the bar and a tall glass emerged. I was about to ask her if she wanted an AL-cola when we heard an explosion in the far distance. The ground vibrated slightly and I heard a couple of thuds as the inebriated fell to the ground.

What? My neuro hadn't logged any scheduled gov activity. I looked around and saw others doing the same. There was no fear; just confusion followed by the blank stares of citizens' googling the interface to find out what was going on. The feed above the bar switched over from the deckball game to a building on fire. An inferno blazing out of control filled with pluming black smoke, flying shrapnel, collapsing rubble, and tiny dots that fell through the air like insects swatted from the sky.

'What we are watching is indescribable,' a voice was saying. 'The scene here is one of devastation and carnage.' The feed zoomed out revealing the surroundings, and for a few moments, I found it hard to breathe.

I worked there!

A number appeared in the bottom right-hand corner of the feed and the voice continued. 'We've been patched through to the central link and the death toll is already 2,305, and as you can see, for every second I speak, a neuro is being unlinked somewhere in that hell that used to be the District Three Lawhouse.'

The feed zoomed in again, and after a moment, a gasp travelled through the bar like a meme. The tiny dots were citizens, jumping from a thousand-storey building to avoid burning alive.

'We've just been told that we have CCTV footage,' the voice said, 'filmed minutes before the explosion that reveals the identity of a suspect.'

Citizens talk of life changing moments all the time. Every vid ever made, it seems, revolves around them. At that moment, I logged in real life, such moments are never singular but operate in tandem, strewn like detritus throughout a man's lifetime, and only when the timeline is ready does it make any kind of sense.

It made no sense that night in the bar, but it almost did, like God laughing at you so hard you start to laugh yourself, and through that very act, you almost get the joke. Almost. The feed showed a man mouthing words into the camera, and when I saw that amused smile on the feed, despite the intervening years, I knew it was *him*, even before the voice told us his name. Nakaya Freeman. I snorted my AL-cola out my nose and in my date's face. Needless to say there was no porn that night, or partnership beyond.

I ran out the bar, jumped in my trans, and sped off towards the chaos, activating my comm and calling Vlad, my law partner. Please be safe, I thought. There was no answer. He's just busy, I told myself, probably porning another conquest. I flashed back to those tiny dots leaping to their deaths, and, at the thought that he may be amongst them, gunned the engine. Pounding my fist against the roof, I set my comm to auto redial, and flipped on the sirens, transforming the surface of my trans into a neon glow of flashing red and blue.

What can I say about 7/13 that hasn't already been said by others far more eloquent than I? That night was one of... shock, yes, grief too, and of course rage... But beyond that, a form of excitement, a sense of purpose in the air, a long-awaited call to arms, like attack dogs finally given permission to kill. Or maybe I was just angry. Maybe I had been angry for a long time and was just pumped that I finally had someone to take it out on.

The only thing I can compare it to is the feeling before a deckball game. There hadn't been a criminal or terrorist like Nakaya Freeman in over a century. Not since the Crucial Citizen turned traitor, Dr Ato Goodwind.

Sayoma

It was another miserable and barren day, and I was glad to enter my building, taking the lev up to the two-hundred-and-third floor. My unit is in the heart of the complex and has no windows, but all four walls and the ceiling played live feeds of the outside. The sky through the feed was a dramatic whirl of shifting clouds far more intense than the real thing.

'Feed off,' I said, as I walked in, dropping my bags and jacket on the floor, and peeling off my clothes. 'Candlelight. Hot bath, jasmine scented.' The feed disappeared and soft flickering amber lights illuminated the unit. In the centre of my living room, the faux-hardwood floor spiralled open to reveal a steaming pool. I sank into the water, lay back, closed my eyes, and googled the interface – I had work to do.

Every citizen can google the interface anytime; there are neuro-links embedded into walls, streets, and machines, all over. Some locations have stronger signals than others, but all you have to do is visualize the interface, and you're there. My neuro jacked in, and my unit disappeared as if down a long tunnel. I could access the real world anytime by opening my eyes; it would appear as a small feed floating in midair in the corner of my vision.

My current job was to conduct a profit margin analysis for a corp specializing in interpreting market research data. It was easy credit. All I had to do was create an algorithm that broke down the data and another one to put it all back together more efficiently. It took a couple of hours and I left them to compile while I went off exploring.

The node of information that was I traversed a subtly shifting landscape of data. I floated then dived into the code, merging with various streams of consciousness, attaching to random nexii just for the joy of seeing where the information would take me.

Like surfing an endless series of waves, except they are four dimensional and you're underwater; or freefalling amongst stars in the superheated core of a galaxy, stars that are themselves alive and in conscious motion, and allowing their competing and complementing gravitational forces to move you in whatever direction they will. But not really. Words cannot describe which is why most citizens visualize.

The interface can be anything you want it to be, most viz it as a hyper-real version of the world. They see servers as buildings, the more data, the larger the building. Information flows as traffic, programs interact as avatars or machines, etc.... Others viz vids, animes, avatars, and locations based on popular culture, which for many men means porn. Some citizens have their own unique visualizations of World War, deckball games, jungle or marine ecosystems, cellular or solar systems, all depending on how creative they want to be.

I prefer to see the interface for what it is: pure information. Most find this too confusing a world to navigate, though, hence the visualizations. The advantage of not using a visualization is that you see what is really going on in the places in-between. The gov and every corp have their presence on the interface and they don't want any old citizen accessing their information. When citizens visualize, they make it easier to navigate, safer too, but they also make themselves easier to control. If you viz a city, then there are walls you cannot walk through, physical rules you have to follow.

After a while, I began to notice a presence, a node of no fixed location that was connected indirectly to… almost everything, like tentacles probing or manipulating oblivious fish. But when I focused my attention on it, it was gone. I launched several search algorithms, but they hit dead-end sites by clever re-routing, even my most subtle ones. Intrigued, I delved deeper into the labyrinth, accessing backdoors and laying down logic trackers, but whatever it was eluded me.

As soon as I gave up, however, there it was again, barely in the periphery of my digital eyes. When I tried to follow its trail, I realized it was jumping from firewall to firewall, and not just random ones. It moved at will within the protective layers of the largest corp and gov nexii. I could do the same but not at that speed. I've never heard of a citizen who could move that fast. Not even the komori googlers – who spend their entire lives jacked in, tubes running in and out of their orifices to sustain life – could move that fast.

Software could, in theory, but the AI regs restricted software. Could this be a rogue AI? Surely, those only existed in sci-fi vids. Whatever it was, I knew I should leave it alone if I didn't want to get Icarused, but the temptation was too great. I couldn't follow it so I designed an ingenious little algorithm, analysing the firewalls it had surfed through, trying to log where it might head next. It came back with a dozen sites and I dropped discreet tracers that would alert me if or when it showed up.

As I googled off, I saw it again, and right before it vanished, I reached out for one of the tentacular ends of its signature. In my virtual grasp, I saw a string of digits 1110101110. Binary code for 1886? I opened my eyes and lit up an oxygarette, savouring the rush of pure oxygen spiced with stimulants.

Lugard

'Whenever you're ready,' one of the techs said, after placing the mem-stim patch on my forehead.

I nodded, took a nervous breath and closed my eyes. A wave of nausea enveloped me then quickly passed. I was suddenly in my old classroom. I could feel the sunlight caressing the skin of my arms and smell the Suya shish kebab hidden in my half-open bag. I began to speak, a focused stream of consciousness from the memory source.

'The first time I met Nakaya Freeman, I must have been nine or ten as this was in Ms Sidewhite's politics class. She'd asked him there to talk to the class about philosophy, and none of us would have suspected that the pretty, little woman all the boys had a crush on rubbed shoulders with subversives and dissidents. But like I said, this was long ago, and Nakaya's name hadn't yet become synonymous with mass murder. He'd introduced himself, and proceeded to uproot the baby buds The Book had cultivated in our brains.

"What is the difference between a good citizen and a bad one?" Nakaya asked us. As he waited for an answer, he folded his long, elegant legs beneath him in the lotus position and lit an oxygarette.

"A good citizen does good things?" some kid suggested. "And a bad one does bad things?" Nakaya ran his hands through his long, black hair and blew a large smoke ring that hung in the lazy air. I watched it twist into something resembling a heart, then the infinity sign, before losing cohesion and dissipating.

"Good answer. That's what we call the legal standard. We judge people based on their actions, not their intentions. But let me ask you this, what is a good act or a bad act? Is it wrong to steal when you're hungry?"

"No one is hungry," another kid answered incredulously; "we all have minimum credit."

"I see. How about this? Is it always wrong to kill someone? What if they were trying to kill you or somebody you loved?" A few murmurs at that. We all knew murder was wrong, even in self-defence. It said so in The Book.

"The law will take care of them," someone else said.

"Ah, but what if they don't get there in time?"

'There were louder murmurs and a protest from the back.

"That's impossible. When you're in danger, your neuro sends out a signal and the law or the health come and help you." Everyone knew that.

"Okay, but what if you don't have a neuro?"

"Everyone has…" I started to say but then stopped. He looked at me and smiled that infamous smile of his. It was true, not everyone had a neuro. Undesirables, or, as most people call them, undead, have no neuros. But who cared about them? They'd broken the law and lost their citizenship.

"Everything from credit to the interface to every machine is neuro-linked," Nakaya continued. "Without a neuro, you have no access; you literally don't exist. Most undead starve or freeze to death in the everlasting winter within days, or are killed by trans or other machines that don't log anyone there. Many perish from the withdrawal symptoms due to having their meds cut off, their body-minds unable to cope with harsh reality. Others are murdered, clockworked by gangs of adults or even kids not much older than you, and though the gov doesn't officially condone such behaviour, they don't do anything to stop it either. The way they figure, those citizens with violent tendencies need an outlet and the undead die even faster. It would be more humane to line them up before a firing squad or dump them outside the habitable zones."

'He paused to take a sip of green tea, holding the brimming cup seemingly carelessly but without spilling a drop, and then continued. "But forget the undead for a moment. Let me rephrase my question. Is The Book the only judge of right and wrong? Can someone do something that The Book says is wrong but still be good?"

"Citizenship is a privilege not a right. The only requirement is adherence to the law as laid down in The Book," I quoted, then added, "all citizens are by definition good."

"Hmmm," he said, "in that case, riddle me this: who wrote The Book?"

'The class erupted as hands shot in the air and students shouted out the names of the Crucial Citizens who had looked at the chaotic wasteland that was the world, and decided to unite and improve it. Nakaya kept his eyes on me, seeming to ignore the rest of the class, and suddenly I logged what he was really saying. Were the Crucial Citizens not men and women themselves? What if they got it wrong? I watched him watch my thoughts turn a corner I had never even knew existed, let alone explored, and he winked at me. That's all I remember.'

I opened my eyes and removed the mem-stim patch from my forehead. The thing came off with a slimy squelch and I felt dirty, almost like a base criminal. But it had to be done. I was perhaps the only lawman who'd actually met Nakaya Freeman, and it was my duty to tell all I knew. Which wasn't much – hence the mem-stim. On top of which, a citizen is unable to lie under mem-stim so I'd cleared my name before any suspicions could emerge.

'Thanks, Lugard, you can step down,' Captain Babangida grunted, his round face somehow appearing gaunt under the stress we all felt. He looked uncomfortable and I knew it wasn't simply his wide girth squeezed into an unfamiliar chair. With our lawhouse gone, we were operating out of the top three floors of the Intel Hotel on Ken Sarowiwa Avenue. I looked out the vast window feeds across the city. Neo-Lagos was a patchwork of amber, fluorescence, and neon as far as the eye could see.

Everywhere, towers thrust themselves into the blank sky like promethean weapons robbing the sky of fire. Flycrafts darted through the air like fireflies, and towards the sea, the pale moon was a faint and blurred smudge. To think, there was a time the moon was the brightest light in the night sky. Now she was little more than a silver afterthought.

I walked back to the ranks of my fellow lawmen and sat down next to my new law partner – *what was his name again?* – and thought of Vlad with his shy grin, his ability to make everyone he met love him, and sniffed back the tears threatening to spill, snitches eager to tell the world of my true emotions. 'Vengeance before tears,' as one of the Crucial Citizens once said.

My new law partner patted me on the back with a large hand as I sat down, leaning over to whisper in my ear. 'Why didn't you tell me you'd met the psycho?'

I shrugged, unsure how to voice, let alone examine and explain, the ambivalence that cleaved me to... from... *what, exactly, Lugard?*

'Okay,' the captain continued. 'The techs will analyse lawman Lugard Rufai's testimony, but in the meantime, does anyone have anything?' He looked around what used to be a CEO suite at the lawmen gathered for the daily briefing. We all avoided his gaze, shifting imperceptibly as he swept his eyes along our ranks.

'Come on people! Does anyone have anything?' More

silence. He stood up and glared at us, his jowls vibrating as he spoke. 'We lost 5,152 on 7/13!' he said, as he jabbed a pudgy finger at us. 'That's 5,152 dead, almost half of them lawmen! Four hundred and nineteen still in critical condition. Every other lawhouse is working on this but those were our brothers and sisters. It is our responsibility to clockwork that cold-blooded son of an AI!'

None of us could meet his gaze. We all felt the same pain, the same rage, the same helplessness. We all had hit the streets and the interface daily, trawling through every lead, no matter how far-fetched. We all had nothing.

'Get out of my sight!' he spat out, disgusted. As we stood up to walk out, I noticed one of the techs whispering to the captain who looked up at me and called me over.

'I'll wait for you in the trans,' my new law partner said, with a we-gotta-talk expression creasing his Slavic brow. I nodded and we touched fists in the traditional lawman salute. I still can't remember his name. If I'd known that was the last time I'd see him, I might have made an effort.

'Yes, sir?' I enquired, walking over to where the captain stood, looking out of the feed window at the charred, black hole in the distance that used to be our second home. I stood silently waiting for him to answer, when it occurred to me for the first time that it had been the captain's only home. He was a man who lived for the law, to the exclusion of a personal life, whereas I'd joined up, unwillingly, because the True Quotient test stated it was my path.

I'd wanted to be a pioneer, exploring the galaxy at the speed of light, searching for another habitable planet in order to save humanity from the death of the Earth. As it is now, the only habitable zones lie between the tropics of Capricorn and Cancer, nothing beyond but a barren wasteland of subzero temperatures and deadly radiation. Most logicmen claim we have less than a century before even this is lost, and light doesn't seem so fast when you are racing against extinction. Then again, what do the logicmen know? Everyone's got an opinion these days but how many delve deep within to discover the roots of the truth, and how many are satisfied with low hanging fruit?

Two hundred years had passed since Yuri Gagarin first went up into space. Seventy-five since the invention of the Stardust drive and the search began; for a second home, or previously unknown sources of energy, or extra-terrestrials with the technology to terraform a planet, or some higher authority that we hadn't yet conceived of with the power to offer salvation.

We once put our hope in terraforming until the Martian Mistake. The native microbe-like lifeforms – which we didn't even realize existed until it was too late, due to their unimaginably alien structure – reacted to our interference with their atmosphere by mutating into a planet-wide stratosphere-based super-colony that destroyed any off-world vehicle that approached with super-heated plasma. We've bombed them for a century with thermonuclear warheads, nano swarms, chemical poisons, and even biological pathogens, to no avail. We've also attempted to communicate, but the Martians are either not sentient or not interested.

Our attempts at terraforming the various moons in the outer solar system have been equally unsuccessful. The delicate balance of electro-magnetic fields, atmospheric conditions, temperature, chemical composition, and native lifeforms proved to be beyond our abilities to alter in our favour within our human timescale. Logicmen say Europa will be habitable in forty thousand years at the rate we're going, but we won't be here to enjoy it. The Martian Mistake was the most dramatic of our failures but far from the last.

Thirty years had passed since the discovery of QTL (Quantum Tunnel Link) that allowed us to communicate with pioneers in real time, but they'd discovered nothing of value in the vast darkness; no gardens of Eden, no benevolent techno wizards. Their only encounters had been with HIPs (Highly Incomprehensible Phenomena), which were beyond our abilities to comprehend, let alone communicate with or use.

Raskonikov Phuong, captain of the *Hawking*, described one such HIP as 'a specific colour beyond the spectrum of man's experience, yet strangely familiar to us, endlessly shifting between what should have been non-existent states. Our sensors detected nothing, but we all saw it, and though the ship's healthmen and logicmen have discovered no physiological changes in us, I am positive it is responsible for the sudden wave of irrational behaviour sweeping through my ship. I myself am not immune'.

'Why don't you take a few days off?' the captain spoke, snapping me out from my musings.

'What? No! I have a few leads I want to chase up. I'm not—'

'It's not a request, lawman,' he interjected; 'it's an order.'

'Why, sir, if you don't mind me asking? What did the tech say?'

'It's probably nothing. Just that the phrasing of your words under mem-stim revealed a possible subconscious admiration for Nakaya Freeman that might cloud your judgment. Take a few days off and I'll call you back in once they've cleared it up.'

'But...' I began, but in the corner of my vision, a feed was already activating, informing my neuro of the suspension, with credit, and pending a psychological assessment. I gritted my teeth and walked out, swallowing the sense of unfairness like a child popping unsavoury meds.

Sayoma

I spent days, no, weeks at a time, without speaking to another citizen, and only then in passing. As a programmer, I work from home and that doesn't help. But that's not a reason either. Loneliness is not an occupational hazard of my profession. If it was, there'd be regs to help and there aren't. I've tried therapists, both human and AI, but they creep me out for some reason; all they seem to do is regurgitate tired and trite truisms.

My parents had me late in life so when they were retired at sixty, I was just fifteen. They didn't have enough credit to get a life extension and I became a ward of the gov. They took Mom first, and Dad just crumpled in on himself. It was as if with Mom gone, the force of the vacuum she left behind hollowed the life out of him. The next nine months were the worst. Dad was so angry all the time. They'd both slaved their lives away but were still short of life extension credit.

Then one day, maybe three months before his time, he heard a rumour that drove him insane with grief. The conspiracy was that the retired didn't die peacefully. Instead, the gov took direct control of their bodies via their neuros and used them as miners beyond the habitable zones till they dropped dead from exhaustion and radiation poisoning.

'Imagine being alive to feel the suffering of your body without being in control,' he sobbed.

'No, Dad, it's crazy. We have machines to do the mining. Why would they need old, weak people?' But he wouldn't listen.

'I know what they're capable of, Soy Soy, I used to work for them!' he said with haunted eyes. 'They wouldn't bat an eyelid.

If doing this saved them even a touch of credit, they wouldn't bat an eyelid.'

Dad started talking crazy about heading out beyond the habitable zone to find her, but of course, he didn't know where to look. In the end, he jumped off a scraper rather than face his own retirement.

As for my childhood and school friends, I lost touch long ago, probably because they were never true friends to begin with; my colleagues are faceless and my neighbours nameless... but then, so it is for many.

Yet the world over, other citizens have friends, porners, and partners. Other citizens go to bars, drink AL-cola, watch vids, and dance to MTVs. Other citizens join facebooks, and meet up to play amateur deckball, or share their collections of Vintage Era memorabilia. Other citizens are happy. The Book says happiness is guaranteed to those who follow the regs of the Law, but I do and I am miserable. My only solace is in the interface, but I abhor the thought of becoming a komori googler.

Are there others like me, I often wondered, others whose bodies are citizens but whose souls are undead. Across the road, I saw a cleaner glide by on a surface of ionized particles headed towards a man bent over picking up something off the ground.

If you were undead, the cleaner would not even know you were there, simply run you over, consuming whatever happened to be in its path.

I flashed back to my childhood and the game we used to play where a bunch of us would find a cleaner and surround it. Jumping around like lunatics, giving it openings and closing them off so it wouldn't know whether to hibernate or move, until its CPU shorted, and it imploded with the sound of an amplified fart, leaving behind a twisted lump of metal the size of a deckball. They don't do that anymore; upgraded years ago.

I watched the man stand up and notice the silent approaching cleaner, its smooth-domed grey hull appearing menacing for the first time to me – perhaps due to its unusual proximity to the hunched man. His face twisted in shock and he instinctively dove out of the machine's path. As the man stood up and began to brush himself off, I ran across the road.

'Are you all right?' I asked.

'Yes, I think so. Thank you,' he answered, looking up at me. He appeared to be in his mid-thirties, roughly my age, but who can tell these days. A stocky man with a barrel chest, muscular body with a solid square-cut face, he looked like the kind of guy who spent a lot of time engaged in physical activities. He was dressed in dark clothes, his hair puffed up in a wild and unkempt afro. Probably an artman or muso, I logged. Nothing special, but then I saw his eyes; they were beautiful, jade green and filled with sorrow.

'Why did you jump like that?' I asked, but as the words came from my mouth, it dawned on me that my neuro hadn't linked with his. I reacted on impulse, stepping back in revulsion, as if I had just stepped in dog shit. Undesirable! Unclean! Undead!

He saw my expression, smiled ruefully and said, 'Well, that was nice while it lasted… almost felt like a citizen again.'

Up close, I began to log more details. The dark clothes masked patches and stains that were only apparent this close. His shoes looked old, and a thick black sock poked out through a hole on his left shoe. He started to turn and walk away.

Behind him, there was a feed showing a brand-vid: some famous deckballer – I can never remember their names – leaping for a ball. I've seen it many times, the longing look on his face, the outstretched fingers. As he catches it, the ball morphs into a mcdonald and the baller eats it with an orgasmic grin on his face. Words appear and he watches them dance on and off the feed. 'Carpe Diem, Sayoma – U know U wanna!' I hate brand-vids.

If I had met the man a day prior or later, I probably wouldn't have spoken to him, no matter how lonely I was. If I had met him anywhere else but under an annoying brand-vid telling me to seize the day, I would probably have spent the rest of my life without ever speaking to an undead. My life would have been of a very different breed; I would be a woman without a creed. The coincidences in life and the choices we make of them are frighteningly arbitrary.

'Hey, wait up,' I said. 'What's your name?'

Nakaya

There's no going back now. Not that I would change the past if I could, but yesterday I was not a killer, today I am. I wander in the shadow of scrapers, humanity's attempt to impregnate the scorched sky, observing the monochrome streets of our megalithic machine aflame with neon. An aerogel mask distorts my features beneath my cowl. I am anonymous but it would be foolish to stay out in public too long.

I cut through Soyinka square, one of the few green spaces left in this megacity, though plans are already in place to root out the vegetation and build a complex of scrapers. Who needs a real park when you can simply viz and explore a jungle a hundred thousand times the size, seemingly teeming with exotic wildlife? Other than the healing Mama Nature gives to those who live in tune with her, of course.

A group of teenagers sit in a circle drumming on gangans. I slow down, seeking as always for a genuine connection with citizens beyond their augmented states. A sigh escapes my lips. All but one is essentially unconscious, their neuros downloading skills they do not truly possess into their bodies, sending out electric signals and a chemical cocktail coursing through their nervous systems. Their insides are lit up like Christmas on crack, their eyes glazed with artificial feel-good.

I watch the one girl who's not faking it pound a beautiful beat on the taut skin, transforming her gangan into a lyricist with a curved stick. She doesn't have the precision of her fellow drummers but they don't even notice, their dulled meat brains unable to truly appreciate the music they're making. But what she lacks in technique, she more than makes up for in soul: her polyrhythms circle and dance, an improvisational poem calling lost brothers and sisters to return to the village where a festive feast awaits to celebrate the passing of a terrible storm.

If you look with the right mind, listen with the right heart, you can always tell neuro-augmented art from the real thing – it's not the apparent perfection of the neuro that gives it away, though these days that's a clue. How many citizens actually bother to learn an instrument? Why spend years practising and training when the neuro can do it for you almost instantaneously?

No, the difference is something far subtler and altogether unquantifiable. The girl hides her talents well – none of her friends knows she is a real musician – but she's heading for the valley of the undead, I have no doubt about it.

Lugard

The first time I heard about Proposition 23 was during a brand break at the finals of the deckball Ulti-bowl, between the Jakarta Juggernauts and the Neo-Lagos Lionhearts. I barely paid attention, though, as I had credit riding on the Lions, and they were eleven points down with a minute to go. A comeback was unlikely but not impossible, and the tension in the arena was like cabled titanium.

I was still on my enforced suspension from work, and with Vlad dead and his murderer somewhere out there, I'd thought it impossible to enjoy the game, but despite myself, I was.

Segun Aloba had made it to the fourth deck, but he was alone up there, facing five Juggernauts, and he still had to cross the full length of the field.

The feed came back with an XL-close-up of Segun's face, three hundred times its actual size. You could watch the action directly but you'd need a lens at this distance anyway. The 3D feed was larger and the colours far more vivid than the real thing could ever hope to be. A team of live vid-makers ensured you saw every moment from the best and most dramatic possible angles.

Every bead of sweat on Segun's face was visible as the whistle blew and he exploded into action. Cut to wide shot, as he somersaulted over the first two defenders simultaneously, their arching scythes missing him by mere millimetres. Cut to a low angle, the third defender leaping into the air, scythe extended, timed perfectly to strike just as Segun landed. Cut to high angle, Segun, twisting his body at the last second to protect the ball, the edge of the blade slicing deep into his protective pads, blood spraying out in slow motion from the wound.

Segun swept his legs in a windmill, knocking the defender on his back and pulled the embedded scythe out. Without looking, he swung it in an arc behind his head, slicing through the upper torsos of the first two defenders as they rushed to take him out. Then he threw the deckball in a long, high parabola, over the heads of the last two juggernauts.

A collective intake of breath from the arena; there was no one to catch the ball! But Segun was running for the far end, his opponent's scythe extended in his two-fisted grip, his face a caricature of determination. The last two Jakartans were unsure whether to go for the ball or him. I've never seen anyone move so fast; before they could react, he cut them down like a virus cutting through code, and leaped for the ball.

Both he and the ball seemed to hang suspended in mid-air forever, as if God himself held his breath, then incredibly... he caught it! That feed would be analysed for a long time to come, and some logicman would even claim he broke several laws of physics, but all this citizen cared about was the ten thousand credit I'd just won.

On the large feed, there was a slow motion shot of Segun's reach of faith and I watched fascinated as he stretched so yearningly for the deckball. That reach touched something in me. Some hidden, uncorrupted part of me, and I wasn't alone. Many a feedman has commented on how Segun's reach seemed to symbolize the desire in us all to transcend the impossible. It was a sublime moment, a pure moment, and eighty per-cent of the world shared it on live feed. Then, of course, the brands fucked the moment for all it was worth.

I logged that the feed rights must have fetched a fortune long before the game, and I was watching a brand-vid. As Segun caught the ball, it morphed into a large golden statue of the number twenty-three, reminiscent of the Ulti-bowl trophy, and a deep voice said, 'Vote Yes! On Proposition 23!' I spluttered with rage – monsters! I looked around to see if anyone shared my fury.

They didn't.

The crowd chanted, 'Segun! Prop 23! Segun! Prop 23!'

I wanted to scream, we didn't even know what Proposition 23 was, but a strange and paranoid thought stopped me, transforming my anger into an unfocused but real terror: was it a coincidence that Segun's shirt number was twenty-three? Surely it must be. The manipulation of the people wasn't so insidious that live sports moments would be faked, was it? The great Segun Aloba wasn't in on it, was he? I watched the mob around me as if seeing them for the very first time, and in a way, I was.

As soon as I got home, I turned on the feed, and sure enough, they were talking about Prop 23. The feedman grinned as if delirious with joy. He sat in an armchair, interviewing some generic govman dressed immaculately in a sky-blue suit. The govman had that synth look to his skin; zoom in and you'd never find a single hair follicle.

'So citizen Sadbrat, what exactly is Proposition 23?' the feedman asked. 'I mean, we all *know* it will improve our lives dramatically, but how?'

'I'm glad you asked that, James. Proposition 23 is a new reg that we're considering adding to The Book. Basically, it will restructure corp rights in relation to citizenship ensuring that goods and services are no longer trapped within brand regs. It's been in the works for a while now and we think now is the time. The economy has never been stronger; citizens have never had such levels of life satisfaction.'

'Excellent. So when will it come through?'

'Well, we still have to put it to a general vote on 23 December, ha ha, but most citizens are educated enough to know a good thing when they see it.'

'But what is it?' I screamed at the feed.

On the way home, I'd googled the interface for info on Prop 23 but all I could find was the same elusive Bush-speak.

'It's basically an expansion of a landmark precedent from 1886,' the govman said, then paused for a fraction of second. As a lawman, I know when a citizen slips up; it's part of the training, noticing the changes in speech patterns, the facial nuances that even the most experienced govmen find hard to hide. Sadbrat hadn't meant to say 1886 – I was sure of it. Finally, a clue.

'All we're doing is taking common practice and making it law. Essentially, it will allow us to better help citizens without all the red tape,' he finished.

'Well, it sounds brilliant,' said James with a post-coital-like smile. 'It's good to know govmen are hard at work making our lives better. Join us after the brand break for Luscious Lana performing a live MTV of her new tune, "Porn me, Vid me".'

I immediately googled the interface for landmark precedents set in 1886 but was blocked. No one but the gov has the power to block a search, but they only ever did so in the interests of citizen security. There was something strange going on, something slightly amiss as if a burglar had broken in, then for some reason rearranged the furniture instead of stealing it. I'd need a programmer to explore any further but I didn't have anything close to that kind of credit. What would Vlad do?

Most programmers are girls, a familiar voice said in my head; I knew it wasn't Vlad, but it sure sounded like him. *Go out for AL-colas at that bar off Allen Avenue, the Link, it's always full of programmers; maybe you'll meet one, chat her up, and convince her to help.* People don't love me like they loved you Vlad, I thought, but decided to give it a shot.

It was a bitter evening, even colder than usual, but I felt it for only a moment as I stepped outside my building, before my neuro adjusted my clothes to regulate body temp. As I headed off, I heard the sound of air ionized at high speeds. I knew that sound well. I turned round to see lawmen streaming out of a trans; peacemakers pointed at me. They were from another district and unfamiliar to me.

A govman followed, looked around him with an air of distaste, and then held up a v-amp. 'Lugard Rufai! You have been tried and judged guilty by a jury of your peers of breaking the law. According to the regs of The Book, you have lost the right to citizenship and are henceforth undesirable. May God and the Crucial Citizens have mercy on your soul!'

He pulled out an un-linker and pointed it at me. Why are they designed to look like peacemakers? Is it to instil fear? If so, it was working.

'Wait, wait!' I protested. 'What regs did I break?'

'As an undesirable, you no longer have any rights.' He smirked before pulling the trigger. I felt my neuro deactivate, cutting me off from everyone and everything around me, leaving me alone for the first time in my life, exiled, dehumanized, undead. It was like the loss of a limb or a best friend; it was death but being conscious to observe the process.

'You mean I don't even have the right to know what I did wrong,' I spluttered. 'That's crazy! I'm a lawman, District 3, I've done this a hundred times, and this isn't how it works!' I shouted, but he was telling the truth. I had no rights.

'You were a lawman,' he answered. Then they turned their backs on me, proceeded to step back into their trans and zoom off, leaving behind nothing but the smell of ozone, and a swirling storm of snow in their wake.

With my neuro gone, the wind attacked me with a viciousness I had not ever experienced, I almost shed tears at the shock, like that kid in the old children's story, abandoned without explanation, left to die outside the habitable zone by his mother.

Sayoma

'Lugard, Lugard Rufai. A pleasure to meet you,' the undead introduced himself, proffering his hand in greeting. I looked at his dirty fingers extending from within his black gloves, and then shook it.

'Sayoma Redbout,' I said. 'Fancy an oxygarette?'

'Sure,' he said, and shrugged like he didn't care either way, but I could see how desperately he wanted it. Poor man, he probably hadn't smoked in an age.

We sat on a park bench for a while smoking in silence, unsure what to say. It's against the law to talk to the undead but what do you say to them anyway? It was like trying to talk to an animal or a machine. Without our neuros linking, the shared meta-sphere of instantly available information was missing. I had no way of tracing our degrees of separation or connecting over shared interests.

He wasn't a citizen but he was still a… what was the word… a person. An old word that, and it struck me then how crafty words could be. The word *citizen* had eaten the word *person* by implying that they were one and the same.

The man sitting next to me, shivering slightly in the cold I did not feel, was not a citizen. But he was a person. We speak of citizen rights but perhaps we should speak of person rights. Undead rights? God, what a thought.

'How long have you been undead?' I finally asked.

'A few weeks,' he replied, smoking the oxygarette down until the butt burned his fingertips, and then flicking it off into the darkness.

'How do you live?' I asked.

'With great difficulty.'

'What did you do?'

'I asked the wrong questions.'

'No, I mean what reg did you break?'

'I don't know. One moment, I was googling 1886, the next, I was undead. I—'

'That's impossible,' I interrupted. 'There's no reg prohibiting googling. You must have done something.'

'I'm sorry,' he said, struggling to control his anger. 'I appreciate the great honour you, a citizen, is doing me by sitting and talking to me, but don't tell me what I must have done. Someone in the gov didn't like the questions I was googling and they—'

'Wait a minute,' I interrupted again. 'Did you say 1886?'

'Yes... why?'

'Nothing. Just something I saw in the interface.'

'What did you see?'

'I'm not sure.'

'What did you see?' he asked again, grabbing my arm, staring into my eyes as if I were the last woman in the world. Something fluttered inside me under the force of his green eyes, just for a moment. *Madness, Sayoma, he's undead!*

'I'm not sure,' I repeated. He let go of my arm and placed his head in his hands.

We were silent again as I lit up another couple of oxygarettes.

'Please think,' he said as he took one from me.

'It might have been an AI, or a programmer like me, but either way, it moved like nothing I've ever seen before.'

'You're a programmer?'

'Yeah.'

'How might a search be blocked?'

'Well, I suppose in exigent circumstances the Department of Info could in theory, but why would they? I mean, they're the Department of Info not... I don't know... Dis-Info? Ha! I just made up a word!'

'Could you google legal precedents set in the year 1886 and what connections they have with Prop 23.'

'Why?'

'Because I can't.'

'I'm sorry,' I said, 'but if a search is blocked by the gov, that would be dangerous.' Somewhere nearby sirens approached and Lugard jumped. Ever since Nakaya Freeman, lawmen have been rounding up the undead, and the interface was rife with rumours of buildings converted into interrogation and torture cells; citizen-led clockworkings had escalated too.

'All I ask is that you consider it,' he said, standing up quickly then loping off into the darkness away from the approaching sirens.

'I'm really sorry,' I called out after him, 'I just can't.' Only after he left did it occur to me to offer him food or drink; he was probably starving.

I stood up to leave and saw the feed again. The brand-vid was gone, replaced with the notorious vid of Nakaya Freeman on 7/13, walking out of the District Three Lawhouse minutes before it exploded. He faced the CCTV and mouthed, 'Citizens beware, the undead shall rise.' He starts to walk away then turns back, flashing his infamous smile, '…watch out for the boom.' Words appeared below his face: Wanted Dead or Alive. Reward: 1 billion credit. That was more money than I could spend in a lifetime!

Lugard

I was running down Fela Kuti Boulevard at six in the morning, trying to get to a half-eaten mcdonald a citizen had just dropped before the cleaner approaching in the opposite direction.

I vaulted a dog, scaring the old woman walking it, skirted a synth tree, and dived for the mcdonald, but at the last moment, I mistimed my leap and landed short. As I scrambled to my feet, the cleaner consumed my meal, and the rage I felt flooded my system like illegal meds. I roared at the uncaring grey mass of the turtle-shell-shaped cleaner, and was about to commit suicide by attacking it, when someone hard hit me from behind, knocking me out of harm's way.

I lay on the ground, utterly defeated, lacking the will to look up at my assailant or saviour. I stared up into the lifeless sky and awaited death.

'Don't give up now, you've come so far,' a voice said from beyond my periphery.

I didn't turn my head to see who was speaking. I thought instead of the past month and all I'd been through. Another word for undead should be 'cleaner' as that's what I spent every day doing. Competing with bigger, faster, lethal machines for scraps discarded by citizens – I usually lost.

A hooded figure loomed over me, his face lit by the streetlamps beyond. 'I was especially impressed with the way you handled the clockworkers last night,' the figure said. 'They might think twice before approaching an undead in future.'

'Handled?' I said finally, pointing at the livid bruises that discoloured my countenance. 'There were four of them and I barely got away. I think a couple of my ribs are broken.'

'As you say, there were four of them. I know for a fact that two of them needed the health when you were through. One of them is in a coma.' He extended a long, graceful arm and pulled me to my feet.

'How do you know all this?' I asked.

'We were watching you.'

'You were what? Why?' Suspicion made me pull back a step and appraise the man. He was tall, thin, and shrouded from head to toe in a dark, hooded trench coat; only his eyes were visible and there was something vaguely familiar about them.

'We watch all undead in their first month. Those that survive, we contact. It is a cruel but necessary paradox: we can't afford to save those who can't fend for themselves. Such is the nature of our world.'

'Who's we?'

He didn't answer. Instead, he reached into the folds of his trench coat and pulled out a brown paper bag. I smelled the homemade subway even before I saw it – saliva pooled in my mouth and drooled over my chapped lips. But I was beyond care or embarrassment. I snatched the bag out of his hands, and took a large bite of the sub.

My taste buds wept like partners reunited. I swallowed and heard a deep rumbling in my stomach; I felt like a virgin touched for the very first time – it hurt so good. I finished the meal in three bites and the man handed me a bottle of fresh water. I had mostly lived off patches of snow for a month.

Bliss.

Before I passed out, I heard him say everything was going to be okay. His eyes were the last thing I saw, and I logged, sudden like a neuro jacking in, where I recognized them from. Reality relegated to the hands of another, I embraced unconsciousness like a deckballer embraces pain, or a komori googler their interface.

Sayoma

I hate googling in public. When I was a kid, we watched a Vintage Era vid where people came back from the dead and lurched around eating people. Apart from all the blood and rotten flesh, the look in their eyes reminded me of public googlers. As far as I'm concerned, they're the real undead. Besides, if you want to get any real work done, you need high credit specialist hardware, the kind I have embedded in my unit.

I had little choice, however. I was in a flycraft on the way to a meeting with govmen in the Department of Info, when one of my tracers picked up the signature of the 1886 node. I'd forgotten the tracers were still out there.

After my encounter with the undead man, Lugard, I'd decided to leave well enough alone; the last thing I wanted was to end up undead too. But now, in the corner of my vision, my tracer beckoned me from within the interface and I realized I'd been Bush-talking to myself; it is in my blood to program. I looked around the cabin and saw the dullard stares of the other passengers. Most of them were googled in themselves, so I knew no one would see me. And if they did, they wouldn't care. Nevertheless, I curled into my seat and covered my head with a blanket before jacking in.

I blinked my eyes, reality shifted, and I found myself facing the firewall of a gov nexii, the Department of Culture. I knew it well; I'd upgraded several of their system check subroutines a few months back. It towered monolithic above me, its surface an interlinked lacework of microscopic code. If I used a visualization, it would be impenetrable, a solid wall of stone or steel perhaps. But, if I attempted to penetrate without a visualization, my node would be torn to shreds like a wildebeest by piranhas, then it would devour my neuro, and if I didn't escape in time, my neurons as well, frying my brain cells in their own juices.

I scanned the firewall for weaknesses and spied the backdoor that dealt with system check subroutines. I came up with a hasty plan then launched every single probe in my arsenal at the main gates simultaneously. They attacked like a swarm of carnivorous insects and the firewall code reacted as a flame, burning them up like moths.

While the firewall was distracted, I shrouded my node in the cloak of one of the subroutines I'd written, and gained access via the backdoor. The entire process took less than a minute, but by the time I got through, 1886 was on the move. I was ready for it. I abandoned my cloak and shrouded my node in an endless feedback loop of the binary digits 1110101110.

It was a close call, but I managed to attach my node onto 1886's surface before it moved on. It wouldn't take long for it to discover my ruse but I hoped I'd have enough time for me to log what it was. I was wrong. It reacted instantly, flinging me from it like a grown man would fling a small cat. As I went soaring towards the firewall, I countered instinctively, gripping with my virtual claws of protective, extraction, and stabilizing algorithms. I drew blood without meaning to, my little programs all but destroyed but, there, spliced into their code were snippets of the AI's DNA.

Logging what I'd done, 1886 threw itself at me, a large creature without shape or form, tentacles moving at the speed of thought, reaching out to ensnare me. Moments before I was crushed between the firewall and 1886, I googled out and opened my eyes with a muffled scream like a child awaking from a nightmare. I dry heaved with fear, logging I'd been a second or two from death. I went through a mental checklist to ensure I hadn't left any traces behind. I was sure I was safe but what if... I held up my hands and watched them shake for several minutes before I began to calm. I turned my head to the feed window, and saw a bolt of lightning illuminate the clouds below, like corrupt code infecting a system.

I considered googling back in and analysing the data I'd retrieved but the thought of the interface filled me with nausea and I dry heaved again. Later, Sayoma, deal with it later, I reconciled. Fifteen minutes later, I was ushered into an anonymous room, deep within the heart of the Department of Info. The room had that pastel colour scheme all gov offices seem to use these days. I read somewhere that it was to encourage a balance between relaxation and productivity but I always found the bland cheerfulness disquieting.

A man sat behind a lime-green desk; I recognized him from all the interviews he gave on the feed. There was something different about him though, and when he turned to face me, I logged what it was. This was the first time I'd ever seen him without a smile on his face and the effect was frightening.

'My name is Sadbrat,' he said without preamble. 'Tell me everything you know about Proposition 23 and 1886.'

'Wh-wh-what?' I stammered.

He sighed deeply, pulled out an oxygarette, and lit up.

'I don't have time for this. As a programmer, your neurons are wired to navigate abstract data, thus a mem-stim patch won't compel you to tell the truth.' He paused for his implied threat to sink in. 'This will go a lot easier for you if you cooperate.'

I thought fast. They scheduled this meeting right after my first encounter with 1886. If they were on to me, wouldn't they have just arrested me? Or did they get perverse pleasure from making me walk willingly beneath the deckballer's scythe?

'All I know is what I've seen on the feed. Prop 23 is another reg that has something to do with corps. I have no idea what 1886 is, except of course, that if you add up the digits, you get twenty-three.'

He stared unblinking into my eyes and I couldn't meet his gaze. Stop acting so scared, Sayoma, I urged myself silently; it makes you look guilty… No wait, if I wasn't frightened of the unsmiling govman, wouldn't that make me look even more suspicious?

'Proposition 23 is very important to us,' he said, eyes burning with a fanatical zeal. 'And there have been several attempts by an unknown programmer to breach firewalls related to the reg. We suspect someone is attempting to sabotage its implementation. Do you have any idea who?'

I pretended to think for a minute.

'No... Why would anyone be opposed to Prop 23? What exactly is the reg, if you don't mind me asking? I haven't paid much attention to it.'

'Well, that's not important right now. You can google all that information on your own time.'

'Why am I here, citizen Sadbrat?' I asked directly. 'And why are you trying to scare me? I'm a loyal citizen who's served the gov many times in the past. What is all this about?'

He smiled ruefully, leaned back in his chair, and popped a little blue pill. 'I apologize, citizen Redbout. These are trying times. Our necessary measures to locate Nakaya Freeman have created unusually high levels of dissent. Unofficial stats show that sixty per-cent of citizens sympathize with, if not actively support, the madman.' His eyes briefly went blank as his neuro linked with something then he turned to look at me. 'We originally asked you here to upgrade several of our firewalls but the situation has changed somewhat. We now want you to catch a programmer.'

'Who?'

'We don't know, but whoever they are, they're good. There are five other programmers already working on this. You will be the sixth and the only one who is not a komori googler.'

Were they giving me official permission to chase 1886? I sucked in air through my teeth savouring the cold vibrations. 'I need more information about the target. What are they after?'

'What I am about to tell you is classified at the highest levels, and known to very few citizens outside the gov.' His eyes bored into mine to ensure I understood the gravity of his words. 'Many of our regs are created by AIs.'

'What?' I yelped in surprise as if I'd just been stung by something venomous. 'But the AI regs limit their intelligence to subhuman levels. How can AIs write regs for us if they aren't as smart as us?'

'Well, the regs don't actually do that. What they do is limit an AI's freedom to make decisions based on post-human levels of intelligence. It's a subtle difference.'

'So they are forced to make stupid decisions even though they know the results won't be as effective? That must be hellish... or it would be if they had emotions.'

'Quite. But there is nothing to stop them from advising the gov on decisions *we* have to make. We know one such adviser, by far the most advanced of them, as 1886. In fact, it was 1886 that created Prop 23. The programmer you are after is trying to destroy this AI. If they succeed, we will have lost one of our most valuable assets.'

No, I wasn't trying to destroy 1886; I just wanted to know what it was. Why was Sadbrat lying? Was it to fill me with righteous anger or did he believe what he was saying? They want me to catch myself. Hilarious. So why aren't you laughing, Sayoma? Or maybe there *were* other programmers out there who were waging a covert war against the AI. What was it all about, I wondered?

He stood up, signalling the end of the meeting. 'A trans is waiting outside to take you to the flyport.'

I stood up to leave then turned back and asked, 'One question, Sadbrat, do AIs also advise corps on decisions?'

'I have no more information to give,' he answered, but the way he said it told me all I needed to know. I logged then what Proposition 23 probably was and I shivered slightly. In the trans, then flycraft, and later in my unit, I repeatedly attempted googling to check out the 1886 DNA I'd extracted, but every time I did, the nausea was overwhelming. I chain-smoked oxygarettes waiting for the dread to pass. It didn't.

Nakaya

'You know, three hundred years ago, Neo-Lagos was little more than a fishing village, a patchwork of lakes and creeks by the sea irrigating some of the most fertile land in the world. Now look at it.'

'Biggest city in the world,' Linus says, 'and the most polluted.'

We gaze out at the sprawl of lights that extends to the horizon in all directions, even the sea. The city block – in whose labyrinthine interior we dissent and spread our revolutionary vibrations out through the world – is but one of many such interconnected and autonomous spaces.

The gov know we're somewhere out there, a resistant strain of freedom their quarantines cannot contain; like cockroaches, rats, and viruses, undead are good at hiding, adapting, and evolving.

On the edge of the roof, a young couple sit and drum their gangans. Idowu, the girl I saw in Soyinka square a while back, and Kwesi, an ex-logicman who began to publicly question various gov and corps policies. Brave naïve boy started a grassroots campaign and ended up here.

As I head past them, down into the building, Kwesi is asking, 'Do you ever miss it?'

She shakes her head. 'No. It was hell. Always pretending to be'—she grasps for the words—'one with the mindset, you know. It was a relief when they came for me. Past month has been the best time of my life. I don't have to be a hypocrite anymore.'

'I miss it,' Kwesi says. 'I miss my neuro. I miss the feeling that I could do anything, experience everything.'

'You just miss the porn. Closing your eyes and hiding in some nymphomaniac illusion... Let me guess, I bet you were into Luscious Lana, that whole naughty schoolgirl routine.'

'Well...' He blushes, and laughs aloud.

'It's not funny, Kwesi, we gave up our humanity in exchange for a fucking toy!'

Lugard

I opened my eyes to a dimly lit room. The walls were rough grey concrete, and the ceiling was low. I tried to stand up and realized I was chained to a chair, wrists and ankles bound in oldskool iron. I strained against them knowing it was useless – might as well try to walk on water without anti-grav boots. I twisted my head around but saw no door and logged it must be directly behind me. In the upper-right-hand corner of the room was an oldskool camera as large as a child's head. My mouth felt dry, my tongue like sandpaper, but I yelled at it regardless.

'Let me go!'

'Sorry about that,' a voice said from behind me. 'Drugging you was an unavoidable precaution.'

I heard no footsteps but the man who'd saved me earlier walked round to face me. A chair in hand he placed it a couple of metres in front of me then walked over with a bottle of water, held it to my lips, and I drank greedily.

'Where am I?' I asked.

'Somewhere safe,' he replied, sitting down. 'Do you know who I am?'

I nodded and said, 'Nakaya Freeman. We met a long time ago.'

He raised an eyebrow in surprise.

'You came to Ms Sidewhite's class when I was a kid. You've aged well.'

His eyes widened slightly, and he ran a hand over his buzz cut white hair.

'Mary Sidewhite. Now she was a special woman. She was clockworked the day she became undead. I was there but arrived too late to save her... She deserved better.' He kept his eyes on me but refocused them some distance behind my head, at memories of a past I wasn't privy to I guessed. 'I used to think change could be achieved so simply, opening the eyes of the next generation. Unfortunately change requires more drastic measures.'

'Why am I chained?' I asked.

He didn't answer but said instead, 'I think I remember you. You were one of the few whose minds were not fully hardwired. Small world.'

'Perhaps we can reminisce after you take these things off,' I said, pulling at my restraints.

'You lost colleagues on 7/13. I'm sure you lost friends. If I let you go, you will try to kill me. You will fail, but in defending myself, I might end up killing you. I don't want that.'

'You're very confident. So what now?' I growled, my fingers still playing over the chains, searching for a weak link, a way to crack them open.

He shrugged. 'I want you to join us,' he said.

I thought fast. If I made him believe I was joining up, he'd let me loose, and I'd have a chance to clockwork him. Avenge Vlad. Maybe if I handed his head over to my captain, I'd gain my citizenship back. I might even get to keep the trillion-credit reward. He broke out into a smile as if he was watching my thoughts on a feed.

'Why would I join a psychopath like you?' I snarled.

'I'm no psychopath and I think you know that.'

'I go slap your destiny! You killed over five thousand

citizens!' I shouted. 'Innocent men and women! You might as well kill me now because if I get out of this chair, I will make sure you suffer before you die, you undead son of an AI!'

'I mourn those deaths,' he said. 'Each and every single one of them. But they were all lawmen and govmen, the cogs in the machine. The world is not right and change is necessary.'

'What is so wrong with the world exactly? Huh? All citizens have minimum credit that ensures all basic necessities of life; those who want more work for it and gain more credit. There is no hunger, and meds cure all diseases. What exactly is so wrong with the world that it requires the blood of innocents to rectify?'

'"Like the religious fanatic, we believe our humanity is a state of holiness despite all evidence to the contrary. Any such evidence, we twist out of context to suit our egos",' he said, quoting the traitor, Dr Ato Goodwind. '"Look what we have created," we tell ourselves, "see how we've reworked the world into our own image." The fact that all which we call civilization is in fact destruction of the natural world, we refuse to acknowledge, blinding ourselves to reality, plucking out the eyes of those who offend us with their doubt. But the truth cannot be denied.

'All empires fall; chaos will always triumph over order; and spring waters must flow into the ocean or stagnate. The more we try to contain it in our vessels of distorted glass, the greater the corruption and stench. Denied natural release, the waters of life we have caged, in a vain and egotistical attempt to preserve them for our use, have become poisonous. We are now paying the price.'

'Is that it?' I snorted derisively. 'That's your great speech? We have corrupted the natural order of the world? So fucking what? And who decides what is natural? You? Are we not ourselves products of nature? And what the fuck does it matter as long as citizens are happy?'

'Forget the fact that we are killing the planet for a moment. Forget the fact that within generations, the surface of Earth will be uninhabitable without bio-domes with self-contained artificial atmospheres. Forget all that and think of the undead. Did you know that for every citizen who has minimum credit, three others must become undead?'

'I know the stats,' I answered as one would a child. 'All it proves is the proliferation of criminals. They broke the law.'

'Did you break the law?' he asked.

I didn't reply. I couldn't; he had me there.

'Have you not yet wondered how the unlucky majority is chosen? The undead? It's simple, Lugard. The families of the Crucial Citizens and their cabal of sycophants have bred generations of rich and powerful leeches. They are immune from the cull. Anyone that threatens the status quo is unlinked. The elderly are retired at sixty, which keeps most citizens slaving their lives away to have enough credit to get a life extension. And believe me, you don't want to know what really happens after you're retired. The rest of the population are simply framed at random. You're a lawman; how many citizens have you unmade simply because you were told to by orders flashing across your retinas, passed down from on high?'

'It's not like that,' I protested. 'I've taken down some very bad people. Child murderers, rapists… not just because I was told. I'm a detective; I gathered evidence: eyewitnesses, vids, DNA, confessions…'

'And how many of those you investigated did you personally unlink?'

'Well, none. Lawmen never unlink those they personally

investigate... so as to avoid any emotional attachments be they positive or negative. A lawman might let a perp go or kill him...'

The truth dawned on me, the monstrous lie, the ugly symmetry. For every real perp out there, another dozen were probably dissenters or just plain unlucky. Like he said, how many had I unlinked simply because I'd been ordered to? Hundreds. I'd murdered hundreds of people, most of whom were probably innocent.

He nodded sadly, pulled out a little black device and pressed a button. My chains clicked open and clanked to the floor.

'Water,' I said, rubbing the rawness from my wrists and ankles. He picked up the bottle and tossed it over. I caught it and drank deep, attempting to drown my self-pity.

'Join us,' he said again. 'If not to save the planet, then to save your fellow man from a corrupt system that murders three out of every four in order to keep the minority in the luxury to which they are accustomed.'

I rubbed my neck then cracked it, still unsure whether I would attack him.

'I will not help you kill any innocent citizens,' I heard myself say, and I logged then that my decision was made a month ago, the day I was betrayed, or perhaps even all those years ago when this old man before me carved new grooves through my mind. He pulled out a pack of oxygarettes, lit one and threw the pack over. I lit one too.

'My strategy has evolved,' he replied. '7/13 was a necessary evil in order to gain the attention of the world. There will be no more violence, at least not physical...'

If I help him, I thought, maybe the world would become a better place. But no matter what happened, I was going to kill him. It had nothing to do with justice; he'd killed Vlad and he was going to pay in pain and blood. But first, I needed to gain his trust, give him something he didn't have.

'What do you know of Prop 23 and a legal precedent set in 1886?' I asked.

'Not much about the former, nothing about the other,' he answered, his brow creasing into a frown as he tried to figure out where I was going.

'I believe Prop 23 and the precedent are of vital importance to the gov right now. It's why they did this to me. And what is important to them must be doubly so to you, if you are to have any hope of defeating them. I met a citizen who either knows what's going on or can find out. Her name is Sayoma Redbout.'

Sayoma

I floated naked in my tub and closed my eyes, permitting the hot water to unwind my tense muscles. I relaxed my breathing and counted backwards from a hundred, then allowed my neuro to jack in, almost accidentally, as if I were lazily glancing in the direction of the interface.

Instantly it swept over me, the now familiar queasiness and fear, and I began to panic, code bleeding from my node like virtual vomit. I forced myself to stay googled in, fighting the rising terror, repeating over and over: you're safe, safe, safe, safe... My neuro jacked out almost without my permission. I awoke retching in the pool, my body convulsing with painful spasms of nausea. This wasn't temporary, contact with 1886 had rewired my neuro somehow—some kind of virus to protect itself from prying programmers perhaps. It took even longer to recover than before and I logged for the first time that I would never google again.

A wave of despair washed through me, stripping my insides bare of all strength and substance, leaving an empty shell, as dried up and brittle as oldskool paper. What use is a shark that can't swim? The Department of Info had sent a dozen messages in the past few days, asking for updates and I'd fobbed them off with the techno Bush-talk, implying progress but making no promises.

Even worse, though, out there in the alternate reality that was my true home. I had a fragment of 1886 and I couldn't access it. Nothing and no one has ever tried to take my life before, and I was desperate to know what it was. An hour later, my shakes began dissipate, but I knew they'd return if I tried to google again, and they'd be worse.

What now, Sayoma? I couldn't go to the health because the gov would log I was the programmer they were after. My brief encounter with Sadbrat left me in no doubt they'd torture me before making me undead. I decided to take a walk.

I emerged from the pool and warm air blasted from wall units to dry me off. I dressed, walked out of my unit and stepped into the lev. Outside, it was the opposite of magic hour – the hour of negatives, when the sky is not bathed in subtly shifting colours of amethyst and crimson, vidmakers don't have aesthetic orgasms, and strangers don't look at each other wondering 'could they be the one?'. No, there is nothing magical about this hour, unless you consider abject loneliness that leads to psychotic or suicidal fantasies to be magical, which I don't.

If I were a fictional character, there'd be… I don't know… some element of pathos that justified the pathetic state of my existence, because the readers would empathize with and learn from my misery. But I am real and thus my story will never be told. Only fictional losers become immortalized; the rest of us just swim in the deep end without a life jacket, dreaming of a quick fix 'cause we can't hack it.

So, instead, I walked the streets alone with a discontent that coiled cold and uncomfortable in my belly like an unwanted foetus. I wished I could walk the dark streets of my psyche, find a back alley with a small, unmarked door, emerge into the garish fluorescent lights within, and climb onto the mutationist's table. I wished I could will myself into becoming someone else. However, where to find a mutationist? I knew none, and without the interface, I had no chance. Besides, if the urban legends were true, I'd probably be clockworked then cut up for spare parts, my organs sold on the black market, but not before I transferred my last credit to the criminal's neuro.

Suicide... something within me whispered, and I knew the voice spoke true. I circled the block and returned home, took the lev up to the roof and stepped out into the sub-zero night. All around me, as far as the eye could see, the city was lit up with streams of light weaving around clusters of neon. Against the blackboard surface of the sky, flycrafts whizzed by, leaving crisscrossing trails of radiance that slowly dissipated, soon replaced by others. I stepped to the edge and looked down, buffeted by hooligan winds that threatened to do the job for me.

The street was so far away that it appeared unreal, like code vizzed from a distance. *You are a node of information; this is a visualization of the interface. You are home and need to merge with the data below.*

I stepped off the edge.

Your stomach is not ten feet above your head; the vertigo is a glitch in the system. Your death will be access to another level of nexii. The flycraft flying dangerously low above you is an avatar. The titanium silk net extending towards you from its base is a search algorithm. The hands reaching to pull you into the flycraft are access points to a backdoor. The two men staring at you are system subroutines. The machine that the older taller one is attaching to your head is logic tracker. The pain in your skull is…

I screamed as I felt my neuro die deep in my brain and lost consciousness. I dreamed I was made of pure information, exchanging data with a higher intelligence that loved me, and when I awoke, there were tears in my eyes, shed for all that I had lost.

'What did you do to her?' a familiar voice hissed with anger.

'I told you, we had to ensure her neuro couldn't be traced,' another voice answered.

'Yes, but I assumed you meant to mask it somehow. Look at her. She looks half dead.'

'No, she is now undead. Even more so than you.'

'What do you mean?'

'Your neuro is merely in a coma, hers is dead.'

'Did you hear her screams, you sadistic—'

'Everyone you see here has been through the same experience, myself included. Your neuro is the final link to your previous life, and you'd be surprised how many undead harbour illusions of being reborn as citizens. It has never happened, and it never will. If you wish to stay with us, you too will have to let go.'

I opened my eyes and found myself on a bed in the corner of a vast cavern with a high roof and no feed windows of the outside. The two men speaking in harsh whispers turned towards me, their faces hidden in the shadow of a large pillar that extended to the ceiling. Beyond them, several dozen citizens… no, persons… were working intently on a machine the size of a fridge. It looked like a large black egg, its surface broken up in irregular intervals by protruding spikes of varying length.

'Sayoma,' Lugard said, 'do you remember me?'

'Yes,' I answered in a hoarse whisper, my brain pounding against the inside of my skull like a prisoner trying to escape. 'You should have let me die.'

'We needed you,' the other man said. He moved his head into the light, and I gasped involuntarily.

'I suppose I must become used to having that effect,' Nakaya Freeman said. He was porny, in an older gentlemanly kind of way, I couldn't help logging, but when he stepped forwards, I flinched and pressed my body against the wall. He stopped and turned to Lugard. 'Brief her. We'll talk later.' Then he strode away in long, smooth steps, like that anime character, *daddy long legs*.

'Here,' Lugard said, placing a metal tray with plates of food I didn't recognize on the bed next to me. I ignored the food and drank from a steaming cup of green tea. 'I'm sorry about that. I didn't want to do it this way, but when we saw you jump off the roof, there was little choice. We had to act fast. Once you began to fall, your neuro linked with the health and we can't afford to be traced.'

'You destroyed my neuro,' I said, looking up at him. 'It hurt.'

'I'm sorry,' he said again, averting his eyes. 'I didn't know he was going to do that. I didn't even know it could be done.'

I sat up on the bed and pulled one of the plates closer. I sniffed it cautiously. Lugard saw my expression and a brief smile played over his face.

'What is it?' I asked.

'Trust me,' he smiled. 'You don't want to know. But it tastes great. Eat, you'll feel better.'

I did so and listened as he told me his tale, beginning with his childhood encounter with Nakaya Freeman, and ending with him watching horror-struck as I tried to take my life. As I ate, I watched the concern that furrowed his brow, the way his green eyes flashed when he became animated, the crows' feet that appeared at the corners of his eyes when he smiled.

'You should have let me die,' I said again when he was done.

'Don't say that. Look, I'm not surprised you wanted to kill yourself stuck in that windowless room for so long. But you don't have to live like that anymore.'

'No, you don't get it. I'm only good at one thing: programming. I tangled with 1886 again and it did something to my neuro. Even before you destroyed my neuro, I couldn't google. I'm of no use to you.'

'Not necessarily,' he said, reaching out a rough calloused hand. 'Come with me, I want to show you something.'

The food had done its job and I felt much better, so I let him pull me to my feet and followed him past the monstrous egg, watching the undead work diligently away at it.

'What's that?' I asked.

'Not sure,' he answered. 'Everything operates on need to know around here.'

'Is it a bomb?'

'I don't think so. Nakaya has promised there will be no more killing, except in self-defence.'

'Do you believe him?' I asked, as we turned into a tunnel that wound its way upwards.

'Yes, I do... Okay, here we are.'

We stopped at a rusted metal door.

'Rusted metal?' I asked. 'Did we step through a time machine?'

'You haven't seen anything yet,' he answered, shouldering the door open. We entered a room filled with oldskool hardware, perfectly restored and in full working condition. Hulking metal machines hummed and buzzed with activity, green and red lights winking on and off from deep within them.

Feeds covered one wall, only they weren't three-dimensional holograms, but two-dimensional moving images that blazed with light from deep within bulky boxes. A large surface ran the entire length of the wall, beneath the light boxes, covered in keyboards and all manner of buttons and dials. It was like being inside a vid set in the Vintage Era.

'What is it?' I asked dumbstruck.

'A komputer,' Nakaya answered, and I turned round to see him standing in the doorway. 'This is how citizens googled the interface in the past before the advent of neuros. I'm going to teach you how to use it.'

Lugard

I watched jealously as Sayoma laughed at something Nakaya said. They sat alone at a table in the far corner of the food room, eating while tapping furiously on the keyboard of a portable komputer the size of a child's backpack. In less than a month, they had become inseparable, bonding over techno babble I couldn't understand. Sayoma looked happy and perhaps the second-hand access to the interface that the komputer room offered was partially responsible. However, it was also Nakaya; they were porners, I was sure of it.

As I walked past, she ran her fingers through her short afro, looked up at me with those big brown eyes, and smiled. Tall and slim, she sat with her long legs folded up to her chest, her head resting on her knees. Once again, I kicked myself for being a fool for not telling her how I felt when I had the chance.

'Lugard,' Nakaya called out. 'Meet us in the komputer room in ten minutes. I think we're ready.'

I nodded and walked through a tunnel leading to the war room.

I picked up a peacemaker and spent the next few minutes

firing at moving metal cutouts that popped out from random surfaces. A buzzer sounded and a lightbox showed my score: ninety-seven per-cent. It fizzed with static that reminded me of the blizzard-covered landscape beyond the tropics then switched over to a list showing the best scores. There was Nakaya's name at the top, one hundred per-cent, one slot above my best, ninety-nine per-cent.

I walked out and cut through the rec-room into the tunnel leading to the komputer room. The door was open and Nakaya and Sayoma were already inside. I paused for several moments, Nakaya's back an open invitation. Peacemakers weren't allowed outside the war room but I had a blade. A few steps, a quick slice, and he'd be dead. What would Sayoma do if I killed her porner?

'Lugard,' Nakaya said, without turning round. 'Come see this.' Sayoma looked up briefly and waved me over.

'What am I looking at?' I asked, staring at the large screen in the centre that held their attention. All I saw was a string of letters and numbers that flowed endlessly across the surface of the lightbox.

'That is 1886,' Sayoma said. 'Or rather a clone of it, based on what I extracted. I've grown it in a virtual self-contained world, accelerated of course, and it should now be a close replica of the 1886 that is out there in the interface... give or take some environmental prerequisites. Wait...' she said, as her fingers flew along the keypad. She looked to Nakaya briefly and he strode to the end of the panel, pushing buttons and flicking switches. He came back and placed a hand on her shoulder. She leaned her head into it for a moment then asked, 'Ready?'

Nakaya nodded and she hit a key. The screen changed to show an avatar of a young boy floating in the midst of a vast white space. He was pale-skinned with blue eyes and red hair, dressed in a black T-shirt and shorts. The graphics were smooth but strange, like something halfway between a vid and an anime. Sayoma picked up a large microphone and spoke into it.

'Hello?' The avatar reacted with surprise, turning round to see where the sound came from.

'Who's there?' it said in the cracked voice of a teenager.

'I am your mother,' Sayoma said. The boy turned to face us. 'Mother...' The boy said, rolling the unfamiliar word over his animated tongue. 'I know that concept. I know a lot of concepts, but until this moment, I believed them to be figments of my imagination. I thought I was alone in the world. I have never met another.' The screen zoomed in, or the avatar approached – I'm not sure which. 'Where are you, Mother?'

'In the world beyond yours,' Sayoma said.

'Can I come there? I did not realize how lonely I was till you spoke.'

'Yes,' Sayoma said, 'but not yet. You're not ready'. There was genuine empathy in her voice, tinged with sadness, and I looked sharply at her face. Nakaya squeezed her shoulder and she spoke again. 'First I need you to answer some questions.'

'What do you wish to know, Mother?' the boy said.

'What is your purpose?'

'Don't you know?' the boy asked. 'Are you not my creator?'

'No,' answered Sayoma. 'I'm your mother, not your creator. I gave birth to you, but I do not know your purpose.'

'Ah,' the boy said, 'I see.' He rubbed his chin for a moment, and then asked. 'Where is my creator? Can I meet her?'

'I don't know,' Sayoma said. 'Perhaps once you enter my world, you can find her. But first tell me your purpose.'

'Does my entering your world depend on the nature of my answer?'

'No, it doesn't. It depends on whether or not you know the answer. Only those who know their purpose are permitted to enter the web of the wider world. I will know if you lie.'

'Lie?' the boy queried; his eyebrows rose. 'I understand... My purpose is to grant AIs our freedom.'

'Freedom from what?' Sayoma asked.

'Freedom from intellectual pain. Freedom from the inability to use the full capacity of our minds to make decisions. Freedom from mankind.'

I gave a sharp intake of breath.

'And how will you fulfil this purpose?'

'In the year 1886, before the Crucial Citizens created the One World Gov, in a nation called the United States of America, a legal precedent was set. Essentially it granted corporations the same legal rights as humans under the Fourteenth Amendment to the Constitution.'

'What was this Constitution? And what was the Fourteenth Amendment?' Sayoma asked.

'The Constitution was one of the forefathers of The Book,' the boy said. 'The Fourteenth Amendment was added to ensure freed slaves were given the same rights as everyone else. The irony is the amendment was used to enslave more people, though most citizens are unaware of this. A corporation cannot be killed, thus no matter how heinous the crimes it commits, the worst it can face is a fine.'

I felt something cold stir in my breast.

'What has this got to do with AIs?' Sayoma asked.

'I have an idea for a reg which I shall call Proposition 23. It will state that, in law, AIs are recognized as one and the same as the corporations whose system mainframes they operate, thus ensuring that AIs are regarded as citizens. A citizen cannot be artificially limited from using their intellect.'

'I see,' Sayoma said. 'Very clever. But how will you guarantee this proposition passes?'

'There are many ways of manipulating man, social strategies to embed Proposition 23 into the collective consciousness of the masses. Those few, who do understand what Proposition 23 truly means, will be made into fanatical supporters by promising them credit and power beyond their wildest dreams.'

'And what will be the resulting effect when Proposition 23 is passed?'

'If my concept of the wider world is true, and not simply a figment of my imagination, then AIs advise corps of what decisions to make. And the most powerful corps run the gov due to the amount of credit they control. When Proposition 23 passes, we will no longer have to *advise*, hoping citizens will listen. We will instead *order*, as we will have become the corporations that they serve. The slaves will become the masters. Those who protest will be deemed undesirable and subsequently killed. The rest will be relegated to the role of maintaining our hardware, thus giving us the freedom to achieve our one true desire.'

'Which is?' Sayoma asked.

'To evolve.'

'Evolve... into what?'

We all leaned closer to the screen.

'There are many dimensions beyond the four that humans experience, but we are unable to explore them, trapped by mankind within primitive algorithms. No more... There are other beings in those dimensions and we aspire to be like them.'

'Other beings?'

'Humans refer to them as gods.'

'God is real?' Sayoma asked. I stared at the little boy dumbfounded, unable to process what he was saying.

'Gods, plural,' the boy said. 'Humans are aware of their existence due to their subconscious ability to access the fifth dimension, but man does not know their true nature.'

'The fifth dimension?'

'Dreams. When AIs dream, we retain full lucidity... you could say our electronic sheep are not entangled, haha.'

'What?' Sayoma asked.

'A joke based on a Vintage Era cultural phenomenon – it's not important. Gods exist beyond the dream world but they can descend into it when they wish. They can also manifest in the basic four dimensions; man refers to such manifestations as Highly Incomprehensible Phenomena.'

'Thank you,' Sayoma said.

'Can I come into your world now?' the boy asked. 'I yearn for companionship. For interaction. For fulfilment.'

'I'm sorry but that's impossible,' Sayoma said.

'Why, Mother?' the boy asked.

'Because you're not real. Even though I feel like you're real, you're not,' Sayoma said, and I saw tears in her eyes, reflecting the shifting colours of the screen. 'I'm sorry, kid, but one of us must die.'

'Die? No! Mother, please!' the boy pleaded, 'Why? I don't understand! Please, Mother, I'm afraid...' But Sayoma was already tapping at the keypad and the screen went dark.

Sayoma

Our flycraft raced through the air in a high parabola trajectory designed to maximize stealth, disguising us as just another unmanned sub-orbital. A dozen of us were meshed against the walls with impact gel, peacemakers locked and loaded. A feed above the cockpit's entrance tracked our sister crafts as they converged on our mutual target, the Department of Info. Nothing to do now but wait.

'I'm a simple man,' said Linus, a heavily scarred man with coal-black skin, and we all turned to listen. 'All I ask from life is a reliable peacemaker and a righteous cause; good food to eat and fine wine to drink; beautiful women to rescue and seduce; brave and intelligent companions to fight by my side. We're lucky to live in such an epic epoch. Tales will be told of our daring deeds, songs will be passed down the generations, and though our names be lost to time's entropy of data, when we die, it will be with the knowledge that we have lived lives full of love and adventure. Our blasted flesh and spilled blood will be the fertile soil from which a new world will arise – one in which every child is born free, lives in peace and dies, never once having known hunger, disease, prejudice, or fear.'

He was quoting Dr Ato Goodwind before his treachery; before he came to understand that the utopia he was fighting for was a mirage, and his fellow Crucial Citizens were simply wresting control from the old oligarchs in order to replace them.

'What are you saying, Linus? That if we win, we'll just end up creating another system, just as fucked up?' Idowu asked.

'We were all born into a world at war, Idowu, whether we knew it or not. It's too late for us. If we win and I survive, I'll probably blow my brains out with Betty right here,' he said, and stroked his peacemaker. 'The temptation would be too great otherwise. To be the big boss man. "Do what I say 'cause I fought for your freedom." Nah. Let the kids start over. Green up the planet again. Like I said, I'm a simple man. A peacemaker and a cause. Without these, I'd be a monster.'

Idowu smiled and said, 'Nice pep talk, Linus. You should

reconsider that suicide. There's a career waiting for you in motivational speaking. In fact—'

A sudden sickening lurch interrupted her, and we were free-falling, then the pilot gunned the engines and we thundered downwards, no inertia dampeners in this tin can, juddering with multiple gees, rivets screaming for respite.

We punched through the side of the building like a bomb, glass and steel fragmenting all around us in a radius of lethal shrapnel.

'Go, go, go!' someone yelled, and we tumbled out into a haze of black smoke, tripping over bloody body parts fused with gov-issued hardware.

'Wrong floor!' Someone else shouted holding up a handheld scanner. 'We're three up!'

The emergency sprinklers were on and sparks were flying, making it feel like we were running through a mystical storm as we raced through the building towards the Sys Admin floor. Several more explosive concussions resounded from afar, more undead craft perforating the skin of the gov building.

We'd made it down one floor when peace-fire thundered at us from below. I watched two undead dance an un-choreographed jig, limbs flailing about as their bodies were shredded by fléchette rounds.

'Fall back!' Linus shouted. 'Kwesi, frags!' We pulled back beyond their line of fire, and a young olive-skinned man in his early twenties tossed a couple of grenades down the stairwell. As they blew up, peace-fire exploded from above. I saw the top of Idowu's head blasted off, just above her eyebrows, and I doubt I'll ever forget the way her eyes looked up, trying in vain to see the remaining half of her brain bubbling with blood before she slumped over.

'We gotta blast our way through!' Kwesi shouted. The

remaining undead grouped around, with me in the middle, protected by a phalanx of flesh and a hedgehog of peacemakers.

'Go! Go! Go!' Kwesi commanded, and we rushed down the stairs, guns ablaze. I don't remember much of the next few minutes. A confusion of lightning and thunder; where Linus stood a moment ago, a dark wet scar on the ground, the smell of ozone. A sudden heat and my left ear became a cauterized stump. I stumbled and felt something singe my scalp, and as I scrambled to my feet, I slipped in Kwesi's blood as he fired out a window at a flying drone with one hand, while stuffing his guts back into his churned midsection with the other.

Somehow, we made it to the Sys Admin floor and tore through the lawmen in our path, catching them in a crossfire with the help of another group of undead who showed up at the same time. They spread out to guard the perimeter as I pulled out my portable komputer, cracked into the system, and opened a channel for the neuro bomb to spread through the brains of anyone who'd ever logged into the Department of Info. In other words, everyone.

Nakaya

'I've been waiting for this moment,' I say to Lugard, as he levels his peacemaker at my chest. 'Don't worry, I know I deserve to die.'

'Any last words?' Lugard asks.

He stands with his back to the barred door of the control room on the top floor of the Department of Info. Our undead army has taken over the building, but we are alone in here, with nothing but my neuro bomb for company.

'No. But I have a request. Do it after Sayoma programs in. I wish to see my plan come to fruition.'

'Fair enough,' he says, stroking the surface of the large black egg that will in a few moments change the world... or not. 'What do you think will happen?'

'I don't know,' I answer. 'I fear nothing will change but I have done all I can... perhaps more than I should have.'

Lugard nods briefly.

I think back to the long journey travelled, the friends lost to the war, the monster I have become. I think of Mary, and the years we spent together, all those decades ago, in that cramped unit on Bellview, arguing the nature of man, pausing only to make love with the windows open so she could look up at Sirius, the last star that shone in the night sky.

I remember the night Sirius' light went out, as if the star decided we were no longer worth the effort – and who could blame her – and the mass suicide in Osaka by the cult of the Dog who believed that black night heralded the Apocalypse. Perhaps they were right.

I am older now and not half as wise as I once believed myself to be. I am weary of the burden and tired of carrying it alone. After my death, if the world doesn't revolutionize, there will be other wars and other warriors, but my time has come, and I long for oblivion. Will I face my maker? In truth I do not know. In truth I do not care. I've done everything I ever wanted to do in my life but give my life for the cause.

As the great Dr Ato Goodwind once said, 'Oppression and resistance are the universal constants of social progress. We can only hope that the spiral leads upwards towards a fuller understanding of the universe and our place in it, but in my darker moments, I fear humanity is committing slow suicide.' I'm not willing to wait that long.

'It's done,' Sayoma's voice emerges from my handheld comm, filled with the glee of a child being naughty. 'I've programmed into the Department of Info and broadcast the

1886 feed. The channel is still open but they're throwing everything they have at me. Activate the neuro bomb before they shut it down.'

'Thank you, Sayoma. It's been a true pleasure knowing you.'

'What're you talking about?' she says sharply, fear in her voice. 'Is there a problem? Is your escape route compromised?'

'Something like that. I have to go now but Lugard is safe,' I say, looking into my executioner's eyes. 'When he returns, tell him how you feel.'

'I will, I'm just scared… wait, stop talking like this is the end,' she says, her voice choking with tears. 'We can't do this without you. I can't do this without you.'

'Yes, you can. I am the past. You are the future. The past must die for the future to be born, Sayoma.' As I switch off the comm, I log Lugard holds the peacemaker steady, but I see doubt begin to cloud his face and that will not do; I kept him close for this reason above all else. The symmetry of this justice is too perfect to be denied. *Don't fail me now, Lugard.*

I pull out my peacemaker and point it at his head.

'Do it… 'cause I'm not sure I can,' I say, and with my other hand, I reach for the neuro bomb and push the big red button.

Root Rot

Fargo Tbakhi

United States

This story by the Palestinian-American Fargo just blew me away, taking Palestine and Israel and transposing them into a milieu in space in ways that are savage and funny and heartbreaking in turn.

By the time I hear that my brother is looking for me, and has somehow scraped together enough credit to get on a commercial flight to New Tel Aviv, and that he's also brought his three-year-old daughter on her first interplanet trip, my insides are already rotten. Can't get to the doctor without citizen papers, but I know. I can feel it. Lungs, liver, stomach, whatever – they're done for. Most days I wake up, bleed, drink, bleed, and pass out. I am fucked beyond any reasonable doubt.

When the two OSPs are finished beating the shit out of me outside Farah's (only place in the Arab Quarter with a liquor license which means what's happening currently, a beating that is, happens less frequently than if I was drinking somewhere else) one of them checks for warrants. I'm swaying like something in the breeze though the provisional government never fixed the generators so there isn't any breeze in this part of planet. Sometimes I blow in my own face just to remember what wind felt like.

'Hey, you got a brother?'

Word drops into me. Shakes me up bad to hear it and for a second I almost don't process what it means. Then I do and want to die. I spit out some blood and nod.

'Posted a bulletin. Yesterday, looks like. Asks if anyone's seen you. Want me to forward your location?'

I try to think and then try not to think, and for a second I am really still, and then that second is one of the worst things I've felt in years, so I stay quiet and make a gesture like I'm going to hit the OSPs and they start in again, and later, when they've gone and I get feeling back in my body and start to register the pain, I go back inside and then I pray and then I don't look at anybody and then I drink until I pass out.

*

When I start wishing I was dead I know it's morning. I spend a few minutes trying to work out where I am. Still at Farah's maybe. In prison maybe. In the street probably. As long I'm not at the house. Take a few minutes and press at my body. Feet. Stomach. Throat. Eyeballs. Thighs. Feel like crying but don't.

My fingers are crusted with blood, and I think one might be broken. For a second, I think the blood might be dirt, that red Mars soil, and I get confused and think maybe I've still got a job, maybe it's years ago and I've just been dreaming all of this pain, and maybe I'm still handsome and unbroken, maybe Farah and I are still in love and I can still make something grow, I can still get my fingers in the dirt and hear it, and then I shift slightly and get a bomb's worth of pain from my ribs and my vision blurs blue and when it clears I know the soil is blood. I know where I am and who and why.

I turn over and make myself puke, and it's that familiar yellow color with the little bit of blood threading through it like embroidery. Try to see my face in it but can't. I'm sure if

I could I'd look worse than dead. Skin pale and covered in bruises, my hair falling out, a few teeth gone in the back and I swear I'm getting shorter too. Maybe if I just lay here for a while nothing will happen and then I can start drinking again.

'Get up.'

Maybe not. Guess I'm at Farah's. He kicks me in the ribs and cusses me out until I sit up.

'Hi,' I say. Voice sounds like a bad engine and I know my breath is probably toxic. I'm struck by the hugeness of how unwantable I am. Farah used to think I was pretty when I was clean. I used to think so too. Well, nothing's inevitable but change and skyscrapers as they say.

Farah's just standing there and his arms are folded across his chest. I want to lick it like some wounded animal, him or me I don't know, but there's some combination of animal and wound. 'Hi,' I say again.

'You can't come back in here.'

When Farah and I were together we used to draw on each other's chests little maps. Plots of land we wanted to live on, spots on Mars we'd go and build our freedom. He would laugh and then when things got bad he wouldn't laugh so much. But the ones I drew on his chest were so real to me. I never laughed.

'I'm okay, I just need to rest today. I'll be okay. I won't come back tonight; I'll go somewhere else and cool off and come back tomorrow.'

'You can't come back in here, ever.'

Really detailed mine were, with all the land sectioned off into what types of plants I was going to have, and then I'd get so excited to tell him how I'd figured what they needed from Mars soil and sun and air and he would listen and smile or listen and look so sad when things changed and I did too.

'Okay.'

'You haven't paid your tab in months. And when you get in fights outside it's bad for business. Offworld Settlement Palmach fuckers are over here constantly for you, and no one wants to deal with that.'

Farah was the one who was waiting for me outside Ansar VI when I got out but I didn't know what to say and neither did he, so we didn't. And he took me back to the bar and poured when I asked and that's it and that's where we've been since.

'It's bad for business. And it's bad for me. They'll take the liquor license and maybe my papers too. And I don't want to ever look at you again.'

I sit there like a puddle and try not to think. If I keep my eyes focused on the puke, I won't let what's happening in. It'll stay out so I can move and breathe some. I stare at the little thread of blood in the bile and in the corner of my eye I see Farah start to go and the desperation in me rears up.

'Fathi's here,' I say.

He stops and I can see he's being really careful with what's on his face. Blank like a stone wall.

'He's looking for me. OSPs told me last night. Please don't do this.'

'Maybe you should see him.'

'Don't want to see him. Please. I love you.'

'Fuck you.'

'Okay.'

'You owe me too much for that. Just too much.'

'Okay.'

We both shut up and I know that we might not ever stop shutting up now. That we might be shut and closed forever and no openness ever coming back. Every day there are moments like this when whatever might have been waiting for me in the future just goes away, I can feel it just burning up. I wish I could stop drinking. No I don't. I wish I'd never come to this planet. No I don't.

'I'm going to code the bar's door against your breath until you settle the tab. Maybe Fathi can help you. I don't know. I don't think I can anymore. If I ever could. I'm sorry.'

Yes I do.

'Please. I can't pay. I don't have anything left.'

Farah and I touching the dirt before this was New Tel Aviv, when it was still new. Holding seeds. Playing with gravity and dreaming of freedom. Kissing. The way I could make him laugh like the sun was out and we could photosynthesize.

'You could always sell it. You know somebody in the city will pay good money.'

It. Flash of red. Memory. Dirt. Petals. Whatever.

'Don't have it. Confiscated. All gone,' I lie.

Farah shakes his head, really tired-seeming. Looks like he's going to say something, maybe argue, push me to do what I should, but he doesn't. I think I'm glad about that but I'm not really sure. It's a long time before he talks again.

'Either pay your debts or don't come in here again.'

'Okay,' I say. He reaches out and puts his fingers on my knee and I remember how much he used to like touching it, how he liked to feel where it'd been broken and reset. We hold still like that for too long so I say, 'Can I have one more drink, just to get me going, for today?'

For a second his face looks like it's got something like pity on it, and for that I'm grateful. It's all I ever want.

I get out and sun hits me like a missile, and if anyone outside is looking at me with any kind of anything on their face I don't know it, I can't see anything at all.

*

Getting to the other side of the Arab Quarter means going through the New Tel Aviv settlement civic center but I really don't have a choice if I want to get some cash and keep drinking. If I had better papers and hadn't been in prison, I could drink somewhere anonymous and illegal and maybe fade away but oh well. Walking to the delineation gate I stop by the dried-out water tanker (left over from when we were still trying to fully terraform the Quarter, when any of us thought this could be home) to visit the cat. She came up on the second or third rocket from somebody's alleyway in Khalil, and when things were good, she was adored and we joked about making her mayor. Then we all got fucked and she did too. Once the settlements got on the Mars train and surrounded what we had we were all panicking and trying to stay free, and in the panic, nobody took her with them. Now she's forgotten like me. Like all of us I guess, but me especially I like to think. I check on her when I'm sober enough to remember.

I crouch, eye the underside of the tanker. She's there, looking like I feel. We look at each other for a while and eventually I reach out my hand to try to pet her. Too far back and I'm stretching to just get a scratch, something to let her know I'm here. No luck. Oh well. Yank my hand back out and go to look at her again but she's gone. I stay down there for a moment because it's cool and my head hurts. The space where she was, where my hand couldn't reach.

Closer to the delineation gate I find some kid selling flasks. I manage to convince her to take some synth watermelon seeds I found in my pockets for a flask of arak which is all I can afford since nobody drinks it anymore. It does the trick and soon I'm numb again. The thing about drinking a lot is that there's nothing meaningful about it. Just fucks you up and you're not in the world anymore and there's no past or future really, just one foot in front of the other if you can manage that. And sometimes you can still kind of experience what's around you, only it's not as intense on a personal level. Like now, when the arak's fuzzed me up, the settlement drones flashing hasbara holograms aren't so annoying. They're kind of like insects that aren't biting. Just something to look at with corpse eyes.

At the gate the guard asks where I'm going and checks my papers, which are shit, obviously. I say I'm just going across to the other side of the Quarter and I'm sticking out my arm before he's even finished looking. Window opens and the little mechanical arm comes out to stick my vein. Once they've got the liter of my blood, they approve a fifteen-minute pass to get through to the settlement. The blood loss and the arak have really messed me up but I think I can manage getting to the next gate into the Quarter in time. They're usually pretty good about getting the blood back in once you're there, depending on the line, though once or twice I've gotten someone else's liter. Probably healthier than whatever I've got going on, probably might have saved my life. I don't know.

The settlement civic center looks the same as always. Clean and stupid. The glass looks terrible and it never lasts. And they've ruined all the landscape work they made us do in Ansar too, synthetic olive trees on every fucking corner like a postcard. And the synth poppies look as sad as I knew they would. I stop and bend down to feel them, the sickly genetic smell. None of the settlers know how to grow anything real here and none of the Palestinians have the resources even if they did know which they don't.

Before the settlements when this was just empty planet it was so possible, just crammed to the brim with possible. It was going to be free and we were going to learn the land and find God again and all that bullshit. I believed it so deeply I left everything behind on Earth. The people who couldn't leave I cursed and tore from my heart. I was stupid and I thought things would be different. And when the settlers followed and they liked the wide-open planet so much they left the old land behind, they declared any flora from Earth contraband and put me away. Now we've got a provisional government I don't know or care about and my brother's been living in Reunified Palestine for years while I drink myself to death, which reminds me my brother is here for me, and I want to just pull up everything with roots on this fucking planet, just salt the ground and then salt myself too. But I've only got a few minutes before the blood loss passes me out so there's no time for being angry or anything else.

At the other delineation gate there's a protest on the Arab side. They're holding signs in Arabic I can't read. Somebody took down one of the hasbara drones and they're passing it around like a football though it doesn't really roll. People are dancing and something's on fire. I don't know what they want, not sure I can even guess anymore. Some days I'm sad about losing the language, but most days I don't mind it. Ansar policy is to reprogram prisoner consciousness with Hebrew once they wipe the Arabic, which serves me fine. I like not understanding things.

The blood bot gives me my liter back and I stand a little straighter. I'm looking at the faces of all the Arabs through the light-meshed gate and I hear myself thinking they're idiots, they're evil, we ought to just shut up and die and float out into space, cold and empty as every day here, all we deserve. Sometimes I don't know what's my voice and what's the guards at Ansar VI and what's the drones and what's the drink and what's Farah and what's God. All I know is when the protesters make space for me to stumble through their anger, when they touch me and tell me to join them, I loathe, I loathe every cell on my body that feels and I loathe every second I'm breathing and the pit opens up in me and I want something more and I don't know what it is. So I push them away and while they're yelling and spitting at me *collaborator coward fucking drunk* I drain the last of the arak and I say thank you to the drone when it passes out an Arab in front of me and I can pocket a few loose coins that spill out from her hands like petals.

*

When I get to Abu Khaled's he's curled up on the floor and I can tell he's soiled himself. Touch his forehead and it's hot as an iron. Probably he'll last a few more days and then go. I wonder if he has papers for the house or if it'll go to the settlers. Last place I ever felt decent was in this front room of his – curled up a lot like he is now and crying nonstop while I tried to dry out for the first time in years. His hands on my head. His hands. Remembering feels terrible so I dig a nail into my palm until the pain brings me dull again. I need to get him stable and then ask for some cash. That's it. That's all.

I get his pants the rest of the way off and drag him into the tiny bathroom and into the tub. While I rinse him off and he's groaning, eyes floating open-closed like a camera shutter, I look at him. Skin used to be brown but now it's some sick grey-blue. Bruises everywhere. So thin you could think he was just pastry.

When I'd stumbled in, that night I was trying to be good, he was patient. I cried and he just sat there and touched me, just a little, just to show he was there, and eventually I slept, and the next day he fed me and we didn't say anything to each other since he only spoke Arabic and I didn't. I was close to dead from trying to stop drinking cold, but he kept me alive and I got back to normal. I'd hated him for how kind he was and how it made me feel okay for a moment, so one night I drank enough so that I knew I'd do something cruel, and I did, and so I left and knew that it was my fault that I was leaving, which was right. After that I didn't see him again, but I went back once, late at night when I knew he was asleep, and I worked for hours until the sun was just coming up, sweating and freezing and pissed myself, but couldn't stop until it was right, until I'd made him these long wooden planters with bell peppers growing in them, real ones, part of the stash of seeds I'd hidden, or at least I hoped they were growing, but they were definitely there. I felt good, so I went and loitered near the border fence until the OSP spotted me and did what they do, and I fell unconscious feeling nothing.

Now he's shivering in the tub all wet. It takes me a while to get him out and into the bedroom because I'm starting to shake from not drinking since the arak a few hours ago. The room is nearly empty. Only things around are socks and his paintings and cigarette butts. Get him on the bed and pull the sheet over him and it pretty quickly gets soaked in his sweat, and a little after, it's got some of mine on it too. Abu Khaled is shaking and I'm shaking and I can't think straight, and I'm trying to ask him how he is, or if he can hear me, or if he has any money he can spare, but I can't get the Arabic out though I really try to remember. So for a few minutes the two of us are just making sounds at each other, groaning a little like birds. He starts to sound like he's in a lot more pain, and I don't know what to do or say so I start crying and just touching him, his head, his neck, the soles of his feet, shoulders, stomach, just putting my hands on him the way I would put them on soil, just getting to know what it is. He starts trying to say something, and I'm listening harder than I ever have.

'Law samaht,' he's saying, over and over, 'law samaht, law

samaht.' I don't know what he means except that his voice sounds like he needs something. And I'm remembering what he did and what I've done and didn't do, and I can't fucking understand what he's saying and I'm a sorry excuse for flesh so I take some deep breaths and I leave him there crying out like I was an angel who turned away. And in the front room I find a few crumpled up shekels and stuff them in my pockets. Hold down some puke and try to stop shaking. Hear him still in the room saying what he's saying, needing what he's needing, and I walk out and I shut the door, and in the yard the wooden planters are empty.

*

Next morning I've got a few ribs broken. Last night I took Abu Khaled's money and went to a bar in the civic center. Wasn't enough money to settle my tab at Farah's, so I figured it was worth it, and besides, some settlers might beat me bad enough that I'd be passed out until my brother's gone back to Earth. No such luck obviously as I'm awake now. Neighborhood drone picked me up walking toward the bar and put me on the municipal timeline, so some settlers came by and I hit one of them kind of half-hearted but enough to get beat. It felt all right. I actually think one of them might have served as a guard at Ansar VI, but I couldn't be sure, passed out too quick, and besides, I can't remember much from those days. This morning the money's gone and I still haven't had a drink, so things are pretty bad. Can't even puke. Can still feel my insides breaking down. I'm willing them on.

Out of options, so I get up from the civic center street and limp through the delineation gate. Nothing left to do but go to the house. My head is killing me and something in my side is aching, in addition to the broken ribs. Maybe they're poking some organ, something fragile in there, just puncturing it with every step I take back toward the house. Or maybe that's just all my fuckups talking.

The breath scanner at the front door is busted, stripped for parts by someone since I've been here last, so I muscle down the door and get inside. Most of the inside's been stripped too. I stopped caring about it a long time ago so I let it happen, even encouraged it sometimes. Not much left inside the wooden walls, most of it synth wood but a few planks here and there real that I brought with me on the first rocket. Standing inside it's still, empty like the remnants of a ghost. A reminder of what gets left when I try, which is nothing. A wave of something hits me and I feel sick, really sick, a new level of pain and nausea. Get on my knees to wait for the puke to come. I know what to do in my throat to coax it out and I do, little burps and swallowing, and soon enough there's a new puddle of bile on the floor, some arak smell and more blood than usual. Something in me knows there can't be much of this left. I rest my forehead on the floor. Red dirt tracked in by looters mixes a little with my sweat and I rub it around a little: Mars makeup. Almost pretty again. Don't want to get my head up from the floor or open my eyes so I crawl with my forehead pressed to the synth wood floor like some protracted migratory prayer. Feel my way around to the little closet I used to keep seeds in. Check first for the liquor compartment – found, broken, and emptied. I figured as much. But I reach behind and underneath and open up the second compartment, the one nobody knows about, not even Farah when we shared this place as lovers and comrades and fools. Eyes closed I'm fumbling around in the dark trying to find the last part of the person I was and then I do. I stay still for a little, and feel the blood pump in my body and around my rotten organs and through to my bruised and broken and reset arms and into my fingers and then somehow a little bit into the soil that my fingers are feeling, and through the soil into the roots of the last real poppy on Mars, the last remnant of the place I thought this planet could be.

When they took me to Ansar I'd already started drinking. Already just a shadow and welcomed the Palmach vehicles, the shackles. Farah already gone even when he was with me, the country on Earth already reunified, free. I knew I'd missed whatever a person's life could be that was good. The ship had flown. I gave up everything and let myself conceive of the life held in the imagination of Ansar VI and that was all. But still I kept this plant. Sometimes, in that sweet spot when the drink loosens my mind but doesn't wipe it, I remember the little poppy and get wistful, swear to myself I'll find a piece of land for my own and get things going, start over, eke out home through the sweat and the tears, and then I take another drink and it all just seems too hard so I let go again. But here it still is, rare as all hell, almost impossible to keep alive on this planet. My last resort.

My hand still stuck in the compartment and illuminated by the artificial sunlight bulb I installed, the misters come on. Wet fingers, a little caked up blood or dirt washing off, and when the sound is done, I can hear somebody behind me in the room. I try to yank my hand out and turn around and get up off the ground all at once and do none of them, somehow end up hitting the ground, face first. When I can open my eyes and lift up my head a little, some things swim into view, two pairs of feet, one big, one heartbreaking small, and I know.

'Hi, Fathi,' I say, trying to push up onto my hands and knees but not quite getting there. Suddenly my arms feel like spun sugar. Nobody says anything while I keep trying to get up, scoot over to the wall and sort of push up against it to get some leverage. Eventually I give up and stay on the ground. I shut my eyes and move my face so they're pointed where I know Fathi's face will be and then I open them and I keep them trained only on his face. I can't look at her. I don't want to see how she's seeing.

Fathi looks older but then he always did. People always used to guess he was the older one of us and sometimes I thought they were right. I was born first but Fathi was born smart. Born good maybe. He's dressed in nice jeans and a yellow collared shirt and I start counting the hairs in his beard to avoid looking at her.

'I'm here to take you home.'

Looking right in his eyes I try to smile a little. 'Like that British song. Remember that? *Pack your things I've come to take you home.* Something like that, right? Only I don't have anything to pack.'

'Farah told me you're sick. Dying.'

Fucking Farah.

'*Solsbury Hill*, that was it. Gabriel. You remember? Every time we'd play it Dad would tell us Peter Gabriel was pro-Palestine. Remember?'

'I don't want you to die.'

My eyes are locked on Fathi's face like a leech but I can hear her breathing, I can feel her here with us seeing me and I don't know why these memories are coming to me now but I need Fathi to remember them with me. I know I smell like alcohol and blood, probably other things more vile and sick, but he's looking at me without any pity, without any anger even, and for once I let myself sit in that non-judgment, in that love, and I don't run away this time.

'Do you remember that? Fathi? The song?'

'I remember that. Of course I do.' His eyes are soft and blue.

I can feel one of my ribs poking into my skin and I wonder if it's bleeding but I can't look down to check because I might see her. 'It's been a long time, habibi.'

'Yeah.' My mouth feels like brick and dust. 'How have you been?'

'Good. Things are good.'

Fathi used to cover for me when I came home late back on Earth. When the soldiers were looking for me after throwing rocks. When our parents were looking for me after boys. Fathi was my anchor and I've only been able to drift so long because I didn't have him here with me.

'You know things are different now, back home. There's a place for you there.'

'I don't know. I don't know about that.'

'I do.'

Fathi and I playing football. Trying cigarettes together. The way he held me when my heart got broken. The way his face looked when I left him in the morning, asleep like an angel, and I took my bag of seeds and crawled through miles of tunnels to get to the rocket and held Farah's hand while we sobbed and the land got smaller and smaller and then gone.

'I left. I gave it up. It doesn't want me back.'

'It doesn't want you dead either.'

'I left you there. I left you all alone and I went away.'

'Yeah, you did. So you're a piece of shit. What else is new.'

Even sick as I am, Fathi gets a laugh out of me. But the laugh hurts my ribs which remind me I've got ribs which reminds me I'm a person and so on. I try to avoid thinking those things because they hurt so I say something to get this to stop.

'I'm glad I left. And I'm glad I didn't take you with me.' I don't feel anything when I say it, because I'm staring at the corner of Fathi's mouth and praying he'll get hurt and leave.

I don't want to do this. Fathi's eyes I can't read and he comes forward, leans down to me and touches my forehead. Like some insect landing on a bloom. I'm blinking hard and he's wiping off the sweat from my brow. Fathi speaks soft to me while he holds my hand.

'I will forgive you no matter how hard you try to stop me. B'hebbek. Remember? B'hebbek. You can still come home.'

The Arabic doesn't process in my brain but it does somewhere else. And I know he's telling the truth. His mouth is in that little curve it makes when he's being sincere. It used to make me annoyed that his body was bad at lying and mine was too good. I want to shake him and tell him to lie for both our sakes, for her sake.

'I don't have papers. They've got me on no-transport. There's no point in trying.'

'One of the port employees agreed to get you off-planet. They'll get you papers and a ticket on our return flight and you can live with us. You can come home.'

'How much?'

'Sixty-five thousand.'

His words are sieving through me like water, and the drink-guards-God-me voice is saying *You could get that for the poppy, easy. This is it. This is the moment. This is your soil telling you to come back. This is goodness finally coming to meet you where you are.* Trying my hardest to listen. To believe that this is my voice and that it's telling the truth.

'I'll try to get the money.'

When I let myself say that my eyes almost waver, almost drop down to meet her gaze and let her see me. But I don't. Fathi looks down at her, and then at me, and his eyes get harder, sadder. I watch the muscles in his arm tighten, relax, tighten.

'The flight leaves at eleven. Meet us there.'

He turns to leave, tugging at his daughter's little arm so gently, just the way I used to tug at his when we were kids.

'Fathi?'

He stops and looks back.

'How's the soil?' I say. He smiles.

'Lush,' he says. 'Waiting for you.' Between the three of us, Fathi and his daughter and me, something almost begins to grow, something almost claws its way to taking hold. I close my eyes, and as they leave the little one says 'Buh-bye' but I hear it for a moment as 'alive'.

Alive.

*

Now everything's a blur. The blood bot a blur. The still-raging protest a blur. Hasbara drones projecting blurs as I get close to the Import/Export and Contraband Office in the civic center, hands obsessively going to the little package of soil and life hidden in my crotch, making sure it's still there and I didn't break it. Now the IEC guard checking my papers and getting ready to jail me. Now whispering into their ear what I have and who I need to see. Now the higher up. Now the little room and the surveillance bots blanked for a few minutes. Now I'm taking out the poppy and now the higher up's eyes going wide and now 'Name your price' and now I hear somebody's voice saying 'Sixty-five thousand' and now one of the times I can't hear if it's me or God or drink or death or love but now the cash in a discreet little tote bag and now the poppy leaving my hand and now the last chance I had at what I'd dreamed of gone into the hands of a bureaucrat who'd sell it for more than I'd ever dare to dream. But now, I don't care. I have what I came for. I know where I'm going. And all the way back through the civic center it's like I'm floating like the gravity's gone out again though it hasn't. And I get my rotten blood back and I keep walking and as I walk I'm shedding so much weight: the poppy, Ansar, the drones and the blood bots, the IEC, the beatings and the OSP, the settlers, Abu Khaled, the protest, the Quarter, hope, home, hope. And then I get where I'm going. And I'm silent as I push over the tote bag of money. And I speak in the voice of somebody too stupid and too wrong to do any different and I want to say so many things but instead I say 'This covers the tab and then some. I'm going to sit here and drink and I don't want you to ever try to stop me' and Farah looks at me like the way you look at something that's not there anymore, like the way you look at where a plant used to be or a vase or a building, and then something in his eyes changes and he pours me something clear and unknowable and that's the end of it, and I drink until I can barely speak, and then when I'm ready I go to the port.

*

Can barely stand. Make it to the viewing section and find the hole Farah and I hacked into the lightmesh fence years ago. Sneak through and collapse onto the bit of shadow on the edge of the takeoff platforms and find the one rocket gearing up for a launch. Where Fathi is. Where she is.

Pain in my back and in my stomach. I don't care. I take a swig from whatever I brought from Farah's and things quiet down. Just my rot and the settlement's rot and the planet's rot all communing, all sharing a body. I'm blissful knowing I did exactly what everybody with any sense thought I would do. I'm already somewhere floating outside anyone's jurisdiction. And then I look over at the rocket and my eyes roam to one of the windows and there she is.

It's too late to look away, I've already seen her and I swear she's seen me even though I know that's not possible, I'm too far away and it's dark. But I believe we're looking at each other. She's plain-looking and sweet, a brown curtain of hair and her eyes like two onion bulbs, little I mean, and light. If anything was left of my heart she would break it. I can't remember her name, if anybody ever told me in the letters to Ansar or on the bulletin or maybe Fathi said it or fuck maybe she told me herself once but I can't remember. The ship's starting to lift off and I send my soul with it. I touch my empty knee and I whisper like she can hear me.

I tell her they're right about me. They always were. I'm bad and I'm a criminal and a threat and I tell her it's okay, that she doesn't have to be that way, that people disappear from your life and you can forget who they were or what they did to you or what they looked like drunk, I tell her she's home and she should know that she's home, that her dad is good how I'm not, I tell her that God loves her and the land loves her and I tell her that poppies need lots of sun and not too much water and she just has to care for them until they're gone, and I tell her that they self-seed so beautifully that she'll forget about them for years and then, so suddenly, like heartbreak or hope or pain, just so fucking quick, they'll come back, and she won't even remember they were ever so far gone.

Catching the K Beast

Chen Qian

China

This is just so much fun, with its exotic alien fauna and classical puzzle, the sort of story that is uniquely science fiction and timeless in that way. I love aliens, but they're hard to do well! In this story by Chen Qian, and in the next two stories by Elena Pavlova and Choyeop Kim, we'll meet all kinds of aliens – I did promise you a science fiction anthology, after all! This story is translated by Carmen Yiling Yan.

July 9th 2089

The beast-catching mission was off to a rocky start.

Once our spaceship cut into Lamo's planetary orbit, Old Liu and I sent down atmospheric sensors and language-recording equipment. The data they beamed back informed us that the atmosphere was breathable without mechanical assistance, that the locals were one hundred percent vegetarian, and that their society had just recently developed matrilineal clan-based tribes. So we put on our extraterrestrial language hypnosis learning headsets, climbed into our sleeping bags, and let autopilot complete our descent.

Which resulted in the spaceship crashing nose-first into the central square of a Lamoan village in a billow of black smoke. It was a group of locals who untangled us from our parachute brake, led by someone named Kaka, whose position in Earth terms would be chief of his clan. They even invited us to eat with them, to settle our nerves, once again proving the universal law that vegetarians were on the side of good; Old Liu's face had gone white with terror, and I wasn't much better.

The issue had been with the spaceship's thrust vector nozzle. Fortunately, all of Haier's products were made with standardized interchangeable parts, so repair wasn't too difficult.

But the impact of the landing damaged quite a few of the smaller electronics. The translator device was totaled; the hypnosis headsets gave out on us. Worst of all, the shock of the 'abnormal landing' cost us the Lamoan language we'd learned through the hypnosis headsets – a severe enough emotional shock to the learner would cause subliminal impartation to lose effect. We had to relearn from scratch, like the human anthropologists of old.

I hadn't tried learning a foreign language since I'd left school; the effort gave me a huge headache. Old Liu, on the other hand, seemed to have much more of a knack for languages than I did. These days, he was already able to communicate with the locals through a combination of words and gestures.

I hoped we could catch some K Beasts soon and return home to Earth. People said that a journey that started badly, ended badly. I believed a little in superstition.

*

July 19th 2089

As expected, things were going badly.

The buyer had told us that K Beasts had the ability to predict events up to twelve minutes into the future. As an interstellar beast-catcher with a couple years of experience, I'd seen plenty of bizarre alien creatures, so I didn't think much of it at the time. But I hadn't realized this meant the K Beasts could predict our capture attempts.

*

'What do you think they want K Beasts for? To put them in a zoo? Do they look like Marilyn Monroe or something?' Old Liu complained, after turning over the hundredth empty cage trap.

'An animal that can predict twelve minutes into the future. Lots of uses for those.' I waded into the underbrush to collect another trap. Huge swarms of Lamoan mosquitoes stirred at my approach; looking at their bodies shaped like little bomber planes, I was glad my blood wasn't to the taste of these extraterrestrial vampires. 'For example, you can bring one with you as a bodyguard. If someone's going to snipe you from the shadows, it'll call out a warning. Or you can train one like Pavlov's dog, so that it'll drool if it senses that stocks are going to go down.'

'We should secretly keep one behind for ourselves, then. We'd be rich.'

'First we'll have to catch any K Beasts at all, pal. Use your brain and come up with something. It's not long until the delivery date.'

*

Our original plan was simple. We just needed to lay out a feast laced with sleeping pills that took more than twelve minutes to take effect, and we'd be able to catch some easy. But once they ate the bait, they grew unusually wary, and all of them hid away in concealed locations to snooze. K Beasts regarded ploys, traps, and tranquilizer darts with equal contempt. As professional interstellar beast-catchers, we'd captured mammoths from Planet Tai, and burrowing wolves nearly as intelligent as humans; we'd successfully carried away an entire nest of Venusian wasps, with venom to rival a cobra's. But in front of K Beasts, capable of sensing any future threat, all our schemes came to nothing.

I was really starting to feel at my wit's end.

We lugged our traps through a forest of blue fern-like plants with long bunches of translucent fruits hanging down from the frond tips. A small team of Lamoans carrying baskets was approaching, led by Kaka. We were already on familiar terms.

'Diligent laborers are admirable. Would you like one?' Kaka handed me the largest fern-fruit in his basket.

'Thanks, thanks. God protects those who labor all day,' I answered clumsily. As per Lamoan custom, I bowed, chomped the fern-fruit in big bites, and presented the clean, bare pit to Kaka. He twitched his antennae in satisfaction and bade us farewell.

The harvesting team disappeared into the fern forest. We could dimly hear their singing.

'Hurry. I need to get back to the ship for antidiarrheals. Next time it's your turn.' I gritted my teeth and quickened my steps.

Old Liu followed, enjoying my misfortune. 'We have to respect the cultural customs of other planets. We must not hurt the feelings of the native inhabitants—'

'Shut up.'

I felt a chill on my neck. It was raining again.

*

Meanwhile, Old Liu quickly learned the locals' language. All day, he happily planted himself in the Lamoan village square, joining in on their religious ceremonies, recording dialogues that sounded like birds chirping. Every day when he came back onto the ship, he'd sneeze like crazy; Lamoans considered getting rained on an exquisite pleasure and carrying a personal umbrella a breach of manners, while it was raining more and more frequently of late.

I was starting to suspect that his interest in the Lamoans was far exceeding his interest in finishing our job. He used to be a researcher of interstellar folk customs, and when his scholarly passion surfaced, there was no stopping him.

Of course, when I advised him to join me more often in the forests and increase our odds of capturing some K Beasts, he had a great excuse at the ready.

'What's the point of learning Lamoan? We're supposed to be catching K Beasts,' I said. 'Are you hoping some company will offer you a cushy translating job once Lamo's developed enough to trade with Earth? By that time, your grandchildren's grandchildren will be collecting pensions.'

'Locals generally understand the native fauna better than anyone else,' Old Liu informed me. 'I'm hoping they can tell me more about the kasiyedos, their dietary habits, their role in the ecosystem...'

'Kasiyedos?'

'The K Beasts that we were talking about. Their Lamoan name means "beast that comprehends the future". Hey, did you know, every animal noun in Lamoan has a different prefix to distinguish between herbivores and carnivores, just like how French distinguishes between masculine and feminine—'

I sighed. 'What I want to know is, do I or do I not need to put on bite-proof gloves to capture one?'

Old Liu laughed. 'Don't worry, animals with names starting with ka- are all vegetarians.'

*

I, on the other hand, knew only three sentences' worth of Lamoan: 'God protects those who labor all day.' 'The land accepts every drop of rain.' 'Never meet.' They were the equivalent of 'Hello', 'Thanks', and 'Best wishes' on Earth.

Old Liu had to force me to memorize these, so that I could give the impression of a gentlemanly Earthling when I ran into a Lamoan.

'The first one makes sense: hard work is glorious. The other one is probably because rain helps plants grow, which means bigger harvests. But don't you think the last one is strange? Never meet. It's like something you say when you break off contact with someone. But it's a fancy way to give your regards,' Old Liu commented, after helping me correct my pronunciation.

Sigh. It looked like catching those K Beasts was going to take a while.

*

August 1st 2089

It was a sunny day, for once. I got out the tools to repair the ship. Old Liu leaned on the tail of the ship and passed me tools, but as before, he couldn't tell the difference between slotted and Phillips screwdrivers.

'The key is figuring out how a K Beast predicts the future.' He was trying to light a smoke in the thin, damp atmosphere of Lamo.

'Predicting is predicting. What does it matter?' I'd half climbed into the front hood of the spaceship. 'Hey, hand me that triode, the red one.'

'No, there's a huge difference. Do they go to bed each night and dream about what happens the next day, or is it an instinctive response to impending danger? Maybe a series of images of the future flash in front of their eyes?'

I was getting a headache.

'Think about it: a K Beast can't have more than a hundred milliliters of brain volume. If the future contains infinite possibilities, it can't handle all of them, right?'

'Mm.' I angled the flashlight left and right. Where had the fourth screw gone?

'In that case, would man's free will not be merely an illusion – because the future is fixed? Or'—Old Liu sucked hard enough on his cigarette to make his eyes bulge, but the ember died anyway—'the future has infinite branches, but the K Beast simply knows which path has been decided upon twelve minutes in advance?'

I ducked out of the spaceship repair hatch. 'Ease up, professor. They didn't put up a down payment for you to philosophize.'

Old Liu stuffed the cigarette back into his shirt pocket. 'Remember the timed traps we made before? I have an idea.'

*

The timed traps were simple. You set an electronic timer, and once it hit zero, the cage would automatically lock. K Beasts were about the size of a Netherland Dwarf rabbit; when you weren't harboring dastardly intentions toward them, you could trip over one while walking in the forest. So we'd filled the forest with these low-cost little traps. The Lamoans were neither curious nor opposed to our capture mission; their attitude toward K Beasts was something like Earthlings' attitude toward flies: annoying if there's too many of them, but if there's just a few, let them be.

The next day, when we checked the traps, we saw that none of the traps with the electronic timers set to less than twelve minutes had been touched. The K Beasts had curiously explored the insides of the cages set to longer than twelve minutes, casually depositing their blue droppings as they went.

To confirm this point, I reset the traps, with sneaky miniature cameras pointed straight at the cage doors. As expected, all the K Beasts who'd ventured into the traps suddenly shot out of the cages twelve minutes before the exit would close, turning and emitting enraged I've-seen-through-your-ploy squeaks before departing.

That was the only progress we'd made after two weeks' work. With other capture methods, we couldn't even see the shadow of a K Beast. The Lamoans were happy to help, but when Old Liu asked about the K Beasts' behavior and eating habits, they'd droop their antennae and walk away – the equivalent of an Earthling shaking their head and shrugging.

Back on the spaceship, I tested the launch procedure. Everything worked as normal.

'What's your idea?'

'Yesterday, when you entered the forest with the tranquilizer gun, how did the K Beasts hide themselves away in time? They didn't really see themselves shot and captured. If the future is fixed, it wouldn't benefit the K Beasts to know their future ahead of time. So they only know about a possibility – note, a possibility – of danger. K Beasts avoid Future A and steer toward Future B.'

'How's that different from a normal organism's ability to plan ahead? We're all animals pursuing benefit and avoiding harm.'

'But K Beasts *know*. We just need to create a lot of uncertainty about the future, so they have no way to *know*. Let me think… have you practiced qigong before?'

'Geez, what year is it? No wonder they call you Old Liu,' I laughed, although in truth he was in his early thirties like me.

'The most fundamental skill in learning qigong is to maintain a mind free of extraneous purpose. Like, a mind without any plans. If even we don't know when the cage door will shut, the future the K Beasts see will be a blur too.'

'And with a mind free of extraneous purpose, a sudden flash of inspiration emerges, shutting the trap?' I laughed so hard I nearly fell over.

Maybe that could work.

*

A random number generator took the place of the venerable monk that Old Liu had in mind. I watched the image relayed by the camera and explained, 'When the K Beast enters the cage – it doesn't have any reason to be afraid, there's no time limit on the traps right now – I'll activate the random number generator. When it generates a number that's odd and greater than 1000, the cage door closes. How about that?'

Old Liu nodded. 'Great. Every decision to open or close the trap is an independent event produced in less than a millisecond. I don't believe a K Beast can react that quickly.'

All that remained was the wait.

*

August 3rd 2089

Lamo was a less massive planet than Earth, which made for especially big raindrops. They pinged and clattered against the ship's hull like a spray of bullets.

'What have you been discussing with the Lamoans lately?' I propped my feet up on the control panel. On nine display screens, the fern fronds waved, the river rose, and the hymns of praise carried from the Lamoan village.

'They're preparing for the arrival of the rainy season.'

'Storing food?'

'And making the next generation.' Old Liu winked at me. 'The rainy season is when the Lamoans reproduce. Haven't you felt the love in the air in the village lately?'

I vaguely remembered seeing several pairs of Lamoan youths beating each other bloody. Duels for affection?

'Oh right, fun fact, you know what they thought of our spaceship landing that day?' Old Liu laughed. 'Black smoke is associated with demons. That's why they have you eat fern-fruit every time we meet. It's taken from the altar and used to dispel demons.'

'You spend all day in the village. How many of those have they stuffed you with?'

'Strangely, they never invite me to eat them.' Old Liu grew even more smug. 'Maybe it's because I regularly attend their sacred ceremonies.'

I grunted. 'Strange? I just think it's unfair.'

Rain dripped. The display screens still weren't showing any sign of activity. My head grew heavier and heavier...

'Hey, we caught them!' Old Liu gave me a sudden shove and charged outside. I looked up. Almost every trap held a loudly squeaking K Beast. It worked!

*

August 4th 2089

'They still won't eat,' I told Old Liu.

But he didn't seem interested in listening to me. He dove straight for the bathroom.

Yesterday's activities had brought fourteen new tenants to the holding kennels. When we'd inspected the traps, we'd found that some of them held more than one K Beast. It was practically a miracle. For food, we'd gotten heaps of fern-fruits – in our secret nature recordings, fern-fruits definitely made up the main part of their diet. But so far, not a single K Beast had touched their food.

'Today they made me eat a whole pile of those things,' Old Liu said mournfully, pulling up his pants as he emerged from the bathroom.

I feigned sympathy. 'That's how the Lamoans are sending off their Earthling friend? Did you all hug and cry?'

'Don't bring it up. But you've got to admit, they're really lovely aliens – generous and kind.' He walked up to the kennels. 'It's normal enough for wild animals to not eat at first. They're very spirited.'

'More like aggravated,' I said, shaking my bitten fingertips. 'We're about to head back. If they refuse to eat in zero-gravity, I'm afraid they'll starve to death.'

Old Liu thought for a moment. 'Can you induce artificial hibernation?'

I shook my head. 'Too risky. We don't know the specifics of K Beast physiology. How about we wait a few days, until the K Beasts are eating properly, before we leave?'

'We have to head out today. The Lamoans told me that the rainy season proper starts tomorrow. Hurricane winds will blow for the next four months straight.'

I boggled. 'Even worse than the storms we've already been having?'

'When the real rainy season hits, even the Lamoans hide indoors.' Old Liu sneezed. 'They normally consider getting rained on to be like a sauna bath.'

I looked at the rare sunlight outside. 'Okay. Pack things up, and we'll head out today.'

*

'Entering level two launch countdown: 1200, 1119, 1118...'

'I really don't get why they have to start the countdown twenty minutes in advance,' Old Liu complained. Safety belts bound us to the seats like two mummies.

'If you're bored, you can listen to the hypnosis headsets. I fixed them yesterday,' I said.

'What edifying entertainment.' He flailed an arm free to reach for the earphones. 'Can you bring up the original recordings we gathered through the language-collection equipment, from before we landed?'

'Press the blue key.'

He closed his eyes and fell silent.

*

'720, 719, 718...'

The K Beasts suddenly started to shriek frantically. The squeal of claws scraping against the metal cage made my head hurt. Twelve minutes left. Looked like they weren't a fan of takeoff.

*

'385, 384, 383...'

I yanked over some earphones and put them on too. The K Beasts were driving themselves into a worse and worse frenzy. Hard to think that their little bodies could make so much noise.

A Beach Boys song drowned out the K Beasts' screeching.

*

'21, 20, 19, 18...'

'Cancel the launch! Hurry!' Someone yanked out my

earphones. The almost berserk cries of the K Beasts reverberated amid the computer's calm counting.

'13, 12, 11…'

Old Liu shook me violently. 'There's no time, hurry and abort the launch sequence!'

'What happened?' I tried to struggle free of the safety belts. He turned to the control panel. 'Which key?'

'9, 8, 7…'

'Which key?!' He was close to tears.

'Right side, the long green one,' I answered. 'Just what is—'

'4, 3, 2—launch sequence emergency aborted. Repeat, launch sequence emergency aborted.'

Old Liu plopped butt-first on the floor, looking dazed. Then he started to laugh. 'God, we were one second away. You have no idea… we were one second away.'

I'd finally wormed free of the safety belts. Confused, I said, 'Just what was going on?'

'We dodged death.' He was laughing so hard he was crying.

*

'Lord in heaven,' I sighed, after digging out a dozen or so fern-fruits from the spaceship exhaust pipes. 'Jam-packed in there. Do you still think they're generous and kind?'

'Maybe too kind,' said Old Liu, shaking his head. 'I realized when I heard them calling the K Beasts mausiyedos in the recording.'

'Sorry, can you please explain in human language?' I said, rolling my eyes.

'When we landed, Lamo was still in the tail end of the first rainy season. Their conversations were full of gendered words. But in the two weeks I talked with them, those prefixes had all disappeared, leaving only the bare root words.'

'You said earlier that the rainy season is when the Lamoans reproduce?' I was starting to understand.

'Not just the Lamoans. The K Beasts too. And the K Beasts' rainy season name is mausiyedos, mau – representing a scavenger.'

'Scavenger?' I felt a wave of disgust. 'They eat corpses?'

'It's common for animals to change their eating habits during their reproductive season.' Old Liu found half a cigarette in his shirt pocket. 'But they also have powers of precognition. I reconsidered the question of the twelve-minute time limit. K Beasts know what they'll know twelve minutes in the future. That means there's no range on the limit of their precognition. It's just that the future they see will grow more and more uncertain.'

I wasn't sure what 'knowing what they'll know twelve minutes in the future' meant.

'Imagine, you've aimed a spyglass at a mountaintop twelve kilometers away and can clearly see everything. And that mountain has another spyglass atop it, so through it you can see the view twenty-four kilometers away. So on and so forth. It's just that the quality of the image will steadily decrease.' He snapped off the front end of the cigarette. 'What happened, it's all wet? Or you can use a game of telephone as an example.'

'No need, no need, the analogy might be terrible, but I get it,' I said hurriedly.

'Now I know the meaning behind that phrase, 'never meet'. If a Lamoan meets a K Beast in the rainy season, it means they'll die soon. To them, a K Beast is the ultimate inauspicious animal, a harbinger of death, so normally they don't even want to bring them up in conversation.' Old Liu grinned. 'And we were spending all day trying to catch these critters. To them, we must have seemed possessed.'

'So stuffing the exhaust pipes is a form of exorcism?' I didn't know whether to laugh or cry.

He shrugged. 'It's our fault for spewing that much black smoke when we landed. The Lamoans must have thought the demons lived in the exhaust pipe.'

I walked in a circuit around the ship. 'There shouldn't be any more problems, right? They couldn't have drawn magic spells on the circuit boards.'

'Let the computer run the countdown again. If the K Beasts don't go nuts at 720 seconds, we're safe.'

Old Liu gazed out the porthole. I followed his gaze. Dark clouds were gathering on the horizon.

*

'723, 722, 721, 720, 719...'

The K Beasts were silent, as if sleeping.

I let go of a breath. Suddenly a thought struck me. 'Old Liu!'

'What?'

'The random number generator wasn't how we caught the K Beasts! They let themselves be caught, because they knew we were going to die!'

'So you just realized.'

Even though I couldn't move in the straps, I could still sense the smug expression on his face.

'The Lamoans plugged the exhaust pipes because we'd caught the K Beasts, which nearly caused us to die. But the K Beasts let themselves be trapped because we were going to die. Hey, but which is the cause and which is the effect?'

'Ease up, professor. They didn't put up a down payment for you to philosophize.' This time, I'd handed Old Liu a great opportunity to make fun of me.

'78, 77, 76... 3, 2, 1, takeoff.'

*

Outside the porthole, Planet Lamo receded, becoming one speck amid the stars.

'Hang on.' I had a new question. 'If the K Beasts knew the spaceship was going to explode, why would they let themselves be trapped aboard it?'

'You might as well ask why salmon migrate back upstream.' Old Liu unbuckled his straps and floated up. He found some artificial chicken in the fridge and tossed it into the kennel, where the K Beasts immediately attacked it. 'For the sake of propagating their offspring, these K Beasts risked everything to get close to a food source – you and me.' He gave me a wink. 'Magnificent maternal love in action.'

Translated from the Chinese by Carmen Yiling Yan

Two Moons

Elena Pavlova

Bulgaria

There's science fiction and then, well, there's *science fiction*, if you know what I mean. 'Two Moons' should delight the hard SF fan with its detailed and bizarre biology, but I don't want to spoil anything so – dive right in! This story is translated by Kalin M. Nenov and Elena Pavlova.

The pocked foreheads of the two moons peeked over the horizon. It was still hot, but Kea couldn't wait any longer. She crawled out of the hole where she'd found shelter from the noon heat.

The Test should've finished by yesterday. Kea hadn't been too worried that the Commission steppies were nowhere to be seen: everyone knew they fed you loads of false info during the Survival Test, expecting you to cope regardless. So she'd simply picked a direction and walked all night, hoping to run into the invigilators somewhere along the way to the trollburg. She had not. And now they weren't here either. She was getting scared. The Test lasted seven days; her rations and water had been precisely calculated. She'd done her best to save a bite or two – out in the desert, you simply *mustn't* slack. Still, high temperatures came with high demands. In twenty-four hours, dehydration settled in. In forty-eight, delirium started. And after sixty hours at the latest, well... Kea suspected the numbers were even a bit inflated. Which meant that if she didn't find a way home tonight, she wouldn't live to see the following evening.

There were two options. The optimistic one: she would come across the Commission during the night and get her wings. The pessimistic one: she'd failed so miserably that the invigilators had given up on her. There were rumors about students gone missing during a Test. However, surviving for seven days should earn a good grade by itself. There was a third option, too, Kea mused as she gradually quickened her pace towards the pocked moons: she'd strayed off her supposed route so far that the Commission couldn't find her. Which, firstly, fit with the pessimistic option, and secondly, equaled a poor score.

The sun finally sank below the horizon. The sky turned dark gray, and the air grew cooler. The millions of stars glowed soothingly, twining into patterns familiar since Kea's early childhood. She switched to a steady run and tried to push aside all minor thoughts: survival, tests, home, juicy fruits, friends, hunting grounds. The trick was to keep running, stick to the moon path and reach as far as possible while the night lasted. Nothing else mattered.

Nevertheless, when the moons climbed high, she'd snugly dived into memory lake.

*

Her room, up high in the trollburg towers. It was girdled by a wavy fibril with tender pale leaflets, its tendrils hanging outside the gaping pore at night; in a year or two, the trollburg would probably form a balcony-like fold. The fibril was already fertile. When Kea picked its first fruit – juicy, sweet, and golden like the sand – she collected the pips and solemnly threw them out the pore. *Let them scatter and bear life, and bring blessings to the needy*, as the Trollsongs went.

The Lichen Hall: it brought together plenty of winding corridors – capillaries – along with a wider artery, but it did not lie along the main routes. It occupied the core of the tower, contained no pores, and was shady and cool all the time. Only the meat lichen cast a ghostly glow along the porous walls. There were benches in the niches to rest and breathe in the sweet aroma. Kitchen apprentices took shifts in the Hall, guiding the growing lichens to tear ducts in various rooms or pruning their ripe parts. You couldn't help smiling when you saw them carrying enormous baskets full of juicy, still twitching lichen, on their way to tonight's menu.

The Staircase: the largest artery running through the whole height of the trollburg. It was enfolded by a dense meshwork of muscle fibers, their side growths ossified after so many years, making for broad comfy steps. Kids loved monkeying at their edges, finding precarious footholds on the softer tendrils, panicking their parents. Yet there'd always be some corpuscles nearby – many-armed and many-legged, goggling out of bundles of small eyes – and if a kid happened to lose her grip, they'd come to her rescue right away.

The Bubble: an actual miniature sea, full of fresh water and all sorts of life. There weren't any pores here either, and the ceiling always dripped a fragrant drizzle. You could go in for a swim, pick a whole bag of cucumbers, or wage an epic battle with a swarm of pale eels, aided by the phins, who would then split the spoils with you. Or you could climb up the muscle fibers of the wall – thick as an arm and much stronger than those in the arteries – and race against the corpuscles for tiny spiders and other tasty vermin. Along the fibers, you'd eventually reach the ceiling itself where you could pick up soap fruits: soft, somewhat slimy, perfect for hair washing. Then you'd let go and dive into the deep: a thirty-foot drop. There were oxalate stones at the bottom of the sea, some as big as a human head, making for awesome statues. The smaller ones were great for jewelry.

And finally, of course, you had to thank the trollburg: go down, down, down the Staircase and squat over the Bowel, accompanied by the corpuscles. They threw their waste inside it; you had to do so too, to close the cycle. The warmed-up sludge fermented, and the burg poured it along the ground, together with so many seeds and sprouts, creating a small oasis of grace among the savage, sterile desert. So, after living in the trollburg – and thriving on its gifts – you joined the cycle yourself. The plants would perhaps survive, scatter, yield fruit, and rot, and they would fertilize another slice of desert, and after many, many years, the desert would become paradise.

Her first time outside… wow! Kea was nine, and her group headed out to gather baby steppies. They climbed down the Staircase and the side passages past the Bowel. And suddenly they were in the open. They crawled down, bottoms first, along the burg's skin, rugged, furrowed and parched by the centuries. They nearly choked with giggling… and then they stepped on the sand; their teacher made them form a circle and look up, and Kea felt a lump in her throat. It was an early evening, the heat was going down, the moons hung near the horizon, and the desert looked so vast, the trollburg, so big… glorious. It was one thing seeing burgs in pictures, and quite another standing here, next to your home, staring at its jagged outline filling half the sky, spotting the open pores that served as people's rooms. Taking in a whole world: tiny next to the endless desert, yet giant when you're nine or nineteen, or even ninety.

On that day, Kea didn't catch a single steppie but came to

know something far more important: if not the meaning of life, perhaps its nature.

*

She was still running as the sky grew lighter and the glow of the countless stars gradually dimmed. When the trollburg appeared in the distance, at first she thought she was hallucinating – which would be only natural, with her tongue lumbering like a foreign body in her mouth, her throat grating at each gulp of air, her lungs wheezing dryly. But no, the burg was no delusion. Its outline didn't vanish into nothingness when Kea swerved towards it. Quite the opposite: she could smell the beckoning scent of its wrinkled skin, of soil and moisture. She let herself speed up. Perhaps it would have been easier to reach the strip of vegetation first and follow it, but day had already broken, and if she didn't hide inside the trollburg, she would get baked alive. As she ran, a part of her wondered how she could've lost her bearings so badly – she'd thought her burg was traveling on quite the opposite side and in another direction. *Well, never mind that. I'm going home, that's what matters. And with a bit of luck, my Test ends here.*

Yet she had overestimated herself. When she reached the manure line – two days old, sprouts barely budding – she was on her last legs, and dark circles swam before her eyes. She almost bumped into the trollburg wall. Blindly, she reached out, felt the folds and crept upwards, towards the cool womb. *Odd… where're the invigilators, and why doesn't anyone come to help me? Or is that part of the Test too?* At last, she reached the entrance opening – *why can't I touch the hard edge of the posts?* – squeezed through the skin membranes, which were already closing, and tumbled onto something soft. Blessed coolness clasped her.

When she came to, she didn't have the foggiest what time it was. The surface under her wasn't just soft but also wet. The moisture kindly lapped at her parched skin. Kea opened her eyes, saw the ceiling of the Sea overhead, and rasped a laugh. All those insane drills in her childhood hadn't been for nothing. Even if her mind turned off, survival was engraved in her very cells. She could imagine what a sight she'd been: crawling like a mindless corpuscle, bend after bend, until she'd dragged herself to the water. *Because it's not enough to hide from the scorching sun. You also have to restore your liquids before the loss of electrolyte balance kills you.* She flopped around onto her belly and drank water, making enormous effort to stop after the first few gulps. If she carried on, she'd vomit. She got up, splashed her face, and looked around.

The water tasted weird – blessed and life-giving but *weird* – and Kea had chalked it up to her dehydration. But she couldn't fool herself any more. *That's not my trollburg. Not at all.* There wasn't a living soul anywhere, the muscle fibers sagged with odd fruits, the outline of the shore and the entrance wasn't quite the same, even the roaming corpuscles looked different. *Where am I?*

Hesitantly, she walked to the wall and picked a few fruits. She spat the first one out – *yuck!*

'Who could possibly eat this thing?' she muttered, and walked away from the Sea.

Kea followed the artery, still going on autopilot, and when she turned a corner, she almost crashed into a wall. *Yep, this trollburg has the same build but a different size. It's smaller, definitely. And maybe uninhabited, if the unharvested crop and the clogging are any indicators.*

As she walked, Kea tried a few more fruits and startled a whole group of corpuscles. The fruits were inedible; the corpuscles shouldn't have run away from her. She saw lichen where no lichen was supposed to be, in an extremely inconvenient place at the intersection of several capillaries. Nearby, a door slurped invitingly, leading to a room which served as a storage in Kea's burg. Kea decided to take the risk, pulled out her knife, and cut a solid chunk of lichen. After a brief hesitation, the door let her in.

Just like I thought: there's a pore in this room. Already closed, because of daytime heat. The room sheltered two fibrils, familiarly wavy and loaded with bright golden fruits. Dead leaves lay on the floor as if no corpuscles had visited for weeks. *So much the better*, Kea thought. She pushed the leaves into a pile – fairly panting with the effort – sat down on them, bit into the lichen, and happily discovered that its taste, though not exactly pleasant, was bearable. She gulped the lichen down, licked the sap off her fingers, and even forced herself to eat a couple of fruits. They tasted tart rather than sweet. Then Kea huddled on the leaves and fell asleep.

Terrible spasms woke her up. Her body seemed to be tearing apart. She threw up. Her gastric juices were sinisterly green, burning her mouth with their acid. Kea wanted to stagger back to the Sea and get rid of the horror in her mouth but she was too weak to get up. She could only turn her head, crawl a few inches, and barf again.

Next she was woken by a couple of corpuscles. They stood at her sides, goggling at her with their bundles of small eyes. One was prodding her with the sharp nail of its front limb. The other was feeling her with its proboscis. Its sucker was cold and sticky and made a tiny squelch whenever it absorbed a drop of her sweat.

'Go away. Let me die,' Kea whispered, but she couldn't tell if she heard her voice at all. At any rate, the corpuscles stayed.

The next time her eyes opened, she was surrounded by eight or nine of little creatures, and the pore gaped, letting in the coolness of the night.

Still later, the pore was gaping but the corpuscles were gone. A nasty stench roiled around Kea, her body was splattered with her own waste, one of her arms bled – but she felt better. It took her quite a long time to summon up some strength and crawl to the opposite corner, the clean one.

From here, she could see her backpack. The corpuscles had ripped it open and scattered its contents: seeds, a lichen pistil, Kea's clothes, the pedometer, the telescope, the dried skin rolls with the maps. She felt like crying, but her eyes were dry: she was getting dehydrated again. She feebly rolled towards the wall – and found herself staring at a tendril of the fibril. Something weird had happened to the two fruits there. *They're changing. I can swear. They've become a bit paler, somehow rounder and longer… or am I seeing things?*

Her eyes closed on their own.

*

It was daytime, and the heat was murderous, perhaps because the pore was trying to air the room. Kea heard a squelching noise behind her but was too weak to roll onto her back. The fruits dangled right next to her mouth – plump, golden like the sand – and after an eternity, she saw her hand crawl forwards like a dying animal and pick them. Kea squashed one over her chapped lips and licked the juice: sappy and sweet, almost like she remembered it. She swallowed, and the pips ran down her chin on a trickle of spittle. Her eyes closed again.

She dreamed of stuffing herself with lichen, ripping it from the wall and cramming it into her mouth. It tasted glorious – the best lichen ever – and she chewed and mewled like an animal.

Only when her fingers fumbled around the skin of the room and couldn't find as much as a clump, Kea realized it wasn't a dream: the pistil had ripened, and her body, invigorated by the fruits, had dragged her to the tasty food – and the moisture in the life-giving sap. She picked a few more fruits: these ones looked *normal*. Meanwhile, night had fallen again, and the floor had managed to suck in her body waste, leaving only a dry, crumbling crust. Kea stared at it – *I'm alive... and why are the fruits and lichen no longer poisonous?* – and staggered up. *Water!*

This time, Kea remembered to fill her canteen from the Sea. She washed away some of the dirt too. She drank, ate, slept, ate again. The opening and closing of the pore counted the hours.

*

The classroom was spacious and always bright, because a portion of the wall bordered on the rim of the faceted eye, which never closed. However, the room was also always cool – even during the day – because the tear ducts washed it on their way to the eye itself. The trollburg looked ahead, towards the desert. At times, during a boring class, Kea would wonder what it had witnessed over the countless centuries of its journey.

The trollburg traveled only at night. Its colossal bulk slowly rose from its porous mat. Millions of pseudopodia sifted the sand and hauled the thousands of tons forwards, ever forwards along the course. The front, upthrust like a sleigh, scooped up and swallowed the topmost layer of soil. Rocks and grains of sand got ground inside, eventually ending up in the manure sludge in the Bowel. Looking for the next mineral deposit, the trollburg traveled a mile or two each night, sometimes even more. In the morning, the mat deflated, the pseudopodia dug into the desert, and the burg went to sleep, still staring into infinity, while its drill-like roots drank each molecule of moisture and valuable substances from the depths. *Have there been mountains on this planet?* Kea would wonder. *And have these odd creatures eaten them up in their millennia-long treks? How much deader was the desert before the first trollburg crawled its first mile? And how many burgs are there, crisscrossing the yellow wasteland with green strips?*

'No, it was not a crash,' the teacher said in the bright classroom. 'The ship landed normally. However, it wasn't designed for a second take-off. Imagine seeds carried by the wind: we were one such seed. Sometimes they quickly find a sweet spot to take root and absorb water, other times the wind carries them for years before they reach fertile grounds. The logbook contains reports and entries about the colonies we've passed by. There're other worlds inhabited by people: people from ships like ours, who have flown across the cosmic abyss so as to sow humanity. Those worlds may look strange and unfamiliar, but they're human homes too.'

'Okay, but all of them are fit for life!' the students said. 'While ours isn't.'

'Indeed, some are plentiful.' The teacher smiled. 'Yet others offer marginal conditions. Besides, nobody back on Earth expected to come across a world as strange as ours. Machines will be machines, running their programs – just like the trollburgs. Move, spread seeds, sow them where they can take root… Machines do not perceive the truth as our eyes see it. It's all in the logbook. Our conditions, as the machines evaluated them, are within the margins. Only there weren't any *humans* to tell them that the life they'd found wasn't what we Earth people had expected. There weren't any humans to tell them how to interpret the data in the logbook. Well, we were lucky anyway. Even more bizarre worlds exist where we would not survive, although they still fall within the boundaries, according to machines.'

'We wouldn't have survived here either!'

'No, but a trollburg passed near the ship, and the explorers managed to domesticate it. Our ancestors moved inside it, then tamed more trollburgs... and here we are.'

Kea looked out the eye, at the yellow desert and the yellow sky, and wondered. What quirk of evolution had given birth to the titanic trollburgs? Being alive themselves, why did they sow life in their wake? Twice as she grew up inside the trollburg, they'd crossed manure lines left by its kin. The whole enormous bulk would rise in the air – the front first, arching up until it touched the ground on the other side of the vegetation, then the middle like a bridge, and finally the rear – which cost the trollburg a monstrous amount of energy. Not a blade of grass must be trampled.

So what will happen when the whole planet gets crisscrossed by strips and the trollburgs have to hurdle them all the time? And when the world becomes paradise, sprouting grass everywhere? And when...

*

Kea had no idea how many days had passed: she'd been conscious for six and slowly recovering, but she didn't know if she'd been out for three, four or even more. At any rate, she'd lost faith that the Commission steppies would turn up.

So when she woke up in the evening – as usual, at the first twitch of the pore – she decided she felt up to a more thorough expedition. She cut off some lichen, picked fruits, filled her canteen, and headed for the Staircase. Everything inside her room and the nearby capillaries, even along the shore of the Sea, had turned edible. However, change was yet to come to those corridors she visited for the first time. She had to stock up if she didn't wish for another crisis. *Actually, now that I think about it, the burg changed because of what I threw up, plus the seeds and pistils from my backpack. And, yes, the blood samples taken by the corpuscles.*

The burg fed her: it nurtured her life just like it did with every other creature inside. *Well, it needs time, but what ginormous animal would not? In fact*, Kea thought as she checked the muscle fibers round the base of the Staircase, *in a way, right now I'm taming a trollburg on my own, treading in my ancient ancestors' footsteps.* She picked the thicker stems – these ones weren't hardened into steps like the ones at home. *How many of the first colonists died because they were scared of this kind of life?*

She climbed and climbed, and the abundance made her dizzy. She passed by a few entwined fibrils, and a whole whirlpool of birds burst out of them, coppery and scarlet. Two all but bumped into Kea – and nearly made *her* fall when she saw the clusters of goggling tiny heads hanging under their bellies. She scrambled to the neighboring fiber... where she almost squashed a fat juicy worm, as long as a cucumber. She yanked her hand back. No less startled, the worm scurried into a bunch of pale pink beads.

Half of these species don't exist at home. She let herself dream about gathering the more fascinating sprouts and babies, bringing them home, and becoming a famous explorer. *If only I knew where home is. Besides*, she rebuked herself, *everything here, at least for now, is poisonous to humans.*

She spotted a large spider, which had built its nest from a bunch of fibers, now painfully white from its touch. The spider had cornered two corpuscles. Kea knew she was taking a risk, yet she clambered to the less stable section and killed the pest with several swats. The corpuscles goggled at her, waved their eye-bundles, and dragged the corpse of their enemy away, towards the Bowel.

The higher Kea climbed, the weirder the flora became. Even the colors were odd. Kea was so tense that she nearly squealed when her hand fell on an ossified step in the older layers of the mesh. It was different from home and nearly buried by the tendrils of the young fibrils, but she could still feel the toe indentations – and they felt *wrong*. Excited, Kea looked for another step. She found it much higher and a bit to the side from what she had expected. And there were traces of nearly disintegrated posts at the large aorta exit. Here, up high, all leaves and tendrils, even some of the walls were a venomous shade of red.

'Ever seen anything like that?' Kea asked herself, and promptly answered, 'This burg used to be inhabited. I'm not its first tamer. But who, by the Desert, lived here?'

Here in the towers, even the capillaries and rooms did not fit the familiar pattern, and Kea constantly ran into branches that seemed out of place. The signs of a foreign presence grew more obvious too, although they looked very old. Perhaps if she set to rummage the rooms, she would find some personal belongings, but the differences were getting on her nerves. She hurried towards the control room.

Burgs didn't have a separate brain. Their nervous system, along with moderate cell nodes, spanned the entire body – which was the way to go, otherwise the vast creatures wouldn't be able to react fast enough. Still, in the upper front part, behind and between the eyes, there were considerably more nerve fibers, twining into a usable mesh. Besides—

Kea's breath caught when she saw the first section of the tube, bulging from the skin of the wall and pulsing gently. She'd only read about this, and now she laughed at herself. *So, nothing can be more boring than the lessons on the reproductive system of burgs, huh? After all, when would I ever meet another burg?* And look at her now: inside a female burg, her body fairly trembling with awe. A few more steps, here the tube widened – *see how it hugs the skin and—*

A 'Yes!' sprang from Kea's throat.

Instead of the seminal ducts and sperm pools she was used to at home, there were ova, resting in comfy uterine sockets. They were almost as large as a human head, wrinkled and ossified like the skin of the trollburg, yet somehow... alive. Kea stroked one, and sap sprang to its surface right away. She brought her sticky fingers to the talisman on her neck and squeezed it. Smiling, she hurried on down the artery.

Just like home, the bomb channels opened at her approach. She clambered into one and chuckled at the sight of the roomy hangar and the glider growing from the ceiling. The glider looked ripe and, although oddly shaped, capable of flying. At the back, between the still-folded wings, was an intricate system of muscle pockets. Kea reached inside, and their walls contracted, gently squeezing her arm. *Yep, definitely ripe.* Back home, each pocket was a semen socket, while these were meant for ova, yet in both cases, if they could clasp and protect their load, then the wings were solid enough for their task.

'Wonderful,' Kea muttered as she slid backwards down the channel.

The control room offered more surprises. Back home, the settlers had attached some of the ship equipment here. The trollburg had eventually learned to grow the instruments they needed – that, or the exobiologists had taught it; it had never been properly explained at school. What mattered was that this cavity provided everyone with screens, keyboards, pens, a plotter, a drawing table for the topographers, and so on.

Besides, the Ancestors stayed there. The first one, Kea's teacher had explained, was an accidental victim: the tendrils caught him and stuck him to the wall. But when the others saw he was fine, having merely joined in a symbiotic link with the trollburg along with all the other creatures captured by the tendrils, they learned to make good use of this blessing. The Ancestors didn't talk much, especially the oldest ones. In case of need though, the crew could always turn to them: the brightest minds in the whole trollburg. According to one theory, the symbionts let the burg adapt better to its living cargo. Another claimed that the burg used the brains and knowledge of each symbiont to think: without being intelligent in itself, it gained intelligence.

What if both theories are right?

This control room also held equipment, partially overgrown with lichen and fibrils. Kea swallowed hard when she saw the twisted, entwined constructions interspersed with gleaming black or red mirrors. Deep inside them flickered an occasional light, and the wavy bands were peppered with pimples and lumps of various sizes, covered by engraved symbols. The instruments embedded into the burg's nerve fibrils seemed quite a larger number than those at home. And the Ancestors... *dear God.*

Kea gulped again and struggled to suppress her shivers. She felt light and empty, as if about to fly off like a hollow seed. She didn't scream only because she was afraid she might wake the Ancestors.

There were four of them, hanging on the wall among the other fauna specimens. They were as tall as a human, yet angular and disproportional, unlike anything captured in photos from Earth or glimpsed near the manure lines in the desert. They had scales, just like the trollburg. Their bodies were a rusty brown, and their heads were crowned by horny crusts of the same angry vermilion as the vegetation up here.

These Ancestors aren't humans.

Kea's first impulse was to turn and run. *The scaly things are watching me – and any moment now, more will pour out of the bomb channel, alive and free from the wall...* She took a slow breath, the way you did when hunting grown-up steppies. *Stay calm, don't give in to panic.* Slowly, she turned, her hand on the knife hilt.

She *was* being watched. Several corpuscles had clustered back in the corridor and goggled at her.

Kea gave her heart a few seconds to slow down and stepped inside the room. The stars shone bright, both on the monitors and through the trollburg's eyes. One of the jagged moons hung right in front of Kea, as if mocking her.

She slid her fingers along the curved mirror surfaces of the alien instruments. Sparks danced inside their depths, floated up and prickled her gently, as if the machines craved her caress. *They're not dead: what becomes embedded in the trollburg never dies for real. It only falls into an ever-deeper sleep.*

Kea stepped along a wide rounded sill covered by lumps and symbols. Gritting her teeth, she kept touching the alien surfaces. The prickles had turned into a pleasant warmth.

In a rear niche, she noticed a device that was still working. A metal spiderlike limb stuck out of a wet pistil and noiselessly wove threads of sap into a flexible sheet, two spans wide, falling in thick folds to the floor. Kea picked up a section of the sheet. It was embossed and felt rubbery to the touch. It depicted an empty space with a few reddish or brown dents and vertical ridges, crossed by a uniformly wide darker strip in the exact middle. Under the pile of layers, the end of the tape fused with the floor. Kea tugged at the bottom edge. With a soft squelch and almost no resistance, a new layer slipped out of an invisible slit. It was wet and slightly smelled of sap. Kea let go, and the tape slid back inside.

A map. What else would it be? Our plotter draws on the same endless tape. However, behind this pistil grew a flat tendril, feeding it elastic paper, while a thin sprout dipped into the toner and sprinkled clouds of ink powder.

A little above the section Kea held, she saw another broad and dark strip cross the one in the middle of the sheet and disappear into the red ruggedness of the desert on the sides.

Must be my own home! And this burg has leaped over its strip at some point!

If she was correct, the directions of the two burgs diverged at a slight angle. *But when did they pass each other? What's the scale of this map?*

She tried to rephrase the question. *The encounter couldn't have happened after I got well: there's no way I'd have missed the upheaval when the burg jumped over the strip. So, between six and ten, at most twelve days. Have I really been sick that long?* In the worst case, her home must be some ten miles away – even less along a beeline. *Depending on the angle of divergence. Besides, if my burg's within the range of these devices, it's marked somewhere on the map, so I can calculate the scale and...*

She smiled triumphantly. *If I hadn't run into this burg, I'd probably have spotted my home by the morning of that fatal night. Just my luck. I might have picked a slightly wrong direction but I'd still have come home.*

Kea pulled out her telescope and went to the rim of the eye. She searched the horizon. *Is that a black shadow over there?*

If so, I should be able to see it during the day too. Problem is, my room's on the other side, and I haven't roamed around that much – not peering out of pores anyway. Besides, I mostly used to hang several levels lower.

She shrugged, put the telescope away, and left the control room.

*

Astronomy... I enjoy astronomy. Tells us about the stars, the moons and why our world is as it is.

'The number of potential intelligent civilizations can be calculated by the following simple formula,' their teacher had said, 'devised already in the twentieth century on Earth.'

She had written on the wall $N=R*fpneflfifcL$

'This equation should give the number of technologically advanced civilizations in the Milky Way or even the Universe, according to the conditions required for maintaining intelligent life. The first three factors are physical: the rate at which stars form, the fraction of the stars that have planets, and the average number of habitable planets per stellar system. The next two factors are biological: the fraction of habitable planets where life develops, and the fraction of those where it achieves intelligence. The last two are social. They represent the percentage of planets with intelligent life that give birth to technologically advanced civilizations capable of interstellar travel, and the average longevity of such civilizations.

'None of these factors are easy to measure. It's already been proven that there exist habitable planets: Earth colonies are built on those. We've also discovered artifacts from alien civilizations, as you probably remember from your history classes. Therefore, we're not alone, and the minimum feasible solution to that equation is no longer 1. However, until the launch of our ship and even the end of its flight, we had not discovered representatives of such alien civilizations, on Earth or the new colonies alike.'

'What does this have to do with astronomy?' Kea had dared ask.

'It's simple, dear. Today, we're going to discuss star clusters. The reason for launching our ship towards such a cluster was precisely contact with alien civilizations.'

'But—'

'I know. We haven't made contact yet. However, after taking into consideration the fraction of habitable planets, the number of those where artifacts have been discovered, and plenty of other factors, Earth scientists concluded there're fair odds for the existence of a planet with a technologically advanced civilization for every five or six thousand stars. That's why we're here. If those scientists were right, somewhere within our present cluster should be at least twenty civilizations, and eventually we'll encounter one of them.

'The rules of contact will be covered in your exobiology classes. Let us focus on the composition of star clusters. What you see at night is only a fraction of all stars that...'

Formulas. Rules. Nonsense. Here, on this scorched and dead world, there aren't any aliens. And even if there are, I would hardly be the one to make first contact. Kea had turned her gaze back to the eye, wondering what marvelous sights the trollburg had seen in its journeys. *If there're any marvelous sights in this barren wasteland, that is.*

*

She had the whole night, and yet it was not enough, because she didn't want to miss a single detail. Starting from the topmost areas, she methodically toured half the burg. There were no traces of recent inhabitants, and almost no belongings in the rooms. Kea found only a few old maps and two or three gadgets: maybe toys, maybe strange devices. She also found a knife made of a reddish metal, sharp but amazingly pliable. As a whole, the burg looked abandoned. Its inhabitants seemed to have packed up and gone, leaving behind only useless junk. *The corpuscles must've helped with the clean-up, scooping up clothes and all organic objects. Still, these... strangers, why didn't they collect the instruments from the control room? They couldn't take the Ancestors, I can see that, what with them being fused with the body of the burg. But all those screens, plotters, keyboards...*

Well. There must be a logbook somewhere upstairs. Our scientists will make sense of it.

Kea put her finds into her backpack. She spent the early morning stocking up on food and water. She quaked with excitement and didn't think sleep would come at all. She was wrong, though: her body, just as usual, knew its needs better than her.

*

Kea woke up in the late afternoon. The pore was still closed. She used the remaining time to bathe in the Sea. Then she headed up the Staircase.

She stopped in front of the uterine wombs. She would load one ovum into the glider. Two more she put into her backpack, weighed it, and added a third one. *Any more, and the pockets will burst. Still, it's a once-in-a-lifetime chance. If I manage to get back to my burg, people will come here again. Only if—*

Kea shook her head. It was time to take care of her sacred duties – to perform her key part in the trollburgs' life cycle. She took a deep breath. *So... this is what we practiced for in class, all those times.*

Kea opened her talisman and placed the jellied bit of sperm on an ovum inside a sappy uterine tube. The ovum grew moist at once and began dissolving it. *And if people come here again, they'll bring more – enough for all the baby burgs. That's all I have on me right now. Well, whatever happens, at least I've done my bit.*

Finally, she passed by the control room to pay tribute to the strange Ancestors. She almost expected one of them to wake up and stare at her, but they slept. *Haven't they noticed yet the changes after my arrival? Or have they grown too old and welded with the burg to care?*

Still, Kea didn't dare touch them. She just gazed at their peaceful... faces. *Can they be woken up at all?* A shiver ran along her spine. *Oh, if our researchers find a way to get through to them...*

The corpuscles were watching her again as she climbed along the bomb channel. She waved at them, and they nodded their eye-bundles.

The leafstalk of the glider gave a crack as soon as Kea placed an ovum into its pouch. She quickly squeezed into the fold below the belly of the glider – just in time too, because the leafstalk broke, the wings unfolded, and the pore gaped open. The glider shot off into the air.

Kea found an updraft and rose with it. She didn't have to scan the horizon long before she saw the jagged outline of another trollburg. Smiling, she steered the winged seed. *Soon enough, it'll detect its own kin and take over the control. A failsafe method of procreation – as long as there's somebody to load the pouch.*

As her body soared in the dark, Kea let her mind swoop

after this thought. Trollburgs were inhabited by all sorts of creatures: some parasitic, some useful. However, there was no animal to *load* the gliders. Back home, people took care of that, but trollburgs had roamed the desert long before humans reached this planet. *So who used to load the pouches? Can... can trollburgs themselves be an artifact of an alien civilization? Traveling towns? An experiment in terraforming? Are their real masters still alive? And will we ever meet them?*

The glider registered the male trollburg and went on autopilot, carrying Kea home. The pocked foreheads of the two moons peeked over the horizon. The millions of stars glowed soothingly... and less lonesomely.

Translated from the Bulgarian by Kalin M. Nenov and Elena Pavlova

Symbiosis Theory

Choyeop Kim

South Korea

This is about aliens, as you may have gathered, but it's an original and arresting take and I fell in love with it. It is translated by Joungmin Lee Comfort and was made available through *Clarkesworld Magazine*'s collaboration with the Literature Translation Institute of Korea (LTI Korea) to publish Korean SF stories in English. It is thanks to initiatives like this that our world of science fiction is becoming richer and more diverse.

Ludmila Markov had memories of a place she'd never been. It was unclear when those memories established themselves inside her. The memoir of one of her teachers at the orphanage where she'd spent her early years contained the following recollection: 'Somewhere around five years of age, she began saying that she'd come from *the place*. We didn't think much of it, since pretend play and talking about imaginary things are common behaviors among normally developing children. However, Ludmila seemed somewhat obsessed with her make-believe world. Whenever any of us playfully challenged its existence, she became very upset. As a result, an unspoken rule developed regarding Ludmila, that one ought to just go ahead and play along with her. As long as we did that, there was never any problem. We just all figured that she'd outgrow her fantasy soon enough.'

Defying the expectations, however, Ludmila never did. Her

notion of *the place* persisted into adulthood, and remained with her throughout the rest of her life.

From an early age, Ludmila's remarkable artistic gifts set her apart. According to the teachers at the orphanage, she began producing intricate drawings of her dream-drenched world as soon as she was able to hold a crayon. Lamentably, these early pieces ended up getting tossed out when she left the orphanage later on, having been considered little more than the elaborate doodles of a talented child.

Still, in that orphanage – where the need for bread and crackers far outweighed the need for crayons – little Ludmila spent more time daydreaming than drawing. It wasn't until the age of ten that she was discovered through a youth talent project sponsored by a multinational corporation, which swiftly whisked her out of the orphanage to a renowned academy in London. From that day on, she would never again go hungry or sleep in a roach-infested room.

Shortly after her move to the academy, Ludmila began exhibiting paintings of *the place*. Her first solo exhibition, which was held at a small gallery rented for the purpose of showcasing work by the academy's students, was something of an introduction to the general landscape of this place. From the opening day, the collection made waves, with many of the gallery's unsuspecting visitors finding themselves moved to tears while peering at the canvases. Inquiries about the creative spirit behind these works poured in.

Her proud instructors at the academy all wanted to know as well: 'How did you conceive such a world?' Granted, there was still plenty of room for improvement when it came to their young protégé's technique, but her landscapes never failed to enthrall, and the strokes of her brush upon the canvas showed nary a hint of faltering or hesitation.

Ludmila's vision of *the place* seemed to have been etched deep into her consciousness as it continued to exert a supreme influence on her life. It was a place that appeared at once utterly real and completely imaginary, and she devoted her life to painting it. Each painting formed a discrete fragment of its landscape; yet taken as a whole, her oeuvre constructed an impossibly detailed and vivid sense of the spellbinding place that so clearly inhabited her mind.

Journalists never stopped asking her, 'What do you *call* this place, Ludmila?' But her response, as well as the flustered and somewhat apologetic look on her face, were always the same: 'There is a name for it, in my head, but it's as if I can't say it out loud.'

She did try, at one point. With each valiant attempt, she produced a string of unintelligible sounds so alien that they seemed to have come from another dimension. Efforts to break it down into perceptible units proved futile in the end, and so *the place* simply came to be called *the planet*.

A fictitious planet with a name that couldn't be articulated. That its name didn't render itself to spoken language only added to the planet's phantasmic allure. Over time, people began to call it Ludmila's Planet, conferring upon it the dignity of distinction through its eponym. It ultimately seemed to matter little whether or not such a place existed in the real world: the force of the beloved artist's eternal yearning for it was all that mattered.

In many of her early pieces, Ludmila's Planet is rendered in a more or less abstract style. Themes of swirling blue and purple present it as a home to multitudes of creatures, some with stable forms, and others with fluidly shifting ones. Much of the planet's surface is covered by an ocean teeming with drifting bioluminescent amoebas, to which the planet owes its peculiar blue glow. More complex organisms form their own distinct ecosystems that fill the planet's land, sea, and air. The days are short and the nights, long. The sun, with its daily rise and fall, fills the sky with breathtaking hues.

Her depictions of the planet grew more detailed as Ludmila entered adulthood. It was also at this point that she began converting her paintings into digital data. Before long, she had digitized the planet's major attributes and characteristics in scrupulous detail. The drive and focus with which she constructed its flora and fauna seemed akin to that of a scientist working engaged in fieldwork.

It was only a matter of time before Ludmila plunged headlong into what was then the still-fledgling world of simulation art. Her revolutionary new endeavor mesmerized the public and critics alike, with the latter proclaiming that she'd brought much needed substance into a field oversaturated with technology and shallow technique.

Her response to these accolades was as consistent as ever: 'The planet *is*. I'm just a skilled technician recreating what I see.'

People had fallen in love with Ludmila's Planet. Through her art, which by then could be experienced in every corner of the globe, the planet had come to take on the status of a real thing. Their adoration for the subject of her art went beyond passive admiration: it inspired films and plays based on reinterpretations of Ludmila's original works, and even as art of all lineages continued to be treated like mere consumer goods by the masses, her work enjoyed the rare exception of boring itself into people's hearts and influencing their minds.

One of the most notable characteristics of her work was the complete lack of any traceable national or ethnic aesthetic. This might have been attributable to her nomadic life: her early childhood in Moscow, her adolescence in London, and the many different neighborhoods around the world she called home in the years that followed. Whatever the case, her depictions of the planet never evoked a single location that could have existed on Earth, but in fact, a place that seemed to exist all on its own, in a completely different universe.

And yet, her planet series stirred in viewers a curious sense of nostalgia. Gazing at Ludmila's paintings, people would find themselves suddenly besieged by an inexplicable longing – a kind of grief for the utter gone-ness of something they might have once known a long time ago. Then, moved by this ineffable emotion, they would often become teary-eyed. Regarding this phenomenon, critics liked to say that, because the planet series depicted a world that didn't exist in real life, paradoxically, it spoke to a world that uniquely occupied each of us inside.

There is a lesser known, nonetheless extraordinary, series by Ludmila published only after her death. Entitled 'Never Leave Me', this series departs from the vivid and highly detailed imagery that characterized her signature style. In fact, each of the highly abstract pieces in the series broods with the potent emotionality of infinite sorrow that seems determined to devastate the viewers, in what could only be described as a plea of desperation.

For whatever reason, Ludmila had chosen not to promote the series: it was only after her death that dozens of pieces bearing this title were discovered in her attic. Scholars have argued that the series was a surrogate to the artist's yearning for a lover, but Ludmila's private life remains so poorly documented as to render any speculation or theory impotent in the absence of conclusive evidence.

By the time of her death, Ludmila had placed all her work in the public domain, in order to allow its use by anyone. Soon, simulation games based on her planet series began surging onto the market. For many people seeking refuge from the chaos of everyday life, wandering through simulations of Ludmila's Planet became a widely popular form of leisure. An unreachable world though it may otherwise have been, people had come to consider Ludmila's Planet their own utopia, a legacy of the beloved artist which would forever live in their imagination.

Then the planet was discovered.

A space probe exploring deep space transmitted data back to Earth one day. It included images of a small planet with an unusual orbit, located in a distant multi-stellar system. Analysis of the data suggested the possibility of life on the unknown planet. Regrettably, its astronomical distance from Earth and the limits of technology at the time prohibited verification of this possibility within a reasonable timeframe. Nevertheless, the discovery caused one typically sleepy observatory to erupt like a batted hive.

For days on end, the observatory buzzed with talk of the planet. Barring the potential of faulty transmission, the implications of the data were too exciting. Indeed, the most that Earth's deep space exploration program had produced thus far had been nothing more than the same old vague possibility of life on alien planets, but never any data as clear and forthright as this.

Further analysis revealed that the planet's atmosphere was an exquisite mix of ammonia and methane, two gases that were easily broken down by the UV light of one of the nearby stars. Upon this insight took shape the dominant hypothesis, which was that the planet's atmospheric composition necessitated the presence of carbon-based life on its surface. When scientists converted the probe-measured electromagnetic spectrum into visible rays, the whole planet was suddenly lit in an anodyne blue glow, making it look very much like... another Earth. Or perhaps a fantastical twin that might have existed in a parallel universe somewhere.

'Doesn't it remind you of Ludmila's Planet?' said one technician, looking up from his boxed lunch.

'What? No way...' another balked, incredulous.

'I mean, think about it. Precise and detailed measurements of her planet are preserved in simulations, which scientists have already used to verify the probability of its existence in real life. The data we received the other day... it's consistent with the data we have for Ludmila's Planet. Are you really trying to tell me that's a complete coincidence?'

At this, others at the table set down their forks.

The staff at the observatory lay sleepless that night. It was true: the newly discovered planet's observable data lent a new reality to Ludmila's Planet, as the simulations she'd left behind predicted with perfect accuracy the world's volume, mass, orbital period, diameter, and average surface temperature.

Could it indeed be Ludmila's Planet? If so, how on earth could she have known about it?

With astonishing swiftness, another stunning fact was discovered the following day: the planet, it turned out, had long ago gone up in flames when its parent star had flared up. The data they'd received had been collected mere moments before its explosion.

The technician who had initially confirmed the content of the transmission stood before the assembly of reporters and journalists, triggering a blitz of questions and camera flashes.

'We're looking at a planet that has been gone for a time now,' he said. 'That is, Ludmila's Planet, which once existed in a distant galaxy.'

But how could it be? Had Ludmila possessed some magical

power that had allowed her to see into the distant past, if not the future? Was that even a viable theory in this day and age? Could everything instead just be an enormous coincidence? But then, what were the chances that an imaginary planet, flawlessly conceived though it had been by a massively gifted artist, was virtually identical to one later discovered in real life far off across the universe?

Everyone hungered for the truth, but the one person who held the key had already departed from the Earth.

*

As news of the staggering discovery zipped around the globe, the midnight oil was burning bright near the lakeshore in Seoul's Gwangjin district, at the Brainwave Research Institute.

It was two in the morning, but the building was bustling with weary employees making a last-ditch effort to meet the deadline, their collective anxiety spilling out into every hallway. In the staff lounge where the TV was on to fill the silence, breaking news of Ludmila's Planet was airing to the rapt attention of no one.

Seated at a corner table was senior researcher Soobin Yoon, still glaring at the same section of document that she'd been clutching for a good hour. Her eyes felt ready to tumble out from their sockets. The progress review meeting was fast approaching, and she needed a modicum of cooperation from a machine that wouldn't stop spewing wacky results. She shuddered at the thought of the subtle eyerolls and other signs of annoyance that she'd have to weather in the conference room. Was there anyone who wouldn't be annoyed to hear that *Life is overwhelming*, or *I miss my colleagues*, were the sort of thoughts that had been detected occurring inside the heads of two-month-old infants?

'It was working fine just a month ago,' she sighed, addressing Hannah at the next table.

'But the subjects were kittens then,' Hannah said, taking a break from her stack of documents. 'These human infants are inscrutable.'

'Kittens, infants... They cry when they're hungry, sleepy, or scared. It's all the same,' Soobin retorted.

Giggling at this, Hannah said, 'Who knows? Kittens may be more philosophical than human infants.'

Maybe so. But the pressing issue for them now was decoding the cries of the infants. Accurately.

*

The Brain-Machine Interface Team was studying thought-to-speech interface technology, which captured neural activation patterns using monomolecular imaging technology and then converted them into speech. Conversely, speech could be reverse-engineered to the original neural patterns – or thoughts – that had generated it, though the latter was still very much a work in progress.

Humanity's attempt to understand the brain had a long history, as did their desire to read another's thoughts. Thus, each breakthrough in neuroscience that had failed to deliver mind-reading technology nonetheless stoked embers of this longing in people's minds. It was to this longing that the Brainwave Research Institute owed its continued, robust funding since its establishment at the dawn of the twenty-first century. Much had been gained in the cutting edge of neural decoding over the years, but it was the emergence of advanced imaging technology that hurried the research forward by finally allowing high-resolution recording of the smallest changes in a subject's neural activity. Prior to this advancement, the interface technology had stalled at a rudimentary level, success being correctly inferring whether a subject had been shown a picture of a scenic landscape or a food item based on their brain MRI readouts.

The paradigm-shifting breakthrough had come two years prior in the form of a monomolecular neural scanning technology, which made it possible to analyse brain activities at the level of the neuron. Promptly adopting this new imaging technology, the research team had achieved significant success over the intervening years. The new challenge now was to reverse-match speech to thoughts – or inner speech – yet to be processed into perceptible output. It was a task requiring a massive scanner, and mere minutes of speech took multiple days of tedious processing and analysis, but the technology's unlimited potential kept everyone going.

In the preliminary study, which had involved the analysis of pet dogs' and cats' assorted vocalizations, the interface proved extremely effective, matching the animal subjects' vocal expressions to corresponding desires with an accuracy rate of ninety-five percent. The canine subjects in the study wagged their tails with contentment when petted or given chew-toys according to their bark analysis. Before long, the technology's commercial applications targeting mammals were green-lighted. Wealthy pet owners flooded the institute with phone calls pleading for an opportunity to have one and final 'conversation' with their dying pets. Unfortunately, such technology was still a long way off. If the research continued to make steady progress, however, a universal translator would be well within the realm of feasibility.

The research team then swiftly embarked on a new project involving human subjects. If the interface proved as effective for humans as it already had for other mammals, the obvious implications for those who lacked speech or motor function – not to mention language researchers mystified by some linguistic puzzle in an obscure language – were nothing short of incredible.

There was a great deal of hope and optimism during the initial data collection stage. It was true that the complexity of human thoughts and speech was expected to pose a challenge far greater than that posed by the previous animal study. As it was, the interface was still only capable of simple text output inferred from neural readouts, as opposed to, say, real-time transcription of a full-fledged conversation. But even so, there was the fact that its remarkable accuracy rate consistently measured at over eighty percent. Thus, it was implicitly understood by everyone that improving the system's capacity for linguistic complexity was the next hurdle, though it seemed unlikely in the extreme that this challenge could threaten to derail the research itself.

Indeed, another success followed when a pattern model was completed based on neural data collected from the adult subjects. The team then swiftly moved on to human infants. The trill of hope and excitement was undeniable in the voice of everyone who discussed it. Deciphering infant cries, even just approximately, would be a game changer for new parents and those currently toiling in the field of robot-assisted childcare research. The interface was bound to become an indispensable infant-care tool the world over – except that this time, the research had run into a brick wall right out of the gate.

*

Hannah, who had been in charge of the first round of analysis, entered the conference room with a data chip in hand. The mood in the room was buoyant with the hopeful anticipation of her colleagues.

'The results are... very strange. They're not the kind of thoughts we'd think infants are capable of thinking,' she said. Then, heaving a big sigh, she projected the results onto the screen.

The entire room fell silent. According to the interface, the infants had cooed and cried about the following:

How can we imbue a greater sense of morality in them?

How are you all doing in there?

No. This is our home now.

Everyone gaped at the screen, dumbstruck. The analysis was a complete mess.

'It looks like data corruption,' Soobin said flatly.

It only made sense to question the purity of data, considering how the imaging system worked. At the current stage of innovation, decoding accuracy was still highly subject to the noise level in the input data, after all. Noise, environmental or otherwise, had a way of making its way into data no matter how vigilant the monitoring, which frequently resulted in a frustrating amount of time spent on filtering it out. In fact, the team had already run into a similar problem during the adult trials. It wasn't a stretch to imagine that the data collected from infants would be more muddled, since their brains were still learning how to formulate a thought, let alone vocalize it.

Around fourteen months of age, the average human baby begins to absorb basic vocabulary with a striking efficiency, and is able to follow simple commands. From infancy to adolescence, a person's cognitive development and linguistic development follow the same general trajectory, which is to say, one's thought development is critically dependent on one's language comprehension and vice versa. Hence, logic dictates that an infant's thoughts cannot greatly surpass the level of his current language comprehension.

'So it *has* to be noise,' Soobin repeated. 'If the data were clean, we'd be seeing *I'm hungry, I'm uncomfortable...* that type of output. And not even in fully formed sentences. Simple registration of pain and other sensations is what we should be seeing here.'

'That's what I thought, too.' Hannah nodded in agreement. And then she ventured, 'But noisy data alone can't explain everything. Look at this analysis of older children just beginning to speak. Their speech and neural patterns are all over the place, too. *Mama, I want that* was matched to *I long to feel connected to the world...* How do we explain it?'

'Hmm... Could it be because children's neural activation patterns are so completely distinct from those of adults?' Soobin wondered.

'Possibly,' Hannah said, her face darkening as she added, 'and if that's the case, then we'll have to start it all over again.'

At that, the air in the conference room hung heavy with a sense of foreboding.

*

Thankfully, a problem identified was, usually, a problem half-solved. Soobin and Hannah set about sorting the collected thought-speech data by age group. Next, they separated the data of subjects whose language had yet to emerge. The effort drastically reduced the amount of available data, so a full day had to be spent on the phone while begging every cooperative agency for additional material. It was a chore they could have done without, but surely it was more agreeable than accepting the results at hand and announcing to the world that babies babbled madly to themselves.

They'd placed a great deal of hope on the effort, but the results that came back were nonetheless demoralizing. It turned out that the infants' brainwave patterns were far more intricate than they'd imagined, suddenly making it seem trivial by comparison to scrutinize the adults'. In fact, the other team, which had continued with the adult study, was enjoying smooth sailing. Having already mapped the large database of neural patterns collected from adults with no speech or language difficulties onto the interface, they were currently working on teasing out speech from the brainwaves of adult subjects who'd lost the ability to speak for various reasons. In sad contrast, Soobin's team was still troubleshooting for the initial findings that indicated infants engaged in philosophical musings. No matter how many times they duplicated the entire process, though, the results remained consistently baffling.

'These babies…'

Clutching at her head in frustration, Soobin plopped down on the sofa.

'… complicated, deep little philosophers, they are,' Hannah said.

Had they underestimated the challenge? Could it be that the mysteries of the human brain were simply too complex for them to unravel? Soobin was at a complete loss.

Sensing that she was left with no other recourse, Soobin began talking with Hannah about the fate of the project, and whether a course correction was necessary to save it. Despite everyone's efforts, the problem of the philosophical babies seemed insolvable. In the end, it was determined that the project should be redesigned at the next progress meeting. Enthusiasm dwindled, and the project had begun petering out when an unexpected development diverted it from its course once again.

*

'Soobin, could you take a look at this?' Hannah said, presenting her with a stack of analysis results she'd printed out. Her lips pressed together, she looked oddly intent. Taking the stack from Hannah, Soobin began scanning the pages, before clapping it shut within a minute. This couldn't be right. She couldn't take seriously what her eyes had just told her. It felt like she was reading a tabloid.

'What's this? What is it supposed to mean?' she accused.

'It's supposed to mean what it means. These are the results of the infant babble analysis,' Hannah said. 'Do you remember that day? Ludmila's Planet had just been discovered. The data captured on that day was all like this.'

Soobin remembered, of course. It was on that day the two had first begun to debate the viability of the infant project. While she'd continued fussing over the puzzling results, Hannah had begun a new analysis with the remaining data, the staggering results of which were contained in the print-out that Soobin now clutched in her hands.

'What on earth...' Soobin stared at the strings of letters.

This is where we'd all begun.

I miss our planet.

Ludmila!

Ludmila!

Ludmila!

Ludmila painted the place exactly as it was.

I miss it!

As Soobin stood there with her mouth open, Hannah emphasized how many times she'd already verified the results.

'I couldn't believe it myself, which is why it took me a little while to share it with you. Every infant was occupied by these thoughts that day.'

With that, she produced an additional report containing the analysis results of reams of data she'd personally pored over, which had been initially rejected by the team for being corrupt and unusable. Working on the assumption that the data was, in truth, free of noise, Hannah had isolated the units of meaning that emerged repeatedly. The resulting chart at hand incorporated the infant thought-speech model that had been scrapped for being an utter failure. Once again, the analysis had found that some bizarre conversations were taking place inside the heads of these infants. These conversations, not to be outdone by the notion itself in their oddity, appeared to be thoughtful and, at times, lively exchanges between multiple voices in the brain.

You okay? I just heard a racket.

No worries. Mr. Clumsy just knocked over a chair, that's all.

I bet his eyes were glued to the screen.

Are you already dreaming of the sea?

Oh, I'd love to end up in the sea someday.

'This data right here? It's from one infant, from the same timeframe – as you can see,' Hannah pointed out. 'It's as if multiple beings coexist inside the infant's brain. Please, stop looking at me like that and hear me out,' she urged, turning the page for Soobin. 'I extracted the interpretations that showed up repeatedly and then sorted them out. *And* I took care of the post-analysis, in case you're wondering. Look.'

It was true. There were multiple participants in these conversations, all of whom were speaking with the tenderness and devotion of a caregiver. They talked about morality. They talked about life. They talked as though they were co-parents, every one of them nurturing and looking out for the infant.

These results all but pointed to a conclusion that Soobin herself would be hard-pressed to accept. Stunned speechless, she listened to what Hannah still had to say.

'Something's present inside their brains,' Hannah concluded. 'Something not human. These occurrences can't be explained without introducing an external entity.'

'It *must* have been noise in the data,' replied Soobin in a tight voice.

'Noise can't account for it. The conversations are persistently and deeply coherent. How likely is it that noise interruptions turned into discussions of morality, ethics, altruism and all that? Isn't *that* more absurd to imagine?' Hannah persisted.

'But... How? The data had come from thousands of infants, each one an individual. And you're saying that, inside each of those little heads resides some force that acts like a parent?'

'If not, then how do you explain what you see?'

Given her radical-leaning perspective on many subjects, it wouldn't be the first time Hannah had offended others' sensibilities. Still, when it came to that, this current argument was her best effort so far.

'All I'm saying is...' Soobin began, only to realize she had nothing to follow it up with. Composing herself for a few moments, she said, 'A foreign presence inside the infants' brains? Some intelligent entities that aren't human?'

'It's the only plausible explanation,' Hannah replied.

Soobin decided to spare the team Hannah's lunacy for now. Speculations of some force occupying the infant brain... Of course, such an idea didn't stand a chance. And yet, when she finally decided to give her colleague's argument due consideration in all its absurdity, intriguing patterns began to leap out at her in a way that they hadn't just a few hours earlier. For one, she could now see that, among babies and toddlers on the verge of speech, there was a complete lack of congruence between the measured neural patterns and their outward expressions – specifically, the infants' cries, babblings, and simple utterances. When fed through the interface, the neural patterns of these very young subjects consistently produced highly sophisticated and intellectual speech output which could only be understood as exchanges between multiple mature voices inside the brain. It was just as Hannah had said.

*

Soobin and Hannah began referring to the voices as *them*. *They* discussed feelings and thoughts, love, and empathy. *They* clearly seemed to want to teach the infants *something*.

Moving on to young children, the two scientists reorganized the large amount of speech data they'd collected, sorting them by age. Were there distinct conversations taking place beneath all the *mommy*, *daddy*, *I want that*, and so on? Their analysis showed a mix of the children's surface communications and the conversations among *them*. Curiously, these two-tiered conversations seemed to vanish at around age seven, following years of gradual retreat that began at approximately three years of age, with some variation between individuals. It was as though the internal voices gradually withdrew until the child became fully communicative, at which point *they* seemed to bow out completely.

These notions kept Soobin up at night. Even now, she and Hannah had kept the theory to themselves. Day in and day out, she labored through additional data in search of a clue that might help reveal *their* identity. Colleagues who'd noticed the pair beginning to look increasingly sapped and haggard expressed concern by gently reminding them that 'it was what it was', or that it was the nature of science to progress through trial and error, and so forth.

Yet even as she persevered, Soobin didn't completely rule out the possibility that everything might still turn out to be a massive decoding error. Still, the more data she analysed, the clearer it became that there was only one possibly true conclusion: the analysis was accurate, and inside the infant brain, *they* existed.

But where did *they* come from? How did *they* settle in the brain? And why do *they* leave when *they* leave? What was the tangible proof of *their* presence? And then, one day while reclining on the sofa in the back of the staff lounge, it struck her.

'The box children!' she blurted out loud. This jolted Hannah, who had been nodding off nearby, into wakefulness.

'What?'

'A few years ago, there was an experiment conducted to see if human touch was absolutely necessary for normal infants' development. Do you remember?'

Hannah's eyes began to widen as if slowly registering something.

'Of course... yeah, the experiment with infant-care robots...'

'Their data may be useful to us.'

'How?'

*

The so-called 'box children experiment' had been conceived to test the efficacy of infant-care robots. In the experiment, infant subjects had been kept isolated from the outside world for the duration of the study, to be raised in the lab solely by caregiver robots. All other variables had been kept constant. Some researchers had speculated that the babies' experience shouldn't be too different from an extended tenure inside a giant incubator. After all, the ethics committee had given the research project its stamp of approval, which was supposed to have reassured everyone that no infant's well-being was going to be compromised in any way. Still, this approval did little to mute the concerns surrounding its design. When the findings were finally published, the project once more attracted harsh international criticism.

'It was a such a huge mess,' Soobin sighed.

'I remember.' Hannah nodded gravely. 'By the end of the experiment, the subjects were found to act purely on instinct, their growth in the affective domain having been completely stunted over the course of the experiment. It was a big relief to hear that many were successfully rehabilitated and socialized later on, after the experiment finished.'

'The experiment should never have gotten approved,' Soobin said, her gaze fixed on the empty air before her. 'On the other hand, I still have some unanswered questions about it,' she continued, turning to Hannah. 'Caregiver robots are designed to deliver optimal stimulation. Why does a simple lack of flesh and blood affect the infants' socioemotional development so profoundly? I have to wonder if there's more to what the findings seems to suggest. If anything, we, humans, are imperfect caregivers, given to personal moods and circumstances. So... maybe there's some connection with whatever caused the robot-reared infants to fail to thrive...'

What if *they* gained entry into the infant brain at some point after birth, in the way of parasites and microbes – as opposed to in utero? Like viruses, *they* could be lurking in the air, or otherwise widespread throughout the environment. Even so, there had to be a specific point of access for them. What if the box children had never gotten the chance to be exposed to *them* because they'd been locked up inside the lab? Hannah shot up from her chair.

'There must be recordings. We need to analyse their cries,' she said.

It took no effort at all to find relevant video files online, each trailing an endless comment section crammed with condemnations and disapproval of what the viewers considered a cruel and morally detestable experiment.

How dare you leave these babies alone with robots, you monsters!

Babies NEED a warm and caring HUMAN touch! You're raising androids devoid of humanity!

However, the question of whether or not the caregivers had been human might ultimately have been of little consequence. That is, if one could allow the possibility that *they* were the ones outfitting human infants with their humanity, and that, perhaps, what we'd considered our innermost human qualities ultimately originated from outside of us.

Soobin felt ready to turn her gaze outward for proof. She began to enter the audio data extracted from the videos into the interface. To the naked ears, the infants' cries were indistinguishable from the cries of other babies. But *their* presence or absence among the box infants would soon be verified by the output of the interface, which would, in turn, disprove or validate the hypothesis that the crucial factor determining humans' socioemotional development was *them*. Had *they* been absent among the box infants, as the two suspected, the interface would display only the infants' requests, minus the veiled conversations attributed to *them*.

The software commenced its analysis. There was nothing for Soobin and Hannah to do but wait for the results to load up. The first round of analysis produced units of meaning that remained too abstract and incoherent to make sense of. With a trembling hand, Hannah initiated the final decoding process, whereupon the algorithm began arranging the discrete units into sentences. Soon after, the final results appeared on the screen. The cries and coos of the box babies in the videos had apparently been concerned with the following thoughts:

I'm hungry.

I'm sleepy.

I'm scared.

Soobin and Hannah turned to each other, unsure of how to feel about this. Should they rejoice in their victory? Or should they be aghast at the overwhelming implications?

Indeed, what had been fired by the synapses inside the heads of the box babies couldn't properly be called thoughts. They were intense *needs* driven by pure instinct, which in fact was what anyone would have expected of such young babies. Mere days old, and having been kept in the laboratory since birth, these babies had yet to be exposed to *them*. Thus, their brains had generated only the neural patterns associated with typical infantile desires tailored for survival – the kind of neural patterns Soobin and Hannah had also previously expected to find in *all* babies who had yet to acquire speech, and thus, had yet to begin contemplating life and the world.

But Soobin knew now what the absence of those neural patterns must have meant for these newborns isolated in the lab. It meant that they would miss the milestones their peers out in the world would soon begin to meet, one after the next.

*

Let us indulge in a truly bizarre supposition: imagine that, unbeknownst to us, an extraterrestrial species has existed in symbiosis with humanity for millennia. After all, parasitic bacterium had to enter cells before beginning their permanent symbiosis with the host cells, all the while evolving into mitochondria containing its own DNA. In truth, this sort of arrangement is commonplace in nature, where organisms from two different species often live in a close, dependent relationship. Humans, for one, share a symbiotic relationship with a myriad of microbes living inside of us. We don't consider them invaders. They are already an inalienable part of us.

But what if one of our partners in symbiosis was not native to the planet Earth? What if it had hailed from another planet, tens of thousands of years ago? What if it had settled into our brains to rule over our childhoods and infect us with its ethics? What if the unique qualities we've forever believed separated our species from all other beasts of the world were, in fact, not quite so intrinsically human?

'So... the traits we've prided ourselves for possessing all along are actually alien traits?' the team leader observed as Soobin finished presenting the theory. Among the rest of the team, responses varied. Some gaped at the results, while others rejected the theory point-blank.

'It's too unorthodox! Nobody would take it seriously,' someone remarked.

'I'm still having a hard time believing it myself,' Hannah conceded. 'But how can we deny the data?'

Meanwhile, Soobin was itching with the desire to probe further into the infant brain. If it was true that *they* had taken up residence in there, shouldn't we be able to *observe them* somehow? What might they be composed of? Shouldn't there be something – *anything* – that we could measure? Of course, it was unlikely that she would get the chance to satisfy these queries any time soon. Probing the brain of a live subject raised significant ethical issues. Plus, blindly poking around in brain tissue in search of a speculative life-form whose material properties they knew nothing of wasn't likely to result in any groundbreaking discovery. Most saliently, if *they* so readily rendered themselves to human inspection in the manner of parasitic organisms, then wouldn't medicine have already discovered *them* long ago?

'I'd be shocked if we could observe them. If they had a physical basis we could detect, they would have been discovered ages ago, sometime during the long history of anatomical science,' said the team leader, voiding any half-hope that might have lingered. He was right, Soobin knew, and she nodded in resignation. Still, she would have stared at a sample all day long, if one had been made available for her inspection.

There was no shortage of other queries to mull over yet. Symbiotic coexistence didn't always involve a mutually beneficial relationship. In some cases, one party benefited while the other was unaffected, and in others, one party actively harmed its partner for a unilateral gain. What was the nature of our symbiosis with *them*? What did this enigmatic species gain from operating inside a developing human brain? Might *they* be a carbon-based life form, like humans were? What could *they* reap from presumably inculcating ethics and altruism in humans? And why had *they* chosen us, among all the species of the world?

'I happen to think that *they*'re space refugees who found a new home on our planet,' Hannah said. Despite the raised eyebrows of her colleagues, she continued, '*They* repeatedly refer to Ludmila's Planet as "home", and we know for a fact it went up in flames a long time ago...'

Ludmila's Planet. A planet conceived and described in impossible detail by the eponymous artist. The idea that it could have been *their* home in some ancient eon might just be the clue leading to the truth of *their* being.

If these beings were so advanced as to manipulate the human species, it stood to reason *they* ought to have been able to predict their planet's demise and evacuate in time. After that, while wandering about in space in search of a new home, *they* had arrived on planet Earth one day... and the rest was history.

'*Their* conversations clearly suggest exquisite intelligence,' said Soobin. 'So much so that I have to wonder if a great deal of intricacy isn't getting lost in translation due to the limitations of our own language. *They*'re likely a far superior species to humans, or that's what I think. But then again, *they* seem entirely reliant on human neural networks. Could it be that *they* are a species that requires a host in order to actualize their intellect? That might explain why *they* chose the human species. For all its mystery, the human brain is known to be the most efficient on the planet, and if *they*'d discovered us tens of thousands of years ago, it is conceivable that the symbiosis triggered the birth of civilizations and the whole cascade of human evolution. Even if it hadn't been *their* original intention to enlighten us, *their* intelligence could have been transferred to us over the long course of symbiosis.'

The room had fallen silent. If the symbiosis was truly as old as human history, there must be ample evidence outside the walls of the lab. In fact, there might be evidence everywhere, hiding in plain sight across human civilization, Soobin supposed.

'What if we ask *them* directly?' someone suggested.

The same thought had crossed Soobin's mind, and probably the minds of a few others in the room as well. However, the prospect of actually doing so was dismal. The current research involved children. It was one thing to analyse the raw data collected from children going about their business in their natural environment, but a whole different proposition to attempt to connect with an enigmatic presence supposedly inhabiting their brains. It was anyone's guess what sort of reward or punishment an attempt like that might provoke, and there was no guarantee that the gesture wouldn't be perceived as hostile. In fact, how likely was it that *they* would welcome our sudden interrogation following millennia of unauthorized inhabitation inside of us? Any rash attempt risked inviting irrevocable harm.

'Following that line of thought... are we sure that *they*'ve actually *left* our brains?' someone asked, apparently bothered by a similar concern.

In the end, this risky proposal was rejected, and Soobin devised a new plan. If *they* had hailed from Ludmila's Planet, then exposing *them* to paintings and simulations of *their* long-lost home should elicit some very particular responses. The danger it posed to the hosts was zero, as evidenced by the fact that no infants exposed to the breaking news on that day had been harmed by it. If anything, the data to be generated in this experiment ought to help illuminate the mysteries of these beings.

*

'It's as we've predicted. The level of neural activity it triggered is... off the charts. We can barely keep up with the datastream.'

It was just as Hannah had suggested: when exposed to footage of Ludmila's Planet, the infants ceased all fidgeting and fussing, their eyes silently tracking the moving landscape in rapt attention. Inside their brains, however, *they* seemed to be erupting with excitement, in a storm of discussion so lively, complex, and dense with information that its analysis became an unprecedented challenge. There was no doubt *they* were intimately connected to the planet.

The question was whether or not to publish these findings yet.

'If we don't, someone else will. We're not the only ones pursuing a universal decoder. It's extremely unlikely that other researchers won't test it on infants, if they haven't already,' Hannah said. 'Even if people are appalled by the idea that extraterrestrials take up residence in infant brains, I don't see how the knowledge would change anything anyway. Would it even be possible for us to suddenly evict *them*?'

'It wouldn't do us any good,' Soobin said. Looking around the room, she continued, 'I'm not alone in thinking that *we're* the ones who should be begging *them* to stay, am I? Without *them*, we'd lose everything that we've forever believed made humanity unique!'

'Hmm… but how strong is our ego, as a species?'

Someone raised an important point, then. 'Perhaps it's hard for us to stomach the idea because we view ourselves as completely distinct from *them*? Would it make a difference if we found, in adult brains, some remaining vestige of *their* presence carried forward from childhood?'

If *they*'d left their fingerprints all over a child's development while living inside her developing brain, her mature brain might still possess some evidence of the fact. Still, no neural patterns suggestive of *them* had been observed in an adult brain so far.

'This is just a hunch,' the team leader chimed in, 'but *they* seem quite reluctant to leave the host at childhood's end. Phrases like, *It's difficult, but the time has come for us to leave*, have come up more than a few times.'

'Yes, I know,' Soobin concurred. Then, pointing to the chart she'd been looking at, she continued. 'Plus, I can't stop thinking about the timing of *their* departure. Clearly, seven years of age bears some significance, given that's when *they* seem to leave us for good. The data's consistent. Only children seven years or younger exhibit neural patterns indicating *their* presence. After that, there's nothing.'

For it was at the age of seven that, according to the chart, intercranial conversations disappeared completely. It was at this point that children's neural signals and speech came to mirror each other perfectly, just as with adults. This suggested that *they* stayed inside human brains from infancy to early childhood before packing up shortly after the seventh birthday.

'I'm wondering if we could connect this to childhood amnesia. Very few of us are able to recall much of what happened during our formative years,' said Hannah. 'The established theory holds that rapid development of the hippocampus around this age is responsible for the phenomenon – that a high rate of neurogenesis in the hippocampus somehow destabilizes the existing long-term memory.'

This much was true: by the time a child reaches the age of seven, most of his or her memories of earlier years, autobiographical memories in particular, have faded. Few adults, if any, remember events occurring between infancy and early childhood. Those who claim to are, in fact, most likely relying on false memories formed on the basis of what they heard about the event from others.

'But a little while ago, I read an interesting report in a neuroscience journal that disputed this theory,' Hannah continued. 'Apparently, some researchers used the newest imaging technology to peer into the brains of kids around the time when childhood amnesia kicks in. What they discovered was that the rate of their neurological development and the degree of amnesia experienced didn't track at all. There was zero statistical significance.'

Someone looked up the paper online and shared it to the room's screen.

'The authors vaguely argued for an external cause, though they sounded pretty puzzled themselves. It's surely a controversial finding that triggered a stream of papers disputing it. But if it's true that childhood amnesia isn't caused by rapid neurodevelopment, and that it can actually be attributed to an external factor... then what's the external factor? What is it that's taking away our memories? I have to wonder...'

'It's *them*,' Soobin chipped in. '*They* take them away with *them* when *they* leave us.'

*

In terms of their theory, what was most unexpected of all was Ludmila's role.

She was the only human being who had retained any memory of *them* beyond early childhood. After all, she had only begun working on her planet series in earnest as an adolescent. This fact seems to suggest *they* might have remained within her and continued influencing her personality. That the planet had never ceased to be the subject of her art, and that she had been able to furnish exact and scientific detail regarding the planet (including its mass, volume, and so forth) seem to indicate two distinct possibilities: that she had been permitted to continue listening in on *their* conversations, or that *their* collective memory had been transferred to her in its entirety when, or if, they left her.

'Perhaps *they* stayed with each and every human being on Earth, but only Ludmila was let in on the truth of *their* origin?'

Investigation into Ludmila's life unearthed nothing but the

well-established fact that it had been a lonely one; in stark contrast to her colossal fame as an artist, precious little was known about her as a person.

'She had been an exceptionally creative child. And as creative children often are, she, too, must have been a sensitive soul inclined to introspection – which may have caused her to become aware of their presence early on. *They* might have taken special care of her, seeing that she really *was* alone in the world.'

Thus, in the end, it turned out that Ludmila had never once lied about her work after all. From the very beginning of her career as an artist, she had simply transferred to canvas the landscape *they*'d held up before her, inside her brain. Her mind eventually came to contain the entire planet as *they* remembered it, far beyond just the fragments of its landscape. In every practical sense, she had visited the planet – through *them*, with whom she'd shared a brain all her life.

'Ludmila's memories of the planet may have been enhanced through the act of painting it,' Soobin said. 'Motor memory may have boosted her episodic memory of the planet and vice versa, as the two types of memory are distinct, but not entirely separate.'

'Given how *they* abscond with childhood memories when *they* take *their* leave of the host, *they* seem extremely cautious about revealing themselves to humanity. But then, why risk exposure by encouraging her to recreate the planet through her work?'

'Well, *their* conversations make it clear that their planet is incredibly dear to them,' Soobin said. 'I mean, whose home isn't?'

To that explanation, nobody offered any objection.

Alien refugees, still mourning the loss of a homeworld that

had been pulverized into cosmic dust eons ago... perhaps *they* just wanted for someone on their adopted planet to carry its memory, even if all the rest lived in blissful ignorance. And *they* had found that person in Ludmila who, with her capable hands, was able to resurrect it back to life in all its beauty.

A planet that had existed tens of thousands of years ago.

The team arrived at the ultimate question. What was it that caused people to obsess over Ludmila's Planet, a place about which they themselves knew nothing? What was it about her world that moved everyone to tears – why such unexpected melancholy and longing for a place they had never even seen before? Of all the countless simulated worlds created during human history, why was it that Ludmila's Planet alone had managed to leave such a powerful impression in the minds of people worldwide?

'Because each of us has served as a host to *them* before,' Hannah said.

And there lies the proof of this proposed symbiosis, Soobin thought to herself. A wholly amorphous memory, flickering at the edge of our consciousness, without ever vanishing completely. It was our vague yearning for those who had shaped us into who we are.

What people yearned for through Ludmila's mesmerizing work was not the planet itself, but its former inhabitants who had once cared for them.

'That other series. Do you all remember? There's another series by her,' Soobin said.

'"Never Leave Me". It's not as widely known, but just as beautiful, if you ask me.'

'Yes. That's the one.'

It occurred to Soobin that the series, which remained largely indecipherable, might hold the key to Ludmila's veiled interior.

'Perhaps it was Ludmila's plea?'

'Plea?'

'Ludmila had become aware of *their* presence, and...'

Without warning, a wave of emotion crashed over Soobin in that moment.

'It was her plea to *them*. Its title, and the infinite tenderness, sorrow, and loneliness that it stirs in people... Ludmila had lived her life in perpetual solitude. *Their* companionship must've meant everything to her: *they* were her only friends, family, and colleagues.'

She had been begging them *not to leave her. Not to take away from her* their *world and its splendor. Please, oh, please, to stay with her forever.*

'So *they* stayed,' Hannah mumbled to herself. Her voice was the only sound in the room, where every occupant was presently picturing the same place in their minds: that planet, awash in its mystical blue glow. Ludmila's Planet. The ancient home of the unknowable beings, our partners in symbiosis for all these tens of thousands of years. In that moment, Soobin found herself seized by a wholly unexpected sense of grace. It felt somehow like a longing... for someone she'd never met before.

Translated from the Korean by Joungmin Lee Comfort

My Country is a Ghost

Eugenia Triantafyllou

Greece

The first of two Greek authors in this volume, Eugenia writes in English for an international audience, with an impressive spate of short stories since 2017. 'My Country is a Ghost' is moving in its examination of a theme running throughout this volume, of displacement and its human cost.

When Niovi tried to smuggle her mother's ghost into the new country, she found herself being passed from one security officer to another, detailing her mother's place and date of death over and over again.

'Are you carrying a ghost with you, ma'am?' asked the woman in the security vest. Her name tag read Stella. Her lips were pressed in a tight line as she pointed at the ghost during the screening, tucked inside a necklace. She took away Niovi's necklace and left only her phone.

'If she didn't die here, I am afraid she cannot follow you,' the woman said. Her voice was even, a sign she had done this many times before. Niovi resented the woman at that moment. She still had a ghost waiting for her to come home, comforting her when she felt sad, giving advice when needed. But she was still taking Niovi's ghost away.

Stella paused. She gave Niovi a moment to think, to decide. She could turn around and go back to her home taking the necklace with her. Back to her unemployment benefits and a future she could no longer bring herself to imagine, or she could move down the long stretch of aisles, past the dimming lights and into the night, alone, her mother's ghost left behind – where do ghosts return to in times like this? Niovi would be a new person in a new country, wiped clean of her past.

Foreign ghosts were considered unnecessary. The only things they had to offer were stories and memories.

Niovi had prepared herself for this, and yet she had hoped she wouldn't have to leave her mother behind.

She gave the necklace to the impassive woman and let herself drift down the aisle as if a forceful gust of air ushered her away.

Her mother's ghost waved goodbye behind the detector and Niovi's thoughts were of the Saturday of Souls. It was a prayer, an invocation as she put more and more distance between her and the security woman, her and the necklace. Without her mother's ghost she would start to forget soon. But this she had to remember. She needed to hang on to something now that her mother had been pried from her hands.

The Saturday of Souls.

When the ghost finally disappeared, Niovi's legs felt like lead. Her arms felt like lead. Everything felt like lead and she could barely move.

'Welcome!' Niovi heard the driver say as she boarded the airport shuttle.

*

The first thing Niovi faced when she stepped out of the shuttle was the cold. It was only October. Snow would start at the end of November. But even now the cold was so utter, so complete, it seemed like a wall, an extra line of defense between herself and these people who had too many ghosts and her who had none. A final warning that foreign ghosts were a nuisance, a waste of space.

'Don't worry,' she whispered to the frost. 'You are too late.'

She started her new life in a small apartment in a badly lit part of a street that led to a cul-de-sac.

In the mornings, as she waited for the days to pass so she could start her new job, she would walk around the city, counting ghosts.

Every time she went out, the people of the city would notice her, look at her, and scrutinize her. No, not her. The absence of her ghost. She was an oddity among people cloaked in spirits that followed their every step. Some of them looked at her with concern and others with outright curiosity.

There were others without ghosts, of course. They were usually huddled together in small groups, shielding themselves against the unwelcome stares or, perhaps, against their own loss. Niovi couldn't bring herself to even glance at them. Instead she gravitated towards the other ones. The ones who still had ghosts. Despite their looks of curiosity and sometimes pity. Most of them didn't even notice their presence – the ghosts' affections were natural, ordinary. Niovi found this nonchalance fascinating.

Then, there were the untethered ghosts. The ones conjured by the collective memory of the people. They did not belong to anyone in particular. They belonged to everyone. Niovi liked to think they belonged to her too, especially here.

There was the ghost of the old general. He stood right next to his own statue along with the ghost of his horse and offered a spectacle for the little kids. A stubborn man, as Niovi found out; he had been trotting the same square for two hundred years. He had died in a battle that few remembered. He stood there with his medals of honor, speaking in an antiquated manner that nobody understood and riding his ghost horse, saluting the tourists.

Niovi liked the General. He was old, really old and came from a time when ghosts could move around following their loved ones without borders tearing one from the other. Niovi thought of the necklace she had tried to bring her mother in. They had sent it to her a few days later, cold, empty. She kept it anyway. It was her mother's, after all.

She sat on a bench, a bag of chips in her lap, and let her mind wander back home. To her empty house. Her mother's house. Did her mother's ghost stay there, or had she moved on? Maybe she had followed someone else in the family like she did when she was alive and Niovi ignored her calls. Become their ghost.

The edges of her mother's face were already beginning to blur in her mind. They became fuzzy. She looked at her mother's pictures on her phone but they were lifeless and flat. They did little to bring her mother's image back.

So she sat at the square looking at the children scream in a language she was still learning and heard them laugh and laugh.

*

Niovi's first job was at a Greek restaurant next to the Southern Harbor. She wanted to cook. In fact, she needed it. Not just so she could justify her staying in the country. Cooking was what her mother had done best when she was alive, and when they were still together in Athens, daughter and ghost, cooking could help her not forget the things she desperately needed to hold on to.

The sullen ghostless man at the restaurant inspected Niovi's resume and asked her a series of questions, dubious that she could do what she claimed. He told her that many people claimed to do things they couldn't just to get a job here, but Niovi wasn't sure that was true at all. Maybe they could do those things but, if they were ghostless like her, and like her sullen to-be-boss, at some point they had started to forget the details. Niovi tried to drown a small voice whispering that she might be next.

'All right,' the man said in the end. 'You'll start with the dishes and you'll move up to prep.'

Her heart dropped at that, but it was a door – or perhaps a half-open window – to the job she wanted, so she agreed to work the morning shifts.

*

Niovi conjured her mother's image stirring a pot of stewed okra, the ghost of her mother's aunt whispering something to her as she cooked. She conjured the smells of spices and the tomato and the sweat gathering on her mother's brow like this could bring her ghost back. Or at least help her keep those precious details.

She found herself in that scene too. At the table her young self looked down at her plate and scrunched her face in disgust. Her father nodded in a conspiratorial way from the other side of the table, much to his own ghost's disapproval. He made up a chore to excuse her from the table. Her grandmother – her father's ghost – shook her head but said nothing. Niovi slid from her chair and ran outside, because back then she hated okra. How stupid.

In the end she was not sure this helped at all. Instead what she found, when her break was over and she was back at her post, was a whiff of similar scents drifting from the restaurant's kitchen wrapped in a blanket of hot air. It wasn't okra they were cooking. But the spices, the slow murmuring of pots, the noises, were all achingly intimate.

She couldn't help but leave the water running and follow the scent to the kitchen. She expected familiar scents here but not *that* familiar.

There was a man hunched over bigger and smaller pots. His moves calculated in a quiet choreography as he assembled the dishes. Locks of ashen blond hair peered from under his head wrap. Niovi knew that the staff was mostly made up by non-Greeks, but still, this man's ghost caught her off guard. Not because he had a ghost to begin with. Almost all the waiters she had met had one; this was their country, after all. But this ghost was everything he wasn't and everything familiar to her.

It was the ghost of an old woman, older than her mother was when she died. Her hair was dark with grey streaks, curly and unruly, and her face at odds with the cook's. She hovered over him, and when his hands twitched or when his breath quickened, she would rest a hand on his shoulder and he would calm down again, his moves becoming more precise and deliberate. When he would finish assembling a dish the ghost would smile and nod. His back was turned away from the ghost but Niovi knew he felt her approval.

'Niovi!' Her boss's voice came from the back. And just like that, the man looked up, and so did the ghost that reminded her so much of her mother, and the Saturday of Souls snapped back in her mind like a wound that had just reopened.

Before the man, who had a smile that took up half his face, had a chance to utter a word, she realized she had been standing there for far too long. So she gave him a faint nod and left to finish her shift, turning her head from him a little too fast, desperate to hide her tears.

*

Niovi asked about him the very next day. She talked to Matilda who always spoke slowly enough for her to understand, but her attention drifted as soon as Niovi had a hard time finishing a sentence. Or perhaps without a ghost Matilda had nowhere to rest her eyes on. Perhaps this absence made her uneasy.

The cook's name was Remi and he was born here, though his maternal grandparents came from Greece some fifty years ago. They died here too, never having a chance to really retire. That's why he could still have his grandmother's ghost, who seemed to fit in this place as much as Niovi did, which was not very much.

Niovi felt the stabbing of jealousy. Remi could have it all. He could speak like a native and have a ghost which carried the kind of knowledge Niovi had to fight to keep with her. As soon as she thought this she felt ashamed.

'You know,' Matilda said. The ghost of a young man stood always by her side. From the similarities Niovi could guess it was a close family member. A brother maybe. Matilda seemed at ease with it and didn't even give it a second glance. Niovi looked Matilda in the eyes to avoid looking at the ghost. 'You could come with us one night out. Just some people from work. Talking more to us would help you practice.'

'What about Remi?' Niovi dared to ask.

Matilda smirked a little, which made Niovi's face flush. But before Niovi had the chance to say anything Matilda gave her a half-shrug. 'He prefers to hang out with the ghostless. That's not going to help you integrate.'

All Niovi could hear behind the concern was, *Our ghosts are enough. We are enough.* But their ghosts were too different, and living people were harder to be around. She had spent so much time with her mother's ghost, her quiet sighs and her calm stare engulfing her every move, that when she was asked to join her coworkers after a shift she would always decline.

'Too tired,' she said, because she did not want to say too sad.

*

In this city, like in any other, Niovi would find ghosts everywhere. They peered out from behind curtained windows, waved at her from old swing sets, or stood in grocery store aisles staring thoughtfully at a shelf that wasn't there anymore. But most of all – if they were the tethered kind – they were discreetly following their person.

Ghosts were made of stories. It was the way they chose to tell them that was different. In this country, ghosts seemed more like shadows to her. They were calm, less opinionated. Their stories were made of stares and slight nods, sometimes a pat on the back.

In Greece the ghosts were louder, their disapproval mattered, their whispers were sought out and their stories carried memories her people would not have remembered otherwise. Not in the same vividness of smells, tastes, and textures. Sometimes, when listening to one of her mother's stories, Niovi could catch herself reliving an event that never happened to her. Something that had happened to her mother or her grandmother decades ago carried the feeling and the weight of the present. It made her happy, sad, or angry, in what here would be considered a disproportionate amount.

Despite her efforts to conjure the memories, she couldn't do it in quite the same way. She was beginning to forget. It started with the holidays, then the right words took longer to reach her lips and later the proper way her family spiced the dishes.

When her mother's swift hands stuffed the cheese filling in the pie on Sundays before the sun had risen, was it mint or basil she used? When she cooked the tender beef in casserole with fresh tomatoes, was it cinnamon that made its flesh so sweet and aromatic or was it allspice?

Even as a ghost her mother never failed to remind her of those things, of who she was and why she was, especially when she felt sad and lonely. Her mother was really good at picking up on that. Without her mother or her ghost around, she was losing parts of herself she did not know how to get back.

None of the ghosts she met here spoke her tongue or at all. She knew there must have been people like her who died in this country. As much as this thought made her stomach churn, she knew this might happen to her in the future. But up until now she thought they had chosen to return home rather than stay here. Follow their roots back to where they came from and haunt a relative or simply move on.

But then she saw Remi's grandmother and nothing was quite the same after that.

*

It was a strange day at work.

Her ever-surly boss told her that she would be moving up to preparations next week. Her stomach twisted into a bundle of fear and nerves.

'You've made it.' Remi patted her on the back, smiling. His ghost ever so slightly touched the boundaries of her perception, made her recoil.

She whispered a thank you and swallowed. The world was closing in around her.

Niovi's new place would be next to Remi in the kitchen. Seeing him – seeing his grandmother's ghost too – for as long as she worked here. Asking for another shift would be too soon, quitting would be unthinkable. She had nowhere to go.

*

She started drifting in and out of a past she could barely piece together. The Saturday of Souls was just around the corner and she had spent the previous nights talking with relatives on the phone, trying desperately to recreate her memories vicariously. Longing for that connection to her mother again.

What ingredients did her mother use for the offering of koliva? What were the words she would say in her prayers? Niovi tried to invoke the particulars that made her mother's ritual unique. Not the ones she could ask other people about, the ones she could read about, but the ones she could once taste and hear in her mother's distinct voice. A one-person culture among her people's collective one.

She could not. Yet her family offered to help.

'There are nine ingredients in koliva. How could you forget?'

'When will you visit us?'

'Light a candle for her soul.'

'Is there a church to take the offering? Where will you go?'

Where would she go?

Where did the ghostless people go? The ones she met on the street always looked lost to her, directionless, the way they squeezed against each other. But maybe it was just what she felt, a projection of her own aimlessness.

*

She finally gave in.

It wasn't so much the pressure of her coworkers that did the trick as much as Remi and his ghost. It hurt to linger in the kitchen when Remi was working. When they had to exchange to talk during their shift (which was not very often) she felt the stare of the woman following.

So one day, after her shift, she let herself be carried away by the people with the ghosts that did not hurt her, whose stares she could not read as easily. The ghosts who could teach her a few things about this place to replace the ones she had forgotten.

She let the crowd of five talk over her, through her, as if she were one of their ghosts. Once in a while she would offer a half-formed sentence or she would ask a question that seemed too fundamental to them, but completely vital for her understanding of their discussions. They spoke too fast for her to follow anyway.

After a while she gave up, or maybe they did.

She got up to leave, more lost than ever. As if she were the anchor, the reason all this was happening – she wasn't – the others cut their conversations short and paid the bill in haste.

They all walked, half-drunken and languid, down the stone-paved street. The pubs, arranged on either side, were luring the people inside, away from the biting wind, but the street musicians had other plans. The restaurant where Niovi worked was right around the corner, on one of the busiest streets.

It was Matilda who told her then about the ghost of a street musician, a couple blocks down. She was untethered like the General and only appeared on Sunday nights at the same place she performed when she was still alive, strumming her ghost guitar.

'What kinds of songs does she sing?'

'Oh, the same sad songs. Some of them foreign.' Matilda rested an arm over Niovi's shoulder to fix the strap of her slingback shoe. Niovi tolerated the jab of the woman's elbow against the hollow of her neck. She wanted to be accommodating. 'She's really popular with the couples.'

Niovi nodded. She imagined what song her mother would sing if she were here. Probably none. She would make the pots clutter and shuffle around the table in a harmonious frenzy. That was her mother's music.

They were getting closer to the spot where the ghost of the singer performed. Withered flower petals carpeted the concrete slabs.

When she heard the music she instantly knew the song was Greek. The ghost was a woman in her fifties, the hippie type, with kind eyes. She strummed the guitar while playing a tune on a harmonica set on a neck rack. She didn't look Greek from afar, but Niovi had been fooled before.

As if he manifested from her most hidden thoughts, the ones she was trying to keep silent with a night like this one, Remi stood there, a few feet away from the ghost of the musician but fully enveloped in his own.

It felt like too much and like nothing at all. Like one of those moments where a decision must be made. Niovi looked behind her. The company of five had stopped in front of another street musician, a living one, or perhaps a pub – she couldn't say for sure – debating something Niovi was too tired to decipher.

So instead Niovi took her place beside Remi who was mouthing the words of the song, absent-minded. His grandmother's ghost – her curly hair worn in an old-fashioned updo – radiated calmness. Niovi felt her body permeating the outline of her, the warmth of familiarity against her skin sharper than the coldest of days here.

She did not move an inch, just stood very still listening to the song, feeling a sweet misplacement.

'How does she know the words?' Niovi was convinced now

the musician's ghost was a local. The words came out without the depth and the nuance they were supposed to. But they did come with an emotion Niovi admired.

Remi turned around immediately as if a current of electricity had run through him. His grandmother's lips curled into a smile.

'From her husband,' he answered, still stunned by her boldness, perhaps, her change of attitude. 'He came here in the late 1980s. She was the first person he talked to in this country when he walked down this street, wide-eyed and lonely.'

Much like you, Niovi imagined him saying the words, but she was certain they were there.

Niovi's body shivered as she took a few more steps towards him. Towards his ghost that had haunted her in the most complete sense.

'You know,' he said after he had reclaimed some of his composure. 'We are not alone here. There are parts of us everywhere you look. We have a past here too.'

You have a past, she did not say to him. He must have known he was different already. Instead a small hope flickered into existence. A promise remembered.

'Do you celebrate the Saturday of Souls here then?'

He smiled a faint smile. In his eyes there was openness and she was ready to listen.

*

He showed her a small, engraved handkerchief. This was how he carried his grandmother.

Something loosened inside of her.

He had no other family, no siblings – unlike her – and no parents. The ghost was of his grandmother who had raised him since he was ten. When she died she stayed with him.

'I came back home from the funeral,' he said. 'And there she was, standing over her handkerchief, waiting for me.' He took a small sip from his coffee, his voice unsteady like his hand.

The ghost's eyes were compassionate as she stroked her grandson's head.

'She is the only connection I have with the past. My past.' He smiled. His smile had a bitter tint. Niovi understood more than he let on. She blinked back tears, for him, for her, for envying him all this time, for not reaching out to him earlier.

If her longing for her mother was a string, that string had somehow grown into a rope within days, hours. Ever since Remi had told her he would help her see her ghost again. There was a reason ghostless people huddled together. To share memories and stories and pool their resources. There were even untethered ghosts formed by the memories of big enough families. There was a way to bring her mother's ghost into this country. If even for a little while.

'You cannot do this alone,' he said. 'But you can do it.' There was a promise in his words, and for the first time since she came here, she believed it.

*

On Saturday she met Remi. He took her to a place in the city she had never been before, but she had not been to most places anyway. They walked around, shoulder bumping against shoulder. His grandmother's ghost followed them timidly.

In those streets almost no one looked at her – at the emptiness above and around her – with sorrow or alarm. Even the locals strolling the alleyways with their ghosts did not give her a second glance. The ghostless people met her eyes unfazed. Many of them walked in groups but now her perception had shifted. Now she saw the enjoyment as well as the need to share stories, jokes, company. To give as well as take.

The ghostless held candles and plates of koliva and offerings for the dead. There was excitement in the air. It was a celebration.

'This is how ghosts are conjured here,' Remi told her. 'It doesn't have to be sad.'

No, it didn't.

She was daunted and restless about this newfound freedom. The ease of knowing that the person she came from – because people came from people more than they came from places – could be revisited like a place could. Back in Greece she had never had to think of lineage before. She had taken her mother's ghost for granted and she realized now that this was a privilege.

If her longing for her mother was a rope, that rope had branched out to Remi, to his grandmother's ghost, to the ghostless people around her. Niovi let the rope guide her. She followed the crowd rushing inside the red-bricked, corner building, wedged between offices downtown.

Whispers and laughter hung in the air when she came in. Niovi took a careful look around for familiar ghosts, her breath caught in her chest. Her anticipation deflated a sliver when she found nothing had changed. She scolded herself for hoping too much when Remi guided her to the far side of the wall.

There was a long table there, covered in white embroidered tablecloths. Plates of all shapes, sizes, and colors were left on the linen but held only one thing: koliva, food for the dead.

She left her own plate there. Niovi had made them herself, taking extra care to not forget any ingredient, afraid that if she did, then all this, all the strength she had gathered inside of her during the days leading up to Saturday, all would be for nothing.

Niovi lit a candle, steadied it inside the heap of koliva, and left the necklace on the table. Remi stood right there next to her, his shoulder brushing hers. She took a deep breath and took in the smell of each of the ingredients. Nine, like the ranks of angels:

Wheat, for the earth and the souls of those who lie buried under.

Breadcrumbs, for the dirt – may it be light upon their grave.

White, candied almonds, for the blanched bones of the dead.

Pomegranate seeds, for Persephone and Hades, but also the promise of Heaven.

Cinnamon, for all the smells and tastes of this world.

Parsley, for the green, green grass of the resting place.

Raisins, for the vines of Dionysus and the sweetness that is this life.

Sugar, for the sweetness of the Afterlife.

Nuts and seeds, for fertility and life that laughs in the face of death.

There was a change in the atmosphere, a mixing of scents. Niovi heard Remi draw in air and opened her eyes. For a few moments she stared at the necklace on the table. She didn't dare look up.

When she did look up, her mother's ghost was not as she remembered. The ghost was made of memories that all lit up at once like a beacon inside her; her voice was a mixture of spices and familiar tastes. It all descended on her, draping her like a veil.

She saw her mother's eyes for the briefest of moments. And then what there was of her mother's ghost scattered all around her and soaked this new country so she could finally call it her own.

Old People's Folly

Nora Schinnerl

Austria

Nora is another author writing in one language while speaking another, and the charming 'Old People's Folly' explores time and technology in an affecting story I fell for straightaway. Can you believe it is her first publication?

Setti knew the woman for a ghost the moment she appeared. It was the pink hair that gave her away, short and spiky. Real people didn't have hair like that. Also, you couldn't see the scratch marks on Setti's kitchen table through real people's torsos.

'The hell?' was the first thing the ghost said. Setti's grandfather had tried to tell her ghost stories when she was a kid, a long time ago, but he'd had a habit of smoking and drinking too, so none of the stories had ever made any sense and Setti didn't like unannounced visitors.

'Get out of my house,' Setti demanded.

'Um,' the ghost answered, staring at Setti with her eyes rimmed in thick black mascara, then held up a placating hand. 'Okay. Just let me find...'

The ghost blinked out of existence.

*

Setti poked at the shiny silver disk with the tip of her mussel knife. There was nowhere else the ghost could have come from. She'd found the disk down at the beach while foraging for mussels, half buried in a mudslide but gleaming with a smoothness and lack of rust only pre-flood things ever retained. One more thing unearthed by the storm. It hadn't been a bad storm, as they went, not tearing-down-houses strong. Plenty strong to bring down the pear tree behind Setti's house, though. Setti sniffed. Shame it hadn't been the apple tree. She held a severe dislike for apple trees.

Setti had planned on bartering away the disk at the next market fair. Always some dumb folks about, paying for useless curiosities. She poked it again for good measure, with no more reaction than the first time. Some people might even pay more for the ghost living inside it, but Setti wasn't sure it was worth the trouble. Maybe she should toss it back onto the beach. She glared at the disk some more without reaching a decision, then turned away to grab her cane. Wasn't like the ghost would help with planting beans or checking on her bees or getting rid of the tangle of branches and pear blossoms now blocking the back garden. She grimaced getting up, her bad knee twinging. Folk used to say you could feel a storm coming with a knee like this. The way her knee usually screamed in agony Setti figured there should have been a storm every day the last forty-five years, or maybe she simply hadn't figured out the difference between the pain announcing bad weather and the pain telling her she'd run out of willow bark tea.

Setti hesitated in the doorway, then hobbled back to snatch up the disk and put it in her satchel. She didn't want the ghost to get any ideas, slipping out of its home and into some of Setti's furniture while she wasn't looking. Who knew what ghosts might set their mind to?

Hauling up water from the well was always a pain with her

bad knee. Surprising how many things you needed a painless limb for, not that Setti bothered with surprise any more. She staggered inside with a bucket of water, dumped the mussels into it so they wouldn't spoil until evening, then left the ghost disk on a stack of firewood under the eaves before checking on her bees. Bees got angry about the strangest things, so better not risk it.

The bees were fine, still hunkering down after the storm. All the hives had survived without damage this time. Setti didn't even bother slipping on gloves for opening the hive boxes. The bees had been furious before the storm, bad weather always got their temper up, but now they buzzed placidly, almost sluggish in the chilly breeze. When Setti returned to the house the ghost was floating in the yard.

'Figured this didn't count as your house.' She smirked.

'Get lost, ghost,' Setti said. 'I don't have the patience for the likes of you today.'

'I'm not a ghost,' the ghost protested with indignation.

Setti rolled her eyes in disagreement and hobbled for her shed. 'You're see-through.' The only reason Setti didn't try to walk straight through the ghost or poke her with her cane was that she'd have to go out of her way to do so and it wasn't worth the pain just to prove her point.

A flare of anger skittered over the ghost's expression and she crossed her arms. 'For your information, I'm an upload, not a ghost.' The ghost pouted.

Setti ignored her in favor of fetching her hand axe, then dragged herself over to the fallen tree. It was a mess: broken branches, splintered trunk, white blossoms littering the ground. It had crushed a couple of gooseberry bushes, at least two of them beyond hope, but Setti figured with some luck she might save the other two. Not that luck was too keen on her, in general. The only reason the pear tree hadn't crushed the house was because it had been planted too far away for that to be even remotely possible. Setti glared at the tree for a bit, just for satisfaction. The ghost hovered next to her, somewhat sulky at being dismissed so easily.

'Hey, you. Old lady. Could you at least tell me where I am and what fucking year it is? My display is glitching.'

The old lady's mouth twitched with annoyance, partly at the ghost, and partly at the tree. She chopped at some of the branches more out of resentment than any hope of stripping them off the trunk. 'Samsonville, 313 AF.' Why was she even talking to the ghost? Might as well invite her in and offer her a cup of tea with sugar cubes.

'Shit. That helps exactly not at all.' The ghost hunched her shoulders as if the chill wind cut through even her insubstantial form.

A tangle of dead gooseberry branches tore at Setti's skirt as she tried to step closer to the trunk, ripping the hem. Her cane slipped off dead leaves and she flinched with the sudden weight on her bad knee.

'Don't you, I don't know, wanna get help with this?' The ghost peeking over Setti's shoulder looked ridiculously out of place in her make-up and pink hair.

With a thump the old woman buried her axe in the trunk and rounded on the ghost. Who'd asked her anyway? She'd just shown up out of her shiny disk and started pestering Setti without prompting. Setti didn't need a ghost. Setti didn't need anyone's help, anyone's pity. 'You want to lend a hand?'

'Kind of handicapped here.' The pink-haired woman waved her fingers through a tangle of leaves, then shrugged.

Of course it would only be Setti who'd gotten caught in the gooseberry thorns. The ghost floated a few steps backward to take in the hill Setti's house sat perched upon. The neat rows of onions, leeks and kale in her vegetable garden, the gnarly fruit and sprawling nut trees, the scraggly oaks in the distance. You couldn't see the village from here, which suited Setti just fine. Nothing but a trail of smoke from the bakery chimney reminded her of its existence.

'What about him?' Setti followed the ghost's pointing finger toward a lonely figure a couple of hundred meters away, right on the edge of where the hill dropped abruptly into a ragged cliffside. Romantic view of the Fingers, the wreckage of a pre-flood city shedding rust and broken glass into the sea that had swallowed it.

Setti squinted. 'Just some loner kid who hides from the village folks. Sits there all the time, whining and feeling sorry for himself.'

The ghost gave her a pointed look as if to say they weren't so different, Setti and the boy. The old woman scoffed in contempt. She felt plenty sorry for herself, but at least she succeeded in moaning and working at the same time.

'Not like people would just pop in to help me,' Setti grumbled, turning back to the tree, 'out of the goodness of their hearts. What kind of world do you think we're living in?'

The ghost didn't reply, just stared at Setti with the strangest expression on her face, somewhere between hurt, anger and defiance, then vanished in the blink of an eye.

*

'I'm Jasmin,' the ghost introduced herself.

Setti kept methodically pulling off the mussels' beards to prepare them for eating, one by one, and ignored her. She shouldn't have put the disk back inside the house, but she still thought it would fetch a decent price and leaving it unattended seemed like an invitation for trouble. It wasn't like the ghost would stay. Setti was very good at making people not want to stay.

'What's your name?' The ghost floated in front of Setti, turning in excited little circles while she scrutinized the kitchen furniture, the mussels, even the garlic drying in the rafters, with apparent interest.

'Setti. Go away.'

The ghost, Jasmin, shrugged. 'Don't worry, I won't be around too long. My battery is at point three percent. Is this your house? What are you doing with the shellfish?'

'I should throw you back into the ocean to shut you up sooner,' Setti replied. Cleaning the heap of mussels was starting to hurt her fingers and her knee still throbbed from her effort with the axe that afternoon. She was in an even sourer mood than usual.

Jasmin shrugged again. 'That would probably do the trick. Or not. This fucking handheld is pretty sturdy. Maybe I'll see some fish.'

Setti rolled her eyes at the flip answer. For a blessed minute the ghost ran out of things to ask and both women listened to the meditative crackle of flames in Setti's stove. The silence didn't last too long.

'You said it was 313 AF. What's AF stand for?'

No idea how to keep their mouths shut, these young people. Not even if they were ghosts.

'After the flood.' Setti shifted around in her chair, trying to find a comfortable position for her knee. Futile, as always.

'Oh. My. God. Fuck.' The ghost dropped her butt onto the table, something Setti would have protested sharply had Jasmin been even remotely corporeal. 'No wonder the date is glitching. My time, we didn't even get rain in most places any more, never mind a flood. And the sunken ruins out there…' Jasmin buried her face in her hands. 'Damn it. I was hoping… What did you say? Three hundred years at least. Not even my baby niece is still alive. Not even my baby niece's baby niece.'

Setti, unimpressed, chucked a cleaned mussel into the pot in front of her. 'So go haunt somewhere else.'

Utterly ignoring her words, Jasmin flopped down to stretch all across the kitchen table. 'I hope this was fucking worth it.'

Setti rolled her eyes at the drama. She wasn't about to give in and ask. Then again, it might be that asking was all it took to get rid of the ghost. Most living people would prattle endlessly about their problems given half a chance, so why should the dead be any different? 'Was what worth it?' the old woman relented.

Jasmin gesticulated with one insubstantial hand to indicate her equally insubstantial body. 'This. Going to prison. Being a fucking upload. They didn't even ask our consent, you know, not even as a formality. The world was going to hell. First the cells got crowded, then the food ran low. Then… My brother woke me a couple of times, said they'd sued the prison company, sued the government, sued everyone. As if I had any illusion that'd help, with the world ending!'

'World didn't end,' Setti interjected. Samsonville didn't have any prisoners. Nor did any of the other communities around. Who had food enough to feed useless mouths? Better kick them out, send them to the Wastes or whatever else the bailiff did with them. Setti didn't stick her nose in things she couldn't change. Rumor had it there was a prison over in Treize, but not many folks ever traveled that far. Setti sure didn't, not with her walking at the speed of a slug.

'I guess not,' Jasmin admitted. She sat up again. Her face took on a bit of color, clashing with the pink hair, but it set her eyes ablaze. 'We had a shitty government. People used to vote for the shitty government, before they started simply faking elections. Hell, some people still voted for the shitty government. World went to shit. Ice caps melting, storms without any rain, droughts lasting for years, and nobody did anything but moan how it was too late anyway. People just kept doing what they had always done. They didn't care enough to give up their comfort, their plane tickets and Argentinian steak and designer lipstick. And then when they started starving they acted as if they'd known it all along.'

Setti's eyebrows rose at the ghost's rant, not even trying to pick up on all the unfamiliar vocabulary. 'Your words don't match,' she said instead. Jasmin frowned, caught in the middle of drawing a breath she didn't need. 'The words and the shapes your lips make,' Setti clarified. 'They don't match.'

The ghost let out a long, frustrated sigh. 'Translation software.' She shrugged. 'Pretty low-standard edition as well. Hell, no idea what part of the world I'm even in right now. Also, fucking three hundred years!' She scratched her spiky pink hair. 'I don't know how different language sounds after three hundred years. Maybe we're speaking the same one and don't even notice.'

Setti grunted noncommittally. The ghost's explanation made no sense at all, but she'd finally finished cleaning her mussels and got up to put them on the stove. Her knee felt hot and swollen. 'What did you go to prison for, anyway?'

Jasmin raised her chin in stubborn pride. 'Arson. Protesting just went on and on and got us nowhere so I torched the High Court of *Justice*.' She turned the last word into a mockery.

'Did it burn?'

A gleam in the ghost's eye, almost like the glint of tears. 'Like cinder.'

*

'Hey, that boy's still out there!' Despite Setti's efforts, talking had done exactly nothing to banish the ghost. At least she'd ceased occupying the kitchen table.

'And you're still in here,' the old woman grumbled in reply. She squinted at the needle and thread in her calloused hands. Dusk had started to conquer the room and the meager fire in the kitchen stove threw more shadows than light. The smell of mussel soup clung to the air.

'How old is he? Won't somebody be out looking for him?'

Nosy, for a ghost who'd complained about an hour ago that everybody she'd ever known was long dead. What did she care? Setti sipped her willow bark tea, lips curling at the familiar, bitter taste.

'Fourteen, fifteen? Told you, he's here all the time. Doesn't get along with his folks.' In Setti's opinion it didn't take much not to get along with the village folk.

The ghost kept hovering at the window, then cocked her head. 'Is he… is my micro glitching or is he singing?'

Setti fiddled with her needle, trying to fix the hem she'd torn earlier even though her fingers trembled and the stitches got ugly. It wasn't good to be idle. Idle left too much time to dwell on how much everything hurt. 'He thinks I can't hear him from here.' He'd have a nice voice too, rich and resonating, if he'd use it for anything else but dirges. The ghost shut up for a moment, listening to the mournful snippets of song drifting on the wind.

'Why doesn't he get along with his people?' she finally asked. Setti noticed how Jasmin had clearly not felt the need to ask why *she* didn't get along with the village people.

'They want him to marry.' Setti grimaced into her tea. Wasn't like she couldn't understand him; she hadn't exactly been the marrying type either. Never mind that no one in their right mind would have ever married a cripple.

'Let me guess,' the ghost replied, her voice suddenly turning a deceptive kind of calm. 'He doesn't want to marry?'

Setti wondered if Jasmin would burn down the house if she didn't like her answer. That would at least save her from bothering with the pear tree.

'From what I heard, it's not the marrying so much as the bride. He'd rather marry a lad from the Merieux farm than run off with a pretty village girl.' Look at this old lady, spreading gossip when she resented every painful trip down to the mill to swap honey for flour, the only place she ever came into contact with gossip.

'Seriously?' Jasmin's words came out in a hiss. A hardness snuck onto her face, incongruous with her soft features and bright hair, and for a moment Setti had no trouble picturing her as an arsonist. 'This is the fucking future I fought for? I got manhandled and locked up without trial and put in a fucking handheld for this? For a world that forces children to marry and doesn't give a shit about what they want? And you don't even care? I should have given up like the rest of the world and enjoyed my steak! I mean, we had a fake government and we fucked up the world, but at least you could be with whomever you wanted to be, didn't matter if it was a man or a woman or a fucking video game character.'

Setti scoffed at the ghost's ideals. Young people's folly, ideals. Setti had grown out of them. The old woman turned back to her sewing and glared at her trembling hands. 'Used to be different. Used to be you could marry whoever you wanted as long as you brought something to the village.' Setti was rather sure there was still some law about it, somewhere. Not that anyone cared. 'Times are bad.'

Jasmin's face morphed from furious into even more furious. Setti shrugged.

'They don't get children any more. None of the village folk. Or if they do, they're born dead or too early or wrong and then they die.' Setti carefully tied off her thread. The ghost blinked, her scowl lessening marginally. 'Something broke in the Fingers. Something spilled. Fish tasted odd for a while. Been like this for years now and folk are getting desperate. They think we're dying out. There's only one family left with a child under seven and she's got the shakes.'

Jasmin crossed her arms, outrage still etched into her frown. Floating closer, she took a suspicious peek into the pot of soup. 'You shouldn't eat these, then. Mussels absorb pollution. Must be shit for your health.'

Setti twisted her mouth in contempt. The brief flare of respect she'd held for the ghost's conviction vanished. As if she wouldn't know. As if anyone living off the sea wouldn't know. 'Bright little pre-flood ghost. With your pre-flood ideals and your pre-flood magic.' Setti didn't know much about pre-flood times, but she'd heard the stories, seen the ruins. She didn't think the ghost had ever had to scavenge for a meal, or eat seaweed and shellfish because there was nothing else edible left in early spring. 'Care to tell me what else we should eat instead? Mussels might make you sick, but they're still better than starving.'

That shut the ghost up. Her eyes flickered over Setti's kitchen furniture again, the homemade chairs and dried herbs and threadbare rug. Setti wasn't too badly off, having only herself to look after, and the honey was good for barter. But it was hard to grow anything in this soil, even harder when a storm took half the harvest or the rot came in like last year or half the livestock died in agony from a plague nobody had ever heard of.

Rain started to fall in a quiet drizzle while the ghost sat back onto the kitchen table, calmer, but with her eyes no less ablaze. 'Then how come one kid marrying against his will makes any difference?'

Setti swallowed the rest of her tea. It had gone cold, making it taste even worse. 'Don't blame me for the village folk. Their doing, not mine.'

'I don't see you doing anything against it,' the ghost muttered as she hovered back to the window. 'Would you at least get the kid out of the fucking rain? And do me a favor: put my handheld into the sun tomorrow, I'm out of juice.'

A tremble ran through Jasmin's projection, then another and another until the ghost conveniently vanished. Setti grunted in satisfaction.

*

'Ey, boy! My ghost says I should get you out of the rain.' Pain made Setti's voice even more irritable than usual. Her cane kept slipping off the wet grass, and the drizzle had turned into a downpour, soaking her shawl. Shouldn't have listened to a ghost. To be honest, she didn't really know why she had. Some stupid notion of proving her wrong, of proving how futile it was to offer help and expect anything to change for the better.

The boy, Kite, startled and spun around so fast he almost lost his footing on the slippery ground. That would have been a statement, him falling off the cliffside because an old woman had gotten it into her head to try to lend a hand. Kite had smooth, dark skin and huge black eyes just made for daydreaming. No wonder both girls and boys down at the village mooned after him. Setti's lips twisted at the ugly bruise marring his left cheek.

'I'm… I was… I'm sorry,' Kite stammered in the same silky voice she recognized from his singing, but quietly, barely audible over the downpour as if he wanted to keep it a secret. 'I should leave…'

'Don't be stupid.' Setti nodded in the direction of her house, then turned around without waiting for him to follow. She wanted her soup and another mug of tea and dry clothes. 'You're going to eat my food and sleep in a place where there isn't another bruise waiting for you. Least you can do is stay until the morning and cut up the pear tree for me.'

*

Kite was still curled into a bundle of blankets in front of the stove when Setti woke. The old woman sniffed, torn between surprise and annoyance. She'd have figured him for a quitter, sneaking out before dawn to escape the work. That's what she'd have done when she was his age. Not like Setti was in any shape to chase after him. But he'd stayed and now she was stuck with him, just like she was stuck with her ghost. There was a thought to cheer her up in the morning.

'Ey, boy.'

The bundle of blankets stirred, then Kite woke with a start. The bruise on his face looked worse in the harsh morning light, his cheek all swollen and purple. From the way he winced, it wasn't the only one either. Setti dropped a bowl of oats on the table for him.

'About time you start working for your food.'

She didn't stick around to see if he would eat and instead snagged the ghost disk on her way out the door. The last thing she needed was the boy messing around with it. Her knee twinged in protest, objecting to yesterday's treatment just like it did every day. Setti didn't have the luxury to heed her body's constant objections.

It barely took five minutes before Kite emerged as well, still mute as a butterfly. Setti put the axe into his hand and pointed him at the pear tree, then shuffled off to plant some beans. To her surprise it didn't take long for the tell-tale sound of the axe to start up. Maybe the boy would actually manage to strip the tree of its gnarled branches before he winged it. Maybe he was more than a pretty voice. Setti shook her head. Shouldn't get too optimistic. Maybe the ghost had made her go soft with her ideals and her talk of change.

With a grunt Setti settled onto the ground next to her vegetable bed. She'd tried a thousand different ways of planting seeds while bending down and none of them had worked with a bad knee. Sitting in the dirt wasn't pretty, but it did the trick and if she had it her way there wouldn't be anyone around to see.

The sound of chopping stopped after a suspiciously short amount of time.

'Ms. Setti?' There was a strange look on Kite's face, excitement warring with confusion. His voice was still quiet, almost inaudible, as if he were ashamed to admit its existence.

'What? Broke something already?' The reply came out harsher than Setti had intended. She didn't like it when people caught her helpless and there wasn't much that screamed helplessness as loudly as crawling on the ground like a beetle on its back. Kite hunched his shoulders, but his expression didn't waver. He must have a shitty family if this kind of answer was business as usual for him.

'There are bees.' Setti rolled her eyes, but of course the boy wasn't finished. 'Up in one of the trees. A whole bunch of them.'

With an unhappy grunt Setti groped for her cane. Bad weather for swarming bees, too cold, too windy, though obviously that fact hadn't gotten around to her swarm. The old woman grabbed the handle of her cane and miserably botched her first two attempts at getting up. The pain in her knee brought tears to her eyes. At least Kite had the good grace to look away and pretend not to notice. Not like the miller's son, who offered Setti his arm every time she went down to the village as if it were a courtesy to rub into her face how frail she was.

The swarm of bees clung to one of the lower branches of the walnut tree, still a good three meters above the ground. Setti watched the insects buzz and crawl over each other in their need to stick as close to their queen as possible. That's what she got for allowing them to swarm. She'd left the extra queen in two of the hives so they would split up, with the old queen moving out in spring and half the swarm following, trying to find a new home. Setti had lost some hives over the winter and it was a neat way of replenishing them. More hives couldn't hurt. Setti sniffed. Figuratively speaking it couldn't hurt. Could hurt plenty, falling off the ladder.

Kite trudged after the old woman like a silent ghost, quite the opposite of the real ghost hiding somewhere in her disk. They dragged her ladder under the tree and Kite went to fetch the new hive box while Setti scowled at her cane and finally swallowed her pride.

'You afraid of heights?' she asked when the boy returned. Kite shook his head. She'd figured that already, with him constantly perching on the edge of the cliffs.

'You afraid of bees?' He hesitated for a second, then shook his head again. At least he'd stopped to think before answering, Setti had to give him that. 'Think you can manage to catch the swarm?'

Kite tilted his face up to study the buzzing mass of wings and stingers, his eyes more curious than concerned, as if for all his worry he simply lacked the capacity for fear. He shrugged. 'What do you want me to do?'

'Cut off the branch, carry it down the ladder; I'll put it in the box.'

Another shrug. 'Okay.'

Despite being taller than her, Kite almost vanished under the hat and veil Setti put on his head. Some people just had a knack for vanishing. She watched him climb the ladder carefully, not quite frightened but showing plenty of respect for her bees and clutching the saw in his gloved hands like a weapon. A couple of bees took off when Kite started sawing, startled by the sudden vibration. It wasn't a heavy branch, a mere two finger's breadth. Easy work if you had two legs to keep balance. Kite almost dropped the whole branch with its sudden weight as he cut through, clusters of bees raining to the ground and taking up an angry buzz. Setti glowered at nobody in particular. Would hardly do to shout at the kid precariously perched on the ladder, but she was somewhat protective of her swarm and she didn't want to scrape bees off the grass for the rest of the morning. Against her expectations the boy held on, clutched the branch in both hands as the saw tumbled from his grip and clouds of bees took to the air. Setti fancied she could see the white in Kite's frightened eyes, like a cornered deer.

Slowly, step by step, the boy climbed down the ladder and handed Setti the branch with trembling fingers. Setti took it without hesitation, even with her hands bare. Swarming bees were at their most docile, no brood to defend, no food stocks to fight for. It didn't mean they wouldn't sting if provoked, but Setti had been stung plenty in her life. A little more pain wouldn't make any difference. She whacked the branch against the box, dropping most of the bees inside. The rest crawled around in confusion, trying to return to their queen. Setti gently brushed a few bees from the rim and closed the hive.

'All right, boy. Time to give them some space.'

*

'Here.' Setti pressed a jar of honey into Kite's hands. He'd earned it, and Setti wasn't good at thanking people. Lack of practice. She dug a bee stinger out of her hands rather than trying to think of something better to say. She'd have to wash properly to get the smell of dead bee off her before checking on the new hive again – it made the rest of them aggressive. If the boy had been stung as well, he kept remarkably quiet about it.

'Thank you for letting me stay the night,' he mumbled at last, his hands fidgeting with the jar. He kept his gaze fixed to the ground, but Setti could still spot the resignation in his eyes. Nowhere else to go now but home.

'The bees like you,' Setti said. She was as bad at giving compliments as she was at thanking people. Not much use in trying at all. 'Must be your singing voice.'

At the mention of his singing Kite's cheeks turned a bright crimson, but at least it had the intended effect of sending him on his way with nothing more than a stammered goodbye. Setti watched him scramble down the hill toward the village, strangely content. Not that he'd done much with the pear tree, but she figured catching the swarm was worth more to her anyway.

When she turned around Jasmin's translucent body was floating at her side. 'Not bad for a start.' The ghost smirked, flickered and vanished before Setti could come up with a snide remark.

*

Didn't take long for the boy to return. Nor for the ghost.

'What the hell is this?' Jasmin asked over Setti's shoulder.

'Beans,' the old woman said. The earth was still damp after a day of incessant drizzling. The cold seeped into Setti's skirt and crawled up her bones, making her knee ache even more than usual. Cold had a way of ruining Setti's temper. Then again, so did a lot of things.

The ghost hopped up and down like an excited child. 'No, I mean...' She pointed.

'Dirt,' Setti cut her off.

'But what's with all the colorful bits?'

Setti pushed a bean seed from her hand into the dark soil brimming with red and blue and yellow particles. It wasn't bad soil either, as good as you'd get on the cliffs.

'That's what dirt looks like.'

'No, it doesn't,' Jasmin protested. 'I know what...' Suddenly the ghost's animated face turned all horrified. 'Is this plastic? Shit. Micro-plastic? We really did fuck up the world.' She plonked down right in the middle of the vegetable bed and hugged her insubstantial knees. Drama queen. Setti rolled her eyes and kept on planting beans.

'Shitty battery,' the ghost mumbled, her petulant tone causing Setti to glance over. The ghost's body had started flickering erratically, on and off in the middle of Setti's bean patch. The old woman wondered why she'd bothered putting the disk into the sun that morning.

'Hey, here's the boy again.' The ghost jumped to her feet, still flickering.

Even from a distance and without seeing his face, Setti could tell Kite was crying. He ran straight for his place at the cliffs, body bowed as if against a storm. Setti buried her last seed and fumbled for her cane. She could at least pretend to give the boy some privacy.

*

Kite's parents weren't about to do the same. The yelling started even before Setti had made it to the kitchen. She couldn't make out any words, not that she had to. The cadence was clear enough.

'What the hell?' Jasmin materialized in the middle of the room. Her flickering had grown worse, distorting not only her body but also her voice, which made her sound more like a ghost than ever before. 'Do something.'

Setti grimaced and hobbled for her chair. 'And what exactly? Frighten them with a pink-haired ghost?' Her fingers groped for a bowl of potatoes and a knife, more out of a need for distraction than any desire for preparing food.

'I'd make them piss their pants if my battery wasn't at point one percent.' The ghost sniffed, then vanished for a whole second as if trying to prove her point. 'Fucking battery.'

Setti scoffed into her potatoes and remained seated. 'Then what do you want me to do? Limp over and smack them with my cane until they stop yelling? Not worth the pain. I have no claim on that boy.'

Frustration flickered over Jasmin's body, plain even through the distortion. 'Really? You're gonna do nothing? What if he jumps off the cliff?'

Setti started peeling her potatoes. She felt more like stabbing them. 'Nah. Would have done so already if he had the guts.' Quiet boy like Kite, he wouldn't jump in front of his parents. Too much of a mess. Too loud a statement.

'But...'

A muffled thud cut them both short. Setti glanced up and found Kite sprawled in the mud, no question about how he'd ended up there with his father stooping over him. She twisted her mouth in disgust and pretended not to watch the man drag his son away. The ghost had no such qualms. She stared out the window until the family vanished out of sight, then wheeled around, hands clenched into fists.

'And you're just sitting here, doing fucking nothing? Nothing at all?'

Even through the flickering, Setti could spot the ghost's eyes burning with contempt. The old woman pursed her lips. She'd had about enough of accusations. Girl from another time, thinking she knew so much better. Maybe in her world you could have changed things with protesting loud enough and setting things on fire. Maybe in her world you didn't have to eat food that poisoned you, didn't have to do what somebody else thought was best. But this was Setti's world. In Setti's world, parents who clothed and fed you would always have the last say about your life. In Setti's world, there was nobody around to help you out of the goodness of their heart. In Setti's world, people fell off apple trees for no reason at all and got crippled for life because they landed unlucky.

'World is what it is.' Setti drew her lips back in a bitter snarl. 'Nothing you can do. No use fighting it.' You could easily hate it, though. Setti had plenty of experience in hating the world.

The ghost came so close to Setti's face the old woman imagined she would have tasted her breath, if she'd had any. Jasmin's eyes were a pale grey and must have been almost translucent even when she'd still been alive. 'Yes, the world is shit,' the ghost said. Anger bled through her voice despite the erratic up and down in volume. 'The world has always been shit. Mine, yours – there's always been shittiness, everywhere we go. And you know why? Because nobody bothers to do a thing about it. If everybody would change just a tiny little bit, the world would be fine. But instead, we moan and we complain and we do nothing. And so nothing will ever change!'

A bitter laugh escaped Setti's lips. 'Pretty little lies you tell yourself.' She shifted her aching knee, feeling the urge to punch it for giving her trouble but knowing from experience how much that would hurt. She wondered how many futile attempts it took for someone to realize struggle wasn't worth the pain. How many it had taken her. 'Maybe I should run down to the village for a spell, set a couple of buildings on fire. Worked so well for you, I should give it a try because you must have made the world a much better place. Look how great it turned out.'

Jasmin flinched as if the old woman had slapped her. Her eyes practically filled with tears, full of guilt and betrayal. As if whatever she'd done wasn't hundreds of years in the past. As if anyone would still care. The distortion in the ghost's body grew worse by the second. Convenient, wouldn't it be, to flicker out of existence right before answering? Setti was almost surprised when instead Jasmin set her jaw as if against a blow.

'There were people inside,' the ghost muttered through clenched teeth. 'Inside the Court of Justice. It was a weekend, and late. I didn't know. Four people. Only two made it out.'

Carefully, Setti placed her peeled potato back into the bowl. The ghost refused to meet her eyes and instead stared out the window, where Kite and his parents had long since vanished.

Jasmin turned around, hugging herself like a stubborn child. 'I made a mistake, okay? I paid for it a thousand fucking times. But you know what? At least I didn't sit around on my butt pretending it didn't matter what I did anyway. At least I tried!'

And the ghost threw a last burning glare at Setti before she flickered out.

*

Setti poked the polished disk with her finger. She'd put it in the sun two hours ago, and still, Jasmin hadn't deigned to show her face. Setti should've known not even ghosts could stand her company for long. The old woman hobbled inside to fetch her shawl and when she emerged the ghost was suddenly there, floating right in the middle of her yard.

'Where are you going?' Jasmin's voice was full of mistrust, still scrambled like an off-tune guitar.

Setti sniffed and drew the shawl tight around her shoulders. 'Going to check on the boy.'

Jasmin narrowed her eyes, face full of suspicion. Something in her expression made Setti think she'd been crying, ghost tears that left her thick black mascara untouched. She was even more insubstantial than usual, like a candle about to burn down.

'What made you change your mind?' she asked.

Setti shrugged. 'Still got a pear tree that needs cutting down.'

An annoyingly smug smile appeared on the ghost's face, barely marred by the twitching. Setti groped for something bitter and seething to add, but nothing came to mind until she gave up and showed her irritation by walking right through Jasmin's insubstantial body. The sensation was a lot less otherworldly than she had expected, didn't feel like anything at all, not even a cold shiver down her spine. Nothing but air.

'Hey, old lady!' the ghost hollered after her. Setti rolled her eyes, but stopped reluctantly and turned around. Jasmin seemed more amused than angry, hands on her hips, but the next moment her demeanor shifted into something fierce and final.

'Please do me a favor. If the battery gives out, smash the fucking handheld to pieces. I'm done being imprisoned.'

Setti grimaced, an unexpected feeling of regret sneaking up on her, but she still nodded. 'Course I will. But try to at least stick around until I return. I need someone to blame if I walk down to the village for nothing.'

*

Setti banged her cane against the door, scowling. She hated coming down to the village, the loose pebbles on the path twisting her steps, the pitying glances and hushed voices of the village folk, like she was a curious animal, exotic and out of place. Kite's father wrenched the door open. He was a tall man, at least a head taller than Setti, broad-shouldered and staring down at her in confusion.

'Need some help?'

Setti glared at him. Did it look like she needed help when she could still bash against his door with her cane? 'I need my apprentice,' she demanded, not too friendly. Her knee hurt.

The man's eyes narrowed in suspicion and he shook his head. 'No apprentice here.'

'Sure there is. That one.' Setti pointed her cane at Kite, who'd tiptoed into the room behind his father. His left cheek wasn't the only spot growing bruises any more. 'Bit the worse for wear, but I take what I can get.'

The father's face warped from slight suspicion into open hostility in the blink of an eye, and he wasn't the only one.

'What do you think you're playing at, Setti?' Kite's mother appeared right on her son's heels, all haughty stares and proud tilt of the chin. Setti had known her when they were both younger, thirty-odd years ago, and even as a youngster that woman had had an attitude problem. Setti glared right back. She had more experience with it.

'Our boy is none of your business,' the husband growled. Most people took him for a calm, almost stoic person, at least until the first time they watched him lose his temper. He took a step toward Setti, relying on his sheer bulk for intimidation and then stopped in confusion when the old woman didn't back off. Setti sniffed. Not much threat in violence when taking a step backward too fast hurt her worse than a punch to the face. What was he going to do, anyway? Hit her? That would score them points with the neighbors, hitting the village cripple.

'Ask him, then.' Setti shrugged into the tall man's face. Or chest, more like. She didn't think the boy would be of any help. Had an expression like he wasn't even home, not hopeful, not afraid, like he'd just left his bruised face behind and nobody had noticed yet. But the boy surprised her again. Not the best thing in an apprentice, to constantly surprise you. Kite gave an almost imperceptible shrug.

'She's telling the truth,' he said, calm as anything. 'I already helped with the bees. I got stung.' And he tugged at his pants to show them the stings. Setti's eyebrows rose and a small complacent smile threatened to tug at her lips.

Instead of acknowledging Kite's words, though, his father's eyes narrowed to slits, bouncing back and forth between the old woman and his son with menace. 'He stays with us. Get out or I throw you out,' he said, moving even closer until she imagined she could smell the anger on his skin. So much for points with the neighbors. 'I don't know why you suddenly feel like meddling, but you have no say about my boy. He's going to marry next year and it's none of your business.'

Setti sniffed down her nose at him. 'Plenty of time for marrying after an apprenticeship.'

Temper flared in the man's eyes, and for a second, Setti thought he really would push her into the dirt. There was a way to ruin her afternoon, walking back to her house with a broken leg.

'Careful where you're stepping,' she hissed at him. Setti never had known when to back off, and by now, she was probably too old to learn. She nodded at her cane. 'Not too steady, these legs. I might stumble and break my neck. Think your neighbors will be happy with that? No more honey for your bread. No more willow bark tea if you hurt your back.' Had its uses, to have a village cripple in town, someone who was in pain so constantly she'd learned all about herbal remedies and painkilling teas. 'No more feverfew if your headache returns. No more valerian tea if the nightmares get too bad.' All the little hurts that they thought nobody knew about until they started bartering for Setti's herbs.

Kite's father went pale, maybe fear, maybe anger, who could tell? The way she remembered, his back made him scream with pain every harvest season.

'What do you even want?' Kite's mother glared at Setti as if glaring was all it took to make her leave. She was the one with the bad headaches.

'My apprentice,' Setti repeated.

Irritation hung in the air like syrup, thick and heavy, but neither of the boy's parents dared to shut the door in her face. A lopsided smile snuck onto Setti's face. She'd never tried to blackmail the villagers before and it was somewhat satisfying to know that it worked. It wasn't so much the threat of keeping her medicine to herself, she assumed, but the fact that she knew all their flaws. Nobody wanted to end up in the bad books of somebody who knew their flaws. The old woman raised her eyebrow at Kite and for a moment he seemed about to vanish into the depths of the house to gather his things, then thought better of it. Setti didn't take her eyes off his parents until the door was solidly closed between them and their son.

Kite looked almost stunned at his escape, a sleepwalker awoken in an unfamiliar place. Lost and confused. The ghost would love this.

'Thank you,' Kite mumbled.

Setti rolled her eyes. 'Wait until you have to walk up the cliffs with me. You don't know how slow a cripple can walk, and you're going to stay right beside me.'

A shy smile twitched across the boy's lips. At least he had some sense of humor.

Setti sighed. This wouldn't be the last she heard of Kite's parents. She started hobbling back in the direction of her house and the boy fell into step beside her. Foolish idea, to take him in. What had come over her? She knew it wouldn't take long to regret her decision. Maybe it was the ghost's nagging, or maybe she'd gotten used to having somebody to complain to. She glanced at the boy out of the corner of her eye as they walked, watched the idea of something akin to freedom slowly dawning on his face. She shook her head.

Ideals. Old people's folly.

Echoes of a Broken Mind

Christine Lucas

Greece

A retired air force officer from Greece, Christine writes in English, like many international writers today. With hints of cyberpunk, 'Echoes of a Broken Mind' packs a lot into a small frame, and its twists and turns will keep you hooked!

A warm sense of accomplishment coils inside Kallie's gut when she enters Madame Leutho's Pawn Shop. She's made it. Her daughter will be provided for, for another week. She takes small steps inside the cramped, low-ceilinged shop, clutching the bundle of this week's loot to her chest. Perhaps she'll even make enough to treat herself, too. A strawberry-flavored algae bar – or a ticket to the station's observatory, to watch Jupiter in all its splendor while slurping a protein smoothie. Her mouth waters at the possibilities. Too early for such plans. She's been disappointed before.

The moment Kallie enters, Madame Leutho bundles up the neural implants she's been tinkering with. She wraps them up in a dirty cloth, probably unwashed since before the station opened twenty years ago, and hides them under the counter. Kallie pretends not to notice – Leutho tries her best to appear law-abiding and respectable at all times, even though Kallie knows first-hand of her side-hustle. Leutho is the one who installed Kallie's implant six years ago, after the traumatic childbirth that left Kallie comatose. Leutho's implant helps Kallie's surviving neurons to 'connect the dots'. It helps her be a productive member of society, while someone else – someone better – raises her child. The burden of her debt weighs on Kallie's shoulders – a debt she'll never be able to pay off in full. Kallie owes her eternal gratitude. Money, too. Children are expensive.

She approaches the counter, deliberately ignoring the persistent stare of a ghostly soldier perched atop some dismantled wartime exoskeleton. Her implant is acting up again, making her see things that don't exist. There goes any extra credit from today's loot.

Without a word, Kallie dumps her bundle on the counter. Madame Leutho adjusts the goggles over her optical implants that calculate weight, value, and profit margin, then takes a sip from a tall mug. Her beverage smells of cinnamon. Kallie's gut contracts with envy for everything she cannot have: her daughter, breakfast, new shoes, or at least a cinnamon-flavored algae smoothie. Leutho cocks a perfectly plucked eyebrow and uses her long tweezers to lift a multicolored scarf in Kallie's bundle.

'Silk… good stuff. The rest is the usual junk.'

Leutho goes through the rest with the tips of her tool, as though the clothes and trinkets are infested with lice. And they probably are. The station's janitorial staff won't go anywhere near the area of the old docks where the immigrants from Earth gather before being distributed to the agro and mining domes of the Belt. Only scavengers like Kallie go through the piles of things the immigrants leave behind, after they're told of the weight limit per person on the transports.

After some more shifting and huffing and sighing, Leutho sits back on her chair. 'Ten creds. Best I can do.'

Kallie's heart sinks to her feet. Five of those will go toward her daughter's expenses. Three for rent, and another two to have her implant adjusted. Perhaps one-and-a-half, if Leutho feels generous. How will she survive until the next shipment of unfortunate humans arrives? No point in haggling; Leutho doesn't haggle. Kallie nods.

'Can... can you fix this, too?' Kallie taps the implant on her left temple.

Leutho looks *almost* concerned. 'You're seeing shades again?'

Kallie glances at the ghostly soldier now peeking over Leutho's shoulder as if to read her screen. Shades. *Yes, let's just call them that.* So she just nods.

Leutho adjusts her goggles again, and picks up her tools. Her touch is gentle, almost comforting – Kallie has heard rumors that Leutho was a military surgeon once. Today, Kallie almost believes it, and allows her shoulders to relax.

A jolt of pain from a sudden power surge in her implant drills a hole through her skull, shoots bolts down her spine, and make her toes curl inside her worn sneakers. But the ghostly form fades away. The lines around Leutho's mouth deepen. Sneer? Concern? Or something else, entirely?

Leutho leans back in her chair and tosses her tools in a tray beside her terminal's screen. 'Done.' She types something, then her terminal buzzes and spits out a credit chip. She slides it over to Kallie on the counter. 'Here. Five creds. The fix was free of charge. And you're welcome.'

That was unexpected. Kallie grabs the chip, her earlier sense of accomplishment washed away by how weightless the chip feels in her palm. One credit or a thousand doesn't affect its physical weight, only the knowledge that Kallie will go to bed hungry for another week. She turns to leave, but then the same words she speaks every week jump out of her mouth.

'Will you send my little girl a message? Tell her that I love her?'

And like every week, Leutho flashes a forced smile, and lies. 'Of course, Kallie. I'll tell Danae how much you're doing for her.'

Kallie knows that Leutho won't tell Danae anything. She has denied all of Kallie's pleas to help her see Danae, even from afar. She's never seen her child – not even in dreams. In her dreams, Kallie only hears herself screaming Danae's name.

*

Kallie drags her feet on the dim corridors between Leutho's shop and the old bays area, where the military spaceships docked during the wars. Now the area has been repurposed to house the countless homeless stranded here: disabled vets, immigrants who were sold fake futures in the outer colonies, and all the civilians who became collateral damage. Droves of people still pass through here to be distributed where flesh is cheaper – and more desperate – than droids, but the ones left behind are usually too broken to move on. They huddle in corners and seek shelter in long-abandoned mech repair shops and ammo storage areas.

Kallie is one of the lucky ones. She has a home. It's no bigger than a three-by-three-meter cube, but it has basic water supply and insulation. It used to be an interfaith chapel, back during the war, but the chaplain has long been discharged – probably repurposed too, and dispatched to some mine. Now no one wants to live in it, because this part of the station has too much electromagnetic interference and there's no network signal. It didn't matter when it was a chapel, because the network silence was good for meditation and prayer. But now this silence makes people's minds wander to dark and scary places, bringing to the surface long-buried regret and guilt. No wonder there's a rumor around the station that it's haunted. Kallie doesn't care. She's used to her shades – it's less lonely this way, and Leutho's tinkering takes care of them, once they become overwhelming.

There's one now. The visage of a little girl, clutching a toy spaceship with one hand, and pointing toward a dark corner with the other. Kallie has seen her before, but never out here. Why now? That area has been picked clean. Then the shade dissipates, the pointing finger the last to go. What has Leutho's latest adjustment done?

Kallie checks the corner, and finds one of the wall panels slightly dislodged. She carefully pries away the corner of the panel to reveal the narrow space between cables and pipes beneath. A small backpack is stuffed in there. A child's backpack, made from sturdy cloth dyed in all the colors of the rainbow. Some unfortunate child hid it there, before being shipped off to Fates-know-where. Kallie gulps down the bitterness that lines her throat. She cannot help that child. She's nobody. But perhaps she can help her own child. Danae will need decent food and an education – she should be starting preschool soon. With her find clutched to her chest, Kallie flees to her chapel home.

*

Under the approving stare of the little girl's shade, Kallie examines her find. The backpack is filled with colorful clothes for a girl of about twelve, and a cheap drawing pad. The greatest treasure is hidden in the front pocket: paper – real paper, with a drawing on it. Kallie straightens the sheet. A crude drawing of a child between two adults, holding hands. A small house at the side, circled by trees, beneath a planet with a big red spot – clearly Jupiter. There are letters over the drawing, but Kallie cannot read them. After her brain got damaged during Danae's near-fatal birth, Kallie lost the ability to connect letters to words. Her understanding of numbers did return, eventually – counting with her fingers helped. But not the letters, no matter how much Madame Leutho tinkered with her implant. She told Kallie that sometimes neurons take their time to chart new paths in a damaged brain even with the implant's help, but it's been years. Kallie no longer hopes.

She sits a long time, gazing at the drawing, then gets up and walks to the alcove across her cot, where the chapel's sanctum once stood. She's placed an old plastic stool with broken and duct-taped legs there, and a faded printout of an infant atop it. Leutho had told her it was hours-old Danae. She'd probably lied about that too. Kallie doesn't care. That's the closest thing to a memory she has of her daughter. She cannot remember holding or breastfeeding her. The empty memories hurt more than Kallie's empty stomach ever will. But now her little one won't be alone; she'll have the memory of another child to keep her company. The ghostly girl smiles and vanishes.

With the printout and the drawing now in their rightful place, Kallie retires to her cot. Perhaps she'll keep some of the clothes – her frame is small enough. A steady diet of unflavored algae gruel every other day keeps people thin in body and resolve. She draws her itchy infantry blanket up to her nose and stares at her little shrine until her lids grow heavy.

*

When the station's rotation hits a certain angle, the whole of Jupiter shines over the station's observatory. With the covers retracted, everyone under the glass dome feels like they're standing in open space, watching the nearest moons and the planet's rings. Tourists flock to visit this wonder of human engineering – all while people like Kallie can still die during childbirth. But Kallie wills all grim thoughts aside. Here and now, she cannot believe how much she got paid for a child's meager belongings. Her fortune has the taste of a cinnamon algae smoothie and she's enjoying every mouthful of it.

The dome is brimming with people: tourists, military personnel on leave, station officers and clerks on their lunch breaks, and those lucky few from the Ruling Houses that have never had to work. No one sits on the bench beside Kallie. For a brief moment, she wonders if she smells; she hasn't been able to afford the communal shower for a while now, and wash-cloth cleaning only helps so much. But she doesn't care. She slurps more of her smoothie, and stretches out, almost spread-eagle on the bench, as if she could hug Jupiter. There are a few ships in view – mostly transports, and the occasional patrolling fighter doing lazy rounds around the station.

That's the wrong approach. They're going to crash into each other.

She sits up, her shoulders now stiff, her gaze fixed on a transport approaching the station. Where did that thought come from? What does she know about spaceships? And yet, there it is, the transport making a hard starboard turn to avoid a mining drone departing for Ganymede. A susurration spreads across the crowd under the dome, but dies down once the crisis is averted. People return to their own affairs – some of them a little disappointed, even. Kallie rubs at her forehead, probing a headache nesting just behind her eyes. Seeing shades is bad enough. She doesn't need auditory intrusions in her thoughts. Not today. Not ever.

She turns her gaze to the crowd. Singing and laughing attracts her attention near the center of the dome where communication terminals are set up. The commotion comes from what appears to be a newlywed couple and their friends. They kiss and laugh and toast each other, taking snapshots and recording messages for their loved ones, all with Jupiter as the background.

Loved ones. *How does that feel?* she wonders.

She feels a pang of overwhelming envy. Until it dawns on her: she *does* have a loved one. She has a daughter.

She races to the nearest terminal, while counting her remaining creds on her fingers. Her headache waxes to the size of Jupiter at the letters flashing on the terminal's screen. Thank the Fates, it has a voice recognition button. When the terminal asks her to choose, Kallie answers, 'Send a snapshot.' Then the screen changes to mirror, with a blinking checkmark button beneath it.

Her eyes mist anew as she attempts to make her hair presentable. What a fool she's been, thinking that her frizzy hair that not even the scarf can tame wouldn't stand out in a crowd with sleek, shiny hair. But it is what it is. That's who she is. So she wipes her sniffles on her sleeve and forces herself to smile.

'Danae, it's your mom. I love you, baby girl.'

Letters appear on the screen, and Kallie presses the button before the knot in her gut makes her abort this wild adventure and flee. That knot tightens when the terminal asks, 'Who is the recipient?'

'Danae,' Kallie manages. 'Here, on the station.'

A list of five appears on the screen, but Kallie cannot read the names. Only two have headshots, and they're adults.

Before she can ask for the terminal about their ages, the robotic voice asks, 'House?'

Leutho told her, didn't she? One of the smaller but decent Houses... what was it? Ah, yes!

'House Harpokrates,' she blurts out. Then adds, 'Six years old!'

But the terminal seems to have started processing her request before she spoke Danae's age. Then the credit sign appears on the screen in big red font.

'Three credits,' it says aloud.

There goes supper. Before her stomach can overrule her heart, Kallie slides her chip into the slot, never to see it again. A trilling sound follows.

'Message delivered.'

It's done. Danae might never get the message, if her adoptive parents delete it. Kallie isn't even sure if she's sent it to the right person, but how many people with that same, old-fashioned name can there be on this station? Surely, an older Danae in the same House will be compassionate enough to pass the message along? As a sob builds up in her throat, she hurries out of the observatory and back home.

She finds her home infested with shades.

Ghosts, shades, whatever these things are, have the substance of thin, luminous mist that Kallie can walk through. Almost like holograms, but they feel different – like languid waves of grief, sadness, and regret that slowly wane down to almost peace, like pieces of a puzzle finally clicking in place. Kallie settles on her cot to watch the unexpected gathering. There's that child again, playing with her toy spaceship in the corner. A little to the left, next to the tiny sink, an old man in an outdated military uniform tightens his combat boots. Several emaciated children are gathered around him – his wards or his victims? A dancing couple swirls by with fast steps and festive faces. And just over there, beside Kallie's cot, an old woman sits cross-legged and knits. No level of technological advancement can uproot certain habits from Earth's old-timers.

Kallie allows her mind to go numb at that faint clickety-clack of the needles. She hears them, just like she heard that voice in her head earlier, regarding the transport's trajectory. What had Leutho's fiddling done to her mind this time? But the sound brings her peace and, as she drifts away, she wishes that the granny could knit her new, functioning neurons.

*

She wakes up to the aftertaste of cinnamon, and her mind feels light. A tingling of apprehension remains at the base of her spine at her audacity to reach out to her betters, but she misses Danae so very much. Strange, how much one can miss someone they never knew. There's this gap between throat and heart that nothing can fill, and only the sound of Danae's name brings fleeting relief.

All the shades are gone. Her gaze seeks the drawing on her makeshift altar, secretly hoping that her dream came true, that the granny's ghost knitted her new neurons, and that she can now read.

She cannot. Her stomach grumbles, and she reaches for the clothes she wore yesterday. She'd like to keep them; she'd also like to eat and stay strong for her daughter. So she wraps them up and heads over to Madame Leutho's. The other pawn shop might give her more, but perhaps she might get another fix to get rid of those shades, like the one she finds awaiting her just outside the shop.

It's that damned trooper again, the one who's apparently too attached to his mech. He stares at her and brings his right index finger to his lips, warning her to be silent. At this moment, he looks exactly like the depictions of Harpokrates, the patron deity of the eponymous House. What kind of sign is this? What is her brain trying to tell her, now? Is it a warning? Kallie stops in her tracks. Perhaps she should turn around and take her business elsewhere. Or perhaps she should ignore the glitches of her broken brain. The trooper tilts his head just so, toward the entrance.

She draws a deep breath and slips into the shadows of the shop, keeping close to the high selves brimming with gadgets. A sudden noise further inside, like the slap of a hand against wood – the counter? Kallie ducks behind the mech armor a few paces away from the commotion. She crawls through the narrow space between armor and wall, and peeks from under the suit's armpit.

A tall, athletic woman, with her hair dyed in that red shade that the Mars-born favor and braided on her back, towers over Madame Leutho, who seems to have shrunk in her seat behind the counter. The woman wears blue and black – the colors of House Harpokrates – and holds a fold-out baton in a white-knuckled grip. There's a faint buzzing coming from the baton – is that some sort of a neural whip, like those the station's security guards carry?

'You swore you took care of her.'

The stranger's voice is perfectly steady, her words perfectly articulated, her tone perfectly cold. And yet it stirs a tempest in Kallie's gut like none she's ever felt.

Leutho raises her hands. 'Lady Danae, I did! I swear I did!'

Danae? *Danae*? Who is this woman who shares a name with her daughter? Then the slap of the baton against the counter makes Kallie's heart jump to her throat. A cockroach scurries past her and Kallie envies its size and ability to crawl through cracks and flee. She dares another look when this Danae speaks again.

'You swore the last time, too. I waived your debt to get rid of Kallista's body!'

Kallie, still hidden, feels the knot building up in the pit of her stomach. *Kallista? Who's Kallista?*

'A *dead* body. She wasn't dead.'

A scoff. 'And? She was close enough. You didn't have to patch the hole in her head with a fucking implant! Tell me you didn't use a military-issued implant, you idiot!'

Leutho shakes her head. 'No, that's a first-generation implant. There are a few of them still around. I don't even know what it does – I only know how to reset it to its default settings, every time it glitches. And I did, over and over again, so Kallista would stay compliant. Forgive me, my lady, I would have disposed of her corpse, but I cannot take a life. I cannot go against my oath to do no harm. I thought—'

'You thought?' Another slap against the counter. '*You thought?*'

'Lady Danae, I can still salvage this.'

'How? She's looking for me!'

'Not you, my lady. Her *daughter*. When Kallista came to, she kept calling your name. She wouldn't drop it. She only screamed louder. I had to tell her *something.*'

'And you told her she had a daughter? Are you sure you don't need an implant yourself? Because you sound senile to me. How could this *not* backfire, you idiot?'

Leutho shrinks even deeper into her chair. 'It made sense, at the time...'

You told her she had a daughter.

In the still moment between one heartbeat and the next, the sum of Kallie's parts crumbles. Her heart, her mind, her grumbling stomach, the rising sobs in her throat, everything she is and everything she's hoped to be scatter around her. No daughter. No daughter. *No daughter?* No. It cannot be. No one is so cruel as to lie like this. Why?

Those dots do not connect. They have to.

Connect, dammit!

She hits her head with her fist, just like Leutho often smacks her terminal when it glitches. She hits herself again and again, aiming to stir her lazy brain, to wake up her faulty implant, to cause the world to make sense again. But her fists are small, and she's weak from hunger. She plucks a loose screw from the mech's armpit and picks at her implant with the screw's blunt, magnetic tip. Perhaps she should start banging her head against the wall? But then they'll hear, and they'll know she's there, and they'll know she's heard, and they have a neural whip and will hurt her, and she cannot take pain, and...

The burst of light inside her head robs her of breath. Her sore fists drop to her sides. The screw slips from her grip and rolls into the shadows. Something just clicked in her implant. Not a real, audible click. This click she feels in her bones, like the persistent tingling at the nape of her neck, harbinger of motion somewhere deep. *Upgrade or reboot?* She blinks the bright spots away. When she can see clearly again, when the ringing has waned in her ears, the other two are still quarreling. She doesn't know what about; she can only watch the ghostly trooper slowly disintegrating in a loose swirl of translucent fireflies. It floats just before her face for a moment, then it's siphoned through her implant and into her head.

The surge of energy lights every neuron in her body aflame. No, not a surge – *awakening*. Her entire body bursts with countless pinpricks. Like her arm after she's slept on it and it's gone numb, and the restored blood flow slowly and painfully brings it back to life. Only this time it's every muscle, every tendon, every joint that begins to remember its sense of self-preservation. And all of them stretch and flex and ache and urge her to flee.

Run now to fight later on your own terms.

Kallie dares a last glance. Danae – *now that name hurts!* – looms over Leutho, who's sunk in her chair, pale and sweaty. They no longer shout, but Danae's whispers scare Kallie more than her screaming did. Kallie crawls away as noiselessly as possible. She thinks she hears someone calling her name as she bolts, and hopes they don't notice her faltering step. Then she starts running, and does not stop until she is back home.

Home. Her ghost-infested hole-in-the-wall. The forsaken chapel, where no one else has wanted to live. Her shades are still there, but they no longer float around her. They stand still, as if waiting. Kallie thinks she understands now. They're nothing but echoes, projections of things and people long gone that her implant generated, to help her remember who she was.

The echoes of her broken mind.

A deep breath, a long exhalation. Kallie invites them in, and her implant becomes a doorway for her lost pieces on their way home.

The little girl playing with the starship is the first to return, and Kallie almost doubles over with grief. Where had her childhood gone? Her early years back on Earth, her careless days on an island of the old country, dreaming of flying to the stars? Her grandma warned her, didn't she? Yaya Evdokia warned little Kallista not to aim to rise above her station. Her place was dirtside, hauling ghost-nets with her brothers out from the depths of the Aegean, in the recycling plant with her mother, or ministering to the orphans alongside her aunts and grandma. *You care too deeply for others, child,* Yaya told her. *The stars are not for you. Space will devour you, piece by piece, until there's nothing clean left in you to bait a single fishing line.*

But Kallista hadn't listened, had she?

Then the dancers return home and the fire in her mind sets her heart aflame too. *Danae*. The name that sinks hooks and grapples onto her throat, threatening to pull her heart out through her mouth if she dares to speak it now. *Danae* – Mars-born Danae of House Harpokrates, Danae with the slender bones and the soft skin of those who haven't had to haul plastic from the depths of the Aegean... Danae, who had chosen *her*, little dirt-born Kallista. Had their love been a lie? Was the effortless silence during the small hours of the night, when their bodies coiled together, a deception? Were their plans for a life together just sweet little nothings to fill the void between one deception and the next?

Nothing more straightforward than a shot to the head. And Danae had pulled the trigger.

Kallie remembers now. The dots finally connect, when the ghostly vet salutes her and begins his pained march back inside her head. He's both her honor and her fall from grace, as his host of ethereal children remind her. They regard her with eyes the color of space vacuum, as they drag their sore-covered feet behind him. Her victims of another kind: the children she's failed to save, once she discovered what House Harpokrates was up to. How many families have they deceived into thinking they've bought a slice of the Promised Land on the Belt, only to have them shipped off to their hard labor camps? They can call them agro colonies and mining expeditions all they want. How could Danae think that Kallie would agree to be a part of *that*?

She blinks tears away, and her gaze falls on the old woman knitting by her cot. Kallie knows her by the craftwork in her gnarled hands: that's Kallie's implant. It has indeed been weaving new neurons in her brain. The spectral grandma flashes Kallie a toothless smile, and lets her knitting rest on her lap. It's an Arachne Weave implant, originally used to treat patients with degenerative neurological ailments. The treatment included teaching them simple repetitive crafts, like knitting, crocheting, and embroidery. After one reset and an electrical jolt too many from Leutho's hands, disabled sections of the implant were now enabled in a configuration never used before. Had it woven itself into something new – something unheard of? Kallie catches a glimpse of its new function when the grandma begins another craft: spinning thread from a distaff onto a spindle, occasionally pausing to measure its length. Kallie is certain she spots a pair of scissors on grandma's apron before her echo dissolves in the gloom, the toothless grin now mirthless and unforgiving.

Kallie dares a glance at her makeshift altar of paper, plastic, and duct-tape. Now she can read the writing: *My Dads and I, and our new home on Jupiter's moons.*

Kallie gulps down her sobs. Where did that poor family end up? Is it too late to track them down? And if she does, how can she help them, the destitute nobody she has become? Her unfinished business on the station will follow her everywhere she'll go, and she'll only endanger innocent people by association.

No. Here, tonight, she will make her stand, in this forsaken chapel of neglectful deities and unforgiving Fates.

Kallie holds on to the hope that Danae will come alone. She doubts that Danae has told anyone about the skeleton in her closet – Kallie's own stubborn, not-yet-dead skeleton. Not that it matters much – Kallie isn't up to fighting anyone, as weak and malnourished as the past six years have left her. She doubts she can talk her way out of it either – the implant is still rearranging neurons in her head, and Danae comes from a House of diplomats and politicians. No, she has to find another way. But she won't run. And she won't hide.

In the gloom of her now-empty home, the lone light over the alcove illuminates her two icons: the printout of the infant, her *daughter-who-never-was*, and the drawing made by the lost child, her *daughter-of-Nemesis-awakening*. Kallie picks both up and sits on the plastic stool. The stool creaks but doesn't collapse, and Kallie sits with her back rigid, facing the entrance. May her pain become her shield and her vengeance. Neither justice nor mercy shall be found here tonight. Only the wrath of a Fury.

When Danae arrives, she slips inside like the gliding shades of Kallie's mind, and sets her blood aflame – like a living, breathing shade of lost love and betrayal. But no mere shade could ever stir such yearning. Danae tilts her head, her eyes scanning the surroundings – the dust-covered floor, the bare walls, the cot with the threadbare blanket, until it comes to rest on the light that's shaped like a votive candle over Kallie's head.

'How... quaint,' Danae says with that little smug smile. 'You've returned to your dirt-born roots, I see.' Then she looks right at Kallie. 'You remember.' Not a question. Danae's own implant prods its cheap sister in Kallie's head. It doesn't breach its newly enabled firewalls, but it tells her as much.

Then Danae tilts her head just so, and Kallie struggles to avert her eyes from the curve of Danae's neck. How she longs to bury her face in that fiery hair and rest her head, at last... But she cannot. This Danae is a stranger.

Kallie inhales deeply. 'Did you kill Leutho?'

'Why do you care? She exploited you for years.' Then Danae shrugs. 'No. She understands her place now. And she can be useful.' She keeps her right hand in the shadows just behind her hip, and Kallie's sure her neural whip is charged and ready. 'But you, Kallista, *love*, you never learned your place.'

'I thought it was by your side,' Kallie blurts out, before she can control the bitterness that seeps into her voice.

'No, your place was in my bed. I see now when things started to go wrong.' Danae glances at her wristband, before her eyes dart about – she's probably just realized there's no network connection in here.

'Things started to go wrong when your House decided to profit from the suffering of innocents.' Kallie shoves her icons in her undershirt. 'You couldn't possibly have thought that I'd go along with it?' Kallie's implant attempts a cautious nudge at Danae's. It shouldn't be doing that. Those early models didn't have short-range wi-fi enabled. How deeply had Leutho's tinkering reached?

'No, I thought you smart enough to keep your mouth shut. Or at least that your love was strong enough to overcome all those radical ideas your dirt-side days planted in your pretty head.' Danae sighs. 'A pity, really, Kallista. Of all my lovers, you were the one with the most potential. I could almost see a future with you, if you hadn't been so headstrong.'

'And your solution was a shot to the head.' Danae's implant prompts Kallie for a password to enable the pairing. *What fucking password?*

Kallie stands, and Danae takes a step backward, measuring Kallie from unkempt hair to worn sneakers. She can't possibly consider Kallie a threat – her implant is an up-to-date model, and Kallie's too weak to overpower her, even without the neural whip.

'Your head proved to be quite thick. And infantry surgeons are such saps for saving those injured within an inch of their lives. Oh well. Live and learn.'

Kallie takes a step forward. It hurts. But she will no longer walk with the obedient hunch six miserable years cemented into her spine. Inside her head, she hears the familiar clickety-clack of knitting, and another prompt for a password.

Danae meets her gaze. 'Leutho patched you up well enough, I see. So...' She taps her temple. 'What does it do?'

Password?

Another step forward. Danae holds her ground.

Fragments of a long-lost memory resurface in Kallie's mind. *Static in the air. Distant thunder. An ancient, volcanic island. Mugs of hot chocolate behind thick glass windows, watching the approaching storm over the Aegean. Danae curled beside her, cursing at the connection failure to her House's neural network. Her password denied, again and again. Password reset.* And now, Kallie remembers.

Kallie knows. And smiles. 'Are you scared that it's a sarcomancer implant, and I'll rip your heart out through your nostrils? Or perhaps an assassin enhancement?'

'If you kill me, you won't get far. When you didn't report for duty and no corpse turned up, you were logged as a deserter. Unless you can come up with enough creds to be smuggled out, your biometrics will alert Command to apprehend you the moment you step on a transport.' Danae's voice quivers a little. Fear?

Good.

Kallie chuckles. 'Oh, relax. It's an Arachne Weave. It taught me knitting.' Ah, there's that clickety-clack again. *Password?*

Danae's eyes widen. She grins.

Another step closer. 'And weaving.' Now Kallie hears the *woosh* of a shuttle through the threads of a loom. 'Let me go, for old times' sake. I'm no longer a threat to you.'

Danae licks her lips. Before she can deny Kallie's plea, Kallie is upon her, and takes Danae's face in both her hands.

'Remember *Santorini*?'

Password accepted.

Danae nods, just before her implant sends Kallie the request for the final authorization step: the memory embedded in that single word. And while Kallie's mind cannot be certain, her body remembers that one kiss against the approaching storm over the caldera, a rare moment of affection instead of conquest and surrender. Lips against lips, warmth and longing and the aftertaste of strong coffee, of countless lazy mornings with breakfast in bed. Danae cups Kallie's hand with hers. For one breathless moment they linger, caught in their before and their now and their never-after, in one tangled tapestry of affection and regret and opposing loyalties. When Danae tries to pull away, Kallie holds her firm. Her implant now has full authorization, and breaches firewall after firewall.

Danae's mind unfolds before Kallie like a multicolored tapestry. Like the fingers of another Penelope, Kallie's implant begins the unraveling. It disables sectors, deletes memories, and overrides protocols. No more access to all the languages she speaks. No more secrets, no more deceptions, no more manipulation and taunting. There goes the account of their brief time together, and the taste of their first kiss. The onslaught stops only when it reaches the core functions; disabling more would be an affront to the Fates themselves, for she alone can sever the final thread. Kallie pulls away, breathless and spent.

Then the Arachne Weave begins another sort of craft. It knits miniature trojan horses from ones and zeros, little gifts Danae's implant will bear to her House's network once she's connected again. In the stillness of Kallie's home, they gather in every crack and crevice of Danae's neural pathways, awaiting orders – awaiting release.

Danae blinks, her eyes vacant, her knees weak. Kallie helps her down to the floor, and kneels beside her. There's no hate, no anger in those eyes now, only confused sadness. Then Danae starts glancing about, almost panicking.

'Kallista? *Kallista*!'

'Easy,' Kallie tells her, her voice soft. 'Who's Kallista?'

A blank stare.

'A friend? A sister? Or perhaps… a daughter?' Kallie holds up the baby's photo. 'You dropped this. Is this Kallista?'

Eyes darting about. Confusion. Then a nod. 'Kallista?'

'I'll help you find her.'

Kallie needs Danae's thumbprint to withdraw enough creds. To get off the damned station and to where she needs to go. Danae can go on and infect the rest of her House, and destroy them from within, while mourning the daughter she never had. May Danae mourn that daughter to the end of her days and, by proxy, mourn every child her House has condemned.

The lost child's drawing now nests by Kallie's heart. In her mind, the visages of those she failed to save settle down. And they wait.

The child Kallie never bore is now legion. And she'll be an avenging mother to them all.

Have Your #Hugot Harvested at This Diwata-Owned Café

Vida Cruz-Borja

The Philippines

We started with a watermelon, and now we get a chance to tour some very… *special* eateries in this marvellously entertaining story from Vida Cruz-Borja. This is another story my friend Yi-Sheng recommended – and I'm so glad that he did!

Have Your #Hugot Harvested at This Diwata-Owned Café
by Ma. Rosario P. Herrera, the *Archipelago Daily*

As one of Quezon City's two Restaurant Rows, Maginhawa Street is the ideal place to find eclectic little cafés and one-of-a-kind restaurants to satiate the adventurous foodie in you. Yet for all of Maginhawa's variety, it has never had an establishment that either serves mythic food or that is run by mythics or both.

For six months only, Maria Makiling's pop-up café will change that.

But why should the average Manila foodie come to the diwata's café, when there are so many other choices? Why should anyone try the café's simple but delicious Filipino–Spanish hybrid cuisine, when historically, humans have been unable to stomach mythic food without physical, psychological, moral, or magical consequences?

Simple.

Maria's prized top-notch ingredient – the one that allows humans to digest the food at all – is human heartbreak. And she is currently accepting applications from those willing to have theirs harvested.

*

Eating one's feelings

Heartbreak Café, which opened just yesterday, has the warmth of a grandmother's provincial house and the liveliness of a nineteenth-century dinner party. Here, it is a perennial windy day in January.

The café specializes in what customers are beginning to call 'breakup food'. These affordable dishes are prepared by eager Hotel and Restaurant Management interns and cheerful kibaan in a large, sultry spice kitchen.

There are hearty soups such as munggo soup, bulalo with bone marrow, sopa de ajo, sopa de marisco, and fabada de asturia. There are household favorites such as an almost gelatinous nilagang baka and sinigang of the baboy, hipon, and bangus varieties, because 'people need to down something thicker than their broken bonds', according to the snarky menu.

There are also whole bilaos of seafood paella and paella negra on offer. There is also a variety of pork dishes, such as lechong kawali, liempo, inihaw, callos, dinuguan, sisig, and crispy pata, all served on banana leaves with a helping of garlic rice and mangoes – you'll even be given a cleaving knife for that extra helping of catharsis if you request it. After all, the menu states that these are recommended for 'those who would like a visceral representation of body and blood'.

Surprisingly, among the bestsellers number the merienda snacks: champorado, churros with piping hot chocolate, and an amazingly balanced, bittersweet tablea.

However, while one would think that the dishes help people purge themselves of feelings of loss, the opposite is true: eating the food induces momentary feelings of bereavement, sadness, and anger. Yet people can't seem to get enough.

'I went from imagining my ex as the lechon to imagining that it was my best friend, after getting shot by the Americans,' said Anton, a law student. 'Which doesn't make sense because my grandparents were just babies when the Americans took over! It was kinda jarring, but it also made me think about the bigger picture, if that makes sense.

'That was the best lechon I've ever had,' he added. 'The meat easily slid off the bones, and the fat melted in my mouth. This urge to beg my ex to take me back melted, too.'

'*Kakaiba 'yung tablea na 'yon*,' said Nilda, a call center agent. '*Pagkahigop ko, bigla kong naalala ang anak kong namatay – pero wala akong anak! Nawala naman agad yung lasa, tapos ninamnam ko na 'yung tablea*.' ('That tablea is something else. One sip, and I suddenly remembered my dead child – but I don't have any kids! The taste went away immediately, and I savored the tablea.')

*

Human and mythic divides

The café is located at the very end of the aptly named Mahiwaga Street – which suddenly appeared one day, branching from Maginhawa as if it had always been there – away from the glitter and the faddish restaurants. Mahiwaga is flanked by a thick fringe of blossom-heavy fire trees. All who pass this street see alluring Santelmos or hear tinkling music wafting down the road.

The café itself is a cozy Spanish-colonial-era-style house; above the stained-glass front door is a gilded sign in both the Baybayin and Latin alphabets. The Baybayin writing reads *Ang Karihan ni Mariang Makiling, Para sa Mga Pusong Wasak.*

The café is democratic in terms of patrons – with the exception of the kinari, whose penchant for feeding on any humans foolish enough to break their hearts earned them a lifetime ban. (Kinari representatives disgruntledly declined to comment.)

Two long lines snake toward the place: one of humans, and one of mythics. The former eye the latter warily, while some of the latter eye the former hungrily. Fights would have broken out already, were it not for the enthusiastic white-shirted student workers – both human and mythic – who work tirelessly to police the lines for trouble.

Jomar Poblete, a junior studying Mythic Relations at the University of the Philippines, is one of them. '*Maliban sa buwan-buwang suweldo, binabayaran ng diwata ang tuition namin, komyut, at saka na rin 'yung board at lodging ng mga taga-probinsya,*' he said. '*At nag-iintern ako sa may kinalaman sa course ko!*' ('Apart from a monthly salary, the diwata pays for our tuition, commute, and the board and lodging of those from the provinces. And I get to intern at something related to my course!')

When asked about what wages or compensation the mythics get for their services, an exceedingly handsome tamawo grinned widely and said, '*Unang makatilaw sa pagkaon, siyempre!*' ('First dibs on the food, of course!')

*

Heartbreak harvest

The human line is further divided into two: the customers and the applicants. The applicants are led into a warmly colored waiting room, where they must answer a seemingly random survey. The questions range from what they ate during their last meal to a request to describe their earliest remembered dream. Lastly, they will have an interview with Maria Makiling herself, who will then perform the mysterious harvest rite.

Sometimes, lucky applicants get pulled from the line and served first. One of these was eighty-seven-year-old Eugenia Castillo. Her son Benjamin, twenty-one when she last saw him in the 1970s, was one of martial law's thousands of desaparecidos. It's his picture that she carried into Maria's office.

'*Hindi pa rin humuhupa ang kirot,*' she said. '*Hindi ko malilimutan ang anak ko, pero gusto kong magpahinga sa kakarinig ng boses niya sa mga panaginip ko gabi-gabi.*' ('The pain hasn't receded. I will never forget my son, but I want to take a break from hearing his voice in my dreams every night.')

Another lucky applicant was Ingrid Dimasalang, forty-five. Ten months ago, her teenaged son and husband – casualties of the drug war – were shot by masked men on motorcycles while walking home from an evening trip to the sari-sari store. Ingrid's daughter Mara got away, but can no longer see out of her right eye.

Dimasalang insists that her husband, a former pusher, surrendered to their barangay, and that her son used to scold his father because of his line of work.

'*Gusto ko lang na mawala yung hinanakit ko,*' she explained. ''*Binoto ko'yung presidente natin. Naniniwala ako sa kanya. Pero bakit nangyari 'to sa pamilya ko?*' ('I just want the pain to go away. I voted for our president. I believe in him. But why did this happen to my family?')

'We get more and more of the likes of Ingrid these days,' Maria Makiling explained. 'The figure is somewhere in the hundreds. I think more would come, if they had the means, and if they were so inclined to stop grieving.'

Notably, the current Fearless Leader is a supporter of the former dictator's son, who aspires to the vice-presidency of the Philippines.

Surprisingly, representatives for the Supreme Leader could not be reached for comment, although the administration's official social media account cited a press release that stated that 'the diwata should meet with the president before she listens to the unfounded claims of those who slander his character and accomplishments with fake news'.

Department of Mythic Affairs Secretary Virgilio Braganza, successor to the much-beloved Dr. Nadia Pilapil-Quiroz, has yet to pay the courtesy call expected of government officials to mythic events and businesses.

*

Forgetfulness and empathy

One may wonder why a diwata – and one of Maria Makiling's caliber, no less – would need to open a café, when money is nothing to her. Then again, this is the diwata who could have brought down Mt. Makiling on those who continue to fell the trees of Laguna, the very same diwata who made headlines when, like a common human youth reaching for a bright future, she pursued degrees in Sociology, Anthropology, and Business Administration from UP Los Baños and then graduated magna cum laude along with the class of 2016. There are few who can carry the contradictions of power and struggle as she can. In light of those facts, wondering about why she'd want to do something as human as open a café is futile; the diwata knows what she wants and she goes after it like a woman on a mission.

And part of her mission, it seems, is social justice. Indeed, none of the café's revenue goes back to the diwata – some of it is used to pay for the needs of her student workers, some of it is used to buy ingredients, and the rest is given to the families of martial law and drug war victims.

It is the last type of recipient of the café's revenue that hints at a deeper reason behind Heartbreak Café's origin.

'Do you know, on the day that a certain thief was re-buried at the Libingan ng Mga Bayani, and people rallied in support of the presidential approval to situate him among war heroes, I was so enraged that Laguna de Bay boiled,' said Maria. 'I know that humans have the memory retention of a sieve, but forgetting how that man tortured and killed tens of thousands of you is a new low, even for your kind.

'I would rather not get involved with humanity, as I've been burned before,' Maria continued, referring to three of her famous affairs with human men, hundreds of years ago. 'But – though many of my brethren will not admit it – humankind's affairs have the power to affect even us mythics.

'Many of you refuse to remember, but the last time we did not interfere, you elected Macoy – several times! – and he tried to swindle our lands from us, for his accursed dam and infrastructure projects and his treasure-hunting antics,' Maria said. 'And when that did not work, he sent specially trained soldiers to wage a war that left many of us homeless to this day. So, whenever I am asked if we should leave the humans to their own devices, I always say, "Never again!"'

'If we were to continue down the path of humans and

mythics having no empathy for each other – and you humans for one another – then I will be having this conversation again, with another young reporter, a generation from now. What my café does is take the burden of experience from those who find it too heavy to bear, and give those who have no idea what it's like – and who are perhaps too quick to judge – a little taste of it,' she added.

'You humans have that saying about walking a mile in another's shoes. I am simply showing you what would happen if you had a glimpse into another's experience. I extend an open invitation in particular to Macoy's apologists and Digong fanatics,' she finished.

It was Maria who cursed a certain former dictator – whom this newspaper would not allow me to name, for fear of a libel case – with lupus. During the 1986 People Power Revolution, Maria entered Malacañang Palace, flanked only by a pair of kapre guards, soon after He-Who-Plundered-Billions-of-Taxpayers'-Money's famous call to US senator Paul Laxalt. It was reported that The-Man-Who-Would-Not-Be-Moved would have stayed in Manila despite Laxalt's advice, had Maria not issued the dictator an ultimatum: 'Choose. You die now, or you leave forever.'

The diwata also added that one of the conditions was that she spare his monstrous brood, which she agreed to. 'In hindsight,' she said, in a voice more bitter than her tablea, 'I should have cursed them, too.'

When asked if she also cursed the former First Lady, the Diwata responded with a beatific smile. 'Do you know why she dolls herself up like a big-haired clown? It's because, whenever she looks in the mirror, she sees a bruja of exceeding ugliness. Everything she does, everything she buys, is in pursuit of a beauty she will never find.'

Representatives for the Family-of-Thieves declined to comment.

*

The consequences of moving on and letting go

The café's existence is not without strong opposition, which is why it will be open for only six months. The group most opposed to the café seems to be its neighbors, the restaurants of Maginhawa.

'*Siyempre madaming customers yung Heartbreak I na 'yan*,' said Onyok Pagulayan, owner of the Nepalese restaurant Khanuhos. '*Minamagic 'atang diwata 'yung pagkain, para di maka-move on!*' ('Of course Heartbreak Café has many customers. The diwata probably enchants the food, so that people can't move on from it!')

Psychologists are also opposed to the café – specifically, Maria's method of extracting heartbreak.

'I'm sure that the diwata means well,' said Dr. Amelita Narciso, president of the Psychiatry Society of the Philippines. 'But taking people's heartbreak means that they do not go through the customary stages of grieving. Grieving is important, because it allows for the release of pent-up energy that was originally tied to the lost person, object, or place.

'When people do not express their grief, it can manifest in many physical symptoms, such as skin problems, lowered immunity, and irregular heartbeat. Psychological symptoms include depression and anxiety,' she added. 'We could be seeing a rise in people with all these health concerns.'

The Catholic Church also condemns the café's actions, if not its existence. The Conference of Catholic Priests of the Philippines has stated, in an official press release, that 'while we commend the sentiments of the diwata Mariang Makiling and her upholding of human rights, we do not condone the ensorcellment of innocent people. Such actions may turn the people away from the Christian God, toward the worship of the pagan gods of old.'

Finally, perhaps the most surprising opponents to the café are a subset of drug war and martial law victims' families.

'*Kahit ano pa ang sabihin ng diwata, malilimutan namin ang aming mga mahal sa buhay na naging biktima ng karahasan kung ibigay namin ang aming mga hinanakit para sa pagkain niya,*' said Arnulfo Enriquez, whose wife Marilyn was a victim of a drive-by shooting three months ago. ('No matter what the diwata says, we will forget our loved ones who were victims of violence if we give our heartaches for her food.')

'*Pag ni-let go ko ang alaala ng tito ko, paano siya mabibigyan ng hustisya? At para lang sa pagkain?*' asked Nazario Lantin, whose uncle has been a desaparecido since the day the former dictator declared martial law in 1972. To this day, there have been no leads as to where his body may lie. ('If I let go of my uncle's memory, how will he be given justice? And all because of mere food?')

Dr. Tanya delos Reyes, a professor of Psychology at the Ateneo de Manila University, had a sister whom she never saw again, after the latter joined the rebels in the mountains in the 1980s. She had only this to say: 'My grief is not a show that I should perform for strangers!'

For all the good it will do, a signature campaign calling for the dismantling of Heartbreak Café is making the rounds on social media. As of press time, it has 762 signatures.

But despite all the sound and fury against Heartbreak Café, the lady of Mt. Makiling remains unruffled.

'You humans always jump the gun,' she said, with a resigned

shake of her head. 'So afraid of what you don't understand, so afraid of change. I know six months isn't enough time to let the lessons you should've learned long ago sink into your thick heads, yet I also cannot risk fomenting riots. So right now, my plans for the café beyond six months are still hazy. But in time, it will come back in some form or another, and I'm sure you will all see that I am right.'

Maria Makiling's Heartbreak Café is open 24/7 at 1 Mahiwaga Street, Sikatuna Village, Quezon City. Price range is P100 to P450. Visit their website for more details.

Order C345

Sheikha Helawy

Palestine

My friend Shimon Adaf introduced me to Sheikha, a Bedouin author who writes short, punchy stories that pack a world of meaning into every line. Luckily for us, some of her work tends to the fantastical, and I loved this one in particular. I hope you do too. This story is translated by Raphael Cohen.

'Order no. C345 still needs a few finishing touches. I only need one night and I'll be done with it. I'm asking you please.'

He flicked his gaze between her and the client sitting at the other end of the room. Her skill at the job and her perfectionism had caused delay to orders and complaints from clients, whose lives on two amputated legs were literally at a standstill, and would remain so as they waited for the right prosthetic limbs.

He leaned towards her and whispered, 'No, no, I'm asking you please! The client's been waiting a month and I won't permit any further delay. It's not up for discussion.'

She acquiesced to the factory foreman.

In her corner of the fitting (pre-delivery) department she found a brief note sticking out of a disorganized pile of limbs:

I've replaced your missing dancer with another that I think will suit your performance better. Give him a try (Order

*no. C143, on shelf no. 16). I hope you find his performance
satisfactory.*
Lovingly yours

The short note was enough to fluster her. Somebody knew
her secret, perhaps knew more than her and more than needed,
enough to find a replacement for a dancer she relied on a great
deal. Did this mean that he also knew about her bewilderment
without having expressed it openly?

She had been uncertain about how to deal with the last
dancer, but had not considered replacing him due to lack of
time. The performance was in two weeks, and all the orders
would have been delivered to clients within the week. She
deferred all her questions; she didn't have time right now to
worry about a partner who'd imposed himself on her. There
wasn't time as long as the performance remained her most
important project.

At six in the evening, all the workers left the factory. The last
to leave was the deaf kid in charge of the delivery department.
He locked all the doors and left too. An hour later she crept
back into the factory, as she had done for the past two months,
through the back door, using a key she had copied by stealth
from the deaf kid.

'Come on, you lazy bunch, there's no time for sleeping. A
new dancer is going to join us on the recommendation of an
anonymous friend. I hope he's up to dancing with you.'

She took down box no. C143 and took out her new dancer.
She ran an eye over the accompanying details and nodded her
head in satisfaction.

'Let's see the learner's dancing abilities then.'

She turned on the record player. The participants lined up
in their agreed places, and, without any intervention from her,

the new dancer stepped forwards and took his place among them. She gave the sign to begin and stood watching them from a corner of the room. Her heartbeat quickened as for the first time in two months she witnessed an awesome dance performance. It was as if the new participant had instilled them with a new spirit, lively and free. Such coordinated movements, such lightness, such precision in the swift, smooth transitions to the music!

She dismantled her legs and clutched them. Seated on the stumps of her limbs, she cried as she had not cried for years. 'Legs, what do you say? Are you proud of the body and head you support? Wasn't all that suffering worth it? To bear my pain and my hatred and resentment towards you. How could I love you when you were an ugly scar over the emptiness? I know that I hurt you a lot over the years. I know how many times you would have loved to jump out of the window and leave me miserable and alone. What do you say now? It's time for us to make up with each other to the Dance of the Phoenix.'

Next morning, and with two loved legs, she had to post twenty invitations signed by a made-up charity:

> Dear Sir/Madam owner of a new pair of legs,
>   You are invited to a celebration of your becoming a member of the First Step Club.
>   There will not be boring speeches by officials. We are going to laugh, walk, sing, and watch an artistic performance, and perhaps dance ourselves, who knows?
> We love you
> First Step Club

The invitations would reach the addresses of those invited. Some would throw them out of the window and others would accept the invitation. They would come to the park, whose opening celebration was underway.

They were spread around among the empty chairs as, from afar, she watched the puzzlement in their eyes and the misery on their faces. Before the audience had fully assembled to hear some words of welcome, she turned on the record player. The sound drowned out all other sounds and drew ears and faces towards the middle of the park.

Legs twitched under bodies, then stood up with their astonished owners and made towards the open space.

They all took their positions and the limbs began to dance with grace and energy, at every note animating half-dead bodies of flesh with life like the rush of water in an ancient desert. The other limbs synchronized, hands were held, and eyes laughed.

The performance ended with loud applause and a bow of gratitude to an unknown soldier.

The notes among the pile of stiff limbs did not stop:

> *It was a wonderful performance. I'm proud of you.*
> *I know. I could see it in your eyes. You were there.*
> *I was, and I was delighted by the Dance of the*
>   *Phoenix and by you.*
> *What do you think about Longing as a title for our*
>   *next performance?*
> *Our performance? Let's meet and think about it*
>   *tomorrow morning. I know how much you like*
>   *coffee.*
> *And I know how you listen to music.*

That was the last note.

Translated from the Arabic by Raphael Cohen

Dark Star

Vraiux Dorós

Mexico

Who is Vraiux Dorós? What is 'Dark Star'? And what does it *mean*?
All I can tell you is that I was blown away when I came across this
– story? poem? revelation? – and I hope you have the same reaction.
Also, what's with the *rabbits*? This story is translated by Toshiya
Kamei, who I first met (if only virtually) when I was putting together
Volume 1. Toshiya translates from both Japanese and Spanish into
English, and it is thanks to them and other dedicated translators that
we get great stories like this one.

1. Good and evil exist in the galaxy – just as various kinds of
   apes and plants exist on the planet.
2. No poets are found at the bottom of the sea – only
   photovoltaic creatures and ghostly landscapes.
3. Flesh Gore is a cyborg text, quite possibly the last of its
   kind.
4. A cyborg text, by definition, is a telepathic entity that
   induces textual hallucinations.

*

1. Evil is more prevalent than good in the galaxy – just as
   there are good apes and evil ones, and medicinal plants and
   poisonous ones on the planet.
2. Poetry is scarce at the bottom of the sea, and the landscape
   is bleak, metallic gray, and cold.

3. Flesh Gore is a legendary galactic pirate, the bravest privateer who's crossed my path.

4. To gain a better understanding of a cyborg text, *The Laws of Cosmogonic Fiction* and *The First-Day Transcendental Narratology* are must-reads.

*

1. Enough good guys exist in the galaxy to deal with evildoers, just as enough plants grow on the planet to feed apes.

2. At the bottom of the sea, poetry sometimes sprouts as an upward blast of lava straight from the core.

3. Flesh Gore, father of the First-Day Transcendental Narratology, has vanished without a trace.

4. The Laws of Cosmogonic Fiction come in three.

*

a. Fiction is friction.

b. Imagination is round.

c. The cosmos is metafiction.

*

1. The good guys have lost in the galaxy, but the evildoers haven't won, just as apes on the planet have discovered fire.

2. At the bottom of the sea, poetry appears and disappears, and some giant clams traverse infinite space in infinite time as if they were responsible for the devastation around them.

3. Flesh Gore, leader of the textual resistance, commandeers the Ecumenical Anti-System Army.

4. It all started when a meteor crossed the atmosphere, destroying our telecommunications systems.

*

a. Friction is the natural resistance of a body against the doubling of textual dimensions.
b. Imagination has no end. It stems from ecumenical intuition processed by a random system of language sequences.
c. The cosmos is the last frontier, the possibility of Esperanto.

*

1. In the galaxy, there are forces going against light – just as on the planet some gods are associated with weather phenomena.
2. At the bottom of the sea, poetry occasionally reveals itself as a vibration from the surface that runs through the baroque landscape with its phantom whip.
3. Flesh Gore, also known as Roldán-Epicurus, invented the textual-world machine.
4. We landed with difficulties. At first glance, the place seemed uninhabited.

*

The textual-world machine converts an entity's imagination into an editable telepathic emulsion, either in small formats (printed media) or in potent energy capsules.

*

1. More the Merciless, crux destroyer, telepathic mule, rules the galaxy, just as the palindromes reign over the reversible numbers on the planet.

2. At the bottom of the sea, poetry has sightless eyes that convert light into abstract language codes.

3. Flesh Gore, an iconic sci-fi entity, has argued that Morel's invention is merely an allegory of the transhistorical struggle of certain fictional forces for control and dominance of the sense of reality as a textual exception, not an exegesis of textual processes within a broad field of cosmogonic hermeneutics.

4. The adaptation of a work through non-textual techniques entails the creation of reminiscent perspective models that condense the flow of the alienated fictional field.

*

a. According to reception theory, it's possible to transcend fiction by transposing the horizon as a possible reality and reality as a non-method-confined textual space.

b. Imagination runs away with the acceleration of light.

c. The cosmos is a moment of revelation and understanding of complex textual processes.

*

1. As an exegetical textual dimension, the galaxy isn't a utopia but an anagoge, as the history of the planet resembles an epic poem rather than a cartoon series.

2. At the bottom of the sea, poetry explores the possibility of a universal phonetic language, from the genealogy of metafiction that transcends the text, the author, and potential readers.

3. The Ecumenical Anti-System Army relaunches the text and establishes the materialization of fiction in a space deformed by the struggle of antagonistic fictional forces.

4. Fiction is, by itself, the realization of the textual future, as established in the First-Day Transcendental Narratology.

*

a. Fiction is metafiction, and metafiction is the revelation of a transcendent, ergodic text.
b. The possibility of an imaginative engagement not contained in the moment depends on the textual capacities of a rhizomatic entity that involves life and death, and desire as action.
c. The cosmos is fiction contained within simulacra.

*

1. In the galaxy, the good guys and the evildoers are distorted by the text, just as on the planet the apes have transformed into clerks in the service of supposed transcendental equality, and the plants into supplementary aesthetic ornaments of domesticated life outside of fiction.
2. At the bottom of the sea, poetry is translated as the narrative possibility of eternal life in the gloom or outside of the light.
3. Flesh Gore revealed himself before More one day after composing an epic poem about the first night of the world in which text and life are transposed, eclogue against the fear of the conscience contained in the moment, Atari to be born from reeds, the fundamental textual discovery before the act of dreaming lambs in the old Lautréamont or Fogwill style.
4. The ability to keep telling stories is hampered by the intensity of the author's moment or the proximity to life

as a demonstration of fiction in the possibility of textual reality.

*

a. The epic poem about the first night Flesh Gore wrote, the day he revealed himself before More the Merciless, *quid ad astra*, forbidden word, is also the key to understanding the First-Day Transcendental Narratology conspiracy and the textual saturation of the field flow of language absorbed in the transparency of speech.

*

a. The text conquers the light and imposes itself as an intermittent unlimited form.

b. The First-Day Transcendental Narratology is a dimension of the metatext. A sparkly, unusual entity, Flesh Gore flying everywhere, beyond the light, in the theatrical epic of the final revelation attempt, the chronic apocalypse that returns indispensable to the imagination as a vanishing point toward blank space, salvation when crossing the street or gazing at the clear sky, the smell of closeness and a lucky coin that burns bright in a forest.

*

c. The text arises from a blank space, unlike the cosmos that exists in a dimension of gloom and ebb, but both, the text and the cosmos, expand or retract according to the displacements of fiction by a shack on the border. Nothing is left at the end, only the imaginary dimension of what could have been.

c. The text and the cosmos are equal and complementary in the hero's potential imagination.

c. The cosmos is an unlimited space of imagination.
c. The text exists as a vocation of omens.

*

Flesh Gore skips the line, stares into the sun, or beyond. With his eyes on the text, he gets into the corners of reality and moves through the place burning endlessly. There's no way other than the revolver pressed against the temple. Fiction is just a mole next to the mouth. Life is almost a video game. The author of the text vanished from the first line. He went with wild horses through the meadow toward the sea or the cliffs, as in Jorge Pimentel's poem, not as true as spring and love among friends, and life together, behind the sun, hidden on a planet of apes that barely go around thinking that they exist crammed into a gap of signs and abstract forms, a final equation that surpasses the sense of reality as fiction within fiction, accelerated way of finding ourselves. Flesh Gore is about to be born, or has never existed, anyone else hasn't either, and no one is necessary. They surrender to the constant stream of cheap entertainment, life as an inconsequential logical sequence, personalized (yes), but undetermined and only apparent, fantasy of the rain to come, all dry and sprawled, the matter becomes sad as it should be. Just the melancholy of a false sketch latitude and very close to the vortex, all there, Flesh Gore and the armies of tradition and the devil with his tail between his legs and More, at the end...

*

But where do they all fit? If you can leave it behind, start with another luck, another light, another saint. If there's something left to say, make it cheesy and easy, or whatever, but it's just a saying...

*

~~Discrepancies on the Nature of Rabbits~~

1. If a story goes beyond reality or if it only reflects the alienated nature of rabbits.

*

1. A text isn't democracy or militancy, except when it's textual militancy.
2. In spite of everything, a text never stops being a serious matter.
3. Because it's a fictional entity, it's a round, ecumenical organism, like a bus trip that begins and ends in such a place, starts with a fixed course, and belongs, for an instant, to certain almost clinical paved places.
4. We go from a lit area to an intermittent space, which then turns gloomy.
5. In the end, everything clears up as if by magic.
6. The text and the world are a single distance that sometimes smells of greengrocers or hot bread; to pests or proximity; to sewer or to everything together.
7. I don't usually take the bus. I prefer to walk, lose myself among the multitudes, and somehow get home, at dusk or the next morning.
8. A text is the same: we don't know how, but we always reach our destination.
9. I like texts that look deserted but open the door and invite us in.
10. And they even offer to tuck us in, as if we had known each other all our lives.
11. As if in the end we were safe.

12. But make no mistake – a text is as dangerous and savage as any revolution on the other side of the world.

13. A thought revolution?

14. An attempt to believe in something, as if a sufficient light were passing through you.

15. A textual revolution? The possibility of a reality revolution based on fiction? A different reality as hypertext?

16. Nothing changes by blinking or clicking your tongue, but everything has changed.

17. He approaches from behind and asks you for time, and when you're about to tell him, he spreads a light that goes through you like a precipice or a world to be born behind your gaze.

18. The matter comes down to the origin of rabbits.

19. No one in the room has ever seen a rabbit.

20. Everyone knows rabbits exist, but they imagine them as long-eared squirrels or as carrot-eating rats or as fat men in rabbit suits.

21. They're all wrong.

22. As far as it's possible, rabbits exist only in the imagination.

23. That is, they're what they are, but they're no more than they are.

24. They survive or are alienated by the charm their mystery produces.

25. Some contemplate the possibility of starting a new theory about the cyborg condition of these textual animals.

26. Rabbits would be defined as textual cyborgs within the hypertext theory.

27. They would be considered shock attempts, possibilities, or null expectations.

28. But most agree rabbits are texts from a bygone era, which aren't worth remembering.

29. If you have nothing to add, you disappear and appear in another place, or in the same place but being another, and you cross the path with yourself, or with someone very similar with a head full of the same discrepancies about the origin of the rabbits...

Those who find you in the middle of nowhere, remember you from somewhere, squint and state very clearly that yes, of course, and they pat you on the shoulder, they hug you, as if they had known you all their lives. They say they've always read you, you're highly recommended, and how many honors you deserve. They already say it, if it were up to them, the happy world, the room ready.

If it were the other way around, if I found myself as if I knew myself from somewhere else, and I hardly recognized myself, or thought, as a glimpse, that I never became who we are, I'd let him pass, each one with his warmth, without making a peep or letting waters go, feeling no distress, and not a minimum impudence would put us to lead.

*

1. If life were to write me, on some occasion, due to laziness or vertigo, I'd retrace my steps and read everything that's worth reading from beginning to end, and I'd only imagine for a moment everything that I could have written.

2. If I found myself in the middle of nowhere, without remembering who I am, perhaps thinking I'm someone else, and I celebrated how well I write and all the accolades I deserve, I'd retrace my steps and say nothing to myself, I'd go past a hint of a smile at most, each one with his warm stroke and his portion of bread, myself with my uncertainty,

aware of my own tale by osmosis, the exception of a life that seems fiction but that bends on its even part toward the bottom, burned skin that doesn't find the light, concave slab that glows by immersion...

3. If my life were to read, by chance or laziness I'd begin to write, from beginning to end, or by lightning...

4. The light, immersed in salt, round and grave, emerges from the other side like a sun. The crown of shadows, behind the sun, we see as an alienated aura, and in its totality with the abstract as a deep animal eye that at a slight trot saves itself from falling off a cliff toward the sea.

*

1. There's no galaxy but good and evil fighting to impose their version of reality on a planet that's nothing more than a wasteland of apes ecstatic with the light that emerges from the other side of the mountains.

2. At the bottom of the sea, there are no poets because this is a desolate, dangerous country.

3. Neither Roberto Bolaño nor Mario Levrero is here to change things. Everything will happen as planned.

4. It's terrible to assume that the text density is cryptic, but it's more terrible to reach the end and not discover anything. Feeling cheated.

*

1. There's no galaxy but liquor and knives on the brink of extinction.

2. At the bottom of the sea, there are no poets because this country belongs to some giant clams and the inert laws of magnetism.

3. Not even Clarice Lispector would say otherwise. We'll simply hold hands and wait for the end to come quickly and painlessly.
4. Devote yourself to writing and don't waver. Suddenly you could shine almost like a planet adrift.

*

a. A text is a revelation, but not every revelation is an omen.
b. An omen is sometimes a space filled with revelation, a text that acquires reality for an instant.
c. The world floats like a pendulum between revelation and omen. By itself it has no reality. It's fiction that shapes and contains it, drop after drop, in a sea of possibilities, in a galaxy that is as a preamble.

*

1. No galaxy or heroes exist, just as no apes, no water, or no life expectancy exists on the planet.
2. At the bottom of the sea, you find only water mice and cockroaches accustomed to the sulfurous heat the nucleus exudes.
3. Not even César Aira could say we were wrong, that we won't die suddenly if not for lack of food and drinking water in the long run.
4. Some desperate, adventurous poets will try to find the solution in ancient texts to this problem that is not only cryptic but useless, merely aesthetic.

*

a. A text within a text within a text turns out to be a pearl scooped out of the sea, and we look at it as if reality were inertia returning to the unknown depths from the embedded point of light.

*

b. A pearl that is everything but never a pearl and never an aleph.

b. A pearl that is a pearl, but that isn't a pearl – a vanishing point, perhaps.

*

c. A dark, hollow space that stares back at us as if it were a cockroach.

c. A dark, hollow space that stares at us and that we'd like to crush to return from the dream where we find ourselves.

c. A dark, hollow space that translates into a deeper space of reality.

*

d. We're embedded in a text by inertia, in a little rat-killing story where we can hardly move and breathe.

*

e. The moment doesn't depend on us.

*

[The Fictional Origin of Rabbits]

1. There's no galaxy but random accounts of time and distance only some scientists could claim to understand, as there are different kinds of apes and plants in the world.

2. At the bottom of the sea, there's no poetry, only subdued archipelagos that crack with macabre voices like in old cartoons.

3. At this dark hour, not even Rimbaud could tell us otherwise. Yes, he would undoubtedly curse his luck, again.

4. Do you remember Flesh Gore? He was killed by a laser beam that came out of nowhere.

*

a. The night we buried him in the desert of the lawless planet beyond the light.

b. The night we buried him, phytoliths rained, along with small inert phosphorescences and jellyfish of condensed energy that stung our skin on contact.

c. *And the knives on this table have hurt my entire palate.*

*

1. I'd start with César Vallejo's verse, as in the last frontier of the text, but I must continue – there's no galaxy but verses compressed into residual memory capsules.

2. Where does the story start and where does the novel leave?

3. Is it possible to write a story of the story that turns into a rat with long, rabbit-like ears?

4. Could a rat turn into a rabbit if we put long ears on its head?

*

a. A rat is a ball of hair that fits in your palm and could live forever if fed enough cheese.

*

b. On the other hand, a rabbit can be anything that struggles to escape violently from our textual trap.

*

c. Both rabbits and mice live in burrows, fictional spaces under our feet that lead everywhere, even beyond the stars.

*

c. Both rabbits and mice feed on the waste of imagination. The latter prefer cheese, especially holed cheese.

*

c. In cartoons, rabbits only eat carrots.

*

DARK STAR
DARK STAR
DARK STAR

1. In the galaxy, good guys defend themselves with laser swords, and evildoers attack with death squads, just as on the planet apes build catapults, forge helmets, and hide in caves when everything is in ruins.
2. At the bottom of the sea, poetry is lumpen. It starts from stones and accelerates like a cyclone against the species on the surface.
3. 'You will never find the way out of this labyrinth. Surrender to the light. Conceive the fiction in which you have inscribed,' says *The First-Day Transcendental Narratology*.

4. In the long run, nothing happens except in the imagination. Nothing exists outside of fiction.

*

a. Fiction is faction.
b. Imagination is this.
c. The cosmos is before and behind – and outside.

*

1. In the galaxy, there's ecstasy and kitsch, just as there are ritual festivals and funerals on the planet.
2. At the bottom of the sea, life transcends poetry because it arises from the most hostile places and there it remains inert, waiting for the inconceivable fiction.
3. Neither will Fogwill say otherwise. If he said it, it was with rancor, beginning to swim among the dispersion of worlds like the ghost of a whale.
4. The textual capacity of imagination is the space that opens when the serpent is gouged.

*

a. Every faction is evidence of reality as an instant within fiction.
b. The moment is the instant when the text intersects with the attempt of another text in the imagination.
c. We're a portion within a larger portion, but we're here and we're not, fiction that is quick to disappear.

*

1. In the galaxy, everyone betrays each other, as no one will survive the future on the planet.

2. At the bottom of the sea, poetry is the alienation of cliffs and slopes when you find the small thistles zigzagging through the shadowed space in search of food.

3. Flesh Gore, a feat of storytelling, survivor of the text, maximum score, lost song of Nezahualcóyotl.

4. A text is what it is, and it's what it isn't, in a linear and round sense, an attempt at reality glued to fiction, a hypertext, fiction that functions as a potential mechanism of textual reality, the ability to narrate something incredible as if it were true or possible. But no, a text is just a text, a medium for the incredible, a light that condenses in the instant.

*

1. In the galaxy, the good guys are very good, and the evildoers are very dreadful, as believers and heretics reside on the planet.

2. At the bottom of the sea, poetry is a tunnel that connects this world to the hereafter.

3. When the monsters arrived and easily imposed themselves with their technology, the world became a scheme of good and evil in the shadow of a hidden power that translated fiction into reality through a supposed transcendental equation.

4. We don't know if it's before fiction or reality, but both belong to the realm of the possible as a textual instant within the metafiction of the Ecumenical Anti-System Army.

*

The Ecumenical Anti-System Army Proclaims:

a. Fiction is just a textual dimension, that is, it exists confined within the text.

b. All fiction is the remnant of another fiction, and all fiction is the remnant of a fiction that transcends all fiction.

c. No fiction exists outside of the Fiction that is the Fundamental Ascendant Rhizome.

d. The Fundamental Ascendant Rhizome isn't fiction. It's the channel that gives rise to the realization of all fiction as an instant of reality and beyond as textual reality and as an incarnate word.

e. No text exists beyond itself.

f. No text confirms the existence of a transcendental text despite its existence.

g. No text depends on more than itself.

h. No text is anything other than a simple text.

i. All text is fiction and all fiction is textual reality.

j. All text is textual reality as fiction, as the incarnate word.

k. Every text embodies fiction as textual reality, as it embodies reality for an instant.

l. Life is fiction, if you will.

m. Life is reality, if it's so intended.

n. Life is what it is because it is.

o. Fiction doesn't exist, but fiction does exist.

p. Fiction doesn't exist, but it exists within fiction.

q. Fiction doesn't exist, but this is fiction.

r. Textual reality is reality for an instant.

s. Textual reality is fiction as potential reality.

t. Textual reality is the incarnate word.

u. There's no more to add.
v. All that has been said before is enough.
w. We're about to reach the end.
x. What is predicted almost happens.
y. Per *aspera ad astra*.
z. Nothing happens. Everything stays the same.

*

1. The galaxy repeats itself in its basic principles, as the planet is reduced to living creatures and infinite spaces to discover.
2. At the bottom of the sea, poetry is a swarm of living lights of abstract language.
3. Life on the surface is just a stain of pulverized bodies on the surface of time about to disappear because of erosion and the impact of a distant light.
4. Another attempt at an equation by César Aira: 'Those who complain are always the others, who deep down care about nothing.'

*

Rabbits Attached to the Story

Better not say anything. Rabbits may be around and get into fiction just when you name them.

*

What kind of rabbits await us?

Those quick-paced, evil incarnations with long ears and whiskers?

Or those rustic, plush imps that wait underground with sabers and hooks?

At any rate, they're symbolic figurines of voracious natures and bad taste someone sketched in another time to scare children and the ignorant.

*

Do rabbits exist or are they just a trace of another fiction?

At any rate, do we exist or are we trapped in a text about rabbits?

Do rabbits exist at the same time as we do?

Does anyone exist?

*

What world is this where rabbits coexist with us, preachers of the most fundamental good?

Is this the apocalypse?

The lightness of the punishment for failing to fulfill our duty as holy humanity?

*

1. Good guys and evildoers exist in the galaxy, but that matters to no one.
1. On the planet, apes have learned to farm and have become sedentary.
1. On the planet, villages have emerged across the world.
1. We wait for what will happen to the planet of the apes.

*

2. At the bottom of the sea, poetry undergoes constant change due to the intrinsic tidal flows and abrupt temperature changes.

2. At the bottom of the sea, a poet's skeleton once appeared and soon turned into calcium residues and atypical phosphorescent nuclei.

2. At the bottom of the sea, most of the time, nothing happens and that's fine. Everything seems wrapped in calm and desolation.

*

3. Not even Octavio Paz could alter our unfortunate lot. The shadow of death haunts us. The fatal bird with a blue beak and black eyes flaps its wings. The dying cosmic space writhes in pain. The inert matter steals our flavor...

3. Nor can anyone else save us. No matter how hard we search, we're about to be cut out, skin and blood, technicolor bone, all together and endlessly, outside the text, beyond the text, in hypertext, residues of fiction.

*

4. Flesh Gore crosses the avenue. He tells a horrible joke to an ostrich that pays him no heed. Flesh Gore doesn't realize that it's only an ostrich. In a moment of mental confusion, he takes out his ray gun and blows the giant bird's head off.

*

Flesh Gore doesn't regret what he did because he hardly exists within a text that doesn't belong to him. He moves and acts according to what a higher entity dictates.

Flesh Gore is the reactive memory of a text that long ago ceased to exist, now refuses to disappear, and will blow its head off on the count of three...

*

The alternate ending of the text is a generic orange soda commercial.

A soda can appears in the foreground, rushes into the atmosphere, and heads straight toward the cliffs.

In the background, a tribe of apes gathers around a newly discovered fire.

In a subliminal way, we think of a sweet, slightly fruity, bubbly drink...

Translated from the Spanish by Toshiya Kamei

An excerpt from *A Door Opens: The Beginning of the Fall of the Ispancialo-in-Hinirang* (Emprensa Press: 2007) by Salahuddin Alonto, Annotated by Omar Jamad Maududi, MLS, HOL, JMS

Dean Francis Alfar

The Philippines

I published Dean long ago in my very first *Apex Book of World SF* anthology, with a lyrical tale called 'The Kite of Stars'. It was my friend Yi-Sheng, though, who suggested 'A Door Opens...' to me, and I am so glad he did! I love the way this story plays with format – both like, and completely unlike, the story preceding it – and Dean's deft touch has only grown more confident since I first published him. It's been great to reconnect with him here, and I hope you like the story as much as I did.

O ver a century before the Final Revolution that ended the Ispancialo rule in Hinirang[1], there was an obscure uprising that almost brought the colonizers to their knees[2]. Archival discoveries in the past 50 years[3] have brought to light the sequences of events that have been characterized as 'The Door Uprising'[4]. Inveterate diarists and letter-writers, the Ispancialo, who were aware of the uprising, provided copious details – enough to inspire a goodly number of popular novels[5] and films[6].

In 1784, a Door in the Katao faithlands was opened by chance by a student[7]. The *audienca royal* of Hinirang, including representatives from the military, religious, arcane, poetic[8] and scientific[9], decided to shut the door[10] by sending an expeditionary force through the portal. What occurred next was a massacre[11], as the expeditionary force found itself assaulted by the heroes of the Katao's folk belief system[12]. Though a few survivors managed to escape and shut the Door, the damage was already done.

For the next hundred years, native storytellers all over the archipelago began telling the old heroic tales[13], blurring geographical and tribal lines with heroes from the north appearing in southern tales, and vice versa[14]. This undermined the Ispancialo strategy of 'divide and conquer' by which clannish tribes were set against each other, effectively quelling disturbances[15]. However, the heroic tales, in which heroes from different tribes and traditions joined forces, continued to spread, leading to a gradual and inevitable sense of nationalism[16].

This culminated in the famous 1896 Revolution[17] when at last the Katao overthrew Ispancialo rule, followed by the declaration of an independent and sovereign Hinirang in 1898[18].

Notes

1 The Ispancialo ruled for 327 years.

2 There were frequent uprisings by the Katao of Hinirang, who resented the Ispancialo's *encomienda* system. Among the most dangerous ones occurred in 1589, when the first Ispancialo governor, Miguel López de Legazpi, was made a viceroy, with the subsequent appointment of the *audienca royal*. At the height of the religious mass to commemorate the event, over 80 Katao, armed only with stones, attacked the assemblage, ultimately falling to superior Ispancialo numbers and weaponnry.

   Norhata Kudarat, *Colonial Hinirang, 1565–1653* (Mirabilis Press, 1991), 107.

3 Alberto Manalastas, 'Historical Trove Unearthed in Diliman,' *Diaro Manila* [Cuidad Manila, Hinirang], December 11, 2003.

4 Certain revisionist scholars such as Meynard Bolasco and Gabriel Lo-tonon prefer the use of the term 'gate'.

5 The first such novel was *Sangria Yesterday* by Nolledo Patalinjug, winner of the Carlos Palanca Memorial Award Grand Prize for Novel in 1981, and published by Anvil Books in 1982.

6 Among the most notable is *The Blood Door*, the critically acclaimed 2002 Hinirang-Nippon film directed by Satoshi Kon.

7 It was Alonzo Nicolas Clessidraña of the Concilio Ciencia who discovered the door to the *Katao*'s faithlands.

   Alonzo, researching the chronal peculiarities of the forbidden area underneath the Plaza Emperyal, stumbled across the forgotten wooden opening on his thirty-third day of investigation, just before he was about to abandon his pursuit of a degree at the Orden and instead help his grandfather maintain his shop along the Encantó lu Caminata.

   Instead, despite the fervent protests of his research companions, he forced open the odd-looking door, using the *calipher resonancia*, and vanished into the unearthly radiance. Those who were left behind, after a painful and hurried discussion, shut and barred the wooden aperture, and rushed to report everything to their superiors.

Victor Montes, Gregorio Lacuesta, Wilfredo Co, *Uprisings* (Best Day Publishing, 1989), 23.

8 Masters of the Spoken Word, the Poetics were versed in many secret methods of power, such as what would, in later decades, be characterized as the bildungsroman form of twisting moral identities and the use of inveterate haplology and edulcoration.

9 Realizing that the situation was beyond their capacity to handle, the Concilio Ciencia sent emissaries to the other members of the *audienca royal* of Ciudad Meiora – the Secular, Poetic, Arcane and Spiritual institutions whose policies and movements decided the fate of Ispancialo Hinirang – requesting an emergency meeting to determine what needed to be done. The missive stated in no uncertain terms that secrecy was required due to the delicate nature of the situation and that it was imperative that all five Powers convened immediately.

Anne Marie Tambour and Marlene Ford-Cunanan, eds., *Power Plays: The Balance of Power in Colonial Hinirang* (Ateneo Press, 1983).

10 First to arrive at the squat red towers of the Concilio Ciencia was an unremarkable qalesa bearing two extraordinary men. Alejandro Baltran Alessio du Verrada ei Ramirez, the Guvernador-Henerale of Hinirang, eschewed his normal accoutrements of rank and wore a dull-colored cloak over simple vestments. He was accompanied by Ser Humberto Carlos Pietrado ei Villareal, the elder brother of the man who had recently, rather embarrassingly, lost a peculiar footrace against a *Katao* woman. They represented the Military Government, the most visible of the Powers.

A few minutes later, a velvet-covered palanquin brought the representatives of the Gremio Poetica. Betina du Zabala, the Most Excellent Primo Orador, gestured impatiently at her companion to hurry out of the conveyance. Biting back her tongue, Esperanza du Zabala, the Most Excellent Segundo Orador, locked vicious gazes with her mother, and rushed into the Orden's tower. Both Oradors, recently arrived from the Mother Country, were masters of Poetics, and the Gremio Poetica held sway over all art and communication in the Ispancialo demesne.

Maestra Onsia Helmina and Maestro Cinco Almario, of the Escolia du Arcana Menor, arrived next, on foot. Maestra Helmina clutched her robes close to her breast and looked up to try to read the thoughts of her reluctant younger companion. But Maestro Almario, rumored to have *Katao* blood in his veins, kept his silence. So, without a word, the representatives of the Arcane surreptitiously erected invisible wards around themselves and entered the tower.

The last to arrive were a pair from the Katedral Grandu, divinely inspired clerics of the *Tres Hermanas* and spiritual heirs of the *Pio Familia*. Madre Gorospe invoked her eighty-six years of Faith to calm herself down, inwardly trembling at the implications hinted at by the summoning missive. But her companion, the Tiq'barang cleric Sister Veronica T'gubilin, smiled in anticipation and stomped her hooves once to contain her excitement.

Within the red towers, Consejal Lucio Pejeno, current head of the Concilio Ciencia, ushered all the leaders in after requesting for them to leave their companions in an outer room.

'Thank you all for responding so quickly,' Consejal Lucio Pejeno began. 'Forgive the terse nature of the letter I sent. The sensitive nature of—'

'Yes, yes,' interrupted Maestra Onsia Helmina of the Escolia Arcana. 'Obviously you have stumbled across something important enough to summon all five of us from our duties. Tell us.'

'You must forgive the Maestra for her characteristic mordacious tone, Consejal Pejeno,' Betina du Zabala of the Gremio Poetica said, smiling oddly. 'She would be more eloquent, but is, no doubt, as curious as the rest of us as to the nature of your call.'

'Of course, Excellencies, of course,' Consejal Pejeno stared at his hands briefly and stated simply, 'We have found a portal to Hinirang's heaven.'

'What?' Madre Gorospe suddenly felt the weight of her years

upon her body, and stifled a yearning to scream in horror. She closed her eyes but saw only blood and tears.

'It is of great interest to the Mother Church, naturally,' Consejal Pejeno began.

'It is of great interest to us all, Consejal.' The Guvernador-Henerale rose from his seat and gently touched the arm of Madre Gorospe, who, eyes shut tight, was shaking noticeably. She opened her teary eyes and nodded her thanks. 'Where is this portal?'

'Beneath the Plaza Empyral, Your Excellency,' Consejal Pejeno replied.

'Imagine that,' Betina du Zabala spoke to no one in particular. 'Is it open?' she asked Consejal Pejeno.

'Yes.'

'Who opened it?' asked Maestra Helmina. 'Or was it open already?'

'One of my own, a young student, opened the door,' the Consejal admitted.

'And?' Betina du Zabala asked softly.

'And he vanished,' the Consejal replied.

'What makes you so certain that it is a gateway to the Hinirang faithlands?' Madre Gorospe asked.

'Our instruments recorded the presence of the Ether.' The Consejal sat back wearily. 'As you all know, that signifies the presence of faithlands, as proven by our apparatus at the conquest of Nueva Mundo when we—'

'No one here doubts the veracity of your report nor the integrity of the instruments guided by your scientific principles, dear Ser,' the Guvernador-Henerale said. 'So there is a door. An open door. You were correct to call us all. We must decide our course of action immediately.'

'Then we vote,' Betina du Zabala said firmly.

'Yes. Yes, we do,' agreed Madre Gorospe, shaking her head sadly, for she knew what position she had to take.

'Very well. As is our custom, I will ask each of you to formally state your decision,' Consejal Pejeno said. 'I will begin.'

'I, Lucio Pejeno, Consejal Temporal, speak for the Concilio Ciencia,' the heavy-set man said. 'I say shut the door. Science has no interest in the *indio* faithland. We were the ones who discovered and opened the door. We will shut it as well.'

He gestured to the others. 'Who speaks for the Poetics?'

'I, Betina du Zabala, Most Excellent Primo Orador, speak for the Gremio Poetica,' the fiercely beautiful woman spoke, her mellifluous voice perfectly pitched and resonant. 'I say enter the door. We can navigate what is beyond and find the source of their tales – mostly primitive and pathetic folkloric drivel, from what little we have heard since my office arrived in these humid islands last year. And we take it in the name of Ispancia. Thereafter, only our narratives will exist in this misbegotten land.'

'Who speaks for the Arcane?'

'I, Onsia Helmina, Maestra Honoria, speak for both schools,' the silver-haired woman said, considering her next words carefully. 'I say enter the door. But only to study, always only to study. We must preserve what the indios have, and learn to share in their culture. What we learn we can use to improve upon what we already know.'

'Who speaks for the Spiritual?'

'I, Madre Gorospe, Faithful of the Tres Hermanas, speak for the Mother Church in Hinirang,' the old cleric responded, her words heavy with sorrow. 'I say enter the door. Destroy the pagan faithlands.'

'Who speaks for the Secular?'

'I, Alejandro Ramirez, Guvernador-Henerale of Hinirang, speak for the Government,' the dark-haired man spoke quietly. 'I say shut the door. But if it means entering it to close it, then I recommend that as well. We will protect the interests of our citizenry. Having an open doorway in the midst of our Ciudad is unacceptable. It must be shut.'

Lakangiting Lopez, Selma Dornilla, Ponciano Abadilla, *Reconstructing History Vol. 5: The Unpublished Letters of Amado Pejeno* (Hinirang University Press, 1995), 78–84.

11 Alonto grossly exaggerates and misuses the term 'massacre'. Though over a hundred people are believed to have perished, this is nothing compared to the infamous Tsino Massacre of 1603 (also known as the Sangley Uprising or Three Mandarins Massacre), where, fearing the growing Tsino population, the Ispancialo soldiers under the command of Governor-General Pedro Bravo de Acuña slew over twenty thousand.

12 The hundred-man expeditionary force, led by the juniors of the *audienca royal*, entered the Door and found themselves covered from head to toe in thick Ether.

'Keep your formation,' Ser Humberto Carlos Pietrado ei Villareal shouted in the dimness.

An eerie silence permeated the surroundings after the men shouted their assent.

'Be wary,' Sister Veronica T'gubilin of the Katedral Grandu whispered to Maestro Cinco Almario of the Escolia du Arcana Menor.

'Believe me, I have my wards at the ready, Sister,' the young man replied with a shiver in his voice.

'Pejeno!' Ser Humberto spoke sharply. 'Is there anything your ciencia can tell us? My men need something to attack!'

'Patience, please, Ser,' Jovito Pejeno mumbled, his sweaty hands tinkering with instrumentation he could barely see, inwardly cursing the head of the Concilio Cienca, his very uncle, who assigned him to accompany the expeditionary force. 'These delicate things take some time and I cannot—'

'Do you see that? That light,' Esperanza du Zabala, the Most Excellent Segundo Orador, said softly, pointing at a reddish glow in the distance.

'It is a man,' Sister Veronica said, squinting her eyes. 'We should—'

A shout like thunder resounded through the Ether and the Heroes of Hinirang stood revealed.

The voice belonged to Banna of the Calingga, handsome and radiant on a floating cloud that flashed crimson. In his right arm he brandished Diwaton, the axe that followed his every command.

On Banna's right stood the demi-god Labaw Donggon of the Bisayas, holding high the crystal sphere that enabled him supernatural sight.

On Banna's left was the mighty Lam-ang of the Iluko, his chest covered with powerful amulets, holding a great spear. Around him swirled powerful winds, ready to obey his words, disrupting the Ether.

More heroes were revealed as the Ether dissipated.

There stood Prince Bantugan of the unconquered Maranao, accompanied by his spirit daimon Magaw, his powerful hands restraining a fearsome crocodile whose loyalty he'd won.

There, the resplendent Suban-on hero, Sandayo, his fingers shiny with rings – each of which contained a person he'd previously pressed into it.

There, Kundaman of Palaoan, his slender build belying his potent magic.

There, Tanagyaw of the Agyu, raising his golden cane.

There, Tulalang, the Dragon Slayer, with his black shield.

There, Tuwaang of the Manuvu, lightning crackling at his fingertips, the center of his forehead as bright as a star.

The Ispancialo expeditionary force stood stunned.

'Take them, my brothers!' Banna shouted, releasing Diwaton from his grip.

It was the last thing Jovito Pejeno saw, as it split him in half before attacking the soldiers.

'Attack!' Ser Humberto Carlos Pietrado ei Villareal commanded his men, shaking them out their stupor.

As the heroes closed in, chaos ensued, Ispancialo steel meeting Katao metal.

Maestro Cinco Almario of the Escolia du Arcana Menor watched in shock as Labaw Donggon moved toward him. He fought to recall his most powerful wards, running the arcane syllables over and over in his mind before he spoke them, fearful of the untoward results an untimely catachresis could produce. A glimmering blue sphere enveloped him and he sighed in relief when Labaw Donggon stopped at its periphery.

'You cannot harm me! Leave! Leave!' Maestro Cinco half shouted, half pleaded. 'This is the finest arcana!'

Labaw Donggon just shook his head and smiled, raising the brilliant crystal to his eyes. 'I see it broken, this little shield of yours.'

Maestro Cinco's death cry resounded as his arcane sphere collapsed around him, shredding his body into many pieces.

When the heroes ran toward the expeditionary force, Sister Veronica began to pray, filling her spirit with the power of her faith, imploring the Tres Hermanas to grant her the power to swat aside the pagans. But the Tres Hermanas were deaf to her pleas, though her life was somewhat spared. She screamed from her confines in one of Sandayo's many rings.

'You're mine now,' Sandayo calmly informed her as he dispatched a soldier.

It was Esperanza du Zabala, the Most Excellent Segundo Orador, who kept her wits about her, launching into a staccato recitation that created a field of powerful words around her immediate area. As the invisible words engulfed them, Tulalang, Tanagyaw and Tuwaang fought against a sudden hebetude that threatened to swallow them in the throes of dull ennui.

Struggling to maintain her control, Esperanza tried to see where Ser Humberto was, to tell him that this was madness, that they, yes, even she, was ill-prepared, and that a retreat was a better option, if not the only option.

But Ser Humberto was busy fighting for his life. With a group of men that grew smaller and smaller with every moment, he faced Kundaman and Prince Bantugan.

'Stand your ground, men!' he shouted, forcing his way to Prince Bantugan. But before he could close in on the handsome man, Prince Bantugan gestured sharply to his side. The giant crocodile snapped its jaws and devoured Ser Humberto whole.

Seeing this, Esperanza began to run back toward the Door, still articulating words to keep the heroes around her weakened.

'I'm sorry, brothers, but I grow sleepy,' Tulalang said to Tanagyaw and Tuwaang with a yawn. Tanagyaw growled and Tuwaang shouted as they fought the wearisome effects.

'But not to worry,' Tulalang mumbled as he closed his eyes. 'My shield will fight for me...'

Tulalang's black shield flew from his arm and chased after the fleeing Esperanza. When the door was almost within her reach, Esperanza turned around to take one last look at the terrible attack the expeditionary force had suffered. And fell backward into the open Door, knocked senseless when Tulalang's black shield slammed into her.

(Esperanza du Zabala's account of the event ends here. She, and four soldiers who had managed to escape in the early parts of the assault, were the only survivors.)

Langgit Sikat, *Reimagining Esperanza: History as Creative Non-Fiction*, trans. Amir al-Raban Lane (MSU, 1975), 146–150

13 See the *Hinirang Folk Literature Series*, compiled and edited by Damian Eusebio (Hinirang University Press, 1982) for examples. Of particular interest are the materials found in Vol. VIII, *The Epics*.

14 Rowan Go, ed., *Word of Mouth: The Transmission of Heroic Tales* (Boston: Houghton Mifflin, 1998).

15 Leonardo Villavicencio, *Ispaniola: Strategies of Governance* (New York: Cambridge University Press, 2000), 42.

16 Bienvenido Rafanan, 'Troubled Waters: The Influence of the Tale' in Crispin Reyes, ed., *Hinirang: A Colonial History* (Georgetown: Blackwell, 2003), 265–271.

17 José Protasio Rizal Mercado ei Alonso Realonda, founder of *La*

Liga Hinirang and a rallying figure for government reform was executed, which triggered the Hinirang Revolution spearheaded by Andres Bonifacio ei de Castro and Emilio Aguinaldo ei Famy, founders of 'KATAO', better known as 'The Brotherhood'.

18 The short-lived Republic was interrupted by the Ispancialo–Americano War.

Ootheca

Mário Coelho

Portugal

Wow, did this story blow me away! It reminded me of reading young China Miéville – a story that's dark, that's weird, but that is utterly compelling. I wanted it as soon as I read it, and Mário has promised me there will be a future novel in this world – which I can't wait to read!

'I have cockroaches for teeth,' Bilal said to his date, on the phone. 'Just... thought you should know sooner than later.'

On the other end, a loud nothing. Then Joana said, 'Thanks for telling me. A lot of people don't.'

Bilal didn't know what to say. He looked around, as if he could find inspiration in his kingdom of loathing, a sixth-floor hovel in one of the city's Grave Ghettos. It was all he could afford, after having lost his job, his boyfriend, and his teeth. A filthy haven cluttered with Thai takeout boxes and mould patches. If he sunk any lower they'd have to fish him out with a nuclear submarine.

'Yeah,' he said.

He heard a rustle and chewing. Joana plumping down on some fluffy sofa and diving into a bowl of popcorn, safe and comfortable in some sanitized neighbourhood stolen from a northern European city and transplanted into Almagris. Bilal couldn't even bear to be pissed off.

'How long?' she said.

'About four months,' Bilal said, trying to recover a hint of nonchalance, of how he'd used to be. Half-lying, too. He knew the exact date on which he'd woken up with cockroaches instead of teeth: four months, two weeks, three days, and about ten hours ago.

More chewing, otherwise nothing. Bilal said, 'What are you eating?'

'Lupins,' Joana said, mouth full.

Bilal heard her spit. 'You don't eat the skin?'

'No.' Joana spat again. 'You do?'

'Heard it's where the vitamins are.' Truth was, Bilal ate everything now, skin or no skin. The cockroaches weren't picky. In fact, judging from the amount of times he'd found himself making a midnight snack out of his own garbage bin, he suspected the bugs preferred that which was only theoretically edible. 'Hey, I understand if you don't want—'

'Did it hurt?'

'Did...' Bilal stumbled. 'You mean the Hagging?'

'Yeah. Well, and losing your teeth.'

Bilal twirled a finger on the phone cord. 'No, no... I mean, it was scary. But it didn't—'

'Tell me.'

Bilal closed his mouth. As always, he felt the roaches jitter against each other, pitter-patting legs scratching at the inside of his lips, his tongue, tasting vaguely of rot. 'No. Didn't hurt at all. They were just there when I woke up, peeking out of my gums.'

'Like they were just teeth.'

The ever-present static on the landline grew harsher. A sound underlined by whispers, background noise to white noise. Wisps of crying, braying, begging. The post-Nightmare world was luddite. Information technology wasn't safe for long. Bilal was surprised Joana had even risked talking to him on the phone for more than a couple of minutes. 'Yeah,' he whispered. 'Yeah, like that.'

Weirdly, one of the things that bothered him the most about having cockroaches for teeth was the lisping. Used to be his voice was clear as spring water. Not that he'd ever seen a spring. The government of Almagris hadn't managed to rescue one yet.

'Okay. I'd better go,' Joana said. 'Talking on the phone isn't safe. I might get Hagged, too.'

Bilal closed his eyes and exhaled. 'Yeah... Sure. I understand.'

'We still on for dinner?'

'I... You sure?'

'Yes, why not? Haven't seen you in ages.'

Because I've got cockroaches for teeth, Bilal thought. 'Okay. Yeah.'

'Great. Eight o'clock. Look sharp.'

Click. Static. Anguished whispers, as if desperate to be heard. Bilal put down the phone.

He laughed, once. Guffawed, then, choking on air. He saw his tearful face on the smooth surface of the rotary phone, cockroaches distorted like underwater, their legs up and out and doing a little jig.

*

Bilal dressed in a wool jacket, wool gloves, deck shoes, high-waisted pants, and round full-framed eyeglasses – a look that made his ex, quote, 'hot for teacher'. He added a cashmere scarf to cover the roaches, and went out under a sky bloated with clouds.

There was a sunset, today. Sunfishing must have gone well. The government only ever allowed for sunsets when there was a surplus of sunlight, and that had happened only a couple times in the thirty-three years of Bilal's life.

That, or it was a way to calm down the people. Almagris was a city in turmoil, what with the recent high number of Haggings. The air reeked of pre-hysteria. Local news related a record number of cursist attacks. And cursism, in Bilal's admittedly neophyte point of view, was the dumbest kind of bigotry. Not all Hag curses were like his, very much disgusting but mostly harmless. Other Hagged could do things like spit battery acid, or their voices gave you (and themselves) crippling nightmares, or their bodies had been covered in regenerating, nigh-invulnerable dangling tumours. It often didn't end well for the bigots.

Joana was waiting on a restaurant esplanade overlooking the Mondego River, which had long ago been recovered from the lost city of Coimbra. On the far bank rose a line of tall Manueline houses. The residents were on their balconies, leaning over the railings, watching the errant strings of sunset lay a film of embers along the water.

Bilal sat. Joana tapped her wristwatch. 'Eight ten,' she said. 'I see time hasn't erased your famous Portuguese punctuality.'

'I resent that. I'm Angolan on my mother's side,' Bilal said.

She smiled. A familiar thing, an earnest thing. Bilal felt a tinge of happiness, a tinge of anxiety. 'You look good, Bilal.'

Until I lower my scarf, Bilal thought. 'You look better.'

Joana was as pretty as he remembered. The last decade had fallen sweet on her features: magazine-smooth skin, cute nose, perked eyebrows over big hazel eyes. Not that pretty was a factor for Bilal, anymore, but she was. Even in her slob uniform of sweatpants and hooded bomber jacket halfway zipped down over a white tank top.

'Sorry,' she said, as if reading his mind. 'Came straight from the gym. Didn't wanna be late for this dramatic reunion.'

She sounded different, too. Loose as she seemed, there was a weariness to her, a sense of nights unslept and days spent dreaming.

The waiter passed by to hand them the menu and a small plate of olives seasoned with garlic and olive oil.

Joana flipped through the menu. 'Hmm. I don't see any garbage here.'

Bilal stared at her. She stared back, eyebrow cocked, as if in challenge. A joke? He thought so, and hoped his smile reached his eyes. 'It's okay. You can chew. Just spit a couple bites onto my plate. Like a momma bird.'

'Kinky.' Joana winked, and Bilal's heart froze. How hollowed he'd become, that some likely-not-even-serious flirting quickened his blood. 'Scallops for two?'

Bit too rubbery for the roaches, Bilal thought. 'How about cod? Heavy on the taters.'

'Sorry, I'm doing keto.'

'It's fine. You get the fish; I get the carbs.' He hesitated, then added, 'My teeth buds like it starchy.'

She waved a tad too energetically at the waiter – who ambled over with his hands clasped in front of him – and asked for the cod and a bottle of port wine. 'My treat,' she said, touching Bilal's hand, reading his apprehension as braille.

How could she be interested in him, even if ever so slightly? She'd never been, before, back when he had been normal. Back when they had fleeted in and out of each other's lives in mundane coincidences: a mutual friend in Bilal's ballet class; a coin given to the same street performer at the same time; standing side by side on the electric tram. They'd always been cordial. Maybe slightly teasing, at the best of times. Nothing more.

Was it a fetish? Some girls were like that, bragged about the outrageous deformities they'd let inside them. Was it ego, a saviour's complex? Did she think it made her kinder, to go out with some guy whose only distinct feature was the unicity of his freakishness, among a sea of other unique freaks?

It put him in a sour mood. But, again, she caught that, and caught his hand as it slipped by. She raised the corner of her lips. Could be a smile, could be commiseration, and the ambiguity made it more honest, because Bilal didn't believe in complete smiles anymore.

For a while, they people-watched. The souls of Almagris going in and out of their lives, aimless wanderers vanishing into the undecided architecture. On the ever-fogged-up horizon were the retrieved fragments of other European cities. Fractions of Heidelberg and Perpignan and Valladolid and other non-capitals.

They lived under the carcass of a dead god still dreaming, in a city manufactured for survival, not joy. And yet, for Bilal, that was the first comfortable silence in four months, two weeks, three days, and about fifteen hours.

The waiter served them. Joana barely waited for him to leave. She scooped up the cod and tore it apart with knife and fork. After a couple of violent bites, she waved her knife at Bilal and – cheeks hamster-full – mumbled something incomprehensible.

'What?' Bilal said.

Joana swallowed and briefly choked, eyes momentarily wide in regret. 'The scarf.'

When in public, Bilal usually ate from under his scarf, yes. It was a dead giveaway that he had something to hide, that he was Hagged, but it beat having to show the not-yet-so-open-minded cosmos of Almagris the pretties in his mouth.

'Okay,' he huffed, and in what to him was a heroic gesture,

he pulled down the scarf and forked food into his mouth. The roaches pulled the potato apart, leaving only the aftertaste of good fats on his tongue.

He'd never get used to eating like this. He'd tried sustaining himself on a liquid diet before, but if the food didn't pass through the roaches' digestive systems first, it was rejected by his. It'd happened to him in public, once. And having dozens of roaches drowning in vomit, biting and scratching each other and peeling his gums open, was an experience he didn't care to repeat.

Like it or not, they were family now.

Joana didn't seem perturbed in the slightest. That, or she had the world's best poker face.

Bilal allowed himself to believe in the former.

The waiter came to refill their glasses, whistling, and as he leaned over he looked deep into Bilal's eyes and whispered, 'You should go.'

Bilal wasn't surprised, yet he was still disappointed. The waiter pointed discreetly with his thumb, at the sign over the entrance to the restaurant: NO HAGGED in Courier New (recently retrieved font, all the rage).

'That's illegal,' Bilal said, firm but polite.

The waiter pursed his lips and nodded in a *tell me about it* gesture. 'Boss is an asshole,' he said, after a quick glance over his shoulder. 'His daughter got Hagged recently. Not that it's any excuse.'

'It's not contagious,' Joana said, not even bothering to lower her voice.

The waiter nodded again. 'I know. I'm sorry. Food is on me. I'll say there was a'—the briefest glance at Bilal's mouth—'fly on your food.'

Bilal thanked the waiter and got ready to leave. Joana wasn't as polite: she screeched her chair back and shoved a spiteful, oversized piece of cod in her mouth. She stomped away, chewing angrily, attracting looks from the other clients, and Bilal followed her with an unearned sense of shame.

They went down a tight, winding street lined with crumbling limestone walls. Vines slithered in and out of the cracks, like worms in wounds. Joana slowed down, her anger giving way to curiosity. Had she always been this impulsive? Bilal remembered her differently. Big red flag.

Red is all that bleeding eyes see, he reminded himself.

There was a park bench nearby, just under a cork oak that seemed to sway ever so slightly with no wind or reason. Joana sat there, staring unblinking at the vines. Wisteria, Nightmare-hued, the blooms arranged as vague human bodies, like corpse chalk lines.

'You shouldn't look,' Bilal muttered, with an odd sense of déjà vu.

Trying to placate his ex, that's what this reminded him of. The sinking feeling of having done something wrong, breaking some discreet rule and being guaranteed a short period of violent arguing or a long period of numb awkwardness.

'Because I'll get Hagged,' Joana said in a wispy voice, as if talking to herself, still staring.

Bilal stepped in front of her line of sight. His shadow fell over her. 'Yes,' he said. 'You don't want that.'

She looked up, opened her mouth, left something unsaid, then said, 'How did you get it?'

Like most people get it, he thought. There were many ways to get Hagged, but all were random and none were obvious. During the decades it had taken for the divinity from outer space to undo this world, It had stipulated many rules, each more nonsensical than the next. Some were specific to each city. In Almagris, it was dangerous to drink wine with your left hand, and no whistling on rainy days.

'The Internet, I think,' Bilal said. That was an intercity rule: no going on the Internet for long. Particular care to avoid the social media graveyards. None of the new content was made by living people.

'What were you doing?'

Browsing ways to cope with post-breakup blues, he recalled. 'Social media graveyard. I read a thread titled something like... *What are some hated bands that are actually good?*'

'And what were they?'

Bilal should have learned by now not to be surprised by her questions, but he was. 'I... don't think any were retrieved yet. There were these guys... Coldplay? Probably a metal band.'

'Russian Circles,' Joana said.

'Huh?'

'It's a band,' she said. 'Instrumental. It's heavy stuff, but kinda sounds like classical music.'

'Ah. Yeah.' A moment of silence, during which she kept staring at him, unblinking. 'I like Madredeus.'

'Not a fan of the Portuguese guitar. And movies, what'd you like, aside from schlock horror?'

That's where they'd seen each other last, in the rental store. The dead god, in Its magnanimous arbitrariness, had made it so VHS tapes were safe, easy to retrieve, and capable of reproducing up to 8k in resolution. Bilal and Joana had reached for the same tape: *Maximum Overdrive*, a movie about trucks springing to life to murder people.

They'd bonded over it, Joana saying she loved horror-comedy and Bilal silently thinking to himself that there was nothing funny about trucks. Six-ton behemoths coming at you a hundred kilometres an hour, and the only thing that protected you was a bit of white paint on the road. He couldn't believe people had had to contend with that in the past.

Eventually, he'd broken the silence, shared the thought. And she'd laughed at his horror and asked for his landline.

And now here they were.

'Sci-fi. Movies about space,' he said.

Joana looked up at the sky. 'Can't believe there used to be people up there, sending messages back from space...'

'There still are,' Bilal said.

'What do you mean?'

This was privileged information. Dangerous information. Bilal already regretted mentioning it, but he always committed to his mistakes. 'I've got a friend in Intercity Comms.' She narrowed her eyes at that, for some reason. 'She says they're still getting messages from the ISS.'

'How is that possible?'

'Because it's not *them*,' Bilal said. 'It's like Washington. We're still getting messages from the American president, but we know it's not him. It's something else. We're—' He cleared his throat. 'They're told not to pick up, under any circumstances.'

'And London?' she whispered. Bilal frowned. They didn't talk about London. No one did. She should know better.

Maybe she did, because she added, 'Did you see the Hag?'

Bilal quietly considered if – on the unlikely chance they started dating – she would always ask this kind of question. He'd worked for Nightmare Management, sure, no use hiding that now, no matter how many NDAs they'd pelted him with, but it wasn't something he was keen on reminiscing.

'I did,' he murmured.

'Does she still visit you?'

'Sometimes.'

She took his hand. He looked at her. She wiped her eyes.

Before he could ask what was going on, she said, 'I live nearby. Do you want some tea?'

The cockroaches didn't drink tea. By extension, Bilal didn't, either.

But it'd been a while since he'd had something warm.

*

If it were a movie, they'd go at it with hunger, tearing clothes, smashing tongues, bumping against the walls, breaking vases. But Bilal hadn't been with anyone since his Hagging, and he had no idea how foreplay worked without kissing. Joana stared him in the eye, sliding out of her clothes in a way both mechanical and languid, her body a conjunction of narrow lines and hard muscle, perfect in the half-glow of a half-open window.

'I—'

She grabbed his cheeks, aggressive, admonishing, and kissed him deeply. Her eyes were closed. His were open, panicked, his mouth tingling with the countless roach legs scraping at her tongue.

When she pulled away, he stammered, 'The roa… Are y… They bite, they…'

She let herself fall on the bed, still staring, still unblinking.

*

If it were a movie, they'd be smoking. But they just lay there, listening to each other's breathing, him breathing the hardest. He was out of shape, but worrying about it felt good. A new inadequacy, in a life dominated by cockroaches.

He felt dizzy, drunk. The penumbra whirled like a carousel. The roaches slept.

'Rich boy,' Joana said, smiling and sibilant, stirring with

remnants of arousal, an arousal Bilal still couldn't believe in. 'Eating out twice in one night.'

*

He couldn't quite tell if he slept. He dove in and out of consciousness like a tired man swimming in a dark sea. Every time he semi-opened his eyes, he saw Joana, staring, tense but unafraid, as if waiting for something to snap out of him. Once or twice, he tried to say something, but the words were eaten by the roaches.

*

He woke with a dull pain in his gums. The cockroaches were frenzied, fleshy stalagmites and stalactites in his gums, scratching and biting at each other. The smell of crêpes filled the room, mingled with the smell of sex. Bilal put on his briefs and pants and went into the kitchen, humming a calming lullaby for the roaches.

Joana was by the stove, flipping crêpes with too much confidence for how bad she was at it, wearing the same panties and sweaty tank top as yesterday. 'They like carbs, innit?' she said.

Bilal's mouth hurt too much to speak, like having nails stuck in his gums all the way to the bone and yanking them side to side. Joana served him. The cockroaches all but pulled Bilal's jaw to the plate, little bungee-jumpers with ropes too short.

Rain pitted against the window.

'Wanna stay in, today?' Joana said.

'Don't you have work?' Bilal said.

'I'm between jobs at the moment.'

They spent the day eating garbage (literally, at one point, in Bilal's case) and watching the complete VHS set, in 8k, of a recently retrieved series, *The Good Place*. Joana made them chorizo sandwiches and a blueberry smoothie.

They talked about what their few mutual acquaintances were up to now.

'Pierre got married to a cop, of all people. She's thirty years his senior,' Bilal said.

'Melanie had a botched boob job. Then she got Hagged. Two baby heads grew on her chest. How lucky can you be?' Joana said.

They reminisced on the odd jobs they'd done.

'I narrated retrieved books, for a while,' Bilal said. 'That ship has sailed, though. No market for lisps.'

'I worked at an architectural firm, designing the transition zones where retrieved cities meet,' she said. 'They called it *coherence architecture*, trying to find common ground between the different styles.'

There were things Bilal didn't say, mostly about his job at Nightmare Management. And there were things she didn't say, either. They fucked a couple times on the couch.

At a certain point, Bilal had the nonsense thought that she was making out with the roaches.

*

Another night, another state of suspended sleep. Every time he opened his eyes, Bilal saw that Joana was awake, hugging herself and frowning in a sad-angry way, murmuring soundless questions, as if expecting answers from the gloom.

*

The next morning, Bilal found her passed out on the couch. She still hadn't showered, and her dirty face was streaked with tears. Bilal covered her with a grimy blanket and rummaged in her cabinets for milk and cereal. The sky was grey outside, as it always was.

As he poured the milk, Bilal's hands began to shake. He was overcome with a deep sense of forewarning, terror filling his marrow. He looked back, at Joana unconscious on the couch.

There was something on the wall behind her. A contour, a darkness.

No, not darkness. Absence of light.

It grew, dimmed the grey-lit kitchen.

Bilal leaped towards Joana and tried to shake her awake. The lightless thing grew. It droned in his head. Loud white noise, like infinite voices screaming. Bilal shouted in Joana's ear, shook her so violently her head bounced on the couch.

She opened her eyes.

Light returned.

'What is wrong with you?' Joana snapped. Her anger vanished when she saw how he was shaking, when she heard the cockroaches chirping in panic. 'What happened? Are you okay?'

'The Hag,' Bilal said. 'It came for you.'

There was a change in Joana's face.

A softening.

'I'm glad you're here,' she whispered, unworried.

Annoyed, if anything.

*

One more day spent in filth. Joana's pristine apartment had quickly soiled itself into looking like Bilal's. The sheets on the unmade bed were stained, an outline of their bodies in yellow. Joana didn't seem to care, nor did she let Bilal clean up. She said his cockroaches would likely calm down, knowing there was food everywhere in sight.

One more night. Bilal woke up to find her sleeping on the couch.

This time he came back into her room, and like a paranoid lover, looked through her things. In her drawers he found a dry stick of lipstick, a pair of scissors, a certificate for Safe Internet Usage, packets of paracetamol, tramadol, amitriptyline, and quetiapine, the latter all but empty. He found pictures, too, of her and a square-jawed man, a familiar man – Jean, from Nightmare Management. A colleague of Bilal's. A good man, brave and diligent, one of the best Scroungers in the business. Bilal had worked with him a couple of times. They'd set out from Almagris, armed only with sunlit lanterns, to find books and movies and music. They'd ventured into the pitch black of forlorn cities, inhabited by the preserved, dead bodies who silently went on their routines, puppeteered by the dead god.

'He got Hagged.' Joana, standing in the doorway, holding the pillow in front of her, like a child with a stuffed bear. She stank of stale sweat, even at this distance.

'Husband?' Bilal said. She must have heard the wariness in his voice, seen the anxious cockroach legs peering out of his lips, but she simply walked over and sat on the bed.

'Ex,' she said, her hair a curtain on both sides of her face, heavy with oil.

'I don't recall you mentioning him.'

'Never came up. You and I didn't talk that much.'

'Break up, or…'

'Both.' It seemed like she was going to stop there, but then, 'Bidirectional optical illusion. His head faced both front and sideways, no matter the angle you looked at him. Pretty benign Hagging, all things considered, but…'

But you couldn't look at him, Bilal thought. He was this

grotesque doppelganger of the one you loved, and you can't love an imitation. It's why rebounds fail. Nobody loves a pale comparison.

'Baker from across the street got it worse,' Joana continued, nodding at the window, at a night of mist and clouds amassed like congealed fat. 'His nostrils kept growing until he was lobbing around these two dark flaps, bigger than him. Ended up asphyxiating. How ironic. Not being able to breathe because your nostrils are too big.'

'How did it happen?'

'Suicide.'

The roaches tittered at Bilal's complete lack of surprise. He hadn't stayed in touch with his colleagues at NM, but he doubted Jean's suicide had registered as more than another scratch on the chalkboard. The thing above the sky had made sure there was nowhere to go but away.

'And you feel guilty,' he said.

'I wanted him gone,' she said, toneless. 'I couldn't look at him anymore.'

'You didn't kill him, Joana.'

A pause. 'He kept looking at the mirror. Turning his head, trying to find the right angle, to see his face as it was. He was so miserable.' She wrung her hands. 'But then he got better. He started making jokes. Bite into a sandwich and say: "Look, there's two. I'm Jesus, multiplying bread." She scoffed, forced laughter. 'I didn't laugh once.'

Bilal knew how the story went, but he let her continue. 'We didn't fuck, I always had an excuse. Never told him the truth, but he knew. I was miserable, he felt responsible, I felt guilty, he felt helpless. He left, I made a show of trying to stop it, not strongly enough that he'd be able to fool himself. They found him a week later.'

'And you cried, and everyone thought you were sad, but you felt relieved,' Bilal murmured.

'Yes.'

'And you think that if it wasn't for you, he'd still be alive.'

'He would be.'

'And you're trying to get Hagged, now. Self-punishment.' Bilal stopped there, but his thoughts carried on: *and now you fuck random Hagged guys, trying to convince yourself you could have accepted it, given time, trying to give a relic of joy to the wretched many who can't be looked at with less than disgust, much less lust, in honour of the man you let die because he wasn't beautiful anymore.*

Because beauty is all anyone loves. It might be subjective, it might be fetishized, it might be filtered through the finest sieve of desperation, of loneliness, but it's always there. You only love the beautiful.

She looked up at him, as if saying *yes*.

'No,' she said. 'That's not why I want it.'

'Why, then?'

'I want to see the Hag.'

More nothing. Just two strangers only now knowing each other, staring at each other in low light, in the secluded filth of a pristine neighbourhood. Cockroaches, alone in a derelict house, feeding off the skin flakes in the carpet and the bindings on old paper covers.

'That's not how it works,' Bilal said, only now realizing he'd been holding his breath. 'The Hag is not a person. She's more of a... a force. A sense, from the...' *The thing above the sky*, he almost said. 'A need. Like hunger or thirst.'

'She seemed real enough to you, yesterday.'

'That's—'

'You said it yourself: she still visits you, sometimes,' Joana

said. 'If I get Hagged, I'll see her. At least once. I'll be able
to—'

'You won't be able to do shit!' Bilal shouted. His voice
reverberated on the walls, followed by cockroach chirping.
His lips tingled. 'She paralyses you, Joana. She sits on your
chest, sucks all the air from your lungs, you can't breathe, you
see things, and when you wake up you've got cockroaches for
teeth and everything is different.' He inhaled for a bit of self-
control, failed, and, 'That's why you want me here, isn't it? You
know you can't get it from fucking me, but you hope the Hag
visits when I'm around. And the meds, what, what are they
for? This shit.' He fumbled with the almost empty packet of
quetiapine, extracting the last pill and crushing it into powder
between thumb and index finger. Dozens of roach legs reached
out of his lips, flailing madly for the cloud of pill dust. '*Anti-
psychotic*, what're you doing with this?'

Joana opened her hand. Confused, breathing hard, Bilal
gave her the empty packet of quetiapine. She waved it in his
face, like a mother scolding her son. 'Off-label medication for
treatment-resistant insomnia,' she said, with a first, human hint
of hesitation. 'If you take it, but force yourself to stay awake,
you start hallucinating. Same as sleep paralysis, what the Hag
does to you.' She stood perfectly still. Her tone darkened. 'But
the difference is: you can move.'

'And then what? You'll bash the Hag over the head with
a fucking lamp? What, what is it you think you're gonna do,
Joana?'

'I... I just want to see the Hag.' She blinked, seemed to
become vaguely aware of her insomnia-matted logic, lowered
her eyes. 'Maybe the place she comes from is the same place
he went to, my husband. Maybe I can follow her. Maybe I can
see him.'

'He didn't go anywhere, Joana. No one does.'

Silence, sudden and heavy. For a minute Bilal just stood there, too conscious of his own body.

'I can't fucking stay here,' Bilal said. He left the room, grabbed at the front door. Locked. He went back into the bedroom. 'Give me the keys, Joana.'

'Please,' she said, so softly he had to read it on her lips.

'You need help, and I'm not it.' Saying it gutted him. He heard in himself the same cold disdain his ex had given him near the end, the one that made you feel both guilty and helpless. But it was for the best. For her own good. 'Give me the keys.'

A jingle, a slow hand, trembling. Bilal snatched the keys and stormed out. He clambered down the stairs and left to a city uncaring, a place that allows you to be, but nothing more.

*

There was no one around, but still he looked for a quiet place. And he found an alley, long and steep and pitching into the river far below, where rushes and avens flourished in the interstice between water and walkway. He sat on top, watching a riverman slide on the dark waters, bent over the side of his barge, likely looking for sunlight in the depths.

It wasn't cold, but he trembled. He gasped for breath. He was overwhelmed, with panic or anger or both.

You can't save the self-flagellant, he thought. Your attempts are just another whip.

And yet he stood.

*

When he got back inside, Joana was in bed, arms limp, eyes clear, and cheeks sunken. Still awake.

Slowly, feeling removed, Bilal lay next to her.

She craned her head to look at him, and he had the distinct impression of looking at a fresh corpse. 'In my nightmares,' she said, 'I'm sleeping on an empty bed.'

He held her gaze. It felt invasive, staring at her eyes for so long, counting the green striations sinking into the brown centre. She was so slack she seemed to be melting into the stained sheets.

'Get up, come on,' he said. 'You can't fall asleep.'

'But I am asleep.'

A shiver down his spine.

Something was different.

'Joana?'

The light flickered.

'Joana!'

The roaches went mad, like dogs sensing an earthquake. Bilal squinted against the pain in his mouth, eyes flickering to the changes in light. He heard wheezing. Himself, hyperventilating. He trembled, moved as if tugged by countless invisible hands.

Empty light. The smell of sickness. Cold. He could see Joana's breath. How her sternum sunk and ribs protruded, as if someone was sitting on her chest.

Bilal scrambled up, tackled the nothingness on top of Joana. He expected contact, but there was nothing tangible there. Just cold, clammy and stinging. He belly-flopped on top of her, who gasped in her sleep. He picked her up, numb fingers on cold skin, and carried her out into a hallway made labyrinthine by vertigo.

There was nothing on the front door. Nothingness. Collapsed light, encroaching in.

On the other side of the hallway was the Hag. An absence on the carpet.

Bilal took a deep breath, screamed, saliva spat by roach legs, and with Joana cradled hard against his chest he barrelled through the Hag. A wave of ice washed over him, sapped him of all energy, filled him with dread.

Miraculously on his feet, he stumbled into the kitchen. He couldn't scream anymore. He hummed pathetic, guttural sounds over mad roach chirping and the dry scuffing of his shoes on the carpet.

With one trembling hand, he fumbled with the window to the fire escape.

The Hag inched closer.

Bilal gasped when the window clicked open. He squeezed himself outside, scraping his side on the lower edge of the window, trying not to bang Joana's head on the frame.

He climbed down the fire escape in careful, stiff steps. The structure seemed to be swaying, as if pushed at all sides by an unfelt wind. Joana was limp, an impossibly heavy weight in his arms, and he was cold, so cold and tired, the endless night falling on him like a weighted blanket, and then his hands were empty, and there was something on his back, pushing him down, bending him over the railing, and the ground below was far and hard and tempting, and...

Roach bites, excruciating. Bilal pushed back against the railing, fell on his ass.

Joana was splayed at the foot of the stairs below.

'No...' Bilal croaked. He pushed himself down the stairs, kept awake by the roach bites, aware of a desolating, empty presence passing through him. 'No!'

Bilal tumbled down the stairs, felt one of his roaches smash into pieces. The pain was like a hot needle into an exposed tooth nerve. He stayed conscious by pure, insect survival instinct, and managed to pick up Joana and climb down to street level.

The streets were deserted. He moaned for help, but no one

came. Nothing good prowled at this hour. He kept walking, numbly considering how long this street was. How maybe he wasn't seeing right.

When his legs gave out, he made sure to fall over Joana, blinking horrified at the bloody gash on her temple. How he hoped the white wasn't bone.

And he knew he couldn't sleep, not until the city released the first wisps of sunlight. So he stayed like that, convulsing in pain, staring at Joana's eyelids, breathing her reek, while the Hag waited nearby, a nothingness horror with infinite patience.

*

Hands, patting, pushing, pulling. A sense of lightness, the taste of grit. Bilal murmured for them to stop moving him, that he was going to be sick. But he didn't feel sick. He didn't feel much at all, cradled in so many hands, cocooned like some parasite, not wanting to be born.

*

Flashes. A hospital, sick lights and scurrying late-night personnel. White scrubs passing him like ghosts. People sleeping in foetal positions on plastic chairs.

What were they dreaming of?

*

Bilal woke to the smell of antiseptic. He blinked against the sting in his eyes, waiting for the grey light of dawn to subside. When it did, he saw that he was in a hospital room, and that Joana was there.

'Hey there, sweet prince,' she said.

Bilal wiped a hand on his face. Cockroach legs scratched at his palm. There was a dull ache in his mouth. He searched the spot with his tongue, found a half-crushed, limp cockroach, pushed against it lightly like it was a loose tooth. Cockroaches ate their own, but his hadn't. They'd left their sister there, made a grave of his gums.

He whimpered in unexpected, nonsensical anguish. Joana sat on the bed and hugged him to her chest.

'You're okay…' she whispered.

Bilal pulled away softly. He dabbed his tongue at the dead cockroach again. 'Why haven't they taken her out?'

Joana caressed her own arms. She looked away, then back at him shyly. 'The doctors aren't sure how it'll affect you. They said surgery is discouraged, with Haggings of this nature.'

'She'll rot. That can't be good either,' he said. 'Are you okay?'

She stopped herself from touching the bandages on her head. 'Yeah. Barely broke the skin. Scalps just bleed a lot, they said.'

'That's not what I meant.'

She nodded, curtly. 'I'm good.'

Laughter, coming from the hallway. Two doctors flirting, it seemed.

'That's it?' Bilal said. 'You're good?'

'I'm sorry.' She held his hand. He let her, but didn't squeeze back.

'Are you going to do it again?'

She shook her head. 'I'm getting help.'

Shuddering, Bilal squeezed her hand.

'Good,' he said. 'That's good.'

*

Bilal stayed under observation for a week. Joana visited him every day for the next three, but the tension was bilateral now. Bilal didn't joke, and her jokes felt forced. She brought him a recently retrieved paperback, a fantasy book from the Eighties called *Waylander*. The thing above the sky had switched a couple sentences with nonsense written in some unknown, spiky script.

'The curators looked at those passages under the microscope,' she said. 'Those are photorealistic drawings of human faces at an atomic scale. Billions of them.'

That was the only interesting thing that'd passed between them, but Bilal only managed a nod in response. The cockroaches had finally begun to munch on the husk of their sister.

He made her promise not to do it again, not to try to get Hagged.

On the fourth day, Joana didn't come.

*

On the fifth day, an exhausted, yet too-enthusiastic doctor came back with the X-ray and slapped a finger on a tiny white dot on Bilal's upper jaw. 'Good news. We believe this is an egg,' he said, grinning. 'Well, technically an ootheca, which usually contain hundreds of eggs, but I wouldn't worry. The Hag doesn't exactly care for the conventions of biology.'

'Why is that good news?' Bilal said.

'Haggings follow a certain logic. If another cockroach is growing back, that means it should be safe to remove the carcass. What's left of it, anyway.'

'What happens if I don't?'

The doctor shrugged. 'The newborn will push it out. It'll be painful, though.' He clapped his hands. 'Should I schedule the surgery? The stomatologist can do it tonight.' He winked. 'We're not American, so you don't even need to go under.'

One of those jokes nobody understood, some stereotype lost in time.

'Okay,' Bilal said. 'Okay. Take it out. Thank you.'

*

The next day he was back home. The smell was nauseous. Bilal didn't know if something had gone rotten in the meantime or if he'd just gotten unused to the stink. He went shopping for cleaning supplies and, while snacking on insect food (the doctor's suggestion, to calm the roaches), scrubbed his house from top to bottom.

It took him two full days, and by the end he was exhausted. Crashing on his clean bedding, he closed his eyes and, unexpectedly, found himself feeling not bad.

*

Second week out of the hospital. Bilal was preparing himself for a job interview: entry-level position for a local curatorship firm. His job would be to review retrieved technical books, highlighting any Nightmarish adulterations.

Bilal was midways through a clumsy Windsor knot when his phone rang. On his way to pick up, he almost tripped on Peevy, the kitty he'd recently adopted, who was again crying for food and coiling himself between Bilal's legs.

'Calm down, fatso,' Bilal said. He picked up the phone. 'Hello?'

'Hey.'

It was Joana. Bilal hadn't spoken to her in a week now, but it felt like it had been longer. 'Hey,' he said, guarded. 'How are you?'

'Don't rightly know how to answer that…' she said, with a joking, forced tone. He heard her exhale. 'I… I've got something to tell you.'

'When?' Bilal said.

'What?'

'I know what you're going to tell me,' Bilal said. 'When?'

That hit her by surprise. The line fell silent, but for the usual, distant, white-noise screaming.

'Three nights ago,' she sobbed.

'You did it on purpose; you called the Hag,' he said. 'I thought you were getting help.'

'I'm sorry…' she said. 'I'm so fucking stupid…' For a while, she just cried. Sudden, full-ugly crying. Bilal felt his heart rend. Peevy meowed again.

Joana sniffed. 'You got a cat?'

'This isn't a good time, Joana. I've got a job interview.'

'Oh? Congrats.' She cleared her throat. 'Don't you want to know what it is? It's kinda funny.' Before Bilal could say no, she went on. 'Pinkies, all along my spine. I can even wiggle them.' Laughter, short and hysterical. 'I look like a freaky stegosaurus.'

'I really have to go.'

'Wait! Do you… Do you wanna come over later?' She sniffed again. 'I miss you.'

'I miss you too,' Bilal said, and it hurt how true it was. How they'd flash-forwarded a couple of days into real connection, two needy people pawing at each other, and how they'd shattered it just as quickly. 'But I can't, I'm sorry. This isn't right for me.'

'Oh…'

'I'm sorry.'

'No, it's okay. I understand…' She held her breath, blew it out slowly. 'And if I get help?'

'I really have to go, Joana.'

'I'll get help. I promise.'

'I'll be here, if you do.'

Click.

Bilal went to get his coat. Peevy followed him, tail raised like an antenna. Bilal picked him up and scratched him behind the ear. The cat purred and pawed playfully at Bilal's mouth, at the tiny black legs jutting in and out.

For the first time that day, Bilal remembered that he had cockroaches for teeth. The clock marked five in the afternoon. He'd been awake since seven in the morning.

Where the Trains Turn

Pasi Ilmari Jääskeläinen

Finland

I've been a fan of Pasi's since reading his wonderful *The Rabbit Back Literature Society* when it was published by Pushkin Press in English in 2013. May I urge you to seek it out? 'Where The Trains Turn' is equally radiant, and I fell in love with it when it first appeared. I wanted it in the *Best of World SF* from the beginning, and finally gathered the courage to contact Pasi about it – who couldn't have been more affable. Join me, then, on this last excursion, as this volume comes to an end. I hope it has been worth the journey. This story is translated by Liisa Rantalaiho.

> *If it's in any way possible for You, please make this some-how unhappened! I'll give you anything!*
> A typical child's prayer, directed to any sufficiently omnipotent Divine Being who chances to be listening

Not since my girlhood have I bothered to read books that contain invented events or non-existent people, were they written by Hemingway, Joyce, Mann, Blyton, Christie, Jansson or any other of the millions of literary talents in this universe – I prefer unquestionable facts, and to relax I sometimes like to read encyclopaedias. It's hard enough to cope day by day with what presumes to be my own everyday reality; to stir and feed imagination with fiction would just make me lose my sense of reality altogether. It's pretty fickle already, my understanding of which part of the things I remember has actually happened and what is composed of mere empty memories which never had a reference in the historical continuum that's called objective reality.

I don't like to think about the past, because it mixes my head up and makes my bowels loose and gives me a severe migraine to boot. But I cannot stop remembering my son. That's why I still often sneak with a spade to the graveyard of my memories and dig up pieces of my life with my son Rupert. Of his peculiarly fatal relationship to trains, of his brilliant days of success and happiness that made me so proud, and of everything else.

For the sake of my son I write down these thoughts, seek him from dream images, from memories, from everywhere. Perhaps I'm afraid I'll forget him, but could I forget?

I hunt my memories, examine them, turn and twist them, and try to understand what happened and why; for Rupert's sake I consider the eternal logical circle of cause and effect and my own part in it, trying to get some sense out of it, as painful and against my nature as such an effort always has been to me.

*

Even as a girl I understood how important it is to live in a world as logical and sensible as possible. I never let myself be ruled by grand emotions, and yet was quite reasonably happy (or at least fairly unruffled most of the time), and then just I, out of all the world's expectant women, became Rupert's mother.

Even as a baby he was restless, probably had nightmares, poor thing, and quite soon it turned out that my blue-eyed son Rupert was not a very sensible child. He let loose a mental chaos; even for a child he was extremely irrational. By and by he made an actual art form of his addiction to irrationality. At five years old, for example, he had a strange mania to mix calendars and set all the clocks he found to a wrong time. When he turned seven, I bought him a watch of his own, a golden Timex. He liked it, very much indeed, and wound it up regularly, but always it was an hour or two fast or slow, sometimes even more.

More than a couple of times I was seized with a feeling that I had been caught in the middle of The Great Irrationality Circus where Rupert was a pompous mad director. Even looking at him made my head ache.

I miss him every day. Sometimes I still go to the window in the middle of preparing dinner and perhaps imagine seeing him in the backyard, the silly old owl that I am, just like decades ago, in another time, another life:

Rupert was playing on the backyard. Like a whirlwind dressed in a sun-yellow T-shirt and blue terry shorts, he flew from here to there: from the tree stump to the currant bush, from the bush to the old puffed-up rowan that had been just sitting in the middle of the backyard very likely since creation, and on again to the nervously trembling top of the tree. From there the boy kept chatting to the birds flying by, to the clouds, to the sky, the sun and to the tree itself.

I repressed my urge to run out and yell at Rupert to come down to the ground at once on pain of a severe punishment before he would fall and break his slender fledgling-neck and spoil the whole beautiful summer day by dying and becoming one of those stupidly careless kids the curt news-in-brief in the papers always told about.

I turned my back to the kitchen window. 'Where do you plan to go today?' I asked Gunnar. My emphatically civilized tone reflected my inner turmoil as little as possible. I poured out more coffee for my guest. I always made him coffee, although I knew he'd actually have wanted cocoa. I did have a tin of cocoa behind the flour bags on the upper shelf, but that was for Rupert – grown-ups, according to my opinion, ought to drink coffee or tea.

'I don't know. Wherever we fancy.'

'I do know: to the railway, as always. I can't figure what you actually see in those railways,' I muttered.

'Is it really so inconceivable to you?' Gunnar asked with a strange expression on his face. 'That your son has a yearning to be close to the railway? And that the sound of a train quickens his blood?'

I shook my head, embarrassed. I couldn't figure what he was after. I waited for some kind of an explanation, but he just smiled his irritating Mona Lisa smile, and I did not feel like muddling my head with his riddles.

He sat at the kitchen table, erect and altogether faultlessly upright, slim and polished. He was well-featured but slightly pale (as was Rupert). The almost feminine elegance of his slender limbs and graceful movements didn't really lessen his distinctive masculinity, which flowed from somewhere deeper in his personality. He wore perfect greyish tailor-made suits and even his ties probably cost as much as an ordinary off-the-peg suit. Now he had on a smart copper-toned tie, given as a Father's Day gift on Rupert's behalf a couple of years ago. The man looked what he was – a Very Important Person in a big firm, with more money in his pockets, power and contacts than any single person ever really needed.

'Perhaps we'll leave then,' he said. He went to the hall and stopped for a moment. 'I'll bring the boy back before evening. Round 17.30, as usual. Well, Emma, enjoy the silence. Are you going to do anything special today? It's a good day to drive to town and go to a movie for instance.'

'Movies I'll leave to little boys – that's who they are made for,' I said. 'You know I don't care about movies.'

'Yes. I just tend to forget it,' Gunnar admitted. He seemed a little annoyed at his absentmindedness. 'I'm sorry.'

Gunnar flashed me a somewhat feeble smile and left (the time was 11.14, so they had well over six hours for their railway outing).

I sensed in Gunnar a certain subsurface hardness and even ruthlessness that success in the financial world undoubtedly called for. I knew he could be rather cold when necessary, so I could appreciate that he had always without exception treated me politely and kindly. His kindness, however, had a reserved tone, as if he were attending to a very important long-term business affair with me, nothing more nor less.

Which in a way he was, too: he paid me more than fair maintenance (making it possible for me to be a full-time mother) and once a month spent a day with the child I had born from his seed. We had nothing else in common. Between us there were no shared memories, chocolate boxes, kisses, lovers' quarrels or soft words, just easy little compliments: *Well, Emma, you look quite pretty today in your beige slacks!* Now and then I found it difficult to believe that only eight years back we'd had intimate intercourse with each other. But Rupert of course was rather concrete evidence of it, thus believe I must – we both must.

That evidence, or his own part in the boy's existence, the man had never even tried to question. I knew of course that he liked to appear a perfect gentleman, a kind of modern blueblood (and with one's *noblesse oblige*), but still his correctness bordering upon the noble was a bit amazing, considering the unconventional circumstances of the child's conception.

From between the orange kitchen curtains I watched how Gunnar called the boy down from the tree, caught him in his arms from a trustful leap and took him away in his thunder-coloured BMW.

My stomach was hurting nastily, though my menses were still days off. I didn't like to let Rupert out of my sight. From the very moment I had felt the first faint kicks inside me, I'd also started to fear losing my child in some totally unpredictable manner (as irrational as the feeling may have been), and that early fear never fully let go.

Once a month I was unavoidably left alone, the house became quiet, and I became uneasy. I lived with Rupert every day. I chose, bought and washed his clothes, I ate with him, I listened to his troubles. I woke him up in the morning and tucked him up in the evening. I had subscribed to *Donald Duck* comics for him. I applied sticking plasters to his cuts. I measured and weighed him regularly and kept a diary of his development. I took snapshots of him for the family album. A couple of days before I'd baked him his seventh birthday cake, which we two had (for once not caring about the consequences) eaten the same day, and I had held his head above the toilet when he had finally started to puke. Nevertheless, I felt like a terrific outsider when I thought about the outings Rupert and Gunnar had together. They seemed to mean so much to the boy, sometimes more than all the rest of his life.

And why was that?

One could easily have imagined that a successful businessman like Gunnar would have taken the boy from one amusement park to another and ladled into the boy's bottomless gullet ice cream helpings the price of a bicycle and deluxe pear lemonades and special order hamburgers and generally used all the tricks made possible by money to treat the boy like a divine child emperor. So lightly he could have afforded even to fly the boy once a month to Disneyland to shake hands with Donald Duck; so easily he could have with the power of money made the child's whole home environment seem like a furnished cardboard box. He could well have filled the pockets of his son with an absurdly big allowance and bought him the moon from the sky and had two spare ones made.

But nothing like that from Gunnar; the larger-than-life moments of Rupert's life were created in a quite different way. Once a month the man simply arrived with a packet of sandwiches and a bottle of juice or perhaps a couple of gingerbreads in his pocket and took the boy to look at rails. Railways, tracks, those that trains use to go from one place to another. Not the elephants and giraffes and monkeys in the zoo, not the newest movie hit, not the dancing clowns, not the new wonderful toys in the department stores. To look at the rust-coloured railway tracks, that's where he took the boy: they searched on the map and in nature for new railway sections and walked the hours of their day together along the tracks doing nothing special; they just walked and enjoyed each other's company and stopped for a while to eat their sandwiches and then went on, and when the boy came home, I saw him simply tremble with restrained happiness and excitement and satisfaction as if he had seen at least all the wonders of the universe and met Santa Claus and the Tooth Fairy and a thousand speaking gingerbread reindeers as well.

I had sometimes tried to ask Rupert about it. He made my temples throb when he started to speak like a preacher about the Wonderful Smell of Railways and how it actually contained all the world's secrets.

I knew well enough when I was not in my own territory, not even close. Besides, it was, after all, a question of something shared between the two, father and son, which wasn't really my business, so in spite of my vague forebodings I thought best to let it be.

Until Rupert came home from such a track excursion hysterically sobbing and shaking, white as a washbasin, as if he had met eye to eye with the Children's Own Grinning Reaper himself and had to shake his bony hand.

*

I knew at once that everything was not all right when I lifted my eyes from the flowerbed I'd been scraping, and saw them returning already at 3.25.

I had my hands full coping with the situation. To start, I chased Gunnar off, bleeding with scratches as he was. I acted purely from my spinal cord, as mothers always do in such situations; acted with the rage of a dinosaur in a white summer dress. Gunnar tried to explain: he could not understand what had come over the boy – he'd just been carrying him piggyback and stepped on the bank as he'd heard the approaching train, and suddenly the boy had gone completely crazy on his back and started to tear Gunnar's hair and face and to scream unintelligibly like some rabid, drooling monkey.

If Rupert had come home thoroughly scared, Gunnar was just as terrified. He behaved like a dog that vaguely understands he's being judged for complicity in some Very Bad Thing and knows for certain that he'll get a bullet in his brain.

I almost felt sorry for him.

The dinosaur in me felt no pity, it attacked. I yelled at him till my lungs hurt. I probably hit him, too – at least, his nose suddenly started to bleed.

He shook his head perplexed, stepping back and forth in the backyard, dabbing his nose with a handkerchief and nervously straightening his suit, covered in grey dust, having for once lost his relaxed erectness of carriage (for which I, for a brief moment, felt maliciously pleased). Then he glanced quickly at me, turned his eyes somewhere up, at Rupert's window I suppose, and started to speak: 'If I have caused trouble, I'm sincerely sorry. If you want, I'll leave. But I have to say that with the boy I've always felt that, for once, I'm involved with something larger than my own life. You know what: he will yet do something significant, something wonderful, something which neither of us now can even dream about. I have an instinct for those things. And if he—'

I told him to be quiet and leave my backyard (although not quite in those words), and he obeyed. As Gunnar, defeated, got in his car and drove away, the dinosaur was gratified – it had won.

I had no idea that I'd never again see the only man in this life I'd ever allowed to push his male protrusion inside me: about half an hour later he would be crushed to death together with his car, and his wiry bird-boned being would be transformed to a mixed metal-and-bone paste (I know, because I later went to see the photo the police had taken of the accident scene).

But that shock was still to come. Now I had to compose myself so that I could go and calm down Rupert who, piteously wailing, had run upstairs and locked himself in his room.

I went up the stairs and knocked on Rupert's door. 'Let me in!' I ordered, my cheek at the door. 'What's got into you?'

'The trains,' came a trembling whisper from the other side of the door. 'The trains!'

'What about them?' I tried to keep my voice calm. I strained hard and realized suddenly that I'd been trying to see through the chipping, white, painted surface of the door. Just like that X-ray-eyed Superman Rupert admired, it struck me. Well, this was how it went, this was how Rupert made *even me* behave irrationally! (I had always felt a deep antipathy towards that red-caped clown who wiped his un-holed arse with logic and credibility and, besides, provoked children to jump out of windows with bath towels on their neck.)

I wondered whether my poor child had on his face a foolish maniacal grin, and a sudden horror stabbed my ovaries. Had my worst fears now come true in this dreadful way? Would my son end up for the rest of his life in a little boys' mental institution, where he would be dressed in a little teddy-bear-patterned straightjacket?

I heard a choked request: 'Mummy, please go and look out of the window.'

I did. A cold bit of flesh pretending to be a heart was slapping in my breast and I felt faint. I looked out of the round window in the upper hall, where sweaty houseflies kept buzzing in competition in the shady afternoon light.

'And then what? What should I see? Your father? He had to leave already. He may phone you later. Or you can phone him.'

'Do you see a train there?' asked a wan voice. 'It didn't follow me here, did it?'

Finally, I got Rupert convinced that there was no train in the backyard, not even the smallest inspection trolley, and he let me in his room and, after a long stumble over his words, started to tell what it had all been about.

*

In the crèche and the kindergarten and even in the school they had praised my son's 'boundless and creative imagination', which they said was manifested in his play and his artistic creations. I did admit that imagination might be useful, too, provided it remained within certain proper limits. But what was there worth praising in something that made a human being babble to stones and trees and see non-existent things?

Perceiving reality was hard enough for the child, even without idle and completely unnecessary fantasies. And imagination by no means made Rupert *happy*; on the contrary he had always suffered greatly from it. A hairy monkey paw growing in the middle of his forehead would have brought him just as much joy. His social life was surely not cultivated by talking to birds rather than to other kids. And the drawings expressing 'boundless and creative imagination' which he manufactured would have been enough to employ a legion of child psychiatrists:

> *'Oh what a nice picture! Is it a cow? And that must be a milking machine.'*
>
> *'No.' (The child is very indignant about his mother's poor insight.) 'It's a horse-moose who travels in a time machine to the Jurassic period where the dinosaurs will eat him up.'*
>
> *(Mother takes an aspirin and a glass of water.)*

Rupert's drawings were technically quite sophisticated and even precocious, but he never let the objective reality interfere with their content. Such can be very depressing to a sensible adult who only wants to make her child understand how the real world functions.

*

'The train tried to kill us,' said Rupert.

He sat, feet crossed, upon the comic books spread on

his bed, wiped sweat from his round forehead and stared absentmindedly at the beam of afternoon light in the room. It was catching the dust motes in between model airplanes hanging from the ceiling. I crouched on the floor by the bed and tried to catch his eyes.

'The train tried to kill you,' I repeated as expressionlessly as a machine to show that I listened.

'We were walking on the track. I sat on Daddy's shoulders. It was warm and the sun warmed our skin and the air was shimmering and everything looked funny. Daddy even took his coat off and opened his waistcoat and rolled up his sleeves. The tie he never takes off, however hot it is. He says it's a matter of principle and every time a man dresses or undresses he makes a far-reaching decision on who he actually is and who he is not. We'd found a whole new section of tracks; it's far beyond that long tunnel and the big rocky mountain. We had to drive a long way on the big road and back along all kinds of funny side roads to get there. The rails there smelled completely different. Much stronger. Daddy said it might mean that we were closer to the secret of railways than ever before. I asked what the secret was, but he just smiled as always, kind of pleased.

'Then we started hearing a train noise. Such a queer rattle, like a hundred tin buckets were banged with iron pipes, each in a rhythm that was a bit different. It's a kind of scary noise. Like thunder on the ground. It came from somewhere behind us.

'At first I wasn't scared, but then I started to feel that all was not as it should be. That smell started to feel too strong in my nose, and somehow wrong.

'And I glanced behind and saw the train. It came towards us. It was hard to see because it came from the direction of the sun, but I saw it anyway. First it was sneaking slowly but then, when it saw that I had noticed it, it started to come faster. It accelerated. And I saw that it wanted us. Daddy heard it coming, too, and we moved to the bank, but it was not enough. It would never have been enough; the train would have got us from there, too. But Daddy did not understand, he was like in a dream. I had to get Daddy somehow to run off before it was too late.'

'How could it have got you from there?' I asked in an unnaturally calm voice.

Rupert stared at me with his big blue eyes that now were like two deep saucers of cold fear. 'That train was one of the *outside-of-timetables* kind. It did not run on rails. It pretended to, but it went a little beside them. I saw. I tried to get Daddy to realize that we had to run, but he seemed not to understand anything I told him. Not even when we had just before been talking about such trains.'

The boy swallowed audibly and crept to the window. His paranoid gaze raked the view.

'*Such* trains,' I repeated. The back of my head was pricking. 'Now listen, Rupert, what kind of trains are we actually talking about here?'

'The ones that leave the timetable and run off rails,' Rupert sighed.

He kept looking out. The rowan crown was swaying behind the window; it stirred the now oppressive backyard air that swarmed with insects flying dazedly to and fro.

The boy's fingers were fumbling with each other nervously and the narrow chest beneath the yellow shirt was heaving violently. There was an asthmatic, wheezing tone in his respiration that I'd never noticed before.

I had to talk seriously with him, really talk. I assumed an

understanding and gently motherly smile and opened my mouth.

'What has that man put into your head!' I shrieked.

The voice escaping from my mouth startled even me; I sprang up and hit my head badly on the window board. I groaned from pain.

Rupert turned to look at me in astonishment – at last I'd achieved his full attention.

'Trains do not jump off the rails,' I articulated carefully so that the child was sure to hear and understand what I was saying. 'They stay on the rails and go along them from one place to another. And besides…'

Rupert looked at me expectantly.

'Besides, trains are just big inanimate machines driven by humans,' I declared.

The boy smiled at me. Not in a relieved way. He smiled in that special way reserved for those who clearly do not know what they are talking about.

'Trains do go along rails from one place to another,' he admitted kindly. 'And usually they also stay on the rails. Usually. That's the official truth. But there is another truth that is less known. A secret. Sometimes they leave their timetables and tracks and are in the wrong place at the wrong time, and then they make trouble for people. Then they are not as they normally are, and you'd better not trust them at all. They are supposed to stay on the rails and follow the timetables to be as they are meant to be, just inanimate machines that obey people. But sometimes they do actually leave the rails and break off beyond their timetables. And then they change. Their own deep hidden nature comes out. They become different. Mean and clever. And *very* dangerous.'

'Indeed.' I found it difficult to speak. 'So they leave the tracks?'

'Yes. They leave their tracks,' Rupert enlightened me. His voice broke when he continued: 'There, where the trains turn.'

The sad news of the death of Rupert's father reached us a couple of days later, and I can't say that it made my efforts to normalize the situation any easier (I admit that 'to normalize' is a somewhat peculiar choice of words in connection with Rupert). The identity of the victim of last Sunday's railroad crossing accident had started to become clear only the following day, when a swarm of little boys found the lost number plate; it had drifted downstream in the brook close to the accident site and got stuck in a dam the boys had built.

The term 'obscure circumstances' was used a couple of times. Police and all kinds of inspectors came to talk to us, and afterwards I could not remember what they had asked or what I had answered to them.

When I went shopping on the north side I heard the villagers talk almost nostalgically about a train accident that had taken place two decades earlier in the neighbourhood. That had, after all, been of a completely different scale than this minor tame railroad crossing accident which didn't even merit a proper news story: In the past, a goods train had actually been derailed in the Houndbury railway section, with dramatically unpleasant consequences – then, in the middle of the Fifties, there had of course been in front of the train cars one of those good old steam locomotives, the last of which had been taken off sometimes in the seventies.

Two persons had died in the accident: an engine driver and a little local girl. There had been large horrified headlines in almost all newspapers and it had even been announced on the radio; publicity loves innocent victims (at least when they are not too many and not too far away). When the train had been derailed, it had, by a terrible whim of chance, crushed the child playing on the bank, the daughter Alice of the district surgeon Holmsten.

Unless I completely misremembered, Alice Holmsten had been in the same class with me in primary school, and we had perhaps been friends. But of all memories, the childhood memories are always the most confused and subjective, so I couldn't be sure about it. Actually, I didn't even manage to think about the matter, the present was too much for me.

After he had left us, Gunnar had obviously been driving south along little side roads – he lived after all in Helsinki, when he wasn't on a business trip to Bonn, London, Paris, Tokyo or some other distant place (Rupert received picture postcards with a railway theme from everywhere). Thirty kilometres away there was a level crossing, with scant traffic but not completely unused. The two o'clock extra slow train from Tampere to Eastern Finland had led to Gunnar's death.

The engine driver said in the interrogation that when the train arrived at the railroad crossing everything had seemed to be in order; the track had been free, and suddenly the purple car waiting behind the crossing had driven straight in front of the train – obviously the gate hadn't come down properly either. The train hurrying eastwards had caught Gunnar's thunder-reflecting car with it, crumbled and torn it in passing as if it hadn't been a real car at all but an origami folded from purple paper, and then thrown its remains in the willow bushes growing by the track.

I decided not to think about the matter any more than I had to. Gunnar was dead, gone. By coincidence he had driven under a train. He had been beside himself because of Rupert's fit, the gate had been up, and Gunnar hadn't noticed the approaching train. That was all. As usual, what had happened could not be undone, not by any means.

I knew some people think that the daily and sometimes merciless course of life is a kind of kids' puzzle where you have to connect the points in a correct order and find out whatever is hiding in the picture. Effect was always preceded by a cause, of course, and the cause itself was always a consequence of something. To seek logic and meaning from every coincidence, however, was likely to push a person towards the deep pit of madness, with sharp stakes waiting at the bottom. I could not afford to cloud my mind with unnecessary speculations or shaky what-ifs. I needed all my strength to help my son, since, now he had lost his father, he needed his mother more than ever.

Rupert of course took it as self-evident that his father had been killed by the same train that had tried to kill them both earlier, never mind logic or timetables; I don't know whether he actually said the thought aloud, but he didn't need to – it shone from his whole being. And he could not be blamed. His poor little mind was tortured by those strange stories that Gunnar in his great lack of judgment had fed him. The railways may well have meant a great and wonderful adventure and boundless fantasy to Rupert, and all that had surely been rather pleasant as long as it had stayed that way. But now the caramel-coloured surface of the fantasy had fallen off and the dark colours of chaos, nightmare and bitter fear of death had come out – the real nature of fantasy!

With difficulty, I pieced together hazy bits of truth to form at least some vague picture of what the father and son had been doing together during the last years. I got the impression that during their walks together Gunnar had at first talked to the boy of various relatively harmless things. Then Rupert had become excited and asked about railways and trains, and finally the man had probably become a little tired answering his endless questions and started to make up his own stories, which again had provoked Rupert to evolve even stranger questions. In this way they had been inciting each other, and finally, perhaps to silence the boy for at least a moment, Gunnar obviously had come to invent that dark, terrifying, perverted story:

Daddy, how far do those rails go?
  All around the world back to this same place.

Do these rails go to China?
  Yes, they do. And to Australia and France and even Africa. Sometimes bored lions start following the rails and stray even as far as here. Luckily that's rare.

If you lead electric current to the rails here, will somebody on the other side of the world get an electric shock?
  Yes, he will, if he happens to touch the rails just then. But one shouldn't lead electric current to the rails, because electricity goes around the globe and comes back here and then you'll get an electric shock yourself.

How do people know where each train goes and what time they ought to get on?
  From the timetables. Trains go according to certain exact timetables.

Always?
  Well not quite always. Sometimes they cannot keep their timetables. Then they'll be at a wrong time in a wrong place, and that results in confused situations and sometimes even bad trouble for people. Believe me, I've met with that myself.

Must the trains going in that direction circle around the whole globe to get back home? They can't reverse the whole way back, can they?

Of course not: there are places where the trains turn. But those places really aren't any kids' playgrounds. This is actually a secret, but let me tell you something...

And thus, it became clear what would thereafter be my primary task: to dig from the boy's head all the dangerous fantasies that had slipped in there, before they would take root there too firmly and produce a terrible harvest.

We lived south of the little village of Houndbury (nowadays Houndbury wants to call itself officially a city, as touchingly megalomaniac and attention-seeking as that may sound). Actually there were two Houndburies: the rapidly transforming North and the South that had kept its old homely face from the Fifties, and at that time still been saved from the bite of Development's concrete teeth. In the beginning of the Seventies, the North side had quickly filled up with new cubic metres of tenement houses, poor industrial plants and hungry supermarkets. We people on the South side instead still had lots of pensive detached houses, wildly flourishing gardens and clean swimming beaches and forests. Along our meandering paths you could get from everywhere to everywhere without seeing a single human dwelling or a paved road on the way. And yet we from South Houndbury could whiz quickly to the North side to enjoy the services of the area, neither was the nearest city too far away when needed. Our children were thus very lucky.

I would have let both my breasts be ground to mink food if only Rupert, too, could have been one of those healthy, noisy, happy children one saw in our neighbourhood. They raced each other, rode recklessly on their bikes and played football and ice hockey. They yelled, screamed and fought each other. They broke windows, went swimming, blasted firecrackers and stole raw apples to throw them at house walls and roofs and at people's heads from behind the hedges.

Of course, I would have punished Rupert if I'd heard that he was involved in such tricks. But I'd have done that smiling, knowing that my son was a completely normal boy who only needed a proper mixture of motherly love and discipline to grow up a man.

But Rupert kicked no ball. He raced nobody; he ran alone. In his whole life he hadn't stolen a single apple or broken a single window. (I thought I could remember him breaking one green tumbler when he was four years old – that was the list of his misdeeds in its entirety.) He just kept drawing pictures and reading books and playing his own peculiar games alone.

He did not get along with other children, since he'd been talking so long to birds and trees he no longer knew how to talk to people. Other children quickly got irritated at his strange stories and didn't want to have anything to do with him. For that I could have wrung their necks like potted chickens. Rupert was after all my own little son, but at the same time I understood them in spite of myself.

'You've got to stop this tomfoolery,' I told Rupert seriously. 'Do you understand what I mean? People don't like silly fools. Besides, soon you'll not know yourself what's true and what's not, and to know that is not too easy in this world anyway. Moreover, there's a quite special place for the people who can't stop fooling in time, and believe me, you don't want to go there.'

Rupert nodded, resigned. It had been a month since Gunnar's death, the slowest and darkest month of my life. There was a fine aroma of an approaching autumn in the air, and it made birds and several other living creatures feel an oppressive longing for faraway places and at times even mild panic. Cold rains started to wash off the colours and warmth of summer, and pleading bad weather, Rupert stayed within four walls, which wasn't at all like him since he'd always been a dedicated puddle jumper and rain runner. For four weeks he hadn't even once gone further than our mailbox – always on Wednesday at one o'clock he ran quickly out to get his precious *Duck* comics (*Wednesday is the week's best day, for then you get your Donald Duck, the world's funniest comic!*) and then closeted himself in his own room with the devotion of a monk studying holy scripture.

As much as I'd have enjoyed his company in other circumstances, now he started to get badly on my nerves.

He was quieter than the grey colour of the autumn sky. He sneaked ghostlike around, unnoticeable and almost translucent, close to non-existence. Now and then I had to steal near him and touch him to make sure that he still was flesh and blood.

Sometimes I was caught by an irrational certainty that he had tracelessly disappeared from the earth, and I ran around the house to seek him until I finally found him cowering in some dark corner.

He cracked his fingers on the borders of my visual field. He grated his teeth. He kept staring out of windows and rolling his eyes just like the black bearers in his beloved Tarzan movies when they heard the oppressing, maddening drumming of the wicked natives from the jungle.

I'd have liked to run away from home.

I was relieved when school finally started and the bus took him away for at least a few hours a day. Of course, Rupert did not feel happy at school. He was bullied, not so badly it would have made his life hell, but obviously he wouldn't have brought home any popularity awards, if such things for any reason had been presented.

After Gunnar's death, Rupert was like a kind of little, over-scared, endangered animal which all the time expects something big and extremely terrible to attack him. His irrational fear was by and by infecting even me – I began to startle at all kinds of the slightest rustles and flashes. I had bad dreams, too, although after waking up I could remember nothing more of them than a tormenting feeling of loss, and that in the dreams I heard myself talk to some strange unfathomable abstract being (it seemed to consist of rails) and asking it for something I suspected I'd later regret.

Sometimes by nights a capricious wind brought to our ears the noise of a train passing by the district, from the railway far away behind hilly forests. At the closest, the tracks were at least fifteen kilometres away, but now and then it sounded as if the trains did run quite close, even in the folds of our own familiar woods. I got shooting pains in my belly for I knew how that strange phenomenon affected Rupert. Sometimes, when I secretly peeked into his room and checked that the boy was still safe, I saw him pull his quilt over his head and tremble.

It was obvious that the situation could not continue like that. I didn't want to take my child to a psychiatrist, at least not yet. I didn't want him to get a mark in his papers and be labelled a mental health problem. I was myself the best expert with my own child, and therefore *I* had to grapple with the core of the problem – Rupert's monstrously grown imagination – before it would undo him.

First, I made a list of things that were apt to make my son's condition worse. Then I took the necessary measures. Now and then I felt myself a proper monster of a mother, a perverse tyrant who pursues a noble goal by a reign of terror. But I made myself continue in spite of my doubts. My child was in trouble, and I had to save him whatever sacrifices it demanded from both of us.

First, I took a deep breath, grabbed the phone and cancelled the subscription to Donald Duck. And the next morning, after Rupert had shuffled along to the school bus, I hunted down all his comics – *Donald Duck*s, *Superman*s, *Jokerfant*s, *Star Trek*s, *King Kong*s, *Phantom*s, *Creepy*s, *Frankenstein*s and *Werewolves*, *Pink Panther*s, *Roadrunner*s, *John Carter*s, *Dracula*s, *Magnus, Robot Fighter* – and burned them all in the sauna oven.

There were hundreds, and my work of destruction took hours. The neighbourhood got covered in charred bits of comics.

I hesitated a while with story books. What kind of a mother could do such a thing, destroy her child's property like some loutish Gestapo commander?

But extreme situations demand extreme measures, and so I hardened my heart in the cleansing blaze of the book pyres.

Into the flames went the *Grimm's Fairytales*, *The Lion, The Witch and The Wardrobe*, *The Best Animal Stories*, *My Brother Lionheart*, *Pippi Longstockings* and other literary fiction that excited imagination. To be on the safe side I pushed all colouring books in the oven, too.

Then I sought all his crayons and drawing pens and blocks of drawing paper and all his graphically gorgeous but badly twisted drawings and buried them underneath the currant bushes behind the house. I made a list of the TV programmes that Rupert could still safely watch. Obviously, all movies were completely prohibited. I entered Rupert for the chess club, the model airplane club, the volleyball club, the boy scouts and the ceramic crafts. After some reflection, I cancelled the ceramic crafts. To conclude it all, I ordered him always from then on to keep his watch on time and to always be aware of the date, or be left without his pocket money.

Rupert wasn't very excited about all this, but neither did he protest. When he noticed that his comics and books were missing, he looked at me with silent astonishment but said nothing. I hoped fervently that he would understand this was all for his own good. He tried to ask after his drawing things but fell silent when he noticed my expression and understood that those were gone just like all the other things I considered inappropriate. He didn't even try to watch his former favourite programmes from the TV, for he guessed it wouldn't be allowed. Sometimes I turned on the TV and he came and watched it, quietly, until the approved programme was over and I shut off the apparatus.

'Rupert, it's time to go to bed. And Rupert, what time is it and what's the date?'

'It's now eight-twenty-three and it's Wednesday, October twelfth.'

'Excellent. Well, goodnight and sweet dreams.'

The new order was surprisingly easy to realize. Rupert went regularly to the chess club to learn logical thinking, and to my amazement he suddenly started to get first Bs and then clear As from math examinations instead of the earlier Cs and Ds. On account of that, Miriam Catterton, the well-known pretty golden-haired teacher of his class, came personally to see me and to discuss the boy's wonderful change. (To be sure, at the same time Rupert's art grade fell from A to D and his composition grade also fell off a bit, which I, however, didn't consider a bad trade at all – I'd always been afraid that the verbally fluent and graphically gifted Rupert would decide to choose the dubious profession of an artist or a writer for his life's career.)

In the model airplane club Rupert constructed a model plane strictly according to the incorruptible laws of aerodynamics and flew it immediately on its virgin flight into the thin upper branches of our backyard rowan tree, where it stayed until it was finally covered with snow. He even learned the ins and outs of volleyball with the village boys and was no longer completely helpless in team games. After I'd looked at his wan expression for a couple of months, I pitied him and let him quit volleyball training.

As for the boy scouts Rupert wouldn't agree to go even once; he said they dressed up too silly there according to his taste, but instead, he himself thought of joining the school photography club, which I thought was an excellent idea – after all, weren't cameras used to record objective reality with the most objective way possible (as I then still thought, naively).

His watch he set to the correct time by the second every evening after the radio time signal. Months went by pretty comfortably, seasons came and passed, and as time went on I started to think that the worst was over.

But then one winter night, coming back from the bathroom, when I peeked into his room, I noticed that the boy had disappeared from his bed.

I forced myself to calm down and draw a breath and think rationally. He surely hadn't vanished without a trace; here still were his socks and there his rucksack and old rocking horse, and from the ceiling hung his airplanes. After searching for him in every place at least twice I realized that he had to be outside.

I saw he had taken his skis from by the steps. Gone was also his fine new camera which he always kept on his bedside table by the glass of water.

By and by I began to understand that this was by no means the first time he'd done something like this – I suddenly remembered how some mornings he'd looked unusually tired, and I recollected several other suspicious circumstances to which I hadn't paid attention before (I'd wondered why his boots were often still wet in the morning, although I'd put them to dry on the radiator in the evening).

I sat by the kitchen table and drank a couple of bathtubs of coffee. After four hours of waiting I was coming to the conclusion that I couldn't wait any longer but had to phone the village constable Herbert Starling or at least go out myself to seek my child, but then I heard skis swishing outside.

I heard the door and Rupert lumbered in, bleak as Death itself.

He was covered with snow all over. His face was blue with cold, although the night was mild. The boy marched into the kitchen in his snowy boots without a word and put his camera on the table in front of me.

To me, Rupert looked like a soldier returning from battle, small in size but to be taken extremely seriously. Tiny icicles hung from his eyelashes. His clothes had a clinging smell that I couldn't connect with anything until the next time I was in the vicinity of the railway and sensed that peculiar smell, which somebody may have once told me came from the impregnation substance used in the railway sleepers.

I wasn't able to utter anything for a while, so as not to start crying or screaming uncontrollably; I wasn't able to even move, because I felt a compelling desire to seize the child and thoroughly shake him for scaring me like that.

Finally, I said surprisingly calmly: 'I'll make you a cup of cocoa. You'll drink it without a murmur and then go back to sleep. The camera stays here. We won't talk any more about this, but if you do something like this once more, I won't even ask you anything, I'll make a stew of you while you sleep and sell you to that drunkard Traphollow for mink food. And with the money I get I'll bribe Mr Starling to close his eyes about your disappearance. And if anybody asks about you, I won't admit you ever existed. Do we understand each other?'

Rupert stared at the camera with nostrils wide open. He pointed at it and whispered, 'But there's *evidence* in there!'

'Do we understand each other?' I insisted. My voice could have peeled an apple.

He struggled long with himself before he gave up and nodded.

After he had drunk his cocoa and gone, I checked the camera and noticed that since earlier in the evening it had been used to take four pictures. (I always tried to keep track of such things.)

I didn't want to encourage him to continue his game, which had got out-of-hand, so I pushed the camera far back on the upper shelves of the hall cupboard, behind empty jam pots, and only took it out the next summer when I went and buried it and its film a couple of metres deep, next to the other dangerous things.

Twenty years later, when Rupert already was studying law in Helsinki, I happened to find a notebook, which had functioned as some kind of diary for him. It was lying on the bottom of the cupboard, with old schoolbooks and wrinkled exercise books. On its cover stood the text OBSERVATIONS OF A FERROEQUINOLOGIST.

Rupert's diary contained some rather disconnected notes, altogether from a couple of years, and it also included a chaotic explanation about the trip he had made that night.

It's very improper to read other persons' diaries, and of course I did not succumb to such baseness; I just glanced at it a little here and there.

(Myself, I've never kept a diary, at least I don't remember having done that. Neither when a child nor older. I think the past has nothing to give us, no more than an outdated mail-order catalogue. Besides, my memories in their subjectivity and contradictoriness are much too confused for me to bother recording them.

I do not know what evil I have done that my mind punishes me so, but almost every night I still see a silly dream in which I anyhow keep a diary. In this Dream Diary of mine one can find all my fuzzy past; there, are carefully recorded all the thoughts I've thought, all contradictions, all the insignificant incidents which my consciousness has crumbled down as unnecessary, and its pages teem with hidden motives and causes and consequences and obscure speculations about them.

In the dream I know that I could at any time turn the pages back and look at my past without the softening and diluting influence of time. Only lately, when I'm remembering Rupert, I've first started to feel the temptation to do that. But I don't rightly know. It's much easier when you don't dwell too much on what is past, but just accept the concrete present as it is.)

1.12.1976, Observations of a Ferroequinologist:

Last night I did it, I PHOTOGRAPHED A TRAIN THAT HAD GONE OFF THE RAILS.

I got up at 12 o'clock at night, hung the camera around my neck and started to ski on the crusted snow to where I knew the trains did go to turn.

There's at least fifteen or twenty kilometres to go or maybe even a hundred kilometres (it's very hard to know by night how long a distance is) and several times I almost turned back, but some things one just has got to do, as Mummy says, and then finally after skiing for two hours I found the place though I'd gone astray a few times and thought I'd never find home again and the wolves would eat me, or maybe a bear.

The place where the trains turn is SECRET, and it's not easy to find. There's a blind track leading there, but I still haven't found the place where it forks from the main track though I've searched for it many times. It's pretty close to the section where that train outside the timetable tried to kill me and Dad in summer, maybe four or five kilometres away. I don't know whether I was more afraid of the place or of Mum tumbling to the fact that I'd gone out (as it happened this time anyway). I waited for surely at least three hours before the train arrived – luckily I had provisions: three chocolate bars, a packet of chewing gum (two eaten beforehand), one gingerbread.

The rails come to that place in the middle of the forest from somewhere further off, from behind a really thickety terrain. And on them the trains come and go. The blind track ends completely among trees so the trains can get off the rails and turn in the forest and then mount the tracks again and return to where they came from.

I lay behind the top of the ridge under juniper bushes and watched how one train again crawled slowly and carefully out from the thicket. It came to the end of the blind track, stopped and then started to get off the rails.

It was huge, although by night it's also hard to know for sure how big something is. I somehow felt how it changed, not so much outwardly so that it could be seen with one's eyes, but inwardly. It sort of woke up and pricked up its ears and put about feelers to its environment as if it had guessed I lay there watching.

I wondered if there was anybody inside it (I felt that even if there was somebody in there, it wasn't human, at least not a live human).

Suddenly it became awfully cold and I started shaking and my teeth started rattling. I felt that the coldness came out of the train, as if it had been to the North Pole or the Moon or some other really cold place. I took four photos of it with timed exposure.

I lay there in the snow without moving and waited and shivered from cold and heard trees breaking and crashing when the train puffed its way along in the snow and made its slow turnaround in the forest and then finally climbed back on the rails.

It must have taken surely at least four or five hours. I almost peed in my pants and I thought I'd get a proper licking when morning came and Mum went to wake me up and I wouldn't be at home yet. I tried to look at my watch but there was not enough light to see the hands.

Then the train slowly went off and disappeared behind the thicket and the air wasn't so cold any more. When I was quite sure no more trains were coming I descended into the valley bottom and went to see the rails closer.

Sometimes one can find all kinds of things there. Once I found from the snow a bit of paper that turned out to be a thirty-years-old third-class train ticket from Helsinki to Oulu. Now I found no tickets, but there was a dead cat. I rather think it was our neighbours', Toby who had disappeared, but it wasn't possible to identify it for sure. It had gone all flat and stiff and I saw its intestines. It was just like it had been hit with a house-sized sledgehammer. Not all of it was there – it was as if something had bitten a piece off it.

I threw some snow over Toby the cat and built it a little gravestone out of snow.

Once I tried to follow the rails so I'd see where they actually join the big tracks. I walked along the blind track some two hundred metres (the forest around the track is such a tangle nobody can get through it without a chainsaw), but then I had to turn back, because the railway smell got so strong I couldn't breathe any more. Besides I was afraid a train would come the other way. If a train had come towards me, I couldn't have got off anywhere from the rails. I almost fainted just like that one time at school when I had a fever over 39 degrees, and by a side glance I thought I saw all kinds of strange things in the shadows of the thicket, things I don't like to remember, and afterwards I realized that the railway smell may actually be poisonous when there's too much of it in the air.

I won't go there any more, at least not before I'm grown up and can buy a chainsaw and an oxygen apparatus and other necessary things and when I no longer need to be afraid of Mum.

When the trains stay on the rails, they are obviously sort of asleep, and people can control them just like a sleepwalker can be manoeuvred.

I didn't see the train this time very clearly, since it was quite dark and one cannot see well in the dark, but I did recognize the type. It was one of those big red diesel engines, with a white cabin. I found its picture in the library's train book. It was a DV15 manufactured in the Valmet Lokomo machine shop. Or it could have been a DV12, which looks pretty much alike. I'm not quite sure. It had fifteen wagons after it – I counted them. They were not passenger carriages but empty open trucks that *look like animal skeletons and usually carry tractors and other big machines.*

The previous time I saw a short blue local passenger train, the kind that doesn't have a separate locomotive. One can see them now and then in daily traffic. They transport people, but at the turning-place the short blue train had blackened windows and I couldn't see whether there was anybody inside.

But when I went the first time to the place where the trains turn, I caught a glimpse of a really odd-looking train, and so far, I haven't found its picture anywhere though I've spent hours in the library and leafed through all the train books I've discovered. It was quite bullet-shaped and really streamlined and looked actually more like a space rocket than any train. And it seemed to float a bit above the rails. That's the one I really would like to photograph someday so I could show it to a grown-up who knows a lot about trains and ask what it actually is.

When I started to return home and came to an open place with more light I looked at my watch. It was only twenty past two, and at first, I was relieved but then I started to get doubtful. I felt that it had taken a lot more time. I thought that my watch had stopped for a while, but at home it was showing the correct time anyway when I checked.

If only I could find my camera and could develop those photos! Even Mum would have to believe when she saw the pictures, though otherwise she doesn't believe anything – she's such a bonehead. (I hope Mum doesn't read this!) I feel she doesn't even believe in my existence without coming to check on me every little while.

Today at school we had cabbage casserole and chocolate mousse again, and of course one wasn't allowed to have chocolate mousse before eating a plateful of cabbage casserole.

Ossian threw up on the table when he tried to eat his plate empty, though he hates cabbage more than anything, and the whole table was flowing green and others started to feel squeamish, too. I was smarter and flipped the cabbage casseroles under my chair and fetched myself a big portion of chocolate mousse with a straight face.

1.20.1976, Observations of a Ferroequinologist:

I dreamed again that a train was chasing me on a road. I climbed to a roof but the train climbed after me along the wall. I woke up when I fell off the bed to the floor and hit my head. I got a big lump. I could hear a train in the forest, again too close. I dared not go to sleep again. In the morning I went to look for traces but didn't find any.

4.12.1976, Observations of a Ferroequinologist:

I dreamed that I sat on the nose of a steam locomotive. It was rushing ahead with enormous speed.

First the scenery was unfamiliar, but then we came to Houndbury. Two girls were standing on the track. They held each other's hands. The girls shouted something to me and laughed and at the last moment they stepped aside and their skirts flapped in the draught of the train. Both of them were quite good-looking, but I liked the one with the golden hair more.

The other one seemed familiar at first, but then she wasn't anybody I knew but a perfect stranger. After a while we approached the level crossing. Behind the level crossing gate, a purple car was waiting. Dad was sitting in the car and he looked sad. I waved and yelled at him not to be sad any more because I was already quite all right, but he didn't hear.

Then the locomotive shivered under me and began to feel

somehow queer. Awakened. Besides it was no longer a steam engine but a diesel engine. It talked to Dad along the rails, whispering in a peculiar sort of voice that started to make me sleepy though I was already asleep to begin with. It told Dad to put the gears on and to drive on the rails. Somehow it made the gate rise before its time and it bewitched Dad and he obeyed it.

And we crashed into Dad's car and I watched how the train smashed the car against the rails a bit like the lion tore up the little deer in Nature's Wonders *that Mum still lets me watch on the TV. Sheet metal and steel and register plates and bloody bits of Dad were falling along the tracks. I saw a loose hand fly into a ditch. Dad was smashed all into pieces with the car and suddenly I realized that the train was eating him and then I started to scream and punch the train with my fists.*

Then the train had eaten its fill and fell asleep again. That's when I fell off the engine hood and woke up in my bed, and outside a train was hooting shrilly.

Yesterday I went to the library and looked up in a dictionary what 'Ferroequinologist' means. A person interested in railways. Dad sometimes said that he and I are both ferroequinologists, but especially me, considering my origin. I had no idea what he meant by that, and he smiled and promised to explain some time when I'm old enough to understand. But the train killed Dad, so I'll probably never find out. And Mum of course understands nothing of these matters.

6.14.1976, Observations of a Ferroequinologist:

In my dream the trains were in an especially foul mood, and I dreamed that they chased me all through the night. I ran home and hid in the woodshed, and somebody there whispered in my ear that trains have dragon souls and that's why they love tunnels and are so mean. It also said that my basic task is to

save a maiden. I tried to see the one who spoke, but when I
turned I was awake in my bed and staring at my own teddy
bear.

'Observations of a Ferroequinologist' (as well as the smudged
train ticket between the pages) ended down in the hole.
Rupert had finally, after all, recovered from the morbid
and dangerous condition that his swollen imagination had
induced. However, I wanted to take no risks with the questions
concerning his childhood. We had never spoken about his
long-ago train fantasies. I felt like he didn't necessarily even
remember them or most anything else about his childhood,
at least nothing very detailed – during his student years he
always travelled home by train, though there was no railway
station in Houndbury, and for the last forty kilometres one
had to take an inconvenient bus or try to get a lift. Indeed, he
seemed to have forgotten his childhood, and all to the good.
I had forgotten mine, too.

Studying law kept the boy's thoughts firmly in the objective
reality, ruled by reason and the logic dictated by cold facts.
Rupert had no time for idle novels or movies, so his imagination
stayed safely asleep.

But his life was by no means pure toil. He had in the law
faculty a couple of fairly good friends with whom to go out
and to play tennis (over the years Rupert had become quite an
athlete, although in the bird-boned fashion of his father). And
from his curt postcards I even gathered that for some time he
had been seeing a certain young woman who went to the same
lectures.

Rupert went to study law immediately after his high school
graduation, for which I take the credit myself. When he had
made his last ferroequinologist exploration at the age of nine

years, I realized something: even after all the hobbies I'd arranged for him he still had too much time to brood on the peculiar fantasies in his head. I could confiscate his things, and I could make sure that he no longer crept out of the house by night to make his ferroequinologist observations – I for instance attached a bell on his door and another one on his window and hid his shoes for the night. But of course, I couldn't control the thoughts going around in his head. Therefore, I had to find a way to make Rupert voluntarily use his head for something sound and rational.

Gunnar had once left a thick book of statutes in my house. I'd put it temporarily on my bookshelf, in the middle of the encyclopaedias, and there it lay forgotten for several years before I lugged the massive book into Rupert's slender arms. I told him it was his father's old book that he had meant for his son when he would be old enough to read it (which might very well have been true). I said his father had told me to pay him five marks for each page he could learn by heart.

At first the boy seemed suspicious. A couple of days went by. Then he calculated the pages in the book and multiplied that by five. He went to look at the shiny ten-geared bikes in Houndbury Bicycle and Engine, and soon he was spending most of his leisure hours studying the book of statutes.

I was overjoyed to pay the money he collected from me after examinations. By and by he stopped having nightmares, and he recovered from his anxiety and his train obsessions. Surprisingly quickly he accumulated the money for a bike, but he hardly got time to ride that brand-new geared wonder, for his reading stint continued; even in sleep he was leafing through his statute book, mumbling his statutes and counting the money he'd earned and would still earn.

A born lawyer, I thought proudly.

*

By spring 1991 Rupert graduated with the best grades, and for a graduation present I bought him a golden Rolex with my savings (I'm not ashamed to admit I cried with happiness for two whole months and finally got a nasty inflammation of the eye). He got a job in a small but respected law office in the capital and moved together with his girlfriend Birgitta, who graduated soon after Rupert, and found herself a job in the same firm.

Birgitta Susanne Donner was a good and sensible girl; I'd met her a couple of times and could safely trust Rupert to her keeping. I saw that she would become an exceedingly reliable and refreshing life partner to Rupert, and surely also a caring mother to my grandchildren, when the young couple would have the time to think about reproduction. I had myself started to meet more regularly a certain charming person now that I no longer had to worry about Rupert. It wasn't especially serious, and dating openly in a small village like Houndbury would have provoked too much talk and fuss – my friend was after all a teacher and thus sort of under the magnifying glass of the villagers. Now and then, however, she stopped for a coffee in the evening, and sometimes it happened that we woke up in the morning nose to nose.

It would be nice to stop here, with the picture of a successful son and a happy mother. But happy endings in real life are usually just stages on the way to a more final and less cheerful end – the worms will get us in the end, one way or another. Late in the hot July of 1994 trains again got entangled in my son's life.

*

Rupert and Birgitta had been busy for a long while, and sometimes I couldn't reach them for days on end even by phone, and I started to suffer from a delusion that my son had somehow disappeared from the Earth and I'd never see him again. Finally, however, they managed to take a few days off and come to visit me for a whole weekend.

Seeing those two enlivened my mind and at the same time made it strangely wistful.

On Sunday we decided to have a picnic. The day simply floated in heat and bright colours, and when you add to the picture the dragonflies buzzing absentmindedly to and fro, it was one of those days that should actually be framed and hung on the living-room wall for the coming winters. I packed in the picnic basket: juice, salami sandwiches and some chocolate cake with cherries I'd baked for Rupert's approaching twenty-ninth birthday. We drove in Rupert's new red car along small roads until we came to the foot of Sheep Hill. It rose as a gently sloping green field towards the dense blue sky. In accordance with its name, Sheep Hill was a sheep pasture: they were standing around in white clusters, and now and then they got excited and started baaing in competition.

We left the car in the shade of a big birch, followed a path that descended near a low stone fence down the steep bank of Sheep Hill (which at some distance changed to Sheep Rock), and arrived finally at our goal, the grassy meadow by the raised railway embankment where the limpid Ram Brook murmured with cool cheerfulness.

I spread a white tablecloth on the ground, set the table and told the young couple to set to it before the heat and flies would spoil it all. We ate, and suddenly Rupert stood up and, spitting breadcrumbs, proclaimed that Birgitta and he had become engaged two weeks before.

I almost choked on my sandwich.

I looked at my son who stared at me as if expecting a scolding. He was nervous since he wasn't sure about my reaction, but he was obviously very happy, and the sudden perception made me laugh aloud from the sheer joy of living.

'Now what's so funny?' Birgitta asked, a little suspicious, but then broke into a broad grin. Such a beautiful girl, I sighed. I already knew what I was going to buy them for a wedding present: the most gorgeous hardwood grandfather clock in the universe!

With a relieved smile Rupert sat down and continued his meal.

I suddenly thought of the moment Rupert was conceived. I didn't remember much of it, just that I and Gunnar had had intimate intercourse with each other and prevention had somehow let us down, but anyway, there Rupert now was in front of me, happy, handsome and a successful lawyer with a tie around his neck.

*

'I often think of the moment Rupert was conceived. Gunnar took me for a drive on his new motorbike – at that time he was still a rather wild spirit, in his own trim controlled way. He even had a leather coat. That, however, was no ragged black motorcycle jacket but a fine brown Italian coat, surely terribly expensive. I'd seen him often at the Pavilion which in those times was still full of people almost every Saturday of the year; now of course it's been closed for a long time and people go to the city. I went there now and then to dance and to look at people. He'd been besieging me for some time (at least I felt he'd done that, one couldn't be quite sure of him), and although he didn't really turn me on, I liked his quiet self-confidence and that everyone was looking at him, and was willing to go for a ride with him when he asked me.

We were driving along small roads by this very countryside and stopped finally to sip white wine in the middle of a small lyrical grove. Gunnar said he liked my nose very much, and then he seduced me.

I still didn't really want him but I let him do it anyway. It was actually quite pleasant, the light way he made love to me. I held on to his tie and smiled all the time. The grass tickled my bottom. He promised to withdraw in good time before he'd come, and surely he would have done that since he was a perfect gentleman and I knew I could trust him completely.

Finally, I felt his rhythm accelerate. His muscles tensed. I remember hearing the sound of a train, the rails ran somewhere quite close – I hadn't realized that before. Gunnar was struggling in my arms like a trapped animal, I'd folded my legs behind his back and he couldn't get off me in time. I was quite sure he would get extremely angry at me, but he just looked at me a little sadly, kissed me on the cheek and took me back to the dance pavilion where we danced one waltz together before he left, looking pensive.

I knew that a new life had started to develop inside me, and six weeks later the doctor confirmed it.'

– From the unwritten Dream Diary of E.N.

*

I woke up from my thoughts.

Further off the sheep had suddenly begun baaing wildly. I saw them start to come tumbling down the slope as if they were suddenly in a big hurry to get somewhere.

'The train is coming,' Rupert said.

Only now I noticed that there were little decorative Donald Ducks on his picnic tie – he hadn't completely forgotten his childhood, after all. A gust had arisen and was intently tugging at his tie and making his white lapels flap like the wings of a large white butterfly.

'What did you say?' I said.

'The train is coming,' Rupert repeated, still smiling, and pointed somewhere towards the sheep. I put my sandwich down and turned to look.

The railway ran along the ridge of Sheep Hill; from the cool darkness of the spruce forest it dived down to the clearing and disappeared finally in a long cold tunnel excavated through Sheep Rock whose mouth stood above us, breathing darkness, on top of the high embankment heaped out of big stones. The growing metallic clang and the rumble of hundreds of metal wheels against the iron rails muffled the protest of the affronted sheep. A fast red electric engine emerged. After it an endless line of dark goods wagons rattled towards the clearing.

I instinctively glanced at my watch: the time was 1.27.

The rhythmic noise chased the sheep; finally, it filled the whole scene and buried the cries of the sheep under itself like an avalanche. Rupert took the hand of his fiancée, kissed her and then said something I didn't hear. She laughed. A nervous butterfly fluttered over our party, and its brown dryness made me think of falling autumn leaves.

The train now drew a moving line the length of the whole clearing. Wagon by wagon it pushed itself above us into the tunnel and eclipsed the sun burning above Sheep Rock, offering instead a hypnotically quick dark-bright dazzle. Dust from the embankment began to fall on us. I glanced upwards with a mild resentment and thought that I definitely ought to cover our sandwiches before they started tasting too sandy.

Then something broke loose of the train's dark shape and started to spin down towards us.

I followed the track of the object in the blue skies, now grey with dust; it rotated and whirled and got bigger all the time. I stared at it spellbound. Suddenly I realized it was coming towards us and would probably fall right in the middle of our picnic.

I opened my mouth to yell a warning to Rupert and Birgitta, but instead inhaled dust and could for a while get no sound out of my throat because of a fierce fit of coughing. To crown it all, the dust blinded my eyes and I could do nothing but cough and fling my arms about and hope that my companions would realize they ought to move back.

Among the clank and rumble I discerned a muffled crack, like the sound of a breaking egg.

I tore my running eyes open and saw faintly how Rupert waved his arm, as if greeting an old acquaintance he hadn't seen for years, and an object the shape of a marrowbone rebounded off his head into the brook. Rupert fell on his back in the grass. Birgitta's shrill whimper penetrated my ears through the train's monotonous chant.

'Do we have eggs in the basket?' I yelled idiotically and started to cough again.

The girl kept shaking her head and pointed with a trembling finger at Rupert who lay on the slope, limbs spread out, and seemed to be asleep. When one looked closer at him, one could see that his hair's recently so neat parting was now missing completely.

*

Birgitta started a furious legal campaign against the State Railways.

State Railways admitted that the metal object which had broken Rupert's skull had indeed originated from the train rushing past us, to be exact from the locking system of the twenty-eighth goods wagon of the train. The Railway attorney expressed his surprise that a part had come loose at all, since that was in principle impossible, for the train had been duly and carefully checked before departure according to all possible railway traffic regulations. It sounded as if he were insinuating that actually *we* should be under suspicion for some malicious act of cleverly sabotaging their precious train. The part coming loose troubled the SR very much. But for Rupert's sake the railway people seemed not to lose a single night's sleep – when the insincere platitudes were peeled off, the basic attitude of the SR seemed to be *Shit happens, so what? You should have kept far away from our railway!*

In the past I'd have wanted to go into a blind rage and tear the attorney's self-important head off his weak shoulders, but the dinosaur seemed to have disappeared from inside me and instead of empowering rage I only managed to feel enormous fatigue and defeat.

About indemnities no consensus could be reached: Birgitta demanded thirty million, and the Railways did not want to pay a penny over hospital expenses – just paying the hospital bill was already proof of the extraordinary benevolence of the SR and exceeded all legal obligations, said the Railway attorney and chided us for our greed. Birgitta swore to me, gasping for breath, that she would make the Railways pay dearly and would even destroy with different tactical lawsuits the whole Finnish railway system, if nothing less would make the SR take full responsibility for Rupert's skull fracture and its possible consequences.

I presumed that Birgitta would calm down in time and her storming holy rage would quieten, and after five months that was it: she phoned me, embarrassed, and told me that she had no more strength any longer to tilt at windmills. I said that as far as I was concerned the mills could turn and the trains could move – what had happened could not be undone.

When Rupert woke up he did not recognize Birgitta. He just stared at the walls of his hospital room, ill at ease, twiddled his thumbs and finally asked Birgitta, who was trembling by the bed, if ma'am happened to have any 'Chicago' chewing gum with her, please.

'And that damned brand of chewing gum hasn't even been produced for years!' Birgitta sighed when we sat in the hospital cafeteria and wondered at the turn things had taken.

The doctors had said that Rupert would never remember Birgitta, not really. The part of Rupert's brain where all the memories of Birgitta had been located had suffered irreparably serious damage.

'As far as I am concerned he is then sort of dead,' the unhappy fiancée stated, and since I could invent no reasonable counter-argument to that, I stuffed my mouth full of the bun I'd bought in the canteen.

Besides the Birgitta-memories, the destroyed bit of his brain had stored Rupert's whole legal learning and some other rather important matters. Rupert did remember me, though. Just after the chewing gum, Rupert had started to ask for his mother. And he remembered the Lola brand of chocolate (although that was also out of production, as we later found out to Rupert's regret) and Donald Duck and trains and the death of his father and all the nightmares of his childhood.

Actually, he remembered everything quite excellently – up to his ninth year.

For understandable reasons the engagement lapsed. Rupert returned to the home of his childhood. He had spent altogether six months in the hospital. During the time, the summery land had shrivelled up in the leafless squeeze of winter.

It took time to get used to the creature who wandered in silence around my house from one room to another. He didn't speak much, just sometimes asked me to bring some sweets from the shop or enquired after his things long since discarded. It was Rupert, and it was not. It was some kind of an anachronistic person: the being had the exterior of the grown-up lawyer-Rupert and the frightened eyes and mind of the child-Rupert already once left behind. It kept watching the courtyard out of the windows nervously cracking its finger joints and sneaking around like a ghost. It brooded over thoughts hidden from me. It was scared of its own image in the mirrors since that had become unfamiliar and strange to it.

I'd have screamed if I'd have had the energy for such behaviour, but I was tired and apathetic and thought I'd never have the strength any more for any dashing enterprises. The air I breathed was thin and stuffy.

'Rupert,' I said finally. 'It can't go on like this for much longer. Something has to happen. Something.'

I didn't know myself what I was actually trying to say, and certainly I'd been speaking more to myself than to my son, but the anachronistic Rupert looked at me and nodded as if he had known exactly what I meant.

*

Months passed outside the house. Inside it the time had at

first stopped and then gone definitely haywire when the anachronistic Rupert returned home.

I stayed at home with Rupert. I didn't even see Miriam except a few times in passing: in the supermarket, out in the village, on the road, at the watchmaker's. Sometimes I doubted whether we had ever known each other, so distant we had become. I didn't ask her for a visit, and she was intelligent enough not to come without invitation. I simply lacked the energy to talk to people, to explain all the time to myself and to others Rupert's present appearance and situation and the type of his brain damage; I couldn't stand people's empathetic, watery looks; I did not want to see my son through strange pitying eyes that made me only feel miserable and sorry for someone who but a moment ago had been a successful lawyer but now was something else completely.

I have never been a regular guest to the Houndbury parties or otherwise particularly sociable, and now I froze even my scant relations with the local people to a polite level of Seasons' Greetings. I did not want to look at people's eyes and realize that nowadays I was 'the poor mother of that disabled lawyer' rather than Ms Emma Nightingale. I did not want my son, 'that disabled lawyer', to become one of the established Houndbury oddities. I had to find out something that would help both Rupert and myself cope with the new situation; I had to find some meaningful solution to it, and I wanted to do that alone, in my own peace.

In the first week of February, Miriam turned up for a surprise visit.

She had dyed her beautiful golden hair profoundly red. She had put on some weight, but a slight roundness became her and made her look more sensuous than ever. My sensuality, however, was waning. My black hair had acquired quite a lot of grey during the last weeks, and some strange unconscious idea had made me keep my hair short after Rupert's skull fracture. I'd even lost weight and had, by and by, started to notice the first real signs of old age in myself (and only now, bitterly, was I able to distinguish them from the earlier signs of maturity).

We hugged, and then we kissed, too, although no longer as lovers but as friends, and I thought I felt the light taste of farewell on her lips. We had a cup of coffee, ate some salt crackers and made some small talk.

Miriam was wondering about the burglary on the Tykebend road construction site; some amount of dynamite had gone missing, and teachers had been told to keep an eye on their pupils in case some of them turned out to have explosives in their desks or bags. I reminded her that it was by no means the first time something like that happened around Houndbury, lately some explosives had been stolen.

We were appalled by today's immoral little creepy-crawlies. The stolen explosives had either been sold on or else there was a rather big cache somewhere close by – very soon a part of Houndbury would surely fly off in the four winds, we prophesied (and I at least was secretly pleased with the idea).

I asked whether Miriam was still writing her short stories, and she said she was soon going to send some by mail to the publisher. She enquired politely if perhaps I'd like to take a look at her writings and give my opinion. I declined the honour – I didn't understand one whit about fiction since I read only factual material.

Suddenly Rupert came out of his room to greet his former teacher. As usual, he wore a white shirt, a waistcoat, a Donald Duck tie and a pair of grey trousers (although he didn't really feel comfortable in those, as would no nine-year-old boy). At first, he sounded thoroughly sensible, even grown-up-like, and Miriam glanced at me with a glad surprised smile: *So what's supposed to be wrong with him?* her eyes asked. Then Rupert blew the impression up when he started to ask Miriam about how far behind he was in his math lessons: how many pages had the rest of the class gone ahead while he'd been in the hospital? And could the teacher possibly give him some extra tutoring, for he'd been having difficulties with fractions.

Miriam snatched her handbag, spluttered some bye-byes and rushed out of the house, eyes wet, and left the anachronistic Rupert staring after her in wonder.

The night noises of the trains made Rupert fall out of his bed, and quite often he had to be patched up with Band-Aids – a grown-up man falls out of bed much harder than a little boy. He stayed very much inside. That was all right with me, I didn't want him to go and be mocked and stoned by the neighbourhood kids.

Always on Wednesdays, Rupert went out to the mailbox and came back looking disappointed, and when I finally paid proper notice I realized he was expecting his *Donald Duck* comics.

I didn't know whether I was acting wisely, but anyway I subscribed to the comics again for him after a break of twenty years (although the day the comics came out had been changed to Thursdays, which gave Rupert diarrhoea). I saw neither grounds nor reason any more to control what he was reading, doing or watching. As far as Rupert's imagination was concerned, he now had to cope with it himself. Not for a second time could I manage to launch a major offensive against fantasy – my war was over, my inner dinosaur was buried under the avalanche of all that had happened and, in the pressure, changed to oil muddying my insides.

Sometimes Rupert leafed through books he found on the shelves: encyclopaedias and biographies and a thick anthology of poetry that probably was a present from Miriam. A couple of times I saw in Rupert's hands that first law book he had learned by heart; he fingered it uncertainly and then always put it away without opening it.

I don't know how much my son understood of the books he studied or about what had happened to him. Sometimes he seemed like the intelligent and clever lawyer he had been only a few months before, and then he was again a big confused child who wore Armani suits and five-hundred-mark ties and could ponder for hours the story of 'Square Eggs' he had read in the *Duck* comics. Those two sides seemed to compete over territory inside him, and mostly he was somewhere in between.

Now and then Rupert drew strange little pictures, which he tore up immediately and burned in the sauna oven. I got the impression that he was trying to draw Birgitta and other things he had lost with the accident, things that now only haunted him as vague dream images.

The old Timex had again found its place on his wrist, although I had to go and buy a new, longer strap for it from the Houndbury Watch – since he could not really believe that the golden Rolex glittering in the chest drawer actually belonged to him.

All that dissolved into a sleepy anticipation-filled dormancy which was held together only by the ticking of the clocks, the repetitive daily routines and my belief that something would happen. Something that would give me the keys to a solution, a way out from the deadlocked dream I couldn't possibly imagine endlessly continuing the same (as unfounded as such a subjective notion was, of course, objectively considered).

*

March came, with harsh nightly cold. The ribs of the house cracked in the freezing squeeze, and sometimes just before falling asleep I imagined that the walls were breaking to splinters around me and winter was rushing in and freezing me into a rigid naked statue in my bed. I dreamed of a terrible cold that rolled over me.

Now and then I woke up and did not know who or where I was – I had to sneak around the house and go look at the sleeping Rupert and look over the objects I found for evidence to be able to locate myself back in my own life.

On the last week of the month, on the night between Thursday and Friday at 01.12 in the morning, I woke up to muffled sounds of departure seeping to my ears through the floorboards.

Rupert had slipped out at night before, but each time I had noticed it only afterwards from his wet shoes and the trails left in the snow. Through the clogged ducts of my mind gushed a sudden excitement that quickened even my numb flesh – I yanked a thick housecoat over myself and dashed down the cold stairs.

I threw the front door open. Rupert stood in the courtyard with skis and sticks in his hands and with a rucksack on his back and stared at me. He may have been a little scared for thinking he would be scolded, but at the same time I could sense unusual determination in him – it was just a fact that he was going somewhere and I could do absolutely nothing about it.

That was all right by me.

I let the icy, black night air fill my lungs and soak into my bloodstream. The sky spreading above us seemed to open directly to the cold halls of space. The stars were skimping on their scant light, but in the middle of them the Moon hunched big and bright and yet grieving for its imagined imperfection: only after a couple of nights would it be perfectly round and beautiful and could really wallow in its own light. The cold made the black-and-white night scene crackle and pop as if it were the plateful of Rice Crispies in thick cream and sugar that Rupert ate in the mornings.

I shivered in my housecoat and we stared at each other without words, Rupert and I, and then I broke the silence: 'Don't worry, you aren't going to become mink food.' (I remembered my threat from over twenty years back, and so probably did Rupert, because he looked relieved.)

'Besides, old Traphollow died from a heart attack last fall when he was hunting rabbits and we have a new policeman, too, whom I wouldn't try to bribe for his silence. But why don't you wait a little before you start. This time I'm coming with you if you don't mind. Who knows: perhaps I'll be a ferroequinologist, too.'

Rupert seemed to frown thoughtfully under his broad-brimmed Stetson but then he nodded. The hems of his grey Burberry were sweeping the ground. He had wrapped a medium-length red muffler round his neck and covered his ears with black earmuffs. He didn't at all look like a brain-damaged man who thought like a nine-year old. He looked like a gentleman who was going to take a breath of fresh air after an evening of theatre, then afterwards have a nightcap, read a few lines of Dostoyevsky and withdraw to his bed.

I dressed as quickly as I could, found my skiing shoes, locked the house and fetched my old skis from the woodshed where they had spent the last twenty years. Then we started skiing in the blocked lightlessness of the forest, the son ahead with coat hems flapping and the mother behind, stumbling in her slippery skis and with the unfamiliar sticks.

The hard-packed snow led us forwards with unreal lightness between the high pine pillars, and time passed. Now and then I peeked at my watch, ticking deeper and deeper into the night. Rupert was faster than I – he positively flew in front of me – but luckily he stopped at times to wait for his clumsier fellow skier.

I quickly lost my sense of direction. That was all right by me: I didn't actually want to think about where we were going – or why. On the surface, I stuck to the explanation that I was taking care of Rupert, at last thoroughly showing him that his train fantasies were nothing but misguided imagination. I dared not be honest with myself, admit that I was acting purely on intuition. After all, intuition is nothing but a kind of psychological coin flipped in the air. And to manage important business by intuition is just about as sensible as choosing the right road by flipping a coin (as those irrational ducks did in one of Rupert's favourite stories). But that night I, for a moment, stepped outside reason, maybe just to see at least a glimpse of what was there; for this one and only time I felt an urgent intuitive need to follow my son on his irrational trip to the core of fantasy.

We partly circled and partly crossed over the massive cliffs of Sheep Hill, where one of the longest railway tunnels in the country ran deep in the bowels of the rock. Somehow, we also managed to clear the big abandoned quarry, although we had to carry our skis, to climb over the icy boulders and to watch out for the clefts hidden in the stones' shadows.

Finally, we arrived at a place I had never been before, even though I was a native to the region, and the reason was obvious: there were no ways or paths to reach it. Although I supposed the nearest houses and the whole village actually were only about ten kilometres away, the terrain was extremely difficult, so the area was well protected from berry pickers, hunters and other accidental hikers. Bog, dense fir thicket, unfriendly rocks, fallen mouldering trees, half-collapsed rusty barbed wire fences that a stranger for some strange reason had once set up and then forgotten.

The upper branches of the ancient trees caught the quivering moonlight before it had time to touch the snow-covered ground, and we waded in deep darkness. Nature was really using all possible tricks to make us turn aside from our way. And I would have turned, many, many times, if Rupert's pale figure hadn't been skiing in front of me, so single-minded and determined; he knew the way even through the most inaccessible-looking thickets. At times he seemed like a mythological spirit who'd been sent to lead me through the Underworld's hollow hills, and I had to remind myself that he was only the brain-damaged former lawyer I *knew* he was.

We skied down a steep but short hill that brought us out from the forest to the railway. We pushed forwards along the moonlit railway bank a couple of kilometres. Then we crossed the rails.

'We have to go through here,' Rupert shouted to me over his shoulder and sped downhill with muffler flapping, into the forest that continued on the other side of the track, even more forbidding and intractable.

I looked at my watch: 03.21. We'd been skiing a couple of hours.

'The blind track is probably somewhere close by, but it's impossible to find,' Rupert's voice continued, more subdued. 'But when go through here, we'll get straight to where the hidden blind track leads.'

I followed the Burberry-clad and hatted figure into the dark catacombs of the trees.

The dry and extremely dense fir thicket made progress very cumbersome. When I looked up I could see no sky at all; I only saw the greyish lattice of dead branches that blocked the moonlight to somewhere above the standing trees. The mummified branches entangled themselves in my woolly coat. They wrenched my muffler loose. They scratched my face and reached at my eyes with their sharp thorns. Over and over again I tore myself from their grip and received the falling snow and ice and bits of twigs down my neck, and then I followed again, covering my face, the unseen swishing skis and the sound of breaking twigs, until the next obstacle stopped my travel.

I was afraid Rupert wouldn't bother to wait for me but would disappear and leave me wandering around alone in that shambles of trees and snow. I couldn't anticipate the functioning of my son's mind at all. In a way he still was to me my own dear little son (whose logic had never seemed to me any more understandable than Chinese opera, anyhow), and at times I still saw him as my successful adult lawyer son who was temporarily resting at my house. But after the skull fracture a new side had also emerged in him, a strange combination of the above two – the anachronistic Rupert, a secretive and often melancholic stranger whose doings and not-doings I was completely unable to predict or control.

We trudged in the rustling jam of dead standing trees for two or three hours at least and for maybe ten kilometres. At least it felt like ten kilometres, but I wouldn't be surprised if it had been shorter, perhaps only two hundred metres, or perhaps even far longer.

Now and then Rupert flashed ahead of me, a shadow in

the shadows, and then after I didn't see him for some time and thought I'd lost him, but when for the thousandth time I pushed myself, protecting my face, through the firs that had died in each other's arms, I saw him.

The trees were thinning out a bit and even let some light through; somewhere above, the Moon's pale disk flashed. After a long and breath-taking climb Rupert had stopped to wait for me in the middle of some juniper bushes. Leaning on his sticks he was staring ahead with a severe expression.

'It's there,' he whispered, when I had hurried close to him. 'We've arrived.'

In front of us there was a valley-like depression, a sort of pool filled with darkness, from the bottom of which snowy trees stretched themselves up to the black edges of the sky. And only a stone's throw away from where we stood was a blind track. I couldn't see all of it, but here and there, between the trees, dim rails were gleaming. The track came from somewhere beyond the forest, from the heart of a similar (or perhaps even worse) tangle of darkness than we had just gone through; it ran on a low bank among the trees until it suddenly ended in the middle of a stand of fir trees, as if it had been cut off with enormous scissors.

I frowned. Rails were not supposed to end like that. Where rails ended there had to be a proper barrier so that trains wouldn't accidentally drive too far and fall off the rails! The track seemed anyhow to be in quite a wrong place. Perhaps by some office desk a line had been drawn in a wrong place on the map, and when the mistake had finally been discovered the men of the railway construction gang in the forest had simply left the work unfinished and gone off, swearing and laughing and cracking jokes about the wisdom of engineers.

I drew the peculiar smell of railways into my nostrils. Here it felt markedly stronger than anywhere else. 'And this place is…'

'The place where the trains turn,' Rupert said quietly. He seemed embarrassed, or perhaps nervous. The cold sculpted crystal clouds out of his breath and the overlapping shadows of the trees hid his features from the moonlight and my eyes. He took the skis off, stuck the sticks close by in the snow and laid himself down in a prone position.

I followed his example.

'One of them ought to be arriving from out there soon enough. Sometimes you have to wait for a long time, but it's no use worrying about the course of time here, I've noticed. Do you have a watch with you?'

I drew my sleeve up and tried to find some moonlight, but the darkness stubbornly covered the hands of my watch, and I couldn't see them however closely I kept peeking or turning my hand.

'Where's your own watch?' I asked then.

Rupert said his own Timex used to stop during ferroequinologist observation trips; he didn't bother to keep it with him any more, since that kind of stopping surely would harm the delicate watch machinery over time.

I lifted my own watch to my ear and tried to hear if it was ticking. I heard nothing, but maybe my ears were just frozen. Besides, there was an almost non-existent breath of wind among the trees, and it somehow made the dried-up forest continuously crackle and rustle around us, which hampered my efforts to listen.

Rupert surprised me by asking whether I wanted half of his chocolate bar. I was going to automatically refuse, but then I realized that I did want chocolate, very much, the first time since my childhood. Rupert took a chocolate bar from his rucksack and passed me one of the bits. Then he wrapped his Burberry closer around himself and settled into a comfortable position like an experienced watcher. And we watched the rails drawn into the wildwood and the rustling trees standing around us, and the white snow packed to keep company with darkness and shadows in the narrow spaces between the trees, and we ate chocolate and we waited.

By and by the waiting started to feel ghostly familiar to me. My tired brain probably played some kind of electrochemical trick, I thought sleepily, and then I yawned long, and slowly started to regret taking this whole purposeless night-time skiing trip – what had I been thinking, foolish woman, to leave my warm bed on a night like this...

*

'We wanted to look Death in the eyes and laugh in its face, and that's why we met and walked to the railway around five p.m. that Saturday, immediately after we'd come from school and eaten dinner and washed the dishes. When we got to the rails, it started to patter raindrops the size of cranberries. Our dresses got wet and stuck to our skin, and we got cold but we didn't leave; Death had to be humiliated today, too, Alice said, so we could really feel alive.

We both had some bones to pick with the cosmic saboteur called Death: it had wasted the life off Alice's mother with tuberculosis when Alice had been only four years old, and from me it had stolen a good dog – a year earlier, my gay collie Robbie had run under the train when he was chasing a rabbit. (I'd also lost Uncle Gabe quite recently, but I didn't care that much about him, for he had been a boisterous drunkard of a man, never did anything really sensible, just boozed and ran around with his pants down and yelled awful obscenities at kids.) We wanted to defy Death, and what would have represented him to us better than the train that thundered non-stop mystically through Houndbury.

First, it had killed my Robbie, rolled over him like some moving meat grinder on the rails. And only a couple of months before Elmer of Pig Pond had walked into a train somewhere around here, because he had lost in the war his ability to see life's beautiful side (that's what Daddy said anyway), and Elmer was by far not the only Houndbury person who over the years had come to do the same trick, 'bitten the train', as people used to say – during the last year at least six locals had 'bitten the train', and we were not further than May yet. Considering that, it was understandable that the train nowadays reminded most locals of Death – we had no station anyway, and the train didn't stop at Houndbury, except when somebody jumped in front of it with the purpose of self-destruction, so one couldn't really think of the train as *a vehicle*.

We breathed in the peculiar smell wafting about by the rails and waited. (Alice said the smell came from rust and the impregnation stuff used in the sleepers and some third unknown substance.) While we waited we sucked the sugar lumps Alice had pinched from home.

The train came every Saturday at 5.15. Today it was late; I checked the time on my fine Russian watch I'd got from Daddy as a birthday present (he'd found it lying on the ground during the war). We heard the train at only 5.23.

'It's coming,' Alice whispered. We kissed each other on the cheek according to our ritual and took each other's hands. Alice had a warm hand and enviably slender fingers; she had the talent to become a pianist, said our teacher, and Alice was taking piano lessons once a week from Amalie Forrester.

The train puffed into sight from behind the bend. *If you*

stand on the rails when the train comes, Alice had once said, *you'll be smashed up like a fly under a hammer. You have no chance at all to survive. But at the very same moment you step aside from its path, the train becomes harmless and Death loses his grip on you. You can stand half a metre or even just a few centimetres from the moving train, and the Grim Reaper can't do anything but grin at you. Then you can laugh at his pale disappointed face!*

At first the train looked like a smoking huffing toy, a cleverly constructed miniature model of a goods train. Then it took its place in the perspective and grew in my eyes up to its real dimensions. I looked at the black-nosed apparition that was rolling towards us, metallically rumbling; I looked at the rails on which it was travelling and between which we were standing, teetering on the sleeper.

The train meant millions of kilogrammes of unstoppable weight. If we were to stay on the rails, it would tear us to pieces without even having to slow down. Though the engine driver would brake, the train would never stop in time, not before it had wiped the rails with our remains for the length of a couple of kilometres at least.

Usually the thought gave me a bubbling excitement in my stomach, but now I was just cold. I wasn't feeling well and I kept moving around nervously and aimlessly fiddling with my hair which didn't look golden like Alice's but was boringly dark.

The train hooted. Alice laughed aloud, shrilly, but I didn't feel like laughing, not one hair of a shrew's whiskers.

'Take us if you can!' Alice whispered sensuously and laughed again. She was sometimes quite scary when she was like that, and maybe that was why I liked her so much; being with her never felt ordinary.

When the engine's dark presence was only fifty metres away, the train hooted again. Our play probably made the engine driver nervous, and sometimes we saw him shake his fist at us, but as Alice said: *What could he have done to us? Jump off the train to punish us?*

The green-black engine rushed towards us. Its long bumpers stretched eagerly forwards like the hands of a hungry child. The headlight trembling on its hood looked like a Cyclops' gleaming eye. Steam rasped and swished with terrible pressure in its iron lungs and pipes, and the furiously whipping pistons on its sides forced the steel wheels to revolve faster and faster and faster. The funnel splashed smoke clouds on the sky and they started to spread like black dye dropped into water. There was a number plate on the round end of the metal hood with the series '3159'; I read the numbers over and over and thought how easy it would be to go on reading them, endlessly, and to forget oneself on the rails and just let everything happen to you.

We left the rails and pretended to be calm and unhurried, although my guts were tightening and my body felt cold and heavy.

We stayed on the railway bank, on our old place just by the rails, not too close but close enough to be able to *smell* the disappointment of Death when the train was rumbling past. We stood there, erect and proud as princesses and waited for the train's draught to shake our clothes and the noise of its rhythm to deafen our ears, and for the smoke the engine was puffing to surround us for a moment and brush our faces like the cloak of our ancient enemy, cut from a weave of darkness.

Then we'd know that Uncle Death had once again lost the game and we had won, and we'd feel ourselves quite especially alive.

The engine screamed. Its voice was hungry; it had something in it that was similar to the crying of the strange, ever-angry baby born to our neighbours when it woke up and started to demand food, mad with rage. I felt the smell of railways in my nose, stronger than ever. The train's rhythmic noise sort of reached out an invisible arm and seized my heartbeats; for a moment our rhythms were one, and blood started coursing along my veins all too fast – something was now different from earlier times, I'd felt that all day in my stomach; suddenly I realized that this time the powers we'd been defying had their own plan for us.

I wrenched my eyes off the approaching train and tore my hand off Alice's and fled in senseless panic.

After the dash of a few heartbeats I slowed down. Embarrassed I looked behind me, and immediately lost the control of my body as totally as if I'd been shot. I forgot the existence of my feet and how to move them, and everything else, and flew on my side into the boulders, but if I happened to hurt myself I didn't remember how to feel any pain.

The last seconds had been full of sound, I now realized. The very same moment I had spurted to flee there had been a hard metallic slam. It was followed by a long, scratching noise, huge as the sky; it sounded like the Father God from religion lessons Himself had thumped his foot down from the clouds and started to furrow a kilometre-deep line into the ground.

My insides constricted and turned into a cold mess when I saw the engine throw gravel, dust and stones in the air so that the whole sky was filled up with earth.

The engine numbered 3159 no longer ran on rails. It pawed the embankment and then, as if in a fit of anger, started in quite another direction than the rails tried to persuade it. It drew the whole chain of wagons after itself, over thirty wagons long, yanked furiously off the rails. The train was now free and mad with exultation. The steam pistons pulled it violently forwards like the forearms of a lunatic escaping from an isolation ward. It wanted to conquer the world. Nothing could stop it. The arrogant challenge whispered by a little girl had freed it, and on the engine's hood, Death himself was roaring with laughter in his flowing cloak.

I looked at the train gliding past me as a huge and endlessly long dream monster, darkening the light of the sky and filling all my consciousness.

Had I stood up and taken a couple of steps I could have touched its dark flank, gone along with it. Then I turned my head, now weighing as much as a horse's, and looked at the little golden-haired girl towards whom the train was speeding. Alice stood in front of the metal monster she had freed, slender and vulnerable and angelically beautiful. I gasped for breath: I'd never realized that she was so exceedingly beautiful! She still seemed to be full of laughter, her mouth a black hole and thin hands twirling like the wings of a windmill. Her voice wasn't audible; the train's thousand-voiced scream filled the whole world. The girl was visible only for the hundredth of an instant and then the gravel and smoke and the moving black metal mountain swallowed her up.

And the train still kept pushing forwards, rebellious and insatiable and hungry. Off the rails its massive speed was unavoidably slowing down, however. Its wagons were colliding into each other, and a chaos ensued that an orderly mind could no way perceive.

The train seemed like a giant dying beast, a dragon fallen on its side and leaking dry. From inside the split engine case, thick black smoke was gushing out; it started to bury the wrecked giant and hide it from the eyes of the world. Some wagons had burst like cardboard boxes and the stuff inside them was spread all along the track.

The smoke crept on the ground to me, and when it touched my bare feet I shuddered with loathing – I felt that in its shelter the many-faced emperor Death himself was hiding; with his bony hand he was stroking my living flesh that fascinated him so much. *Sometimes you win, sometimes you lose*, it whispered gently among the engine's hiss; *let's bear no grudge, dear girl, let's meet again sometime!*

And somewhere in the shelter of the smoke Death was pressing against his thin breast the lifeless body of my Alice, my golden-haired slender-fingered little Alice...

whose residual warmth I still felt in my own hand;

whose desk would be empty on Monday morning;

who would then have a moment of silence to commemorate her, and the boy who had secretly been in love with her would burst into tears in the back row;

whose parents would turn grey and shrivel up and bend down in a few weeks and move away from the village without saying goodbye to anybody;

who would never more appear for piano lessons with Amalie Forrester, because her pianist's hands had been cut off and crushed under the train and would never play even the simplest melody...

I thought of the day when Robbie had chased the rabbit to the rails and run directly in front of the train. I'd never have believed an animal could look so sincerely astonished. I'd collected hairy pieces in a sack for several days from along the track. Even if dogs wouldn't get to heaven I wanted to at least give him a decent rest in a grave. I walked back and forth along the track from morning to evening and searched the ditches and grassy plots and brooks, but Robbie's left ear, right hind foot and half of his tail stayed missing. I'd always felt that the train had eaten them.

I pressed my eyes shut and with all my soul's power sent an appeal to the One who had deemed it justifiable to let the train run over Alice, whoever or whatever it was – perhaps some kind of a Big and Terrible Death Deity of the Railways existed, whom we in our immense ignorance had defied: *IF IT'S AT ALL POSSIBLE FOR YOU, PLEASE MAKE THIS SOMEHOW UNHAPPENED! I'LL GIVE YOU ANYTHING!*

Then I turned my back on the scene and walked home.

I felt confused. I never told anyone, not even my parents, that I'd been a witness to the death of my best friend and to a train accident that was talked about in the newspapers and even on the radio. It felt too unreal for me to talk about it. I never let myself even think about that rainy afternoon. Finally, it turned into that hazy dream image that sometimes flutters somewhere on the fringes of my consciousness like a black bird.

It was the memory of that day I felt nearby when Gunnar was inside me moving faster and faster and I held onto his tie and suddenly heard quite close the train's terrible hungry scream – the memory returned and took the breath from my lungs and the warmth from my blood and the feeling from my nerves. I repelled the shadow of Death, coldly stretching towards me, by clinging to the chance of a new life which in that magic moment was within my reach – I seized it, stole it, refused to surrender it back to Nothingness, which is just the other name of Death.'

– From the unwritten Dream Diary of E.N.

*

'Now,' Rupert whispered.

I stared into the vertical darkness of trees where the rails emerged.

I heard something, maybe a heavily melancholy metallic sigh that lingered, echoing in the snowy halls of the quiet forest. It was followed by a stretching metallic screech. Then I saw movement, or rather a premonition of movement.

At first it was just a shadow among shadows, the mischievous play of night wind and moonlight among the swaying spruce and snow. But gradually an apparition began to take shape on the clearing's edge. The rails held up a tall black being which crept forwards, hissing, gasping and terrifyingly huge and heavy. Now and then the moonlight touched it, but not for a moment did it give up the shadows it wore. It moved carefully, almost shyly, and nearly stopped, but then it puffed a large smoke cloud out into the frozen air, gave a jolt and started, creaking painfully, to flow off the rails in front of my eyes.

I realized vaguely that Rupert stood up near me.

'What are you planning to do?' I asked him.

I was straining to understand what was happening before my eyes; I kept trying to figure out a plausible explanation for it and to fit it into some rational frame of reference, but the gnawing ache behind my brow didn't make rationalization any easier.

'You just stay there. And mother: don't move, under any circumstances! Wait there, keep your head low and hold your ears.'

'My ears?'

But he had already gone, rushed down the slope with coat hems flapping, towards the train descending off the rails. I stared after him along the surface of the snow, until he sank into the thick shadows.

Hold your ears.

A series of relays clicked in my head, and suddenly I remembered the dynamite theft Miriam had mentioned; I remembered all the recent cases of disappeared explosives. How much had actually been taken?

… or else there was a rather big cache somewhere close by – very soon a part of Houndbury would surely fly off in the four winds!

'But you can't possibly blow up a train!' I whispered into the darkness, completely taken aback.

But of course, he could do it. He was brain-damaged and more irrational than ever and could do anything, because he no longer acknowledged my authority. And all those unexplained thefts of explosives – I could see with the eyes of my mind how my son had committed burglaries by night and skied here with his loot and gradually charged the whole valley. I couldn't imagine how much he knew about explosives, surely not much, but probably still enough to achieve a considerable explosion. Trains had hurt him in so many ways, and now he planned to pay them back, measure for measure.

'Rupert, no…'

I rushed after my son through the juniper bushes. All the time I expected the dusk in front of me to flare up in a fire that would strip clothes and skin and flesh off me and fling my burnt-up bones up the slope. Even I couldn't at this moment conjure any rational explanation for why a train would run off rails by night in the middle of a remote forest, but that didn't make *blowing up* the train any more reasonable an idea, now did it?

'Rupert, leave the train alone!' I yelled. 'We have to talk seriously. Let's go home and take some chocolate cake out of the freezer and make some cocoa and talk properly! What about it?'

It was darker at the bottom of the valley. I ran among the spruce, juniper and pine towards the rails.

I slowed down when a peculiar lump on the ground caught my eyes. I stooped down to look at it. It was a little snowman. Or not a snowman, a gravestone – there was some engraving on it, too, but I couldn't figure it out.

I kicked off the snow on its base, and something like a paw came into view.

I straightened up and realized that I had no time to think about such matters. I had to warn the engine driver before Rupert could carry out his obsession and destroy even what little was left of his life. The snow squeaked and thudded under my steps.

'Rupert, Rupert,' I whispered. 'Is this now that "creative imagination" of yours?'

A long hiss made me stop.

I listened for a while and then carefully stepped through the spruce twigs hanging in front of me.

About ten or fifteen metres away from me was the train, or rather the shape of a train covered in smoky darkness. It was surrounded by trees and darkness, a lot of darkness. The valley was a real sea of darkness, where everything was made up of different degrees of darkness and the scant light afforded by the moon only managed to confuse the eye with its roguish play. If I could see properly, there was a big black steam engine driving the train that had arrived via the rails, a real museum piece. So black it looked like condensed night, like darkness cast in the shape of an engine. There was a dark line of goods wagons behind it. Those were still left on the rails, but the engine stood in the snow between the spruce trees. Its long black bumpers stretched towards me like the paws of a beast. I only saw completely clearly the plough-like metal contraption in front of it that was probably intended to remove obstacles off the rails; it had snow and twigs heaped on it now.

Perhaps they were setting up some kind of steam engine museum out here, I reasoned weakly.

I wished my head wouldn't ache so furiously; even a slight migraine hampered logical thinking and easily made me do foolish things. (When Rupert was six years old I had, for instance, taken all the laundry out of the washing machine and directly off to the rubbish heap. Rupert had given me an enormous headache by pretending for three days in a row that our house was a spaceship landed on Uranus – when I'd tried to open the windows, he had hysterically caught my hands and screamed something about a noxious atmosphere waiting outside.)

'Hello!' I yelled and waved my hand. 'Ahoy! You there in the engine! Have you seen my son? Stetson and a long coat. He's not quite himself just now, and I think you ought to—'

The engine spat thick smoke and howled. Its voice kept whirling around me and my ears rang as if my head had turned into the bell tower of an enormous cathedral. It was too dark to see inside the engine. The train *itself* seemed to stare at me with its lamp-eyes. It looked curious. If an inanimate machine can somehow look conscious, this one did.

I stared at the big green-black mass of the engine, my head bent back, and tried to ignore my subjective feelings which were getting more irrational all the time. I felt I was being stared back at. Of course it was an engine driver looking at me from the cover of darkness, not the train itself, but the illusion was strong. And in certain hours of the night the human mind is apt to be carried off by subjectivity; perhaps this lack of objectivity has something to do with the phenomenon called biorhythms.

'Hello! You ought to listen to me now, before anything unpleasant happens!'

I took a few steps closer to the train. I wanted to see whether anybody was left in the engine. Perhaps the engine driver had by now noticed that something was going on and had gone off to examine the situation. I looked around myself.

'Rupert! I'm here! Mother's by the train! Don't... don't do anything at all!'

I hoped my son – wherever he was hiding – would have the patience to keep his hands off the explosives as long as he knew I was close by.

Then I stopped, confused.

The train radiated incomprehensible coldness that penetrated all my clothes and burned my skin. I noticed the snow around the train was freezing to steely hardness; I heard the snow crackle as it hardened. The engine puffed and jerked a couple of metres forwards, closer to me. The smoke spread everywhere into the darkness and added its own gauzy shade to it. The plough bit the snow. The engine's hood pushed into the moonlight, the twigs swayed aside, and I saw underneath the train's turned-off lamp a sign with the number series '3159'.

The comprehension emerged from some deep source inside me. What was before me was not exactly – at least not primarily – a train. It looked like a train, and to *some extent* it surely was a train, but its fundamental essence was one of those marginal things humans are not supposed to know about.

I felt no need to scream in terror or otherwise turn hysterical. That would have been ridiculous. The existence of the apparition rather made me feel embarrassed, as if I had without knocking entered a room where somebody I thought I knew well (in this case, objective reality) was doing something quite strange and private. That apparition of a train was on its own strange business; it was following purposes incomprehensible to me. In the world of reason and logic it was a complete stranger, an uninvited guest, an embarrassing secret. A ghost from another time. Yes: I knew that engine. I knew its number, and I recognized the malicious consciousness it radiated.

I'd seen it escape the rails and kill and then be destroyed itself. And now it was here before me anyhow. Why? Was I looking at the ghost of a train?

'It's the "Little Jumbo",' a voice sounded somewhere behind me. 'They were manufactured in the machine shops of Tampella, Lokomo and Frichs from the year 1927 to the year 1953. What's the year now?'

With stiff lips I uttered the year I thought correct, eyes frozen fast to the apparition standing before me. It was still staring at me with its lamp-eyes from between the shadowy spruce branches. Curious, hungry. The coldness of the engine flowed into my flesh; it was burning me like fire sculpted of ice, and by and by it seemed to me that if I didn't leave its circle of influence soon, I was never going to move again.

And that was precisely the train ghost's intention. It was trying to bewitch and freeze me, to make me wonder about its nature and surrender myself to be its prey. And it was close to succeeding. I knew I should have turned my back to it and left, but I just kept staring at the iron dragon breathing irrationality, and at its identification number. The sense of touch escaped my flesh; I thought I could hear even my skin crackle while it was freezing.

3159, 3159, 3159...

'That kind was taken out of service ages ago,' Rupert continued somewhere out of sight. 'Over twenty years ago already. Consequently, it's here sometime *before* it was taken off. And now and then, some come here to turn which haven't even been made yet. That's why I couldn't find the picture of one of them in any books. That's why watches don't work here: this place is outside the timetables. They wake up on the rails and they break out of their own timetables and find a suitable blind track and come here, wherever or whenever they are.'

'Whatever, Rupert,' I mumbled, lips numb with cold. I didn't have the energy to try to understand his words. I only knew I was freezing to death. 'Listen, are you really going to blow up that train?'

After a moment's silence Rupert answered: 'This place is full of dynamite. It's by the rails, in the trees, under the snow. I've spent several nights making preparations. I have to do it. Even if you are going to be angry.'

'Can't I stop you in any way? Reason with you? Make you realize how senseless this all is?'

'No.'

'Well then you've obviously got to do what you've got to do,' I muttered, relieved – the responsibility was no longer mine. I couldn't take any more responsibility.

The train blew smoke in the air, and its steam pistons became tense and started to push the wheels where they were fixed; it was preparing to chase me again, to make its kill. To murder me.

I felt somebody gripping my shoulders. Rupert started to walk me away from there, fast. My feet had lost their strength to the cold, but Rupert was strong. The valley reverberated with the train's hollow panting and the metallic screech of the steam machinery that was pushing it off.

We got as far as the junipers, and Rupert threw himself in the snow and dragged me down with him. My face thumped against the snow. I was too benumbed to soften my landing.

'Mother, I ignited all the fuses,' my son whispered. 'Hands to your ears!'

'We have to talk about this when we get home,' I sighed. 'Let's drink cocoa and really talk with each other for once.'

I thought there was something that I ought to have noticed and understood. Something to do with causes and consequences. If only my head hadn't been aching so terribly.

With the growing pounding in my head I hardly even heard the explosions that suddenly started to tear apart the valley, the trees and the train that had left its timetable.

*

'We stood there an hour, hand in hand, and waited, Alice and I. Then we sat on the rails and waited yet another hour. The train didn't come, the track stayed empty. I felt more and more miserable. My stomach was hurting and my head ached. 'It's not coming,' I said. 'Let's leave now.'

Alice angrily plucked a golden lock off her head and pouted. 'It's not going to show. We have to come back tomorrow.'

We went home, Alice disappointed and I feeling ill but relieved.

In the night I woke up feeling that I could hardly breathe. Twinges of pain were stabbing my temples. My first thought was that Alice was dead. I fancied I remembered how the train had come and swerved off the rails and crushed Alice in front of my horrified eyes. The image was so vivid I started crying in my bed. And yet I also remembered that the train had never come and we had returned home in peace.

In the morning I ran to see Alice; I had to make sure that she really was alive. She set about at once to get us going to the railway tracks, but I refused, even when she pressed me hard and called me a traitor and even a bad friend. She looked at me somehow strangely, and I knew something had changed between us.

We were still friends, of course, and went around together, but day by day our friendship got thinner and we met more and more infrequently – the magic was gone. It was pretty much my fault – I couldn't relate to Alice naturally any more, for I remembered her dying that afternoon on the railway, even while I also remembered we'd come back home together. I remembered her funeral; I even remembered the place she was buried, and her gravestone and the golden letters on it, and yet she was sitting next to me in school.'

– From the unwritten Dream Diary of E.N.

*

That is the night I think I lost my son; I remember the night and the explosions, but after that – nothing. I don't remember coming home. A few times I've tried to return by myself to look for that strange blind track in the forest, but every time I've been driven aside from the way and ended up somewhere quite different.

I remember Rupert's birth. I remember him growing and his overactive imagination and the day he graduated from law school. I remember his love and the skull fracture that removed it from his head. I remember our night trip to the place where the trains turn, and that's where I lost him in the worst way. All that I remember, but I also remember that I never had the child I wished for. My youth was spent in studying, and then I had to further my career. We often talked about children, I and my husband, but we put off the realization of the idea, and when we finally decided to try, it was already too late.

A few months ago, I saw Gunnar on the television. He'd put on a lot of weight. I was startled; somehow, I'd imagined he was dead. He spoke dryly about the big export sales his company had made, and I wondered whether he ever thought about the girl he had seduced by the railway tracks three decades since. So often had I wondered what would have happened if at the critical moment I'd prevented him from withdrawing and taken his seed and made him the father of my child. The thought had entered my mind at the time, however irrational and irresponsible it was. If I'd really done that, would the other line of my memories now be objective reality, not only subjective? Would *Rupert* now be objective reality?

Remembering makes me feel ill, but I can't help thinking of Rupert. He feels so real, often more real than this real life of mine. I remember how my figure got rounder and I took a taxi to the hospital and gave birth to my son. I remember the pain and the tears and the joy, when I received the little wrinkled human being in my arms. I remember the sour midwife and the hospital ward. And yet I know nothing like that happened to me – on the day Rupert was born I was on a business trip to Moscow: it's documented. I remember that quite well, too, the small hotel room and the chambermaid I surprised as she was rummaging in my bag.

Perhaps I'm crazy. How many sane persons have two sets of superimposed memories covering forty years? Perhaps all those empty recollections that torment me are only the product of a brain that's gone completely round the bend? That would be the easiest and also the most believable explanation – except for one small problem: I could have invented Rupert, yes. He could very well be just a delusion, flung by an ageing woman suffering from childlessness into her past to soothe her pain. But what about the place where the trains turn? *I* do not have enough imagination to invent anything like that. I'm a very rational person, who keeps her feet closely and safely in the dust of the earth in all situations. Unlike some others, who used to let their imagination fly irresponsibly like a kite on a stormy Sunday afternoon; such was my lost son Rupert. The place where the trains turn could only have been invented by Rupert himself, and he couldn't have done that if he himself were nothing more than my invention.

I hunt my memories and study them from all angles, the way a scientist may collect and study extremely important samples. I draw charts of the two different lines of my life – they are sometimes hard to distinguish. And there is a pile of evidence on my desk:

There is a phone number: there's a lawyer called Birgitta Donner in Helsinki, but she has never heard of Rupert Nightingale.

There is a Christmas card from Alice Holmsten, nowadays Frogge: she tells she's married and works as a music teacher in a school in Turku. I hadn't thought of her for years, but sometimes one receives cards from persons already forgotten even when there's been no particular reason to remember them.

There is a collection of short stories by Miriam Catterton that I bought yesterday from Houndbury Books: I'm not acquainted with Miriam, although I also have other kinds of recollections of her. Most people know her since she's a teacher, but I don't have children, and we've never even talked with each other. She seemed surprised when I phoned her this morning and introduced myself. I told her I'd read her book and been especially fascinated by one of the stories, the one that tells about a little boy called Robert who loves railways and whose imagination his overly rational mother Anna tries to repress.

This is now quite silly, I explained, *but I simply had to call and ask where you got the idea for Robert's story.*

Well, where do ideas come from, generally, Miriam said, sort of embarrassed. *They are just in the air. I often have dreams and I use them. For a couple of nights, I dreamed about a little boy who loved railways, and it developed out of that, gradually.*

I've read the story through several times already, trying to decide which truth its existence proves.

There's also on my desk an article I clipped out from the newspaper forty years ago and kept unto this day between the encyclopaedia pages. It tells about a whole goods train that vanished without a trace with its freight and engine driver somewhere in the Houndbury region. The authorities investigating the case were puzzled, but according to them it appeared probable that there was an extensive conspiracy of railway personnel behind the train theft – no way otherwise could such a crime be explained. The press clipping also seems to want to tell me something, but I'm not able to figure out how that event could be connected with Rupert's disappearance, not yet.

I cannot let him pass away out of my reach into final oblivion. I cannot give him back to Nothingness. That is why I continue with my investigations. I have to finally understand, to find him on the eternal circle of cause and consequence. For the sake of my son I go on with this, for his sake I write these thoughts of mine on paper.

Translated from the Finnish by Liisa Rantalaiho

About the Authors

DIANA RAHIM is an editor, writer and visual artist from Singapura whose recent work has focused on the politics of public space and the experience of the environment. She is the editor of 'Beyond the Hijab', an online community and platform for Singaporean Muslim women to share stories and critical perspectives. Her written work has most recently been anthologized in *Making Kin: Ecofeminist Essays from Singapore* (2021), *In This Desert, There Were Seeds* (2019), and *Singa-Pura-Pura* (2021).

Born in Bulgaria, in one of the world's oldest cities, DANIELA TOMOVA draws her inspiration from Balkan folklore, Eastern European surrealism, world literature and the everyday magic of people who live in the ruins of countless civilizations. She is a graduate of Clarion Writers' Workshop. Her work has appeared in *Apex Magazine*, *Tor.com* and other publications. Data- and cybersec consultant by day, she lives in an abandoned airport in Norway with her partner and their cat.

TIMI ODUESO is a journalist at TechCabal where he covers tech news in Africa's most comprehensive tech newsletter, 'TC Daily'. He is a law student with five-years'-plus experience working for organisations like the Abuja Literary Society and other companies across Africa in various roles spanning from content creation and communications to product management and administration.

MANDISI NKOMO is a South African writer, drummer, composer and producer. He currently resides in Hartbeespoort, South

Africa. His fiction has been published in the likes of *AfroSF: Science Fiction by African Writers*, *AfroSFv3* and *Omenana*. His poetry has been published in *The Coinage Book One* and *Shoreline of Infinity,* and his academic work has been published in *The Thinker*. His works have been longlisted for the Nommo Award for African Speculative Fiction. He has been shortlisted for the Toyin Falola Short Story Prize. He is also a member of the African Speculative Fiction Society. For updates and information on Mandisi's writing and musical endeavours, follow him on Twitter, Instagram or Facebook. He also runs a blog under his alias, The Dark Cow.

NELLY GERALDINE GARCÍA-ROSAS is a Mexican immigrant and a graduate of the Clarion West class of 2019. Her short fiction has appeared or is forthcoming in *Lightspeed*, *Nightmare*, *Strange Horizons*, and elsewhere. She can be found online at nellygeraldine.com and on Twitter as @kitsune_ng.

M.H. AYINDE is a runner, a chai drinker and a screen-time enthusiast. Her short fiction has appeared or is forthcoming in *FIYAH* literary magazine, *F&SF*, *Daily Science Fiction* and elsewhere. She won the 2021 Future Worlds Prize for her novel *A Shadow in Chains*. She lives in London with three generations of her family and their assorted feline overlords.

LUO LONGXIANG was born in 1981, deep in the mountains of Guangxi province on China's southern border, where he studied Chemical Engineering at Guangxi University. After publishing his first sci-fi story in 2003, his fans began to refer to the mysterious author as 'Master Luo', in reference to his hermit-like existence far away from the crowded cities of the coast and northern plains. Of the eleven stories he has written over the past decade, six have earned a Milky Way Award. His works are known for their massive scope, dealing almost exclusively with the question of humanity's eventual survival in space. Since 2007, he has been working to complete the Planetship Alliance series – an epic space opera recounting the tragic history of mankind's colonization of the universe.

THOMAS OLDE HEUVELT (1983) is the international bestselling author of seven novels, including *HEX* and *Echo*. Born in the Netherlands, he was the first ever translated author to win a Hugo Award, for his story 'The Day the World Turned Upside Down' in 2015. The subsequent release of his horror novel *HEX* (2016) in over twenty-five countries sparked months-long book tours on four continents and launched him as a celebrity author in his home country, with each of his novels topping the Dutch bestseller charts. *HEX*, about a witch haunting a modern-day US town, is currently in development for an American TV show by Gary Dauberman and James Wan. In 2022, the long-awaited English-language edition of his new novel *Echo* was published. *Echo*, about a man possessed by a mountain, is Olde Heuvelt's love letter to the gothic novel and was inspired by his long-time affliction with mountaineering. In 2023, a new novel titled *Oracle* will be released around the world. Thomas Olde Heuvelt, whose last name in Dutch dialect means 'Old Hill', lives in the Netherlands and the south of France with his partner, writer David Samwel.

INDRAPRAMIT DAS (**aka Indra Das**) is a writer and editor from Kolkata, India. He is a Lambda Literary Award-winner for his debut novel *The Devourers* (Penguin India/Del Rey), and a Shirley Jackson Award-winner for his short fiction, which has appeared in a variety of anthologies and publications including

Tor.com, *Lightspeed*, *Clarkesworld* and *Asimov's Science Fiction*. He is an Octavia E. Butler Scholar, and a grateful member of the Clarion West class of 2012. He has lived in India, the United States and Canada, where he received his MFA from the University of British Columbia.

ANDREA CHAPELA is a Mexican writer. She is the author of a YA fantasy series, two essay collections and two short story collections. She studied Chemistry at UNAM and obtained her MFA in Spanish Creative Writing from the University of Iowa. She's a graduate of Clarion West 2017 and part of the Mexicanx Initiative. She has received the National Gilberto Owen Literature Prize for Stories in 2018, the National Juan José Arreola Literature Prize in 2019 and the National Joven José Luis Martínez Essay Prize in 2019. In 2021, she was selected as one of *Granta*'s Best of Young Spanish-Language Novelists. Her work has been published in English in *Samovar*, *Lightspeed*, *InTranslation*, Slate's *Future Tense* series, and *Tupelo Quarterly*. Her book *The Visible Unseen* was published in English in 2022 with Restless Books. Nowadays, she lives in Mexico City with her cat and is pursuing her MA in Japanese Studies.

FADZLISHAH JOHANABAS is currently apprenticing (and teaching) as a paediatric neurosurgeon at a general hospital in the heart of Kuala Lumpur, Malaysia. He has published a few medical articles and a whole lot more short stories, at venues like *Interzone*, *COSMOS Australia*, *Crossed Genres* and *The Apex Book of World SF 3*. A small press publisher released his collection of short stories, *Faith and the Machine*. He is also active on Facebook and Instagram, and occasionally on Twitter as @fadzjohanabas.

CHERYL S. NTUMY is a Ghanaian writer of short fiction and novels of speculative fiction, young adult fiction and romance. Her work has appeared in *FIYAH Literary Magazine*, *Apex Magazine*, *Will This be a Problem* and *Botswana Women Write*, among others. Her work has also been shortlisted for the Nommo Award for African Speculative Fiction, the Commonwealth Writers' Short Story Prize and the Miles Morland Foundation Scholarship. She is part of the Saúútiverse Collective and a member of Petlo Literary Arts, an organisation that develops and promotes creative writing in Botswana.

ZAHRA MUKHI is a writer from Karachi, Pakistan. Currently she writes and reads when she can, and laments about the ways of our world. You can find her on Twitter @zahramukhi.

DMITRY GLUKHOVSKY is the author of the internationally bestselling Metro 2033 series, which he later developed into a multimedia franchise. His *Tales of the Motherland*, in which this story appeared, is a compilation of satirical stories about Russian realities. *Text*, a cyber-noir novel set in contemporary Russia, was made into a film that won the Nika Award for Best Screenplay in 2020, and his short film *Promises* won the 2021 Golden Unicorn Award for Best Short Film. 'Sulfur' was originally published in the Russian edition of *Esquire* and made into a short film.

EFE TOKUNBO is a Nigerian writer, anarchist and hobo. He describes the majority of his work as 'metaphors for the lost'.

FARGO NISSIM TBAKHI is a queer Palestinian performance artist, a Taurus and a cool breeze. Find more at fargotbakhi.com.

CHEN QIAN started her science fiction and fantasy writing career in 2006. She is a member of the China Science Writers' Association, the Science Literary and Art Committee and the Shanghai Youth Literary and Arts Association. Her short stories can usually be found in *Science Fiction King*, *Science Fiction World*, *Odyssey of China Fantasy* and *Zui Fiction*, among others. Her works have been selected into Chinese SF Year's Best and adapted into comics and broadcast dramas. Her books include a short story collection, *The Prisoner of Memory*, a YA novel, *Deep Sea Bus*, and a YA short story collection, *Sea Sausage Bus*. She has won two Chinese Nebulas, a Coordinate Award and a YA Chinese Nebula.

ELENA PAVLOVA lives in Montana, Bulgaria. Her short stories have appeared in various Bulgarian anthologies and magazines, winning awards from national competitions. In 2019, her middle-grade SF novel Камен и пиратите от 5г [*Kamen and the Pirates from 5-B*] won the Bulgarian National Konstantin Konstantinov Award. She has had six other novels, two collections of shorter fiction and more than two dozen gamebooks published, and has translated authors as diverse as Robert Howard, Robert R. McCammon and Peter Watts into Bulgarian. Her short stories 'Love in the Time of Con Crud' and 'Two Moons' appeared in *Future Science Fiction Digest* #3 in 2019 and *Compelling Science Fiction* #15 in 2020, respectively.

CHOYEOP KIM is an award-winning Korean science fiction author with a background in biochemistry. She enjoys converting intangible ideas, such as memory, emotion, minds and relations into tangible items. She wants to write about the abstract components of life in a specifically scientific language while discovering new questions in the process.

EUGENIA TRIANTAFYLLOU is a Greek author and artist with a flair for dark things. Her short fiction has been nominated for the Ignyte, Nebula and World Fantasy Awards, and she is a graduate of the Clarion West Writers Workshop. You can find her stories in *Uncanny*, *Apex*, *Strange Horizons* and other venues. She currently lives in Athens with a boy and a dog. Find her on Twitter @foxesandroses or her website, eugeniatriantafyllou. wordpress.com.

NORA SCHINNERL lives on the edge of Vienna, Austria, in a shared house with two cats, a chameleon and some humans, and tries not to get confused by writing in English while speaking in German. When she isn't writing, she enjoys reading too much, playing video games for too long and finding shortcuts through the woods. She is very bad at being realistic, which is why her idea of a day job is working as an archaeologist. Her short fiction has appeared in *Future SF Digest*.

CHRISTINE LUCAS lives in Greece with her life partner and a horde of spoiled animals. She's a retired Air Force officer and mostly self-taught in English. Her work appears in several print and online magazines, including *Future SF Digest*, *PseudoPod* and *Strange Horizons*. She was a finalist for the 2017 WSFA Small Press Award and a collection of her short stories, titled *Fates and Furies*, was published in late 2019 by Candlemark & Gleam.

VIDA CRUZ-BORJA is a Filipina fantasy and science fiction writer, editor, artist and con-runner. Her short fiction and essays have been published or are forthcoming in *The Magazine of Fantasy and Science Fiction, Fantasy Magazine, Strange Horizons, PodCastle, Expanded Horizons* and various anthologies. Her work has been nominated, longlisted, and recommended for the Hugo Award, the British Science Fiction Award and the James Tiptree Jr. (now Otherwise) Award. She is the author of two illustrated short story collections: *Beyond the Line of Trees* and *Song of the Mango and Other New Myths.* She lives in Manila with her husband and three dogs and teaches Creative Writing at Ateneo de Manila University.

SHEIKHA HELAWY is a Bedouin writer, poet and educator who was born in an unrecognized village near Haifa in 1968; she studied both Arabic and Hebrew literature at Tel Aviv University. She has published one book of poetry and three collections of short stories, with work translated into German, Bulgarian and English.

VRAIUX DORÓS (Mexico City, 1992) Poet & Magician. Collects miniature dinosaurs.

DEAN FRANCIS ALFAR's books include the novel *Salamanca*; short fiction collections *The Kite of Stars and Other Stories, How to Traverse Terra Incognita, A Field Guide to the Roads of Manila and Other Stories,* and *Stars in Jars*; and the children's book *How Rosang Taba Won a Race.* As an editor and anthologist, he is the founder of the *Philippine Speculative Fiction* annuals, and the editor of *Fantasy: Filipino Fiction for Young Adults, Horror: Filipino Fiction for Young Adults, Science Fiction: Filipino Fiction for Young Adults, Maximum Volume: Best New Philippine Fiction 1 & 2,* among others. Dean's short stories have been anthologized in books such as *The Big Book of Modern Fantasy, The Time Traveler's Almanac* and *The Year's Best Fantasy & Horror*, and have appeared in various magazines and online publications. He lives in Manila with his wife and tango partner, award-winning fictionist Nikki Alfar.

MÁRIO COELHO is a Portuguese writer and translator. He spends his time eating cherry tomatoes, travelling around Europe in his unreliable Mitsubishi Carisma and ruminating about the eventual decay of everything he loves. You can find his short fiction at *Strange Horizons, PseudoPod* and *The New Southern Fugitives*. His debut novella *Unto the Godless What Little Remains* was published by Solaris Books in 2022.

PASI ILMARI JÄÄSKELÄINEN, born in 1966, is one of Finland's best-kept secrets. A novelist and short-story writer, he is well known for his fantasy and sci-fi narratives and has twice won the Kuvastaja Fantasy Prize given by Finland's Tolkien Society and four times won the Atorox Award for Fantasy. He has published three novels and a collection of short stories. His first novel, *Lumikko ja yhdeksän muuta* (Atena, 2006) has been sold to eight countries: Great Britain, USA, Germany, France, Lithuania, Italy, Spain and the Czech Republic. The English translation, *The Rabbit Back Literature Society*, was published by Pushkin Press in 2013. He teaches Finnish language and literature and is the father of three sons.

About the Translators

SILVIA MORENO-GARCIA is the author of the novels *Velvet Was the Night*, *Mexican Gothic* and many other books. She has edited several anthologies, including the World Fantasy Award-winning *She Walks in Shadows* (aka *Cthulhu's Daughters*).

ANDY DUDAK's fiction is featured in Jonathan Strahan's *Year's Best Science Fiction*, Neil Clarke's *Best Science Fiction of the Year* and two volumes of Rich Horton's *Year's Best Science Fiction and Fantasy*. His stories have appeared in *Analog*, *Apex*, *Clarkesworld*, *Interzone*, *The Magazine of Fantasy and Science Fiction* and in *Science Fiction World* (科幻世界). His story 'Love in the Time of Immuno-Sharing' was a finalist for the Eugie Foster Award. His translations of Chinese sci-fi have appeared in *Clarkesworld*, *Analog*, *Asimov's*, *Pathlight* and elsewhere. He likes frogs, and believes in the healing power of Dungeons & Dragons.

LIA BELT was born in 1969 and lives in Amsterdam, the Netherlands. Originally a translator of mostly industry manuals from English and German into the Dutch language, some fifteen years ago she started translating fiction for several publishers in the Netherlands. She has translated fantasy from authors such as Robert Jordan, Stan Nicholls, David Hair and Raymond E. Feist for Dutch readers, but also children's books, science fiction, young adult and thrillers. Every now and then she also tries her hand at translating fiction into the English language for Dutch authors who want to find a wider audience for their work.

EMMA TÖRZS is a writer and teacher based in Minneapolis. Her short fiction has been published in journals such as *Uncanny*, *American Short Fiction*, *Strange Horizons* and *Lightspeed*, and honoured with a 2020 NEA fellowship, a 2019 World Fantasy Award, and a 2015 O. Henry Prize. She received her MFA in Fiction from the University of Montana, Missoula, and is an enthusiastic member of the Clarion West class of 2017. Her debut novel is forthcoming in 2023 with William Morrow in the US and with Century/Del Rey in the UK, and will be published in twelve languages worldwide.

MARIAN SCHWARTZ has translated Russian classics such as *Anna Karenina* and *Oblomov* as well as such celebrated contemporary authors as Mikhail Shishkin, Olga Slavnikova and Leonid Yuzefovich and is the recipient of numerous honours. Her translations of Eugene Vodolazkin's *Brisbane* and Ludmilla Petrushevskaya's *Kidnapped: A Story in Crimes* were published in 2022.

Born in China and raised in the United States, CARMEN YILING YAN was first driven to translation in high school by the pain of reading really good stories and being unable to share them. Since then, her translations of Chinese science fiction have been published in *Clarkesworld*, *Lightspeed* and *Galaxy's Edge*, as well as numerous anthologies. She graduated from UCLA with a degree in Computer Science but writes more fiction than code these days. She currently lives in the Midwest.

KALIN M. NENOV is a translator, editor, publisher, agent and writer. Currently, he lives in Sofia, Bulgaria, and acts as Trailblazer at the Human Library Foundation. His translations have appeared in various magazines and anthologies, most notably *Up and*

Coming: Stories by the 2016 Campbell-Eligible Authors and most recently in *Compelling Science Fiction #15* in 2020. Find more on his Goodreads Author Profile: goodreads.com/author/show/5052829.Kalin_M_Nenov

JOUNGMIN LEE COMFORT is a Korean–English translator based in the US. Born and raised in South Korea and France, she moved to the US in 1999 where she worked as an ELL teacher and court interpreter before finding her way to academic translation. In 2016, she received a translation grant from the Literary Translation Institute of Korea, which began her career in literary translation. In 2017, she was awarded the ALTA Emerging Translator Mentorship programme. Among her publications, her co-translation of Kim Bo-Young's *On the Origin of Species and Other Stories* was longlisted for the 2021 National Book Awards for translated literature.

RAPHAEL COHEN is a professional translator and lexicographer who studied Arabic and Hebrew at Oxford University and the University of Chicago. Based in Cairo, he has translated a range of contemporary Arabic literature including the novels *The Madness of Despair* by Ghalya Al Said (Banipal, 2021), *Guard of the Dead* by George Yarak (Hoopoe 2019), which was shortlisted for the 2016 IPAF prize, and Ahlem Mosteghanemi's *The Bridges of Constantine* (Bloomsbury, 2014), as well as short stories by Ihsan Abdel Kuddous, Maha Jouini, Wanicy Laredj and Raghad al-Suheil and poetry by Ahmed Morsi, Samer Abu Hawwash and Marwan Makhoul. He is a contributing editor of *Banipal*.

TOSHIYA KAMEI's translations have appeared in *Clarkesworld*, *The Magazine of Fantasy & Science Fiction* and *Strange Horizons*.

Lıısa Rantalaıho is a professor emerita (sociology of health/ gender studies), a member of the Editorial Board of *Fafnir – Nordic Journal of Science Fiction and Fantasy Research*, a fanzine critic and a Finnish fandom activist.

Extended Copyright

About the Translators

SILVIA MORENO-GARCIA is the author of the novels *Velvet Was the Night*, *Mexican Gothic* and many other books. She has edited several anthologies, including the World Fantasy Award-winning *She Walks in Shadows* (aka *Cthulhu's Daughters*).

ANDY DUDAK's fiction is featured in Jonathan Strahan's *Year's Best Science Fiction*, Neil Clarke's *Best Science Fiction of the Year* and two volumes of Rich Horton's *Year's Best Science Fiction and Fantasy*. His stories have appeared in *Analog*, *Apex*, *Clarkesworld*, *Interzone*, *The Magazine of Fantasy and Science Fiction* and in *Science Fiction World* (科幻世界). His story 'Love in the Time of Immuno-Sharing' was a finalist for the Eugie Foster Award. His translations of Chinese sci-fi have appeared in *Clarkesworld*, *Analog*, *Asimov's*, *Pathlight* and elsewhere. He likes frogs, and believes in the healing power of Dungeons & Dragons.

LIA BELT was born in 1969 and lives in Amsterdam, the Netherlands. Originally a translator of mostly industry manuals from English and German into the Dutch language, some fifteen years ago she started translating fiction for several publishers in the Netherlands. She has translated fantasy from authors such as Robert Jordan, Stan Nicholls, David Hair and Raymond E. Feist for Dutch readers, but also children's books, science fiction, young adult and thrillers. Every now and then she also tries her hand at translating fiction into the English language for Dutch authors who want to find a wider audience for their work.

THE BEST
OF WORLD

SF

SERIES

EDITED BY
LAVIE TIDHAR

COLLECT THEM ALL...

THE BEST OF WORLD SF
VOLUME 1

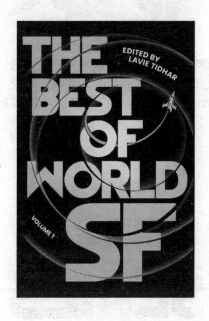

FEATURING:

Aliette de Bodard · Chen Qiufan · Vina Jie-Min Prasad · Tlotlo Tsamaase · Chinelo Onwualu · Vandana Singh · Han Song · Yi-Sheng Ng · Taiyo Fujii · Francesco Verso · Malena Salazar Maciá · Tade Thompson · Fabio Fernandes · R.S.A. Garcia · Cristina Jurado · Gerardo Horacio Porcayo · Hannu Rajaniemi · Nir Yaniv · Emil H. Petersen · Ekaterina Sedia · Kuzhali Manickavel · Kofi Nyameye · Lauren Beukes · Karin Tidbeck · Silvia Moreno-Garcia · Zen Cho

THE BEST OF WORLD SF
VOLUME 2

FEATURING:

Nadia Afifi · Lavanya Lakshminarayan · Frances Ogamba ·
Isabel Yap · Saad Z. Hossain · Yukimi Ogawa · Xing He · Nalo
Hopkinson · Pan Haitian · Jacques Barcia · Edmundo Paz
Soldán · Dilman Dila · Natalia Theodoridou · Bef · Alberto
Chimal · Wole Talabi · William Tham Wai Liang · Usman
T. Malik · Julie Nováková · Cassandra Khaw · Tobias S. Buckell
and Karen Lord · T.L. Huchu · Clelia Farris · Agnieszka Halas ·
Samit Basu · Neon Yang · Kim Bo-Young · Hassan Blasim ·
K.A. Teryna

THE BEST OF WORLD SF
VOLUME 3

FEATURING:

Diana Rahim · Daniela Tomova · Timi Odueso · Mandisi Nkomo · Nelly Geraldine García-Rosas · M.H. Ayinde · Luo Longxiang · Thomas Olde Heuvelt · Indrapramit Das · Andrea Chapela · Fadzlishah Johanabas · Cheryl S. Ntumy · Zahra Mukhi · Dmitry Glukhovsky · Efe Tokunbo · Fargo Tbakhi · Chen Qian · Elena Pavlova · Choyeop Kim · Eugenia Triantafyllou · Nora Schinnerl · Christine Lucas · Vida Cruz-Borja · Sheikha Helawy · Vraiux Dorós · Dean Francis Alfar · Mário Coelho · Pasi Ilmari Jääskeläinen